第十四届亚洲艺术节
暨第二届海上丝绸之路国际艺术节
The 14th Asia Arts Festival
The 2nd Maritime Silk Road International Arts Festival

第三届亚洲文化论坛

论文集

主　　编／贾磊磊　李树峰
副 主 编／郑长铃　程永生
执行主编／王巨川　张敬华

PROCEEDINGS OF
THE 3RD ASIA CULTURAL FORUM

文化艺术出版社
Culture and Art Publishing House

图书在版编目（CIP）数据

第三届亚洲文化论坛论文集/贾磊磊，李树峰主编．
—北京：文化艺术出版社，2016.12
ISBN 978-7-5039-6220-2

Ⅰ.①第… Ⅱ.①贾…②李… Ⅲ.①文化研究—亚洲—文集 Ⅳ.①G13-53

中国版本图书馆CIP数据核字（2016）第287157号

第三届亚洲文化论坛论文集

主　　编	贾磊磊　李树峰
副 主 编	郑长铃　程永生
执行主编	王巨川　张敬华
责任编辑	帅　克　赵　月
装帧设计	姚雪媛
出版发行	文化藝術出版社
地　　址	北京市东城区东四八条52号　100700
网　　址	www.whyscbs.com
电子邮箱	whysbooks@263.net
电　　话	（010）84057666（总编室）84057667（办公室） （010）84057691—84057699（发行部）
传　　真	（010）84057660（总编室）84057670（办公室） （010）84057690（发行部）
经　　销	新华书店
印　　刷	国英印务有限公司
版　　次	2016年12月第1版
印　　次	2016年12月第1次印刷
开　　本	787毫米×1092毫米　1/16
印　　张	30
字　　数	536千字
书　　号	ISBN 978-7-5039-6220-2
定　　价	68.00元

版权所有，侵权必究。如有印装错误，随时调换。

目 录

大会致辞

在第三届亚洲文化论坛开幕式上的致辞 ………………………… 李书磊 3
泰国前副总理披尼在大会上致辞 ……………… [泰国] 披尼·扎禄颂巴 5

主题演讲

亚洲文化交流之我见 ………………………………………… 莫 言 9
日本茶道文化发言纲要 …………………………… [日] 千玄室 10
亚洲合作对话 …………………………… [泰国] 班迪·林沙军 12
"和而不同"是中华文化的大智慧 ……………………… 刘梦溪 15
以"一带一路"建设为主题的演讲 ……… [柬埔寨] 萨姆闰·卡姆森 19
三大特征和三大责任 …………………………………… 余秋雨 21
亚洲国家文化的作用和"一带一路"合作
　　………………… [孟加拉国] 穆罕默德·阿尔塔夫·侯赛因 22
加强跨文化研究,增进亚洲各文明间的互惠性理解 ………… 王铭铭 31
在第三届亚洲文化论坛上的演讲 …………… [斯里兰卡] 伯纳德·瓦桑塔 32
非遗保护与"一带一路"建设 …………………………… 田 青 34
文化在21世纪海上丝绸之路经济带建设和文明对话中的作用
　　……………………………… [科威特] 拉马丹·沙拉哈 35
突破文化孤岛,打造文化共同体 ………………………… 尹 鸿 36

1

分论坛中方论文

（按作者姓氏汉语拼音排序）

标题	作者	页码
华侨华人在"一带一路"民心相通中的作用	陈奕平	39
中华文化影响世界的两种路径：不应被忽视的民间文化	陈支平	48
从文化视角看"一带一路"建设	方长平	58
"丝绸之路"上的瓷器贸易与世界文明再生产	方李莉	59
从敦煌文化的形成看亚洲文化的融会发展	高德祥	88
对话视野：国际关系中文化差异的管理之道	郭惠民	94
"一带一路"与亚洲文化空间秩序的新关系	胡惠林	99
考古发现所见早期丝绸之路中外交往史迹钩沉	李 青	101
重建艺术与生活之间的联系 ——重新认识东方"艺道"观的未来价值	李新风	107
云南跨境民族母语文化融入"一带一路"战略发展意义研究	李 瑛	109
"一带一路"沿线民间文学与民族关系研究	林继富	115
海上丝绸之路、海丝文化与闽南	刘登翰	116
中韩电影合作共赢的途径	刘 藩	123
"方寸世界·天人合一" ——中国篆刻艺术的艺术特色和文化功能	骆芃芃	129
作为文化线路的"海上丝绸之路：福建史迹"遗产保护研究	骆文伟	133
重拾东方色彩传统	牛克诚	142
法国人的"丝路"理念与运作实践 ——以"第九届里昂国际舞蹈双年节"为个案	欧建平	144
"一带一路"框架中戏剧交流的回望与前瞻	宋宝珍	155
从《红楼梦》中的某一个案来看中日学者的相互影响	孙玉明	162
中国传统戏剧中的文化基因与文化对话	王 馗	163
丝绸之路的艺术交流对古代中国乐舞发展的影响 ——以宫廷乐舞为例	王宁宁	164
钱锺书释"老健春寒秋后热"	王人恩	168

元代海陆丝绸之路文化汇合点
　　——以希腊文化东渐泉州为例 ················ 吴幼雄　173
在音乐文化交流中保持文化特色："一带一路"的思考 ········ 项　阳　183
创建亚洲新文明华侨华人的作用不容忽视 ············ 谢必震　189
两岸歌仔戏艺术合作之回顾与瞻望 ··············· 谢雍君　194
弘扬丝路精神，深化文化交流 ················· 徐玉梅　199
区域性对外传播中如何做到"民心相通"
　　——以在滇东南亚留学生对"云南"的幻想主题分析为例
　　··································· 杨姣　吴玫　202
生态文明时代的文化精神 ···················· 于文秀　233
闽南文化在"一带一路"中的纽带与桥梁作用 ······ 袁勇麟　涂怡弘　238
敦煌与丝绸之路文明 ······················ 郑炳林　246
海丝文化概念及其生成内涵
　　——兼论海丝文化与闽南文化之关系 ········ 郑长铃　王巨川　248

分论坛外方论文

（按 ACD 国家顺序排序）

在日本正仓院仓库中新发现伊朗纹饰织锦 ·········[日本]影山悦子　257
亚洲文化合作的共赢之路 ················[韩国]柳在沂　259
"一带一路"建设和亚洲文化对话 ············[缅甸]吴吞翁　261
丝绸之路：跨文化之融合 ················[越南]阮氏玄　267
求同存异 ····················[孟加拉国]卡伦南舒·巴鲁阿　272
家庭为根，社会为本
　　——斯里兰卡文化发展项目 ·········[斯里兰卡]伯纳德·瓦桑塔　275

Context

Address

The Address in the Opening Ceremony of the 3rd Asia Cultural Forum
.... [China] Li Shulei 285

The Address at the 3rd Asia Cultural Forum ...... [Thailand] Phinij Jarusombat 287

Key-note Speech

My View on Asian Cultural Exchange .... [China] Mo Yan 293

Outline of Speech on Japanese Tea Culture .... [Japan] Genshitsu Sen 294

Keynote Speech at the 3rd Asia Cultural Forun
.... [Thailand] Bundit Limschoon 296

Harmony with Diversity: Great Wisdom of Chinese Culture
.... [China] Liu Mengxi 300

To Attend the 3rd Asia Cultural Forum on "the Belt and Road"
.... [Cambodia] Samraing Kamsam 305

Three Characteristics and Three Responsibilities .... [China] Yu Qiuyu 308

The Role of Culture in Asian Countries and "the Belt and Road" Co-operation
.... [Bangladesh] Md. Altaf Hossain 309

Strengthen Transcultural Studies and Enhance the Reciprocity Understanding
among Asian Civilizations .... [China] Wang Mingming 321

Speech ·················· [Sri Lanka] K. P. Bernard Vasantha Silva 323
Protection of Intangible Cultural Heritage and Construction of
　"the Belt and Road" ····················· [China] Tian Qing 326
The Role of the Culture in Building Economic Belt for the Marine Silk
　Road in the 21st Century and the Dialogue of Civilizations
　················· [Kuwait] Ramadan AlSharrah 327
Break through Isolated Culture, Build Cultural Community
　················· [China] Yin Hong 329

Speeches of the Sub-forums from China
(In the order of surname Pinyin)

Role of Overseas Chinese in People's Communication of "the Belt and Road"
　················· Chen Yiping 333
Two Paths of Chinese Culture Influencing the World: the Important Civil Culture
　················· Chen Zhiping 346
See "the Belt and Road" from the Perspective of Culture ······ Fang Changping 348
Integration Development of Asian Culture Seen from the Formation of
　Dunhuang Culture ····················· Gao Dexiang 349
Cultural Dialogue: Management of Cultural Difference ············· Guo Huimin 357
New Relations between "the Belt and Road" and Asian Cultural
　Spatial Order ····················· Hu Huilin 359
Research of the Silk Road and North-west Ethnic Art History ············ Li Qing 361
Rebuild the Relation between Art and Life ····················· Li Xinfeng 362
Significance of Integrating Mother Tongue Culture of Yunnan
　Cross-border Ethnic Groups in "the Belt and Road" Initiative ······ Li Ying 364
Research on Folk Literature and Ethnic Relations along "the Belt and Road"
　················· Lin Jifu 374
Maritime Silk Road, Maritime Silk Culture and Southern ············ Liu Denghan 375
Win-win Paths of Sino-Korean Film Cooperation ····················· Liu Fan 376

Unity of Heaven and Man in Square Inch World	Luo Pengpeng	377
Heritage Preservation Studies on the Cultural Route	Luo Wenwei	378
Revive Traditional Oriental Colors	Niu Kecheng	380
French Concept and Operation Practice of "Silk Road"	Ou Jianping	383
History and Prospect of Drama Exchange in "the Belt and Road" Frame	Song Baozhen	397
Take an Example of Translation in *A Dream of Red Mansion* to View the Interaction between Scholars in China and Japan	Sun Yuming	407
Cultural Genes and Dialogues in Chinese Traditional Operas	Wang Kui	408
Impact of Silk Road Art Exchanges on Development of Ancient Chinese Music Dance	Wang Ningning	409
QianZhongshu Interprets "The Health Status of the Elderly is Unstable, Like Spring Chill and Autumn Heat"	Wang Ren'en	411
Point of Cultural Convergence for Marine Silk Road and Land Silk Road in Yuan Dynasty	Wu Youxiong	412
Exchange and Integration of Chinese and Foreign Music: Reflection on History and Development of "the Belt and Road"	Xiang Yang	413
The Role of Overseas Chinese is Crucial to the Creation of New Asian Civilization	Xie Bizhen	415
Review and Expectation of Cross-strait Cooperation in Hokkien Opera	Xie Yongjun	416
Building of "the Belt and Road" and Xinjiang Music and Dance Art	Xu Yumei	417
How to Achieve "People-to-people Bonds" by External Communication in the Region?	Yang Jiao / Wu Mei	418
Cultural Spirit in an Era of Ecological Civilization	Yu Wenxiu	419
Southern Fujian Culture Functions as the Bond and Bridge in "the Belt and Road"	Yuan Yonglin / Tu Yihong	426
Dunhuang and Silk Road Civilization	Zheng Binlin	428

Concept of Maritime Silk Road Culture and the Connotation
.... Zheng Changling / Wang Juchuan 431

Speeches of the Sub-forums from Foreign Countries
(In the order of ACD countries)

Newly Identified Iranian Motif of Brocade in Shosoin Storehouse in Japan
.... [Japan] Etsuko Kageyama 435
The Win-win Solution for Asian Cultural Cooperation
.... [South Korean] Ryoo Jae Ky 438
The Building of "the Belt and Road" and Cultural Dialogues in Asia
.... [Myanmar] U Tun Ohn 441
The Silk Road: Multicultural Integration .... [Vietnam] Nguyen Thi Hien 448
Unity in Diversity .... [Bangladesh] Karunangshu Barua 455
Family Based Socio-cultural Development Project in Sri Lanka
.... [Sri Lanka] Bernad Vasantha 459

大会致辞

在第三届亚洲文化论坛开幕式上的致辞

福建省委常委、宣传部部长　李书磊

（2015 年 11 月 9 日）

尊敬的丁伟副部长、王文章院长，

尊敬的披尼·扎禄颂巴主席和各国来宾，

尊敬的莫言先生和学术、文化界的各位老师、同仁，女士们、先生们：

上午好！

今天，各方嘉宾相聚泉州，参加第三届亚洲文化论坛，称得上是群贤毕至、少长咸集。受尤权书记的委托，我谨代表中共福建省委、福建省人民政府，向论坛的举办表示热烈的祝贺！向出席论坛的海内外嘉宾表示诚挚的欢迎！

因为论坛在泉州举办，我很高兴有机会向大家介绍泉州。在宋元时期，它曾是各国商人云集之地，是中国文化开放的象征。泉州的开放不是在列强压迫下被动的开放，而是主动、自觉、自由的开放，表现了中国文化包容、向新的品质。今天泉州还保存着当年外来文化的丰富史迹，这些史迹往往让人很吃惊、很感慨。

泉州还是伟大思想家李贽的故乡，今天的古街区还保留着李贽的故居，院落、老屋、碑刻尚存。李贽的思想活力、文字锋芒相信也和泉州的多元文化传统有关。弘一法师晚年择居泉州并在这里圆寂，他留恋的可能是泉州的古城氛围和良风美德；弘一法师曾专抄朱熹赞美泉州的对联："此地古称佛国，满街都是圣人。"这副对联也激励我们做好今天的文化建设。

我们感到特别庆幸的是，泉州还保存着 6、7 平方公里的老城区，其街巷房舍还保持着古老的格局、机理与风貌。不少老街区居民充实、业态丰富、生活完整，是存活下来而且很有活力的中国传统城市文化。特别是在早市、晚集的时候，走在沿河的古街上，很有历史穿越之感。这得益于泉州市一直延续了"新旧分治"的理念，一以贯之地保护古城。我们已计划在南城一处叫聚宝街的区域作整体的保护与整修，理念是保存古建筑的本体、老胡同的尺度、老居民的生活。

也向大家报告一下，现在古城保护也面临着许多困难和压力。第一还是要强力遏制各方的利益冲动，制止要在寸土寸金的古城开发房地产的念头。第二是要努力解决因产权不明不细带来的维修滞后、房屋衰败问题。第三还有一个技术性难题,就是如何处置近年来在老街中盖起的新房子问题,在新旧杂错的街区如何最大限度地延续古城风貌。这些也都是想向各位学者请教的问题。

在泉州城内还保存了许多家老工厂的厂房,既作为承载城市记忆、见证中国现代化进程的工业遗产,也作为文创产业的基地。这些老工厂的厂房特别有艺术感,特别适合用来做文创,也特别吸引年轻人、吸引"小资"创客。推荐大家去参观"领 show 天地"和"源和 1916"两个老厂房文创园区,这两个地方给古城带来了巨大的生机和能量,"源和 1916"园区中老面粉厂的车间、麦罐今天看来仍很惊人,其高大雄伟的风格堪比古罗马的神殿。

文化遗产保护和文化建设使城市有了独特的风貌和魅力,是城市吸引力和城市价值的重要源泉,现在泉州和全福建的各级政府、市民越来越认识到了这一点。泉州的文化保护可以说是我们竭尽全力在做的一个实验,我们努力在延续、发扬传统中推动古城的复兴,这里面有成功、有成就,也有失败、有挫折,特别希望各位文化学者也将此作为一个案例,以泉州为田野调查范式做些研究。文化研究若选一个有特色的城市作为对象,也是一件很有趣味、很有意义的事。

最后祝论坛成功!

谢谢!

泰国前副总理披尼在大会上致辞

[泰国] 披尼·扎禄颂巴

各位来宾，女士们、先生们：

大家好！

我非常荣幸应中国文化部邀请，代表泰国来到中国福建省泉州市出席"第十四届亚洲艺术节·第三届亚洲文化论坛"，在此谨向中方主办单位表示最诚挚的谢意！

本届文化论坛的主旨是，以共同建设丝绸之路经济带和21世纪海上丝绸之路为契机，为亚洲国家之间文化交流搭建高层平台，增进理解、互信和友谊。泰国地处东南亚中南半岛，与中国陆地直线距离仅200多公里，同时也是海上丝绸之路的途经国之一，自汉代始即与中国频繁交往，中国的瓷器、丝绸、手工艺品，包括传统节日和习俗都对丰富和促进泰国文化发展产生了重要影响。当前，泰中关系全面深入发展，泰国理应积极加入"一带一路"建设，为促进中泰及亚洲各国之间和平发展和文化交流做出应有的贡献。

我曾担任过泰国政府两任副总理和七任部长，主管过经济工作。任何一个有远见有智慧的政治家都懂得，维护本国利益是对外关系的出发点和原则，但一国的国家利益必须在融入国际社会的共同利益中才能找到国际间合作的基础，才能真正发展自己、惠及本国人民。中国国家主席习近平阁下代表中国政府提出的"一带一路"倡议，顺应了当今和平、发展、合作、共赢的时代潮流，受到沿线各国广泛重视和支持。

"一带一路"跨越疆土，绵延千年，自古以来就是一条商贸通道，又是文化之旅。经济与文化密不可分，经济的发展只有跟文化联系在一起才能长久，才能可持续发展。我以前一直从事政治、经营商贸，对文化重视不够，我对文化的认识和重视是从担任泰中文化经济协会会长和泰中文化促进委员会主席之后开始的。通过与中国文化部、中国对外文化交流协会、中国驻泰国大使馆和曼谷中国文化中心等共同举办和参加一系列泰中文化交流活动，我深切感受到文化软实力对促进两国关系发展、加深人民之间友情发挥了独特的重要作用。可以毫不夸张地说，国与国之间交往，即便谈的是政治、做的是商贸，真正交流的却是文化，是心灵的沟通。今天，我们亚洲各国代表出席亚洲文化论坛，我们要讨论要交流的中心思想就是在共建"一带一路"的过程中，如何发挥文化的功能。亚洲国家间文化交流也要搭上"一带一路"的快车，就像乘坐上中国的高铁，为亚洲文化旅游产业发展加速提速，开拓新契机、新途径。

在此，我想结合泰中文化交流实际提出几点建议：

1. 加快与中国互建文化中心，泰国将尽快在北京建立泰国文化中心。在亚洲国家已建成的中国文化中心要扩大功能，通过新媒体等手段扩大受众面和覆盖面。

2. 建立亚洲国家间历史档案、信息、资料共享机制。中国历史悠久，虽经战乱，许多历史文物、档案资料仍传承有序。泰国和周边一些国家，历史上一直与中国交往频繁，在民族、宗教、文化、习俗等方面互鉴交融，结下很深的渊源，但缺少可资研究的遗留资料，如中方能给予协助，将会拉近中国和"一带一路"沿线特别是邻近国家民众距离，增进文化认同，夯实"一带一路"利益共同体的社会和历史根基。

3. 亚洲文化论坛办得很有成效。在论坛大框架下，可单列一些研讨项目，便于各国专家学者更具体更有针对性地研究解决一些交流中存在的实际问题。

4. 在政府支持下，更多地发挥民间文化机构和社会力量的作用，更多地举办双边和多边文化交流活动。像在泰国举办的"欢乐春节"，朱拉蓬公主倡导、两国政府举办的"中泰一家亲"音乐会等具有较大影响力的品牌项目还要继续办好。今年11月16日，以"新丝路开启新旅途"为口号的泰中旅游文化友好车队将从新疆发车，行程15000里至泰国曼谷结束，将为宣传中国和泰国旅游、文化开辟新的渠道。明年，泰中双方将共同制作一档泰中明星参与的熊猫主题娱乐节目，在泰国清迈出生的熊猫林彬也将在电视中亮相。这是一个面向两国民众特别是两国青少年的节目，得到泰国副总理和泰国国家旅游局、泰国电视三台等机构的积极支持。无论是友好车队万里行，还是熊猫明星秀电视节目，都是对传统文化合作项目的创新，希望能够做成泰中两国乃至"一带一路"文化合作的示范项目，开启文化交流新的里程。

各位与会代表、各位朋友，新时期"一带一路"建设已经起航，这是我们亚洲大家庭共同的使命，经济和科技等合作有些项目需要谋划、筹备，文化交流可以先行，让我们携手合作，迎接亚洲文化发展更加璀璨美好的明天。

谢谢各位！

第三届亚洲文化论坛论文集

主题演讲

亚洲文化交流之我见

中国艺术研究院文学艺术创作研究院名誉院长　莫　言

一、在亚洲各国乃至世界各国的合作对话中，政治对话是为了处理各国之关系，经济贸易是为了各自之利益，文化交流是为了丰富各国人民乃至全人类之生活。

从来就没有单纯的政治对话，政治博弈是为了经济利益。而所有的经济贸易都同时包含着文化的交流，就像丝绸不仅仅是可以制作服装的纺织品，陶瓷不仅仅是可以盛物的容器，许多商品本身就是文化的载体、艺术的精品。因此，丝绸之路从根本上讲是一条文化之路，它的经济利益性是暂时的，而文化意义是深远久长的。

二、传统文化是我们最宝贵的财富，是取之不尽用之不竭的宝藏。文化的交流应该建立在各自的传统的基础上，从传统的文化中选择最灿烂最优秀的部分展示给别的国家的人民。

三、文化交流是互相吸引、互相学习的过程。亚洲各国的文化，早已是你中有我、我中有你。

四、文化交流的最根本的目的是文化的创新，是继承本国传统中有价值的，学习他国文化中最优秀的，创造出最能反映当代现实、满足人民精神需求的新的文化形态，使人的情感更丰富、人的生活更美好。

日本茶道文化发言纲要

日本茶道里千家前家元 千玄室

《神农本草经》中写道:"神农尝百草,日遇七十二毒,得茶而解之。"这是人类尝试茶叶的第一步。公元780年前后,唐代陆羽著有《茶经》,完整地介绍了茶叶生产的历史、源流、现状、生产技术以及品水和饮茶的技艺。饮茶的习俗最早从中国传到日本也是在这个时代,而饮茶文化在日本真正传播开来则一直要等到400多年后的镰仓时代。

抹茶在唐朝、宋朝达到顶峰,特别在宋朝,已经有了完整的寺院抹茶点茶仪式。明朝之后,中国开始流行用叶茶汤泡的小壶泡法,发展到如今有了绿茶、黄茶、白茶、乌龙茶、红茶、黑茶等六大茶类的品饮方式。古代的抹茶点茶逐渐失传。

公元9世纪末(日本的平安中期)抹茶随日本遣唐使进入日本,点茶被日本人民所接受并推崇。公元1191年日本僧人荣西将茶种从中国带回日本,从此日本才开始遍种茶叶。在南宋末期(1259)日本禅师南浦昭明来到中国浙江的经山寺取经,交流了该寺院的茶宴仪程,首次将中国的茶道引进日本,成为中国茶道在日本的最早传播者。日本《类聚名物考》对此记载:"茶道之起,筑前崇福寺开山南浦昭明由宋传入。"南浦昭明由宋归国,把茶台子、茶道具一式带到崇福寺。

之后的足利义满将军时期出现了"宇治六园"的记载,说明茶叶的栽培在宇治一带已经初具规模。室町时代日本中世生活文化发展迅速,村田珠光、武野绍鸥以及千利休的出现,把日本的饮茶文化推向了被称之为"侘茶"的茶汤文化,奠定了今天日本茶道的基础。后人把千利休的茶道思想总结为:和、敬、清、寂四字,并在茶道的实践中把它总结为以下七条:

> 点茶要口感好,添炭是为了烧水,花要像在原野中盛开一样,准备茶事要冬暖夏凉,要守时,凡事要未雨绸缪,关怀同席的客人。

与此同时,抹茶的制作工艺在之后的江户时代日渐成熟,每年4月中旬开始,大约30—40天间用稻草、苇秆或者寒冷纱等材料将茶树遮荫至5月中旬采摘，以增加茶叶中叶绿素和多种氨基酸的含量，减少涩味。抹茶每年只在5月采摘一季，传统茶园全部手采。茶青在采摘后会经过蒸汽蒸青停止发酵，之后迅速冷干脱水制成粗制碾茶。碾茶需要在冷藏库中存放一段时间之后，才会开始精制过程，最后用石臼碾成粉末成品。

茶道在利休之后，也在其后人和弟子的传播下继续深化，完整的茶道过程称之为茶事，全部做完需要4个小时的时间，包括添炭、怀石料理、中立浓茶、添后炭、薄茶。它是包含陶瓷、书法、建筑、插花、闻香、饮食等多方面内容的综合的生活艺术。通过习茶、饮茶，可以接触到许多日本传统文化的侧面。

茶道既不是一个哲学概念，也不是一个美学理论，把茶道中的实践扩大到从日常生活的点滴去实践，开启自己的感官，感受自然大美，敬畏生命的伟大。茶的艺术就是从体贴生命的伟大之处而来。茶道的实践会让我们学会：只致力于做一件事，至于其他，不去想，也不去做。在一杯茶道中，找到自己心灵可以安住的角落。

再次感谢大家，让我们在此共度了有茶的时间。

亚洲合作对话

[泰国] 班迪·林沙军

尊敬的中国文化部副部长丁伟先生,

尊敬的中国文化部前副部长、中国艺术研究院院长王文章先生,

各位尊敬的代表们,女士们、先生们:

大家好!

我非常荣幸能够代表亚洲合作对话的33个成员国,就"新丝绸之路"在文化全球化方面所起的作用发表演讲。

尊敬的各位来宾,自人类文明起始,文化发展从未停止。人类是文化的载体,随着人与人之间的互动,文化也在不断变化。长久以来,全球人类社会的联系变得愈加紧密,近几年更是迅猛发展。

目前,随着交流与信息科技的进步,全球化在世界范围内为各种文化价值观的交流做出了自己的努力。随着现代化交通工具和经济关系的发展以及跨国公司与全球市场的形成,文化全球化加速了世界体系的整合趋势。然而,由于全球化进程过于迅猛,文化的同化现象变得日趋严重。

麦当劳和可口可乐随处可见,这种现代化可能导致文化认同和文化多样性的流失,其中最受威胁的就是文化处于"弱势"的发展中国家。全球化的破坏导致出现文化弱势,这对每一种文化认同都十分危险,对发展中国家的威胁尤为突出。因此,我们所处地区的人民对自身文化特性和认同的保护问题非常关心。

然而,文化交流的好处在于它能够产生强大的协同作用,最大限度地促进建设性交往。因此,在通过社会互动应对全球化加速同化的问题时,不应排除文化交流,而是应通过实施战略计划来加深国与国之间的相互理解,加强跨文化沟通和合作。

为此,我们已做出了巨大的努力,以寻找平衡当地文化的其他方式,从而避免盲目跟从主流文化或被西化。

因此,尊敬的中华人民共和国主席习近平阁下提出的"新丝绸之路"倡议正适于应对这一全球化问题。"新丝绸之路"的特点在于它不限于贸易和经济合作,通过丝绸之路进行的文化合作也将对增进区域和谐起到至关重要的作用。

"新丝绸之路"在文化层面的合作将有助于创造建设性交往，亚文化可以就此展现自身特点，平等互动，从而避免主流文化的冲击。

以古丝绸之路为例，5000年前，丝绸之路不仅是一条简单的贸易之路，也是周边群体相互交流的渠道。互不相识的人们在这条丝绸之路上进行交易，异国与当地的文化得以交流。这种联通是和平的精神、是和谐的发展，有些甚至传承至今。

这条丝绸之路具有独特的连接性，它不仅成为了各群体之间繁荣发展和贸易来往的源泉，也促进了艺术音乐等知识发明和智慧文化的交流。对我来说，丝绸之路不仅促进了国际贸易往来，也推动了人类文明互动，从而形成了亚洲的独特之处。

丝绸之路上的陆路与海路不同，在陆路行进的商队途中不免要与其他群体和文化进行互动。因此，在贸易驱动的交流中，沙漠中最小的村落也加入这种互动，他们不仅接触到了先进的文明世界的产品，也获得了思想、知识、经验和信仰的交流。

由此可知，丝绸之路上不仅有贸易往来，经济文化活动也十分频繁。丝绸之路上的商业活动也使互相敌对的群体以和平的方式开始了互动，这就是和平的沟通。

因此，这条历史性的丝绸之路为现代国际商业做出了榜样，即"学习交流文化艺术形式和规范的现代典范"。

如今，如果想通过地区合作产生最终利益，就要为丝绸之路搭建一个平台，从而为亚洲国家之间更加顺畅地进行文化交流提供支持。

为促进人类文明的繁荣发展和相互理解，我们亚洲合作对话组织就是最佳的平台，它拥有近距离的地理优势，便于地区文化交流。亚洲合作对话的区域性合作是加速经济发展和社会发展的必要机制。在以丝绸之路精神和文化为基础的文化互动的推动下，我们可以为拥有不同信仰和背景的人民搭建一座沟通的桥梁。通过成员国之间的紧密联系，合作与对话将更加便捷，同时减少对立与冲突。亚洲合作对话将在文化合作层面通过各种形式增强亚洲文化的力量。

由此，亚洲合作对话的成员国建立了一个文化合作机制来加强亚洲各国的文化联系，即亚洲合作对话文化协调中心，这个机制将深入地对各类文化问题的探讨进行审视。这个提案是由伊朗伊斯兰共和国提出的，他们还提出了承办2016年将在德黑兰举行的第四届亚洲合作对话文化合作的部长级会议。明年的文化部长会议将确保文化倡议和项目的具体化和实施，并最终使亚洲各国间的文化政策制定协调一致。

紧密的合作和建设性交往将带领亚洲迈向可持续的经济繁荣发展，并应对全球化的同化问题。在这一点上，我想引用尊敬的习近平主席在联合国教科文组织总部的发言，他曾说："历史告诉我们，只有交流互鉴，一种文明才能充满生命力。只要秉持包容精神，就不存在什么'文明冲突'，就可以实现文明和谐。"

尊敬的各位来宾，最后，我想说，亚洲是古代文明的摇篮。从中东到远东，由于当地优质文化特性得到良好的保存，因此区域性繁荣已得到充分的发展。亚洲的特点就是多样性。无论国家大小，发达不发达，都十分重视当地特点，任何保卫和维护国家尊严的努力都未妨碍亚洲各国和平共处。

亚洲虽然存在多样性，但仍保持互动。我相信，如果我们加强不同文明之间的共识与宽容、增进交流和互相理解、加强不同文化之间的协同作用，那么，通过"一带一路"计划和亚洲合作对话论坛，亚洲就会在互相尊重和公平交流的基础上对建构求同存异的和谐世界起到重要作用。

"和而不同"是中华文化的大智慧

中国艺术研究院终身研究员、中国文化研究所所长　刘梦溪

中国文化倾向于不把人与人之间的关系弄得那么紧张，不主张世界上的事都那么不可调和。"和而不同"是中国人面对这个世界的总原则，也是中国文化贡献给人类的大智慧。"和"的关键，首要在承认不同。如果都相同，就无所谓"和"了。不同，也能共处于一个统一体中。

不过，我想追寻的是，人与人之间的差异，南方人和北方人的差异，中国人和外国人的差异，真的有那么大吗？从学理上来分析，我认为差异是第二位的，相同之处是第一位的。所以中国最古老的《易经》有一句著名的话："天下同归而殊途，一致而百虑。"意思是说，尽管方法途径不同，人们最后总还是要走在一起的。

宋代的思想家程颢和程颐，即二程子，他们把为人处世致力于"求同"还是"求异"，看做是一个人的"公心"和"私心"的问题。他们说："公则同，私则异。"[①] 并说"同者"是"天心"，意即上天的旨意。在另一处他们还说："圣贤之处世，莫不于大同之中有不同焉。不能大同者，是乱常拂理而已；不能不同者，是随俗习污而已。"[②] 不承认人和事的不同，二程子认为是没有修养的人的胡言乱语；但如果否认"大同"，就是"乱常拂理"，十分荒谬。就其错误的程度而言，二程子认为不能求大同的性质更为严重。

我国当代已故的一位学问大家钱锺书先生，早年写了一部著作叫《谈艺录》，1948年该书出版的时候，他在序言中写下两句点题的话：

东海西海，心理攸同；
南学北学，道术未裂。

在钱锺书先生看来，东西方文化虽有不同，但不论东方人还是西方人，其心理的反应特征和指向常常是相同的。

---

① 《二程集》下册，第1256页。
② 《二程集》下册，第1264页。

这也就是孟子说过的："口之于味也，有同耆焉；耳之于声也，有同听焉；目之于色也，有同美焉。"孟子说到这里，提出一句反诘——他反问道："至于心，独无所同然乎。"难道人的心，就没有相同之处吗？孟子的结论是："心之所同然者"，是"理也，义也"（《告子上》），也就是认为人的理性良知必有所同然者。所谓人同此心，心同此理，即为此义。人类原初的情感和理想期待，本来都是这个样子。只不过由于意向与行为的交错，造成了诸般的矛盾。古今贤哲启示我们，应该透过人类生活的矛盾交错的困扰，看到心理期许的一致性轨则，看到不同背后的相同。

上世纪末，1999到2000年，我有一段时间在哈佛大学做研究。我和哈佛大学的很多教授都有对话，其中一个对话的对象，是哈佛大学费正清中心的史华慈教授。他是一位法裔犹太人，懂七八种文字，早年研究日本，后来研究中国，林毓生先生告诉我，见到史华慈，可以看到西方的大儒是什么样子。他的一个重要学术理念是"跨文化沟通"，主张人和人之间、不同的文化之间、不同的族群之间，是可以沟通的。他跟我谈话中，提出一个理论，他说语言对于思维的作用，并不像人们想象的那么大。这个我以前从没有听说过，因为语言是思维的工具，没有语言，人还能思维吗？当然我们了解，不会讲话的小孩子，会画图画，画图画也是一种思维。史华慈教授为了倡导跨文化沟通，试图在理论上有新的建构。他的这个理论想证明一个问题，即语言不通，也不见得是人们交流的完全不可逾越的障碍。当时我说，我能够给你提供的一个例证，是语言不通也可以发生爱情。当然语言不通谈恋爱，容易发生问题。可是语言相通谈恋爱，照样发生问题。可见问题的主因，不一定是由于语言。

不同的文化可以沟通，不一定那样对立，这是中国文化一向的主张。宋代思想家张载（字横渠），一个非常了不起大学者，关中人，他有名的四句教是："为天地立心，为生民立命，为往圣继绝学，为万世开太平。"这四句话气象大得不得了。试想，"为天地立心"、"为生民立命"，这是何等怀抱！大家知道中国文化当中有民本思想的传统，关注生民的利益，是每个知识人士、每个为官的人必须做的。所以过去的县官叫做"父母官"，民之父母，他当然要关心民的利益。张载讲的"为生民立命"，来源于孟子的思想，因为孟子讲过"正命"，即人要正常的生，正常的活，正常的死。不要让民众过不正常的生活。"为生民立命"的意思在此。最后的指向，是"为万世开太平"。这是张载很有名的四句教，叫"横渠四句教"。

但是张载还有另外的四句话，我叫它"哲学四句教"。这四句话是：

> 有象斯有对，对必反其为，
> 有反斯有仇，仇必和而解。

这四句话讲的是哲学，是一种宇宙观，是对整个宇宙世界发为言说。这个世界上，有无穷无尽的一个个的生命个体，可以称作"象"，这些"象"，有动物的，有植物的，每个"象"都不同，真是万象纷呈。"有象斯有对"，说的就是各个"象"的不同。即使是美丽的女性，也有不同的美。所以古人有一种说法，叫做"佳人不同体，美人不同面"。西方也讲，世界上没有完全相同的两个生命个体。

"对必反其为"，是说一个一个的"象"，不是静止的，而是流动的。由于各个"象"的不同，其运行流动的方向也不相同，甚至有时候会背道而驰，所以会出现"有反斯有仇"的情况，发生互相间的纠结。这个"仇"字，古代的写法是"雠"，左边一个"鸟"，右边一个"鸟"，中间是个言论的"言"。隹（zhui）是一种尾巴很短的鸟，"雠"字的本义是两只短尾巴鸟在叽叽喳喳地讨论、争论、辩论。人有人言，鸟有鸟语。这个"雠"字，就是"校雠"的"雠"。我们都有过校书的经历，那是很难的事情，所谓无错不成书，很难一个字都不错。古人的"校雠"，更是一件大事。你拿这个本子，我拿那个本子，一点一点地校，互相讨论、争论，难免面红耳赤。但两只短尾巴鸟互相讨论、争论、辩论的结果，并不是这只鸟把那只鸟吃掉，而是达成共识，或达成妥协，求同存异，走向"和而解"。

这个世界有差异，但差异不必然发展为冲突，冲突不必然变成你死我活，而是可以"和而解"的。你想，用这个思想来看待世界，不是可以减少很多不必要的麻烦吗？当然，不是一方的问题，而是彼此双方乃至多方的问题，所以需要沟通对话，需要多边商量。"有反斯有仇"，就是沟通、对话、商量、研讨、互相校正的过程。

但对话需要智慧，需要对话者具有异量之美。孔子讲的"己所不欲，勿施于人"，就是中国文化的异量之美。一个是"和而不同"，一个是"己所不欲，勿施于人"，这两句话都是孔子在世时说过的话，时间在公元前5世纪，当时正是世界文化历史的轴心时代。我想我们有理由把孔子这两句话的思想，看做是中华文化解决人类生存之道的一种大智慧。

21世纪已经过去十几年了。20世纪是纷争的世界，发生了两次世界大战。21世纪人类还要被这些灾难吞噬吗？人类不可以用自己的理智和智慧，使这个世界变得更好些吗？中国文化里面的"和而不同"的思想，"己所不欲，勿施于人"的思想，就是要我们正确认识这个世界的生存状态、正确认识人类自己，并事实上给出了危机的解决之道。我主张这个世界应该更好些，应该更和谐，应该没有恐惧，应该有话好好说。

这里的关键词是两个：一个是"和"，人人都乐于接受而向往的境界；另一个是"不同"。"不同"是"和"的条件。承认不同、容许不同、欣赏不同，才能走向和谐。如果一切都相同，穿衣相同、走路相同、思维相同、说话相同，这个世界就令人窒息了。孟子说："充实之谓美，充实而有光辉之谓大。"试想，能够使之充实起来的东西，能够都是完全相同的东西吗？不同物的组合，才能称之为"充实"。不同的合乎审美规则的组合，才能创造美。所以，"和而不同"既是世界本来的样子，又是创意的源泉；是美的出发，又是充实而有光辉的起点。

但是不要忘了，还有一句是"己所不欲，勿施于人"，这是指示给我们的处理人类的不同的最合乎人类本性的理性方式。

以"一带一路"建设为主题的演讲

柬埔寨王国文化艺术部国务秘书　萨姆闰·卡姆森

各位尊敬的来宾，女士们、先生们，
亲爱的朋友们：

我很荣幸今天能来到这里，代表柬埔寨王国文化艺术部参加第三届亚洲文化论坛，这是一个亚洲各国进行文化交流与沟通的高层平台，在中华人民共和国福建省泉州市，此次论坛给各位亚洲的专家、学者和艺术机构提供了多种渠道和机会来增加对彼此的理解、信任、交流和合作。

首先，我想借这个特别的机会向中华人民共和国，尤其是中国文化部，在这个重大的日子，组织以"一带一路"为主题的第三届亚洲文化论坛表达我深深的谢意和感激之情，同时也非常感激论坛组委会对我们的热烈欢迎和热情款待。

作为论坛参加国之一，柬埔寨坚定地支持中国政府最近提出的"新丝绸之路经济带和21世纪海上丝绸之路"的倡议，即"一带一路"，该倡议敦促相关各国建立互利共赢的"利益共同体"。同时，这些举措也帮助各国建立共同发展繁荣的"命运共同体"。

柬埔寨深信，面向未来的"一带一路"举措一定能够加强我们的连接，促进和平、合作和共同利益的发展，这既是本世纪的精神，也是全世界人民的唯一心愿。

本届论坛将讨论：亚洲合作对话中文化的角色与作用、从亚洲文化的特性看"一带一路"合作、亚洲文化合作共赢的路径。

柬埔寨代表团坚信论坛将成功举办。

借此机会，在这个重要场合，请允许我与大家分享一下目前柬埔寨在保存和保护文化遗产上的文化合作情况：

在合作和保护文化遗产的框架方针内，作为在世界上物质和非物质文化遗产丰富的国家，柬埔寨为保护、重建和振兴我们的文化遗产，包括柬埔寨文化和历史名城、名刹古寺、宗教历史遗迹以及文化表达形式和多样性，在制定国家文化政策、战略目标和行动计划上做出了许多努力。

的确，随着人民教育的发展、人民参与保护历史遗迹意识的觉醒和相关法律法规框架的建立，我们有效地保存和重建了很多历史遗迹并成功保护了非物质文化遗产。为了这一目的，加强亚洲各友好国家之间的文化合作也因此变得非常密切和热忱。

最后，我谨代表柬埔寨代表团，在此号召我们"第三届亚洲文化论坛"能够做到以下几点：

坚决信守我们对加强文化合作所做出的承诺，为了亚洲和全世界的相互理解、共同利益，彼此信任、沟通以达到稳定、和平与繁荣；共同努力保护我们的文化遗产，反对非法贩卖文物，抵制文化全球化的负面影响；坚定地执行"第三届亚洲文化论坛"的成果，建立互利共赢的"利益共同体"；进一步加强我们"命运共同体"的和平、共同进步和可持续发展。

最后，我谨代表柬埔寨文化艺术部，再次向各位表达我深切的感激和美好的祝愿，各位尊敬的来宾，女士们、先生们，祝大家幸福安康、吉祥如意！

感谢您的关注！

三大特征和三大责任

著名文化学者　余秋雨

在全世界的各种文化中,亚洲文化有三个共同特征,因此产生了三个共同责任。

第一,亚洲文化历史悠久。在公认的人类四大古文明中,亚洲占了三个,那就是:美索不达米亚文明、中华文明和印度文明。此外,亚洲还有希伯来文明、波斯文明、阿拉伯文明、蒙古文明等均对古代世界产生过重大影响。它们的强盛、衰落和奋斗积累了大量正面和反面的历史经验,需要向当今世界系统讲述。

第二,亚洲文化极为多元。亚洲文化由于生态环境远比欧洲、美洲复杂,文明型态的丰富性、奇特性、自足性也居世界之最。因此,亚洲文化最有资格证明:文化差异并不是冲突之源。历史上一切重大的恶性冲突有可能打着"文明"的旗号,其实全都出自于一切文明的反面。因此我曾在参加研讨《联合国人类发展报告》(2004)时,与其他学者一起否定了亨廷顿先生的"文明冲突论",并用图图大主教的一句话作为报告的结论:"Delight in our differences."(为我们的差异而欢欣)

第三,亚洲文化有待阐述。与欧美文化相比,亚洲极为悠久又极为多元的文化大多缺少近代化的全球认知,常常处于被猎奇、被误读、被妖魔化的困境。因此,发掘亚洲文化的珍贵内涵,使它们充溢人类的共同价值系统,是当前面临的重大责任。在这过程中,亚洲文化的跨空间大流通必将是最好的出路。古代的"丝绸之路"在这方面已经做出了成功示范,我们有理由展现更宏大的现代形态。

亚洲国家文化的作用和"一带一路"合作

孟加拉国文化部辅秘、文物局局长　穆罕默德·阿尔塔夫·侯赛因

简　介

2000多年前，亚欧大陆上勤劳勇敢的人民，探索出多条连接亚欧非几大文明的贸易和人文交流通路，后人将其统称为"丝绸之路"。千百年来，"和平合作、开放包容、互学互鉴、互利共赢"的丝绸之路精神薪火相传，推进了人类文明进步，是促进沿线各国繁荣发展的重要纽带。进入21世纪，在以和平、发展、合作、共赢为主题的新时代，面对复苏乏力的全球经济形势、纷繁复杂的国际和地区局面，传承和弘扬丝绸之路精神更显重要和珍贵。

文化是一种工具，它让不同国家的人民紧密相连，文化没有诸如边界、宗教和社会的区分。

从亚洲文化的特性看"一带一路"合作之前，我们首先讲讲丝绸之路——"丝绸之路经济带"和"21世纪海上丝绸之路"。我们必须了解紧密相连的网络系统，如中巴经济走廊（CPEC）和孟中印缅经济走廊（BCIM），官方称之为"与一带一路倡议紧密相连"。

丝绸之路

丝绸之路，简称"丝路"，是一条古代的商路，连接中国和西方国家，承载罗马和中国这两大文明古国之间物品和思想的交流。丝绸运往西方，而羊毛、金子和银子则运往东方。通过这条商路，中国也受到基督教和印度佛教的影响。

丝路始于西安，全长4000英里（6400千米），一个商队曾经经过中国的长城，一路向西北方，通过塔克拉玛干沙漠，爬上帕米尔高原（山脉），穿过阿富汗抵达黎凡特，从那商品经过地中海运输。很少有人能穿越整条道路，货物总是通过不同的中间商逐步运送。

随着罗马帝国在亚洲的领土逐渐丧失和阿拉伯势力在黎凡特的抬头，"丝绸

之路"日益失去安全，直至行人绝迹。13、14世纪，丝绸之路由蒙古人复兴，那时，马可·波罗沿着丝路一路前往至契丹（中国）。

现在，部分丝绸之路建有连接巴基斯坦和中国新疆维吾尔自治区的高速公路。在这条古老的道路上，联合国推出了建设亚洲高速公路的计划。

"一带一路"

2013年9月7日，中国国家主席习近平对哈萨克斯坦进行了国事访问，作为其国事访问的一部分，习近平主席在纳扎尔巴耶夫大学提出了"丝绸之路经济带"。"新海上丝绸之路"则是习近平主席在对印度尼西亚进行国事访问时在印尼国会上提出的。

这两大倡议表达了建立互利共赢的海上和陆地经济走廊、整合欧亚市场和进行文化合作的愿景。《推动共建丝绸之路经济带和21世纪海上丝绸之路的愿景和行动》中阐述：

> "一带一路"贯穿亚欧非大陆，一头是活跃的东亚经济圈，一头是发达的欧洲经济圈，中间广大腹地国家经济发展潜力巨大。丝绸之路经济带重点畅通中国经中亚、俄罗斯至欧洲（波罗的海）；中国至东南亚、南亚和印度洋。21世纪海上丝绸之路重点方向是从中国沿海港口出发经过南海到印度洋延伸至欧洲；从中国沿海港口出发过南海到南太平洋。

"一带一路"倡议包括多个经济和一些非经济因素，其中文化是重要的部分。也许最频繁提到的一个经济因素是，为提高经济实力和加强"一带一路"沿线各国与中国西部地区间的联系，中国将重点投资基础设施项目。习近平主席说，中国必须与相关国家携手努力，共同加快基础设施建设和互联互通的步伐，建设好"丝绸之路经济带"和"21世纪海上丝绸之路"。在这些国家相互联通后，各国的文明将相互传播。

共建"一带一路"旨在顺应世界多极化、经济全球化、文化多样化和社会信息化的潮流，秉承开放的区域合作精神，致力于维护全球自由贸易体系和开放型世界经济。共建"一带一路"旨在促进经济要素有序自由流动、资源高效配置和市场深度融合，推动沿线各国实现经济文化政策协调，开展更大范围、更高水平、更深层次的区域合作，共同打造开放、包容、均衡、普惠的区域经济文化合作架构。

共建"一带一路"致力于亚欧非大陆及附近海洋的互联互通，建立和加强沿线各国互联互通伙伴关系，构建全方位、多层次、复合型的互联互通网络，实现沿线各国多元、自主、平衡、可持续的发展。"一带一路"的互联互通项目将推动沿线各国发展战略的对接与耦合，发掘区域内市场的潜力，促进投资和消费，创造需求和就业，增进沿线各国人民的人文交流与文明互鉴，让各国人民相逢相知、互信互敬，共享和谐、安宁、富裕的生活。

进一步发展中国与中亚国家间的联系具有现实意义，区域合作进一步深化。通过政策沟通、道路联通、贸易畅通、货币流通、民心相通，使欧亚各国经济联系更加紧密、相互合作更加深入、发展空间更加广阔。丝绸之路经济带是世界上最长的经济和贸易走廊，具有最大的发展潜力，沿线各国的经济发展和文化合作将获得新动力，也将获得共享合作成果的新机遇。

共建原则

恪守联合国宪章的宗旨和原则。遵守和平共处五项原则，即尊重各国主权和领土完整、互不侵犯、互不干涉内政、和平共处、平等互利。

坚持开放合作。"一带一路"相关的国家基于但不限于古代丝绸之路的范围，各国和国际、地区组织均可参与，让共建成果惠及更广泛的区域。

坚持和谐包容。倡导文明宽容，尊重各国发展道路和模式的选择，加强不同文明之间的对话，求同存异、兼容并蓄、和平共处、共生共荣。

坚持市场运作。遵循市场规律和国际通行规则，充分发挥市场在资源配置中的决定性作用和各类企业的主体作用，同时发挥好政府的作用。

坚持互利共赢。兼顾各方利益和关切，寻求利益契合点和合作最大公约数，体现各方智慧和创意，各施所长，各尽所能，把各方优势和潜力充分发挥出来。

框架思路

"一带一路"是促进共同发展、实现共同繁荣的合作共赢之路，是增进理解信任、加强全方位交流的和平友谊之路。全方位推进务实合作，打造政治互信、经济融合、文化包容的利益共同体、命运共同体和责任共同体。

"一带一路"贯穿亚欧非大陆，一头是活跃的东亚经济圈，一头是发达的欧洲经济圈，中间广大腹地国家经济发展潜力巨大。丝绸之路经济带重点畅通中国经中亚、俄罗斯至欧洲（波罗的海）；中国经中亚、西亚至波斯湾、地中海；中国至东南亚、南亚、印度洋。

孟加拉国 & 中国的文化交流历史

孟加拉国和中国都是世界文明古国。我们无法确切知道这两个国家是从什么时候如何开始文化方面的交流的，但我们知道，自从开始有人类历史以来，它们并行发展，共享文化特质，这一共享传统一直延续至今。

甚至在佛教传播之前，公元前 1500—1000 的商周文明和古吠陀文明就显示了文化和语言的交流迹象。例如，汉语"无名指"，用梵文和巴利语都是 anamika（无名指），孟加拉国一些古文献中提到"chinas"，指中国人。公元前 5 世纪的《摩柯婆罗多》中也提到了中国。孔雀王朝的考底利耶大臣（前 350—前 283）在他的《政事论》中指中国丝绸为"chinamsuka"（中国丝绸衣服）和"chinapatta"（中国丝绸包）。同样，张骞和司马迁在《史记》中也提到了"Shendu"，可能指代梵文的"Sindhu"。

公元前 6 世纪，孔子和释迦牟尼的诞生开创了两个文明之间交流的新时期。阿育王在公元前 256 年继位后对佛教的传播使两个文明古国联系更加紧密。阿育王两种语言（佉卢文和希腊语）的法令中规定扩大佛教在中国和中亚的传播。这一措施一直延续到公元一世纪色迦王统治时期。在他统治时期，首都位于 Purushpura（即现在的巴基斯坦白沙瓦），佛教朝圣者和学者沿着历史上的"丝路"前往此处。迦叶摩腾和竺法兰居于洛阳的白马寺。沿着丝路，和阗、吐鲁番和库车成为著名的佛教和印中交流中心。著名的学者鸠摩罗什开始在长安（即现在的西安）的佛堂搜集和组织翻译重要的佛经，一直到公元 413 年他圆寂之前，他将 98 本重要的佛教经典作品翻译成了汉语。因此，是他将大乘佛教和中观派学说带到中国的。公元 5 世纪，印度佛教学者昙无谶来到中国，带来了"大乘涅槃经"，并在公元 415 年翻译成了汉语。与此同时，中国朝圣者 Fa Hein 沿着丝路前往印度，并于公元 405 年抵达。Batuo（464—495）和菩提达摩曾访问过中国；玄奘（604）和义净是著名的纳兰达大学的学生。总之，丝绸之路在促进孟加拉国和中国的文化、商业和技术交流中扮演着重要的角色，它同时将我们与古波斯和地中海的人民相连。

中孟合作的新机遇

2015年9月26日，中国国家主席习近平在纽约会见孟加拉国总理哈西娜，两国元首同意加强双边在各个领域的合作。

习近平指出，中孟两国是好邻居、好朋友、好伙伴。中方视孟加拉国为南亚和印度洋地区重要合作伙伴，愿同孟方保持高层交往，拓展贸易、产能合作、能源开发、基础设施建设等重点领域合作。

他强调，继续办好两国建交40周年纪念活动，推进教育、广电、高校合作，便利双方人员往来，给两国人民带来更多福祉。

双方还要保持在重大国际地区问题上的沟通和协调。习近平说，中方愿为孟方应对气候变化提供力所能及的支持。

习近平指出，当前中国人民正在致力于实现中华民族伟大复兴的中国梦，提出建设"一带一路"和"21世纪海上丝绸之路"的倡议，希望同包括孟方在内广大邻居和朋友共享发展机遇。

中国支持中国企业赴孟投资，愿为双方商定的重大合作项目提供融资支持。

中方重视孟方为推动孟中印缅经济走廊建设发挥的建设性作用，将同各方保持密切沟通，推动走廊建设早见成效。

哈西娜表示，孟中建交40年来，两国已建立起紧密的伙伴关系。孟方感谢中方长期以来对孟经济社会发展给予的帮助。孟方愿加强同中方在经贸、金融、基础设施建设、人文领域交流合作，积极参与孟中印缅经济走廊框架下合作。

自从1975年双方建立外交关系以来，中国和孟加拉国在完全平等、互相尊重和相互信任的基础上，一直是好邻居、好朋友、好伙伴。2010年，两国元首宣布他们将致力于建立"更紧密的全面合作伙伴关系"。2013年，双边关系维持了良好的发展势头。

此外，孟中印缅经济走廊取得了重大进展。

孟加拉国的6座友谊桥已经落成，第7座正在建设中。在中国资金和技术的支持下，许多其他的基础设施大项目也在进行中。

由于孟加拉国在地理位置上毗邻中国，有更廉价的劳动力、友好的投资环境和秀丽的风景（如考斯巴萨），可以说，孟加拉国有更多的优势利用"中国机遇"。完成孟中印缅经济走廊后，孟加拉国将占据更有利的条件。

4个国家一致同意应把重点放在孟中印缅经济走廊的建设上，主要关注以下领域，包括交通、电信、电力&能源、贸易和投资、可持续发展和人员交流的区域联通。因此，中国和孟加拉国应加强在以下方面的彼此互动与合作：

促进区域互通。历史上古代丝绸之路就将我们联系在一起。孟加拉国应努力恢复该区域的道路联通，探索铁路、水路和航空联通。最近，孟加拉国政府已决定快速完成六大项目，包括帕德玛桥建设、深海港和地铁建设。这充分说明致力于加强交流的决心，位于南亚、东南亚和东亚之间的孟加拉国具备成为区域交通枢纽的潜质。

扩大人员交流。作为世代友好的邻居，中国和孟加拉国应努力实现交通的联通以及两国人民之间的相互理解，加强双方的友好合作。

改善跨境交通基础设施，即众所周知的互联互通，是孟加拉国实现经济效益的重要工作。这是中孟两国途径缅甸进行道路联通的重大倡议。你怎样评价目前该联通的进展？2010年，孟加拉国总理访问中国时，中孟同意继续讨论两国间道路和铁路建设的可能性。自此，双方在这方面保持了紧密的合作。2013年5月，中印共同倡议建设中印缅孟经济走廊，推动中印两大市场更紧密的连接，最终推动中印缅孟区域内贸易、经济和文化的交流。中孟的道路联通将成为中印缅孟经济走廊框架下的重大工程。中方将继续与孟方合作，致力于该框架的快速实施。

"一带一路"的文化魅力

2013年，中国国家主席习近平在他的海外国事访问期间提倡建设"一带一路"，包括丝绸之路经济带和21世纪海上丝绸之路。

这一倡议作为北京振兴古代"丝绸之路"（1000多年前的主要商路）的计划，连接了欧洲和中国地区，促进了沿线各国人民的经济和文化发展。

"一带一路"包含了中国丰富的文化内涵，以及在新的历史时期中国的和谐文化的内涵。"一带一路"策略的光明未来将与其历史渊源和文化魅力紧密相连。

首先，"一带一路"追求和平。和平是世界各国人民的共同愿望。"丝绸之路经济带"和"21世纪海上丝绸之路"包括50个国家44亿人民和各区域经济总量21万亿，它们大多是具有不同历史、不同国情和发展水平的发展中国家。它们的基础设施薄弱。这些国家间的交流也不是很顺畅，但作为后发优势，它们将拥有巨大的发展空间。

对这些国家来说，最大的诉求就是在和平的国际环境下赢得发展机遇。"一带一路"的建设有助于加强国家关系，维持地域稳定性。毋庸置疑，它为这些国家享受经济繁荣和人民享受幸福生活提供了有利的条件。

其次,"一带一路"重视合作。任何一个国家都不可能单独地实现发展。"一带一路"沿线的各个国家,有些资本过剩、有些资源有余、有些劳动力充足、有些市场潜力巨大,简而言之,它们可以优势互补。因此,建立一个合作的多元化平台迫在眉睫。

最近几年,有些国家通过上海合作组织(SCO)、中国—东盟(10+1)和金砖四国平台加强了彼此间的合作。中国和"一带一路"沿线国家的这些双边、区域和多边合作机制进一步改善。中国在促进基础设施建设方面做出了重大贡献,建立了亚洲基础设施投资银行和丝路基金,为相关发展中国家提供了巨大帮助。与此同时,其他金融平台的构建,如金砖四国新发展银行和上海合作组织开发银行,稳定推动和保证了"一带一路"策略的实施。

第三,"一带一路"倡导双赢合作。双赢合作已成为了全球发展的一个趋势。在发展的强劲势头的带动下,"一带一路"不仅连接了东亚经济圈,而且与发达的欧洲—北美经济圈相连。

"一带一路"主张政策沟通、设施联通、贸易畅通、资金融通、民心相通,坚持共商、共建、共享原则。"一带一路"策略是开放包容。随着该策略的逐步实施,"一带一路"将开通丝路沿线的渠道,促进区域经济实体的共同发展,并将加快新海事秩序的构建。"一带一路"将对全球地缘政治结构以及崭新的基于双赢合作的未来世界秩序的建立产生影响。

中国有几千年的和平文明史,中国人民深刻了解和平和双赢合作的重要性。通过这些充满历史智慧和传统中国文化的理念的指导,"一带一路"必将为世界的和平、稳定、发展和繁荣注入强大动力。

促进文明多样化和保护亚洲文化遗产的措施

亚洲有丰富多样和完整的有形和无形文化遗产。特别是在南亚,尤其是孟加拉国、不丹、印度、尼泊尔和斯里兰卡,有 35 个联合国教科文组织确定的文化遗产。其中 15 个是佛教遗址,包括如来佛祖的出生地和尼泊尔的蓝毗尼(释迦牟尼的出生地)。

印度次大陆(包括孟加拉国和巴基斯坦)以及斯里兰卡、缅甸和其他毗邻国家拥有可追溯至 5000 年前的独特的文化遗产。在这片区域的所有遗产中,印度教有重要的作用。在笈多、Sen、Pal 和其他王朝有众多古老的寺庙和纪念碑。此外,在穆斯林帝国,尤其是在莫卧儿时期,有上百个代表这一地区伊斯兰文化的雄伟的纪念碑、堡垒和建筑，蕴含出色的建筑设计理念的大量清真寺则展示了那些时期灿烂的文化和创新意识。

文化在亚洲国家间的作用

沿线国家间需互办文化年、艺术节、电影节、电视周和书展；合作开展广播影视剧精品创作及翻译；共同申请和保护世界文化遗产，我们应该增加沿线国家间的人员交流和合作。

我们应该加强旅游合作，扩大旅游规模；互办旅游推广周和宣传月等活动；联合打造具有丝绸之路特色的国际精品旅游线路和旅游产品；提高沿线各国游客签证便利化水平。我们应该推动"21世纪海上丝绸之路"邮轮旅游合作。

推动文化多样性，保护孟加拉国的文化遗产

根据1968年《古物法》（1976年修订版），文化部文物局负责孟加拉国的物质文化遗产。

目前，在孟加拉国有451个受保护的文化遗产和纪念碑。其中一些著名的遗产包括：

PaharpurMahavihara，Noagaon

Mahasthangarh fortified City，Bogra

巴盖尔哈德塞特·昆巴德清真寺 & 邻近清真寺

Kantajiu Temple，Dinajpur

达卡拉勒巴堡城堡

索纳尔冈巴拿马城

ChotoSona Mosque，Chapai Nawabganj

锡尔赫特巨石

达卡亚美尼亚教堂

JagaddalaMahavihara

LalmaiMainamati，Comilla

2012年，伊斯兰教科文组织将达卡列为伊斯兰文化之都（亚洲地区）。孟加拉国致力于保护和保存这里历史悠久的清真寺和纪念碑。

2015年，印度民航局和旅游局、孟加拉国与联合国世界旅游组织（UNT-

WO）共同出席了为期 3 天的国际会议，会议主题为"发展南亚佛教中心可持续和包容的佛教遗产和朝圣者线路"，这将促进跨境的佛教交流、推动朝圣旅游以及这一地区的和平与和谐。此外，它将帮助提高人民保护佛教遗址的意识。

在孟加拉国 Parjatan 公司和文物局的帮助下，孟加拉国旅游局努力促进自然和文化旅游的发展，为私营和国际旅游组织提供支持。

同时，正在努力帮助当地居民提高保护遗址的意识。

2010 年，在南亚经济合作（SAEC）框架下已经启动一个南亚旅游基础设施发展项目。通过这个文物局项目，四个重要的遗址和基础设施得以保存，从而推动文化旅游的发展。

结束语

"一带一路"的建设是一个系统的项目，各国应相互协商，共同建设，以满足各方的利益；沿线各国应共同努力，将各国的发展策略相融合；加强东西方之间的交流与合作，丝路精神是世界各国共享的历史和文化遗产。

秉承"共商、共建和共享"的原则，促进"一带一路"的建设，不应仅仅积极推动区域经济的交流与合作，同时应该重视文化遗产和人文精神。进一步深化丝路沿线国家间友好、非政府和务实的合作。丝绸之路经济带和海上丝绸之路沿线各国可以通过跨境和跨文明交流活动，推动思想的交流和整合，加强对话，实现繁荣和平的欧亚区双赢。

"一带一路"建设应打破传统的区域经济模式，重塑新的高效模式。在不同国家公认的思想和原则的指引下，需要推动更高水平更广泛领域的合作，包括产业转型、贸易深化、增加投资。同时需要深化在人文、教育、文化、科学和技术、生态、环境等领域的合作，以实现政策沟通正常化和贸易投资自由化。

在一个知识和经济深入融合的时代，高等教育已经成为推动社会和经济发展的关键力量。为了推动沿线各国间教育的更好交流，特别是高等教育的交流，建设"一带一路"显得尤为重要。沿线各国应通过更频繁更高水平的教育资源共享、科技和技术合作以及人员交流，进一步推动高等教育领域各种形式的人才交流，从而为建设"一带一路"提供更多专家和人才。

加强跨文化研究,增进亚洲各文明间的互惠性理解

北京大学社会学系教授　王铭铭

"丝绸之路经济带"和"21世纪海上丝绸之路"战略构想提出以来,建设跨越地区、民族、国家的利益、命运、责任共同体,成为一个富有时代特征的号召。

跨越地区、民族、国家的利益、命运、责任共同体的形成,有赖政治互信和经济融合。然而,缺乏文化包容,政治互信不易确立,经济融合不易实现。故而,开拓文化自信、包容、共荣的园地(即费孝通先生所说的"各美其美、美人之美、美美与共、和而不同"),通过对话交流,促进不同文明、文化和宗教的相互尊重,都有着高度的必要性和紧迫性。

文化自信、包容、共荣,既需引起国家与社会的进一步重视,又亟待人文社会科学界加以深入研究与广泛阐述。

跨文化的相互认识,出现甚早,在古代知识与宗教领域中,都存在丰富的案例。但是,基于文化人类学泛文化研究法形成的跨文化研究(transcultural studies),则于1990年代形成于欧洲,其主旨在于"寻求在文化之间的空间里实现知识互惠和相互理解"(Alain Le Pichon语)。按我个人理解,"知识互惠和相互理解"构成某种"互惠性理解"(reciprocal understanding),亦即在文化之间的相互认知中实现或部分实现的、同时有益于互动中的文化双方自我认同与相互认同的理解。

跨文化研究在20年的传播中渐渐演变成一门人文社会科学综合性学问(如,德国海德堡大学已建立跨文化研究研究学位)。过去20多年来,国内亦有学者参与了欧洲跨文化研究院的活动。

然而,作为一门综合性学术门类,跨文化研究在国内方兴未艾。

展望学术发展的未来,我们相信,亚洲各国之间的合作对话,不仅要依赖各国文化的自我认识,而且还要更多凭靠各国对他国文化的他者认识,亚洲各国学者亟待紧密合作,创建跨文化研究学术基地,提升各自跨文化研究水平,将理论与各国文化历史与现实相结合,提出互有裨益、相互关联、共同繁荣的观点,以之促成文化自信、包容、共荣的知识沃土。

在第三届亚洲文化论坛上的演讲

斯里兰卡内政、西北省发展和文化部辅秘　伯纳德·瓦桑塔

首先，请允许我向中华人民共和国政府、中华人民共和国文化部、福建省以及中国艺术研究院邀请我们参加本次重要论坛表达衷心的感谢。中国和我的祖国斯里兰卡的联系可追溯到几百年前，我在此很荣幸地说两国关系从古至今一直是诚挚而友好的。无论何时，每当我们遇到困难时，中国总是义无反顾地对斯里兰卡提供支持。

在此我非常高兴地看到除了中国还有很多其他友好国家，尤其是印度，与斯里兰卡一起参加此次论坛。

此行我代表的是斯里兰卡文化事务部，我们知道文化是两国建立强大关系的纽带，斯里兰卡文化事务部与多国在文化领域签署过备忘录（Mou）。

尽管我们来自不同的地方，说着不同的语言，有着不同的宗教和信仰，但是我们有着同一个，两个或多个文化起源。我们无法忽视印度流域文明，也不能忘却摩亨焦达罗哈拉帕（Mohendejaro Harappa）文明，以及昊万厚（Howang-ho）文明。

斯里兰卡文化事务部迄今为止已与多国共签署了58个备忘录，建立文化联系。为了实践所签署的备忘录，斯里兰卡文化使团前往备忘录国家参加文化活动，同时我们也邀请各国文化使团来斯里兰卡参加文化活动，这种友好而快乐的文化交流为斯里兰卡与这些国家建立强大而真挚的关系铺平了道路。

在此我还想说我们有很多备忘录（Mou）计划有待实施，我大概列出了以下几个：

文化知识交流；

民俗艺术交流；

针对文化推广创建的项目；

知识语言共享；

在国内组织不同的文化发展会议；

组织外国文化领域的专家访问；

在国外举办文化展；

组织国内文化盛会；

政府官员和文化使团参加国外培训和研讨会；

通过两国儿童和青少年交流扩展知识与理解；

让友好国家学者有机会研究成员国的珍贵档案和历史文献资料；

发展旅游业，获取成员国文化和宗教知识。

如上所说，这些备忘录并非只与亚洲国家如印度、巴基斯坦、马尔代夫群岛等国签署，同时我们也与很多亚洲地区以外的国家签署。

斯里兰卡政府也同意并乐意与目前没有建立文化联系的国家签署备忘录，也愿意与已签署备忘录的国家进一步扩大现有的文化关系。

在此我想说一下2014年为努力扩展文化关系而实施的一项特殊项目。那就是为纪念中国航海家郑和而建的美术博物馆，郑和曾在15世纪航海时到达斯里兰卡，该博物馆目前位于我国加勒博物馆内。2014年许多中国游客来斯里兰卡旅游，今年他们将能够到加勒博物馆的郑和将军美术馆参观。美术馆展示了郑和和他的船队从他们的大型战舰上靠岸登陆的情形，同时也展示了加勒省南部的社会和文化风貌。

斯里兰卡政府拨出专项资金用于项目建设，中国政府提供了航海家郑和将军的雕像，斯里兰卡民族遗产部长、斯里兰卡南部省省长和中华人民共和国政府高级官员参加了博物馆开幕式。相信斯里兰卡的中国游客在参观加勒博物馆里的郑和美术馆后一定会不虚此行。

另一个项目是斯里兰卡文化事务部实施的2012年印度安德烈邦项目。该项目在安德烈邦文化主题公园建立了一个斯里兰卡著名佛祖雕塑的复制品。

在两国双边和文化关系引领下，我们与尼泊尔和泰国也共同实施了多个项目和计划。

为提高斯里兰卡文化中心的功能，一项特殊项目已进入计划阶段。该项目将于2016年开始实施。我们期待着，通过找回斯里兰卡文化传承的珍贵品质，建立一个更美好的社会。

我相信此次参加论坛的各国都为此有着相同的努力。各友好国家可以共同实施上面提到的这些类似项目，以加强亚洲国家的文化联系。

"文化"在增强一个国家的实力过程中，有着不可估量的作用，我们今天的论坛对于各国分享这些经验起着至关重要的作用。请允许我再次感谢中华人民共和国政府、福建省、中国国家美术学院、论坛组织方和所有参会者给予我这个机会。

谢谢大家！

非遗保护与"一带一路"建设

中国艺术研究院研究员、中央文史研究馆馆员　田　青

"一带一路"（the Belt and Road，B&R），是指"丝绸之路经济带"和"21世纪海上丝绸之路"。"一带一路"是中国政府提出的一个有创意的合作发展理念，旨在借用古代"丝绸之路"的历史符号，高举和平发展的旗帜，积极主动地发展与沿线国家的合作伙伴关系，共同打造政治互信、经济融合、文化包容的利益共同体、命运共同体和责任共同体。

"一带一路"相关国家，都有着悠久的历史文化，有着丰厚的非物质文化遗产资源。保护好这些非物质文化遗产，在今天有着特殊的意义。非物质文化遗产是人类的共同财富，是民族精神文化的重要标识，内含着民族特有的思维方式、想象力和文化意识，是一个国家一个民族文化生命的DNA。它不仅展现出世界各国人民无限丰富的创造力，而且也体现了世界文化的多样性。在全球化和现代化进程中，世界的文化生态正发生着巨大的变化，尤其是"一带一路"沿线的大多数发展中国家，其蕴涵民族精神家园的非物质文化遗产无不受到西方强势文化的猛烈冲击，面临着消亡的危险。因此，提倡并做好"一带一路"国家非物质文化遗产的保护工作就显得极为重要和迫切。

在非物质文化遗产保护方面，中国虽然起步较晚，但步子大、速度快、成果多。中国政府和社会，积累了许多被称为"中国经验"的非遗保护的方式、方法，与"一带一路"国家共享这些经验，让千百年来在"丝绸之路"和"海上丝绸之路"沿线传承至今的人类祖先的天才创造重新被重视和欣赏，让这些独特的民族文化在"现代化"的大潮中继续传承并发扬光大，是"一带一路"建设的重要内容。

文化在 21 世纪海上丝绸之路经济带建设和文明对话中的作用

科威特管理学和经济学教授、投资公司联合会秘书长　拉马丹·沙拉哈

新丝绸之路延伸大约 11000 公里（8000 英里），起点为中国上海，终点为德国首都柏林。但是项目的更新信息显示，新丝绸之路将延伸至西班牙的伊比利亚半岛。

中国国家主席习近平在 2013 年初即已提倡要振兴这条道路，2014 年又倡议启动亚洲基础设施投资银行计划，有大约 58 个国家参与这一计划，包括北大西洋公约组织（NATO）的 12 个成员国，中国为项目首期出资 470 亿美元。

"丝绸之路"名称的由来可追溯到中国的机织丝绸。约公元前 3000 年，丝绸业依赖织造、刺绣等高端技术获得了发展，丝绸成为世界其他地方颇为紧俏且价格不菲的商品。

项目涉及约 65 个国家，项目的主要目标之重要性在于推进政治关系和基础设施发展、增加商品流动、增加收益和鼓励人员交流。同时，项目对陆地运输、海洋运输和航空运输都非常重要。

本项目在全球范围和科威特国在经济上是可行的。

随着科威特经济水平的提高，我们发现丝绸之路城市项目和科威特丝绸城之间的联系。我们认为，我们基于 20 年后的战略远景，通过 5 年大型项目规划的执行助力国家的发展，包括丝绸城市群项目。该丝绸城战略性工程的地址经仔细挑选，连接穆巴拉克和新机场，使它成为海湾地区、伊朗和中亚国家的十字路口。这些足以让我们找到一个城市来协助历史上丝绸之路的邻邦，恢复科威特作为全球金融和商业中心的地位，使它成为连接东西方的十字路口。

"丝绸城"项目不仅仅是一个投资项目。该重要的战略性项目与各层次的众多项目一起实施，包括贸易、旅游、投资项目和商业发展。它已被设计成一个自由区，将为公司提供更好的设施，为地区商业的开展提供在科威特的地理优势，因为科威特是海湾地区和中亚国家的商业枢纽。

"丝绸城"项目的理念和愿景及其未来的前景在于效仿联合文化与投资的理念，这即证明，在文化的交流和传播过程中，"丝绸城"项目在过去、现在和未来都在重振"丝绸之路"精神之间有一个连接点。

突破文化孤岛，打造文化共同体

清华大学新闻与传播学院常务副院长　尹　鸿

"一带一路"思路，是借"丝绸之路"之传统、举和平发展之旗发展沿线国家的经济合作伙伴关系，共同打造政治互信、经济融合、文化包容的利益共同体、命运共同体和责任共同体。文化在其中发挥着重要作用，沟通情感、创造共信、民心相通才能路通带和。

第一，现状：应该尊重文化差异，突破孤岛现象。"一带一路"涉及东亚、中亚、西亚、北亚、南亚几十个亚洲国家和欧洲、非洲相关国家。这些广袤的区域，由于六大原因，形成了某些交流障碍，文化孤岛现象比较突出。这六大原因包括：（1）经济发展水平差异；（2）社会制度差异；（3）宗教信仰差异；（4）地缘关系差异；（5）语言文化差异；（6）东西方文化传统差异；（6）民族文化差异。

一方面是亚洲各国各地区存在不同程度的文化"孤岛现象"，另一方面欧美文化因为整体的发展水平的优势，对亚洲国家产生了越来越大的影响。亚洲国家内部出现了所谓的本土文化与外来文化的文化阶层圈子差异。

第二，策略：借助大市场的力量，发展"有文化"的商业。"一带一路"首先是贸易之路。古代丝绸之路是商品贸易之路，科学技术文化借助商品贸易得到传播。物质商品和贸易由于其实用性、必需性、轻意识形态性更加容易传播，文化应该首先借助贸易进行传播。（1）应该重视打造"有文化的商品"，如同中国古代的瓷器、茶叶，传播的不仅是物质，也包括美术、书法、生活方式、哲学观念、价值观念。（2）应该注重通过时尚、旅游、休闲、设计、工业品、工艺品的贸易，注入更多的文化元素，促进相互交流和理解。（3）应该加强文化创意设计、指导、培训，打造品牌，推动中国传统文化与现代生活的有机结合，体现具有时代感的民族性。

第三，发展：从文化交流走向文化交易，从文化产品走向文化产业。（1）通过文化交流培育市场需求，最终通过交易使文化传播效果最大化；（2）先合作产品，然后合资企业，最终出现跨国企业；（3）开掘共享文化资源、打造区域文化共同体；（4）形成商品文化、文化商品、小众文化、大众文化的文化整体链条。

第三届亚洲文化论坛论文集

分论坛中方论文

华侨华人在"一带一路"民心相通中的作用

暨南大学国际关系学院、华侨华人研究院　陈奕平

2013年9月和10月,中国国家主席习近平在访问哈萨克斯坦和印度尼西亚时,先后提出共同建设"丝绸之路经济带"和"21世纪海上丝绸之路"的战略倡议,一般简称"一带一路倡议"。中国政府提出"一带一路"战略构想,倡议通过"政策沟通、设施联通、贸易畅通、资金融通、民心相通",建构"命运共同体"。建构"命运共同体"的关键在于民心相通,而实现民心相通的基础在于人文交流、相互理解和尊重。古代丝绸之路既是商贸之路,也是人文交流之路,沿线沿岸国家共同的历史记忆和文化遗产以及互利共赢的经贸合作是"一带一路"建设的基础。如何推进人文交流与合作、促进民心相通,是摆在决策层和学界的一个重大课题。本文以海外华侨华人在中华文化传播、中国国家形象建构等方面的作用为个案,探讨"一带一路"文化交流的路径、机制和平台。

一、华侨华人在"一带一路"民心相通中的作用

目前海外华侨华人已超过6000万人,分布在全球198个国家和地区,其中在"一带一路"周边沿线地区就超过4000万。他们祖祖辈辈在当地生存发展,拥有一定的经济实力、广泛的人脉关系以及融通中外的文化优势,在"一带一路"民心相通中能发挥独特且重要的作用。

(一)传播中华文化

作为沟通中国与居住国桥梁和纽带的广大海外华侨华人,建立类型多样的社团组织,创办各种华文学校及华文媒体,创作多种类型的华文文学,开展多种华文教育活动,积极传播中华传统文化,维护、塑造中国良好的国际形象。同时,海外华侨华人还在吸收当地文化元素的基础上,发展中华文化,形成了颇具特色的海外华人文学与艺术氛围,为当地人民所乐见并接受。

海外华侨华人传承和发扬中华文化,大体表现在三个层次:一是表层的器物文化,如茶具、灯笼、对联等;二是行为文化和习俗文化,如春节、元宵节、清明节、端午节、中秋节等各种节庆,华人婚礼等;三是华侨华人身上展现的

中华传统文化价值观。①

（二）介绍中国的现实国情和发展道路

改革开放 30 多年来，中国经济飞速发展，国内生产总值年平均增长 9%，为世界所罕见。中国经济快速发展的关键在于中国的经济制度和发展道路。就中国国情和发展道路的介绍方面，中国政府开展了多方面的工作，也取得了一定成效。但是，对海外华侨华人和归侨侨眷在这方面的巨大潜能还重视不够。事实上，"海外华文媒体、华人社团、文化中心和华侨华人热心人士都在不同程度，以不同方式介绍中国的国情现状和发展模式，尤其是海外华文媒体近年来普遍增加了对中国新闻的报道，不断扩大版面和报道力度，介绍中国政治昌明、经济发展、文化繁荣、社会稳定"②。

表1.1　马来西亚华人在介绍中国方面的作用

	您的朋友、邻居或者同事是否曾经通过您了解以下有关中国的事项？	您是否曾经通过您的华人朋友、邻居或者同事了解以下有关中国的事项？
中国文化或艺术方面	72.8%	82.7%
中国经济发展和现状	46.6%	62.5%
中国政治发展和现状	38.4%	42.8%
	您的朋友、邻居或者同事是否曾经通过您了解以下有关中国的事项？	您是否曾经通过您的华人朋友、邻居或者同事了解以下有关中国的事项？
中华价值观方面（如重视教育和家庭、孝敬老人，等等）	76.8%	73.5%

笔者主持的海外问卷调查也证实了这一点。以马来西亚调查为例③，为了解马来西亚华人在介绍中国方面的作用，我们针对华人和其他族裔（主要是马来族人）分别设计了两道题目："您的朋友、邻居或者同事是否曾经通过您了解以下有关中国的事项？""您是否曾经通过您的华人朋友、邻居或者同事了解以下

---

① 陈奕平主编：《和谐与共赢：海外侨胞与中国软实力》，暨南大学出版社 2012 年版，第 192 页。
② 陈奕平主编：《和谐与共赢：海外侨胞与中国软实力》，暨南大学出版社 2012 年版，第 7 页。
③ 2011 年，笔者率领的本课题组利用在马来西亚进行学术交流的机会发放问卷，也委托马来西亚大学教授协助发放问卷，成功收回 429 份问卷，其中来自华人受访者和马来人受访者的问卷分别为 242 份和 187 份。

有关中国的事项?"从调查结果看,马来西亚华人在介绍中国文化或艺术、经济发展和现状,传播中华价值观等方面发挥了重要作用。值得注意的是,或许出于敏感性的原因,马来西亚华人在介绍中国政治发展和现状的作用稍逊。(详见表 1.1)

(三)侨务公共外交与中国外交政策的理解、支持和解释

公共外交很早就受到中国政府的重视,在当代更成为中国总体外交的重要组成部分。2009 年 7 月 17 日,胡锦涛在第十一次驻外使节会议上明确要求:中国"要加强公共外交和人文外交,开展各种形式的对外文化交流,扎实传播中华优秀文化"①。而中共十八大报告也明确指出:"我们将扎实推进公共和人文外交,维护我国海外合法权益。我们将开展同各国政党和政治组织的友好往来,加强人大、政协、地方、民间团体的对外交流,夯实国家关系发展社会基础。"②

中国发展的历史与实践表明,华侨华人是中外交流重要而不可或缺的桥梁与纽带,也是中国海外利益重要的开拓者、承载者和有力的维护者。华侨华人曾为新中国打开外交局面、化解外交僵局做出了重要贡献。比如:名闻遐迩的陈香梅女士对中美关系发展进程产生重要影响,在过去的几十年中,频繁地穿梭于中美两国之间,为促进中美友好做了许多工作;祖籍广西北流的马来西亚华人曾永森先生,在 20 世纪 70 年代开始了中马外交的"破冰之旅",为促成中马建交立下汗马功劳,被人们誉为"马来西亚的基辛格"。

二、华侨华人参与"一带一路"民心相通的路径和机制

(一)华侨华人传播中国传统文化的渠道和路径

1. 海外侨胞的行为文化、观念文化渠道

海外侨胞的行为文化和观念文化渠道,包括海外侨胞的节庆习俗以及海外侨胞的经营理念、管理模式,使中国传统文化的特殊魅力在当地社会乃至国际社会中得以展现。华侨华人遍布世界各地,所谓"有海水、有阳光的地方就有

---

① 《胡锦涛等中央领导出席第十一次驻外使节会议》,新华网,2009 年 07 月 20 日,http://news.xinhuanet.com/politics/2009-07/20/content_ 11740850_ 1. htm。
② 《十八大报告》(全文),新华网,2012 年 11 月 19 日,ttp://www. xj. xinhuanet. com/2012-11/19/c_ 113722546. htm。

华侨华人",他们是传播中华文化的使者。遍布世界各地的唐人街、中餐馆、中医诊所、华文学校、中华武馆等成为展示中华文化的重要场所和路径,而春节、中秋等节庆及华人的婚丧习俗活动,则让西方人有了"零距离接触"中华文化的机会。

2. 华社"三宝"渠道

华人社团、华文媒体和华文学校并称华社"三宝",是传承中华文化的重要平台。

春节期间,海外华侨华人社团都会举办舞龙舞狮、春节大游行、花车表演、美食节、联欢晚会等各种喜庆的活动。2010年的春节期间,在美国首都华盛顿,大华府地区同乡会协会举办的庙会吸引了众多人的目光,既有中国各地美食供品尝,也有民族舞蹈表演,而歌曲联唱、小品、戏曲、武术、民乐演奏等节目相继登场,将文艺演出的气氛推向高潮。

同时,华侨华人社团举办的活动不限于唐人街,也常常走出华人社区。之前,海外华侨华人庆祝春节,主要基于文化的无意识,是华侨华人自娱自乐的行为,或为故国怀乡,或为教育子女,基本上都在华人社区举行。随着在住在国影响力的提高,海外华侨华人为展现悠久独特的民族文化的各种庆祝活动,在春节期间,走出华人社区,走向住在国的标志性地段。

海外华文媒体人向来以传播中华文化为重要使命,成为传播中华文化的重要渠道。随着中国的崛起和国际地位的提高,海外华文媒体也进入了一个新纪元。国务院侨务办公室原副主任赵阳在2007年第四届世界华文传媒论坛闭幕式上曾说:"海外华文媒体正处在蓬勃发展期,华文媒体行业具有光明的前景。""华文传媒是传播中华文化的重要力量,是扩大中国与世界交往的文化使者。"[①]如《美南日报》关于中国内地的678篇报道中,政治类报道185条、经济类报道196条、社会类报道226条,而文化类报道71条。[②]

华文学校是海外华侨华人社会的重要支柱。自20世纪80年代以来,由于中国的国际影响增大、中国政府对华文教育的重视和海外华社对华文教育的需求,华文教育进入一个新的蓬勃发展时期。海外华文教育既为华人社会和所在国家培养了懂华语的人才,为维持和增强华人社会的民族认同和文化认同提供了重要的平台和手段,也为传承和发扬中华文化提供了重要的渠道。笔者负责的本

---

① 赵阳:《前景光明 海外华文媒体正处在蓬勃发展期》,中国侨网,2007年9月4日,http://www.chinaqw.com/zgqj/qjdt/200709/04/86285.shtml。
② 闫欢、王琳琳:《华文媒体的中国国家形象报道研究——以〈美南新闻〉大陆版块报道为例》,《新闻界》2012年第15期。

课题组走访美国、加拿大、法国、缅甸、菲律宾、马来西亚、印度尼西亚等多个国家的华文学校,亲身感受到这些学校传承中华文化的积极努力和卓越成效。比如,印度尼西亚巴厘文桥三语学校近年来几乎每年都举办春节晚会,在学校老师的组织下,英文小主持人和中文小主持人搭配得当,从幼儿园到中学的各年级学生积极参加、努力表演,舞蹈、唱歌、书法、诗朗诵、乐器表演应有尽有,而家长们也积极投入,活动更吸引当地民众观看。

3. 海外华商和华人精英渠道

海外华商也是中华文化的重要传播者。在这里,"华商"特指活跃在世界经济舞台上的海外华侨华人群体。全球华商总资产达到数万亿美元,已成为全球化时代的一股重要经济力量,既是中外经济合作的重要桥梁和推动力量,也是展现和传播中华文化的推动力量。华商独特的经营理念、管理文化其实源自中华传统文化,如:华商在企业管理中强调"诚信"、"以人为本"、"和气生财"、"勤俭节约"、"量入为出"等价值观,"对家庭和睦、增强企业凝聚力,乃至社会稳定和发展,无疑都具有积极的作用";"华人企业凭借血缘、亲缘、地缘形成了广泛的人际关系,这种人际关系网在华人企业的成长和发展中发挥着重要作用",并在此基础上逐步形成现代商务网络。① 华商活跃于国际经济舞台,不但成为我国侨务工作的重点对象,也成为世界各国发展经济争取的对象。

而海外华人精英则通过学术著作、学术活动及媒体文章等形式传播着中华文明特有的思维方式、哲学观念、道德伦理、文学艺术等文化内涵,并探讨和宣讲中华文化在推动人类文明进步中的作用。比如,作为现代新儒家学派代表人物的杜维明,长期致力于儒家文化的研究与传播,诠释中国文化、反思现代精神、倡导文明对话,在海内外享有很高的学术声誉。2013 年 2 月,在联合国"文明联盟"第五届全球论坛上,杜维明成为唯一的主题发言人,论述了"跨文化对话在我们所处时代的意义",受到绝无仅有的崇高礼遇,突显出华人学者在世界讲坛上的话语权和影响力。

(二) 中国道路和对外政策的传播渠道和路径

中华文化的传播渠道也是中国道路和对外政策的传播渠道。

首先,华侨华人的个人渠道、海外华文媒体、华文教育及华人精英的著述

---

① 陈卫平(香港安达控股国际集团董事长):《华商在中国—东盟自由贸易区建设进程中的优势》,中国侨网,2004 年 7 月 26 日,http://www.chinaqw.com/node2/node116/node119/node162/node2222/node2542/node2545/userobject6ai184523.html。

和演讲，介绍中国国情和发展模式以及中国的对外政策和侨务政策。中华民族的凝聚力是中国最大的软实力，五千年的文化传承使海外侨胞对祖（籍）国具有较强的认同感，他们对于祖（籍）国的发展及其取得的成绩感到自豪。自新中国成立以来，尤其是改革开放30多年来，海外侨胞在促进我国对外交往、协助我国开展外交工作方面发挥了重要的作用。华侨华人通过个人渠道、华文媒体、华文教育及著述和演讲向世界解释和宣传中国，成为加强沟通理解、推动友好合作的"民间大使"。

第二，华侨华人社团，尤其是定期举行的世界华商大会这类世界性的组织网络和社团活动，密切了华侨华人与中国的联系，推动了华侨华人居住国与中国的交流合作。

近年来，海外华侨华人社团逐渐走向国际化，形成了不少世界性华侨华人组织及网络。这些世界性华侨华人组织及网络不但是华侨华人贸易合作与文化交流的平台，也是密切华侨华人与祖（籍）国联系、加深对祖（籍）国了解与合作的重要渠道。成立于20世纪90年代初的世界华商大会（World Chinese Entrepreneurs Convention，WCEC）就是这样的组织，它于1991年8月在新加坡召开了首届大会。经过20余年的发展，世界华商大会已先后在新加坡、中国香港、曼谷、温哥华、墨尔本、吉隆坡、汉城（今首尔）、神户举办，规模也不断扩大，影响力与日俱增。2013年9月，第十二届世界华商大会在中国成都召开，出席大会的代表来自104个国家和地区，人数近3 000名。世界华商大会"成为世界各地华商促进经贸合作的纽带和桥梁，有效地促进了华人华商服务当地经济，推动了所在国家和地区经济的发展"[①]，也密切了华人与中国的联系，加深了对中国的了解。

三、影响华侨华人参与"一带一路"建设的因素

华侨华人在"一带一路"文化交流和国家形象建构中占有重要的地位，也起到重要的作用，但发挥海外侨胞的作用也面临着一些困难和挑战。

1. 国家间关系直接影响华侨华人生存发展。华侨华人住在国与中国之间关系友好、受挫或交恶都会影响对华态度，影响当地华侨华人的生存和发展。

2. 影响华侨华人住在国对华侨华人的政策。比如，东南亚和欧美国家对华

---

① 《世界华商大会》，新华网，2003年6月25日，http://news.xinhuanet.com/ziliao/2003-06/25/content_ 936409. htm。

侨华人的政策，影响华侨华人的生存环境；即使是东南亚国家对华侨华人的政策也不相同，华侨华人的政治地位也不一样。

3. 由于历史原因，海外华侨华人之间在不少问题上看法不同。中国大陆和台湾地区的华侨华人之间的关系会受到海峡两岸关系的影响；不同华侨华人社团之间的隔阂；老一代华侨华人与新生代华侨华人之间存在代沟和对中华文化认同上的差异。

4. 华侨与华人认同上的差异。中国政府一再强调，华侨与华人同为侨务服务对象，却有明显的政策界线区别。作为中国公民，华侨有责任维护中国国家利益，有义务为促进祖国和住在国的发展、为祖国和住在国的友好合作发挥积极的作用。而作为外国公民的华人自然应效忠属籍国，为属籍国国家利益尽责，如何把握、保持、发展与外籍华人的关系，关系到侨务工作的科学发展和可持续发展。

四、政策建议

1. 合作共赢思维：民心相通的原则

现实主义权力观强调竞争性和排他性，追求相对收益，即使欧美软实力理论也倾向从竞争性视角看待中国软实力的建构与运用①，"大部分都持一种零和观点，以消极而非积极的心态看待中国软实力的发展"②，"着眼点还是为提醒西方政府如何应对中国软实力上升可能带来的问题以及西方政府的应对之策"③。

海外侨胞在居住国的表现力、影响力是祖（籍）国感召力和影响力的重要一环，是促进民心相通的基础之一，但要发挥海外侨胞的作用，我们认为还要有共赢思维。过去，我们更多地强调华侨华人对中国在经济、科技等方面的贡献，但随着中国的强大，西方某些国家政府和民粹分子总是戴着"有色眼镜"看中国，危言耸听地渲染"中国威胁论"，华侨华人有时被诬蔑为"第五纵队"和"黄色间谍"。④ 为驳斥这样的诬蔑，消除华侨华人居住国政府和民间的顾虑，

---

① 陈奕平、范如松：《华侨华人与中国软实力：作用、机制与政策思路》，《华侨华人历史研究》2010 年第 2 期。
② ［美］约瑟夫·奈著，王缉思译：《中国软实力的兴起及其对美国的影响》，《世界经济与政治》2009 年第 6 期。
③ 方长平：《中美软实力比较及其对中国的启示》，《世界经济与政治》2007 年第 7 期。
④ 陈奕平、范如松：《华侨华人与中国软实力：作用、机制与政策思路》，《华侨华人历史研究》2010 年第 2 期。

我们应当强调作为软实力的海外华人资源的"共赢性"①,即对华侨华人、居住国和中国等多方的贡献②。同时,我们还要注意软实力话语的内外差异及国际传播内容和方式。

其实,中国政府一向强调"三个有利于"的原则,就是要在有利于海外华侨华人长期生存和发展及当地社会经济文化的发展,有利于发展我国同华侨华人住在国的友好合作关系,有利于推进我国现代化建设和祖国统一。

2. 文化认同:民心相通的基础

文化认同是一种身份认同,是对相同文化的认可,并由此产生深层次的心理积淀。通过使用相同的文化符号、遵循共同的文化理念、秉承共有的思维方式和行为规范,进而形成一种亲近感和归属感。

华人由于在住在国长期的生活过程中形成了独特的文化,华人文化为适应当地生存的需要,与中华文化有些不同,但是与中华文化同宗同源,与中华文化有无法割舍的联系。优秀的中华文化是支撑中华民族绵延发展的精神支柱,是维系海外侨胞的重要纽带。海外侨胞是中华文化的重要传承者和传播者,在推动中外友好交流、传播中华文化的积极力量、增强中华文化国际影响力等方面都扮演着重要的角色。

当然,我们应注意到如今大多数华人都已加入住在国国籍,成为住在国公民,在政治上效忠于住在国。侨务工作要尊重华人对住在国的政治认同和效忠,引导海外华人立足本地,努力促进当地社会经济的发展,增强自身在住在国的社会地位,充分融入当地社会并为住在国民众接纳。在这样的前提下,华侨华人才能更好地为中国发展及居住国和中国关系发展贡献力量。

3. 公共外交:民心相通的着力点

华侨华人推动民心相通,首先是发挥其桥梁作用。费丽莫(Marrha Finnemore)等建构主义学者曾指出:国际组织等非国家行为体在传递和扩散国际规范以及说服国家去评价国家利益目标中的功能意义③;人们在互动中建构了共有观念,观念形塑和改变国家行为体的对外政策,所以人际良性互动足以架起两

---

① 高伟浓:《软实力视野下的海外华人资源》,吉隆坡:学林书局,2010年7月,卷首语。
② 2006年在联合国首届"国际移民与发展高层对话会"上,大会明确提出的"各国政府合作营造移民自身、移民原居国、移民接纳国三方共赢"的目标已在政治层面上得到越来越多国家的认同。参见 General Assembly of United Nations, Globalization and interdependence: international migration and development, A/60/871, 18 May 2006, http://www.un.org/esa/population/migration/hld/Text/Report%20of%20the%20SG(June%2006)_English.pdf, p.5.
③ [美]玛莎·费丽莫著,袁正清译:《国际社会中的国家利益》,浙江人民出版社2001年版,第6—7页。

国间的沟通桥梁。①

　　侨务公共外交是中国特色公共外交的重要组成部分，它服务国家总体外交，是国家外交主体资源日益拓展的显著标志。侨务公共外交强调的就是以侨务工作为渠道的公共外交，它的目标是既要反映中国和中国政府的真实形象，也要注重释疑解惑、消除误解和客观传达等过程。我们认为，在当前复杂多变的国际形势下，通过华侨华人开展公共外交，促进住在国与中国的友好交往与合作，化解外交僵局，向住在国政府和民众传达和介绍真实中国，构建良好的中国国家形象，应当是当代中国外交一个富有价值的新命题，也是包括各涉侨部门和涉侨工作者的重要任务。

　4. 国家形象构建：民心相通的重点

　　国家形象建构是国家软实力建设的核心组成部分。构建良好的国家形象，是我国历届政府的重要国策。构建新型大国形象，需要社会各方面的共同努力。作为反映华人诉求、承传中华文化的喉舌，华文传媒从早期缓解华人思乡情绪，发展到现在积极参与政治选举，成为当地社会生活一股不可忽视的力量，在政坛产生了愈来愈大的影响，从而在复杂的国际政治关系和全球化的背景下，重构了华人与当地人之间的敏感和复杂的种族关系，同时在某种程度上维护了中国国家形象，促进了中国与当地国的政治关系的发展。

---

① Juyan Zhang, Exploring Rhetorie of Public Diplomacy in the Mixed-motive Situation：Using the Case of President Obama's nuclear-free world's Speech in Prague, *Place Branding and Public Diplomacy*, 2010, (6): 294.

中华文化影响世界的两种路径：不应被忽视的民间文化

厦门大学国学研究院　陈支平

近年来，随着中国改革开放的深化和国际地位的提升，人们在探寻促进中国文化对于世界文明进步有着更大影响力之道的同时，也感叹近代以来中国文化在世界文化整体格局中的式微。从文化传播史的角度来考察明清以至民国时期中国文化与世界文明的碰撞与交流，以及这种碰撞与交流的历史走向和经验教训，无疑对于我们全面客观地了解中国文化对于世界文明进步的贡献，从而以更加广阔的视野来审视明清以来中华文化与世界文化的相互影响及其历史地位，有所裨益。

迄今为止，学界对于中华文化对于世界文化的影响，习惯性地局限在上层文化即中华经典文化特别是儒家文化的对外传播史之上，而忽视了中华民间文化特别是中国东南沿海区域民间文化对于世界的传播。这种看法无疑是十分偏颇的。事实上，从明清以降，中国东南沿海区域民间文化的对外传播，已经逐渐成为中华文化对外传播的主体。

一、明代中后期至清代前期：中西文化的平等交流

我们要厘清这一问题，首先应该把中国明清时期的历史放到世界历史的发展进程中去考察。明代中后期即公元15、16世纪之后，是中国历史从"区域史"迈进"世界史"的关键时期。换句话说，明代中后期历史揭开了中国历史与世界历史相互交融的新篇章。具体地讲，在15、16世纪以前，世界上的不同地域与国家，基本上是相互隔离的，虽然有时断时续的经济与文化交流，但是这种交流尚未形成世界性不可或缺的格局，从这个意义上说，15、16世纪之前的世界各地，基本上还只是"区域"的历史。而这个"世界史"形成的时期，就是公元15世纪至18世纪，也正是中国的明代中后期。明朝是汉族地主阶级建立的最后一个王朝，它把专制主义中央集权的官僚政治推到了一个新的高度，社会经济恢复并超过宋元时代的最高水平，延续几千年的中国封建社会进入了晚期发展阶段。也是在这个时期，中世纪的欧洲发生革命性的变革，向资本主义社会转变。早期西方殖民主义势力与中国航海势力在东南亚和中国东南沿海

的相遇，使中国的历史发展进程再也不能孤立于世界历史发展之外了。这些与以前历代王朝不同的境遇，造就了明代中后期以来独特的历史地位和丰富多变的时代风貌。①

在明代中后期中国社会经济激烈变动及其与早期西方殖民主义势力的碰撞过程中，东西方之间的文化交流也不可避免地发生了前所未有的态势。虽然说，中国的文化对外传播，可以追溯到汉唐时期，但是那个时期的中国文化对外传播，主要局限在亚洲的相邻国家，对于欧洲等西方国家的影响，极其间接且相对薄弱。但是到了明代中后期，情形就不一样了。双方不仅在贸易经济上产生了直接并且带有一定对抗性的交往，而且由于西方大批耶稣会士的东来，在文化领域也产生了直接的交往。

然而遗憾的是，在我们中国的一般明史通史教科书中，人们更多谈到的是明代的科技成就是如何地吸收西方先进的思想文化与科学技术，而很少涉及中国文化也在这一国际相互碰撞的过程中向西方传播的。固然，明代中叶之后，伴随着世界地理大发现和新航路的开通，西方思想文化及科学技术，也日渐向外传播。而明代嘉靖、万历时期社会经济的发展，海外贸易所引起的传统商品扩大再生产和改革工艺的要求，迫切期待着科学技术的创新和总结。欧洲耶稣会士传来的西方科技，如天文、历算、火器铸造技术、机械原理、水利、建筑、地图测绘等，又以其新奇和实际应用刺激了讲究实学的士大夫的求知欲望。在这双重因素的交互推动下，出现了一股追求科技知识的新潮，产生了一次小型的"科学革命"②。这种思想文化与科学技术的变化，充分地体现了这一时期中国文化与西方文化直接碰撞和交融的初步成果，同时也折射出当时的中国社会，在面对新的世界格局调整的过程中，是以一种包容开放的心态来与西方的思想文化科技展开交流的。

正因为如此，尽管当时西方耶稣会士的东来，是带着宗教传教目的的。传教士对于所谓"异教徒"的文化，往往带有某种程度的蔑视心态。但是在较为开放的中国社会与文化面前，这批西方耶稣会士们敏锐地意识到中国传统文化的博大精深，很少有人用轻视的眼光来对待中国文化。由于有了这种较为平等的文化比较心态，明代后期来华的耶稣会士们，在一部分中国上层知识分子的协助下，开始较为系统地从事向欧洲译介中国古代文化经典的工作。入华耶稣会士先驱利玛窦所撰中国札记以丰富的资料，向西方"开启了一个新世界，显

---

① 陈支平：《从世界发展史的视野重新认识明代历史》，《新华文摘》2010年第18期。
② 杨国桢、陈支平：《明史新编》，人民出版社1993年版，第427—432页。

示了一个新的民族"①，成为西方世界了解"神秘东方"的重要文献。利玛窦还将"四书"译成拉丁文寄回意大利，金尼阁于1626年将"五经"译成拉丁文。意大利耶稣会士殷铎泽和葡萄牙耶稣会士郭纳爵合作，将《大学》译成拉丁文，以《中国的智慧》为名于1662年出版。1687年，柏应理、殷铎泽等人还编译了《中国之哲学家孔夫子》一书，该书在巴黎出版后，风靡西方世界。殷铎泽还翻译了《中庸》，取名《中国之政治道德学》。此外，还有巴多明的《六经注释》、钱德明的《孔子传》和《孔门弟子传略》等。到17世纪末叶，已有数十种中国经典译本在欧洲流行。法国国王路易十四还曾专门诏谕皇家印刷厂大批印制传教士从中国带回的"四书"译稿。②

在这种较为平等心态的中西文化交流与文化传播中，中国的文化在西方受到了应有的尊重。据说到了17—18世纪欧洲哲学与政治启蒙运动的时候，欧洲的一部分哲学家以及政治家和文人，一度用孔子的名字和思想来推动他们的主张。启蒙思想家在继承古希腊、罗马以来西方理性主义精神遗产，尤其是近代实证论、经验论的同时，又把眼光投向了中国，发现了在两千年前就无比清晰地阐述了他们欲发之言的伟大哲人——孔子。莱布尼茨兴奋地宣布："全人类最伟大的文化和文明，即大陆两极端的二国，欧洲及远东海岸的中国，现在是集合在一起了。我相信这是有命运的安排。"在耶稣会士从中国带回的各种知识中，没有哪一样像有关中国哲人孔子的思想那样引发欧洲知识界的热情研究与讨论，而与之相关联的对于中国的理性主义、政治制度中的文官制度、科举制度和法律的探讨，更是直接成为欧洲启蒙运动的重要灵感。在西方哲人对古老的中国制度的赞颂中，我们感受到的，其实更多是地理大发现与文艺复兴时代西方对国家—教会一统性社会秩序的怀疑。宗教改革、文艺复兴、资本主义经济、绝对主义政治，动摇了中世纪教会一统型社会结构，近代西方社会分化与危机造成的恐慌与焦虑，有意识或无意识地表现在对大中华帝国的羡慕与颂扬中。

孔子及其所代表的中国政治哲学对于欧洲启蒙运动的影响，使我们可以看到一个有趣的现象：整个18世纪所有有关中国的重要著作和西方思想文化史上的重大事件，大体上都是同步出现的。孟德斯鸠的《罗马盛衰原因论》（1734），杜赫德的《中华帝国论》（1735），伏尔泰的《中国孤儿》、《风俗论》（1756）

---

① ［意］利玛窦、［比］金尼阁著，何高济等译：《利玛窦中国札记》，"英译者序言"，广西师范大学出版社2001年版，第21页。
② 方豪：《中西交通史》（下），上海人民出版社2008年版，第725—728页；王杰、冯建辉：《欧洲启蒙主义者是如何汲取儒家思想的》，载《北京日报》2007年8月13日。

和《百科全书》的第一卷（1751），几乎是同时出版的。而使中国的哲学与知识在欧洲获得最大声誉者，有著名的伏尔泰、莱布尼茨等人。伏尔泰从儒学的"人道"、"仁爱"思想和儒家道德规范的可实践性中看到了他所寻求的理想社会的道德理论和道德经验。具有道德教化作用的孔子儒学在伏尔泰眼中，简直就是其自然神论的现实版本，所以他认为"世界上曾有过的最幸福、最可敬的时代，就是奉行孔子的律法的时代"。德国哲学家莱布尼茨惊呼："从东方的中国，竟然使我们觉醒了。"孟德斯鸠从中国的儒学中看到了伦理政治对于君主立宪的必要性。莱布尼茨甚为感叹中国哲学的内在联系和深刻思想，他强调中国文化的悠久："中国是一个大国，它在版图上不次于文明的欧洲，并且在人数上和国家的治理上远胜于文明的欧洲。在中国，在某种意义上，有一个极其令人赞佩的道德，再加上有一个哲学学说或者有一个自然神论，因其古老而受到尊敬。"同时代的法国思想家魁奈，是法国重农学派的开山鼻祖，他十分推崇孔子重农抑商、以农为本的思想，并仿行中国皇帝所行的"亲耕礼"，被誉为"欧洲的孔夫子"。以法国狄德罗和达朗拜等为代表的"百科全书派"，也试图从中国的道德理性中获取养分，他们曾经赞扬中国是世界上唯一的把政治和伦理道德相结合的国家。[①]

我们回顾历史上中国与西方的文化交流历程，不能不得出这样的结论：明代中后期以至明末清初，是中国文化对外传播的黄金时期。而这种黄金时期的出现，正是建立在明代社会应对世界变化所持有的包容开放态势的基础之上的。

二、清代中期以至民国时期：中国东南沿海地区民间文化的对外传播

研究中国文化对外传播史的学者，更多地把这种文化传播局限在以儒家学说为核心的带有意识形态意味的政治文化之上。事实上，仅仅有意识形态意义上的文化是远远不能涵盖明代中后期以来中华文化对外传播的固有面貌的。我以为，明代中国文化的对外传播，至少还应该包含一般民众的生活方式即民间文化对外传播的这一路径。

明代中后期是中国传统朝贡贸易向民间私人海上贸易变迁的重要转折时期。16世纪初叶，西方葡萄牙人、西班牙人相继东航，他们各以满剌加、吕宋为根

[①] 陈支平主编总纂：《中国国学中心·中外文化交流特展馆文本》之四《明清时期·全球格局下的文化碰撞》，国务院参事室国学中心主持编写，2014年12月。

据地，逐渐伸张势力于中国的沿海。这些欧洲人的东来，刺激了东南沿海地区商人的海上贸易活动。伴随着明代中期社会经济特别是商品市场经济的发展，中国的商人们也开始萌动着突破传统经济格局和官方朝贡贸易的限制，犯禁走出国门，投身到海上贸易的浪潮之中。于是从明代中叶以降，中国沿海海商的足迹几乎遍及东南亚各国，其中尤以日本、吕宋、暹罗、满剌加等地为当时转口贸易的重要据点。他们把内地的各种商品，其大宗者有生丝、丝织品、瓷器、白糖、果品、鹿皮以及各种日用珍玩等，运销海外，而换取大量白银以及胡椒、苏木等香料回国出售。由于当时的欧洲商人已经染指于东南亚各国及我国沿海地区，因此这一时期的海外贸易活动，实际上也是一场东西方争夺东南亚贸易权的竞争。中国的沿海商人，以积极进取应对的姿态，扩展势力于海外各地。

明代中后期不仅是中国的商人们积极进取应对"东西方碰撞交融"的时期，而且还随着这种碰撞交融的深化，中国的对外移民也形成了一种常态的趋向。我曾接触过许多福建沿海地区的民间族谱，其中记载的从明代中期开始向海外移民的资料不在少数。这里仅举一部族谱为例，就足以说明当时沿海商民向外移民的一般情景。

石狮市的《容卿蔡氏族谱》：

> 八世正晓，讳日明，生嘉靖癸亥年（1563）十月初二日，万历癸卯年（1603）十月初七日卒于吕宋。正施，讳一恕，生万历壬午年（1582）十月初三日，卒□□戊午年十月初九日，殁于吕宋。九世景道，生□□丙申年正月初一日，卒崇祯己卯年（1639）十一月初九日，在吕宋。娶永宁干氏。景辉，生万历壬辰（1592）八月初八日，卒失详，殁在吕宋。景夫，生万历乙未年（1595）二月初三日，卒□□戊辰年四月十五日，殁在吕宋。景进，生万历癸未年（1583）十一月廿六日，卒失详，殁在吕宋。十世茂甫，生万历辛卯年（1591）正月初六日，卒于吕宋□□年六月十四日。申甫，讳廷绅，号拱北，生万历庚寅年（1590）二月廿八日，卒崇祯己卯年（1639）十□月初九日，在吕宋。康甫，生万历乙巳年（1605）十二月廿一日，卒□□己卯年十一月初九日，在吕宋。实甫，生万历丙子年（1576）四月十五日，万历丁未（1607）十二月十五日卒于吕宋。觐夫，生万历乙酉年（1585）六月廿五日，卒于吕宋。懋琰，生万历癸卯年（1603）十二月初三日，卒□□己卯年十一月初九日，殁在吕宋。安甫，生万历戊申年（1608）九月十二日，卒失详，殁在吕宋。节甫，讳光宁寞，生万

历庚寅年（1590）四月廿七日，卒□□年二月廿九日，没在吕宋。□甫，讳廷梓，生万历庚戌年（1610）三月初七日，崇祯己卯年（1639）十一月初九日卒于吕宋。延甫，生万历丁丑年（1577）七月初四日，卒万历丁未年（1607）四月初六日，在吕宋。西甫，生万历己未年（1619）四月十一日，在吕宋卒，不知年月。聚甫，讳克萃，生卒失详，卒于吕宋。璋甫，生万历壬辰年（1592）正月初一日，卒在吕宋。平甫，生天启癸亥年（1623）闰十月廿六日，顺治丁酉年（1657）三月初十日卒于吕宋。十一世鸿极，生万历甲寅年（1614）十月十四日，卒吕宋。鸿嘉，生万历庚子年（1600）十二月廿二日，卒天启丁卯年（1627）二月廿二日，卒吕宋。鸿远，生万历癸巳年（1593）十月初八日，卒崇祯己卯年（1639）七月初八日，在吕宋。鸿敬，生万历壬寅年（1602）九月初八日，卒失详，殁于吕宋。鸿宪，生崇祯癸酉年（1633）十月初一日，卒失详，殁在吕宋。鸿□，讳维岳，生天启乙丑年（1625）正月片八日，卒吕宋……①

类似的记载在福建等沿海地区的民间文献中可谓不胜枚举。从以上引用的这些民间族谱记载中可以看出，这些向海外移民人数较多的家族，基本上是处于明代私人海上贸易最发达的地带，家族成员向海外移民，往往是父子辈、兄弟辈相互连带的。当1571年西班牙殖民者进抵菲律宾群岛并构建了以马尼拉城为中心的殖民据点后，积极开展与东亚各国贸易，采取吸引华商前来贸易的政策，前往菲岛的华商日渐增多，其中不少人定居下来。据当时明代福建官员的描述："我民往贩吕宋，中多无赖之徒，因而流落彼地不下万人。"② 有的记载则称这些沿海商民，"流寓土夷，筑庐舍，操佣贾杂作为生活。或娶妇长子孙者有之。人口以数万计"③。至于明代后期聚居在马尼拉的华人，据1574年西人Hernando Riquel写道："中国人每年继续扩大他们的商业，提供给我们许多物品，如糖、小麦、面粉、胡桃、葡萄干、梨、柑桔、丝绸、瓷器、铁器，以及其他我们在这个岛上所缺乏的小型物品。"④ 此外，一部分华人还从事建筑、裁缝、

---

① 石狮市的《容卿蔡氏族谱》扫描本现藏厦门大学国学研究院资料库。该族谱修撰时间不详，大约在清代后期至民国年间。石狮市原属明代福建泉州府晋江县，容卿即今石狮市灵秀镇镜内。
② 张燮：《东西洋考》卷5，《东洋列国考》，中华书局1981年版，第91页。
③ 顾炎武：《天下郡国利病书》卷93《福建三》，广雅书局光绪26年刊本，第13册。
④ Alfonso Felix, Jr., ed., *The Chinese in the Philippines*, Volume I, Manila, Bombay and New York: Solidaridad Publishing House, 1966, p. 21. （此资料由张先清教授提供，特此致谢）

印刷等各类手工劳作，一部分人则开设商铺、饭馆、药铺，行医等。①

　　这种带有家族、乡族连带关系的海外移民，必然促使他们在海外新的聚居地较多地保留着祖家的生活方式。于是，家族聚居、乡族聚居的延续，民间宗教信仰的传承，风尚习俗与方言的保存，文化教育与艺能娱乐偏好的追求，都随着一代又一代移民的言传身教，艰难存继，而得到了顽强的生命力。

　　应该特别提到的是，这些有民间自发迁移到东南亚及世界各地的华侨及其后裔们，为了在当地取得良好的社会活动空间，以及不忘家国根本的文化传承，许多人在留居国和留居地进行着华文的传播与教育。紧随近代传教士创办华文报刊的脚步，华侨群体也开始在海外创办了华文报刊。其中，由华侨独资创办、存在时间长、影响也较大的正规华文日报，要数薛有礼于 1880 年在新加坡办的《叻报》。《叻报》至 1932 年 3 月停办，存在了 52 年。"南洋第一报人"叶季允在任新加坡《叻报》主笔期间，以"惺噩生"为笔名发表了数百篇社论和评论，在《论教子弟》（1887 年 9 月 2 日）、《论诚实乃为人之本》（1887 年 10 月 12—13 日）、《论傲字为处事大病》（1887 年 10 月 14 日）、《论交友勿事戏谑》（1887 年 10 月 19 日）、《论报恩》（1887 年 10 月 29 日）等社论或评论中，叶季允十分强调对子弟的家庭道德教育，提倡人与人之间的以诚相待，倡导谦虚谨慎、以德报德等，不但向华侨华人宣传中华民族优秀的传统道德观念，同时也向当地人民传播中华民族优秀的传统道德文化。

　　在南洋地区，随着华侨长期滞留海外，移居南洋的华侨妇女开始逐年增加，且有相当一部分华侨在有了一定的经济基础后与当地妇女通婚，这些行为使南洋华侨社团的二代侨民数量不断增加。渐渐地，一些有经济实力的华侨私人聘请家庭教师教育子女，进而有子女的几户人家联合起来共用一个教师，租赁或借用一个共同的场所，最早的华侨教育机构——私塾就这样产生了。它完全仿照中国旧制建成的传统私塾，教学内容主要是儒学经典，诸如《三字经》、《千字文》、《百家姓》、"四书五经"等，数学则是珠算、尺牍等实用内容。

　　20 世纪初，海外开始出现新式华文学校，首先是普遍开办小学（初等学堂）。1902 年，中华学校于马来亚槟榔屿创立，为马来亚办新式学校之先声。1906 年，吉隆坡尊孔学校成立。与此同时，先后兴办的有越南堤岸漳闽学校和中法学校、柬埔寨新民学校、砂劳越诗巫黄乃棠垦场学校、朝鲜仁川华侨学堂、

---

①　关于早期华人在马尼拉的社会生活，见李毓中、季铁生：《图像与历史：西班牙古地图与古画呈现的菲律宾华人生活（1571—1800）》，刘序枫主编《中国海洋发展史论文集》，第九辑，台北：中央研究院人文社会科学研究中心，2005 年，第 437—477 页。

缅甸仰学中华义学和益商学校、新加坡各帮办的道南学校、端蒙学校和启发学校等。1918年6月，著名华侨领袖陈嘉庚联络养正学堂等16校总理发起筹办新加坡南洋华侨中学。陈嘉庚首先捐了3万元，在他的带领下，各帮侨领共计捐款50余万元。新加坡中华总商会召开捐款侨众大会，通过董事会组织章程，公推陈嘉庚为总理。董事会成立后，即以5万元购置小坡利民律15号陆寅杰洋楼两座，作为最初的校舍。又写信给上海江苏教育协会会长黄炎培请其代聘涂开舆为校长。1919年3月21日，南洋华侨中学正式开学，是新马地区第一间华文中学，广招南洋各地高小毕业生。该校的创立，标志着南洋华侨教育已从基础教育走向了中等教育阶段，进入了一个新的发展时期。自此之后，南洋各处不但中等学校继起设立，小学也发展得更快。

随后，新加坡华侨还带动英殖民地政府筹办了最早的高等教育机构。当时，英属马来亚以新加坡为首府，英政府起初对华侨教育抱着漠不关心、敷衍了事的态度。对历史、地理、化学等文化知识很少教授，学校教科书只教服务、公役、书记等科目。后来。美属菲律宾等地的教会学校提高很快，因此英政府所设之政府学校也不得不做了相应的改善，但与菲律宾美国人所设的学校相差甚远。英属马来亚华侨虽然有了中等学校，但就整个英属殖民地而言，尚没有与中等教育衔接的高等教育。因此，积极关注华侨教育的陈嘉庚又开始试图筹办高等学校。1918年，陈嘉庚答应捐助美国教会在英属马来亚创办大学，但他提出该所大学必须兼教中文，他所捐的10万元作为该科基金，教会校长应允了他的要求，并与其签订了付款的具体事宜。在陈嘉庚的带领下，华侨们踊跃捐款，很快就募捐了50万元。可惜由于英国政府的阻挠，未能实现。新加坡华侨真正参与创办的高等教育机构是著名的新加坡国立大学医学学院（Faculty of Medicine, National University of Singapore），这是新加坡乃至整个马来半岛最早的医学院。1904年，华侨领袖陈若锦（1859—1917）代表华侨向殖民地总督请愿，要求自创一所华侨医科学校，总督认为只要筹到所需资金，即可向殖民地立法委员会和马来联邦提出创办方案。陈若锦当即率先捐款1.2万元，并四处奔走筹款，侨商们大力支持，不久即募得9万余元。在华侨们的共同努力下，1905年7月3日，医科学校正式成立，定名为海峡殖民地及马来联邦官立医学院，开创了马来半岛医学教育的先河。后来，随着华文教育的进一步发展，闽籍华侨陈六使秉承陈嘉庚的意愿，在新加坡主持创办南洋大学，为华人历史上第一所海外大学。①

明清以来这种由民间传播于海外的一般民众生活方式及其文化传播,逐渐在海外形成了富有中国特色的文化象征。因此,我们在回顾中国以儒家经典为核心的意识形态文化在明代后期向西方传播的同时,绝不能忽视明代中后期以来一般民众生活方式即民间文化对外传播的文化作用及其意义。

三、清代中期以至民国时期:中华民间文化对外传播逐渐成为主体

综上所述,明代中后期以来中国文化对外传播具有两个层面与两种途径,即由西方传教士及中国上层知识分子翻译介绍到欧洲的以儒家经典为核心的意识形态文化,以及由沿海商民迁移海外所传播过去的一般民众生活方式的基层文化。随着时间的推移和世界文明格局的变化,这两种文化传播层面与途径,并没有殊途同归,形成合力,而是经历了不同的艰辛挣扎的发展历程。

以儒家经典为核心的意识形态文化对外传播,经历了明清易代之后,其开放的局面还继续维持了一段时间。然而到了清代中期,政府采取了较为保守封闭的对外政策,尤其是对于思想文化领域的交流,逐渐采取压制的态势。在这种保守封闭的政策之下,中国文化的对外传播,受到了一定的阻碍。更为重要的是,随着西方资本主义革命的不断胜利和工业革命的巨大成功,"欧洲中心论"的文化思维已经在西方社会牢固树立。欧洲一般的政治家和知识分子们也逐渐失去了对于中华文化的那种平等的敬畏之心,延至近代,虽然说仍然有一小部分中外学人继续从事着中国文化经典的对外翻译介绍工作,但是在绝大部分西方人士的眼里,所谓的中华文化,只能是落后民族的低等文化。尽管他们的先哲们,也许在不同的领域提及并且赞美过中国的儒家思想,然而到了这个时候,大概也没有多少人肯于承认他们的高度文明思想,跟远在东方的中国儒家文化有着什么样的瓜葛。时过境迁,从19世纪以后,中国以儒家经典为核心的意识形态文化在世界文化整体格局中的影响力大大下降,其对外传播的作用日益衰微。

反观由沿海商民迁移海外所传播过去的一般民众生活方式基层文化的这一途径,则相对地通畅一些。清代政府虽然采取了较为保守封闭的对外政策,但是对于海外贸易,一方面是相对宽容,另一方面也无法予以有效的禁止。在这

---

① 陈支平主编总纂:《中国国学中心·中外文化交流特展馆文本》之五《近代时期·欧风东渐下的文化重构》,国务院参事室国学中心主持编写,2014年12月。

种情景之下，沿海居民从事海外贸易和移民的活动一直被延续了下来。特别是在向海外移民方面，随着国际间交往的扩大和资本主义市场的网络化，其数量及所涉及的地域均比以往有所增长。到了近现代，中国东南沿海向外移民的足迹，已经深入到亚洲之外的欧洲和美洲各地，甚至于非洲。

如前所述，中国沿海商民向外移民的一个重要特征，就是能够在相当高的程度上保留和传承其在祖籍的生活方式。于是，经过数百年来中华海外移民的艰难挣扎、薪火相传、生生不息，世界各地逐渐形成了具有显著特征而又不可替代的"唐人街"、"中国城"。我们走遍世界各地的"唐人街"、"中国城"，其充满着中华文化浓郁气息的建构与特征，几乎都是一致性的。这种一致性的建构与特征，正显示了由沿海商民迁移海外所传播过去的一般民众生活方式基层文化在海外的成功传播与发展。到了20世纪上半叶，在一般西方人眼里的中华文化，基本上就是等同于分布在世界各地的"唐人街"、"中国城"了。即使是到了今天，遍布在海外各地的"唐人街"、"中国城"，依然在传播中华文化的道路上，发挥着极其重要的桥梁纽带作用。而这一重要桥梁纽带的形成与发展，是由明代社会奠基起来的。

从文化传播史的角度来考察明代社会，以往被人们所忽视的由沿海商民迁移海外所传播过去的一般民众生活方式基层文化的文化传播途径，实际上成了18世纪以后中华文化向海外传播的主流渠道。我们只要认识到这一点，那么我们对于明代历史在中国历史和世界历史上的重要地位，就不能不有了一个更加广阔的崭新体会。

从文化视角看"一带一路"建设

（摘要）

中国人民大学国际关系学院院长　方长平

"一带一路"的研究目前主要集中在经贸和安全领域，学界和舆论界从文化视角探讨的比较少。笔者拟从文化视角考察"一带一路"建设。中国外交传统在这个问题上有三种认识：第一，在"一带一路"建设乃至中国外交领域中，要注意提供公共产品。这些公共产品不仅是物质性的，更包括观念、制度等文化形态的东西，也就是说要把我们的文化、价值以公共产品形式传播到外部世界；第二，与上述观点相对，文化的本质和活力应该是它的多样性，文化不能讲一体化，越是经济一体化就越需要强调文化的多样性。因此，在"一带一路"建设中要避免讲文化一体化，尤其中国要避免讲文化传播。笔者超越了以上两种观点，认为"一带一路"建设中跨文化的沟通和人文交流确实重要，可以起到民心相通的作用。但最终结果不是某个国家文化、某个民族的文化去同化其他文化，而是在文化平等交流过程中，形成一种带有共同价值的东西，如和平、开放、平等、包容、合作、共赢等，这些东西可能也是我们自己倡导的，但它们超越了国家性和民族性，更多体现的是人类共同价值。从文化交流模式看，文化交流不要受国内"文化搭台，经济唱戏"的模式影响，文化交流有自己内在规律和自主性，不要过于强调文化交流为经济服务的功利性。

"丝绸之路"上的瓷器贸易与世界文明再生产

中国艺术研究院艺术人类学研究所所长　方李莉

一、中国瓷器贸易的世界话语

"一带一路"的国家战略让在遥远过去由于贸易在海上和陆地上产生的丝绸之路重新开始受到关注。实际上在这条路上被贩运和销售的不仅有丝绸，还有茶叶、瓷器、漆器等许多的中国制造的产品，当时的中国制品具有世界公认的优越地位。美国学者罗伯特·芬雷曾在他的书中写道："人类物质文化首度步向全球化，是在中国的主导下展开。在绝大部分的人类历史时光之中，中国的经济都为全世界最先进最发达。"① 但今天的我们，似乎忘记了我们这段历史的荣光，还忘记了在历史上，中国不仅是一个"黄色"的农业文明的国家，也是一个"蓝色"的海洋贸易非常发达的国家。

为此，本文选择"一带一路"上的中国陶瓷贸易作为主题，希望能通过讨论当年在海陆两条丝绸之路上所发生的，有关中国陶瓷贸易而带来的世界文明互动的历史，让我们重新确定中国的物质文化在世界文明再生产过程中所起的作用，以及其所占有的位置和所处的坐标。中国是世界上最早发明瓷器的国家，从东汉开始中国的瓷器走向成熟，在唐代被销售到世界各国。在一千多年的历史中，它始终居于世界文化交流的中心，是全世界最受喜爱、羡慕，也是最被广泛模仿的产品。其成为一大物质媒介，跨越遥远的距离，促成了许多不同文化间艺术象征、主题、图案的同化与传播。但是有关这样的历史却并没有受到研究者们的广泛关注，即使关注也很少从更广泛的文化政治经济的角度来进行深入的讨论。正如罗伯特·芬雷所说，瓷器是一种敏感度极高的人与事物之间的测压计，比其他任何商品都要来得敏感。因为它记录了来自种种面向的冲击，包括传统艺术手法、国际贸易、工业发展、政治纷扰、精英阶层思想、仪式礼

---

① ［美］罗伯特·芬雷（Robert Finlay）著，（中国台湾）郑明萱译：《青花瓷的故事：中国瓷的时代》，海南出版社2015年版，第16页。

俗和文化接触等。①

在国际学术界，世界的物质文化交流史越来越受到关注，如美国人类学家西敏司所写的《甜与权力》，关注的就是糖的贸易及生产是如何与早期资本主义原始积累、奴隶化生产，乃至国与国之间的政治经济关系联系在一起的，其已经成为一本世界名著被人们所阅读。而陶瓷所能牵连出的内容会更多，因为，其不仅是一种"物"，还是一种被抽象提炼和象征隐喻的符号载体，这一器物远比其他的物质产品更接近文化和艺术的境界。而且其文化功能繁多，如，想象力的运用、传统习俗的体现、社群意识认同的陈述、社会凝聚力的彰显、身份地位的载体、自我物象化的呈现、社会价值的具体表达等。因此，讨论中国陶瓷贸易所带来的世界性文化冲击，可为世界文化和艺术史的书写提供极具启发性的种种思考。

瓷器还有一项特殊之处，丝绸之路上的茶叶、香料、丝绸，走的都是单向旅程，自东而西，最后在终点处被人消费使用而难以留下踪迹。只有陶瓷，不仅历时长久，还被永远保存在博物馆和家族传承中，由此，在文化的相互影响上发挥着长久的核心作用。另外，其所呈现的世界贸易造成了艺术图像和造型的普世性冲击也是很值得我们去讨论的，而且在这样的过程中，我们还看到世界不同国家的艺术图像的不断相互影响及不断再生产的过程。如取自中国瓷器的中国艺术母题与图案，被远方社会接纳拥抱、重新组合、另加诠释，成为其他商品上面的装饰，然后作为异国风情再送回它们当初所来之处。另一方面中国陶瓷工匠经常改造异国图饰，用于自家产品，然后又由商人运送出口，使之归返几代以前这些图案的原产地。因此某一受到中国影响的纹饰版本，传到半个世界之外，被当地艺匠模仿，后者却浑然不知这项曾经给予中国灵感、而自身正在被仿效的异国文化，其实始于自家祖先。

在这里我们看到的是，不同文明的再生产，实际上是在相互获取学习资源的过程中发生的。在全球化加速发展的今天，我们越来越意识到，每个社会都是全球的组成部分，都不是孤立存在的，社会与社会之间互为发展条件，相互之间的竞争、交融、碰撞以及力量对比的关系都是推动全球发展的重要动力。这样的情景不仅存在于今天，也存在于历史上。但过去做历史研究的学者，因为过于强调在本土国家的框架内理解问题，很少做这样的跨文化的研究，也很少将研究视野扩大到整个世界，但这正是笔者最感兴趣的问题。

---

① ［美］罗伯特·芬雷（Robert Finlay）著，（中国台湾）郑明萱译：《青花瓷的故事：中国瓷的时代》，海南出版社2015年版，第16页。

另外，受进化论的影响，西方史学家们基于文艺复兴以后，对世界变局的片面认识，认定只有欧洲国家才是不断发展进步的，其他地区则处于"停滞状态"。① 这也影响到了国际学界以多元互动的视野来看待这一欧美以外的全球贸易历史，当然，近年这一研究现象已在改变，一些欧美史学者们也在将视野投向这些非西方的世界，试图以此为目标重新认识世界历史的整体面貌。

作为中国学者更应该主动关注这一研究，以重新定位在欧洲地理大发现之前，中国在世界历史中所起到的重要作用。即使是在地理大发现的近三百年的历史中，中国仍然是世界的领跑者，甚至是西方文艺复兴时期的榜样之国。本着如此的目标，本文试图探讨从中国唐代开始的一千年多年的历史中，中国是如何在与印度、波斯、阿拉伯、印度尼西亚甚至东非等文明区连为一体的"环印度洋的陶瓷贸易网络"中起到主导作用的。另外，15世纪以后，由欧美主导的"跨大西洋和太平洋的全球陶瓷贸易网络"是如何形成的，而且在这样形成的过程中，我们看到的是人类在跨越远距离的商业交换活动中是如何形成一个"世界体系"，并构成一系列交叠互动的多重经济体，一个极其复杂的交易网络。在这样复杂的网络中，中国的陶瓷贸易将欧亚大陆的极大部分串联在一起，最后又借由欧洲链接了美洲大陆，由此，中国成为这个世界体系中最重要的关键枢纽和带动这个世界体系运转的发动机。当然，这一发动机到18世纪以后逐步熄火，到今天，中国启动的"一带一路"战略还能让中国这一发动机重新点燃火花吗？这是一个非常值得思考的问题。

二、漕运开通后的中国水运

中国是世界上最早发明瓷器的国家，中国瓷器的对外贸易在东汉成熟时期也许就开始了，但真正形成一定规模、遍及亚非大陆，应该是从唐代开始的。因为只有到了唐代，中国的漕运才得以完善，并日趋发达，才能使这些瓷器得以大批量地运送到沿海的港口，再由各港口运送到旧大陆的许多国家。

中国漕运的发达，始于隋朝，完善于唐朝。隋炀帝大业元年开凿通济渠，从西苑引谷水、洛水入黄河；又引黄河通淮水，通过漕运将江淮粮秣物资运到京师。到唐肃宗时，又使长江—邗沟（邗沟是联系长江和淮河的古运河）、汴河（古运河的一段）—黄河及黄河—渭水三个交汇处转运仓的建设有所加强，并形

---

① [美]杰里·本特利、赫伯特·齐格勒著，魏凤莲译：《文明的传承与交流1000—1800年》（第5版），北京大学出版社2014年版，第5页。

成"舟车既通,商贾往来,百货杂集,航海梯山,圣神辉光,渐近贞观,永徽之盛"①的场面。

唐代的水上运输发达,促成了造船工业的发展,尤其是长江流域的江南地区造船业之盛,为全国之最。唐代造船材料,多用坚硬耐用的楠木;其次则用樟树、杉树或柯树等,所造船大致可分内河船及海洋船两类。海洋船方面,唐代远航外洋的船甚多。唐太宗时,阎立德在江西南昌造浮海大船500艘。自东海、黄海直上高丽。另一方面亦有远至红海的商船。②

正如亚当·斯密所言:"各行各业可及的市场,因水运而扩大,此为陆运所不及。所以唯有在滨海地区以及可航行内河的沿岸,各类工业才会开始进行分工与改良。"③当时的中国各瓷区,之所以能利用大量生产的技术,正是因为借由"比起尼罗河、恒河,甚至两者加起来更广的内陆航道",使中国的瓷器得以运销遍及各地的市场④。明时期曾经在中国生活过的利玛窦感叹,搭乘船舶来往,是中国一大奇妙景观:"天然河川,人工运河,这个国家的水道如此密布交错,几乎可以乘船前往任何地方。"⑤而这一切都是在隋唐时就打下的漕运基础。

如唐代出口白瓷、三彩制品和青花瓷的重要窑口巩县窑,其位置正处于洛水与黄河交汇的洛汭地带,这里曾是沟通北方大半个中国的漕运枢纽。这里溯洛水向西可达东都洛阳和京师长安;顺黄河东去,可抵郑州、开封,转入大运河向北直通华北大平原,由天津到朝鲜、日本;向南直达当时重要港埠、国内国际商贸城市扬州;再顺长江东去,可直航海外达东亚、南亚与中东地区。陆上,从巩县窑址向西南,经轩辕关即达唐代大都会东都洛阳,洛阳当时是丝绸之路的东端,成为巩县窑产品陆上输往西域和欧洲的重要通道⑥。还有当时的长沙窑生产的釉下彩瓷器远销亚非不同的国家,其地理位置处于湘江附近,其产品从湘江到洞庭湖,然后达长江进入海外。当时著名的瓷器产地越窑,更是属于明州地区,明州是当时的重要港口,可以直通海外。正是这种便利的水运交通,让中国的瓷器通过国内的人工及河流运输到达沿海港口、到达内海,然后

---

① 钱穆:《中国经济史》,北京联合出版公司2014年版,第217页。
② 钱穆:《中国经济史》,北京联合出版公司2014年版,第224页。
③ [美]罗伯特·芬雷(Robert Finlay)著,(中国台湾)郑明萱译:《青花瓷的故事:中国瓷的时代》,海南出版社2015年版,第51页。
④ 钱穆:《中国经济史》,北京联合出版公司2014年版,第217页。
⑤ Smith, Adam. 1976. *An Inquiry into the Nature and Causes of the Wealth of Nations*. 2vols. Edited by R. H. Campbell and A. K. Sinner. Oxford: Clarendon Press.
⑥ 王健华:《浅谈永宣青花瓷器的伊斯兰因素》,《中国古陶瓷研究》第4辑,紫禁城出版社1997年版。

穿过马六甲进入印度洋走向欧亚非大陆。当然，唐代除水运之外，尚有陆运，但作为易碎的瓷器，水运自然要安全便利得多。

三、繁荣的中国港口与对外贸易

唐代中国是世界上最先进的社会，唐代帝王向各方面扩展他们的统治权，扩张到朝鲜和越南（当时称安南），远及中亚的游牧部落和沙漠绿洲中的定居区。同时，唐政府非常重视对外贸易，为了管理市舶贸易，唐玄宗开元年间（713—741），政府在广州设立市舶使①，唐代其他贸易港尚有泉州、杭州及扬州等，唐之广州、扬州，其繁盛可先后媲美于今日之香港与上海。②

唐朝都城长安（今西安）成了差不多有200万人口的世界中心城市，是来自拜占庭和中东各国的商旅荟萃之地。③ 不但是当时中国，甚至亦是全世界的最大城市。④ 当时外国人所到中国著名城市很多，长安、洛阳以及沿海的扬州、明州（宁波）、泉州、交州、广州等地都已成为中外商人聚集的国际都市。

中国自古对外交通要道主要有二：一为西北陆路，二为东南海路。自汉代以来，武帝通西域，西北陆路对外交通日见发达。东汉时班超出使西域，到了地中海，接触罗马等国。中国的丝就由此时传入罗马。至于东南海路，经交州（即越南，当时属于中国）、广州等地，进入海洋。

到唐代时，海运路线得到了扩张。以从明州港出发的航线为例：从明州港出发南下，穿过台湾海峡，向东南到达菲律宾群岛。沿吕宋岛、民都洛岛、宿务岛、棉兰老岛、苏禄群岛西海岸南下，经加里曼丹岛西北海岸至爪哇、苏门答腊岛，越马六甲海峡，进入印度洋，再穿过尼科巴与安达曼两群岛，横渡孟加拉湾至印度东海岸，再从东海岸南下，经斯里兰卡后，又沿印度西海岸北上，循着大陆海岸线，一路直达波斯湾，或由席拉夫登岸，由此深入伊朗内地；或至波斯湾尽头，溯底格里斯河而上至忒息丰、阿比尔塔和萨马腊等地。一路则继续沿阿拉伯半岛南岸经阿曼至亚丁湾，或入红海北上抵达阿伊扎布或库赛尔港，在此卸货后，再向西横穿沙漠到达尼罗河，然后顺尼罗河而下最终抵达福斯塔特；或沿非洲东海岸南下，经曼达岛、吉迪，最后抵达基尔瓦岛。⑤ 唐代，

---

① 钱穆：《中国经济史》，北京联合出版公司2014年版，第228页。
② 钱穆：《中国经济史》，北京联合出版公司2014年版，第228页。
③ [美]费正清著，张理京译：《美国与中国》，世界知识出版社2003年版，第61页。
④ 钱穆：《中国经济史》，北京联合出版公司2014年版，第232页。
⑤ 冯小琦主编：《古代外销瓷器研究》，故宫出版社2013年版，第104页。

除明州港外，还有广州、泉州、扬州三个重要港口。

　　唐初商业运输及海外贸易大增，广州和泉州首度成为重要港埠。当时有人造访广州，看见"来自印度、波斯和南海等等各地的船舶无法计数，满载熏香、药材和珍品，堆积如山。"① 9 世纪以后，中国式大帆船开始主宰对印度洋的贸易，取代了印度洋开来的较小船舶，制瓷业尤其因此获利丰厚。②

　　7 世纪时阿拉伯人征服接管波斯，此时伊斯兰势力在阿拉伯世界建立根基。接下来阿拉伯穆斯林征服了伊拉克、地中海东岸、美索不达米亚、埃及以及波斯，造成西南亚贸易区全面重整，统一在伊斯兰旗下。③ 这样的统一体使这个地区变得日益强大，并以此为力量渗透到周边国家。8 世纪起，西南亚船舶开始来到广州，大批阿拉伯人和波斯人在此定居。④ 有各种外国货轮，名叫"南海舶"者，每年均驶来广州与中国进行贸易。其中以狮子国（即今斯里兰卡）的货轮为最大。船高数丈，置梯以便上下，堆积宝货如山。每有番舶到港时，郡邑为之喧阗。⑤ 可见当时的贸易，一方面是中国的商人走出去，另一方面是西南亚等地的商人也在走进来，形成一种循环的流动。

四、"物"的流动与"人"的流动

　　唐代中国面对的世界不仅是一个"物"的流动的世界，还是一个"人"的流动的世界。当时的首都——长安城尤为繁荣，犹如一块大磁铁，吸引各地杂耍人、画师、舞者、魔术师和乐师纷纷沿着驼路前来。⑥ 另外，还有叙利亚商贾、波斯教士（包括摩尼教、拜火教、景教派基督徒）、粟特工匠、犹太医生、阿拉伯珠宝商、西藏佣兵、维吾尔马商等，络绎往返行走于海上的丝路和陆地上的丝路。现在中国西北及黄河中游至广东省一带，经常发掘出波斯王朝的银

---

① ［美］罗伯特·芬雷（Robert Finlay）著，（中国台湾）郑明萱译：《青花瓷的故事：中国瓷的时代》，海南出版社 2015 年版，第 114 页。
② Hodges and Whitehouse 1983：130-32；Daryaee 2003. The historical coincidence of the creation of the Tang and Muslim regomes is stressed in Hourani 1951: 61-62.
③ ［美］罗伯特·芬雷（Robert Finlay）著，（中国台湾）郑明萱译：《青花瓷的故事：中国瓷的时代》，海南出版社 2015 年版，第 115 页。
④ ［美］罗伯特·芬雷（Robert Finlay）著，（中国台湾）郑明萱译：《青花瓷的故事：中国瓷的时代》，海南出版社 2015 年版，第 114 页。
⑤ 钱穆：《中国经济史》，北京联合出版公司 2014 年版，第 234 页。
⑥ ［美］罗伯特·芬雷（Robert Finlay）著，（中国台湾）郑明萱译：《青花瓷的故事：中国瓷的时代》，海南出版社 2015 年版，第 119 页。

币，可见当时波斯人在中国经商地之广了。① 尤其是横跨亚、欧、非三洲的阿拉伯帝国，中国称其大食国。自唐高宗永徽年间开始，大食人便从海、陆两途来华经商，出售药材、香料、珠宝等物给中国，并将中国的丝绸、瓷器、造纸术、炼丹术和养蚕织丝技术输往欧、非两洲。中国文化及产品传入欧陆，大食起了中介的作用。②

当时往返于中国的除西南亚国家的人们，还有许多周边的东亚、东南亚和南亚的人们。唐太宗时，东亚的高丽、百济及新罗三国均有派遣贵族青年来长安留学。当时中国政府特在楚州等地设立"新罗馆"，以处理两国间之商务。当时在中国扬州、涟水、诸城、牟平及文登等城市，聚居新罗人无数，称为"新罗坊"。③ 还有东南亚的骠国（今缅甸南部）、真腊（今柬埔寨）、林邑（今越南南部）及堕和罗（今泰国南部）、宗利佛誓（今苏门答腊）及诃陵（今爪哇）等国，都与中国建交并通商。他们分别把香料、珠宝、棉布、犀牛、大象等运销中国，并购买中国的丝绸、瓷器及工艺品返国。至于南亚的狮子国（今斯里兰卡）、天竺（印度）、尼婆罗（尼泊尔）及罽宾（今巴基斯坦）等国与唐朝亦有通商。④

笔者曾在美国大都会博物馆，看到许多唐代的陶俑，里面有当时生活在中国的欧洲人、阿拉伯人、波斯人，还有黑人。据说，唐代时，中国有钱人的家中，常养有"昆仑奴"，即来自非洲的黑奴，可见当时的中国是一个国际化程度非常高的国家。

陆地和海上沿途的商人们，不仅把中国的瓷器运到亚非大陆，同时，也将印度和波斯甚至北非埃及的图饰技法以及他们的图画版本传给中国。在唐以前，中国的工艺美术装饰中大多是人物、禽兽和抽象的几何纹样，很少有植物纹样。但在伊斯兰的世界和佛教的世界里，各类植物和花卉才是他们艺术表达的主题。由于商贸的流动，伊斯兰和佛教国家中律动变化、循环连续的"卷草纹"、格式化的花卉，还有自由表现的莨苕、棕榈叶、牡丹、荷花等各色花卉，都被僧侣和各式工匠模仿在无数佛窟、巨墓内，因而进入到中国艺术的主流中，同样也进入到中国的陶瓷装饰中，尤其是唐代以彩绘见长的长沙窑的装饰中。就这样，人和物的流动，也带来了艺术和文化符号的流动及融合。

---

① 钱穆：《中国经济史》，北京联合出版公司 2014 年版，第 239 页。
② 钱穆：《中国经济史》，北京联合出版公司 2014 年版，第 242 页。
③ 钱穆：《中国经济史》，北京联合出版公司 2014 年版，第 240 页。
④ 钱穆：《中国经济史》，北京联合出版公司 2014 年版，第 242 页。

五、宋代的内敛与开放并存

宋朝是中国古代历史上商品经济、文化教育、科学创新高度繁荣的时代，也是陶瓷制作的巅峰时期，当时著名的瓷窑遍布大江南北。但这个时代和唐代比较起来却是从开放走向内敛的一个时代。唐代的疆域阔大，有1200多万平方公里，而北宋只有400多万平方公里，四周被西夏、辽、吐蕃诸部和大理国所包围，到南宋更是偏安一隅。此时的中国对外具有较大的防范心理，在文化上开始产生强烈的自我认同，唐代的那种容纳整个世界的博大胸怀开始收缩。从陶瓷器的表现来看，外来的造型和纹饰开始减少，取而代之的是从本国的传统寻找文化，具有一种复古的趋势。

自宋神宗元丰以后，皇家祭祀天地开始"器用陶匏"，并正式建立官窑。以朴素的"陶匏之器"来体现古礼"尚质贵诚"的精神。其造型仿商、周、秦、汉古铜器中的各式鼎、樽、觚、尊、彝（方彝）、卣、壶、罍、瓿、盉、甗等礼器。作为皇家祭祀的礼器，其是具有宗教意味的，是祭天祭地祭祖宗的神器，陶工们制造它是充满敬意和崇拜的。中国远古时期以玉为祭器，那是因为在中国人的观念中，玉可通神灵，是日月之精华。作为复古盛行的宋代文化的主流，自然在制瓷时将追求玉的质感为最高标准。因此，不仅是官窑产品，就是当时的汝窑、哥窑、龙泉窑、景德镇窑、耀州窑等，也大多是各种类玉般的青瓷。当时的青瓷非常丰富，有天青、梅子青、粉青、蟹壳青等，还有景德镇的青白釉，这些釉质都具有玉般的质感和光泽。这种典雅的如玉般的纯净之色，体现了宋瓷的最高境界，也体现了中国人追求天趣质朴、天地人浑然一体的审美观。如果说，唐代陶瓷的特色是以异国情调为母题、充满活力的自然风格、雄浑的气质与彩绘的装饰。而宋瓷则是以中国的远古传统为根基，追求釉质温润、造型古雅、色泽纯净，体现天然质朴的神工鬼斧之美。在宋代，瓷器逐渐成为用餐、家庭装饰和文房四宝中的固定元素。经由行家的鉴赏、委制和收藏，瓷器文化被整体地纳入到上层社会的礼制与价值观中。在文人士大夫眼中，它代表文雅、教养，集道家隐者的节制寡欲与儒家恂恂君子的谦朴内敛于一身。

尽管宋代实行的是内敛型文化，但朝廷却仍然非常重视海外贸易。北宋初年朝廷就在杭州设立两浙路市舶司，以辖管杭州、明州的市舶事务。太宗端拱二年（989）规定："自今商旅出海外番国贩易者，须于两浙市舶司陈牒，请官给券以行，违者没入其宝货。"① 宋元祐二年（1087），又在泉州设立市舶司，嗣后又设来远驿，以接待贡使和外商。直到北宋，广州仍然是我国最大的港口。当时的主要港口除杭州、明州、泉州外，还有广州港。从唐代起，广州就设立了市舶使，宋代又设立了市舶司，负责掌管海外商舶贸易。

此时的国际海路，有许多中国商人参与，他们和阿拉伯人一起，成为中国与印度洋两地贸易的主导者。此刻来自各地多元族裔的穆斯林商人：埃及、阿拉伯、波斯、东非、印度、东南亚，与中国商人并非两个完全独立不属的类别，因为在这些中国商人中也有人信奉伊斯兰教，而穆斯林商人也有家庭世居中国；两者都对海上运输贸易采取积极主动的态度。考古学家在波斯湾多处港口发现的中国铜币，便多由抵达此间的中国商船载运而来，船主则是居于中国沿海城市的穆斯林商人。② 此时穆斯林商人的陶瓷贸易规模得到了进一步发展，商人们将中国商品带到瑟罗夫与邻近港口，货物由这里转为陆运，通过扎格罗斯山脉，抵达波斯法尔斯与克尔曼两省的城镇。船只向北再行350公里，到达更远的巴斯拉，此城位于底格里斯河和幼发拉底河的三角洲，之后，再通往哈里发王国的其他大城。③ 近年来，在这些城市都发现一些宋代瓷器碎片，并在萨马拉宫及后宫废墟发掘出土了一些餐具和香瓶。

到南宋女真建立的金国征服北中国，结束了宋王朝的第一阶段。接下来金国又击败契丹辽国，几乎切断了宋帝国与中亚的所有接触④，从1126年至1279年蒙古灭宋为止，中国君主只能从长江之南、位于浙江杭州的临时国都，治理他们残存的帝国疆域，统治面积仅余原有中土的三分之二。北方强权横亘阻绝，丝路不再可及，南宋毅然转身，迎向海洋。

正因为如此，整个宋代的出口瓷生产也都转向了沿海一带。唐代的出口贸易瓷，不仅限于沿海一带，还有许多内地窑口，如长沙窑、巩县窑等都参与做出口瓷。但到宋代以后，虽然是大江南北名窑遍布，但出口贸易瓷的生产主要转移到了沿海一带。近年来，在沿海一带，发现了许多宋元时期的沉船的遗址，在这些遗址中我们看到当时出口的产品主要有龙泉窑的青瓷，景德镇的青白瓷，福建建窑的黑瓷，福建德化、广东潮州等仿景德镇的青白瓷等。白礁一号沉船

---

① 《宋会要辑稿·职官》四四。
② So, Billy K. L. 2000. *Prosperity, Region, and Institutions in Maritime China: the south Fukien Pattern*, 946-1368. Cambridge, MA: Harvard University Asia Center. 108-111.
③ ［美］罗伯特·芬雷（Robert Finlay）著，（中国台湾）郑明萱译：《青花瓷的故事：中国瓷的时代》，海南出版社2015年版，第105页。
④ Mote, Frederick W. 1999. Imperial China, 900-1800. Cambridge, MA: Harvard University. 49-71.

遗址出水了一批陶瓷器，大多数是黑釉盏。①1987年在广东台山县川山群岛附近海域发现一艘古代沉船，命名为"南海一号"，已出水完整和可复原的陶瓷器4500余件，分别来自景德镇窑、龙泉窑和福建地区与外销瓷密切相关的诸多窑口，如德化窑、磁灶窑等②；"华光礁一号"沉船遗址位于西沙群岛华光礁西北部，是一处南宋中晚期的沉船遗址③，共采集和出水万余件瓷器。这些瓷器大部分来自福建的各民间窑口，其中的青白瓷器主要是景德镇窑的产品，青黄釉瓷器属龙泉窑。④从这些水下考古发掘的瓷器我们可以看到，宋代中国的外销瓷生产主要是集中在江西、浙江、福建、广东。福建和广东就在沿海，而江西和浙江都可以通过福建入海。如福建东北部与浙江、江西接壤，龙泉窑主要产区的大窑窑区，经过很短的陆路，即可进入闽江水系的上游，景德镇属信江水系，与闽江水系的上游邻近，可经过一段较短的陆路转入闽江，顺江而下出闽江口入海。这样的交通，导致处于福建省的泉州港迅速崛起，成为一座国际性的重要贸易港口。

六、黄色的陆路与蓝色的海路并存

如果说，唐代是中国瓷器出口贸易的第一次高峰，到14世纪初期，在由蒙古人建立的元政府的推动下，中国的对外陶瓷贸易就进入了第二次高峰。之所以如此，是因为当时的蒙古人建立了世界上绝无仅有的最大的帝国，它从东方的朝鲜和中国一直扩展到西方的俄罗斯和匈牙利。蒙古帝国的这种国际规模，使它可与引起文化和制度大混合的欧洲扩张相比。⑤

从11世纪到15世纪，突厥和蒙古民族的帝国扩张行动在欧亚土地上建立了前所未有的紧密联系。通过促进前所未有的规模上的跨文化交流和交换，游牧帝国将整个东半球大部分地区各民族的生活和各个社会的经验融为一体⑥，并把

---

① 栗建安：《福建古窑址考古概述》，《福建历史文化与博物馆学研究》，福建教育出版社1993年版。
② 冯小琦主编：《古代外销瓷器研究》，故宫出版社2013年版，第42页。
③ 栗建安：《西沙群岛水下考古调查发现陶瓷器的相关问题》，《西沙水下考古1998—1999》，科学出版社2006年版，第269页。
④ 冯小琦主编：《古代外销瓷器研究》，故宫出版社2013年版，第43页。
⑤ [美]费正清、张理京译：《美国与中国》，世界知识出版社2003年版，第85页。
⑥ [美]杰里·本特利、赫伯特·齐格勒著，魏凤莲译：《新全球史：文明的传承与交流1000—1800年》，北京大学出版社2014年版，第6页。

蒙古人的控制扩大到东至中国、西至波斯的地区。①

正是因为这样的强国崛起，使欧亚大陆成为一个安全的商业通道，即便是个人也有能力穿越整个欧亚大陆，当年的马可·波罗和他的父亲、叔父就是如此以步行往返于欧洲与中国之间的陆地，于是，中国和西欧这样遥远的土地第一次被直接联系在一起。远距离贸易的影响超越了东非沿海地区，进入了内陆。②

在元代不仅是水路交通，就是陆路交通也开始繁盛起来。由陆路运载瓷器销往国外自然不如海路方便和平稳，但仍然有商人走。有关这方面的文献曾记载："余于京师，见北馆伴口夫装车，其高至三丈余，皆鞑靼、女真诸部及天方诸国贡夷旧装所载。他物不论，即以瓷器一项，多至数十车。余初怪其轻脆，何以陆万里？即细叩之，则初买时，每一器内纳沙土及豆麦少许，叠数十个，辄牢缚成一片，置之湿地，频洒以水。久之，则豆麦生芽，缠绕加固，试投之牢确之地，不破损者，始以登车，临装驾时，又从车上掷下数番，其坚韧如故者，始载以往，其价比常加十倍。"③

虽然元代的陆路安全畅通，瓷器的运输也有不少走陆路者，但海陆还是更安全快捷，所以元代大量的陶瓷贸易还是沿着唐宋时期的海道在进行。近年有关元时期的沉船遗址也不断被发现，"北礁一号"沉船遗物点、"北礁三号"沉船遗物点、"大连一号"沉船遗物点等，都发现了大量当时运往海外的中国瓷器。

七、世界图像符号的交流与互动

元代的出口瓷中，最为引人注目的就是景德镇的青花瓷。在元以前景德镇生产的是青白瓷，而不是青花瓷，但到元以后却出现了青花瓷这一新的品种。这一品种从一开始就不是为中国人所制造，而是为了伊斯兰世界所制造的外销瓷。从15世纪到15世纪中期，中国最重要的港口是泉州。居住在中国的穆斯林人，特别是住在泉州的、以富裕而著称的波斯人和阿拉伯人无所不具，商业上的交易，促进了这些富商和中国艺人们的交往。于是，对中国古瓷颇感兴趣的

---

① [美]杰里·本特利、赫伯特·齐格勒著，魏凤莲译：《新全球史：文明的传承与交流 1000—1800 年》，北京大学出版社 2014 年版，第 6 页。
② [美]杰里·本特利、赫伯特·齐格勒著，魏凤莲译：《新全球史：文明的传承与交流 1000—1800 年》，北京大学出版社 2014 年版，第 47 页。
③ （明）《万历野获编》卷三〇。

伊斯兰国家——波斯和叙利亚商人把伊斯兰国家生产的钴蓝料介绍给景德镇的陶工，并向他们定购大量的青花瓷，这些商人不仅为景德镇的工匠们提供了促使元青花瓷出现的装饰上的材料，同时，也为这些青花瓷的生产提供了广阔的市场。

青花瓷的出现在中国的陶瓷史上是一个重要的事件，因为在这之前，虽然出现过唐代长沙窑的釉下彩瓷、宋代磁州窑、吉州窑的铁锈花彩瓷，但这些彩瓷都不是中国瓷器装饰的主流。从东汉到魏晋南北朝直到唐宋以前，中国的瓷器装饰主要还是以一道釉的素瓷为主。自从青花瓷出现以后，这样的局面得以改变，中国自此进入了彩瓷时期。所谓的彩瓷，就是在瓷器上出现了用毛笔绘制的有具体的装饰主题的绘画及图案。这些绘画和图案，不仅丰富了陶瓷器的装饰内容，而且还导致了一场世界性的图像大交流的产生。

在穆斯林的宗教文化中，一直反对描绘人类、动物或任何生命，因为在穆斯林眼中，只有安拉可以创造生命，艺术家绝不允许模仿安拉。因此，在清真寺的壁砖、地砖上，到处可见的是《古兰经》经文穿梭在生命树枝丫之间，文字交互整合于错综深邃的植物迷宫之内，非常富有装饰性。人们走进穆斯林的清真寺，到处都是装饰性的图案和文字，墙壁和天花板上到处都绘满了各色植物，颜色十分丰富耀眼，使得来访者感到自己仿佛走进了一个到处充满鲜花的豪华花园。除清真寺的装饰外，波斯的地毯也很有自己的风格，所有的空间都被图案挤满而不留空隙，而且一道道的花边图案非常华丽。这样的装饰手段被波斯的商人们带到了中国的景德镇，被描绘在由景德镇生产的青花瓷上。于是，在元青花瓷上出现了类似清真寺和波斯地毯的装饰，这种装饰的特点是，中间一个大圆饰，然后盘子的四围以纵轴向外四散，有时多达六层，彼此精细叠加。中间的主图描绘一株盛放的花树或中式的孔雀、鸭禽、荷花等图像，还常常巧妙借用植物图案，诸如点点的花瓣、起伏的枝茎，构成这些禽鸟的外形轮廓，令这些图像几乎融于整体花样之中，于是一种崭新的装饰风格得以呈现。中国元以前的彩绘瓷，普遍都比较疏朗，留白较多，且写意手法居多。但新产生的元青花瓷，以一种伊斯兰式的标准手法，将中式动植物造像予以扁平化、抽象化，得以无尽连续重复，几乎看不到留白。

而且这类的表现手法，发展到16世纪以后，深受欧洲人的喜爱，大多出口到欧洲的瓷盘，都是在典型的伊斯兰装饰的方形、菱形、条纹形、重叠交错的圆形、辐射多边形、榫接六角形、太阳光芒、四瓣式花卉、星状格纹等等几何图案中，装饰上中式的主题绘画，如佛教的吉祥图案，如菩提树、宝伞、法轮和法螺等，还有牡丹、荷花、松竹梅、假山、玲珑石、孔雀、牡鹿、野生羊、鹰隼等，形成了一种被欧洲人称之为"克拉克瓷"的图式而风靡欧洲乃至全球。

当时，不仅是穆斯林的图案装饰进入了中国的瓷器系统中，其玻璃和金属器皿也来到了中国的瓷器系统中。早在唐代，波斯的饰有鸡首的银壶就翩翩地到达中国（也有可能来自地中海东岸），中国的陶瓷工匠们依样制作，遂使此物大为流行，蔚为时尚。还有西南亚的香客随身带的水壶，被称为"军持"，这是从印度梵语音译过来的，在印度化时代曾盛行于东南亚，到了伊斯兰化时代，成为伊斯兰教徒惯用器物①，是佛教僧侣和伊斯兰教穆斯林随身携带用于贮水、饮用和净水的器物。中国陶瓷工匠将它们转为瓷制品，在这些地区流传。还有诸如大肚深腹的罐瓮、带边柄的大口水壶、弧形喷嘴、大啤酒杯、鱼筐、脸盆架、葫芦形瓶、玫瑰水喷头、穿带壶、大型矩瓶、深碟，等等，这些都是中国陶瓷工匠模仿埃及、叙利亚与波斯等地的金属器造型，这些样本有些是穆斯林商人特意送往中国以供参考，有的是由泉州、广州当地穆斯林家庭提供的。②

文明与文明间的学习常常是迂回反转的。不同国家和民族之间常常在几百年间的彼此影响中，又回到原地。如，到 11 世纪波斯的商人又将唐版的鸡首瓷壶回销到西南亚，那里陶匠或金属匠忘记了这曾是他们老祖宗的东西，纷纷起而仿效。还有一些中式的植物纹饰，原也是唐代由波斯传入的直系嫡裔，经过几个世纪以后又沿着丝路回传，在伊尔汗王朝境内扎根。几世纪间经过改装，被凡事都崇尚中国的伊斯兰上流社会，将其改造得更上层楼，让受波斯卷草纹影响的中式的缠枝莲图案处处绽放，不断再现于织毯、金属器、灰泥壁、书籍装帧、屋瓦墙砖和陶器上。

受伊斯兰文化影响的中国青花瓷，发展到 15 世纪已经非常成熟，并成为埃及、叙利亚与波斯陶工模仿的对象。任何的模仿都不会是机械的模仿，这些伊斯兰国家的陶工们，慢慢地采取了更自由、解放的律动和空间感，他们的图案逐渐开放，融进中式特有的某些生命力与自发性。而在中国方面，则采纳了伊斯兰构图元素，诸如带状纹饰以及更严整的空间规范。他们也变得擅长使用西南亚式的空间组织脉络，传递自身的视觉语汇风格。③ 如此制作出来的青花瓷，由于穆斯林文化的影响形成了中国文化以往所无的新元素，成就了一种新的魅力，这种魅力无论在伊斯兰之地或在全世界都令人无法抵挡，最终风靡世界。

---

① 韩槐准：《军持之研究》，《南洋学报》第 6 卷第一辑。
② Bailey, Gauvin Alexander. 1996a. *The Response II: Transformation of Chinese Porcelain Production and Trade with Iran*. In Golombek, 57-108.
③ ［美］罗伯特·芬雷（Robert Finlay）著，（中国台湾）郑明萱译：《青花瓷的故事：中国瓷的时代》，海南出版社 2015 年版，第 198 页。

八、中华文明威临四海

明代结束了元代蒙古族的统治，曾一度被蒙古统治者所荒疏的儒学传统又开始回到中国文化的中心，一方面是皇家学院和地方学府对儒学的发展提供财政支持，开始编撰《四库全书》等儒学典籍，另一方面还在开始恢复被蒙古统治者荒废了的科举考试体系。

在儒家统治阶级眼中，泱泱华夏最重要的是以文明教化为己任，向域外输出它的文字、典章、衣冠、律令、官制、经典，以及丝绸、绘画和瓷器等。在这所有的输出品中，重要的不是物，而是文化，即使是物，也是承载了文化的物。正是这些承载了文化的物，为中国这个"中央或中央之国"建立了它的古制、先贤与圣典等文化价值观所体现出的文明形象，将自己的文化传扬给其他国家。而那些教化程度较低的四方之民，则以进贡的方式向天子表示臣服感戴。自汉唐代开始，中国就是世界经济的发电厂，因此自古以来即以"中"国自居，亦即世界的轴心。[①] 事实是如此，自汉唐以来，以中国为中心，周边环绕着许多小国，还有那些遥远的西南亚、西亚、北非、东非、欧洲等"蛮戎夷狄"，都在通过文化和物质的流通领受着中国分赐的福祉。

到明代的永乐年间，皇帝为了威临四海，重组"中央之国"与更广大世界之间的关系，采取了一个当时看来非常大胆的作为，即任命卓有战功的太监郑和率领一支317艘船、28000人的舰队出洋，1405年由中国出发。这样的气势在当时来讲可以说是绝无仅有、所向披靡的。

在中国的历史上，将这一行为称之为"郑和下西洋"。这个巨大出行任务一共有7次，从1405年开始到1433年最后一次归国（已是宣德皇帝在位），一共花了28年的时间，时间跨越了整整一代人。永乐皇帝利用海上势力宣扬国威的方式，打破了古代中华帝国只是被动等待各国来朝贡的传统政策，第一次也是最后一次，试图主动涵纳、指挥蓝色中国的海上事业。[②]

郑和宝船浩浩荡荡驶入各国港口的景象，每每令当地人印象深刻，叹为观止。只见大帆染成棕红，船栏上黄色彩帜鲜明，船身漆着巨大的白色海鸟，桅杆高耸入云。然后数千军士开步下船，搭建起强固栈仓。根据郑和旗下穆斯林

---

① ［美］罗伯特·芬雷（Robert Finlay）著，（中国台湾）郑明萱译：《青花瓷的故事：中国瓷的时代》，海南出版社2015年版，第198页。
② Chen Ching-kuang. *Sea Creatures on Ming Imperial Porcelains*. In Scott. 1993. pp. 13-32.

通译官马欢所著的《瀛涯胜览》我们可以看到：大明皇帝使者所到之处，"蛮魁酋长争相迎"。①

15世纪埃及名史家巴耳迪记载："圣地麦加有消息传到（开罗），中国开来了许多大帆船抵达印度港口，其中有两艘停泊在亚丁湾。"② 当时，急于与中国做生意的苏丹，允许中国船进入吉达，这是红海距麦加最近的港口。

在前三次的航海中，郑和率领他的船队到达了东南亚、印度和锡兰。第四次航行到达波斯湾和阿拉伯半岛，而此后的探察冒险沿着东非海岸南下，造访了一些港口城市，最南到达现在肯尼亚的马林迪。在整个旅行过程中，郑和慷慨地把中国丝绸、瓷器和其他商品作为礼物散发出去。其目的并不是为了贸易，而只是为了确立中国人在印度洋地区的地位。单单为了其中某次出航，朝廷就吩咐景德镇烧造了443500件瓷器。如果七次出航次次都携有相同数量，表示1405年至1433年之间，共有高达3104500件瓷器随同三宝太监远赴东南亚群岛和印度洋沿岸的国家。③

在中国的历史中，商业从来都是所有行业里的末业，而以政府形象出行的船队自然是把贸易看成了最不重要的部分，其政治性远远超出其商品性。也许正是这一原因，自永乐皇帝以后，中国政府再也没有组织过如此庞大的船队出海，因为国库没有能力去支持这么奢华而没有收入的政治宣传活动。

在郑和下西洋以后的半个多世纪以后，处于欧洲伊比利亚半岛的葡萄牙和西班牙，开始了欧洲的地理大发现。但他们的船队与郑和的船队相比只是小巫见大巫，葡萄牙达·伽马于1497年率领的船队，只有四只船140位水手，而麦哲伦环球航海的船队只有五只船，但是他们却开拓了整个人类社会发展的现代史，让欧洲一跃成为世界最发达的地区，而中国却错失了这一良机。

九、地理大发现与全球物质交换

尽管从唐代开始，中国的瓷器就在欧亚非旧大陆上贸易和流通，但在这之前，并未踏进美洲大陆还有大洋洲群岛，即使在欧亚非大陆，由于欧洲的路途遥远，中国的瓷器从未真正满足过欧洲人的需求。但自15世纪末到16世纪，这

---

① （明）马欢著《瀛涯胜览》，海洋出版社2005年版。
② ［美］罗伯特·芬雷（Robert Finlay）著，（中国台湾）郑明萱译：《青花瓷的故事：中国瓷的时代》，海南出版社2015年版，第252页。
③ ［美］罗伯特·芬雷（Robert Finlay）著，（中国台湾）郑明萱译：《青花瓷的故事：中国瓷的时代》，海南出版社2015年版，第252页。

一切都得到了彻底的改变。

这一改变是由欧洲的地理大发现开始的，1497 圣诞节前夕，葡萄牙航海家达·伽马率领的船队终于闯出了惊涛骇浪的海域，绕过了好望角驶进了西印度洋的非洲海岸。

1498 年 5 月 20 日到达印度南部大商港卡利卡特。这意味着其只要穿过马六甲海峡就可以进入中国南海，直接登陆中国进行贸易。这也意味着中国和欧洲的遥遥相望的历史结束了，这两个强劲地区的人们终于可以面对面地交流和贸易了。

还有一条航线是由西班牙航海家哥伦开辟的，他从 1492 年开始，四次横渡大西洋，到达了美洲大陆。他的后来者，西班牙航海家麦哲伦，又从 1519 年 10 月开始，花了一年的时间，到达美洲大陆，穿过南美洲大陆南端和火地岛之间沟通大西洋和太平洋的海峡（后来被命名为麦哲伦海峡），由大西洋进入了太平洋，这是欧洲人以往未知的海域。1521 年 3 月，船队到达了菲律宾，在菲律宾的不远之处就是台湾，以台湾为跳板，很容易可以到达中国沿海的泉州、厦门等港口，与中国进行贸易。

这些新的交通网络联接了印度洋、大西洋和太平洋，欧洲的水手们通过不断的探险，终于寻找到了通往亚洲市场的新航路，并建立了联接世界各大洋的贸易路线，开始和世界各地的人做生意。新航路不仅促进了欧洲与撒哈拉以南非洲以及亚洲的直接联系，而且便利了东西半球以及大洋洲之间的互动。

也就是在大约 1500 年至 1800 年间，世界各地区之间建立了广泛的联系，从而把人们带入了世界近代历史的早期阶段。① 欧洲的商人利用这些新航路的便利创立了真正的世界经济体系，农产品、手工业品以及其他各种商品，包括瓷器都可以到达遥远的异地市场。从 1500 年至 1800 年欧洲人虽然征服了菲律宾和许多印度尼西亚岛屿，在全球化进程中获得了最多利益，但这绝不能证明他们是近代早期世界事务的主宰者。因为面对强大的政权，如中国、印度、西南亚和安纳托利亚，甚至岛国日本，他们都毫无威慑力可言。②

但无论如何，欧洲人"终于将马可·波罗所形容的富饶中国，以及那里数

---

① ［美］杰里·本特利、赫伯特·齐格勒著，魏凤莲译：《新全球史文明的传承与交流（1000—1800 年）》，北京大学出版社 2014 年版，第 172 页。
② ［美］杰里·本特利、赫伯特·齐格勒著，魏凤莲译：《新全球史文明的传承与交流（1000—1800 年）》，北京大学出版社 2014 年版，第 173 页。

不清的新奇事物，拉到唾手可及的近距离内"。① 世界上其他地区的民族也在探索着更广阔的世界，然而只有欧洲人把东、西半球和大洋洲的土地与人民联系在一起，是欧洲的地理大发现决定性地改变了世界力量的平衡。

在大西洋和太平洋之间的美洲新大陆的发现，以及绕经好望角前往印度航线的成功，将"寰宇"的范围推向全球规模。世界各地的人都开始身陷与日俱增的交换活动，包括商业、科技和智识。"寰宇"的范围转型扩大，其中一项影响的后果便是亚洲商品可在欧美两洲取得。这是有史以来第一次，瓷器成为一项真正具有世界性身份的商品。所谓物质文化的"全球化现象"。② 自此时开始，中国瓷器的纹饰、色彩和形制，得到了真正的全球化式的首场展示。因为16世纪之前，中国瓷器虽然大量销往亚非大陆，但却很少现身欧洲，屈指可数的几件珍品受到物主高度爱惜。因此，1497年，当达·伽马自葡萄牙出发，展开他绕过非洲前往印度的划时代之旅时，葡萄牙王曼努埃尔一世千叮万嘱，交代他务必带回两样西方最渴求的物事：一是香料，二是瓷器。③

1514—1516年间，葡萄牙大帆船第一次在广东沿海靠岸，自1540年起出现于福建，1542年之后靠泊日本。1543年，西班牙人到达东亚诸海，1553年葡萄牙人取得澳门居住权。从那时开始，欧洲人终于可以直接从中国人那里得到他们梦寐以求的、美丽的青花瓷器。

当时欧洲正值文艺复兴时期，伟大的文化和思想的革命运动需要来自方方面面的启蒙和文化资源，欧洲遥望着东方的伟大帝国——中国，充满着想象与向往：国家盛行读书、讲究礼教人伦，让中国成为欧洲向前发展可以参照的一个先进标杆。但在16、17世纪交通的不便、文字语言的不通，使东西方的相互了解充满了神秘的猜测。当16世纪中国大量美丽的青花瓷开始输入到欧洲，装饰着美丽花草图案和木刻版画中的戏曲故事的青花瓷，使欧洲人对中国这一遥远的国度有了更直观的形象认知。所以欧洲人说，青花瓷是中国送给欧洲文艺复兴的最好的礼物。

---

① ［美］罗伯特·芬雷（Robert Finlay）著，（中国台湾）郑明萱译：《青花瓷的故事：中国瓷的时代》，海南出版社2015年版，第16页。
② ［美］罗伯特·芬雷（Robert Finlay）著，（中国台湾）郑明萱译：《青花瓷的故事：中国瓷的时代》，海南出版社2015年版，第16页。
③ ［美］罗伯特·芬雷（Robert Finlay）著，（中国台湾）郑明萱译：《青花瓷的故事：中国瓷的时代》，海南出版社2015年版，第5页。

十、全球化陶瓷贸易的首次登场

葡萄牙和西班牙由于航海上的优势,使他们在地理大发现的早期成为世界贸易中的佼佼者,葡萄牙人占领了澳门,以那里为据点与中国做瓷器生意,并固定在印度转口装船,一次载运瓷器高达6万件。其与中国建立直接贸易关系之后,每艘船装上20万件瓷器更成常态。①

16世纪晚期,其他国家的投资人开始组织自己的探险队去开拓亚洲市场。跟随葡萄牙进入印度洋的国家中,荷兰和英国最为出色。英国和荷兰的实业家们开始建立起了全球性的商业网络,英国商人集中在印度,在孟买、马德拉斯和加尔各答建立商埠;而荷兰则广泛活跃在开普敦、科伦坡和巴达维亚(现在爪哇岛上的雅加达)建立商埠。比起葡萄牙及西班牙前辈,英国和荷兰的商人有更快捷、更廉价、装备更强劲的船只,使其在经济上和军事上都有竞争优势。英国及荷兰的商人们很快就取代葡萄牙及西班牙的海上霸主地位。

在17世纪初,英国和荷兰商人组织了两个非常强大的股份公司,即英国东印度公司和荷兰东印度公司。个体商人募集的基金支持了公司的启动,亚为公司装配船只和海员,提供贸易所需的商品和资金。虽然有政府的支持,公司仍然是私人所有的企业。政治上畅通无阻使公司代理人可集中精力于有利可图的贸易。②

如果翻开中国的陶瓷外销史,我们可以看到自明万历天启以后,荷兰殖民者步葡萄牙、西班牙后尘,大搞贩卖中国瓷器的行当,他们以印尼的巴达维亚(雅加达)为据点,在中国沿海一带采购瓷器,或者由中国船舶将瓷器直接运到巴达维亚,再由东印度公司转运到东南亚各国及西亚、荷兰本国。数量之巨,出人意料。1602年—1644年,荷兰东印度公司贩运到印尼各岛的明瓷总额在42万件以上。仅1636年一年里,从巴达维亚运到爪哇万丹齐里彭、亚帕拉、第加尔、贝加龙干、桑丹、答里、安汶、苏门答腊詹卑、英德拉哥里、西巴里巨港、苏门答腊西海岸和亚齐、婆罗洲、苏加丹那、马塔甫拉和文郎马神等地的瓷器,

---

① Information on porcelan exports is taken from Ho 1994: 37; Deng 1997a: 276 and 1999: 60; Young 1999: 74; Godden 1982: 57, 60 – 62; Jörg 1982: 93, 149; Volker 1954: 226 – 28; Wästfelt, Gyllensvard, and Weibull 1990: 27; Clunas 1987: 16.

② [美] 杰里·本特利、赫伯特·齐格勒著,魏凤莲译:《新全球史文明的传承与交流(1000—1800年)》,北京大学出版社2014年版,第193页。

总数约达 38 万件，荷兰东印度公司还根据东南亚的需要向中国订购瓷器。①

当时的英属印度公司也不遑多让，在伦敦仓库储放了大量存货。十年之后，一艘英属东印度公司的船只，载走高达 40 吨（约等于 50 万件），1721 年又有 4 艘船各载了 21 万件。根据当年一份销货单显示，1732 年某艘瑞典商船一口气运了约 50 万件中国瓷回航。另一艘瑞典船"歌德堡号"更厉害，1745 年装了 70 万件，连同丝绸、茶叶、藤器、珠母贝和香料等，来回航期足足 2 年，全程 4 万公里，却不幸在母港歌德堡近在眼前的距离处沉没，惊传一时。1777 至 1778 年的航季期间，荷属、英属连同其他欧洲各国的东印度公司，总共 22 艘船舰，从广州运走了 697 吨，约合 870 万件瓷器。

当时的欧洲人到中国来经商，并不仅仅只是为了购买瓷器，他们之所以特别喜欢载送和购买瓷器，是因为瓷器既重又不透水，是最实用的压舱货，可提高船只在波涛汹涌大海中的稳定度。1672 年英属东印度公司驻越南代表回报伦敦总部："此地以粗瓷压舱，极有道理"，全都是运往菲律宾、泰国的现成船货。② 其不仅可以压舱，还可以和其他的货物混装，如"各式有用的中国瓷器，特别是盘碟之类，可以装得很紧密。再买一些大中小各种尺寸的碗、大到可以种橘子树的中国大花盆、种小树小花的小盆……你买来的任何中国容器，都把它们装满西谷、米、椰子、淀粉或其他利润更好的货品"。③ 其实不仅是可以和各种食物一起混装，尤其重要的是其可以跟茶叶混装。如荷属、英属东印度公司都用铅衬的箱柜运茶以保新鲜，再把茶箱放在装瓷的条板箱上方。瓷器可保茶叶干燥，茶叶则提供减震缓冲以减低瓷器破损。由于瓷器有如此的种种与其他货物混装的优点，所以几乎所有来中国购物的船只都会购买上一些美丽的各色瓷器，同时也构成了即使在今天，如果我们去欧美大陆的许多旧房子里或到一些家庭里，都会看到几件祖上流传下来的中国瓷器，可见当时的中国瓷器在市场上的出售量有多么的巨大。

十一、世界瓷都景德镇

在 17 至 18 世纪的时代，可以说没有哪座城市有景德镇在世界的知名度高，

---

① 叶文程：《中国古外销瓷研究论文集》，紫金城出版社 1988 年版。
② ［美］罗伯特·芬雷（Robert Finlay）著，（中国台湾）郑明萱译：《青花瓷的故事：中国瓷的时代》，海南出版社 2015 年版，第 32 页。
③ ［美］罗伯特·芬雷（Robert Finlay）著，（中国台湾）郑明萱译：《青花瓷的故事：中国瓷的时代》，海南出版社 2015 年版，第 32 页。

即使没有到过景德镇，但是它的名字是随着它所生产的瓷器而传遍世界的。景德镇掌控了全球瓷器市场，不仅仅因为产品精良，也因为生产规模与组织先进；它代表了在蒸汽带动的机器年代来到之前，手工艺产业的最高峰，大规模集中制造生产最壮盛的成就。殷弘绪笔下的景德镇夜间景象——全城犹如一座熊熊燃烧的巨炉——并不只是幻象错觉，而是如实反映每日生产运作的真实景象。①

虽然广东、福建沿海数百座窑也产制了相当数额供应韩国、日本和东南亚等地，但欧洲市场上的瓷器却大部分是来自于景德镇，这也是景德镇在欧洲知名度高的缘由。

当时为了获得中国景德镇的瓷器，欧洲大量的银元流入到中国，当时的欧洲人还没有独立生产瓷器的能力。于是景德镇就成为急于掌握中国陶瓷技艺的欧洲人的探访之地，他们需要在这座城市了解到中国的制瓷秘密。

于是，1698年，法国耶稣会派遣一位叫殷弘绪的教士，来达中国景德镇昌江边的一所教会担任传教士。其目的就是为了获得有关景德镇陶瓷生产方面的技术资料，而殷弘绪的确不辱使命，很出色地完成了这一任务，说明他的上级早就看出他极具打探分析的才干。②

当时的殷弘绪，对景德镇悠久的制瓷历史背景一无所悉，而且因为瓷器史向来未曾引起过中国文人阶层的重视，所以当地没有任何书面文献可供他搜集，所以他只能亲自去实地考察，他靠着"出入窑坊之间，自己用眼睛观察、亲口询问参与工作的基督徒"，很显然，他也赢得了许多非基督徒的帮助，包括店东、瓷商，甚至几位官员，尤其是当时的督窑官唐英。③通过考察他获得了惊人的陶瓷知识，他把这些观察到和学习到的知识如实地记录下来，写成一封封长信向中印传道事务部的司库欧里汇报景德镇的制瓷方法。

1712至1722年十年之间，殷弘绪写过多封长信，这些信函很快就收入《耶稣会士中国益智奇闻书简》，全书34卷，是第一部可供欧洲人广泛取得中国相关知识的巨著。这份资料后来又收入《中华帝国全志》，作者赫德曾任路易十四的专职司铎；伏尔泰和其他多位哲学家大力推崇中国，就是深受此书影响。④

---

① ［美］罗伯特·芬雷（Robert Finlay）著，（中国台湾）郑明萱译：《青花瓷的故事：中国瓷的时代》，海南出版社2015年版，第32页。
② ［美］罗伯特·芬雷（Robert Finlay）著，（中国台湾）郑明萱译：《青花瓷的故事：中国瓷的时代》，海南出版社2015年版，第32页。
③ ［美］罗伯特·芬雷（Robert Finlay）著，（中国台湾）郑明萱译：《青花瓷的故事：中国瓷的时代》，海南出版社2015年版，第32页。
④ ［美］罗伯特·芬雷（Robert Finlay）著，（中国台湾）郑明萱译：《青花瓷的故事：中国瓷的时代》，海南出版社2015年版，第32页。

在宋应星的《天工开物》中纪录，景德镇瓷器"共计一坯之力，过手七十二，方克成器"。"过手七十二"，也就是说有32道工序，这在18世纪来说，如此分工细致的流水作业线是非常先进的，殷弘绪看到如此的场面他在信中写道："看到这些器皿如此快速地经过如此多人之手，真是令人惊奇。"[①]

在元代时期，景德镇一代又一代不识字的画工，为了应付来自伊斯兰国家的青花瓷订货，他们一笔笔忠实地描摹着那些复杂美丽的植物图案，还有那些看不懂的阿拉伯书法，这份经验累积到了16至18世纪派上了用场，通过长期的训练，使他们有能力依样画葫芦。当时的来样非常复杂，有在欧洲贵族订制的瓷器餐具上仿绘那些各种不可解的家族纹章，还有来自伦敦或巴黎的各行各业行会，诸如贩鱼业、屠宰业、糕饼业、家禽业、砌砖业和裁缝业的各种行业的纹章瓷器。[②] 面对外来的订单，景德镇的画工除必须解读一大堆令他们困惑不解的各家族、各行业的纹章图像外，还要面对罗马神话、圣经故事、欧洲当前的时事等各种画面的绘制。因为需要特别制作处理，所以，这些饰有西式图案的瓷器价格不菲。广州的荷兰商人转告荷属东印度公司的董事群："欧式画面或人物会比中国本土纹饰贵上一倍。"[③] 面对这些来自欧洲不同国家和阶层所需要的瓷器，景德镇工匠们的绘画能力得到了大幅度的提高。此时，中国所面对的市场不仅有欧洲，还有东南亚、西南亚、东亚、北非、东非等，但景德镇已经没有精力再接受这些比欧洲次一等的市场的需求，因而这些市场的需求就让位给了福建及广东一带沿海的窑口。

在这里我们依旧看到了文明的反复利用的过程，本来印刷术是来自中国，但从15世纪50年代开始，印刷术在欧洲盛行起来，印书商们在不同国家的首都汇集了各方专才：画工、手稿饰工、雕工、金工、金属工以及学者，共为同一种产品效力，最后在全欧创造了所谓的"知识共同体"。[④] 17世纪后期，欧洲的这些冒险创业家们，又开始将这些印制的不同图谱送往中国不同的瓷区和景德镇作为外销的陶瓷纹饰的参考。经景德镇瓷工们描绘的这些图谱被送到世界各地以后，又成为大家争相学习的对象，由此源自于世界各个不同文化的图案、

---

① ［美］罗伯特·芬雷（Robert Finlay）著，（中国台湾）郑明萱译：《青花瓷的故事：中国瓷的时代》，海南出版社2015年版，第27页。
② Bai, Qianshen. 1995. "The Irony of Copying the Elite: A Preliminary Study of the Poetry, Calligraphy and Painting on 17th-centuery Jingdezhen Porcelain." Cambridge, MA: Harvard University p. 127.
③ ［美］罗伯特·芬雷（Robert Finlay）著，（中国台湾）郑明萱译：《青花瓷的故事：中国瓷的时代》，海南出版社2015年版，第22页。
④ ［美］罗伯特·芬雷（Robert Finlay）著，（中国台湾）郑明萱译：《青花瓷的故事：中国瓷的时代》，海南出版社2015年版，第22页。

纹饰与符号开始进入了大规模的全球化的交换混合时代，也由此训练了景德镇一代又一代具有精湛绘画能力的陶瓷工匠，这种传统还一直延续到今。

十二、茶叶与茶壶中的文人气

在当年的一带一路贸易中，最重要的物产还是茶叶，当时的茶叶在欧洲是一种时尚的饮料，当时欧洲人几乎对茶着迷，曾有人写了一首诗："茶，裨益我们的头我们的心；茶，几乎疗治每个部位；茶，令老迈者重新得力；茶，令冷寒者小便得畅。"①欧洲人还认为，茶可强化大脑和胃，具有促进消化、排汗等功能，还可"增强体力以防慢性病，因为它有一项很棒的优点：可令血液变甜而稀释"。② 由于对茶叶的入迷，其对与茶叶相匹配的陶瓷茶具也大感兴趣。

中国的茶壶最有名和最有特点的当属是江苏宜兴的紫砂壶，有人认为，宜兴的紫砂器以泥质细腻、呈色丰富闻名，烧成后的紫砂壶保温性和透气性均十分理想，是沏茶的理想用具。但笔者却认为，它的名气并不仅仅是在于材质，重要的是和其他地方的茶具比较起来其有更浓厚的文人气。据说，这种文人气的出现，是由于一位叫供春的工匠带入的。供春曾是宜兴进士吴颐山家的书童，由于受过文人的熏陶，在他后来从事陶匠的生涯中，就将这些耳濡目染的文人品位带进了自己所做的茶壶中。供春生于明正德年间（1506—1566），1522 年是嘉靖元年，那时供春 16 岁正值青少年，于 1566 年嘉靖末年去世。他的青少年直至去世都是生活在明嘉靖年间。笔者强调这一时间段就是想说明，这段时间正是欧洲人进入中国购买茶叶和茶壶的期间。供春所制作的这种带有中国文人气息的茶壶，被欧洲人一眼看中，并大感兴趣。这种兴趣也推进了宜兴茶壶的行销市场，虽然在中国的陶瓷史尚没有欧洲人定制宜兴茶壶的记录，但在欧洲的文献中却有不少这方面的纪录。

17 世纪中叶，荷属东印度公司开始在运送茶叶的同时也把宜兴茶壶运抵到了欧洲，结果和在中国一样，大受欢迎。③ 欧洲人不仅欢迎宜兴茶壶，还努力地模仿宜兴茶壶，欧洲的银匠们就抄袭了这些中国新颖的设计，并据此造出各式

---

① ［美］罗伯特·芬雷（Robert Finlay）著，（中国台湾）郑明萱译：《青花瓷的故事：中国瓷的时代》，海南出版社 2015 年版，第 22 页。
② Postelthwayt, Malachy. 1774. The Universal Dictionary of Trade Commerce. 2vols. 4th ed. Reprint, New York：Wallace & Company.
③ Coutts, Howard. 2001. The Art of Ceramics：European Ceramic Design, 1500 – 1830. New Haven, CT：Yale University Press. pp. 146 – 47.

变化，知名的英国安妮女王银茶壶造型，便源自一只梨形宜兴壶。

有位荷兰陶匠专门仿制宜兴壶，1678 年在报上登广告吹嘘自己："制作之红色茶壶取得如此完美之成就，颜色、纯度、耐久度，毫不逊于东印度进口原版。"① 宜兴壶在中国也以其自然主义风格闻名，作品常采"象生"形制，如莲花、瓜果、石榴、葫芦、竹子，等等。西方也纷纷模仿这股异国情调，因为这种有机造型令他们的客户着迷。大约在 1670 年，荷兰代夫特的阿里·德·米尔德（Ary de Milde）；大约在 1690 年，英国斯坦福谢尔的约翰和约瑟夫·伊勒斯（Joseph Elers）；大约在 1710 年，德国麦森的约翰恩·弗里德里奇·鲍特格（Johann Friederich Bottger）都成功地仿制出宜兴的紫砂器②。

宜兴紫砂器在英国女王玛丽二世的收藏中占有重要地位。在她的密室"到处填满了中国瓷器，她的披风装饰有中国精美的红色饰物，令人称奇"。③ 长期以来，中国制造各种陶瓷器的方法和材料一直都使西方人感兴趣。荷兰画家也在他们的画作中为这种中国茶壶留下永恒纪念。④ 17 世纪荷兰哈伦画家罗斯彻墩的静物画《茶什》，描绘一张漆器黑桌，上面放了一把宜兴茶壶、一个气派茶瓮、数盏青花瓷杯，还有一块水晶。他的另一幅静物画《银器乌木盒》，则有一只银镶鹦鹉螺，旁边也是一把宜兴壶，盖上还系了金色丘比特像，显然是暗指这种流行的中国饮料具有春药功效。⑤

作为茶的载体的宜兴壶，在欧洲人的眼里不仅是一种器物，而是一种文化的象征物，其仿生的造型，具有文人气的装饰、书法，欧洲人拿起茶壶慢慢品尝其中的茶水时，其实是在体味一种中国的文化气息。这种气息所代表的是一种高雅、深邃、具有东方神秘感觉的心理体验。所以对于当时的欧洲人来讲，他们饮食的茶叶未必对身体有他们想象的那么多的益处，他们使用的宜兴茶壶又未必有多高的审美性，最重要的是其代表了一种时尚的引领潮流的风尚。

---

① ［美］罗伯特·芬雷（Robert Finlay）著，（中国台湾）郑明萱译：《青花瓷的故事：中国瓷的时代》，海南出版社 2015 年版，第 148 页。
② ［美］罗伯特·芬雷（Robert Finlay）著，（中国台湾）郑明萱译：《青花瓷的故事：中国瓷的时代》，海南出版社 2015 年版，第 148 页。
③ ［美］罗伯特·芬雷（Robert Finlay）著，（中国台湾）郑明萱译：《青花瓷的故事：中国瓷的时代》，海南出版社 2015 年版，第 149 页。
④ ［美］罗伯特·芬雷（Robert Finlay）著，（中国台湾）郑明萱译：《青花瓷的故事：中国瓷的时代》，海南出版社 2015 年版，第 148 页。
⑤ ［美］罗伯特·芬雷（Robert Finlay）著，（中国台湾）郑明萱译：《青花瓷的故事：中国瓷的时代》，海南出版社 2015 年版，第 148 页。

十三、瓷器传播与物质文化塑造

在今天的人们的眼中，瓷器是一个再平常不过的物质产品，但殊不知，中国瓷器的发明却是中国人对世界文化的一大重要贡献。中国瓷器的输入改变了许多地方的生活方式、卫生习惯和文化礼仪。

从生活方式的改变来讲，在中国瓷器输入之前，东南亚一些国家没有理想、适宜的饮食器具。在马来半岛洛坤附近、印度尼西亚爪哇岛中部、文莱一带古国，"饮食以揆叶为碗，不施匙筋，掬而食之"①，有的"饮食不用器皿，缄树叶以从事，食已则弃之"②，"以竹编、贝多叶为器，食毕则弃之"③。所以当中国瓷器一经输入，就成为了他们理想的饮食器具，这种器具因其卫生、实用、便于清洁等优点被广泛接受和使用，以致东南亚"寻常人家……盛饭用中国瓦瓮"④。当然那些地方相对比较贫穷落后，所以，中国沿海一带烧制的粗瓷常常被销售到那些地方。

中国瓷器的输入不仅改变了东南亚一带的生活方式，包括欧洲的生活方式也因为中国瓷器的输入得到改变。在17世纪之前，欧洲很少有人单独进食。当时的勺子、杯子、盘子非常稀有，所以，用餐是一种社会性的群体行为，即大家共用碗盘。在当时的风俗画中我们可以看到，集体共食是常态：众人共享一杯、一碗、一盘、一勺吃喝；当时的礼仪手册指示："喝前，切记先用布把你的嘴和手擦净，才不会弄脏杯子，否则同桌的人都不想和你共饮。"⑤其实这种习俗，在今天的某些基督教堂里还仍然保留着，当做完礼拜领圣餐、喝象征基督血的葡萄酒时，仍然是大家共用一个杯子。

当中国的瓷器进据餐桌成为普遍现象之后，欧洲集体共享的进食风俗开始从上流阶层撤退，此时，卫生观念、自我节律、社交礼节也同样发生改变。⑥来自中国的全套瓷器餐具的出现，不仅为每个人的进餐空间画下范围，促使同桌

---

① （宋）赵汝适：《诸番志·登流眉条》。
② （宋）赵汝适：《诸番志·苏吉丹条》。
③ （宋）赵汝适：《诸番志·渤泥国》。
④ （元）周达观：《真腊风土记》。
⑤ [美]罗伯特·芬雷（Robert Finlay）著，（中国台湾）郑明萱译：《青花瓷的故事：中国瓷的时代》，海南出版社2015年版，第303页。
⑥ Elias Norbert. 1982. The History of Manners. Translated by Edmund Jephcott. New York：Pantheon books. p. 56.

互动遵守自制,同时,餐桌礼仪的重点也开始从如何共享公碗,转向如何正确地用刀叉按住烤牛肉、单独使用属于个人的整套杯盘刀叉的餐桌文化,使欧洲人的饮食文化进一步走向高雅化和卫生化。

瓷器不仅是一种用于日常生活的器具,其还具有文化的象征意义。当中国瓷器进入到东南亚的一些区域时,那些地方还处于原始的部落状态。作为从中国一个如此高级文化中输入的瓷器,就被当地土著赋予了一种高深莫测的神秘色彩。这些中国瓷器被土著们用作巫术仪典上摆放高级供品的器具,举行仪典或给人治病时,少不了使用这些瓷碗、瓷碟,一边舞动,一边敲击,或把该病的符写于瓷器上,置水饮之,以求神灵的到来,让百病远离①。这种将中国的瓷器赋予神性的习俗,不仅是在东南亚,在非洲的一些国家也一样,他们用青花瓷装饰城门、墓壁以及墓柱②。

另外,瓷器还是一种文化的礼仪用品。当中国的瓷器到达邻国日本时,其连同茶叶及禅宗一起,形成了茶道文化。直到今天日本仍遵循唐宋旧制的点茶法:以竹筅将茶膏搅成绿色汤花,再端给客人饮用。整个过程和技巧费时、费工,需要大约30种茶具,遂成为"茶之汤"或谓"茶道"的中心焦点。在日本"唐茶"茶叙大受欢迎,常伴有博弈与清酒。雅致寂静的"茶室"自成一隅,与宅中日常起居作息区域分开,成为赏花、诵诗、赛香(参加者辨嗅各式香料)之场所。在这样的茶空间里必备之物包括:漆画屏风、带轴的绘画、带座的瓷瓶、青铜香炉与彩绣锦缎。这些道具和享用这些道具的人构成了一种以茶为中心的文化气氛,这就是茶道。这种茶道是唐宋时期的中国文化,但在其本土的中国这套高度结构化的社交、精神仪式已经消失了,却完整地保存在了日本。今天,其成为了地地道道的日本传统文化。

在这里,我们看到的是,一种物质产品的介入,往往改善的不仅是某种生活中的某个局部的器用方式,其还连带了一整套的文明和习俗的再产生。

十四、被"粉碎"的中国瓷器

当欧洲人第一次进入亚洲市场,并能直接与中国人做生意以来,他们狂热地从中国进口瓷器,透露了自从他们展读了马可·波罗对中国的记事以来,对中国抱持的那份又慕又羡之心。当时整个欧洲的上流社会都以能拥有中国的瓷

---

① 富斯:《菲律宾发掘的中国瓷器》,《中国古外销陶瓷研究资料》第一辑;伊静轩:《菲岛风光》。
② (明)费信:《星槎胜览·彭坑国条》。

器为荣耀，但由于大量的购买中国的瓷器、茶叶、漆器等，导致了欧洲的银元都流入了中国。1571 至 1821 年间，欧洲自南美与墨西哥进口的 4 亿银圆中，有一半供西方诸国购买中国产品之用，其中当然包括了中国的瓷器。由于银元的不足，导致路易十四国王大量融化宫中的银器，以换取中国的瓷器。也因为大量销毁银质餐具，进而造成更多的白银流向中国以购买瓷器餐具。更有甚者，某出法国喜剧曾描绘一位贵夫人打碎了俗称为"荷兰瓷"的代夫特陶，宣称自己今后只用中国瓷器。① 欧洲人如此地喜爱中国的瓷器，被当时的人称之为"瓷热病"，这样的"病"实际代表的是当时的欧洲向这个世上最古老帝国的文化展现的第一波最高敬意。

但这种敬意不久就动摇了。为了摆脱在经济上对中国的仰赖，17 世纪之后，欧洲开始致力于仿制中国瓷器，并进而挑战后者的产业实力。最后终于在 18 世纪末完成了欧洲瓷器生产在商业方面的胜利，一举将中国瓷器逐出国际市场。这项胜利，也预示了西方在现代世界将要获得的压倒性支配地位。与此同时，中国瓷开始在世界市场上全面崩盘，这种崩溃正是与中国在世界事务上划时代的衰退同步进行，也与西方势力上升、前进成为全球重心的时序相互对应。②

中国生产的瓷器在欧洲没落，英法工厂生产的瓷器在国际市场称胜——反映了欧洲和亚洲之间关系的大逆转。此时的欧洲，不再接受理想化的中国形象，拒斥了中国瓷和中国情调。中国瓷器和中国美学，此时引发的都是负面反应。熟悉中国的欧洲商人开始反驳耶稣会士描绘的、被理想化了的中国形象，并详细地指出，他们所认为的中国官吏腐败衰弱的一面。在这里我们看到的是，当年欧洲对中国瓷的狂热，预示了一个崇拜中国时代的到来，而一旦中国从模范榜样的宝座上跌落下来，中国的瓷器也随之一起摔到了地下。

多少世纪以来，景德镇以"天下瓷都"的称号一向雄踞瓷器产业的霸位，此时终于遇到了无法击退的劲敌。景德镇代表工业革命之前手工业的最高峰，它的劳力密集的工作方法、大规模分散化的结构，足以应付来自日本和东南亚大陆的挑战。然而，这一切优势、自信，却在 1800 年之后很快丧失殆尽，因为世界体系的重心移转到西北欧各国，机器代替手工，集约化、规模化代替分散化、多样化的时代终于来临。亚当·斯密在《国富论》中有句名言，点出了世界秩序此番大洗牌的关键前提："美洲大陆的发现，以及经由好望角通往东印度

---

① ［美］罗伯特·芬雷（Robert Finlay）著，（中国台湾）郑明萱译：《青花瓷的故事：中国瓷的时代》，海南出版社 2015 年版，第 218 页。
② ［美］罗伯特·芬雷（Robert Finlay）著，（中国台湾）郑明萱译：《青花瓷的故事：中国瓷的时代》，海南出版社 2015 年版，第 218 页。

群岛航线的开发,是人类史上最重要的两大事件。"①

正是由于这两件大事的出现,使当初最多不过是欧亚大陆一处边陲成员的欧洲,却在近世初期开始崭露头角,攫夺了世界舞台的中心位置。它不仅开拓了全球海运航线,还在南、北美洲植入欧式社会,并将亚洲大部分地区变成了它的殖民地,塑造出新型的政治与经济制度,最终一手催生并主导了现代的诞生。② 在这新的一场较量中,中国的瓷器不仅是失去了长期以来的巨大的海外市场,而且失去了整个国家的文化竞争力。长期以来西方人膜拜的并不真正是中国的瓷器,而是中国的文化和礼仪制度。当这些东西不再能引起西方人膜拜的时候,中国的瓷器也就自然地被西方世界丢弃并摔碎。

十五、"黄色"与"蓝色"的中国选择

尽管中国在历史上曾驰骋海洋,将自己的茶叶、丝绸、瓷器等优秀的手工艺品贡献给世界,但这样威武的业绩和工作,在中国文人的笔下却常被漠视,因为中国是一个重农轻商的国家,在这个国家中,商业向来被视为"末业"。在这样的观念中,代表了中国商业文化的瓷器贸易,自然会拜倒在重视商业文化的欧洲人的手上,这是一场"蓝色"文化和"黄色"文化的较量。欧洲是"蓝色"文化的代表,中国是"黄色"文化的代表。但如果我们翻开中国的历史,包括我们阅读中国瓷器贸易的历史,我们就可以看到,在历史上,中国都长期处于某种可称为"黄中国"对"蓝中国"的紧张关系之中。③ 简单地说,前者代表黄河、长城、农业优先、大陆至上、命令式经济体制、儒家文官制度、漠视海洋世界;后者则意谓着长江下游、市场经济、自给自足、文化互动、长距离贸易、迎向海洋。④ 笔者认为,长期以来,虽然中国趋向于重农轻商,但也向来是"黄色文明"和"蓝色文明"共存,中国人常说自己是黄河的儿女,其实也是长江的儿女,长江是一条通往大海的重要通道。从唐代一直到郑和下西洋为止,中国人都是通过长江到达海洋,从而成为海洋上的强者。只是明中期以

---

① Smith, Adam. 1976. An Inquiry into the Nature and Causes of the Wealth of Nation. 2 vols. Edited by R. H. Campbell and A. K. Skinner. Oxford: Clarendon Press.
② [美] 罗伯特·芬雷 (Robert Finlay) 著, (中国台湾) 郑明萱译:《青花瓷的故事:中国瓷的时代》,海南出版社2015年版,第218页。
③ Mote, Frederick W. 1999. Imperial China, 900 – 1800. Cambridge, MA: Harvard University Press. pp. 14 – 15.
④ [美] 罗伯特·芬雷 (Robert Finlay) 著, (中国台湾) 郑明萱译:《青花瓷的故事:中国瓷的时代》,海南出版社2015年版,第336页。

后的精英阶级才单一地坚持大陆观点,对他们来说,"海洋是商人的场域,是逐利而非逐位者或追求原则者的天下。海洋代表着无法治理的陌生异域,他们往往心怀忧虑而视之,且务必尽可能地避而远之"。①

而这一切的起点正是从 15 世纪末开始的,当中国人从海洋退缩时,欧洲的地理大发现却开始了。于是,一场东西方的相逢导致了世界格局的巨大改变,前者是大陆导向思维,遵奉以陆地为根基的权力中心;后者则属海洋导向,以军事武力为后盾开创海上商贸事业,最后以后者胜利而终结。这一后果到今天都是中国人的心结,这一心结让我们认定,中国只有"黄色文明"的历史,而没有"蓝色文明"的历史。

但当我们今天重新面对的"一带一路"的区域,我们看到的是,在历史上"蓝色"的中国和"黄色"的中国一样强大。我们的祖先曾用他们的驼队、船队走出了一片天地,开辟了举世闻名的陆上丝绸之路和海上丝绸之路;后来,在这海陆的两道上,不仅有了我们祖先的足迹,还有了许多外来者的足迹;再后来,我们不敢再往前走,于是,我们关门了。最后,外来者竟然用炮火打开了我们的大门,走进了我们的家里,让中国曾一度被沦为一个半殖民地的国家。今天,中国的经济发展了,我们不仅要打开大门,我们还要再次出发,但如何出发、是否需要回头看看我们的历史,那是我们曾经向今天走来的路。笔者认为历史是不会死的,它是在不断地游动,只是有时我们会疏忽它的存在,看不到它所蕴含的内在生命力,所以,我们需要了解历史和唤醒历史,并以此来看通往未来的路。

通过阅读这段历史,我们看到的是,瓷器发明于中国、传播于世界,又将世界的文化带回来,滋养了中国。瓷器代表的是中国历史上的最先进手工劳动,是农业文明的高峰之作。今天许多的传统,包括手工艺,在新的历史阶段又再次萌发它们新的生命力,景德镇这座著名的瓷都,在沉寂了 100 多年以后的今天,又开始充满朝气(笔者曾持续研究这座城市 20 年),再次受到全世界的瞩目。也许有一天在新的生态文明中,那些古老的农业文明中积累的智慧还会给予我们新的启示。世界不同地区的文明就是如此地循环反复在进行着新的再生产,今天是中国的发明,明天被中国以外的文明所用,再后天可能又返回其所在地生长出新的文化。

在历史上,中国为世界文化、政治、经济、科技等方面的发展作出过许多

---

① Wang 2000 : 3 - 11 makes the case for the signficance of a maritime focus in western Asia and continental one in China; see also Chaudhuri 1985: 122 - 23, 208; Padfield 2000: 7 - 19.

重要的贡献;在今天,当我们再次出发,踏上"一带一路"中我们祖先走过的山山水水,我们带给世界的是什么样的新的物质和新的思想,这是值得我们思考的。就像当年世界风靡中国瓷器的时候,全世界的人们真正崇拜的并不是中国瓷器,而是中国的文化政治、礼仪风尚等,当这些东西得不到尊重时,中国的瓷器就开始破碎。今天我们在重拾这曾经破碎的瓷器、顺着历史的脉络往前看的时候,我们应该有些什么样的新思考,这是本文和读者们一起要完成的作业,也是这篇文章写作的根本意义所在。

从敦煌文化的形成看亚洲文化的融会发展

敦煌市文化学会　高德祥

敦煌文化博大精深，源远流长，是一种多元文化的产物，在两千多年的历史长河中，发展形成了独具魅力的文化形态。

敦煌位于中国甘肃省的最西端，地处古丝绸之路上的咽喉要地，是古代东西方交流的必经之地，世界四大文化体系（中国、印度、希腊、伊斯兰）在这里交汇，各种文化在这里得以充分交流与融合，因而形成了博大精深的敦煌文化。

以敦煌莫高窟为代表的石窟艺术，集中展示了古代丝绸之路上的多种文化形态。20世纪初，敦煌莫高窟藏经洞被发现，出土了约70000多件珍贵的历史文物，震惊了世界。文献的内容除佛教典籍外，还有摩尼教、景教、道教、儒家典籍。此外，还有天文、历法、军事、地理、民俗、姓氏、账册、名籍、函件、书信、诗赋、辞曲、方言、游记、杂写等，由于藏经洞的发现而产生了一个新的学科——敦煌学。

敦煌文化的形成是丝绸之路多民族、多区域文化传播融合的集合体，没有古代丝绸之路的畅通，没有东西方多元文化的融合发展，就不可能产生举世闻名的敦煌文化。由此可见，文化的发展、创新和繁荣必须走交流融合之路。今天"一带一路"的提出，再度为经济文化的发展繁荣提供了前所未有的发展机遇，亚洲正处于厚积薄发的时代，具有一定的区域优势，经济大发展，文化大繁荣，需要加强合作，增进交流，相互借鉴，共同发展。亚洲又是一个多民族居住地，文化形态各不相同，内容丰富，形式多样，这是亚洲文化的特点和优势，也是亚洲文化交流融合的良好基础，通过广泛的交流，必将对促进亚洲经济发展，文化繁荣，社会进步，推动人类历史的发展产生深远影响。

一、敦煌文化形成的历史背景

敦煌文化的形成经历了一个漫长的过程，有着非常复杂的历史背景，从现在的情况看，主要有三方面的原因：丝绸之路的畅通、佛教的传入和多民族文化的融合。

（一）丝绸之路的畅通

从历史上看，中国很早就与中亚、南亚、西亚和欧洲的许多国家通过陆路交通，有着密切的交往。公元前138年奉汉武帝之命，张骞率领100多人第一次出使西域，于公元前126年回到长安，历时长达13年。公元前119年他带领300多人奉命第二次出使西域，进一步了解西域各地经济和文化发展情况，为西汉王朝开通丝绸之路提供了极其重要的依据，因此，西汉王朝在公元前111年设敦煌郡，并设阳关、玉门关，专门管理东来西往的过客。由于特殊的地理位置，当时的敦煌成为中原与西域交往的必经之地，随着商贸的流通，各种文化也开始广泛交流。古代时期西域的乐舞非常发达，大约在南北朝时期（3世纪）在当时非常有影响的康国乐、安国乐、天竺乐、龟兹乐、高昌乐、疏勒乐、西凉乐从西域传入中原，而且在隋唐时代产生了很大影响，唐代时期盛极一时的"十部伎"就是在吸收融合了外来乐舞的基础上而形成的。"胡旋舞"、"胡腾舞"，以及琵琶、竖箜篌、筚篥、五弦琵琶、羯鼓、腰鼓等许多乐器都是从西域传入的。跳胡舞、奏胡乐、穿胡服、吃胡饭成为朝廷上下的一种时尚，这个时期西域文化极大地影响了中原的传统文化。

无论是中原文化还是西域文化，首传之地就是敦煌。敦煌遗书中除了大量的汉文文献外，还有相当数量的梵文、粟特文、突厥文、于阗文、回鹘文、叙利亚文、西夏文、蒙文、古藏文等。这些珍贵的历史文献充分证实了各种文化在敦煌交流的实际情况。

（二）佛教的传入

可以说，敦煌艺术是佛教的产物，没有佛教的传入就没有敦煌石窟艺术的产生，佛教对敦煌艺术的产生起了决定性的作用。

佛教大约在公元前5、6世纪的印度产生，传入中国的时间大约在东汉初期，敦煌是佛教传最早的地区之一，随着时代的发展，佛教在中原地区产生的影响越来越大，信教者越来越多，在这样的形势下，从南北朝时期兴起了建造佛窟的热潮，由于敦煌地处丝绸之路咽喉要地，这里已经成为经济文化的集散地，佛教在这里迅速得以传播和发展，建窟造佛自然而然成为人们的一种精神追求，随之在敦煌先后建造了举世闻名的莫高窟、西千佛洞和榆林窟。自公元366年莫高窟创建后，历经北魏、西魏、北周、隋、唐、五代、宋代、西夏、元、清十余个朝代，上下历经1000多年，在现存的492个洞窟中保存的古代壁画45000多平方米，彩塑2000余身，是世界上现存规模最大的佛教艺术宝库，1988年莫高窟被联合国教科文组织列入世界文化遗产保护名录。2014年6月丝绸之路被联合国教科文组织列入世界文化遗产保护名录,敦煌境内的悬泉置和玉门关两处汉代遗址被列入丝绸之路的重要文化遗产。

榆林窟石窟现存42个洞窟,西千佛洞现存16个洞窟,这两个石窟也保存了大量的壁画和彩塑,内容和形式与莫高窟基本相同,属同一类型的建造风格。

敦煌壁画的内容除了佛教题材之外,还有许许多多反映现实生活的场景,如收获、耕地、出行、狩猎、嫁娶、丧葬、杂技、武术、歌舞表演等,甚至把刷牙、剃度、婴儿车这样细微的生活场景都淋漓尽致地描绘在壁画中。

从敦煌壁画中可以清楚地看出,早期壁画中的绘画线条粗犷,构图简单,无论是天宫伎乐、飞天伎乐,以及人物形象、衣冠服饰完全是西域风格。而隋唐时期绘画风格完全发生了变化,西域风格的东西逐步在淡化,而中原的传统绘画风格却十分明显,线条流畅,构图细腻,人物形象栩栩如生,不仅追求绘画中的形似,更重要的是讲究神似,这是在佛教传入中原几百年之后发生的根本性变化,这种现象充分展示了敦煌文化的多元性和包容性。

值得深思的是,建造佛窟的初衷是信教者的一种精神寄托,他们花去大量的时间和财物不是为了追求创造艺术,而是为求得来世。而事实这些石窟造像似乎脱离初建者的本意,不再是单一的佛教圣地,而成为名副其实的艺术宝窟,这种结局在当时是任何建造石窟者难以想象的,古代的佛教石窟,成为今天珍贵的艺术宝库,其艺术价值远远超越了佛教的意义,这是一个戏剧性的变化,自古至今多少人在梦寐以求地创造艺术,可最终销声匿迹一事无成,而许多东西当初根本就不是为了创造艺术,千年之后却反而成为举世无双的艺术创造,这样的事例很多,如敦煌的莫高窟,西安的兵马俑,北京的八达岭长城,以及故宫等都不是为艺术而建,而随着历史的发展,这些都成为重要的世界文化遗产。这些典型事例充分说明,任何一种文化的形成,往往不以人们的主观意志所决定,而是需要长期的交流、融合、积淀。

(三) 多民族杂居是敦煌文化产生的基础

可以说,文化史就是人类史,一个地方的文化史就是一个地方的民族发展史。敦煌历来是一个多民族杂居的地方,因此多民族文化的融合是形成敦煌文化的重要因素。

早在新石器时代敦煌就有三苗族生活在这里,秦、汉之际,敦煌为月氏和乌孙的游牧地。月氏,是羌族的一支,乌孙是"戎"的转音。到汉文帝前元元年(前179),北方匈奴的势力强大起来,渐次向南扩张、月氏、乌孙、相继西迁。敦煌和河西走廊的广大地区均为匈奴所据。

张骞两次出使西域，为汉朝对西域有了一定的了解，所以，汉武帝元狩二年（前121）春，汉武帝选派年仅20岁的霍去病讨伐匈奴，匈奴败北后，敦煌以及河西一带归属于汉朝版图，并且大量移民于敦煌，开垦土地发展农业，敦煌由原来以少数民族游牧的地方，成为以汉民族为主与少数民族杂居的地方，这是敦煌文化发生的一次重大的历史性变化。

汉以后，由于北方地区各民族混杂居住，各种文化在这里汇集交融，这个时期北方形成了一部独具特色的乐舞《西凉乐》，这部伎乐不仅在北方有很大的影响，而且隋唐时期在宫廷中也久传不衰，得到了帝王们的高度重视和喜爱。关于《西凉乐》的形成，《隋书·音乐志》记载："西凉（乐）者，起于苻氏之末，吕光、沮渠蒙逊等据有凉州，变龟兹声为之，号为《秦汉伎》。"《旧唐书·音乐志》记载："（西凉乐）盖凉人所传中国旧乐，而杂以羌胡之声也。"从文献记载中可以看出，当时流传盛广的《西凉乐》是以西域的龟兹乐，北方地区的民族音乐，以及中原的传统旧乐基础上融合形成的，这部音乐就是多元文化的产物。敦煌是《西凉乐》的产生和流传地，其影响非常深远，受到人们的广泛喜爱，甚至被画在了佛教壁画中，至今可以从敦煌莫高窟220窟（初唐）北壁的壁画中看到《西凉乐》的精彩表演场景。

公元755年敦煌被吐蕃占领，在吐蕃统治的70多年间，虽然地方居民多为汉民族，但是，由于统治者的强行推行，吐蕃文化成为当地的主流文化。这个时期不仅佛经的翻译中出现了大量的吐蕃文，而且人们的衣食住行也发生了很大变化，久传不衰的《西凉乐》也被吐蕃乐舞所取代。莫高窟156窟南壁所画的出行图，反映的是河西节度使张议潮打败吐蕃收复河西地区，敦煌及河西地区重新归属于中原王朝，人们载歌载舞拥戴欢庆的盛大场景。但是，由于70多年的吐蕃统治，吐蕃文化已经渗透在当地的传统文化中，一时还难以改变，所以，在盛大的出行队中表演的舞蹈依然是吐蕃舞，由此可见，民族的更迭对文化所产生的影响是极其深远的。

公元1036年北方的党项族迅速强大，敦煌被西夏王朝占据，并控制敦煌长达190余年。西夏王朝为了长期巩固自己的势力范围，创造了西夏文字，极力创造新的文化模式，以达到彻底改变人们的传统文化观念，因此，这个时期敦煌壁画中所表现的内容和形式，显然与前代有所不同，其内容和形式具有鲜明的西夏文化特征。

13世纪，北方又一个民族崛起，1227年敦煌属蒙元帝国管辖，敦煌文化中又融合了草原游牧民的文化。公元1368年明王朝建立，由于种种原因，明代在嘉峪关修筑长城设防，放弃对敦煌的管辖，敦煌的原有居民全部东迁，因此，敦煌文化在这个时期随着人口的迁徙而暂时中断。

清朝再次收复敦煌，清雍正四年从甘肃省 56 个州县移民至敦煌，敦煌成为一个多民族居住的地方，多种文化在这里再次交流融合，形成了另一类型的文化形态。

从两千多年的发展过程中可以看出，敦煌文化的形成经历了一个非常复杂而又漫长的历史过程，这是敦煌多元文化形成的主要原因。总结敦煌文化形成的历史原因，有助于我们进一步加深对亚洲文化融合发展的理解。

二、亚洲文化融会发展的潜力

亚洲是全世界几大洲中人口最多，文化传统历史悠久，民族成分最为复杂，文化形态非常多元的一个洲，佛教文化、道教文化、儒家文化、伊斯兰文化形成了亚洲文化的基本形态，不同种族、不同地区的民间传统文化极大地丰富了各民族的精神文化生活。在今天高度发达的信息时代，通过"一带一路"把亚洲各国人民再次紧密地联系在一起，一种多元文化交流的时代已势在必行，亚洲文化的交流融合不仅会极大地丰富亚洲的文化内涵，也必将对人类文明的发展产生重要影响。

（一）人口优势是发展亚洲文化的基础

亚洲居住着全世界三分之二的人口，世界上最大的人口国也在亚洲，而且民族众多，信仰各一，社会制度各有不同，文化类型多种多样。亚洲各国紧密相连、世为友好、心相系、情相连，只有通过各种交流，相互借鉴、增进互信，才能促进经济发展，社会进步。文化传播影响力的大小，往往取决于受众者的多少，因此，人口资源是亚洲文化交流发展的最大优势。文化是人类精神创造的产物，不同的人类种群创造出不同的文化形态，文化又是人类思想沟通的桥梁和纽带，正是基于这种原因，亚洲需要更加广泛的文化交流，通过"一带一路"建设把亚洲的文化发展提升到一个新的高度。

（二）悠久的历史是亚洲文化融会发展的优势

亚洲是人类文明最早的发祥地之一，文化类型多样、内容丰富、历史悠久，几千年的文明史创造出了许多不朽的文化精华。中国文化、古印度文化、伊斯兰文化自成体系，传播广泛，影响深远，在人类发展过程中产生了重大影响，为推动人类历史的进步做出了巨大贡献。从历史上看，早在丝绸之路开通初期，亚洲各国已开始了广泛的交流，东来西往，延续不断，多种文化相互交融、相互渗透，敦煌文化的形成充分证实了这一点。

文化是人们的精神体现，不同的民族、不同的时代，人们有着不同的文化观念，这种观念是随着时代的发展而转变，世界上没有哪一种文化形态是一成不变的，亚洲的文化传统虽然历史悠久，但是在历史的发展过程中，始终在相互交流、相互借鉴、融会发展，既保持了本民族的文化传统，又注入了新的文化内涵，这是亚洲文化久传不衰、兴旺发达的重要原因。

（三）亚洲文化融会发展势在必行

历史在发展、人类在进步、文化在创新，这是人类发展的历史必然。文化的生命力就在于创新，没有创新的文化是无法传承下去的。亚洲文化有着悠久的历史传统，在新的历史条件下，为亚洲文化的创新和发展奠定了良好基础，在亚洲各国共同的努力下，通过"一带一路"紧密联系，加强协作，亚洲文化必将再创新的辉煌，一个丰富多元的亚洲文化将展现在世人面前。

对话视野：国际关系中文化差异的管理之道

国际关系学院副校长　郭惠民

从 20 世纪 70 年代实行改革开放政策以来，中国与世界的联系就开始不断地加深，无论是在经济上还是在政治、科技、文化层面上，中国都积极地在国际范围内与各国进行着互动往来。在此过程中，中国不仅综合国力得到了长足的发展，国际事务的参与程度也得到了大大地加深，开始逐渐地在全球治理中发挥着自己不可替代的作用。

单从参与世界经济发展角度来说，不论是 "一带一路" 国家战略的稳步实施还是 "亚投行" 的正式建立，都不难看出中国已经逐渐掌握了世界经济发展的规则，并且开始对新时期新形势下的复杂挑战主动做出积极应对。然而随着中国企业大规模 "走出去" 已成为可预见的现实，文化差异也成为了中国经济想要在世界范围内大展拳脚中不可忽视的障碍。如何管理文化差异，降低矛盾摩擦、冲突风险不仅成为当前中国深化对外开放必须解决的难题，同样也成为中国更好地加深与世界联系、实现全球利益互惠互利所必须跨越的阻拦。

一、中国与世界的关系日趋紧密

从 2013 年 9 月习近平主席在访问哈萨克斯坦时提出 "丝绸之路经济带" 的构想开始，再到一个月后在亚太经合组织（APEC）领导人非正式会议上提出的中国愿与东盟国家共同建设 "21 世纪海上丝绸之路"，"一带一路" 倡议正式形成。作为一个适应世界经济新格局发展的产物，它力求在依靠中国与有关国家既有的双多边机制基础上，借助行之有效的区域合作平台，积极发展与沿线国家的经济合作伙伴关系，共同打造政治互信、经济融合、文化包容的利益共同体、命运共同体和责任共同体。换句话说，"一带一路" 构想的提出和实施不仅是中国深化对外开放、优化资源配置的需要，更展现了中国 "致力于维护全球自由贸易体系和开放型世界经济"，以及 "将为世界和平发展增添新的正能量"[①]

---

① 新华社：《推动共建丝绸之路经济带和 21 世纪海上丝绸之路的愿景与行动》，新华网，（http://news.xinhuanet.com/finance/2015-03/28/c_1114793986.html）。

的负责任大国形象。从另一个角度说，它的提出昭示着中国经济与世界经济的高度关联，中国的发展已经逐渐与世界的发展融合在了一起。

中国与世界日趋紧密的关系不仅体现在经济领域，在承担国际事务的责任方面表现也十分显著。2016年9月12日G20全球治理指数在北京发布，中国以第四的评估结果跻身全球治理的第一梯队，这项指数细分为四大评估指标："机制"、"绩效"、"决策"、"责任"，其中中国的单项排名分别为第七、第四、第四和第五，整体表现较为均衡。这项指数的发布也更加直观地展现出了中国近些年在国际事务中发挥的作用以及在全球治理中做出的巨大努力。也正是因为中国积极承担着推动世界发展的责任，使得中国自身的发展与世界发展的紧密程度也进一步加深。

二、国际关系中的文化差异

随着中国融入世界体系程度的不断加深，因经济发展程度、现代化发展的成熟度、地缘环境以及制度和认知结构等方面的区别与不同，所导致的文化差异与冲突也变得愈发突出。仅从经济领域来看，近年来，我国"走出去"的企业当中就存在着因不尊重当地风俗习惯而遭到所在国居民抗议抵制；因员工不同文化背景沟通不畅，而产生大量争议和隔阂；因内外部发展环境、经营理念、管理方式发生变化，对文化差异认识不足，从而无法很好整合企业文化，导致投资失败、经营困难，等等，各类问题频显。这对于我国企业扩展海外市场、深化对外开放以及推行"一带一路"的建设都有着很大的负面影响。

另一方面，文化差异对于中国国家形象的塑造也造成了巨大阻碍。在2010年BBC就28个国家对中国国家形象所做的民意调查中，中国仅在巴基斯坦和非洲国家的形象是正面的，而在亚洲、美洲、欧洲都以中性和负面为主。这个调查也证明了巨大的文化差异导致当今依旧有很大一部分国家的人对中国有误解和偏见。不同因素所造成的文化差异及其无法对其进行有效管理不仅会带来人们对中国国家形象的各种误读与偏见，也会导致中国在国际舆论中的形象负面化，更重要的是不利于中国文化的对外传播，阻碍中国软实力的建设与发展，进而影响中国国家话语权的构建和提升。

当今世界因急剧变化充满不确定性，而由文化差异所导致的焦虑、疏离、断裂、沟壑和冲突触目皆是。多元的文化，差异的存在是必然。事实上，遭遇文化差异的阻碍是国际关系发展进程中无法避免的问题，因为文化差异不仅仅会产生于因国别不同而导致的不同的价值观取向抑或是思维方式上的差异，"在人种的基础完全相同的地方也会产生文化上的差异"①。因此，文化差异的存在是无法消除的，如何更好地管理差异，降低冲突风险，努力做到求同存异，寻求对话与信任才是国际关系中真正的文化差异管理之道。

三、对话与信任——文化差异的管理之道

（一）对话管理差异

对于对话理论的研究，早在20世纪60年代的传播学界就已经开始，阿什利·马森更是在其出版的《人类的对话》中将对话称为"传播的第三次革命"。对话理论中所强调的平等开放和彼此尊重，实际上在那时就已经得到了认可。对话式传播中所包含的各方都享有平等的地位，反对单方面的权威压迫和真理独占的平等意识，对于管理当今国际关系中所存在的文化差异有很大的借鉴意义。因为"对话不仅仅是一种传播手段，也包括了人类生存方式的相互参照——对话建立了人与人之间相互开放、彼此依存的关系，是自我与他人共同'在场'的相互审视和相互认证"②。随着全球化进程加深和互联网技术不断发展，人们慢慢发现，世界是一体的，或者说世界已经在逐渐走向一体，处于世界体系中的各国不仅利益共享，面对风险与危机更要共同承担。因此，在国际语境中的相互理解、交流与对话以及彼此信任成为了国际关系中对待文化差异的最好处理方式。换句话说，对话作为一种双向的传播，它是一个互为主体性的过程，参与对话的双方能够拥有同等的主体地位，以达到一种"协商的理解"。这是国际关系中管理文化差异的理想方式，也是不同文化寻求共存、共识和共同利益的必然选择。

随着中国与世界关系的日趋紧密，面对不论是经济"走出去"还是文化传播中存在的各种因文化差异而造成的误解和阻碍时，我们要逐渐改变原有对文化差异的处理方式而选择加强与各国的对话交流，以增进人与人之间、社群之间、民族国家之间的协同，凝聚最大共识。事实上，中国在近些年也已经开始尝试在国际关系中用对话方式来改善我国的国家形象、打造国家品牌，以改善因文化差异而带来的负面的国际环境。最显著的就是完善国际传播体系的硬件设施，以使得在国际传播大环境中，中国的国家媒体拥有与其他国际主流媒体

---

① ［美］罗伯特·路威著，吕叔湘译：《文明与野蛮》，三联书店2005年版，第29页。
② 孙英春：《跨文化传播学教程》，北京大学出版社2015年版，第338页。

相差无几的全球覆盖率。然而，在实际影响力方面，极高的覆盖率却并未带来与之相匹配的实际影响力，中国媒体的国际公信力和议程构建能力并未获得较大的提升，换句话说，对话的成功率并不高，结果是"传而不通"和"通而不受"，造成这种现象的最主要原因就是我们所采取的对话大部分都以自我为中心。实际上，不论是对外交流还是对外塑造中国形象，承认他者，了解对方国的文化和认知特征是必不可少的一步。因为"交流就是承认他者。不仅是一个简单的感知问题，而且是一个建立人的秩序的问题"①。只有了解对话另一方的实际情况，才可以从对方行为背后的态度和原理来理解对方，再进一步寻求互相理解以组建新的对话，并进而通过不断的对话来改善自己的形象。

（二）对话创建信任

国际关系中的交往不论以哪种形式开始，最终最完满的结果都是归结于信任。实现国家间的彼此信任是国家交往过程中始终不断追求的最终目标，而这种信任的产生也建立在不断进行的交流对话和平等倾听的基础上。信任是一种特殊的品质，它无法用金钱来衡量，不能被下载，不能立竿见影，它只能在一次次的来往互动来中缓慢积累，但是它同样可以瞬间消失无踪。个体间建立信任需要日积月累，需要从每一个个体间良好的对话开始，国家间建立信任则更是如此。然而在现实中，西方一些大国的传播战略往往以说服输出代替相互理解成为了其对话理论的主体，讲故事的唯一目的是对抗和征服，这种对话只是披着霸权外衣下的片面价值观宣传，它无法转换为积极信任，也无法延续出下一次对话。积极信任是相对于消极信任而言的。所谓消极信任，指的是对既定路径、规范、制度和权力的接受和遵从；而积极信任指的是主动从他者那里赢得信任。积极信任既是双向、开放、平等对话的产物，又是对话得以持续和升级的前提。

良好的对话意味着倾听和认同，意味着在对话的双方之间建立了一种相互尊重、彼此信任的关系。这样才可以从被认同延伸到到信任，才会催生出下一段良好的对话。换句话说，所有真正有意义的对话最终都归结于信任，信任也由对话的进行而逐渐加深。只有在信任的前提下，国家间的文化差异才能够被理解、被管理，国家间的交流与对话才能通畅，而不再只是"没有被传播、被

---

① ［美］彼得斯著，何道宽译：《交流的无奈：传播思想史》，华夏出版社2003年版，第13页。

分享、在表达中没有得到再生的自言自语"①。在当今时代的传播交流语境里，人类应该摒弃传统的二元对立思维，即不以一元征服另一元，也不放任因对立、分裂可能造成的虚无、终结甚至其他灾难性后果，而是寻求差异的有效管理、风险的积极防控，在富有张力、均衡、持久、多元、多层面的对话中促进相互信任理解（理解并不等于接受）、利益互惠和价值协商，表达和实现多元以及各自的利益关切，构建合作双赢的良好国际关系生态，创造一个多样、有序的美好世界。

---

① ［美］詹姆斯·凯瑞著，丁未译：《作为文化的传播——媒介与社会论文集》，华夏出版社2005年版。

"一带一路"与亚洲文化空间秩序的新关系
（摘要）

上海交通大学、国家文化环境与政策研究中心　胡惠林

一、"一带一路"的空间关系与文化特质

"一带一路"建构了古代亚洲与世界的空间关系和文化特质：大陆文明和海洋文明交相辉映，开放包容，文明互鉴，多元一体。

丝绸之路——古代亚洲的文化对话方式。丝绸之路形成于中国与欧洲大陆和阿拉伯世界的经贸往来和文化交往，但，它的性质是亚洲的。

丝绸——是中华文明的独特语言和表达方式：人与自然、人与社会的精神关系和文化秩序。

丝绸——是中华文明贡献给亚洲的文明成果，也是亚洲贡献给世界的文明成果。

丝绸——是人类文明和亚洲文明对话的共同语言与审美载体。

丝绸之路——是亚洲文明与世界文明的交往、沟通之路，互通互融，互相欣赏和互相借鉴，成果共享和共同发展构成了他的内在本质。

二、亚洲的空间构成与文化秩序

作为文明体系的构成：儒教文明与伊斯兰文明构成了亚洲文化基本的精神空间秩序。

作为文明形态的构成：中华文明、印度文明和阿拉伯文明构成了亚洲文化形成的基本来源。

作为文明主体的构成：多民族融合和文化多样性建构了亚洲文化对话的基本历史。

三、"一带一路"与亚洲文化秩序演化的新关系

"一带一路"给亚洲文化发展提出了新命题,带来了亚洲文化交流交往的新机遇,创新了的亚洲文化对话的新形式。

"一带一路"的古老形式与当代价值。

"一带一路"的古老形式与当代转换。

"一带一路"的现代形式与交往革命。

"一带一路"与促进亚洲文化关系的现代演化,重构亚洲文化新关系。

考古发现所见早期丝绸之路中外交往史迹钩沉

西安美术学院 李 青

在远古时期,中国文明在与西方文明相对隔离的情况下,经历了一个独立发展的漫长历程。在这个漫长的发展过程中,中国文明虽然起源于中国本土,但却不排除与域外的联系和接触的可能。在丝绸之路正式开通以前的一个相当长的时期里,中国与域外的交往实质上出现了一个初步发展的阶段,如"支那"和"赛里斯"名称的出现,即是中外交往所带来的痕迹。而近代以来考古发现的材料,则更进一步揭示了早期丝绸之路中外交往的一些史实。

一

考古材料证明,在俄罗斯外贝加尔地区发现的石核、石锯、石钻及锛形器等,即与山西沁水旧石器时代晚期下川文化的同类器具有高度的相似性。这暗示着在旧石器时代晚期,中国北方即与西伯利亚地区有着某种联系。在新石器时代,中国西北地区以及西藏、内蒙古和东北地区,都曾发现有重要文化标志细石器。这种细石器在中国最早出现于华北地区,它属于游牧狩猎型文化系统,从其石器形制和制作技术来看,通常被称为非几何形细石器。它与欧洲、北非、西南亚的几何形细石器不同,而与北亚、东北亚、南西伯利亚等地区的细石器文化则属同一系统。在蒙古的沙巴拉克、莫尔特因阿姆等遗址,以及俄罗斯贝加尔湖附近的塞尼米尔斯、久克台等遗址,即发现有这种类型的细石器。[①] 不仅如此,这种细石器还有可能通过中国西藏地区对印度东北部的非几何形细石器文化产生了影响。[②] 另外,日本和朝鲜半岛也都曾发现过同类制品。至于这种细石器是起源于中国华北还是起源于外贝加尔湖地区,目前似无定论。

在中国北方新石器时代和早期青铜时代出现的陶器、彩陶和青铜制品等,

---

① 中国大百科全书编委会编:《中国大百科全书·考古学》,中国大百科全书出版社1986年版,第43—44页、第66—67页、第653—655页、第706—707页;陈尚胜著:《五千年中外文化交流史》第一卷,世界知识出版社2002年版,第22—23页。
② 安志敏等:《藏北申札、双湖的旧石器和新石器》,《考古》1979年第6期。

都不同程度的凝聚着东西方文化交往的痕迹。西伯利亚的尖底、圜底罐文化系统陶器在中国北方的出现，中国北方的平底罐文化系统陶器在西伯利亚地区的出现，显示出中国北方与西伯利亚地区的文化联系。山陕黄土高原是仰韶文化的发源地，然而，仰韶文化彩陶的某些纹饰和形制与中亚、西亚的同类制品的相似性，显示出中国彩陶文化与中亚、西亚彩陶文化有着某种联系的可能。辽宁喀左县东山嘴红山文化遗址出土的陶塑裸体残迹，与欧亚大陆发现的所谓"早期维纳斯"塑像有着密切的关系。新疆古墓沟出土的石雕女像，亦无疑与分布于欧亚草原的石人为同一文化类型。在新疆、甘肃、陕西和内蒙古一带不同时期的文化遗址中所发现石质权杖头，则明显为出现于公元前4000年的美索不达米亚文化向东传播的物证。[①] 不仅如此，早期丝绸之路东西方交往的一个重要方面，还体现在青铜文化的传播中。

二

在公元前第4千纪初，西亚最早进入了青铜时代，其后，青铜制造技术便很快传播到远东、欧洲、北非等地。中国的青铜时代始于公元前21世纪，止于公元前5世纪。在新疆古墓沟墓地和小河墓地、甘肃东部的马家窑文化遗址、山西榆次源涡镇的仰韶文化遗址、河北武安的赵窑遗址、辽宁凌源牛河梁的红山文化遗址、山东泰安的大汶口文化遗址中，都曾发现有小件铜器或铜炼渣，标志着青铜工业的滥觞和铜石并用时代的来临。其中尤以新疆小河墓地出土的铜镜和马家窑文化遗址中所出土的青铜刀等，被一些学者认为是中国已知最早的青铜制品。中国早期青铜文化在北方的出现，不排除是通过早期丝绸之路由西向东传播的结果。这种青铜文化上的联系和影响，还体现在稍后的二里头文化晚期的青铜器中。

1980年，考古学者们曾在河南偃师二里头遗址中发现了具有北方系特色的环首柄刀。[②] 所谓"北方系"青铜器，亦被称之为"绥远青铜器"、"鄂尔多斯式青铜器"或"中国——西伯利亚"类型青铜器。这种北方系青铜器不仅分布于中国北方地区，同时在蒙古境内和俄罗斯外贝加尔地区、图瓦地区、米努辛斯克盆地、克拉斯诺亚尔斯克地区、阿尔泰地区，以及吉尔吉斯草原、鄂毕河

[①] 刘学堂：《新疆史前宗教研究》，民族出版社2009年版，第65—68页；李青：《丝绸之路楼兰艺术研究》，新疆人民出版社2010年版，第74—76页。
[②] 二里头工作队：《1980年河南偃师二里头遗址发掘简报》，《考古》1983年第3期。

中游地区直到黑海沿岸一带，都有零星发现。① 早期北方系青铜器的代表器物包括青铜短剑、管銎战斧和连铸的短柄青铜刀。这些器物显示了游牧文化的特征。有学者指出：

  出土这些器物的我国北方地区，当时与西伯利亚等地有着密切的青铜文化联系。而且，北方系青铜短剑和管銎式武器最早起源于伊朗，因此，它也反映了东西伯利亚地区以及我国北方地区与伊朗地区在青铜文化上的某种接触。②

三

  除青铜器外，早期玉器的发现亦昭示着中国内地与域外的交往迹象。中国的玉器最早出现于距今约7000年的新石器时代。在河姆渡文化、大汶口文化、良渚文化、红山文化、龙山文化和齐家文化等遗址中都曾发现有制作精良的玉器。早期玉器大都属软玉，主要产自新疆和田一带。从考古发现的情况来看，自新石器时代以后，新疆和田玉一直不断地向内地输入，在内地不同时期尤其是早期丝绸之路时期的文化遗址中所发现的和田玉器，都无疑成为内地与西域交往的重要物证。1976年，在河南安阳发掘商王武丁配偶妇好墓（约前13世纪末—前12世纪初）时，出土了750余件玉雕制品，其中包括琮、璧、圭等礼器，戈、戚、大刀、钺等仪仗器，以及人物和动物雕像等。这些玉制器均采用浮雕和圆雕的制作手法，雕琢精致。经鉴定，这些玉石均属软玉，绝大部分的产地为新疆和田，它们有可能是通过西北地区的游牧民族特别是月氏人转贩而来的。③ 另外，在先秦文献如《管子》、《山海经》、《穆天子传》中，亦有诸多关于昆仑玉的记载。由此可见，在早期丝绸之路时代，西域与内地之间即存着联系的通道，这条通道亦被一些学者称之为"玉石之路"。内地的丝绸向西方输出，西域的玉石向东方输入，构成了早期丝绸之路东西交往的景观。

  在早期丝绸之路时代，东西方的交往通道除沙漠之路外，主要还包括草原之路。草原之路是指经北方草原游牧民居地至中亚乃至东欧的道路，具体而言，是指从中原北上，经蒙古高原逾阿尔泰山脉和准噶尔盆地，进入中亚北部哈萨克草原，再经里海北岸、黑海北岸到达多瑙河流域的通道。这条通道是古代游

---

① 林沄：《商文化青铜器与北方地区青铜器关系之再研究》，《考古学文化论集》（一），文物出版社1987年版，第134页。
② 陈尚胜：《五千年中外文化交流史》第一卷，世界知识出版社2002年版，第28页。
③ 中国社会科学院考古研究所：《殷墟玉器》，文物出版社1982年版，第11—19页。

牧民族的迁徙之路，亦是早期丝绸之路东西方文化交往的主要通道。如果说早期北方青铜文化和二里头青铜器受到了西方青铜文化的影响，那么，其文化传播渠道除沙漠之路外，更重要的还有可能是草原之路。在公元前 2000 年之际，东欧的印欧语系民族斯基泰人即是沿草原之路由西而东并南下印度或东北行至阿尔泰地区。① 在商王朝建立之前，其先民经常迁徙，活动范围较广。② 在公元前 18 世纪至前 17 世纪，当商部落兴起之时，活动在华北一带的操阿尔泰语系诸语言的北狄族便被排挤到北方。其后，由于殷商王朝的不断扩张，则有可能使北狄族向更北的方向迁徙。③ 考古发现的材料也不断地揭示着草原之路东西交往的史实。

1950 年，俄罗斯考古学者在西伯利亚地区贝加尔湖沿岸发现了格拉兹科沃文化（Glazkovo Culture）墓葬，年代为公元前 1800—前 1300 年，出土的白玉环同商代流行的白玉环、白玉璧的形制和纹饰十分近似。而中国玉器出现的时间应比格拉兹科沃早数千年，因而不排除格拉兹科沃文化受到中国文化影响的可能。

1912 年，俄罗斯考古学者在今下诺夫哥罗德市附近塞伊马火车站旁发现了塞伊马墓地（Seima Cemetery）。年代当在公元前第 2 千纪后半期。墓地的属有者为原始芬兰——乌戈尔人。随葬品有锛、矛、刀、剑等青铜器，同时还出土了白玉环等玉器。俄罗斯考古学家戈罗德佐夫（V. A. Corodtsov）曾指出："塞伊马墓地出土的白玉环是西伯利亚出产的，但年代明显晚于商代玉器。"④ 俄罗斯考古学家吉谢列夫（С. В. К. иселев）认为：

> 白玉的西传完全证实，在塞伊马时期，伏尔加河和卡马河沿岸、西伯利亚、贝加尔湖沿岸和中国北部之间有过联系。塞伊马、图尔宾诺、贝加尔湖沿岸和绥远（内蒙古）等地相似铜刀的形制很可能也是沿玉器之路（即草原之路）传播的。经由此路传播者还有塞伊马出土的其他器物：锛和菱形铤的矛。这类器物现已不能认为只是西部的产品了，安阳出土的锛同塞伊马所出十分相像，同器身较厚、只饰三角纹而无菱形纹的外乌拉尔类型尤其相似。类似的锛在绥远也有。矛头

---

① 张国刚、吴莉苇：《中西文化关系史》，高等教育出版社 2006 年版，第 30—31 页。
② 王国维：《说自契至于成汤八迁》，《观堂集林》，河北教育出版社 2001 年版，第 326 页。
③ ［俄］吉谢列夫：《南西伯利亚古代史》（上册），新疆社会科学院民族研究所 1981 年版，第 88 页。
④ 转引自张广达、王小甫：《天涯若比邻——中外文化交流史略》，香港中华书局 1988 年版，第 10—11 页。

的情形也是这样。塞伊马矛头分布很广，从摩尔达维亚到南西伯利亚，从伏尔加河和卡马河到伊塞克湖都有，因此，现在不能认为它们是这一广大地区某个中心所产。研究西欧和近东青铜时代的矛头类型，没有发现这样的器形。但是远东却发现有类似的器形，如安阳就有带菱形铤的矛头。最后，奥克拉德尼科夫（А. ЛОКЛαДНИКов）在谢片察诸遗址发现的三足陶器也是一个证据，这些陶器同中国鼎和鬲完全相同。①

四

尽管塞伊马文化与殷商青铜文化有着明显的联系，但是，还不能将它们简单看做是一方对另一方的单向影响，尤其是在不同的时期，它们之间的关系则存在着不同的互动状态。如上所引，吉谢列夫虽然认为商文化通过草原之路对塞伊玛文化产生了一定的影响，但是，他同时还指出，商代后期的青铜文化之所以有高度的成就，是由于塞伊马文化影响的结果。② 而林沄则认为，塞伊马文化兼有西方的安德罗诺沃文化和东方的卡拉苏克文化的成分，它本身就是一种包含着东西方文化因素的青铜文化，因此也就无从谈起它作为青铜文化的一种类型而对商文化产生了多大的影响。③ 即便如此，从早期青铜文化发展序列来看，商代青铜文化以及北方系青铜器都直接或间接地与南西伯利亚青铜时代文化，如阿凡纳谢沃文化、奥库涅夫文化、安德罗诺沃文化、卡拉苏克文化以及上述格拉兹科沃文化和塞伊马文化等有着一定的渊源或互动的关系。

考古发现和研究证明，人类用铜最早是在公元前 6 千年的安纳托利亚地区开始，在进入锡青铜时代以前，有过很长一段使用红铜和坤铜合金的时间。从安纳托利亚向世界各地传播金属冶炼技术的时间，大约在公元前 2000 年左右。分布于南西伯利亚叶尼塞河中游米奴辛斯克盆地和阿尔泰地区的阿凡纳谢沃文化，年代约在公元前 3 千纪下半叶至前 2 千纪初，介于当地新石器文化与奥库涅夫文化之间，居民属古欧罗巴人种，是欧亚大陆欧罗巴人种的最东支。该文化用红铜打制耳环、手镯等饰物和针、锥、小刀等用具，文化特征同黑海沿岸竖

---

① ［俄］吉谢列夫：《南西伯利亚古代史》（上册），新疆社会科学院民族研究所 1981 年版，第 71 页。
② ［俄］吉谢列夫：《苏联境内青铜文化与中国商文化的关系》，《考古》1960 年第 2 期。
③ 林沄：《商文化青铜器与北方地区青铜器关系之再研究》，《考古学文化论集》（一），文物出版社 1987 年版，第 134 页。

穴墓文化、木椁文化以及中亚扎曼巴巴文化有不同程度的相似性。① 其冶铜技术有可能是后来出现于叶尼塞河中游米奴辛斯克盆地的奥库涅夫青铜文化之源。奥库涅夫文化为南西伯利亚青铜时代文化，年代为公元前2千纪上半叶，晚于阿凡纳谢沃文化，早于安德罗诺沃文化。出土有较多的红铜和青铜器，有锻制的鱼钩、刀、锥、鬓环和铸造的斧等。该文化居民属蒙古人种，这是一个值得注意的现象。② 在奥库涅夫文化之后，南西伯利亚出现了著名的安德罗诺沃文化，其分布地域西起南乌拉尔，东到叶尼塞河沿岸，北起西伯利亚森林南界，南达中亚诸草原。年代约为公元前2千纪至1千纪初，早于卡拉苏克文化。从考古发现的情况来看，该文化中的青铜制造技术已经达到了一个较为成熟的阶段。金属制品有青铜锻造或铸造的武器、工具及其他日用器具，如斧、矛、镞、刀、短剑、锛、凿、锯、镐、鱼钩、锥、针以及铜箍，也有青铜串珠和饰牌等。该文化居民属欧罗巴人种的一个特殊类型。其文化有可能起源于西部地区，特别是北哈萨克斯坦和外乌拉尔一带。③

在奥库涅夫文化尤其是安德罗诺沃文化时期，中国与南西伯利亚发生了密切的联系。以蒙古人种为主体的民族创造了奥库涅夫文化，该文化消失之后，这些蒙古人有可能向东向南迁徙，从而推动了北方系乃至中原一带青铜文化的发展。此后，以欧罗巴人种为主体的安德罗诺沃人不仅有可能通过草原之路将青铜制造技术直接或间接地向中国北方以及伊犁河流域、阿尔泰山及和中原一带传播，而且他们还越过天山通过沙漠之路来到塔里木盆地，在克里雅河至罗布泊一带定居下来，创造了古墓沟墓地、小河墓地、克里雅墓地等一系列西域早期青铜文化。

中国境内的史前遗址中，虽然也有少量的青铜和青铜遗物出现，但真正进入青铜时代的年代大约在公元前2千纪左右，与奥库涅夫文化和安德罗诺沃文化时代相当，这绝非是偶然现象。然而，在此后由于商文化的不断发展，如前所述中国文化又与安德罗诺沃文化之后的塞伊马文化发生了联系，不仅影响了塞伊马文化的发展，同时也有可能受到塞伊马文化尤其是青铜制造文化的影响。而到卡拉苏克文化时期，中国商周文化通过草原之路对南西伯利亚的影响则愈见鲜明。

---

① 中国大百科全书编委会编：《中国大百科全书·考古学》，中国大百科全书出版社1986年版，第2—3页。
② 中国大百科全书编委会编：《中国大百科全书·考古学》，中国大百科全书出版社1986年版，第23页。
③ 中国大百科全书编委会编：《中国大百科全书·考古学》，中国大百科全书出版社1986年版，第15—16页。

重建艺术与生活之间的联系

——重新认识东方"艺道"观的未来价值

（摘要）

中国艺术研究院研究生院党委书记　李新风

亚洲文化、东方文化具有自己鲜明的特性。这一点如果与西方尤其是西方近现代文化相对比，就尤为明显。我们仅以艺术为例。在我看来，强调艺术与自然和人的生活整体之间的内在联系的"艺道"观便是具有鲜明东方文化特点的根本艺术观念。而它与西方近现代以来的主导性的"自律"艺术观念形成鲜明的对比。

东方的"艺道"观，讲求以艺进道、以艺媚道、以艺明道、以艺载道、以艺求道。用北大楼宇烈教授的话说，即"以道统艺"、"由艺臻道"，都是讲艺不离道、艺不远道，即艺术并不脱离天地自然之道与社会人伦之道，而恰恰是道以艺显、艺以明道，道与艺合、艺与道一，甚至可以说，"艺即道"。这样一种"艺道"观，在中国的道家与儒家的艺术观念中均有充分的体现，尽管对于"道"的内涵的解释或有侧重点上的区别——道家之道更主要的是天地自然之道，而儒家之道更主要的是社会人伦之道。而在佛教及中国化佛教即禅宗中，在东亚日本的传统艺术观念中，也有鲜明的体现。这种艺道观植根于艺术与自然和人生之间原本具有的天然不可分割的联系的基础上，符合艺术创造自身的实际，也有利于艺术自身的实践。这种艺术观念，形成了东方世界艺术人生化、艺术不离功用以及人生艺术化、生活审美化的强大传统，也导致除所谓专业性诗人、艺术家的创作之外，大量的诸如书道、茶道、花道等生活艺术形式的出现。这种理论的合理性与优越性是十分明显的。

然而，当历史进入现代社会以来，在"西风东渐"的总的历史文化语境下，亚洲（东方）各国争先恐后地将来自近现代西方的思想观念、思维方法引入自身文化体系，而对自己的文化传统重新审视乃至重新评价、重新建构。许多东方世界传统的思想、观念遭到质疑乃至批判、抛弃。在艺术观念上，同样是以西方近现代的艺术观念来重新审视、重评重构东方自身的艺术观。其中，居于核心的是用西方以康德为代表的、人为划分真善美三大价值之间的分界、明确切断艺术与自然和人的生活整体之间的内在联系的艺术"自律"观，来否定东方传统的艺术观。在这样的大潮中,东方传统的艺道观实际上被作为一种负面的遗产而受到批判和否定,遭到被遗弃的命运。

今天,西方那种人为割断艺术与自然、人生之间本有的密切关联的"自律"艺术观在整个世界范围内(包括在欧美的西方世界)开始受到重新审视和评价,其罔顾艺术与自然、人生的真实存在的内在联系的主观性、人为性、虚妄性、武断性,越来越清晰地呈现在人们面前,它的使艺术异化的弊端也愈益明显地暴露出来。与之相比,东方传统的艺道观,其对于艺术与自然、人生之真实关系的阐释的真理性将得到重新发现和重新认识与评价,它在未来人类艺术观的重构中必将发挥应有的积极作用而得到高度的重视。

云南跨境民族母语文化融入"一带一路"战略发展意义研究

云南民族大学　李　瑛

云南面向"三亚"(东南亚、南亚、西亚),肩挑"两洋"(太平洋、印度洋),自古就是中国与南亚、东南亚各国的陆上通道,出境公共路20多条,是南方丝绸之路上的重要省份,在国家战略构想"一带一路"建设中具有重要的作用和意义。

云南历史悠久、文化深厚、宗教多元、民族特色鲜明,中国56个民族中,世居云南的民族25个、云南特有民族15个、人口较少民族8个,尤其是有16个民族跨境而居。云南与缅甸、老挝、越南三国接壤,与泰国、孟加拉、柬埔寨印度等国家地缘相接,是跨境民族[①]最多的省份,16个跨境民族(傣族、景颇族、苗族、拉祜族、佤族、壮族、傈僳族、哈尼族、彝族、独龙族、布依族、瑶族、德昂族、阿昌族、怒族、布朗族)分别生活在总长为4060公里的边界线上:中缅边界线1997公里、中老边界线710公里、中越边界线1353公里,他们"山川同脉、江河同流、民族同宗、文化同源",如"傣—泰民族"就包括中国境内的傣族、泰国的泰族(Tai)、缅甸的掸族(Shan)、老挝的老族(Lao)等生活在澜沧江湄公河流域的民族。众多少数民族跨境分布,对云南边疆地区的建设与发展产生着重大影响,正是在这个意义上,可以看到国家发展与少数民族工作的重要联系。

跨境民族是一种特殊的民族现象,尽管跨境民族所生活的国家不同、体制不同、意识形态不同、社会生活环境相异,但相互之间影响很大,彼此在语言、文化、宗教、风俗、经济、血缘(亲属)和地缘等方面的联系不仅难以割裂,且会一直持续下去。作为中国西南的门户,云南跨境民族在"一带一路"发展战略中,无论是打造经济走廊、提升技术应用、旅游开发、生态保护,还是保护物质文化与非物质文化遗产、传承民族传统文化、维护民族团结与世界和平,都发挥着不可替代的作用,尤其是其母语文化作为意识形态的直接和最重要表现,所起到的交流、传播及影响作用更大,必定要融入"一带一路"战略发展

---

① 就地域而论,跨境民族指一切政治疆界与民族分布不相吻合而跨国界居住的民族。

之中，发挥积极意义。

1. 母语交流增进感情、和顺睦邻，是延续和提升母语文化地位、促进边疆地区和谐发展与社会稳定的良好手段。

云南跨境民族母语文化境内外发展虽不平衡，但十分丰富：壮族有中国政府帮助创制并批准推行的壮文（广西）；越南壮族也有政府帮助创制的拉丁字母拼音壮文；苗族则国内主要分布在贵州、湖南、云南、四川和广西等省区，国外苗族分布在越南、老挝、泰国、缅甸、美国、法国、加拿大、澳大利亚、德国和阿根廷等。苗语内部有方言、次方言之分，国内苗族分别使用几种不同的方言、次方言语，国外苗族则只使用其中的川黔滇方言、川黔滇次方言苗语。国内外苗族使用多种不同的文字形式，其中，国内有湘西苗文、黔东苗文、川黔滇苗文、滇东北老苗文、滇东北新苗文等；国外主要有越南苗文、老挝苗文、杨松罗苗文等，国内外瑶族大部分使用瑶语，民间有使用仿汉方块瑶文的传统，同时创制有拉丁字母拼音瑶文，并实现了国内外的统一；彝族国内分布在云南、四川、贵州和广西，国外分布在越南和老挝等。国内外彝族共同使用彝语，内部分六大方言，且差别较大。彝族有老彝文存在，但现在学和用的人不多，四川、云南和贵州分别对本省的老彝文进行了规范，并推行和使用；哈尼族国内分布在云南红河、思茅和西双版纳等地，国外分布在越南、老挝、缅甸和泰国。哈尼语内部分哈雅、碧卡和豪白三大方言，国内哈尼族有政府帮助创制的哈尼文，国外哈尼族有的有本民族文字，有的没有；傣族国内分布在云南德宏、版纳、思茅等地，国外包括缅甸的掸族、越南的泰族、老挝的泰族和泰国的泐人等。傣族使用傣语，分傣那和傣泐两个方言。国内傣族分别使用傣那文（德宏）、傣仂文（版纳）、傣绷文和金平傣文等，缅甸掸族使用傣绷文，越南泰族使用金平傣文，也有新创的拉丁傣文；景颇族国内分布在云南德宏，国外分布缅甸的克钦邦和掸邦。景颇族使用景颇语和载瓦语，文字也有景颇文和载瓦文两种。前者于19世纪末创制于缅甸，1957年国内对其进行改造，缅甸则沿用原形式，后者系国内于1956年创制，且只在国内推行和使用；傈僳族国内分布在云南怒江、丽江、迪庆等地，国外分布在缅甸和泰国。傈僳语分怒江、禄劝等方言。国内傈僳族使用老傈僳文、新傈文等，国外则只使用老傈僳文；拉祜族国内分布在云南思茅和临沧，国外分布在缅甸、泰国、老挝和越南。拉祜语分拉祜纳和拉祜西两种方言。拉祜族原有一套拉祜文，国内于1956年对其进行改革并实验推行，国外则没有改革；佤族国内分布在云南临沧和思茅，国外分布在缅甸、泰国和老挝。佤族使用佤语，过去英国传教士为佤族创制有佤文，称"撒拉文"，但国内于1956年另外创制了一套佤文，国外及国内的信教群众则使用"撒拉文";德昂族国内分布在云南德宏州,国外分布在缅甸。德昂族操德昂语,国内没有本民族文字,国外则使用缅文、掸文字母拼写德昂语;独龙族国内居住在云南怒江贡山县,国外住在缅甸克钦邦独龙江下游。独龙族使用独龙语,过去传教士曾为缅甸独龙族创制有拉丁字母拼音文字,称日汪文,现缅甸独龙族仍在使用,因语音差别,国内于1983年又设计有独龙语拼音方案并试行。

以上多种语言,至今依然活跃在跨境民族群众生活之中,是他们保持联系的一个重要、有效和现实的方式,在平时走亲访友、赶集赴会、民俗节日、歌会歌圩等场合,互相使用母语拉家常、讲故事,长期以来,形成情感上相互联系、经济上相互往来、文化上相互渗透的局面。"一带一路"战略构想中重要的理念内涵是中国与周边国家共同建设、共同发展,云南跨境民族母语文化为其奠定了深厚的全方位交流的语言文化基础;

2. 母语文学强化跨境民族的认同感和历史感,发挥母语文化巨大的归宿力量,是边疆地区民族认同、经济发展的精神基础。

云南跨境民族母语文学是母语文化的重要载体和重要内容,表现为三个层次:一是口传文学、二是古籍文献、三是作家母语创作。口传文学如神话、史诗、传说、故事、诗歌、歌谣、谚语等,很多口传文学都在境内外流传,有的民间文化品种在中国境内衰落和失传,但邻国却保存较好;反过来,有的在境内传承得很好,邻国却失传了。此外,大量有文字记录的古籍资料是母语文化的历史表达,如傣族的贝叶经、彝文古籍等,数万卷堪称民族古籍博物馆,其中彝族长篇叙事诗《阿诗玛》已入选第一批国家非物质文化遗产名录。无论是口传文学还是古籍文献,其母语叙事传统"同源异流"、跨境交流的特点,不仅促进了"一带一路"建设中境内外民族文化频繁接触,同时,带动了跨境民族在经济方面的相互联系,为境内外各民族以及中国与周边国家共同建设、共同发展打下良好的人文环境,是云南面向东南亚、南亚呈辐射中心的重要内容之一。

与口传文学和古籍文献相比较,云南跨境民族作家母语创作起步于新中国成立初期,近二十年来发展迅猛。云南25个世居民族中,22个民族有自己的语言,14个民族有自己的文字,由此奠定了云南少数民族母语文学丰富多样的基础,其中,跨境民族作家母语创作有德宏州的景颇族、傣族、傈僳族,西双版纳州的傣族,怒江州的傈僳族,红河州的哈尼族、苗族,文山州的苗族等,母语文学作品除具有独特的美学风格和艺术特点之外,对中国西南边疆多民族地区文化和谐、民族认同具有特殊的作用与意义,跨境民族作家母语创作彰显出边疆特有的人文精神内涵,提升了母语文化的地位,深化和发展了我国与南亚、东南亚各民族友好关系，有助于"一带一路"战略构想的实施，尤其是在东南亚、南亚地缘政治格局发生变化的情况下，云南跨境民族作家采用各自的母语创作，对境外相邻民族有着较大的影响，是国家认同、祖国统一的精神武器，众多作家的母语作品犹如边疆地区跨境民族文化交流的一座桥梁，担负着边疆和谐文化建设的重任，意义深远。云南跨境民族作家母语文学原创作品不仅在当地人民群众中具有影响力，同时，对境外同一民族特别具有神奇的感召力量。苗语诗人张元奇在文山人民广播电台举办的春节联欢晚会（1987 年）上，朗诵了他创作的苗语诗歌《我们的名字叫苗族》，翻译为汉语是：

> 为什么我们要说自己的语言/为什么我们要穿自己的服装/不为别的什么/只为我们的名字叫苗族/为什么我们要学习自己的文字/为什么我们不忘记自己的历史/不为别的什么/因为我们的名字叫苗族/为什么我们要传承自己的文化/为什么我们要保持自己的风俗/不为别的什么/因为我们的名字叫苗族/我们有自己的血统/我们有自己的骨肉/我们有自己的思想/我们有自己的使命/我们是世界上的一个民族/别人的历史有多悠久我们的历史也有多悠久/我们勤劳/我们勇敢/我们有生存的权利/我们有发展的主张/我们居住在这个世界上/足迹从东方洒满西方/我们从不怕谁/我们不做奴隶/我们不欺弱小/我们爱好和平/我们与其他民族一道/共创和谐美好的社会/无论走到哪里我们是苗族/无论经过多少世纪我们是苗族/我们不会忘记自己的名字——/苗族！苗族！！苗族！！！①

该诗歌受到了广大苗族人的称赞，后来由文山苗族陶永华谱成歌曲，流传到越南、老挝、泰国、美国、法国等国家的苗族聚居区，对促进文山苗族和国外苗族的友好交流产生了积极的影响，激起离散千年、遍布世界多地的苗族同胞共同的民族认同感。

3. 东南亚、南亚在中国对外政策战略中一直居于重要地位，而云南位于中国西南边疆，具有独特的区位优势。目前，强调与周边国家互联互通，加强与丝绸之路沿线国家经济合作、文化交流，而云南跨境民族与周边毗邻国家的很多民族同源异流，由此，借助跨境民族母语文化在云南与东南亚、南亚之间的

---

① 杨桂林：《滇南苗乡苗族当代文学雏议——云南文山苗族当代文学创作回顾》，文山壮族苗族自治州苗学发展研究会编：《中国西部苗族学术研讨会论文集》，云南民族出版社 2011 年版。

天然纽带关系，充分发挥云南跨境民族母语文化的软实力作用，增进互信，促进合作，加深友谊，为"一带一路"建设营造良好的而社会环境和国际环境。所以，从国家层面保护和发展母语文化，全方位展示跨境民族母语生活多层共生的现实状况，契合当代"一带一路"战略发展的文化构想与精神诉求。

  1956年，周恩来总理特批云南德宏傣族景颇族自治州《团结报》社成立，并以傣族、景颇族、傈僳族、汉族（后又增加景颇族载瓦语）五种民族文字出版发行，表现了政治家的远见卓识。云南跨境民族母语文化的发展，除作家们自己发表和出版作品的形式之外，媒体的载体和传播功能如同推进器，使其远播周边的东南亚国家。德宏州文联于1981年创刊主办了德宏傣文文艺期刊《勇罕》、景颇文文艺期刊《文蚌》、傈僳语刊物《W—Ny》（后停刊），西双版纳自治州文联则创办了西双版纳傣语文艺期刊《版纳》，这些刊物长期刊发少数民族作家的母语文学作品，不仅得到境内老百姓的喜爱，也同样受到境外老百姓的欢迎，景颇文文艺期刊《文蚌》除在国内发行，在德宏州景颇族人民中传阅外，还正式发行到缅甸克钦地区，对境外景颇族有很大影响。云南省广播电视台则专设民族语言频率频道，目前建立了景颇族、傣族（包括德宏、西双版纳傣语）、傈僳族、拉祜族等四个民族、五个语种的电台民族语节目部，很多地州也建立了少数民族母语广播电台，如文山人民广播电台有苗语、壮语、瑶语广播，覆盖面主要是越南宣光省、和江省、老街省的部分区域，境外听众达100多万。明尼苏达州立大学教授杨道博士（美籍苗族）1987年到昆明听到文山台带去的苗语歌曲，他感慨地说："世界上有七八个苗语广播电台，文山台才是最正宗的，希望文山电台的苗语广播能给世界人民传播友谊的佳音。"泰国披集省克梅村苗族村长侯宗夸（泰名玛纳）从80年代初，就一直收听文山台的苗族语广播，1991年3月13日，当时文山还没有对外开放，他受两百多户苗民委托，带着美好的祝愿，辗转昆明，绕道前来文山台专门拜访全体苗语采编译播人员。[①]1997年，德宏州建立了"德宏少数民族语言文化电视译制传播中心"，为播出傣语、景颇语、载瓦语（景颇支系）的民族语电视专用频道，其中有"傣族名著名剧欣赏"栏目。该中心的民语节目设计覆盖率约为150万人口，德宏的邻居州保山以及缅甸边境一线地区不同程度地可以收看节目。随着社会、经济、文化的发展，不只是省一级、州一级有条件开设母语电台广播，县一级的广播电视局也逐渐拓展母语广播事业，如屏边县人民广播电台于2012年9月正式开播，

[①] 云南广播电视局宣传管理处：《"油毛毡精神"绽放的民族之花——文山人民广播电台民语频率先进事迹》，2010年9月20日。

特设苗语节目。

当然，跨境民族母语文化在发展中也存在一些问题，如境内外文字使用问题。云南省语委资料显示，云南16个跨境民族中，有12个民族（傣族、景颇族、彝族、哈尼族、壮族、苗族、瑶族、藏族、傈僳族、拉祜族、佤族、独龙族等）在境外有相应的民族文字，境外文字影响现象日益突出，如傈僳族过去国内外都使用外国传教士创制的老傈僳文，国内外不少群众至今仍然使用，但50年代以后，国内认为老傈僳文是外国传教士创制的，于是又另外创制出一套新傈僳文，致使国内傈僳族出现了同时使用新老傈僳文的情况，引发了新老傈僳文之争的一些矛盾。再如，有的人希望境内使用境外的文字，利用报刊、广播、VCD光碟等影响境内民族语言。据调查，仅在德宏州，境外流入的傣文、景颇文、载瓦文和傈僳文报刊书籍达几百种，藏语、傣语、景颇语、载瓦语、傈僳语、苗语、瑶语等民族语广播电台就有几十家，至于VCD光碟，在一些边境民族地区随处可见，估计有200多种40余万片（碟）；境内少数民族经常看境外民文报刊、听境外民族语广播、播放境外光碟，所受影响不小。跨境民族母语文化问题被境外某些别有用心的人拿来做人权讲坛意见，影响了边疆的稳定。

总而言之，跨境民族本民族意识、宗教意识、境内外文化交流的引导和影响首先依赖于语言文字工作，随着"一带一路"战略构想的实施与建设，倡导推动云南跨境民族母语文化境内外交流与对话机制，保护、延续、发展母语文化，有利于增强民族的凝聚力，实现云南跨境民族母语文化与外交之间的良性互动，深化我国与南亚、东南亚各国的友好关系，意义深远。

"一带一路"沿线民间文学与民族关系研究
（摘要）

中央民族大学　林继富

"一带一路"借用古代"丝绸之路"的历史符号，意在共同打造文化包容的利益共同体、命运共同体。在"一带一路"建设中，文化建设先行的理念成为政治家和学人的共识。在"一带一路"文化建设中，民间文学作为沿线多民族流传最广泛、历史最悠久、影响最深远、生活中最活跃的传统文化，在民族发展和民族交往中发挥了重要作用。

"一带一路"沿线民间文学是跨民族和跨地域的生活文化，这些民间文学以多样化的方式存活在民众生活中，并且具有穿越不同民族和地域的特殊力量。不同民族讲述同一个故事，同一个故事在不同民族中流传，意涵着民间文学包含了民族共同价值观、道德观作用下的不同民族情感的流动和文化采借行为，由此凸显民间文学所包含的多民族文化元素背后隐藏的文化交流和民族交往等功能。

"一带一路"沿线民间文学包含了丰富的民族交往关系内容，在历史上，不同民族因为不同的生活习惯，他们在讲述民间文学时具有选择性和倾向性。从现实生活来看，"一带一路"沿线民间文学作为民族交往关系的特殊性不断被演绎。从深层次挖掘民间文学心理上的趋同特点，讨论民间文学的意义和心理结构，寻找"民心相同"与"一带一路"沿线多民族民间文学共同性结构关系。

民间文学是口头讲述、口头传承的文学，这种文学是生活的记录，是情感的再现，因此，"一带一路"沿线民间文学成为多民族生活关系和文化关系的记忆，润滑着不同民族之间的交往关系。

海上丝绸之路、海丝文化与闽南

福建省社会科学院　刘登翰

一、从经济命题向文化命题延伸

中央提出的"一带一路"发展战略，特别是国家主席习近平在 2013 年 10 月访问东南亚诸国时提出的"建设 21 世纪海上丝绸之路"的倡议，这是一个内涵丰富、深刻，在当前世界多极化、经济全球化、文化多样化、社会信息化的时代环境下，指引中国与海上丝路沿线国家实现互联互通、合作发展、经济共荣的顶层战略设计和实践平台。中央发表的《一带一路愿景与行动》的文件指出："'一带一路'旨在促进经济要素有序自由流动、资源高效配置和市场深度融合，推动沿线各国实现经济政策协调，开展更大范围、更高水平、更深层次的区域合作，共同打造开放、包容、均衡、普惠的区域经济合作架构。"

由此可见，建设海上丝绸之路主要是一个经济命题。

但历史经验告诉我们，经济命题从来不仅仅只是经济，它的背后，或它的本身，渗透着复杂的文化因素，甚至本身就是一种文化。因此，经济命题必然要向文化命题延伸和转化，这样的例子，不胜枚举。

这首先因为，一切社会活动——包括经济活动，都是人的活动，以人为主体和由人来主导的，即使在信息时代，也莫不如此。人是文化的创造者，同时又是文化的创造物，因此人是文化的最大载体，也是文化最重要的传播媒介，不管你自觉还是不自觉，人走到哪里，文化便传播到哪里。从这个意义上说，所有经济交往，也都是人的交往，其实质也是一种文化的交往。

其次，广义地说，经济也是一种文化。经济是一个抽象的概念，它是价值的创造、转化和实现。如果我们把价值创造的成果视为一个个具象的"物"，那么每个具象的"物"，都有它从设计、制作到生产的过程。比如历史上大量外销的瓷器，瓷器的最早发现、烧制和使用，是中国人智慧的体现。它包括了物质性的显形文化和非物质性的隐形文化两个层面。一个杯子，从瓷土的开采、烧制到最后成型，是显形的物质文化；而瓷土的发现、配方直到产品的设计、造型、上釉、彩绘等技术手段和创造思维，则是潜隐着制作者智慧的一种非物质性的隐形文化。而它在流通过程中，海路的开通，造船的技术、人际的交往、贸易的方式等，也无不承载着丰富的文化内涵。在经济交往中，不仅是人，"物"也是文化的重要载体。

不同区域、国家的经济交往，可能由于某种原因一时中断或终止；而其在交往过程中产生的文化传播、交汇和遗存，却不会随着经济交往的中断而消失，它还长久地保存在后世的社会生活中，发挥作用。通往中亚的（陆上）丝绸之路，自宋元以后，实际上已经中断了一千余年；但当年融入汉文化中的西域或中亚文化，仍活跃在今天的中国、特别是西北地区的社会生活之中。经东南亚、南亚通往西亚和欧洲的海上丝绸之路，也几度中断，但中华文化的诸多元素，仍在今日的东南亚诸国文化中清晰可见。相对而言，经济比较容易受到外在因素干扰而中断，而文化一经留存，却是长久、永恒的。

经济命题向文化命题的转化，或从文化视角看经济，是对建设海上丝绸之路认识的深入。

二、闽南文化的海洋精神对海上丝绸之路的推动

（一）两种不同的海洋观和海洋价值取向

在地球表面上，海洋所占面积约百分之七十。海洋把陆地分割，但海洋也使被分割的陆地交往成为可能。因此，走向海洋，是人类必然的选择。

面对海洋，东西方有不同的海洋观和海洋价值取向。

西方的海洋观，其理论起点来自黑格尔。黑格尔在《历史哲学》的"历史的地理基础"中提出了与地理相联系的三种文化形态：草原和高地的游牧文化、以陆地为天限的农耕文化、与海为邻的海洋文化。认为以非洲为代表的游牧文化，是野蛮和原始的；以亚洲为代表的农耕文化，是封闭和保守的；唯有以欧洲为代表的海洋文化，才是开放、竞争、勇于冒险和征服的。虽然他承认，"精神文明从亚细亚升起"，但世界历史是从东方走向西方，而欧洲是绝对的"西方"，"绝对是世界的中央和终极"。这样的海洋观，成为16世纪以来欧洲崛起的海洋殖民帝国的扩张性和掠夺性的理论支持。

中国不仅是一个内陆国家，中国还有着漫长的海岸线和沿海岛屿，特别东部和南部疆域，与海相生相伴，有着丰富的海洋文化资源。但中国从不把海洋作为向外领土扩张和财富掠夺的手段和途径，这是和西方完全不同的海洋观和海洋价值取向。15世纪明永乐年间，郑和奉命七下西洋（最后一次由其副手王

景弘率领），比哥伦布发现新大陆还早。但郑和此行，目的只是以宣昭和赏赐来弘扬天朝威仪，结好邻近国家，只有政治目的而无领土扩张和经济掠夺的举措。在此之前，从唐宋到元，无论从陆上或海上来到中国的商人，最初是以"朝贡"的方式实现贸易的目的，即向政府进呈纳贡，然后获得加倍（有时甚至是10倍、20倍）丰厚的"回赏"。随后政府设置市舶司，专管对外贸易和来华洋舶。在朝贡贸易的同时，发展市舶贸易，即民间私商与外商的贸易，由市舶司代表政府监管和抽税。中国的远航海上和对外贸易，是以扩大政治影响和睦邻、互惠（就朝贡贸易而言，惠外更多）为目标。这样的海洋观和海洋价值取向，才可能使海上丝绸之路成为一条贸易之路、合作之路、友谊之路、和平之路。

（二）海上丝绸之路的两条路径

"丝绸之路"的命名是德国地理学家李希霍芬提出的。他在19世纪60年代到中亚和中国考察，发现从公元2世纪的汉代开始，就存在一条从长安、洛阳经河西走廊到中亚、西亚，最后到达欧洲的商道，其主要物流是输出中国的丝绸，便以"丝绸之路"名之。这条沟通亚欧非几大文明体系的商贸之路，最初在汉武帝时代的开通，更多的是出于政治和军事的目的；直到唐代，经济和人文的交流才逐渐繁盛起来。然而这条丝绸之路沿线，诸多国家、民族的矛盾纠葛重重，实际上通少断多。在唐初强盛国力的保障下，曾经一度繁盛，之后便逐渐淹没了。

陆路之不可行，公元9世纪善于经商的阿拉伯商人绕道海上，开拓了通往广州、泉州、宁波、扬州等南中国沿海港口城市的商道，重续与中国的贸易。因此海上丝绸之路从唐代开始，经宋、元而达到高潮，他们带来了珍珠、宝石、犀角、香料和其他矿产，带走的除传统的丝绸之外，更主要的产品是以陶瓷和茶叶兼及其他手工业品为大宗，但仍仿效"丝绸之路"之名，称为"海上丝绸之路"。在经过宋元两代的繁荣之后，明代开国之初即厉行禁海，从政策上把这条海上丝路封杀了。然而到了明中叶，景泰新政，重开海路，"准贩东西洋"。在宋元号称"东方第一大港"的泉州后渚港，因淤塞等原因失去优势，新崛起的漳州月港便取而代之，其"海舶鳞集，商贾成聚"，盛况空前。至明末清初，为防倭乱和明郑的海上政权，重施海禁，实行迁界，使盛况一时的月港海上贸易再次跌入低谷。然而此时这一国际化的海上贸易已趋成熟，不仅有传统的航路，北向琉球、朝鲜、日本，南从菲律宾走向美洲，东经东南亚、南亚而到中亚、西亚、欧洲和非洲；更有新崛起的西班牙、葡萄牙海上帝国等绕过中亚商人，直接进入中国海要求贸易，开放口岸。政府之禁海，迫使成长起来的私商入海寻求与外商交易,并为了利益保障购买武器,成为纵横海上的许多商业武装集团。这些被政府视为"走私"或"海盗"的海上商业武装集团,通过争斗、兼并,最后形成了郑芝龙、郑成功集团一支独大。彼时郑氏集团控制了台湾海峡的黄金航道,过往船只须向郑氏报关、纳税,领取令旗,便可保一路平安畅通。明郑在台湾建立的反清复明政权,其庞大经费多由此来。康熙平定台湾之后,在厦门设立海关,对外贸易的中心便南移厦门。清末民初,战乱频发,社会动乱,民间商人便把资金转向东南亚,大批城市贫民和破产农民也循迹走向南洋,一个浩大的"下南洋"移民潮大都以厦门为出海通道。

从历史上看,中国人踏上海上丝路,实际有两个导向,也是两条路径,一是官方的导向,二是民间的导向。两个导向和两种路径,表现出海上丝路不同的形成过程和贸易方式。

(三) 闽南文化的海洋精神对海上丝路的延续和发展

《山海经》称"闽在海中"。其北,高耸的武夷山屏障了与中原的交通;其南,则面临浩瀚的大海。闽南的滨海地理环境,使早期生息在这里的闽越先民发展了山行水处、饭稻羹鱼的海洋文化。近年有海外学者从 DNA 的对比研究,确认早在 5000 年前,就有古越族先民,从福建沿海出发,经中国台湾、菲律宾,逐岛迁徙,先后南抵新西兰,西到马达加斯加,东达夏威夷和伊斯特岛,并画出抵达这些地方的时间表。公元 4 世纪(西晋末年)以后,中原移民南徙福建而至闽南,带来的中原文化融合土著的闽越文化,在长期的滨海生活中,发展了中华文化的海洋精神。善于舟楫的闽南人早有拓耕海上、经商异域的传统。郑和七下西洋,其副使(后升正使)王景弘即为闽南漳平人,其船队篙师、水手,也不少来自闽南。明清以来,突破海禁在海上与外商贸易而被视为"走私"和"海盗"的商业武装集团,也大多出自闽南。清末民初,频繁的战乱和灾祸,迫使大批闽南人远走南洋,客观上延续了这条曾经中断的海上丝绸之路。迄今移居海外(以东南亚为主)的闽南人超过 1000 万以上。这些主要来自闽南的"南洋客",包括投资经商的生意人、有手艺的工匠和出卖苦力的城市贫民与破产农民,他们实际上从资金、技术和劳力资源三个方面,推动了丝路沿线国家的发展,也把主要以闽文化(闽南、福州)、粤文化(潮州、广府)和客家文化为表征的中华文化,传播到他们足迹所到的地方。

从严格意义上讲,闽南文化并不就是海洋文化。作为中华文化的下位文化,闽南文化涵盖在中华文化的大传统之中。漫长历史的农耕文明及其以儒学为道统的文化传承,深刻影响着闽南社会的建构。不同的是,闽南的滨海地理环境和闽越文化的融入，以及闽南人经商异域的历史传统，使南传闽南的中原文化，拥有迥异于其中原本土的海洋色彩和海洋精神。我曾将此一文化形态称为"海口型文化"①，它既是中华文化向海洋文化过渡的海口，也是外来文化进入中国内陆的海口。它的多元文化双向交汇的丰富性和特殊性，拓展了闽南文化的海洋精神。

闽南文化的海洋精神和闽南人"下南洋"的历史传统，对海上丝路建设的延续和发展，有着不可低估的积极意义。

三、海丝文化的闽南元素

海上丝绸之路是历史形成的。在漫长岁月中，不同地域、国家之间的经济交往，带动了不同文化的交流、互融，使一种融合着不同地域、国家文化元素的新的文化形态——海丝文化，成为一个客观的存在。

但是，当我们进入这个问题的讨论时，有两个前提应当注意：

（1）海上丝绸之路不是一个"点"（某个国家、地区），而是一条"线"，或一个"片"。即不只有两个国家或地区的双边经济、文化关系，还有海丝沿线多个国家或地区的多边经济、文化关系，是丝路沿线国家、地区互通互鉴、共建共荣的一种特殊的经济、文化形态。当然，国与国之间的双边关系，将成为促进整个地域多个国家或地区的多边关系的基础。"点"不能代替"线"，但"点"的联结是"线"的形成。海丝文化也是一样。海丝沿线不同国家或地区的文化，其交会的文化不尽相同，所形成的海丝文化也各具不同特色。华人足迹遍布东南亚，但菲律宾的华人文化并不完全相同于马来西亚的华人文化，马来西亚的华人文化也不等同于印尼的华人文化。一方面，华人移民来自于不同的移出地，如闽、粤、浙等（而闽亦有福州、闽南，粤亦有广府、潮州等之分），其移入地虽泛称南洋（东南亚），但菲律宾、马来西亚、印尼、泰国等文化也多有差异，信仰也各不同，还有其他语言、职业等因素。海丝文化构成元素的复杂、多元，应引起我们注意。对海丝沿线国家或地区的文化形态，必须具体分析，分别对待。

（2）中华文化在海丝形成的历史上，主要是以它在闽粤的地域文化形态作为表征，具体地说就是福建的闽南文化、福州文化，广东的广府文化、潮汕文化，以及主要存在于闽粤的客家文化等参与到海丝文化的交融中来的。尽管今

---

① 参见《中华文化与闽台社会》第六章第一节，人民出版社 2013 年 9 月版。

日的交流更多的是以中华文化的主体来实现，但历史上这些地域文化对海丝沿线国家或地区的影响，仍深刻地存在着，成为今日海丝文化构成的基础。

"海丝文化"的概念，其内涵和形态，是一个有待更深入探讨的命题。但它鲜明的特色，已引起人类学者、社会学者、文化学者、语言学者、宗教学者、民俗学者等的广泛关注。我以为下面互相关联的四个方面，最能彰显"海丝文化"的特质：

（1）海丝文化是一种多元交汇的文化，不是某个国家、地区的单一的文化。

（2）海丝文化是不同文化在互鉴互融中形成的一种"混杂"的文化。

（3）海丝文化的"混杂"是双向互融的，即发生在交汇的不同文化体双方。例如在闽南文化中融入了阿拉伯、东南亚的文化元素，在阿拉伯、东南亚文化中也融入了闽南的文化元素。

（4）在海丝沿线国家，往往存在着一个相对集中的异文化的聚集区。如新加坡的牛车水、吉隆坡的中国城、菲律宾的王彬街等，是早期华人移民的传统聚居区。这些聚居地至今仍集中地保留着较为浓厚的中华文化传统，犹如在异域里保留着的一块中华文化的"飞地"。同样，这种仿若文化"飞地"的存在，也是双向的。如在宋元时期被誉为"东方第一大港"的泉州，曾经是阿拉人、波斯人在远东最大的聚居地，阿拉伯文化、波斯文化在泉州留下许多印迹。今天尚有五万余阿拉伯人、波斯人的后裔居住在泉州，著名的如晋江陈埭镇的丁氏族群、白崎村的郭氏族群、永春县的浦氏族群等，都是当年阿拉伯人、波斯人后裔。虽然历经数百年岁月，其文化上已大部融入汉族文化，但在信仰、祭祖仪式、餐饮食俗等方面，仍保留着阿拉伯的信仰传统和文化习俗，成为开放、多元的泉州文化的构成因素之一。

这种多元文化的互相交融和混杂现象，是海丝文化最重要的特色。考察今天丝路国家的文化状况，仍可以看到以闽南、福州、广府、潮汕、客家等地域形态为表征的中华文化，在丝路沿线国家留下的深刻烙印。马来西亚、新加坡、印尼的峇峇娘惹文化，是最典型的一个案例。所谓峇峇和娘惹，是15世纪郑和下西洋的船队，途经满剌伽（马六甲）、室利佛士国（新加坡）、满者伯夷国（印度尼西亚）沿线留下的中国男子，与当地女子通婚后生下的后裔，男称峇峇，女称娘惹。后来移居而来的汉族男子与当地马来女子通婚的后裔，一般也称为峇峇、娘惹。他们虽然远离故土，数百年来仍保留着中华文化传统，重孝道，序长幼，男主外，女主内，在信仰和习俗上沿袭华人习惯；但在日常生活、饮食习惯和服饰等方面，融合了大量当地的马来文化。他们有自己特殊的语言，以福建话（闽南话）混杂着马来话为特色。他们最初被视为土著，以和后来移民的"新客"相区别。但当地流行的一句闽南话"三代为峇",即把新客与马来女子通婚的后代,也视为峇峇与娘惹。近年由于政治的原因,当局已不再把峇峇娘惹视为土著,而称为土生华人或侨生华人。峇峇娘惹在马来西亚、新加坡和印尼的存在,已成为不同国家、地区的种族、血缘和文化在海丝之路混杂、融合的典型客观事实。利用百余年前一座民居而建的马六甲的娘惹博物馆,其主人身份及建筑形制、陈设装饰、生活遗习等所保留的鲜明、浓郁的中华文化传统及其南洋色彩,提供给了我们观察和分析娘惹文化的充分例证。

闽南人由于临海而居,历史上出海经商、谋生形成传统。在海丝沿线国家,几乎没有不留下闽南人创业、谋生足迹的。闽南人重情尚义,有强烈的乡土故园观念和认祖归宗情结。自古以来形成的泛神信仰和祭祀之风,使之即使远行海外也把祖宗香火和家乡神祇带在身边,每到新地便立庙祭拜,作为不忘祖根和生命的保护神。这一切使闽南文化的种种事象,伴随闽南人下南洋的足迹,广泛传播在海丝沿线国家,并在与当地文化的互相融合中,发展出新的文化形态。闽南文化是中华文化传延海丝的重要文化表征之一,也是海丝文化不可或缺的重要构成元素。研究海丝文化,不能不关注闽南文化在海外的延伸和发展。

建设21世纪海上丝绸之路是个综合性的课题。毫无疑问,在经济合作共赢的主导下,文化将扮演着重要的角色。

现实是历史的延伸,而历史是现实的背影。关注海丝建设,不能不关注海丝的历史和现实。一方面,发掘、研究、保存、传承历史上海丝之路留下的丰富文化遗产,为今日的海丝之路、海丝文化提供发展的基础和助力。就闽南而言,一个可资操作且意义深长的问题是,发掘闽南三大港口:泉州后渚港、漳州月港和厦门港走向海洋的兴衰更迭、承接延续的历史,疏理其在不同历史时段与海外贸易和人文交往中所处的地位、作用和丰富的文化积淀,联合国内其外海丝城市,申报国家级的海丝文化遗产项目;同时联合海丝沿线国家,将海上丝绸之路和海丝文化申报列入世界文化遗产目录。申遗的过程即是重新认识海丝和海丝文化,密切海丝沿线国家、地区关系,加强对海丝和海丝文化资源的发掘、保护和弘扬,进一步发挥海丝文化在21世纪海上丝路建设中的作用。另一方面,21世纪海上丝绸之路的建设,面临一个世界多极化、经济全球化、文化多样化、社会信息化的全新的时代环境,如何在新的环境下丰富、创新海丝文化,是一个新的课题,有待我们深入探讨和实践,这是所有关心海丝发展的实践者和研究者共同的责任。

中韩电影合作共赢的途径

中国艺术研究院文化发展战略研究中心　刘　藩

中韩电影产业合作的方式多样，遍及产业链的上下游，目前主流的有以下几种：（1）影院投资建设，如韩国 CJ 集团旗下的 CGV 公司在中国建设的影院。（2）互相进口电影，如韩国商业片《暗杀》、《鸣梁海战》引进中国，中国的《赤壁》、《北京遇上西雅图》等影片输出韩国。（3）中韩合拍，进行艺术与市场的全方位合作，案例有《分手合约》、《大明猩》等影片。（4）两国电影人才的交流、输出，中国方面有《集结号》使用韩国的制作团队，韩国导演郭在容导演的《我的早更女友》，正在为万达筹备《斗破苍穹》的韩国导演姜帝圭。演员方面的交流更是频繁，例如韩国演员权相佑出演《十二生肖》、张东健主演《危险关系》和《无极》、苏志燮出演《非常完美》。中国演员出演韩国片，如《盗贼联盟》中的李心洁和任达华、《武士》中的章子怡，以及《我的老婆是大佬 3》中的舒淇，等等。（5）故事方面的借鉴与合作，例如韩国导演曹义锡的《监视者们》翻拍自香港电影《跟踪》、《重返二十岁》是韩国电影《奇怪的她》的姐妹片、余华的作品《许三观卖血记》被韩国公司改编成了电影。（6）公司股权合作，2014 年年底华策影视获得韩国 Next Entertainment World 电影公司 15% 的股权，成为第二大股东。（7）中韩还有一种特殊的合作，由韩国演艺公司培养中国籍韩流明星，如从韩国艺人体系中培育出的吴亦凡和鹿晗，现今已成为当红明星。

在上述众多合作方式中，中韩合拍片是最值得研究的，因为合拍片可以直接促进文化交流，促进国民心灵沟通。

一、中韩合拍片的现状和问题

旨在促进两国交流的《中韩电影合拍协议》（以下简称《协议》）已经于 2014 年 7 月签署。根据《协议》，两国合拍的电影若获得"中外合作摄制电影（合拍片）"的认可，在中韩两国都将被看做是"国产片"，享受各自国内对国产电影的保护政策：不受引进片配额限制，从每年 1—2 部韩国引进片到更多具有韩国元素的影片；制片方收益大幅提高，分账比例从 20% 左右提高到 40% 左右,或者从低价买断中国市场版权到韩国合作投资方按照投资比例获得40%左右的票房分账。有了这一政策推动,未来中韩合拍片的前景势必更加广阔。

合拍协议的出台,源于双方合作的可能性、必要性和巨大的发展空间。

从韩国方面讲,韩国本土电影市场太小,迫切需要向外扩张。韩国人口只有约5000万,相当于我国的一个省,影院只有400多家,银幕只有2500多块,市场规模仅有16641亿韩元(约接近100亿人民币,15亿美元,2014年全年总票房)。据韩国电影振兴委员会(KOFIC)统计数据,2014全年韩国国产片观影人次达到1亿770万人次,连续第三年突破1亿大关。全年总观影人次为2亿1500万人次,连续两年突破2亿人次大关。人均观看电影次数为4.3次,已经饱和成熟。平均票价6.74美元,略高于中国的5.55美元,但在韩国属于很普通的全民消费项目。

2010—2014年韩国电影市场数据①

年度	韩国本土电影			外国引进电影			总计	
	票房总额(亿韩币)	观影人次(万人次)	占有率	票房总额(亿韩币)	观影人次(万人次)	占有率	票房总额(亿韩币)	观影人次(万人次)
2010	5084	6884	46.6%	6488	7892	53.4%	11573	147,759,214
2011	6137	8286	51.9%	6221	7685	48.1%	12358	159,724,465
2012	8361	11461	58.8%	6190	8027	40.3%	15513	213,348,254
2013	9099	12728	59.7%	6414	8606	40.3%	15513	213,348,254
2014	8205	10769	50.1%	8435	10736	49.9%	16641	215,056,912

中国则有近14亿人口,拥有7亿多城镇观众总量,这个总量是约2.8万块银幕覆盖到的市场范围,还在继续增长。2014年中国电影票房收入296亿元,2015年超过400亿元,约为70亿美元。

在韩国,一个电影卖得再好,观影人次最多不过千万人次。截止到2015年为止,韩国仅有13部国产片超过一千万人次,最多的《鸣梁海战》累计观影人次1761万,已经创造了韩国影史纪录,累计总票房达1357亿韩币(约合8.1亿元人民币)。排名第二的是《国际市场》(观影人次1425万),第三是《老手》(观影人次1341万),第四是《阿凡达》(观影人次1330万)。但中国最高的国产片《捉妖记》观影人次是6543万,票房超过24.29亿元人民币。观影人次最

① 数据来源于《2014韩国电影市场回顾》,2015年1月11日,时光网。

多的外片是《速度与激情7》,为6245万人次,票房24.27亿元①。中韩同属于东亚的儒家文化圈,没有欧美市场的文化差异,而且地缘相近,理论上有巨大的合作空间。

如果合作,不但可以将韩国片拓展到中国广阔的市场。而且韩国影人,导演、编剧和演员,大量的特效制作人员,灯光、美术、服装、制片等各类专业人才都可以在中国找到更多的工作机会。比如《大明猩》执行制片人孙长铉,刚来中国时,负责的是冯小刚《集结号》的特效拍摄,后来又陆续接拍了《唐山大地震》、《一九四二》、《大明猩》、《登陆之日》等众多中韩电影,已经在中韩合作中打开了局面。

从中国方面讲,中国电影过去13年高速发展,市场规模很快可以追上北美,市场热钱涌动。最近几年,电影成了中国的热门产业,钱虽多了,但有创意的好项目却成了稀有品。每年600多部故事片的产量,大部分都是"烂片",即使是能够在影院公映的200多部中,也是"烂片"居多,好故事、好制作品质奇缺。而且,中国的影人队伍参差不齐,龙蛇混杂,导致制作品质良莠不齐。中国电影对外合作的需求主要体现在两个方面,一个是好的创意和故事,另一个就是专业技术人才。

近年有大量的韩国电影人带着剧本来中国寻求合作,包括《王的男人》和《素媛》的导演李俊益、《观相》的导演韩在林等人。还有的如郭在容、姜帝圭、张太维等则被中国公司聘请,委托创作。《来自星星的你》的导演张太维甚至向任职的电视台申请停职两年,执导中国片《商学院合伙人》。除了"内容",以及能够生产内容的导演和编剧,中国还需要电影工业各个环节上的技术人才、制作人员。韩国的导演、编剧、制作人员的职业化水平较高,能完整按照电影工业的生产标准和流程推出产品。不同于中国导演的艺术情怀、"圈钱"企图,他们是按观众的需求去生产产品,职业化程度更高。

从理论上讲,中韩电影合作一定能够互惠共赢,看上去"天时、地利、人和",大有可为,但在目前的实践中仍存在诸多问题。

(1)中韩文化、国情差异较大,中国观众被好莱坞影片长期熏陶,口味单一,不太接受韩国电影。而且韩国电影的实力远逊于美国,难以争得进入中国市场的权利。在2014年《中韩电影合拍协议》签署前,平均每年只有1.4部被引进中国。比如2011年的《鸡妈鸭仔》、《开心家族》、《深海之战》,2012年的《晚秋》、《铁线虫入侵》等,票房均不够理想。这些因素导致中韩合作面临较大

---

① 数据来源于国家新闻出版广电总局电影资金办截至2015年9月11日的数据。

的困难：文化差异和好莱坞的竞争。

（2）中韩合作创作摄制，操作起来难度大，盈利困难。赚钱的只有《分手合约》（1.92亿）、《我的早更女友》（1.59亿）等少数影片。亏损的不少，如《危险关系》。该片由《八月照相馆》的导演许秦豪执导、严歌苓担纲编剧，中方公司全额出资，号称制作费过亿，邀请到张东健、章子怡、张柏芝三位大牌明星加盟，豪华阵容备受瞩目。虽然声势浩大，但电影票房最终只卖出6000多万，口碑票房双输。由韩国showbox公司和华谊联合出品的《大明猩》，制片成本高达2000万美元。虽然它在中国区卖出了1.11亿元票房，但韩国票房却不理想。中国观众已经习惯于胡编乱造娱乐致死的逃避式娱乐，但韩国观众比较严肃较真，韩国高票房国产片多数具有浓厚的国情背景如《鸣梁海战》、《国际市场》，因为他们更看重电影所能反映出的现实意义、民族情感、文化认同，所以不太喜欢《大明猩》的幻想色彩。中韩观众需求差异较大，众口难调。

（3）在实践中的中韩合作的电影，多数是国产片，而非两国真正的"合拍片"，因为合拍片的要求多，门槛高。合拍片的基本标准有三条：一是双方共同创作剧本，故事要与中国有机关联，当然这也就意味着要在中国取景；二是中国演员至少占主演的三分之一；三是由双方共同投资，利益共享，风险共担。按照这三条标准，《神话》、《危险关系》、《晚秋》等大量影片虽然在一定程度上由两国电影人共同完成，但它们要么是国产片，要么是韩国片，不是真正意义上的"合拍片"。真正的中韩合拍片其实很少，如2000年的《飞天舞》、2013年的《大明猩》。

不过自从2014年7月《中韩电影合拍协议》签署之后，中韩合拍片渐渐多了起来。韩国电影振兴委员会北京办公室首席代表金炑贞说："真正的中韩合拍片时代现在才刚刚开始，过去大部分有韩国工作人员参与的电影，都是中方全额投资的中国电影。符合政策意义的合拍片每年只有一部左右，现在则有两三部，且呈上升趋势。"中韩合拍片项目的韩国公司认为理想的方式是：韩方投资30%，中方投资70%。这样的合作，只能是以中方为主导，但中方公司和从业人员良莠不齐，合作效果有待观察。

（4）韩国影人的职业水平和敬业精神好于中国，双方拍摄电影的行规、习惯有较大差距，在合作过程中还有大量需要磨合的地方：导演和演员的权力分配、拍摄周期、创作自由度等。例如著名的"郭在容请辞《杨贵妃》剧组"事件。除了演员，韩国创作者还要面对拍摄周期的问题。在韩国一部电影通常要拍三个月，而在中国拍一个半月就能杀青。不仅创作周期缩短，韩国电影人的创作自由度也受损。

（5）理想的合拍题材少。中韩两国地域相近，民众的文化和生活习惯也有颇多相同，但要想真正找到两国民众都感兴趣的题材却非常难。

（6）韩国没有审查制度，中国的审查制度也让不少韩国电影人"望而生畏"。中国影人在适应审查方面尚且时常出错，宁浩的《无人区》拍摄完成后搁置多年，在做出重大修改后方才得以公映。对韩国人来讲完全就是从头开始，难免导致创意受限，甚至自我阉割。这一点，对以构思巧妙著称的韩国编剧、导演来讲，无疑具有巨大的杀伤力。很难想像韩国人能在中国拍出《辩护人》、《恐怖直播》等具有批判性的影片。即使是不涉及社会议题的犯罪片《盗贼联盟》，也仅仅把部分场景放在了澳门，主题故事还是韩国化的，所以该片在韩国大热，在中国却反响平平。

二、提升中韩合拍片水平和盈利能力的对策

即使有审查制度的桎梏，但困扰当前华语影业的不是资金、政策、渠道，而是优秀人才和优秀作品匮乏，是怎样才能提升华语电影的艺术文化品质和摄制制作品质。受困于审查制度、急功近利的社会风气、娱乐至死的圈内风气、国民教育和电影教育的教条主义，中方主创迷失在场面、特效、明星、话题、互联网思维和所谓 IP 中，忽视精神和情感，艺术创造力一直滞后于产业发展的需求，也影响了整个华语电影品质的提升。

加大与韩国影人的合作，恰恰可以弥补中国影人艺术创造力薄弱，合作可以产生文化杂糅优势，可以产生品质的进化效果。我们可以尝试提出一些解决目前问题的对策建议：

（1）合拍，就意味着要同时适应两边市场的需求，也意味着要牺牲一些本土特色。如果想要在中、韩两国同时受到欢迎，就不能小家子气，不能固守本土特色，从情节、台词、人物、服装等创作因素到投资、演员阵容、营销话题等运作因素，都能让两边的观众可以接受。尤其是题材选择，必须瞄准中韩观众都感兴趣的题材，由中韩编剧共同创作故事，争取让两国观众都有共鸣。低端的如暴力、惊悚类题材，中端的如两国历史、文化等共通题材，高端的如具备国际视野和国际议题的、同时与两国切实相关的题材，都可作为候选。

（2）一般影片以中国导演为主导，将中方对于主题、价值、正能量等电影内涵的重视，加上韩国影人的类型片技巧和工业水准，结合在一起才能综合创新，才有可能共同缔造出可以和美国好莱坞比肩的世界级的华语电影产业。某些特殊等类型片，比如奇幻、惊悚，不涉及太多国情、"地气"的，以韩国导演

为主，如《笔仙》、《斗破苍穹》。另外，还可探索更灵活的合作方式，如韩国导演担任监制，中国年轻人出任导演，中韩合作编剧。

（3）目标市场主打中国，在内容的取舍上，还是要尊重主打的市场需求，以中国市场为主，兼顾韩国市场。情节编织和人物塑造要考虑到整个华语圈市场的口味，避免两边都讨好，却两边都讨不好的"夹生饭"局面。韩国那些涉及朝韩分裂题材的优秀影片如《太极旗飘扬》、《国际市场》，在韩国票房很高，但中国观众却并不关心。这些题材不是合拍片的理想题材。

（4）对于韩国影人水土不服等问题，笔者认为改良提升中国片场机制，提升职业化水平是当务之急，但同时韩国主创也要适应中国国情，在战斗中适应实战环境并学习战斗规则，让双方在在互相了解中互相适应。

（5）中韩的一线发行公司应当加大发行力度，找到喜欢韩国元素的影迷群体，培养更多的目标观众。

（6）使用中韩都认可的明星，如全智贤、金秀贤，尤其是韩国艺人体系培养出来的中国明星，如吴亦凡。需要注意的是，要将韩国演员的扎实优良作风带到中国，影响中国演员；而不能反过来，让中国演员的恶劣、摆谱、高价作风带坏韩国演员。韩国演员的片酬比国内低得多，在一部电影的总制作费中，通常只占一小部分。比如2012年的《盗贼同盟》的演员阵容在当时被认为是超豪华阵容、"天价片酬"：第一男主角金允石6亿韩元、全智贤3亿8000万韩元、金惠秀3亿7000万韩元、金秀贤8000万韩元。换算成人民币，分别是360万元、228万元、222万元、48万元。金允石和宋康昊这样一线大腕，片酬即使上涨，也仅仅是从6亿韩元涨到了最高10亿韩元（约600万元人民币）①。600万元人民币在国内只能请到二线或三线明星，一线大腕的片酬已经高达3000万元人民币。

（7）在制作上，采取韩国团队主导，中国人员参与的方式。韩国团队主导，可保证较高的制作品质，中国人员参与，可传帮带，学习技术经验，培养中方团队。中国影视制作量足够大，需要的制作技术人员多，这种合作可以逐步培养更多合格的制作人员。

尽管中韩合拍片在实践中面临着种种问题，但办法总比问题多，在两国政府政策的推动下，在双方市场机制的激励下，中韩合拍片会越来越好。

---

① 数据来源于《韩国电影实地调查：产业篇》，腾讯网。

"方寸世界·天人合一"
——中国篆刻艺术的艺术特色和文化功能

中国艺术研究院中国篆刻艺术院院长　骆芃芃

篆刻艺术是以石材为载体，以汉字为主要表现对象并由中国古代印章镌刻技艺发展而来的中国特有的传统艺术。古代印章是行使和授受国家机构的权力、证明个人身份的凭信物。其制作多由工匠采用金属铸造和凿制而成，距今有三千多年的历史。

一、世上独一无二的存续状态

中国篆刻艺术，源于中国古代的印章镌刻技艺，而类似印章模样的印具，在中国之外的一些古老的文明国家同时也有一些从形制到用途都很相似的器物：

（1）美索不达米亚地区的印具（公元前3500年）。高拉时代石印及印迹，约公元前3500年。

（2）西亚北部和中亚地区的印具。公元前15世纪到公元前12世纪赫梯人建立了强盛的帝国，赫梯国王的印章和印迹中间是国王姓名和人像，四周为赞美词。

（3）古埃及地区的印具（公元前3070年）。钤有印迹的古埃及泥块及摹本，约公元前3070年。古埃及第18王朝金印，公元前1552—前1306年。

（4）印度河流域的印章（公元前3745年）。印度最早发现印章样的器物约在公元前3745年至公元前2500年，那时的印已发掘出2000多方了。公元前2300年，印度出土封泥，和中国汉代封泥非常相像。

（5）古波斯地区的印章。巴林岛出土的波斯湾式印章钮式，为公元前2300年至公元前1800年，是波斯地区的印。

（6）爱琴海地区的印。圣甲虫红玉髓金戒指，公元前550—前510年。

（7）古希腊的印章。古希腊时间（公元前450年—前330年），这时的印文多为希腊神话中的英雄人物、人的姓名、肖像，如维纳斯、斯芬克斯、亚历山大等。

（8）欧洲中世纪的印章。欧洲中世纪出现了"纹章"，是欧洲印章的雏形。

公元 4 世纪后，中国的印章文化随着文字逐渐向东传播。传到了日本列岛和朝鲜半岛。

在中国，印章起源于三千多年前的殷商时代。迄今为止，我国发现的最早的印章，是殷商时期刻在龟甲骨上面，类似印章样的东西。人称"商鈢"。西周时期鈢印已开始广泛使用，文献中已经有"鈢"与"鈢节"的记载。

印章作为一种艺术品的出现大约是在唐代。在唐代以前，印章的入印内容大多是官衔、人名，少数的也有吉祥用语。唐代丞相李泌，第一个将其书斋馆号"端居室"的名称作为印文内容。以后的宋元各代，又有了以人名字号、书画鉴赏、诗词成语等为入印内容的印章。这样，印章的用途扩展了，它不仅限于实用，而且还有了被人欣赏的艺术价值。

从唐代开始，印章的发展，便产生了两大分支：一支是继续沿袭古代印章中实用性的一面，以致发展到今天的公章、领钱用或者签字署名用的戳子。今天的这类印章，同样不作为艺术品。印章的另一分支是由唐代书斋馆号等印章发展而来的，直到今天的流派艺术印章。这类印章有实用价值，更有艺术价值。

古代的实用印章，在当时虽然不被当作艺术品，但这些印章，却客观地反映了当时刻工们高超的艺术构思和精湛的技艺，具有很高的欣赏价值和艺术价值。因此，这部分印章，仍然作为极宝贵的艺术财富，载入篆刻学的史册，成为篆刻艺术发展中的一大系统——"古代系统"。

公元 13 世纪之后，艺术家开始选用石材代替金属并亲自动手刻制印章，这一技艺的改变，为篆刻艺术的发展提供了广阔空间。

篆刻家在继承前辈优秀技艺的基础上不断进行创新，出现了自明清以来的皖派、浙派以至今日的流行印风等多种流派和风格，并产生出丁敬（1695—1765）、邓石如（1743—1805）、吴昌硕（1844—1927）、齐白石（1863—1957）等诸多大师。这些艺术家将这门古老而又弥新的传统艺术一直传承、发展并创造至今。

当今，篆刻艺术的现状和发展又是怎么样的呢？

今天的篆刻技艺主要采用叶蜡石一类的寿山石、青田石等；其主要工具是刻刀、印床、印泥、毛笔、宣纸等；主要工艺流程有设计印稿、上石、镌石、钤印、刻款、拓款等；上石的书法功底，巧妙的布局能力，精湛娴熟的刀功，共同构成篆刻艺术的技艺内涵。

篆刻艺术的刻制材料主要采用叶蜡石一类的寿山石、陶瓷等。

篆刻的基本用具有刻刀、墨、印泥、毛笔、印笺。

书法是篆刻的功底；书法的好坏直接影响着篆刻作品的效果。

目前，篆刻艺术在大陆有着广泛的群众基础，从业者从普通百姓到具有综合文化素养和精湛技艺的传承人。当下的专业社团有 500 多家，著名的有成立于一百多年前的西泠印社、有作为中国第一家研究和创作篆刻艺术的国家院体机构的中国篆刻艺术院。中国篆刻艺术院将中国篆刻艺术作为独立学科建设了起来，同时为国家培养一批又一批的篆刻艺术的硕士研究生人才。

综观中外古代印章发展的历史，从两河流域到印度河流域；从黄河流域到古埃及、古希腊、古罗马……历史之悠久，范围之广阔，应该说是古代人类文明的辉煌代表。然而把印章发展成为一门艺术并流传至今的，只有中国。因此，中国的篆刻艺术无疑是世界人类非物质文化遗产的代表作。

二、篆刻艺术的主要特色

中国的篆刻艺术的特色主要表现在下面几个方面：

（1）借用契刻古代文字的方式表现中国传统文化中虚实相生、阴阳合一的审美取向，具有抽象和神奇之美。今天也有用简化字入印的印章了。

（2）融多种传统文化底蕴于一身。作者要在很小的尺寸中表现中国的诗、书、画和构成学，并且真实、准确地表达其思想、情感、学养，追求布局和刀法的精微妙趣，风格各异，可谓"方寸之中表现大千世界"。

（3）篆刻作品是人文与自然的结合，是天然石材、精制钮雕和篆刻技艺"三美合一"的过程。

（4）"天人合一"的完美结合。印材是大自然提供的天然石头，它具有自然之美，天工造物之灵气；印章是艺术家刻的，它具有人文内涵。这两者完美结合真正体现了中国传统文化的核心境界"天人合一"。

（5）现代展厅中展览展示的空间构成之美。从 2006 年起，中国艺术研究院中国篆刻艺术院举办了"金石永寿——中国第一届寿山石篆刻艺术展"、"江山多娇——庆祝中华人民共和国成立六十周年篆刻艺术精品展、中日篆刻艺术展"、"人类非物质文化遗产代表作——中国篆刻艺术精品展"、"天翰云章 金石永年——骆芃芃篆刻书法艺术展"，在这几次重大展览当中，策划及设计者以全新的理念、前所未有的见地将篆刻艺术置于一个展览展示的新空间，让篆刻艺术融于中国传统建筑，传统陈设、传统器乐、传统礼仪当中，构成了篆刻艺术的空间之美。

（6）与生俱来的实用性和艺术性的并存发展。印章艺术从它的起源到发展至今，始终伴随着艺术性和实用性的并存现象。即便是发展成为了独立的艺术——篆刻艺术，它的实用功能仍然无时无刻地存在着。

篆刻艺术的实用功能和艺术功能主要表现在以下几个方面：

（1）人物的凭信价值。今天的姓名章，既是一方完美的艺术品，又具有着人物的凭信作用。把印章盖在公文、支票以及各种契约及合同上，可以起到法律的公正作用。

（2）书画收藏品和图书的从属关系的印证以及品鉴。把印章盖在收藏的字画及图书上，可以印证物品的从属关系，并起到品鉴的作用。

（3）书画作品的款识作用。把印章盖在书画作品上，可以起到作者的款识作用。

篆刻艺术几千年生生不息，而真正使其具有强大的生命力的原因，正是其艺术寓于实用，实用凸现艺术的双重特性所致。

今天，篆刻艺术的这种双重特性在新的历史条件下，又有了新的发展领域。近年来，艺术家将篆刻艺术广泛地运用于现实生活中，如用在邮票、茶壶、瓷器、茶叶、雕塑、公园、建筑及广告标识上。2008年北京奥运会的徽标——"中国印"就是当今篆刻艺术用于生活领域中最好的见证。

三、带有浓郁东方色彩的社会文化功能

篆刻艺术的社会文化功能，集中体现了东方的哲学理念。

（1）是修身、修为、立德和养性的重要途径。

（2）是提高作为一个中国文人素养的重要手段。

篆刻艺术之中包含着众多的学问和技艺，比如文学、哲学、历史、美学、文字学、训诂学、设计学、书法、刀法、绘画等等。从事篆刻的人，需要具有这些学问和技能才能刻好印。

（3）是人际交往和学术交流的有效方式。

（4）篆刻艺术的作品有着审美和收藏价值。

中国的篆刻艺术，是中华传统文化中优秀的艺术瑰宝，是中华民族宝贵的精神和物质财富。而今，中国篆刻艺术已成功列入人类非物质文化遗产代表作名录，这对它的传承、保护和发展提供了有利的条件和良好的国际环境，而它所具有的审美和文化功能，不仅影响了中华大地几千年，而且还一定会影响越来越多的不同国度的民众。

作为文化线路的"海上丝绸之路：福建史迹"遗产保护研究

华侨大学通识教育学院　骆文伟

1993年桑地亚哥·德·卡姆波斯特拉朝圣路（Santiago de Compostela）的西班牙部分被列入《世界遗产名录》。与此同时，一种全新的遗产保护概念——"文化线路"（cultural routes or cultural itinerary）走进世界遗产领域。自1998年国际古迹遗址理事会（ICOMOS）[①]成立文化线路科学委员会（CIIC）[②]，通过了《CIIC章程》等一系列文件；到2003年世界遗产委员会《行动指南》给予"文化线路"明确的定义；再到2005年ICOMOS第十五届大会形成《文化线路宪章》（草案），文化线路迅速成为近年来世界遗产保护界关注的热点。

一、文化线路的定义、特征及发展趋势

2003年ICOMOS提交给世界遗产委员会《行动指南》修订计划的讨论稿里，把文化线路的定义为："文化线路是一种陆地道路、水道或者混合类型的通道，其形态特征的定型和形成基于它自身具体的和历史的动态发展和功能演变；它代表了人们的迁徙和流动，代表了一定时间内国家和地区内部或国家和地区之间人们的交往，代表了多维度的商品、思想、知识和价值的互惠和持续不断的交流；并代表了因此产生的文化在时间和空间上的交流与相互滋养，这些滋养长期以来通过物质和非物质遗产不断地得到体现。"[③]

这个定义概括了文化线路的如下几个特征：首先，它的本质是与一定历史时间相联系的人类交往和迁移的路线，包括一切构成该路线的内容：城镇、村庄、建筑、闸门、码头、驿站、桥梁等文化元素，还有山脉、陆地、河流、植

---

① 国际古迹遗址理事会（International Council on Monuments and Sites）是世界遗产委员会的主要咨询机构，简称ICOMOS。
② CIIC（The ICOMOS International Scientific Committee on Cultural Routes）是国际古迹理事会文化线路科技委员英文简称。
③ CIIC. 3rd Draft Annotated Revised Operational Guidelines for the Implementation of the World Heritage Convention. Madrid, Spain, 2003.

被等和路线紧密联系的自然元素。其次，作为一种线形文化景观，它的尺度是多种多样的：可以是国际的，也可以是国内的，可以是地区间的，也可以是地区内部的；可以是一个文化区域内部的，也可以是不同文化区域间的。第三，它的价值构成是多元的、多层次的：既有作为线路整体的文化价值，又有承载该线路的自然地本身作为山地、平原、河谷等生态系统拥有的生态价值；不仅包括分布在其内部的建筑和其他单体遗产自身的价值，还包括非物质文化遗产所蕴涵的价值。①

文化线路的内涵和外延进一步拓展，体现出世界文化遗产研究和保护朝以下趋向发展：遗产规模由点状向线状和面状发展，保护对象由遗产本体扩展到周边环境、视线走廊；遗产类型由静态同时向动态和活态发展②；由重视帝王将相伟绩与宫廷遗产同时向民间遗产发展；由重视城市遗产向同时重视乡镇、农村遗产发展③；由强调文化内涵同时也强调经济价值和自然生态系统的平衡能力④；由重视历史价值向同时重视现实价值发展；由重视纯文化意义遗产向同时重视反映人地和谐关系复合遗产发展⑤；由单一文化向强调跨国界或跨地区的交流和多维对话，突出文化多样性；利益主体由重视国家意志向同时重视公众参与态度、行为发展⑥；遗产申报由地区独立申报同时向跨区、跨国联合申报发展⑦。

二、"海上丝绸之路：泉州史迹"遗产资源概况和特征

我国是历史悠久的文明古国，中华文明 5000 年传承经久不衰，拥有着十分

---

① 李伟等：《世界文化遗产保护的新动向——文化线路》，《城市问题》2005 年第 4 期。
② 徐嵩龄：《第三国策：论中国文化自然遗产的保护》，科学出版社 2005 年版。
③ 刘小方：《文化线路遗产——旅游的跨文化之路》，《中国西部》杂志旅游刊 2013 年第 1 期。
④ 王志芳等：《遗产廊道——美国历史文化遗产保护中一种较新的方法》，《中国园林》2001 年第 5 期。
⑤ CIIC. 3rd Draft Annotated Revised Operational Guidelines for the Implementation of the World Heritage Convention. Madrid, Spain, 2003.
⑥ Gayle McPherson. Public memories and private tastes: The shifting definitions of museums and their visitors in the UK. Museum Management and Curatorship 2006, 21 (1).
⑦ 刘睿文：《多国联合申报世界文化遗产模式的引入》，《经济地理》2005 年第 3 期。

丰富的文化线路遗产资源①，其中以丝绸之路最引人瞩目，在地区乃至世界经济文化的交流中占有重要的地位。海上丝绸之路（maritime silk route）②，是相对陆上丝绸之路而言的，指古代中国与世界其他地区进行海外贸易的海上交通路线。通过此路将古代中国的丝绸、茶叶、陶瓷、铁器等物产销往欧洲和亚非其他国家，而欧洲商人则通过此路将香料、药材、宝石、毛织品、象牙等带到中国（宋元时期泉州海外交通图，如图1③所示）。海上丝绸之路是连接东西方重要的海上通道，也是一条沟通人类物质文明和精神文明的对话之路。

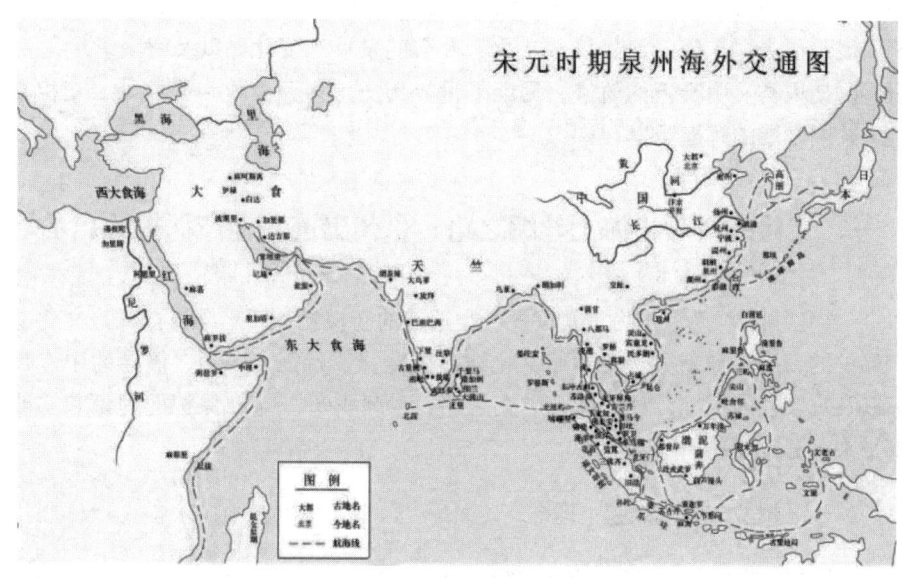

图1　宋元时期泉州海外交通图

泉州是"海上丝绸之路"的起点，中西文化长期在这里交流汇聚，遗留下大量罕见的海上丝绸之路文物古迹和辉耀古今的文化遗存，全市仅全国重点文物保护单位就达32处。根据港口地理、主题与历史的关系，大体可分为：航海

---

① 截止到2014年12月，被列入国家文化遗产的文化线路有丝绸之路、北京中轴线、大运河、蜀道、灵渠等5处，潜在文化线路遗产主要有：茶马古道、秦直道、三峡古栈道、豫晋"朝拜之路"、徽杭古道、藏彝走廊、北京长河、川黔驿道、浙东唐诗之路、滇越铁路、长征线路等。我国现拥有47项世界遗产，但只有"丝绸之路：长安—天山廊道路网"、"中国大运河"两项世界文化线路遗产。
② 海上丝绸之路是由日本学者三杉隆敏在他1967年出版的《探索海上丝绸之路》的专著中初次提及，这个概念如今已被学术界所普遍接受。
③ 图片来自泉州海外交通史博物馆，制图：刘梅。

与通商贸易、城市本身的历史、宗教与多元文化等三大类史迹。同时，泉州也是闽南文化主要发祥地和闽南文化遗产的富集区，具有闽南文化、中原文化、迁徙文化、海洋文化等文化特征，拥有包括方言、口传、宗教、武术、医药、饮食、民俗、音乐、戏剧、美术、习俗、建筑和传统技艺等大量的优质非物质文化遗产。泉州现拥有南音、水密隔舱海船制造技术、传统木结构营造技艺、妈祖信俗等4个世界非物质文化遗产，31个国家非物质文化遗产项目。这些海丝文化遗产真实记录了曾被誉为"东方第一大港"刺桐港的历史原貌，呈现出种类齐全、强聚分布、内容丰富、保存完整、时间跨度大等特征，它们从不同侧面展示了中国东南沿海经济、文化、社会的发展和变化，以及海上丝绸之路全盛时期人类文明交流的轨迹，见证了世界历史上多元文化和平共处、互相交融、共同发展的辉煌历程。

三、文化线路对"海上丝绸之路：泉州史迹"遗产保护的启示

"文化线路"无论作为重新审视人类遗产的新视野和新思维，抑或是文化遗产保护的新类型和新方法，对照文化线路的定义、特征、内涵、倡导的中心目标以及真实性的标准，对"海上丝绸之路：泉州史迹"遗产保护的理论和实践都带来十分重要的启示。

（一）树立"整体性"理念

"文化线路"历史悠久、体量庞大，具有跨文化、多维度、大尺度、生态多样性等特性，这就要求我们从多维视野来重新审视文化遗产，要突出其多维价值及整体价值。对这些在空间、时间、类型维度上相互联系的文化遗产进行保护，应倡导"整体性"和"区域性"理念。

首先，遗产保护运动应从对单体文物的保护，发展到保护成片的城镇、村落、街区景观整体乃至包含独特文化资源的线性景观。以"海上丝绸之路：泉州史迹"为纽带实施的文化线路保护，将有效扩大遗产的保护范围，能极大推动区域遗产的保护。要加大对老城区、古街区、古瓷窑、水下文物的保护和发掘，通过对分散的文物和遗址进行文化线路多元价值评析，讲述各文化遗存与"海上丝绸之路"商贸往来的关联，以论证古刺桐港和"海上丝绸之路"的相互作用和相互影响，在此基础之上形成泉州海丝遗产的完整形象。

其次，丝绸之路是省、部、全国乃至国际上的联合，必须建立起区域间乃至国际间协同创新机制。"海上丝绸之路"是一条跨越上万公里海上线路，仅仅

在国内部分就有数千公里，目前进入国家遗产名单的城市就有 9 个①，也没有哪一个城市可以完成单独申报。在申遗过程中，如果有一个城市或一个点出现问题，那么整个项目就要面临失败，因此必须保证不出现城市短板。要发挥泉州在海丝城市联盟的排头兵作用，争取在国家文物局指导下，建立专门的机构，统筹中国"海上丝绸之路"9 个城市文化遗产立法、保护、利用、研究和联合申遗工作，搭建政府、文物管理部门、博物馆"三位一体"的运作平台，建立信息共享、政策互通、人才共育、品牌共塑、遗产联展等联动协作机制，以保证各申遗城市能够"齐头并进"，努力做好各地海丝史迹的整合以及海丝线路的时空衔接，加强泉州与东南亚、南亚、西亚、东亚等国家海丝城市协同联动，构筑起一个新的、完整的国家性海丝文化遗产保护网络。除此，在国家文物局和联合国申遗职能部门的支持下，尽早启动"海上丝绸之路"申报世界遗产国际协商会，借鉴"丝绸之路：长安—天山廊道路网"跨国联合申遗的成功经验，拓展申报"海上丝绸之路"文化线路遗产，争取早日进入《世界遗产名录》。

（二）坚持"保护第一、合理开发"

"海上丝绸之路：泉州史迹"的遗产保护是泉州遗产工作的重心。首先，要严格对照文化线路的内涵和特征，始终坚持以"保护第一，合理开放"和"社会文化效益与经济效益并重"的基本原则，正确处理好保护与开发的关系，真正实现保护—利用—再保护的良性循环。

首先，应重点做好以下几项保护工作：1. 除重点保护好已公布的国家、省、市三级文物保护单位外，还必须保护好虽未定级但经过评析确有遗产价值的古建筑、历史文化街区、历史遗址遗迹等，还应抢救性保护好已被损害的文物古迹遗存和在城市建设经拆除的古民居建筑构件。2. 整体保护好老城区中的整体格局和历史风貌。这包括：（1）"鲤鱼城"的平面形状、方位、轴线以及与之相关联的棋盘式路网道、护城河和破腹沟两大自然水系；（2）传统民居"红砖白石双坡顶，出砖入石燕尾脊"等营造技艺；（3）骑楼及中西合璧古民居；（4）遍布于城区中的刺桐树和其他各种古树名木②。3. 严格按照"修旧如旧"原则来整治遗产地及周边环境。如规划建设好德济门遗址公园、锡兰王子陵园遗址、

---

① 在最新公布的《中国世界文化遗产预备名单》（2012 年 11 月更新）中，共有福建泉州、浙江宁波、广东广州、江苏南京、扬州、山东蓬莱、广西北海、福建漳州、福州等 9 个城市进入"海上丝绸之路"国家文化遗产名单。
② 何振良、庄小波：《泉州老城区文化遗产现状调查与保护对策研究》，《泉州学林》2009 年第 2 期。

五里桥、洛阳桥中国名桥主题公园、磁灶窑址泉州外销瓷文化公园、法石村"海上丝绸之路"文化旅游街等一批精品景区。4. 积极申报泉州北管、泉州拍胸舞、梨园戏、泉州提线木偶戏、晋江布袋木偶戏、高甲戏、惠安石雕、泉州花灯、惠安女服饰、德化瓷烧制技艺和法属波利尼西亚联合申报"南岛语族迁徙"①等为世界非物质文化遗产；5. 对于泉州海丝文化线路的历史记载、有关于人员组成、旅行证件、文献以及包括民俗、民风、戏曲在内的非物质遗产等方面资料，都应统一进行整理。6. 重点建设好泉州海交馆综合展、磁灶窑址泉州外销陶瓷展、泉州博物馆"世界多元文化展示中心"等一批精品展览馆，同时要通过加强博物馆、档案馆建设，丰富海丝历史文化展示体系和展示功能。

其次，文化线路自身就是天然的"旅游线路"，其构成线路资源内容丰富，类型多样，特征鲜明，具有多功能性，众多线性特征造就文化线路不可多得的遗产旅游优势和开发价值。其旅游功能正因它以遗产保护为目的特性，使以其为基点进行的旅游开发都将着力于遗产的可持续性，这将有利于遗产保护与旅游发展的共赢。自泉州启动海丝旅游专项以来，泉州海丝遗产旅游虽得到一定的发展，各遗产地旅游发展水平也不尽相同，但总体上海丝旅游条块分割严重、旅游开发层次较低，旅游的可进入性较弱，旅游市场开发很不理想。为此，应树立区域旅游合作理念、实施旅游资源统一管理、探索旅游资源专业化、市场化运作的新举措，精心打造海丝旅游品牌。

第三，文化线路同样把历史文化内涵放在首位，但相对于文化遗产，文化线路同时也强调经济价值和自然生态系统的平衡能力。因此，泉州海丝遗产工作还应坚持"社会文化效益与经济效益并重"的原则，实现遗产资源保护和开发对地区经济、社会、文化的综合效益和长远效应。

（三）唤醒公众参与意识

世界遗产体现着"一个国家（地区）的意识形态渊源"，换言之，遗产是一个国家或一个地区的一国、一地区的"文化身份"象征。理清自己的意识形态渊源，确认自身的文化身份，才能在缤纷的世界、地方文化、政治舞台上鲜明地树立自己的形象。文化线路倡导的中心目标就是要借助保护和申报世界遗产这样的机制唤起社会公众对遗产热爱和关注。② 文化线路突出并培育社区的参与意

---

① 《"南岛语族迁徙"计划申报世界非物质文化遗产》，2010 年 11 月 23 日，泉州网（http://www.qzwb.com/mnwhw/content/2010 - 11/23/content_ 3511402_ 2. htm）。
② 李伟等：《世界文化遗产保护的新动向——文化线路》，《城市问题》2005 年第 4 期。

识,把社会公众对建立文化线路的意愿作为辨别文化线路真实性标准之一。当前在泉州,"海上丝绸之路"申报世界遗产已成家喻户晓,但是社会各界尤其是公众,缺乏对世界遗产内涵准确理解,对文物及其保护的意义认识不到位,社区公众参与保护的意识淡薄。要利用各种新闻媒体系统地、分系列地开展遗产资源的普及宣传,通过举办"海上丝绸之路"旅游文化节、"东亚文化之都"泉州活动年、世界闽南文化节、元宵踩街、海洋文化节、中国遗产日宣传等重大节庆活动,唤醒人们对海丝线路遗产的认同感,唤醒全民参与保护的意识,在外围形成严密的"保护带"。要通过制定吸纳社会资金的优惠政策和措施,建立完善的遗产保护投入机制,建立起遗产保护专项基金和非物质文化遗产保护中心,重点用于国家、省级风景名胜区规划、文物古迹和非物质文化遗产抢救保护。

(四) 建构共生理念[①]

共生是指共生单元之间在一定的共生环境中按某种共生模式形成的相互谐调、共存共赢关系。一般而言,共生由共生单元、共生模式和共生环境等三要素构成。[②] 在遗产区域建构共生理念,符合文化线路遗产的特征要求。

首先,要实现宗教和文化的多元共生。中世纪刺桐港繁荣兴盛,商人、旅行家、僧侣及各界各业的外国人汇集于此,带来了佛教、伊斯兰教、基督教、印度教、摩尼教、日本教和犹太教等文化,并和中国本土的儒教、道教和民间宗教互相辉映、相互融合,共同缔造了泉州宗教文化多元并存的局面。由于事过境迁,我们已经很难对泉州历史上的各个宗教文化的历史脉络做出精确无误的复原和现况定位。但是,我们还是可以借助历史文献和田野调研资料,从历史的视野重温泉州多元宗教共存现象,对它们的历史与现况进行了纵向考述和横向比较,随着时间的推演、磨合及对话,而彼此尊重、求同存异,进而融合、相互合作,从而为人类福祉做出贡献。

其次,要实现城市现代化与历史文化遗产的共生。随着泉州经济飞速发展,城市化进程不断加快,泉州海丝文化遗产保护与城乡建设之间的矛盾日益突出。20 世纪 90 年代以来,泉州老城区在全国"旧城改造"的热潮中"全面开花",引发了一场对老城区的"建设性破坏"。文化被誉为"经济发展的原动力",城

[①] "共生"(Symbiosis) 一词来源于希腊语,最早缘于生物学,由德国真菌学家德贝里(AntondeBary) 在 1879 年提出,意指"不同种属的生物按某种物质联系共同生活"。20 世纪 50 年代以后,共生方法开始应用于社会领域。

[②] 张健华等:《闽台旅游合作的共生模式研究》,《福建论坛》2008 年第 3 期。

市历史文化遗产不仅是城市发展的独特见证，同时也是城市促进地方经济、社会均衡和谐发展的重要资源。根据我国现行的法律政策，可以对历史文化遗产实行分层次、并根据不同特点采取不同方式进行保护。[①] 第一个层次是城市单体文物，主要包括古建筑、古墓葬、古遗址、石刻、名人故居和近现代有纪念意义的建筑物等，要遵循不改变文物原状的原则，保存历史的原貌和真迹。第二个层次是具有传统风貌的历史街区，如中山路、西街、旧馆驿、井亭巷、金鱼巷、聚宝街、青龙巷、万寿路、伍堡街，等等，要保存历史的真实性和完整性。第三个层次是历史文化名城，包括老城区的格局旧貌、平面形状、方位、轴线以及与之相关联的道路骨架、河网水系、古城楼等，不仅要保护城市的文物古迹和历史地段，还要保护和延续古城的格局和历史风貌。

第三，要实现文化遗存、自然环境、非物质文化遗产共生。在我国，文化线路往往是文化、自然、非物质三位一体的大型遗产，自然环境在文化线路的历史形成中起着举足轻重的作用，在精神塑造和民族性格形成过程中起到限定和约束作用，众多民族千百年来保留下的非物质文化遗产也为文化线路增添了无穷的韵味。文化线路以线路作为纽带，把线路及其构成部分作为整体资源进行保护，既保护文化遗产自身、也保护其赖以生存的环境，又要保护遗留下来的非物质遗产元素。要注意避免和克服我国遗产保护中长期存在的两种不平衡倾向：一是"重文化遗产轻自然遗产"，二是"重物质文化遗产轻非物质文化遗产"，要把具有广泛性、普遍意义的各类遗产纳入到保护体系中来。因此，"海上丝绸之路：泉州史迹"文化线路保护应尽可能涵盖：（1）文化遗产元素，即前文提及的航海与通商贸易、城市本身的历史、宗教与多元文化等三大类史迹；（2）自然遗产元素，即彰显出人类开拓进取精神的海丝文化线路经过的发源地、传播中的具体场所、发生重要影响地点的地形地貌、自然景色；（3）非物质遗产元素，即包括无形的语言、音乐、习俗、手工艺制作以及人们的生活方式和习俗。

除此，泉州海丝遗产保护还应该实现生活与遗产、传统与现代、人与自然、人与遗产和谐共生的思想理念，在更大的空间范围和最广的地域范围来保护和延续历史文化脉络，更全面、更立体地展示城市的历史文化发展轨迹，在继承历史文化传统的基础上，形成古代文明与现代文明的交相辉映，人文资源与自然资源的相互依托。

---

① 何振良、庄小波：《泉州老城区文化遗产现状调查与保护对策研究》，《泉州学林》2009 年第 2 期。

世界遗产的保护和申报既是申报地梳理、完备、健全、提升形象的过程，也是自觉接受国际规则监督的过程。借鉴文化线路这一文化、自然与非物质遗产保护并举的理念和方法，对于"海上丝绸之路：泉州史迹"遗产保护和申报无疑具有非常重要的意义。我们坚信，只要精心保护，基础工作做扎实了，"海上丝绸之路：泉州史迹"终能昂首进入《世界遗产名录》。

重拾东方色彩传统

中国艺术研究院美术研究所所长　牛克诚

东方式的色彩认知与表现自成体系并源远流长。在亚洲各国的神话传说或史诗中，有大量的色彩词，记录着远古东方人对于色彩的辨识与感受；亚洲各国历史上的彩陶、染织、服饰、建筑、绘画等的色彩应用，体现着东方人色彩感觉的丰富与细腻。然而，近代以来，随着欧洲合成染料的输入，西方的色彩名称与配色方式等也传入亚洲，从而弱化了东方自古以来一脉相传的色彩感觉。另一方面，随着西风东渐而来的西方色彩学，也逐渐覆盖了东方的色彩知识体系。20世纪二三十年代，吕澂、史岩、李慰慈、刘以祥、俞寄凡等的色彩学著作，其概念与体系就基本上是来自西方色彩学的。西方色彩学在日本、韩国、印度等亚洲各国的传入情形与中国相似，甚至它们有的在时间上还要早于中国。陈之佛的《色彩学》（1928年商务印书馆出版）就是以日本为中介而对西方色彩学的转述。从那以后，西方色彩学就一直成为我们学习与应用的色彩学；从认知到表述，也就几乎一直依靠着西方色彩学的词汇、概念与知识框架，而东方传统的色彩感觉、色彩观念与配色经验等，也就越来越被漠视与淡忘。1992年，韩国国立现代美术馆出版了《韩国传统标准色名和色样》，其中很多传统色名已很难为现代人所理解。在中国，缃、绛、赪、缁等色彩词，也连同其微妙的色彩感觉渐渐淡去。这一现象意味着，在亚洲的现代化进程中，与器用层面一样，观念、认知层面也产生了与传统之间的严重断裂，这也造成了东方色彩传统主体意识的不确定状态。

东方式的色彩认知，是将自然万物的复杂色相归纳成几种与最基本物质相联系的原色，这些原色又组合成丰富多样的色彩；它强调物体本身的固有色，注重颜色本身的色相品质，以及各种色彩之间的对比、映衬等结构关系。这与17世纪中叶牛顿对光谱色彩的解析以来，形成的以光色原理为出发点的西方色彩学体系有着巨大的不同，而这终究体现的则是东西方思维方式的不同。西方色彩学是一种科学的、分析的系统，它的背后是西方的科学思维，即以形式逻辑体系和系统实验为主的分析的自然观与方法论，通过实验研究、定量分析、推理求证等建立起形式逻辑公理体系。而在东方色彩传统中，则体现着整体和谐的有机论的思想精髓，以及综合、模糊、直觉、体悟的思维特色。

然而，一直以来，我们总是把羡慕乃至崇拜的目光投向西方，而作为亚洲人的我们反而对亚洲所知甚少。我们此前一直都在关注西方色彩学研究领域发生了什么，而对我们周边国家的色彩研究进展却很少关心与留意。我们又往往把自己国家的色彩资源、状况与西方去对照，而却很少与我们周边国家进行横向比较，这就形成了一个个单独的亚洲国家的色彩体系，与一个整体西方色彩学的不对等的对比关系。

因此，重拾东方色彩传统，首先就要以亚洲为傲，同时更要学会欣赏周边国家，欣赏它们的色彩历史经验，关注它们的色彩研究现状，在此基础上，加强亚洲各国学者的学术交流，通过各国的学会会刊、文集等相互发表论文，相互译介色彩著作，相互引进色彩学术研究成果并借鉴其观念和方法，从而促进东方色彩研究的总体深入。通过对亚洲国家之间色彩传统的比较，找出彼此间在色彩观念与表现上的共同性，从而实现对色彩认知与表述体系上的东方主体的再确认。目前，亚洲已有较具规模的"亚洲色彩论坛"，只是，其每一届的主题词差不多都是亚洲色彩的应用与市场。与应用研究并行，东方色彩传统的基本概念、范畴及体系等的建构工作更亟待进行，因为，东方的色彩应用毕竟要获得来自东方文化的支撑。

重拾东方色彩传统不只是对亚洲各国色彩历史资源的学术梳理，也不只是对东方色彩传统的价值重估，它其实更关涉到一个当代文化的重要问题：在亚洲的现代性进程中，我们该如何挖掘那些具有悠久历史的东方智慧，以让它贡献于新世纪亚洲乃至整个世界当代文化。

法国人的"丝路"理念与运作实践
——以"第九届里昂国际舞蹈双年节"为个案

中国艺术研究院舞蹈研究所所长　欧建平

一、法国人对世界文化艺术做出的重大贡献

在世界文化艺术史上，法国人曾做出过重大贡献。据4卷本的《法国文化史》说，"上中世纪（5—10世纪）'法国'文化史上最重要的一件大事，就是创造了法语，它是罗曼语族中最古老的一种语言"。就世界文学艺术史而言，18世纪和19世纪堪称"法国人的世纪"。在世界舞蹈史上，学院派芭蕾的程式化语言自1700年用法语命名以来，至今没有发生过重大改变。在世界文艺思潮上，浪漫主义运动起源于19世纪的法国，强调本体美学的"为艺术而艺术"的理论与实践也来自同一时期的法国，而浪漫主义芭蕾舞剧处女作《仙女》自1832年首演于巴黎歌剧院以来，脚尖舞技术至今依然是传统女子芭蕾的"法定技术"。

在这200多年的时间里，法国人中间脱颖而出了许多举世闻名的文学家和艺术家，比如文学家巴尔扎克、司汤达、雨果、乔治·桑、梅里美、福楼拜、大仲马、小仲马、波德莱尔、都德、左拉、罗曼·罗兰、戈蒂埃，画家德拉克洛瓦、莫奈、马奈、德加、雷诺阿、塞尚，雕塑家罗丹，音乐家伯辽兹、古诺、德彪西、亚当，戏剧家伏尔泰、莫里哀，舞蹈家诺维尔、维斯特里父子、塔里奥尼、佩蒂帕，等等，可谓灿若群星，数不胜数！

即使到了20世纪，法国文学艺术家中也依然是群星灿烂的。从1901年法国人莱涅·苏利普吕多姆首次获得诺贝尔奖历史上的第一个文学奖，到1985年法国人克劳德·西蒙再次获得此项殊荣，这80多年的历史上，共有12个法国人获得这个奖项，堪称世界第一，比英、德、意、西、俄等其他欧洲文化大国都多出了一倍。在20世纪的世界舞蹈史上，法国人同样是名家辈出的，比如说编导家中素以雅俗共赏独树一帜、仅是给中芭就复排了《卡门》、《年轻人与死神》、《阿莱城的姑娘》、《平克·弗洛伊德的摇滚芭蕾》和《蝙蝠》共5部经典作品的罗兰·佩蒂；比如说曾来中国演出芭蕾史诗《生命之舞》，其舞台张力惊天动地的舞蹈思想家莫里斯·贝雅；在表演家中，比如说巴黎歌剧院芭蕾舞团技艺

俱佳的伊韦特·肖维蕾、被世人誉为"天下第一腿"的西维·纪莲……法国文化艺术的潜力之雄厚由此可见一斑,而这则正是当下法国文化软实力持续高涨的根源所在。

此外,在国际学术界,法国人以及法语文化圈中的汉学家人数据说等于全世界的总和。仅就《易经》的翻译和研究而言,两个最早的西语译本中,就有汉学家夏尔·达尔莱(Charles de Harlez)翻译、首版于1889年的法语译本。1998年,法国时任总统希拉克在中国古代青铜器赴法展览开幕式上提出的一个细节问题,连我们随团的考古专家都回答不了;对此,中外媒体均有报道。2006年,我第四次赴法考察期间,在蓬皮杜文化中心图书馆查找资料时,碰见一位名叫阿伦的法国青年学者主动和我打招呼,原来他曾在北京大学考古学系读本科,其间多次在央视看过我主讲的舞蹈节目,后来则回到巴黎大学,攻读中国文物考古专业的研究生……这些貌似偶然、实则必然的事例,均不仅说明了法国人古往今来、自上而下,对中国文化的研究兴趣之高,而且也证明了这个民族自身的审美情趣和文化品位非同凡响。

二、"里昂国际舞蹈双年节"的30年回眸

"里昂国际舞蹈双年节"(Biennale de la Danse de Lyon)1984年由里昂市的舞蹈宫主任居伊·达尔梅先生(Mr. Guy Darmey)所创办。由于从一开始,便得到了里昂市、罗纳-阿尔卑斯大区,以及法国中央文化与交流部等各级政府的鼎力相助,到2014年为止,它已经成功举办了16届,而参加演出的舞团、舞团的国际覆盖面、舞蹈节的具体内容、各类演出的场次、观摩演出的观众人次,以及在国内外产生的巨大影响诸方面,均不断得到扩大。

从第二届开始,这个国际舞蹈双年节开始走上了一个系列化的发展道路,即每届均选定一个不同的主题。2000年、2002年和2006年,我曾分别应法国驻华大使、文化参赞和该舞蹈节的邀请,三次到访这里,不仅观摩演出、发表评论,而且如约采访了达尔梅主席,用心研究了舞蹈节的创办理念、运作模式和推广方法,具体情况摘要如下:

1984年为第一届,这个舞蹈双年节当时未设主题,参演舞团的数量只有14个,演出的场次为66场,观众数量为39800人次。

1986年为第二届,它开始以让里昂市民熟悉世界舞蹈为目标,设立了这样的主题:《德国表现派舞蹈及其影响》,借此回溯了德国舞蹈对法国现代舞的启蒙式影响;参演舞团的数量为18个,观众数量为42350人次;除演出之外,舞

蹈节还围绕这个主题，举办了包括了展览、电影播映在内的各项活动。

1988 年为第三届，主题是《法国舞蹈 400 年》，借此回顾了法国舞蹈从芭蕾到现当代舞的全部历史；参演舞团的数量为 20 个，并且开始在里昂市区各处，举行露天演出和舞会，故而使得观众的数量增加到 54737 人次。

1990 年为第四届，主题是《美国故事》，目的在于回溯美国现代舞对法国当代舞的重大影响，因而请来了世界知名的所有美国舞团，数量多达 23 个，并且发掘了一批编导新秀，观众人数猛增到 72974 人次。

1992 年为第五届，主题是《西班牙激情》，让里昂市民饱览了这个国家激情万丈的舞蹈传统和多姿多彩的当代发展；参演舞团增加到 27 个，观众数量持续增长为 89000 人次；与此同时，按照西班牙的民俗风情，舞蹈节在里昂市中心举行了以民间舞为主题的集市，由此吸引了 15 万里昂市民前去观看。

1994 年为第六届，主题是《非洲妈妈》，20 个舞团选自非洲和美国纽约的黑人居住区哈莱姆，观众数量多达 75500 人次；而踏着非洲节奏进行的大游行《五彩缤纷的节日》，则吸引了 12 万里昂民众踊跃观看。

1996 年为第七届，主题是《巴西色彩》，31 个巴西舞团参加了演出，500 位舞者、歌手、乐手、令人叫绝的现代舞创作者和流行音乐传统的捍卫者均聚集在里昂，吸引了多达 82559 人次的观众，而首开河的"狂欢大游行"则调动了上千位专业和业余舞者，在为期 6 个月的时间里大跳特跳各种巴西舞蹈，吸引了多达 20 万人次的观众。

1998 年为第八届，主题是《地中海热风》，35 个舞团来自 12 个地中海地区的国家，展演了大量的舞蹈风格，并使观众的数量再次增加，达到 85000 人次。

2000 年为第九届，主题是《丝绸之路》，31 个团体及两位独舞表演家沿着古代丝绸之路的路线，分别选自中国的北京、上海、广州、香港、台北，其他亚洲国家中的韩国、日本、泰国、印度、蒙古、叙利亚、伊拉克，非洲的阿尔及利亚，欧洲的乌兹别克斯坦、克罗地亚、荷兰、法国，等等。

2002 年为第十届，主题是《拉丁美洲土地》，36 个舞蹈团的 600 位编导、舞者、歌手和乐手选自阿根廷、玻利维亚、巴西、智利、哥伦比亚、哥斯达黎加、古巴、墨西哥等 11 个国家，以及作为东道主的法国，总共推出了 37 台演出，观众人数达 93000 人次。

2004 年为第十一届，主题是《欧罗巴》，原因是欧洲各国经过多年的协商之后，依然不能就建立欧洲联盟的大事达成统一。本届舞蹈节邀请了 21 个欧洲国家的舞蹈团在里昂手舞足蹈，其中有 10 台为世界首演，包括如日中天的英国当代舞编导家韦恩·麦克格雷格和荷兰行为艺术家扬·法布雷的两台演出，目的在于用舞蹈的方式，表现欧洲各国同心协力的巨大威力和莫大魅力。

2006年为第十二届，主题结束了以地域划分的系列，而将注意力转向了占全人类50%的城市人口，由此命名为《城市之舞》，意在通过四大洲29个城市舞蹈团的实验性和探索性演出，表现城市人民对人类文明进步做出的重大贡献。

2008年为第十三届，主题转而全力以赴地为当代舞提供舞台，并开始了"舞蹈焦点"的崭新系列。当年推出的新作品共16台，编导家则有德国人苏珊娜·林克，法国人蒙塔尔沃·埃尔维厄、昂热兰·普雷热卡日，美国人卡洛琳·卡尔森，中国人文慧，等等。

2010年、2012年、2014年分别为第十四、十五、十六届，主题继续是"舞蹈焦点"，但重心则分别放在了新生代编导的扶持、业余舞者的提升以及葡萄牙等往届双年节有所忽视的国家舞蹈之上。

归纳起来，里昂国际舞蹈双年节30年来的成功经验有五条：

一是每两年一届，以便有充分的时间做好下一届的筹备工作，包括认真做好相关研究工作，亲自前往主题国家和地区挑选舞团及其节目，签订具有可行性的演出，甚至委约创作合同。

二是每年选择一个国家、地区或以欧洲、城市作为主题，以便向里昂市民形象生动地传播全球化的丰富多彩，深化民众对于建立欧盟、发展城市文化的认知。

三是以里昂舞蹈宫为基地，建立舞蹈双年节的常设机构，确保合同中的每项细则在舞蹈节的开幕前后得到落实。

四是围绕相关主题，举办包括为年轻人在周末下午举办的普及性演出、展览、电影播放、露天免费演出、公开课、舞会、狂欢大游行在内的各项活动，确保舞蹈节成为全体里昂市民——纳税人的节日。

五是加大国内外媒体的宣传与报道工作，使得里昂国际舞蹈双年节成为具有全球意义的国际活动，不仅极大地强化了里昂和法国的国际影响力，而且有效地促进了各国人民之间的相互理解，其重大意义更在于恰如我1988年在纽约访学时接受《纽约新闻报》整版采访时所说："如果人们相互理解，就不会再有战争！"

三、以"丝绸之路"为主题的"第九届里昂国际舞蹈双年节"

"丝绸之路"是历史上横贯欧亚大陆的贸易交通线，史称由张骞通西域时开启，从西汉都城长安出发，经过河西走廊之后，分两路继续西行，最后进入欧洲和非洲,曾极大地推进了中国与亚、欧、非各国经济与文化的友好往来,并因当时的出口商品以丝绸最具代表性,1877年由德国地理学家费迪南·冯·李希霍芬(Ferdinand von Richthofen)在《中国》一书中首次提出,随后得到中外史学家们的赞同,并由各国民众沿用至今,影响深远。

里昂作为中国丝绸进入法国的第一站,拥有一个规模可观的丝绸博物馆,而无独有偶的是,"里昂国际舞蹈双年节"每次开幕期间均租用它的场地作为总部,因此,2000年以"丝绸之路"为主题的这届舞蹈节可谓准备充分且相当圆满。舞蹈节主席居伊·达尔梅先生在节目册的《开篇辞》中热情洋溢且充满诗意地说:"东方、西方、亚洲、欧洲,2000年的里昂国际舞蹈双年节将带着我们踏上丝绸之路。2000年来,这条窄窄的'丝绸之路',却引领着人类从撒马尔干的深处来到了威尼斯的城门,从穿过里昂的罗纳河两岸来到爱琴海两岸。当不同的世界刚刚开始相互学习之际,'丝绸之路'便通过丝绸与黄金的贸易,以及思想的交流,将各种技艺与文化联系在了一起。'里昂国际舞蹈双年节'盛邀诸位踏上这个从中国西安出发,一路西行,穿越中亚、西亚,直至法国里昂缫丝厂和埃及亚历山大港的发现之旅,而800位亚洲舞者、乐手和歌手的表演,将包括各国鼓手们经久不息的隆隆鼓声、中国古典舞的楚楚动人、日本歌舞伎的炉火纯青、泰国皮影戏的妙趣横生、印度卡塔克古典舞赤脚踢踏的踩地有声,这些表演艺术家们将与法国罗纳河-阿尔卑斯地区的艺术家们分享其创造激情。我盛邀诸位前来与他们见面,并分享其各自的文化与宗教、艺术与才情,而'丝绸之路'则会为大家打开知识的大门。让我们携手,将这些知识带上各自的归途……"

在第九届里昂国际舞蹈双年节上,31个团体及两位独舞表演家沿着古代丝绸之路的路线,分别选自中国的北京、上海、广州、香港、台北,其他亚洲国家中的韩国、日本、泰国、印度、蒙古、叙利亚、伊拉克,非洲的阿尔及利亚,欧洲的乌兹别克斯坦、克罗地亚、荷兰、法国,等等;其中,仅是来自中国各地的团体就多达10个,而唯一的两位独舞表演家也都是中国香港的(梅卓燕、杨春江,均为自编自演的现代舞)——中国人和中国文化在整个国际舞蹈节上,可谓出尽风头。

究其原因,既有历史的——众所周知,"丝绸之路"本来就起始于中国的西安,即当年的长安,因此,荷兰国际民间舞团经过实地采风后创作的晚会,就取名为《金色的西安》,其16个舞蹈节目中,包括了6个中国风格的节目:首先是"太极拳",给媒体的说明文字写的是:"西安是中国古代的帝都,同时也是丝绸之路的起点。从当地秦始皇陵墓中出土的兵马俑多达6000尊,其泰然自若的神情和身心合一的特征,可由太极拳这种最具中国身体文化特征的艺术来代表。"第二个节目是"高跷",说明文字是:"高跷是陕西省与西安市每年春节期间的主要民俗活动,其中包括了可为整个表演增添轻松幽默的丑角——'老扛'、崇拜阳刚之气的'狮舞'和祈盼风调雨顺的龙舞,等等。"第三个节目是"扇舞",说明文字认为,"扇舞因为制作扇子使用了丝绸,可谓最能够体现丝绸文化与魅力的舞种";第四个节目是"长绸舞",主办者认为,"这个舞蹈不仅将丝绸的文化与魅力发扬光大,而且将中国戏曲与舞蹈中的古典主义精神发挥得淋漓尽致"。第五个节目是"藏族舞",主要通过"卓谐"(圆舞)和"堆谐"(踢踏)这两种代表性舞蹈表现了生活在陆路南线"丝绸之路"和"世界屋脊"上的藏族同胞们热情奔放的民族性格;节目单上注明了,这是由中国舞蹈家刘友兰编导的。第六个节目是新疆喀什的赛乃姆,节目单上也特别注明,这是由中国新疆维吾尔族舞蹈家帕莎·乌梅尔(Pasha Umer)在1999年为该团编导的,形象再现了维吾尔民族能歌善舞的天性,而新疆当年也是"丝绸之路"的必经之路。舞蹈节组委会对"丝绸"、"丝绸之路"这些关键词与各种舞蹈间的关系做出的这些解读,可谓视角新鲜、简明扼要,不仅可以帮助法国观众更好地欣赏这台演出,而且可以让我们做演出、写舞评的人们受到启发。随后,这台晚会还沿着丝绸之路,接连表演了蒙古、印度、塔吉克斯坦、乌兹别克斯坦、巴基斯坦、阿富汗等亚洲民族,以及里海与高加索地区的阿瓦尔、亚美尼亚、俄罗斯等横跨欧亚民族的传统歌乐舞,仿佛让现场观众在短短的135分钟里,从中国古都西安出发,一路西行,到达欧洲,不仅重走了这条古而有之的"丝绸之路",而且亲睹了沿途的服饰歌舞与风土人情,禁不住感叹世界文化的千姿百态和人类文明的源远流长……

颇有历史感的是,节目册上还提供了一张1570年比利时安特卫普绘制的《亚洲地图》,并将整台舞蹈晚会16个节目按照"丝绸之路"的轨迹逐一标出,让观众看到了对历史的尊重。

在这届以"丝绸之路"为主题的国际舞蹈双年节上,开幕演出由北京舞蹈学院的《长绸舞》、《秦俑魂》,广东现代舞团李宏均和香港舞蹈家梅卓燕的各自独舞,以及日本的鼓舞团、韩国的歌舞团构成。随后的中国晚会还有上海歌舞团的舞蹈服装表演《金舞银饰》和上海师范大学学生舞团的《中国民族民间舞蹈晚会》,这三台晚会集中展示中国传统舞蹈文化的博大精深,均令法国观众眼花缭乱,心旷神怡,纷纷前往后台,找舞者们签名留念。

中国舞蹈在这届舞蹈节上独领风骚的原因中,既有历史的,也有现实的——中国台湾、香港、广州和北京的现代舞近年来在国际舞坛上捷报频传,撼人心魄。

在整个舞蹈节上,林怀民先生和他的"云门舞集"可谓独占鳌头——作为亚洲现代舞的旗舰舞团,"云门"得到了所有舞团中唯一有资格推出《流浪者之歌》(视频《流浪者之歌》)和《水月》共两台演出的殊荣,而由"太极导引"产生的以柔克刚和行云流水等内在张力,配合简约凝重与天人合一的视觉效果,更是令各国观众顿开茅塞、赞叹不已。

台湾方面出场的还有三个优秀团体:陈美娥为"汉唐乐府"创作的《艳歌行》,被法国媒体认为,是"最具东方人文精神和西方现代概念的室内乐舞";林丽珍为"无垢舞蹈剧场"演出的《花神祭》,是为数不多的几部由"里昂舞蹈双年节"出资的委约作品,不仅色彩简约明快,而且极具中国特有的仪式美感;而"优剧场"的鼓舞史诗《听海之心》,则可谓用结实的丹田气,发出的令人振聋发聩的大自然之声。

香港方面的节目也是异彩纷呈——首先是城市当代舞蹈团演出的现代舞史诗《九歌》出手不凡,编导家黎海宁以旅美华人作曲家谭盾那时而古朴悠远、时而撕心裂胆的音乐为契机,释放出压抑过久的感觉激流,搬演出生离死别的人生戏剧,让西方人体验到了中国文化与美学迥异于西方的深层底蕴和内在张力;作为香港现代舞第二代的代表人物,梅卓燕自"回归"以来,便一直以其个人的身份,以及中国传统文化的当代代表,走红于世界各地的大舞台上;此次,她参加了整个舞蹈双年节的开幕演出;杨春江这位当年香港中文大学的毕业生、城市当代舞蹈团夜间课程的学生和城市当代舞团的演出总监,如今已是香港现代舞第三代的代表人物,并且开始活跃在国际舞台上;他的多媒体新作《自然人体的天堂》将精心拍摄的录像与自己灵活多变的身心巧妙地融为了一体,既当众满足了自我欣赏的心理需求,也纵情歌唱了人类肢体的无穷智慧。

内地方面的演出总是气势磅礴的——广东实验现代舞团借助于"改革开放"的东风,1992年成立,成为中国第一个专业的现代舞团,在海内外大批专家学者的调教下,尤其是在创始团长杨美琦和艺术总监曹诚渊的精心培养下,涌现出了大批身心并用、技艺俱佳的现代舞精英,其中的乔杨、秦立明、邢亮、桑吉嘉、李宏钧先后在巴黎国际现代舞大赛上,为中国夺得四块金牌,创造了令法国人疑惑不解的"中国现代舞奇迹",因此,李宏钧也应邀在开幕式上表演了他在巴黎获得金奖的独舞《我要飞》,受到法国观众和各国媒体的众口交誉。

北京现代舞团自1999年张长城和曹诚渊接任之后,在国际舞坛上频频亮相,为塑造古都北京的现代新形象立下了汗马功劳,他们的晚会包括了曹诚渊的《鸟之歌》、高艳津子与滕爱民的《两个世界》、滕爱民的《喃喃而语》、李捍忠与马波的《野性的呼唤》，让西方人领略了中国现代舞的巨大潜力。

在亚洲其他国家中，舞蹈节还邀请了日本、韩国、印度、泰国、蒙古、乌兹别克斯坦等国的舞蹈团和乐团。其中有日本的4台：首先是起源于公元7世纪的"非遗"项目——歌舞伎（Kabuki），以及三个现代舞团：东京伊藤金与光明未来舞蹈团（Kim Itoh and The Glorious Future）的《松南书上的男生女生》（Shonen – Shojo Boys & Girls）和京都单色杂耍舞团（Monochrome Circus）的《京都即景》（Kyoto Scene）。但给人印象最深的演出还是日本现代舞大师敕使川原三郎（Saburo Teshigawara）的舞蹈剧场《绝对的零》（Absolute Zero），因为身兼编导、演员、音乐联席总监、布景设计、服装设计和灯光设计六职于一身的三郎，仅仅通过个人调遣自如的肢体、张弛得当的对比，外加一点视频投影和一个少女的偶尔出场，便把全场观众的注意力紧紧抓住了一个晚上，并且没把自己累得死去活来！

韩国方面，有资深舞蹈家金梅子领衔的创舞会演出和洪尚玉的现代舞演出。

印度方面，有新德里的婆罗多、马德拉斯的奥迪西两个古典舞团，以及新德里现代舞大师乌黛·香卡的亲传弟子——纳南德拉·夏尔马领衔的脚步现代舞团的三台演出。

泰国方面，舞蹈节挑选了传统的叙事舞剧，题材是印度长诗《罗摩衍那》。

蒙古方面，邀请了20世纪80年代曾在里昂跳舞，随后去了克罗地亚的斯普利特歌剧院芭蕾舞团做团长，现在乌兰巴托做舞团团长的吉丽娜·克雷莫纳（Kilina Cremona），创作的这台向里昂丝绸制造者雅克·布罗希耶致敬的舞蹈晚会。

乌兹别克斯坦方面，有来自撒马尔干的民间乐队演出的舞蹈音乐会《乌兹别克斯坦之声》。

伊拉克方面，请去的是大名鼎鼎的巴格达木卡姆演奏团，名称是《丝路上的沙漠商队》。

在东道主法国方面，有四个现代舞团的演出，题材均在不同的方面，同"丝绸之路"的主题直接或间接相关；这种选材的视角，可为我们提供参考：

首先是法国著名当代舞编导家让-克洛德·加洛塔（Jean – Claude Gallotta）为他的格勒诺布尔国立舞蹈中心创作的当代舞剧《马可·波罗的眼泪》（Les Larmes de Marco Polo），笔者一连看了两遍，并应法国驻华使馆文化参赞刘丽华女士之邀，逐一采访了编导家加洛塔、编剧克洛德-亨利·布法尔、旅法作曲家许舒亚、中国笛子演奏家张维良、大提琴演奏家文森特·德布瑞纳、马可·波罗的扮演者路德维希·加尔万，并以书面论证的方式，说服法国使馆，促成了这部非常前卫的当代舞剧在 2001 年秋天来华，于北京、上海各演了一场。

这部舞剧的创作灵感来自举世闻名的《马可·波罗行记》的问世过程——1254 年，马可·波罗出生于意大利的威尼斯，1271 年来到东方，因深得元世祖忽必烈的信任，而在中国为官 17 载，因此得以游遍神州；1292 年，他离开中国，经过 3 年的旅途劳顿之后，终于回到了威尼斯，却在同热那亚的交战中被俘入狱，但却因祸得福，有机会安下心来，回忆并口述了自己在东方，尤其是在中国的罕见经历，并由同狱笔录成书。1299 年，他获释回到家乡，而这部游记则被译成多国文字，在各国广为流传，并对随后新航路和丝绸之路的开辟，产生了重大的影响。加洛塔这部舞剧的意义就在于，面对已有同样题材的歌剧、舞剧、电影、电视片问世这个事实，他轻松地走出了"讲故事"的误区，而将重点大胆地放在了根据情节发展的大致线索去编舞之上。

第二部法国作品是由里昂本地的当代舞编导黛尔芬·高德小姐（Delphine Gaud）为自己的舞团创作的当代舞剧《垂死的蚕蛾》（Bombyx Mori）。作为法国最早的丝绸生产之都，这部舞剧的题材来自 20 世纪初里昂当地发生的一个真实却离奇的故事：一群丝绸厂的女工因对蚕丝甚至蚕茧迷恋得不可自拔，初而产生了恋物癖式的性欲，继而斗胆偷盗丝绸，终而锒铛入狱，或被送进了疯人院……为了跳舞的方便，编导家把洁白透明的丝绸拟人化成了第五个人物，并使四个女人时而像蚕茧那样爬行于地面，时而则成为剧中的传奇人物。由于这个故事一直在里昂民众中广为流传，因此，观众的热烈掌声，甚至喝彩声证明了，他们在理解上没有出现任何障碍，故而能够集中注意力，观看编舞和跳舞。而在动作的传情达意上，高德小姐的手法显然也打破了古典芭蕾舞剧的叙事习惯，主要传达的是主人公的精神状态，因此，在风格上比较接近加洛塔的《马可·波罗的眼泪》。这个作品也是舞蹈节的委约制作，以便体现对本地舞蹈发展的支持。

第三个法国舞团是同样来自格勒诺布尔市的克里斯蒂娅娜·布莱兹（Christiane Blaise）舞蹈团，风格也是当代的，作品名称叫做《小心丝绸》（Alerte La Soie）。同前面两部作品截然不同，这个作品完全不讲故事，而讲哲学——对于诸如丝绸那样表面柔和、美丽的东西，一定要加倍提防，比如叱咤风云的"现代舞之母"伊莎多拉·邓肯，就死于那条长长的、且飘逸的丝巾！而这一切概念则是通过动作在力度、时间和空间等各方面的强烈对比，来转化成的一种感觉。

第四台演出是法国贝桑松与圣普利斯特的 RAP 舞团融西方街舞和印度卡塔克古典舞于一体的《人神之舞》，从本质上体现出东西合璧、古今交融的"丝路"精神。

舞蹈节期间，还举办了丰富多彩的活动，包括安排荷兰国际民间舞蹈团和上海师范大学的学生舞蹈团分别为社会各界人士和在校学生举办的11场演出，"丝绸之路"沿线国家的摄影展、文物展、丝绸歌剧服饰展、云门舞集的"太极导引"公开课、电影展映、埃及亚历山大港和威尼斯两个主题的广场舞会，以及由里昂地区各个移民社区共4500位群众盛装参与的、欧洲规模最大的狂欢大游行。

"第九届里昂国际舞蹈双年节"的观众总人数是79060人次，不算展览、太极导引公开课和其他示范讲座的免费观众和参与者，仅是购票观众便多达71531人，比上一届多出11%，赠票为7529人次，剧场上座率平均为90%，其中包括四场演出、三场演出的成人套票和青少年套票；此外，"狂欢大游行"（Le Défilé）的观众多达20万，而法国国家电视三台的现场转播则吸引了另外的15万观众，总计35万观众。与此同时，舞蹈节还邀请了249位海内外记者，其中包括我在内的外国记者多达96人，并有海内外19个电视频道作了不同深度的报道。

在我们中国政府提出建设"一带一路"这个宏大的战略构想，并在逐步实施之际，我愿将自己亲历亲目、亲身体验的这些法国的"丝路"理念与运作实践条分缕缕出来，并配上精美的图片，与诸位分享……

谢谢大家的倾听与观看！

参考文献：

1. [法] M. 索托、J.‑P. 布代、A. 盖鲁‑雅拉贝著，杨剑、付绍梅、钱林森等译：《法国文化史》，华东师范大学出版社2006年版。

2. [加] J.‑B. 纳多、J. 巴洛著，何开松、胡继兰译：《六千万法国人不会错》，东方出版社2005年版。

3. [美] W. 索雷尔著，欧建平译：《西方舞蹈文化史》，中国人民大学出版社1996年版。

4. 欧建平：《世界艺术史·舞蹈卷》，东方出版社2003年版。

5. 欧建平：《〈马可·波罗的眼泪〉：舞出浓浓诗意》，《人民日报》（海外版）2001年9月18日第7版。

6. 欧建平：《〈马可·波罗的眼泪〉与舞蹈语言的诗意》，《今日艺术》2001年11月。

7. 欧建平：《向世界敞开心扉——里昂国际舞蹈双年节述评之一》，《舞蹈信息》2003年1月15日第4版。

8. 欧建平：《将丝路引入法国——里昂国际舞蹈双年节述评之二》，《舞蹈信息》2003年2月1日第4版。

9. 欧建平：《拉美舞风席卷里昂——里昂国际舞蹈双年节述评之三》，《舞蹈信息》2003年2月15日第4版。

10. 欧建平：《拉美舞风席卷里昂——第十届里昂国际舞蹈双年节述评》，《中外文化交流》2003年2月。

11. 欧建平：《气象万千的拉丁美洲舞蹈》，《舞蹈》2003年3月。

12. 欧建平：《现代舞巅峰的拉美大师——里昂国际舞蹈双年节述评之四》，《舞蹈信息》2003年3月1日第4版。

13. 欧建平：《观念纯舞＋投影——里昂国际舞蹈双年节述评之五》，《舞蹈信息》2003年3月15日第4版。

14. 欧建平：《行为艺术＋环境编舞——里昂国际舞蹈双年节述评之六》，《舞蹈信息》2003年4月15日第4版。

15. 欧建平：《双年节中的斑马舞蹈团及其他——里昂国际舞蹈双年节述评之七》，《舞蹈信息》2003年6月15日第4版。

"一带一路"框架中戏剧交流的回望与前瞻

中国艺术研究院话剧研究所所长　宋宝珍

2013年9月和10月由中国国家主席习近平分别提出建设"新丝绸之路经济带"和"21世纪海上丝绸之路"的战略构想。

"一带一路"作为现代思想理念和跨文化发展框架,旨在促进中国与周边国家的政治协商、经济兴盛与文化包容,在利益共同体原则的基础上,实现亚、欧、非洲不同文明之间的对话、交流与合作,实现中国的和平发展以及周边国家的利益共商、共享、共建。

经济发展与文化繁荣是中国和平崛起的重要保证。"一带一路"构想中的经济腾飞,离不开跨文化的交流、合作、互惠、融通。在这样的时代背景下,中国戏剧如何抓住机遇,应对挑战,发展进步,这是值得思考的现实命题。本文就中国话剧百余年历史发展中,与外来文化的关系进行简单的梳理,以便以史鉴今,抚今望远。

一、中外戏剧的碰撞与交流

中国是一个戏剧大国,传统的戏曲艺术(opera)历经800多年的历史沧桑,演变为300多个剧种,分布在全国各地。在20世纪初叶,却产生了一种源自西方的现代舞台艺术形式——话剧(spoken drama)。

中国话剧,在艺术形式上有别于传统戏曲,它不以歌舞演故事,而主要以对话、形体动作和舞台布景,创造真实的舞台幻觉。

没有中西文化的交汇,也不会有中国话剧的产生。

话剧作为一种现代艺术形式,也是文化创意与交流的载体,在"一带一路"框架中,理应发挥其在各民族之间增进友谊,加深理解、开展合作、谋求共识的作用。

迄今可查的西方戏剧在中国本土的演出,可以上溯到16世纪末。据《澳门圣保禄学院年报》记载,澳门圣保禄学院的师生们曾于1596年1月16日在圣保禄教堂(今大三巴)台阶上演出过西方戏剧:"圣母献瞻节那一天,公演了一场悲剧。主角由一年级的教师担任,其余的角色由学生扮演。剧情叙述信仰如何战胜了日本的迫害。演出在本学院门口的台阶上进行，结果吸引了全城百姓观看，将三巴寺前面街道挤得水泄不通……演出如此精彩，毫不逊色于任何大学的水平。因为主要剧情用拉丁文演出，为了使不懂拉丁文的观众能够欣赏，还特意制作了中文对白……同时配上音乐和伴唱，令所有的人均非常满意。"①

文中提到戏剧，表现的是"信仰战胜日本的迫害"，那么由此推断，这个戏有可能已经不是单纯的宗教剧，而是部分地反映了澳门人民抗倭斗争的故事，这也是这个戏的演出受到市民普遍关注的原因之一。文中还记载，演出中出现了"中文对白"，这说明，当时圣保禄学院的师生，已经具有了良好的中文水平，也有一种可能，中国人参与了这个戏剧的制作、演出活动。

1604 年 1 月 27 日的《澳门圣保禄学院年报》，详细记述了一场喜剧演出的内容与经过，圣保禄学院的学生演出，甚至开始走出校园的围墙，进入了澳门社会的市民生活。年报记载提到了本次演出的社会效果："本来这一喜剧如同往年那样，是为欢迎中国主教莅临而演的，但是今年似乎是为了娱乐本城居民，因为市民们为荷兰人给他们所造成的巨大损失而沮丧，荷兰人刚刚剽掠了澳门的三艘货船……"②

就以上两场演出而言，戏剧观众中都包括澳门的居民，说明有了"公演"的性质。迄今为止，这是有据可查的中国本土最早的话剧演出。

鸦片战争之后，中国被迫打开国门，东西方文化开始交汇。19 世纪末，清政府开始派人赴西方游历，首位远行欧洲的人，是号称"东土西来第一人"的斌椿。

斌椿是第一批由清政府派往"泰西"（欧洲）游历的人。他是旗人，自小并不聪慧，长大后"性更迁"。但是，他也是个"奇人"，是一个喜欢游走的旅行家。他说："九州曾历历，广见堪傲睨。"那时，去往海外被人视为畏途。而他63 岁高龄却"慨然愿往"，有人为他担忧，他写下"天公欲试书生胆，万里长波作坑坎"的诗句，毅然前往。回国后写了《乘槎笔记》，记录了以其好奇的眼光观察到的新鲜事物。

斌椿第一次向国人报道了西方的戏剧演出情景。在剧场里他看到贵族名媛们姗姗而来，穿着华丽，长裙曳地，袒胸露臂，珠光宝气。而舞台上的情景更让他新奇，他赞叹道："女优登台者多者五六十人，美丽者居其半，率裸半身跳舞。剧中能作山水瀑布、日月光辉，倏而见佛像，或神女数十人自天降，祥光

---

① 李向玉：《澳门圣保禄学院研究》，澳门日报出版社 2001 年版，第 1 页。
② 李向玉：《澳门圣保禄学院研究》，澳门日报出版社 2001 年版，第 90 页。

射人，奇妙不可思议。"① 显然，他被西方戏剧的奇妙诡秘迷住了。

中国人最初接触外国戏剧时，最感兴趣的往往不是戏剧本身，而是由于文化差异而引起的最敏感的地方。这从中国最早的一些外交官所写的《西洋杂志》（黎庶昌）、《出使英法俄日记》（曾纪泽）、《漫游随录》（王韬）、《随使法国记》（张德彝）等书中不难看到。

他们感兴趣的是外国剧院的建筑，如巴黎的倭必纳大剧院之"如离宫别馆"，"规模壮阔逾于王宫"等；还有就是中外演剧人员之差别，如说"英俗演剧者为艺士，非如中国优伶之贱，故观园主人亦可与冠裳之列"，甚至感到"习优是中国浪子事，乃西国以学童为之，群加赞赏，莫有议其非者，是真不可解矣"。接触到戏剧本身，最惊叹的是西方戏剧舞台布景真实与奇诡，"千变万状，几乎逼真"，"令观者若身历其境，疑非人间，叹观止矣"。而对话剧艺术的最初概括是"白而不唱"，"既无唱工，又无做工"。西风东渐，一种外来的艺术形式，逐渐为中国人所接受。

二、具有现代性民族性的现代戏剧的孕育与生成

五四时期中国戏剧经历了现代史上一次"西潮"。

中国戏剧界一面反帝反封建，一面吸纳外域的文化营养，探索民族戏剧的发展方向。在人们探索新的戏剧的发展路向的时候，易卜生及其戏剧不仅率先进入国人视野，而且成为了当时的思想旗帜和艺术榜样。

在 20 世纪 20 年代，不仅胡适高扬"易卜生主义"，一些有志于创造中国现代戏剧的青年，如洪深、田汉等，均把"做中国之易卜生"当作自己的人生理想。与此同时，西方的现代主义，包括象征主义、表现主义、唯美主义、未来主义等各种戏剧流派传入国内，为中国剧作家打开了现代人生的视阈。然而排演直接翻译的西洋戏剧，中国人看不懂，甚至不知所云，这就迫使中国戏剧开始探索民族化的戏剧之路。

在 20 世纪 20 年代中期，中国戏剧界曾经出现过"国剧运动"。"国剧运动"实际上是一些自国外留学归来的人，有感于中国文明戏的衰落，而意欲寻找民族的现代戏剧的发展之路，进而掀起的一次戏剧思想讨论。1926 年，余上沅、徐志摩等人在北京发起创办《晨报·剧刊》，并且制定了一个包括创办剧校、剧院在内的宏大的计划，但很多计划落空。而唯有《剧刊》，在徐志摩的支持下得

---

① 钟叔和：《走向世界》，中华书局 1985 年版，第 69 页。

以实现，共发表了有关戏剧的文章约 20 余篇，参加撰稿的有徐志摩、余上沅、闻一多、赵太侔、张嘉铸、熊佛西、邓以蛰、梁实秋等。他们彼此的艺术主张和理论观点，其实是不尽相同的，但创建中国自己的戏剧样式的目的却有着昭然的一致性。

余上沅、赵太侔等人从中西戏剧的比较中，认为中国传统戏曲"重写意"，有别于西方戏剧的"重写实"，因而，应当吸收中西戏剧之长，创造一种"国剧"。但是，何为"国剧"、如何创造"国剧"，在理论上他们仍然处在探索阶段。

在戏剧实践上取得突破性成就的时期，应当是 20 世纪 30 年代以后的事。

经历了"五四"时期的思想解放和文化交融，在广泛吸纳西方戏剧精华的基础上，中国话剧立足本土，走向成熟，出现了以曹禺及其优秀剧作《雷雨》、《日出》、《原野》、《北京人》、《家》等为代表的戏剧成果。这些剧作具有现代意识，利用本土题材，反映了民族精神与中国气派，以其深邃的内涵、圆熟的技巧、成功的形象、完整的结构被认为是中国话剧的经典之作。

三、中俄戏剧交流与中国表演体系的建立

中华人民共和国成立后，从 1953 年开始，在全国戏剧界展开了学习斯坦尼斯拉夫斯基演剧体系（简称斯氏体系）。

首先，以艺术管理方式向戏剧工作者推荐学习斯氏著作《舞台动作》、《演员自我修养》等。其次，聘请前苏联专家普·乌·列斯里、鲍·格·库里涅夫、格·尼·古里也夫来华授课。其三，自 1953 年到 1957 年，在中央戏剧学院和上海戏剧学院，举办培训班和进修班。

推广斯氏体系对于提高中国舞台艺术水平却是具有积极作用。

1957 年老舍创作了话剧《茶馆》，经由北京人民艺术剧院演出，成为新中国戏剧创作中具有里程碑意义的杰作。剧本 3 万字，写了 3 个"朝代"，时间跨度 50 年，写活了 70 个人物。它以高度的艺术概括，浓郁的民族气派，浓重的历史含量和浓厚的生活气息，谱写出一部史诗性的画卷。总导演焦菊隐探索着演剧民族化的道路。他对斯坦尼斯拉夫斯基体系有着深刻的理解和掌握，但是，他更醉心于如何将中国戏曲的精华运用到话剧中来，并且找到把它同斯氏体系融合的契机，打通中国戏曲同西方戏剧相结合的道路。他赞成"内心体验"，"逼真地再现生活"，但更追求戏剧诗的境界，追求高度的艺术真实，高度的艺术概括。

1958 年，以田汉《关汉卿》的问世为标志，出现了一股历史剧的创作热，其特点是，一些老一辈剧作家纷纷执笔。如郭沫若的《蔡文姬》、《武则天》，曹禺的《胆剑篇》，丁西林的《孟丽君》，刘川的《窦娥冤》，老舍的《义和拳》，田汉的《文成公主》和朱祖诒的《甲午海战》等。这批历史剧，有些写得相当精彩，演出后受到观众的热烈称赞。其中，《关汉卿》堪称田汉的绝唱，他以诗的语言、诗的情调与诗的构思，谱出了一曲关汉卿的赞歌，展现了田汉不仅作为一位戏剧家，而且作为一位热情澎湃的浪漫诗人的卓越才华。《关汉卿》浓郁的抒情色彩，伴随着化入其中的元曲的神韵和声律，显现着浓烈的诗情和悲怆的意味。

1959 年，郭沫若为北京人艺创作了四幕历史剧《蔡文姬》，将一个 2000 多年前的古代才女形象，搬上了中国当代的话剧舞台。这个戏经由焦菊隐导演，朱琳主演，上演后获得轰动，至今仍然是北京人艺的保留剧目。

四、改革开放以后的戏剧发展

改革开放以后，西方现代的各种哲学观念、各种艺术思潮和流派引进国内，现代主义关于探索人、探索人心、探索深藏在人的内部的隐秘灵魂的理念，以及表现主义、象征主义手法，意识流、荒诞派的艺术特点，布莱希特的"间离效果"，"史诗剧场"观念，以及"残酷戏剧"、"质朴戏剧"等观念，都给从事话剧的人们带来新的感觉和新的启示。这些现代意念融会在话剧舞台艺术中，通过不断被吸纳、转化，逐渐地实现了民族化，也慢慢被国人所接受。

为了开阔戏剧视野，展示人类优秀的戏剧成果，中国戏剧界以宽广的文化胸襟，独到的审美眼光，与其他国家和地区的戏剧家们开展了广泛的艺术合作。

进入新时期以来，北京人艺演出了大量文本质量良好、艺术水准高超的外国剧目，如《公正舆论》（罗马尼亚）、《贵妇还乡》（瑞士）、《屠夫》（奥地利）、《推销员之死》（美国）、《女人的一生》（日本）、《洋麻将》（美国）、《上帝的宠儿》（英国）、《二次大战中的帅克》（德国）、《芭芭拉少校》（英国）、《哗变》（美国）、《海鸥》（俄罗斯）、《哈姆莱特》（英国）、《油漆未干》（法国）、《家有娇妻》（英国）、《榆树下的欲望》（美国），等等。

长期以来，北京人艺邀请了很多国外的戏剧专家走进剧院，进行艺术合作与交流，形成了多项戏剧成果：1981 年，英国著名导演托比·罗伯森为北京人艺执导了莎士比亚的名剧《请君入瓮》。1983 年，美国著名戏剧家阿瑟·米勒为北京人艺执导了他自己的名剧《推销员之死》。1988 年美国奥斯卡金像奖获得者、美国电影学院院长查尔顿·赫斯顿为北京人艺导演了《哗变》。1991年莫斯科艺术剧院导演奥列格·叶甫列莫夫为北京人艺导演了《海鸥》。2013年莫斯科艺术剧院导演彼得罗夫和北京人艺青年导演王鹏共同执导了意大利作家皮兰德娄的名剧《六个寻找剧作家的剧中人》。

1980年9月至11月,北京人艺的《茶馆》应邀赴德国、法国、瑞士三国进行访问演出,全程50天,访问15个城市,演出25场。所到之处,外国观众反响强烈,他们被中国演员的精湛表演所打动,欢呼《茶馆》是东方舞台上的奇迹。

1983年,《茶馆》应邀到日本东京、大阪、京都、广岛演出。

1986年,《茶馆》赴中国香港,以及新加坡、加拿大演出。

2006年,复排的《茶馆》赴美国肯尼迪艺术中心演出,并在美国其他城市巡演。

上海话剧艺术中心自1995年成立之始,便注重扩大与世界各国的文化交流,学习世界各国优秀戏剧创作的经验。近10年间,中心已先后上演了古今中外作品100余部,并且与英国、美国、法国、澳大利亚、俄罗斯、日本、新加坡、韩国、爱尔兰、埃及、德国等国以及中国香港、台湾地区的艺术家们开展各种形式的合作及互访演出,获得海内外文化界的高度评价,在不同国家和地区的观众中引起了强烈的反响。

中国国家话剧院(NTCC)是中华人民共和国国家表演艺术院团,于2001年12月25日,在原中国青年艺术剧院和中央实验话剧院的基础上成立。

国家话剧院集中了一批最优秀的话剧舞台艺术人才和影视艺术人才,是一个继承传统、努力进取、富于探索,追求高水准话剧表演艺术,创造话剧艺术精品的生产基地。

国家话剧院以创作和演出高质量、高品位的中外优秀话剧艺术为己任,同时不断追求戏剧舞台的经典性和实验性,始终体现世界和民族的先进文化成果。

2002年,创作演出了五台大戏:《萨勒姆的女巫》(美国)、《这里的黎明静悄悄》(前苏联)、《老妇还乡》(瑞士)、《关于爱情归宿的最新观念》、《叫我一声哥,我会泪落如雨》,组织了部分保留剧目赴上海、香港、澳门等地演出,并参加了国际艺术节的展演和中外戏剧的交流活动。

从2004年起,中国国家话剧院与中国对外文化集团公司等单位一起,创立了每两年一届的国际戏剧季。前两届的戏剧季分别以纪念契诃夫、易卜生、莎士比亚,华彩亚细亚、华彩欧罗巴、国际演出季名义,进行国内外戏剧集中展演,促进了国内外戏剧界的交流,推动了中国话剧事业的发展。

近年来，中外戏剧交流的新特点：

（1）从演出外国剧作到邀请外国导演直至同步引进有市场前景和社会影响力的西方名剧。

（2）旨在进行中外戏剧汇演的"戏剧演出季"、"精品展演"、"国际戏剧节"明显增多，一流的国外戏剧家及其团队来华演出频繁。

（3）中国现代戏剧开始走出国门，参加诸如"契诃夫戏剧节"、"阿维尼翁戏剧节"、"中日韩戏剧节"、"爱丁堡戏剧节"，等等。

2014年11月1日至12月25日，第六届"戏剧奥林匹克"在京举行，本届戏剧奥林匹克的主题是"梦想"，口号是"中国的梦想，世界的舞台"，它汇集22个国家上千位戏剧家创作的46部作品，在北京17个剧场进行了百余场演出。

戏剧奥林匹克首先是舞台艺术魅力的视觉盛筵，戏剧奥林匹克主席、希腊特尔佐布罗斯导演的《被缚的普罗米修斯》，以石头圈内歌队演员匍匐在地的身体，烘托普罗米修斯的悲壮兀立；以导演在台边的吟诵和场外传出的爆炸轰鸣，实现远古与现代的对接、互动。

随着对外戏剧交流的增多，中国本土戏剧的发展日益红火。

据北京演出行业协会统计，2014年北京各类营业性演出共计24595场，而话剧类演出4519场，比去年增加5%；儿童剧类演出3134场，其他类型及小剧场演出3200场。其中，包括话剧、儿童剧、相声、杂技等语言类演出占总场次的67.8%。按观众人数统计，话剧类观众147.1万，儿童剧类观众101.5万，其他类型及小剧场观众106.1万。

"一带一路"框架下的戏剧交流展望：

（1）"一带一路"的战略构想是推进中国经济崛起、民族文化振兴的有力举措，现代戏剧作为文化交流的载体，将发挥重要作用。

（2）好的戏剧是无国界的，在世界经济一体化的今天，中外戏剧交流将常态化、有序化、持续化。

（3）中国现代戏剧本来就是"舶来品"，其艺术样态与发展步态，与其他民族不同。

（4）在相互尊重、互惠共赢的前提下，跨文化的戏剧交流将会范围更广，形式更多，效果更好。

法国荒诞派戏剧家尤涅斯库说过，戏剧是人类的本质需要。预祝人类的戏剧乃至世界的文明发展得越来越好。

从《红楼梦》中的某一个案来看中日学者的相互影响
（摘要）

中国艺术研究院红楼梦研究所所长　孙玉明

截止到目前为止，日本已经出现四个一百二十回《红楼梦》全译本。松枝茂夫译本和伊藤漱平初译本出现在中日邦交正常化之前，没有受到中国大陆"红学"的影响。但中日邦交正常化后，尤其是20世纪80年代初期松枝茂夫和伊藤漱平访问中国艺术研究院红楼梦研究所之后，伊藤漱平不仅又依据庚辰本改译了他的初译本，而且在注释方面也明显受到了影响。其后出现的饭冢朗全译本，尤其是去年刚刚出版的井波陵一全译本，受到的影响则更为明显。我们仅以第五回中的《枉凝眉》为例，即可看出这一影响。中国艺术研究院红楼梦研究所校注的新校本《红楼梦》，初版和第二次修订时，均将《枉凝眉》一曲归属宝玉和黛玉，这明显是不符合实际情况的。第三次修订时接受某些学者意见，改为合咏黛玉和宝钗。井波陵一明显采纳了新校本前两次校注的注释。但将来他如果还要修改，不知道能否采纳新校本第三版的意见。

中国传统戏剧中的文化基因与文化对话
（摘要）

中国艺术研究院戏曲研究所所长　王　馗

文化如何实现对话，前提条件是：文化是自信、自足的，文化是宽容、包容的，文化是创造、发展的。在中国一带一路建设进程中，需要展现自信、宽容、开放的民族文化发展观，这是中国重要的文化传统和历史经验。"目连救母"故事源出印度佛教中的多生因缘故事，却在中国佛教仪式与戏曲艺术中得到多元再现，这足以说明中华文化不但作为包容体，接纳了来自域外的各种文化基因，而且作为创造体，也不断地拓展出更加丰富的艺术表现形式。

在广东客家佛教香花仪式中，最动人的仪式内容是对"目连救母"故事的敷衍。这个故事通过横贯中国中西部的丝路，将佛教立足的因果律渗透到中国南北方的传统道德伦理中，展现了佛教因果不昧的终极道理，又有禅宗、密宗等宗派所秉持的供僧功德、中阴救度的世俗伦理，同时也兼容了中国传统家庭伦理与人性关怀。附着于佛教仪式的"目连救母"故事随着华人在海上丝绸之路的向外迁徙，一直流播到东南亚等海外华人社会。同时，故事通过戏剧的敷衍，与中国传统礼乐制度相并生，成为中国戏曲舞台上的重要剧目，并在中国丰富的民族创造、地域创造、族群创造出，形成各种风格迥异的演出形态。

一个故事缘起，连接起文化传统各不相同的地域，创造出丰富多元的文化形态，展现出各具特色的东方智慧。在"一带一路"文化空间中，亚洲文化合作共赢的机制，实际正通过这个故事中折射出来的文化交流历史，清楚地展现出来。

丝绸之路的艺术交流对古代中国乐舞发展的影响
——以宫廷乐舞为例

中国艺术研究院舞蹈研究所　王宁宁

引子：公元前139年，一张榜，一个人，与丝绸之路的缘起

公元前139年，西汉王朝受到匈奴在边境上的骚扰与进犯，另一个部落大月氏（今中亚地区阿姆河流域、土库曼斯坦）在与匈奴的战争中，大月氏王被割头，匈奴用大月氏王的头颅做成饮酒器，大月氏虽愤怨，但无法与匈奴抗衡，被迫西迁而去。汉武帝得知此情报后，决定通使西域"事征四夷，广威德"（《汉书·西域传》），同时展开与西域国家的友好交往。而后，朝廷招募的榜文遍布长安，在张贴的榜文下人们驻足而观，只见簇拥的人群中走出一个人来，此人揭下了榜文，朝着应征的官府走去……这个人名叫张骞，他当时只是朝廷的一个低级官员，名"郎"（郎：帝王侍从官）。

公元前138年，张骞持汉节，带领100多人的团队通使西域。正是这个原本为了抗击匈奴、加强国防的初衷与行动，凿通了古代西域丝绸之路，使东、西方文明碰撞。沿着西域丝绸之路驼队的足迹，异域音乐歌舞不断传入中原地区，深刻影响了古代中国乐舞……

胡乐西来，华乐嬗变

根据《汉书·西域传》记载，汉朝盛行角抵百戏表演，西域大宛国（帕米尔西北，今乌兹别克斯坦一带）使者来汉朝觐见汉武帝时，进献了东罗马杂技艺人。汉朝使者出使安息国（今伊朗），安息国王令二万骑兵在边境上迎汉朝使者；而后安息国使者来汉朝，又带来了西域杂技艺人。汉武帝刘彻曾在海边举行盛大的演出，那些曲折肢体、吞刀吐火的表演场面让汉武帝心情大悦，也使得角抵奇戏表演在汉朝不断地增变。东汉时西域传入的"胡箜篌"、"胡笛"、"胡舞"等颇受汉灵帝刘宏的青睐，一时间爱好"胡乐"成为了时尚，被贵族们

所追捧。

　　魏晋南北朝是古代中国民族交流、文化多样性最突出的时期。因匈奴、羯、氐、羌、鲜卑等"五胡"政权的存在，给中原传统文化造成很大的冲击，这时从西域丝绸之路传入的"胡乐"已经渗透在人们的生活中。比如，三国曹魏皇室贵族曹植就喜欢穿"胡服"，还能自跳"胡舞"。公元382年，十六国前秦皇帝苻坚为了得到当时的龟兹佛教高僧鸠摩罗什，发动了一场战争，这场战争不仅俘获了佛教高僧鸠摩罗什，还得到了西域龟兹乐舞。公元568年，北周武帝宇文邕聘娶西域突厥公主为皇后，随着突厥公主而来的陪嫁队伍浩浩荡荡，其中有西域龟兹国（新疆拜城库车一带）、康国（今塔吉克斯坦、乌兹别克斯坦）、安国（今乌兹别克斯坦布哈拉一带）等国的乐工舞伎，他们带了西域的乐器、歌舞、乐律音调等。北魏、西魏时期，西域《疏勒乐》（今新疆喀什疏勒县一带）、《高昌乐》（今新疆吐鲁番一带）传入中原。1999年在山西省太原市王郭村虞弘墓出土的北朝墓葬石椁浮雕乐舞图，不仅具有浓厚的中亚和波斯风格，还展现了墓主人不同寻常的外来文化背景。山西大同市曹夫楼村出土的北魏杂技俑，人物皆为高鼻深目的"胡人"形象，它见证了这一时期中、西方乐舞的交流。盛行的西域"胡乐"在当时战乱频繁的时局中，潜移默化地改变着人们的观念与行为。

　　隋唐时期是古代中国最为繁荣强大的时期。根据隋朝裴炬《西域图记序》记载，当时西域丝绸之路有南、北、中三条道路，皆可直通印度、罗马和波斯。当时外国使者云集长安，中、西方文化交流空前繁荣，前期传入的各国各民族乐舞，在隋唐燕乐中得到了集中整理和保存。比如，隋唐宫廷燕乐七部伎、九部伎、十部伎，它属于国家乐舞，其中吸纳包容了多部西域外国乐舞，如有《天竺伎》、《安国伎》、《龟兹伎》、《疏勒伎》、《高昌伎》、《康国伎》、《扶南伎》、《高丽伎》等。隋唐燕乐以"有容乃大"的气度，把不同国家民族的乐舞容纳为一体，在风格、名称、服饰、乐器、道具上"原生态"地保持了各国各民族风貌。虽然在数量上外来"胡乐"占多数，但在出场的顺序安排上却都是以中原乐舞，如《燕乐》、《清商》为开篇，这种顺序安排反映了古代"华"正"夷"偏的传统观念。经过长期的中、西乐舞交流，至隋唐时乐舞的观念形式等嬗变突出。

　　在古代传统观念下，宫廷舞蹈是以"文"与"武"来分类命名。文，即文德。武，即武功。即文舞与武舞。这种分类标准影响并约制了技艺表现，因为所有动作的表达与含义，都要明确指归在"文"与"武"的事件及其思想内涵上。有时舞蹈用"大"与"小"来分类命名。大舞，指宗庙祭祖之舞。小舞，指祭祀自然山川神灵之舞。大舞、小舞的分类，又是依据祭祀神系的等级来区别和命名。在这样的思想观念中，舞蹈不仅形式内容与既定思想紧紧捆绑，而且在身体语言表现，以及动作形式的运用上，也被"画地为牢"地限定了。除了用文与武、大与小，来分类命名舞蹈之外，很多时候舞蹈又是以它的歌名、曲名来作为舞名。有时又是以舞者所持道具来命名舞蹈。可见所有这些传统舞蹈分类法，都没有从艺术风格和身体动作本体来考虑。但是，到了隋唐时期，由于受西域外来音乐歌舞的持续影响，在宫廷中开始出现"软舞"、"健舞"的分类。"软"与"健"二字，直指身体动作的柔软度、力度与风格特征，完全不同于以往。很显然，这时古人开始关注身体动作本体以及舞蹈艺术风格的体现，而不只是注重伦理思想观念的传达。

伴随丝绸之路而来的"胡服"在引领中原传统服饰改易的同时，也促使传统舞蹈在身体语言表达上发生了改变。比如，自西周以来，古代服饰是"上衣下裳"或"深衣"，长袖长裙、宽大阔绰。我们古人常说"长袖善舞"，就是指长袖服饰与舞蹈的紧密关系。传统服饰具有封闭性特点，舞者仅有面部或头部外露，一旦舞将起来，舞者的身姿就会呈现出像书法墨迹流线一般的抑扬顿挫。但是到了隋唐时期，受"胡服"的影响和服饰改易，女子服饰出现了"胡衫"细袖、半臂袖、翻领、无领、宽大领口等样式，这种服饰使得女子可以袒露脖颈以至上胸，完全突破了传统服饰的封闭性。于是，身体本然的质感开始进入人们的视线，并受到人们的欣赏，舞者也不再像以往那样——谦恭、低俯，曲蹲、含蓄，而是抬头挺胸，展示其美丽的身姿。再加上这时舞者时兴盛装打扮，脚踏胡靴，肩披长帔，舞蹈完全超越了传统"长袖善舞"单一性表现，有了更丰富多彩的视觉刺激与审美表达。

隋唐时西域各国的乐器、乐曲和音调等传入，也不断刺激改变着传统乐舞的形态。隋唐乐队多采用西域的鼓、笛子、琵琶等乐器来伴奏，如此动感跳跃、节奏鲜明的音乐，一改传统乐器编钟、编磬、笙、竽、琴、瑟的器乐形态和音乐风格，也不断挑战人们的审美经验。可以说，正是来自丝绸之路的乐舞交流、碰撞与融合，推进了古代乐舞的创新与发展。

结语：丝路新声，叩响未来

2000 多年前，张骞先后于公元前 138 年、公元前 119 年两次出使西域，虽然两次都没能达到汉武帝的原本目的：联合大月氏"夹击"匈奴、联合乌孙"断匈奴右臂"，但是由此却带来了"和亲"通婚，以及政治、经贸、文化、艺术、科技等多方位的交流。这不仅深刻影响了古代中国乐舞的发展，同时也深刻影响了中原文化，以及亚洲乃至世界文明的进程。应该说，这是古人始料未及、没有想到的结果。那么，丝绸之路的历史经验告诉我们：历史选择与历史规律，在某种程度上说，它是权力和人类意志难以掌控的，但其中各国各民族的共同利益与共同威胁——此乃丝绸之路各国各民族交流发展的政治生态之共求共需，亦是一把标尺。为了和平友好、互信互利，为了人类快乐幸福的生活，这是古代丝绸之路发展的历史推动力。如果说，我们的古人凿空西域，开辟丝绸之路，其缘起仍然囿于一时一事的战略考虑的话，那么，今天习近平总书记提出的"一带一路"、"复兴丝绸之路"的伟大构想与宏伟蓝图，其善缘而起，在世界胸怀、全球着眼点、造福人类与战略高度上，都已经远远超越了我们古人的思想与心胸。"一带一路"、"复兴丝绸之路"所具有的新的历史高度，它带给中国与世界的福祉将不可估量！而在"一带一路"、"复兴丝绸之路"伟大构想与实现过程中，音乐舞蹈艺术仍然会以它生动、感人、和谐、快乐的优胜性，去感染人心、去化解压力、去传递快乐幸福的讯息，发挥着其他形式门类所不能替代的作用。

钱锺书释"老健春寒秋后热"

集美大学文学院　王人恩

"老健春寒秋后热"一语出自《红楼梦》中的紫鹃之口,第五十七回"慧紫鹃情辞试忙玉　慈姨妈爱语慰痴颦"写紫鹃与黛玉夜间说话:

> 夜间人定后,紫鹃已宽衣卧下之时,悄向黛玉笑道:"宝玉的心倒实,听见咱们去就那样起来。"黛玉不答。紫鹃停了半晌,自言自语的说道:"一动不如一静。我们这里就算好人家,别的都容易,最难得的是从小儿一处长大,脾气情性都彼此知道的了。"黛玉啐道:"你这几天还不乏,趁这会子不歇一歇,还嚼什么蛆。"紫鹃笑道:"倒不是白嚼蛆,我倒是一片真心为姑娘。替你愁了这几年了,无父母无兄弟,谁是知疼着热的人?趁早儿老太太还明白硬朗的时节,作定了大事要紧。俗语说,'老健春寒秋后热',倘或老太太一时有个好歹,那时虽也完事,只怕耽误了时光,还不得趁心如意呢。公子王孙虽多,那一个不是三房五妾,今儿朝东,明儿朝西?要一个天仙来,也不过三夜五夕,也丢在脖子后头了,甚至于为妾为丫头反目成仇的。若娘家有人有势的还好些,若是姑娘这样的人,有老太太一日还好一日,若没了老太太,也只是凭人去欺负了。所以说,拿主意要紧。姑娘是个明白人,岂不闻俗语说:'万两黄金容易得,知心一个也难求'。"[①]

何为"老健春寒秋后热"?颇具权威性的《红楼梦大辞典》解说云:

> 春日渐暖,虽寒也不会持久;秋后转凉,再热也是短暂的。比喻老年人的健康正如春寒秋热,不能长久。宋·太平老人《袖中锦》谓:"世间四事不可久恃:春寒、秋热、老健、君宠。"此语系紫鹃指贾母

---

① 本文所引《红楼梦》原文均据中国艺术研究院红楼梦研究所校注本,人民文学出版社 1982 年版。

而言。①

《红楼梦大辞典》引用《袖中锦》的资料作注大致正确，比起一些排印本或简注、或误注、或避而不注要好得多，虽然未臻于完美，亦未指出其最早出处。

其实，早在《谈艺录》（补订本）出版的1984年，学贯中西、纵观古今的钱锺书先生就在书中指明了"老健春寒秋后热"这一词语的最早出处及流传、引用情况，其所昭示的文献资料弥足珍贵，而且昭示了先进的研究方法，值得后人珍视。据笔者所见，首先指出钱锺书引用"老健春寒秋后热"作比喻并且认为"钱先生为注红专家提供了很好的借鉴"者是沈治钧先生②，但是因限于题旨，沈先生未再做追踪。笔者多年来也一直留意、思考着这一问题，今遵循钱先生论批评赏析的观点即"立异无当，不如照钞，依样葫芦，犹胜画蛇添足"③之告诫，故不揣浅陋，拟循着钱锺书指出的线索梳理一下相关文献资料，以为后来注释《红楼梦》者和"红学"爱好者提供一些帮助。

钱先生指出：

> 吾国古来俗语以"春寒、秋热、老健"三者喻"终是不久长之物"，早见欧阳永叔《文忠全集》卷一百四十八《与沈待制》，太平老人《袖中锦》增"君宠"而成四事；诗歌、小说皆沿袭之。（如李天生《受祺堂诗集》卷一《朝雨谣》、姚春木椿《通艺阁诗三录》卷四《春雪席间》、《封神演义》三十五回黄飞虎语、《红楼梦》五十七回紫鹃语、《儿女英雄传》二十一回褚大娘语）。明人《三报恩传奇》第六折有诗，踵事增华："老健春寒秋后热，半夜残灯天晓月，草头露水板桥霜，水上浮沤山顶雪"；又土风本色之"九如"也。④

钱锺书著作素以高瞻周览、言简意赅、源流清晰、金针度人著称，这段文字首先点明"老健春寒秋后热"这一说法"早见欧阳永叔《文忠全集》卷一百四十八《与沈待制》"，博涉多通的钱先生将这一说法出现并见于文献的时间确定在北宋，这是溯源。欧阳修《与沈待制》："某启：数日不奉问，苦暑非常岁之比，少壮者自不能当；衰病之人，不问可知焉。辱教，承体气清安，甚慰。

---

① 冯其庸、李希凡主编：《红楼梦大辞典》（增订本），文化艺术出版社2010年版，第30页。
② 沈治钧：《无端说梦向痴人——钱锺书谈〈红楼梦〉》，《贵州大学学报》2000年第2期。
③ 钱锺书：《管锥编》第一册，中华书局1979年版，第369页。
④ 钱锺书：《谈艺录》（补订本），中华书局1984年版，第617页。

俗以立秋日卜秋暑多少，据今日之势，犹当更猖狂耳。然世言春寒、秋热、老健，为此三者，终是不久长之物也。"① 考《与沈待制》作于庆历三年（1043），时欧阳修年不足四十而叹衰老，这是常见的文人的叹老嗟贫的"狡狯笔法"。② 钱先生还敏锐地发现"太平老人《袖中锦》增'君宠'而成四事"这一现象，考太平老人（张仲文）《袖中锦》："世间四事不可久恃，春寒、秋热、老健、君宠。"③ 张仲文大概生活在宋元之际④。对于后来"诗歌、小说皆沿袭之"的情况，钱先生仅做指示发踪，未引具体文献资料，这是明流。今尝试做一梳理：

> 李天生《受祺堂诗集》卷一《朝雨谣》并序："闻之田畯'朝雨虽雨不雨，老健春寒秋雨'。"⑤

李天生，即明末清初陕西人李因笃（1632—1692），字子德，一字孔德，号天生，为明清之际的音韵学家、诗人、思想家、教育家，被时人称为不涉仕途的华夏"四布衣"之一。

> 姚春木椿《通艺阁诗三录》卷四《春雪席间示张伊卿席冠甫二子》："落灯风后兴阑珊，骤觉严威意外干。一琖醇醪才子劝，漫天春雪老夫寒。（自注：谚云：老健春寒秋后热。友人多以予为强健，故有

---

① 《欧阳修全集》下册，中国书店1986年版，第1274页。
② 古代文人未老言老、未衰言衰、未愁言愁、未贫言贫、未醉言醉者屡见不鲜，最经典的例证如：屈原作《离骚》时尚在中年，然《离骚》中反复叹老："汩余若将不及兮，恐年岁之不吾与"；"老冉冉其将至兮，恐修名之不立"。杜甫《杜位宅守岁》："四十明朝过，飞腾暮景斜。"白居易《隐几》："行年三十九，岁暮日斜时。"欧阳修做滁州太守时虚龄四十，而《醉翁亭记》写道"而年又最高，故自号曰醉翁也"，"苍颜白发"；苏东坡三十八九岁时任杭州通判，其《正月二十一日病后述古邀往城外寻春》诗云："老来厌逐红裙醉，病起空惊白发新。"清人姚莹《识小录》卷六有"文人喜言老"条，罗列甚多，可参。
③ 张仲文：《白獭髓》，《丛书集成初编》（补印本）之《白獭髓及其他四种》，商务印书馆1939年12月版，1959年10月补印，第2页。亦可参《说郛》卷十二下，影印文渊阁《四库全书》第876册，上海古籍出版社2003年版，第622页。
④ 关于太平老人张仲文的生活年代，方健先生《久佚海外〈永乐大典〉中的宋代文献考释》一文指出："今考方回《桐江续集》卷33《送张仲文教谕还宣城序》称：仲文，名炳。乃张雄飞（字宏甫）之长孙，其叔张鏐（字以洪），与方回同生宝庆三年（1227）。则张仲文已是宋元之际人。如果方回所记的张仲文就是《白獭髓》的作者，则显然其文抄自俞文豹《唾玉集》（即《吹剑录》），虽已加补充改写，但反不如俞氏之文简而传神。"见《暨南史学》第三辑。
⑤ 清康熙年间刻本《受祺堂诗集》三十五卷，福建图书馆藏。

此戏）……"①

"姚春木椿"即姚椿（1777—1853），字春木，一字子寿，姚鼐弟子，著述甚多。

> 《封神演义》第三十五回黄飞虎语："纣虽强胜一时，乃老健春寒耳！"②

又《儿女英雄传》第二十一回：

> 褚大娘心里想的是："……纵说我随了老父朝夕奉养，比他强些，老人家已是'老健春寒秋后热'，'譬如朝露，去日苦多'。那时无论我心里怎样的孝顺，难道还能派定了人家褚家子弟永远接续邓家香烟不成？"③

钱先生认为"明人《三报恩传奇》第六折有诗，踵事增华"，信然！考明人毕魏《三报恩》传奇第六折："（净）老健春寒秋后热，（小净）半夜残灯天晓月，（丑）草头露水板桥霜，水上浮沤山顶雪。"④正如钱先生所言，由欧阳修倡言的"老健春寒秋后热"这一说法在《袖中锦》中增"君宠"而成四事，而到明人《三报恩传奇》中踵事增华为九种，五彩缤纷而后出转精。以上资料中，只有姚椿《通艺阁诗三录》卷四《春雪席间》、文康《儿女英雄传》晚于《红楼梦》，其余均早于曹雪芹创作《红楼梦》的时间；博大精深的《红楼梦》是一部百科全书，曹雪芹乃旷世奇才，善于向前代的文化遗产汲取养料，"老健春寒秋后热"之进入曹雪芹的笔下就是顺理成章的事情了。

我曾经说过，钱锺书虽不以"红学家"名世，但借用一句钱锺书评论孔颖达的话来评价钱锺书在"红学"方面的贡献，即"红学"史"当留片席之地与"钱锺书⑤。不劳多征，仅从他解释"老健春寒秋后热"的发轫、发展、流变来看，即可窥见钱学包罗富厚之一斑；就研究方法来看，钱先生特别留意戏曲、

---

① 姚椿：《通艺阁诗三录》，《清代诗文集汇编》第522册，上海世纪出版股份有限公司、上海古籍出版社2010年版，第193页。
② 《封神演义》，广东人民出版社1980年版，第307页。
③ 《儿女英雄传》，上海古籍出版社1991年版，第239—240页。
④ 《郑振铎藏古吴莲勺庐抄本戏曲百种》第4册，国家图书馆出版社2009年版，第242页。
⑤ 王人恩：《钱锺书与〈红楼梦〉》，《文学评论》2007年第2期。

小说、随笔、谣谚中的谈艺资料，如欧阳修《与沈待制》是书札，太平老人《袖中锦》是随笔，李因笃《朝雨谣》是谣谚，《封神演义》、《儿女英雄传》、《红楼梦》是小说，《三报恩传奇》是戏曲，只有姚椿的《春雪席间》是文人诗，这让我们想起钱先生在《读〈拉奥孔〉》一文中的一段名言：

> 一般"名为"文艺评论史也"实则"是《历代文艺界名人发言纪要》，人物个个有名气，言论常常无实质。倒是诗、词、随笔里，小说、戏曲里，乃至谣谚和训诂里，往往无意中三言两语，说出了精辟的见解，益人神智；把它们演绎出来，对文艺理论很有贡献。①

这一段话可以看作钱先生"演绎""精辟见解"的经验之谈、夫子自道和经典例证。在对"老健春寒秋后热"的"演绎"中，钱先生往往将常人不经意、不重视的"谣谚和训诂"揭示出来，"解难如斧破竹，析义如锯攻木"②，"三言两语"而"谈言微中"；如此的演绎要比某些质木无文的长篇大论而解释不了一个具体问题的所谓论著不知高明和有用多少！而重视废话一吨，轻视微言一克的做法应该摈弃。

我还在"训诂"中发现了一条资料，兹附骥之尾，权当作猪八戒随孙大圣打仗"放屁添风"而"助些胆气"③，清人魏荔彤撰《大易通解》卷十一即引"谣谚"解经：

> 谚云："老健春寒秋后热"，俱言不能久耳。④

魏荔彤（1670—？），字赓虞，号念庭，又字淡庵，号怀舫，直隶柏乡（今河北省邢台柏乡县）人，清代理学家、易学家、医学家。著述甚多。他的这条资料为钱锺书的说法提供了绝好的注解。

可以认为，钱锺书先生将"老健春寒秋后热"这一小小的、但多年来无人能够解决的学术公案做出了高明的破解，后来的学人应该尽量明白钱锺书已经说过什么，以避免浪掷精力的闭门造车、重复研究。

---

① 钱锺书：《七缀集》（修订本），上海古籍出版社1994年版，第33页。
② 钱锺书：《管锥编》第4册，中华书局1979年版，第1421页。
③ 钱锺书：《小说识小》，《钱锺书文集》，北岳文艺出版社2003年版，第639—640页。
④ 魏荔彤：《大易通解》卷十一，影印文渊阁《四库全书》第44册，上海古籍出版社2003年版，第412页。

元代海陆丝绸之路文化汇合点
——以希腊文化东渐泉州为例

泉州师范学院　吴幼雄

引　言

元代福建泉州是世界东方贸易大港,也是国内江浙、淮湖贸易网区的中心,江浙行省和福建行省的省会曾设置于泉州。元初,"四海舶商,诸蕃琛贡,皆于是乎集"。[①] 宋末元初,仙游人林蒙亨作《螺江风物赋》,形象记载元初泉州港舶来货贸易盛况,是"胡椒、槟榔、玳瑁、犀象、殊香百品、异药千名、木帛之裘、葛布之筒,重载而来,轻赍而去者,大率贸白金而置青铜"。这些舶来货品,待"扶桑日出,阳候波暖,舳舻衔尾……瑕琛远货不可殚名者,辐辏于南北之贾客"。这些国内市场的贾客"自远方而来,徙家者复多于穴之蚁、巢之蜂"。[②]

长江中下游地区遂成为泉州港海外贸易商品供应的后方基地和舶来货品的倾销之区。伴随着海内外经济和文化的交流,泉州成为多种宗教传播的地区,又是世界多种宗教文化的辐射点。本文以元代泉州遗存宗教石刻,证实欧洲希腊文化艺术如何借印度犍陀罗式艺术,通过海上丝绸之路东渐泉州;同时,通过遗存泉州元代古叙利亚文字基督教墓碑,揭示希腊文化借基督教从陆上丝绸之路传入泉州之事实。结论是元代福建泉州是海上丝绸之路和陆上丝绸之路文化的汇合点。本文以元代遗存宗教实物,证实欧洲希腊文化和艺术,如何通过"海丝"与"陆丝"交汇于福建泉州。

一、希腊艺术借印度犍陀罗式艺术传播中国

所谓犍陀罗式艺术,即是希腊系艺术和印度佛教艺术相接触、相吸收而产

---

① 乾隆《晋江县志》卷16,词翰,庄弥邵《罗城外壕记》。
② 弘治《兴化府志》卷32,礼纪、艺文志、辞赋类,林蒙亨《螺江风物赋》(有序)。

生的一种新型的雕刻艺术。也可以说是希腊化了的佛教艺术。因为它在古代西北印度的犍陀罗地区（今白沙瓦）为中心发祥，所以后来被称为犍陀式雕刻艺术。犍陀罗艺术雕刻根源之深，波流之广，不但影响了印度固有的雕刻艺术，而且分海、陆两路波及中国。其一，是随着印度佛教从海路传播南洋群岛和东南亚进而传播中国东南沿海地区；其二，随着印度佛教通过陆上丝绸之路传播西域各地，越葱岭，经天山南路，分两道入玉门关和阳关，并东渐中国内地。或直接随佛教经喜马拉雅山传入中国西藏，然后借藏传佛教（喇嘛教）流播西北、内蒙古和华北地区。犍陀罗式的雕刻艺术，对中国的雕刻艺术起了不小的影响。

公元前327年，希腊马其顿国亚历山大王东征波斯，占领当时为波斯的一个行省的印度西北地区。希腊占领者在被征服的地区建立不少希腊式城市，因此希腊的文化经波斯等地源源流入印度。公元前305年，亚历山大王的部将塞留古建立条支国。公元前250年至公元前249年，条支国分裂为希腊人在阿姆河南建立大夏国；波斯人在其故地之西建立安息国。严格说，这时期已属罗马期了，希腊文化一方面为罗马所继承，另一方面传播到东方后，与东方文化交融而被称为"东方希腊文化"。安息、大夏均受希腊文化深刻影响，尤其大夏国是东方希腊文化的集中地。所谓东方希腊文化，是以希腊文化为主流，概括了罗马、东罗马、波斯、大夏等的文化。西北印度在受了希腊文化的洗礼之后，经过长期的酝酿，于大月氏贵霜王朝迦腻色迦王时，绽放出璀璨瑰丽的艺术花朵——犍陀罗式雕刻。

二、佛教、印度教和犍陀罗式艺术

印度的偶像崇拜导源于希腊。印度古婆罗门教是继承吠陀教的传统的，没有偶像崇拜。后来，婆罗门教有神祇造像是导源于佛教的。婆罗门教的建筑和造像最早不超过6世纪，它是属于新婆罗门教——印度教的产物。也就是说佛教是古婆罗门教的分支，但它比婆罗门教先有石质材的建筑物与造像。印度教的雕刻艺术，是从佛教艺术演变而来的。所以，犍陀罗的佛教偶像崇拜是导源于希腊；印度教的偶像崇拜是源于犍陀罗[1]。

但是印度教的神祇造像有着它的特殊风格，即多头多臂的形态。多头多臂的艺术造型也影响了印度的大乘佛教，以及密宗（真言宗）的艺术，如多头多

---

[1] 丁文光：《犍陀罗式雕刻艺术》，人民美术出版社1959年版，第4—5页。

臂的珂梨底天、观音菩萨、降三世明王诸像的出现。佛教的造型艺术虽然在漫长的岁月里有了不少的变化，但是佛像自从犍陀罗式雕刻艺术对它有了基本定型以后，这种多头臂的形态不论在什么地方都曾扩展到佛像身上来。

印度小乘佛教是不主张偶像崇拜的。待希腊系艺术在犍陀罗地区兴盛后，佛教方才逐渐流行偶像崇拜。开始很可能是造菩萨偶像，后才延及佛本身的偶像。印度的佛菩萨造像之肇始，最早不超过公元1世纪。犍陀罗式雕刻的出现，佛教艺术进入了一个新的重大的发展阶段，其影响还通过陆路和海路波及中国的西南、西北、华北、内蒙古和东南沿海地区。

三、泉州佛教的犍陀罗式雕刻艺术

泉州佛教的犍陀罗式雕刻艺术有两种，一为圆雕，一为浮雕。泉州南俊巷承天寺观音阁祀奉一尊3米多高的元代十一面千手铜铸观音，同属犍陀罗艺术作品。观音宽肩、隆胸、束腰、跣足，跌坐在有花饰的圆台之上，其三对大手臂分别为：下对手臂的手心朝内作愿心印；中对手臂手心上翻；上对手臂特长高高举起。这三对六只手臂皆饰有臂镯、腕轮。颈上有璎珞，胸部有胸饰。观音背后则加饰象征性的"千手"。十一面观音皆隆鼻，脸部丰满，表情慈祥，眼半闭，耳有珥珰饰物，头戴莲花、火焰装饰的花冠。这是一尊典型受印度教影响的犍陀罗式多头多臂观音铜质圆雕艺术品。

泉州清源山碧霄岩有摩崖三世尊佛浮雕坐像。三世佛跣足，并排跌坐在仰覆莲台上，中间为现在佛，手施触地印之降魔印；左尊为过去佛，手亦施触地印之降魔相，但左手掌上托钵；右尊为未来佛，作施定印之禅定相。三尊一列浮刻于长方形龛内，龛长6.5米、高3米。

碧霄岩的三世佛像，皆袒露右肩，宽肩、隆胸、束腰、面庞圆润、丰满，头上有三层螺结，耳长垂肩，罗纱披左肩，胸腹部衣襟直垂，袒露的右臂肌肉丰满圆润。左臂及两腿有罗纱褶纹，显露出丰满的肌肉，后有背光，属吐蕃式佛教石雕。雕工精湛，造型优美，是犍陀罗式的雕刻艺术精品。

据碧霄岩元初摩崖石刻记载："至元壬辰（至元二十九年，1292年）间，灵武唐吾氏广威将军阿沙公来监泉郡。登兹岩而奇之，刻石为三世佛像。饰以金碧，构殿崇奉，以为焚修祝圣之所。仍捐俸买田五十余亩，入大开元万寿禅寺，以供佛赡僧为悠久……至正丁未（至正二十七年，1367年），福建、江西等处行中书省参知政事般若帖穆尔公分治东广，道出泉南，追忆先伯监郡公遗迹，慨然兴修，再新堂构……郡守新安郑潜拜手书，同游行中书省理问官忽纳台、广东道宣慰使司同知副元帅阿儿温沙哈儿鲁氏、泉州路达鲁花赤元德瓮吉剌氏、讲资寺教寿讲主智润及广威公外孙同安县达鲁花赤寿山与焉。"①

碧霄岩崖记里"唐吾氏"、"哈儿鲁氏"和"瓮吉剌氏"等，皆元代的部族名称。如"唐吾氏"，即唐兀、唐古特，亦称党项，亦即西夏（西方书籍称Tangut）。三世尊犍陀罗式佛像为灵武唐吾氏广威将军阿沙，于1292年来监泉郡时所刻。灵武在山西省，原为西夏之地。至元二十九年，西夏人阿沙到泉州任鲁花赤（地方最高行政长官），乾隆《泉州府志·文职官》有其名。②

据碧霄岩崖记载，元初三世尊佛像是"饰以金碧"的，即在石雕原型的基础上，饰以灰泥、金碧。迨至75年后的至正二十七年（1369），由蒙古人忽纳台和创建三世尊佛像的西夏人阿沙的外孙同安县达鲁花赤寿山等，多位元朝行省、地方高级官员和僧人重修。

1988年，重修前的"饰以金碧"的碧霄岩三世尊佛像，与现在见到三世尊佛像的形象有很大的区别。虽然三世尊佛像依然袒露右肩、右臂，但是三世尊佛像都饰有披肩，且披肩长垂遮盖右臂及肘，而左肩的披肩则短得多。左、右二尊佛像的左胸及腹部的袈裟褶纹是斜向的而不是原型腹部垂直的袈裟褶纹，且左臂袈裟遮及肘部。此外，中间的佛像是穿菩提树叶的袈裟。记得1958年摄此照片时，菩提树叶是银白色的，而袈裟底色是金黄色的。这种服饰的佛像是从未见过的。不知多少年前，暴雨过后，山体滑坡，庙堂随山体塌落，三世佛像高悬20多米的山崖上。1988年，清源山风景区修缮碧霄岩，依山势建钢筋混凝土支架，分三层，第三层为敞开式阁楼。重建佛堂时，从三世尊佛像身上剥落的灰泥洞里，发现灰泥塑佛像里原型是石刻佛像。于是剥去灰泥，重现犍陀罗式三世佛像雕刻的原型。

那么，碧霄岩的犍陀罗式雕刻艺术是如何传到泉州的呢？西藏的喇嘛教是公元8世纪印度那烂陀寺大德莲花生，以印度秘密教（密教）教旨与西藏的巴思教教旨互相融混而产生的一种适合西藏社会的新教。"喇嘛"，藏语意谓"无上"，即汉语的"上人"。蒙古人信仰神佛茹荤，其僧侣又食肉，他们的日常生活多以"肉乳为食"、"毡帐为居"、"皮毛为衣"。③他们的日常生活近西藏人的生活方式，所以喇嘛教容易被接受。蒙古戡定青海、川藏、吐蕃，僧侣声势大振，西藏的喇嘛教为大汗忽必烈所接受，于是蒙古族遂成为黄衣佛号之民族，

---

① 吴幼雄、黄伟民、陈桂炳主编：《泉州史迹研究》，厦门大学出版社1998年版，第120页。
② 乾隆《泉州府志》卷26《文职官上》。
③ 冯承钧译：《马可·波罗行纪》上册，第69章《鞑靼人之神道》。

在关外时如此，入关后还如此，上自帝王，下至吏民，多愿倾囊建庙，以资焚修。

元统一中国过程中，把喇嘛教带入华北（以北京中心）、内蒙古和西北地区。泉州清源山碧霄岩的犍陀罗式雕刻三世尊佛像，即为藏传佛教喇嘛教遗物，它是希腊、印度、西藏雕刻艺术的混合作品；它是由蒙古的官员（西夏人）带入泉州的；它是由陆路传入泉州的犍陀罗式雕刻的艺术珍品；它是我国江南地区少见的喇嘛教的遗址。

四、泉州印度教的犍陀罗式雕刻

1934年，泉州城南的南校场出土一尊石雕立姿神像。当时人们误认为释迦佛像。[①] 1957年吴文良著《泉州宗教石刻》确认此神像为婆罗门教（印度教）的毗湿纽石刻造像。[②] 毗湿纽石雕立像高115厘米（包括石座）。头部戴一高顶的帽子，帽子分三层，上有饰物，两眼下视，鼻梁高耸，耳长几及肩上。有四只手臂，上两臂食指上套一个圆形法宝；下两臂右手小臂伸出（但已断毁，可能作无畏手印），左臂下垂撑一根棒形物。毗湿纽石雕像的上体裸露，宽肩、束腰，腹部两块肌肉突出；下体有透明罗衣束住，膝盖关节明显，直立在半月形的莲座上，座底有榫卯。石质系辉绿岩，雕工简朴、圆熟，充分表现人体的健康美。就毗湿纽整体的雕刻形式，近似印度尼西亚玛琅、梭罗的印度教塔婆的人体雕像。这是泉州典型的印度教犍陀罗式雕刻。

吴文良《泉州宗教石刻》第四部分"泉州古婆罗门教"（即印度教），图版111、112、113、114，是四幅印度教的壁龛石刻。

图111全体刻成一屋宇，形如龛状。屋顶有脊，屋脊分两层。上层的左右角，各浮雕螭首；下层屋脊分向左右倾斜；正中刻一个如钟形的宗教标识。钟形顶有佛焰，中刻一个圆环，四周绕以图案花纹。屋宇下面左右各刻有一根石柱，柱头系希腊式雕刻。柱旁各立一座葫芦形小塔，塔下的两根柱子也是希腊式的雕刻。龛内正中刻着一尊四臂神像，头发向上直竖，前两手合十于胸前后；后两手，一持圆鼓，一持兜矛，跌坐在一个仰覆莲台上。神像耳长垂肩，束腰，手臂裸露，带有手镯。神像右边的莲台上，竖立一个"磨盘"（linga，印度教崇拜的性器官）。图112刻一神像跌坐莲台上，两手合十于胸前，束腰，有背光。

[①]《晋江文献丛刊》第一辑，1946年版，第111—121页。
[②] 吴文良：《泉州宗教石刻·泉州古婆罗门教石刻》图115，中国科学出版社1957年版。

其他雕刻与四图大同小异。图113龛中雕一个四臂神像，面貌丑恶，怒发冲冠，右脚下踩一个小鬼，另一足高高踢起，四手各持法宝。神像两旁各侍立一位女神，上体裸露、乳房丰满、束腰。这种女神形象雕刻皆源于受犍陀罗艺术雕刻影响之佛教珂梨底和女药叉雕像。右旁女神头发竖直，手下垂，手心向前。图114其雕刻与前三幅相同，唯龛正中刻一女神像跌坐在一朵绽放的莲花中，神像有四臂，后两臂持矛和圆圈，前两臂已残断，头有螺结，耳长垂肩，宽肩、束腰、上体裸露，乳房丰满。

20世纪80年代，在泉州南门外池店乡（属晋江）的一座小庙里，发现一方印度教石刻，全部没有图案雕刻，龛中仅刻一位女神像，头上有冠，耳上有耳珰，有四只手臂，各持法宝，宽肩、丰乳、束腰，坐在仰覆莲台上，左足垂在地上。左、右各立侍随从，头上有螺结，亦宽肩束腰。

此外，泉州开元寺大雄宝殿后廊西边石柱之西面上部的印度教之希腊式石柱上，亦有毗湿纽的化身石雕，在石刻的圆圈内，刻着一个四臂的毗湿纽，端坐在仰覆莲台上，两旁各有Saktis丰乳女神，坐在座旁生出的开放的莲花上。

还有，泉州开元寺大雄宝殿前露台下须弥座束腰部分的石刻，系辉绿岩雕成。其雕刻内容，均以印度古代传说为题材。露台南面的束腰上，浮刻狮子37只和人面狮36只。各石埵间有间柱隔开，须弥座的上下，则刻斜形莲瓣。

人面狮身的艺术雕刻，导源于埃及的人面狮身石像，以后传到希腊，再由马其顿王亚力山大向东传至印度，再由印度从海路传入泉州。石刻中的人面狮身雕刻形状各不相同，有的头发蓬松，两耳垂肩，耳上有饰环，四足立地；有的头上有三层螺结，用前右肢持一枝莲花或其他花朵。狮子的状貌也不一样，有的昂首张爪，作欲噬状，有的向前弛突，有的回首顾盼。此外，泉州还发现许多印度教寺庙的希腊式柱头石雕和希腊式十六面石柱。

1956年，吴文良先生在泉州南门伍堡街发现一方断裂为二的印度泰米尔文字和汉字的石碑。1981年，经日本大阪大学斯波义信教授翻译，泰米尔文字内容如下：

  向庄严的褐罗致敬。愿此地繁荣、昌盛。时于释迦历1203年哲帝莱月（注：即公元1281年4月），港主抱伯鲁马尔，别名达瓦浙哈克罗·瓦帝格尔。由于察哈台—罕的御赐执照，据此，乃被庄重地把乌帝耶尔·厮鲁迦尼—乌帝耶—那依那尔神灵敬请入座，并愿吉祥的察哈台一罕幸福昌盛。①

同样的泰米尔文字石碑，日本国东京大学的辛岛升的认读有些差异。他认为立碑人为"圣班达·贝鲁玛"，建庙的目的是承"蒙契嘎察伊汗的御赐执照"。② 如果按第二种译文，则"契嘎察伊汗"为谁无可稽考。而斯波义信译文的"察哈台——罕"，即元世祖忽必烈。碑文的纪年为公元 1281 年，正是元世祖忽必烈在位的时间。

元初，泉州与马八儿国的交往是十分频繁的。马八儿国在南印度，是泰米尔人的居住区，流行泰米尔文字。日本学者斯波义信认为石碑文里的"褐罗"（辛岛升译为"合罗"），即印度教的湿婆神。联系泉州发现的刻有"御赐佛像"的印度教门楣石刻（现在置于泉州开元寺大雄宝殿大门楣上），它们可能同出于一座湿婆神庙。

综上所述，元初泉州有一座印度教湿婆神庙。以上所列的印度教神像和人狮石雕艺术，皆源于受希腊雕刻艺术影响之犍陀罗雕刻艺术，它是自印度取道经南洋群岛及东南亚，从海洋传入泉州的。

五、泉州伊斯兰教和基督教之犍陀罗式雕刻

前文已述，犍陀罗艺术也可以说是希腊化了的佛教艺术，犍陀罗的佛教偶像崇拜是导源于希腊，印度教的偶像崇拜是导源于犍陀罗。那么，元代泉州伊斯兰教和基督教雕刻艺术又与犍陀罗雕刻艺术有何牵连呢？

犍陀罗雕刻艺术的种类，还有一种塔婆的雕刻艺术。较典型的如坦叉始罗地方的萧里昂塔院、白沙瓦的亚立斯泰提塔群、油撒孚择伊发现之塔婆，以及喀布尔河北面的他库契巴伊伽蓝遗址等地的塔婆雕刻。③ 这种犍陀罗式的佛教塔婆雕刻艺术也随着佛教传入中国，在长期衍化过程中逐渐被中国的伊斯兰教、基督教雕刻艺术所接受，而以须弥座式和须弥座祭坛式的雕刻形式定型，宋、元、明时代传布开来。如新疆喀什的伊斯兰教圣贤墓、扬州的伊斯兰教先贤墓、广州的先贤墓、南京的郑和墓、福州的先贤墓、泉州的灵山圣墓和泉州众多的

---

① 吴幼雄：《泉州宗教文化》，鹭江出版社 1992 年版，第 309 页。
② ［日］辛岛升：《十三世纪末南印度半岛与中国之间的交流》，副标题《围绕泉州泰米尔石刻与"元史"马八儿等国》，昭和六三年，汲古书院出版。
③ 史岩：《东洋美术史》卷上，《犍陀罗之建筑》，商务印书馆 1936 年版，第 136—145 页。

古伊斯兰教、基督教须弥座式和须弥座祭坛式石墓。

泉州伊斯兰教、基督教的须弥座式石墓有两种类型，一种是三层一种是五层，一般是五层为多。五层石墓一般前四层为一石块雕成，第五层墓顶石由另一石块雕成。少数为四层石墓，亦有一墓由多块石头构成。

五层须弥座式石墓之底层都为六足如意状之中国式雕刻。第二层为希腊式连续传枝之图案雕刻。第三层为佛教之莲花瓣雕。第四层如果是伊斯兰教石墓，则刻阿拉伯文字，内容多为《古兰经》章、节或圣训，有的则刻死者的名字、籍贯和死亡时间。如果是基督教石墓，则多为空白，而天主教则于正面用拉丁文刻死者的姓名。第五层称墓顶石，一般由另一石块刻成。墓顶石正面，多刻尖拱型，亦有刻圆拱型的。如果是伊斯兰教，则浮刻"云月"，如果是基督教，则浮刻莲花承托十字架。以上石墓雕刻同属犍陀罗式雕刻艺术。

六、深含希腊文化的古叙利亚文字拼写突厥语之基督教墓碑

近百年来，福建东南沿海文化古城泉州，先后发现来自陆上丝绸之路的十方古叙利亚文字拼写突厥语基督教墓碑，一方回鹘文基督教墓碑和四方蒙古八思巴文字基督教墓碑，其数量之多为全国之最。

此十方墓碑的墓主人，均来自陆上丝绸之路，几乎都使用"马其顿城的菲利浦汗之子亚历山大大帝纪年"。下面列举两方墓碑说明，一方是基督教神职人员——神父；另一方亦是神职人员，又是一位将军的夫人。译文如下：

> 以圣父、圣子和圣灵的名义，直到永远，阿门！马其顿城的菲利浦汗之子亚历山大大帝纪年1630年，突厥语纪年羊年十月初八，神父乔治完成了弥施珂的使命，愿他的灵魂永远在天堂安息吧！怀念他吧，阿门！[①]
>
> 以圣父、圣子和圣灵的名义，直到永远。马其顿城的菲利浦君王之子亚历山大帝王纪年1608年，突厥语纪年猴年腊月初十，幸福的女牧师阿依——库都尔夫人……完成了上帝的使命。愿这位将军的伴侣

---

① 牛汝极：《中国元代叙利亚文景教碑铭文献研究》，铭文4，上海古籍出版社2008年版，第130—136页。

的灵魂在天堂永久地……安度，愿她流芳百世，阿门！①

"亚历山大大帝纪年"，即希腊历。始用于塞留古王朝。王朝以叙利亚为统治中心，以朝代纪事法，创造希腊历。以公元前312年10月1日为起始纪年。

希腊历1630年，即公元1318年（延祐五年）；希腊历1608年，即公元1296年（元贞二年）。"弥施珂"，即救世主、耶稣基督。马其顿城，位于巴尔干半岛马其顿王国境内，南邻希腊。

公元前378年，菲利浦二世建立马其顿国，其儿子亚历山大在位时（前336—前323）向东方扩展波斯。前327年，到达印度河流域，建立亚历山大帝国，把希腊文化带到东方印度，形成所谓的"东方希腊文化"，犍陀罗式艺术即由此而来。那位神父和将军的夫人（身份牧师），是随蒙古大军南来福建泉州当属无疑。这是希腊基督教文化从陆上丝绸之路东渐福建泉州的物证之一。顺便提一下，泉州还保存六方刻着古阿拉伯文字的中亚布哈拉（今乌兹别克斯坦）、西亚格兹威尼（今亚美尼亚）等地人的墓碑，这些都是元代陆上丝绸之路文化延伸到福建的物证。

结束语

历史文化名城泉州保存着许多元代犍陀罗式艺术石雕刻，它们分别属佛教、印度教、伊斯兰教、基督教和和天主教。泉州元代的犍陀罗式艺术是分别由陆路、海路传入的。元代泉州宗教门类之多，犍陀罗式艺术雕刻之盛行，是因为它为当时世界东方最大的海港之地位决定的，也是与当时泉州是江浙、淮湖国内贸易网络的中心地位所决定的。元代马可·波罗正是由陆上丝绸之路来中国，然后由泉州港起航回意大利的；元代福建行省省长亦黑迷失（畏吾儿人）也是来自陆上丝绸之路，然后从泉州四次出洋至印尼、印度；高昌城畏吾儿人契玉立任泉州郡守，将汪大渊《岛夷志略》附《清源郡志》之后出版。这里特别要指出的是，在看到元代海外贸易对泉州宗教文化艺术影响的同时，千万别忽略陆上通道对元代泉州宗教文化艺术的影响。所以，元代泉州是海上丝绸之路和陆上丝绸之路文化和艺术的交汇点。

我想本文可以用下面一段对话作为结束语。

---

① 牛汝极：《中国元代叙利亚文景教碑铭文献研究》，铭文8，上海古籍出版社2008年版，第146—149页。

2011年9月27日，卡塔尔首都多哈阿拉伯现代美术馆馆长瓦桑·阿尔·库戴里女士，受邀到泉州海外交通史博物馆参加蔡国强中东"灵魂返乡"仪式新闻发布会。她在对我40分钟专题采访后，我陪同她参观了泉州海外交通史博物馆宗教石刻陈列馆，她突然惊奇地问我："这些刻有阿拉伯文字石墓和墓碑的艺术造型，怎么在阿拉伯和我们国家（她是伊拉克巴士拉人）都未曾见过？"当我回答："这些都是融合了埃及、希腊、阿拉伯、印度、中国的艺术，且出自福建泉州匠人之手的石刻，现存的每座须弥座式石墓，都是融合多国文化艺术的珍品。"她大为吃惊，为福建泉州文化积淀之深厚，赞叹不已。

在音乐文化交流中保持文化特色:"一带一路"的思考

中国艺术研究院音乐研究所所长 项 阳

中国制定了"一带一路"的发展战略,沿着这带与路定会带动相关国家与地区经济上长足发展,互利共赢,与此同时促进区域间的文化交流。音乐为交流的重要选项之一。历史上中国与外来音乐最重要的交流一是西域,二是西方。西域音乐自汉唐以降沿丝绸之路文化传播带对中土音乐文化造成深远影响,天竺、安国、康国、龟兹、疏勒、高昌等多部乐进入中原,造成"洛阳家家学胡乐"的盛景,继而融入中土礼乐和俗乐两条主导脉络的用乐形态之中;"海上丝绸之路"由来已久,但对中国音乐的影响是从明清以降集中显现,传教士成为传播与交流的先声。进入20世纪,始于学堂乐歌,无论国人留洋还是西人入中土,中国对西方音乐从一种被动接受到主动汲取,这其中有着诸多复杂的因素。西方音乐对中国的影响侧重城市,但作为重要传播群体的传教士却非限于城市,在中国西藏、云南、贵州、四川、广西等许多偏远地区都有传教士持续性的活动,西方教会音乐也逐渐渗入,甚至对一些少数民族地区的音乐都造成实质性影响。此后由于从国家意义上特别是音乐教育主动接受西方专业音乐创造的诸种理念,以致数千年所形成的中国音乐传统多有淡化。

随着社会的发展与进步,中国与世界多样化的交流越来越多,及至当下,人们足不出户,多媒体技术引领遥远的双方既面对面又畅游世界,这种开放与交流在一个世纪之前不可想象。我们需要思考的是,中国有着数千年文明积淀,历史上对外多有交流,但呈主导与渐融之别,显现中华文明之特色构成和开放胸怀。我们应该认知中国音乐文化的传统或称特色,加强对中国传统音乐文化历时性积淀梳理的力度,将音乐文化的深层内涵"讲清楚"。"优秀传统文化是一个国家、一个民族传承和发展的根本,如果丢掉了,就割断了精神命脉。"(习近平)音乐文化是为中国传统文化的有机构成,明确哪些形态和应用方式彰显中国传统音乐文化特征,西域和西方音乐对中国音乐文化有哪些实质性影响,在国家发展战略"一带一路"实施进程中,顶层设计者应从不同层面把握传统文化的意义,在守成中发展,在文化交流过程中采取相关策略,无论音乐还是多种文化形态不至于随波逐流陷于文化迷失。

"一带"交流：丝路乐舞与中原乐舞分工有自

我们先看历史上这"一带"。一般意义上丝绸之路是汉代以降形成，但实际上中原与西域的交流比丝绸之路要早得多，近年来考古工作者在对安阳殷墟墓葬之古玉分析的基础上探求和田玉石东进、在 3500 年之前即形成古玉之路，中原与西域之交流绝非仅是汉唐以降的事情。从音乐形态讲来，我们应该把握在丝路形成之前中国音乐有怎样的传统，如此方能认知在丝路开通对音乐文化有怎样的影响与演化。

周代，中国音乐有了国家制度下的规范意义，形成礼乐与俗乐两条主导脉络的用乐方式，作为国家礼制仪式用乐，更是形成了既有核心为用又有多层次为用的整体礼乐观念，即在国家最高礼制仪式中以雅乐为重，其乐队组合（所谓"金石以动之，丝竹以行之"，编钟编磬领衔，中原乐器分金石土革丝木匏竹八类为用）、乐律、乐调诸多层面一定为中原自产，形成所谓"华夏正声"的意义，其他类型的礼制仪式中则可以吸收社会上存在的多种乐制类型为用，这种礼乐文化传统是在国家体制下从宫廷到各级地方官府整体为用的样态，形成中国礼乐多类型、多层级的体系化，这种样态延续了数千载，这是中国传统音乐文化的特色构成，亦成为中华礼乐文明独步世界之林的显著标识。

在中国礼乐文化中间也有外来文化融入。乐在中土与礼制、礼俗仪式相须且固化为用，以应对国人情感多层次多类型的仪式诉求，所谓"礼乐相须以为用，礼非乐不行，乐非礼不举"[①]。在中国礼乐体系中，除雅乐之外还有多种乐制类型，诸如汉代以降的鼓吹乐（不同时期乐队组合之领衔乐器有差异，早期以觱篥和角为主导，其后则引入唢呐与笙等并用）等形态。汉唐间丝绸之路文化传播带以战争、礼贡、商贾等多种方式进入中土的西域音乐，有明显标识，所谓多部乐的意义。在进入之初可能就是在宫廷中单纯用于表演，然而，当这些乐部被纳入国家用乐体系必有相应的机构以为承载。这些乐部多为歌舞乐三位一体，且曲体庞大，成为国家用乐体系一道亮丽的风景。《唐六典》云：

> 太乐署教乐，雅乐大曲三十日成，小曲二十日。清乐大曲六十日，大文曲三十日，小曲十日。燕乐、西凉、龟兹、疏勒、安国、天竺、高昌大曲，各三十日，次曲各二十日，小曲各十日。高丽、康国一曲。

---

① （宋）郑樵：《通志》。

鼓吹署捆鼓一曲十二日，三十日一鼓，一曲十日，长鸣三声十日，铙鼓一曲五十日。歌、箫、笳一曲各三十日。大横吹一曲六十日，节鼓一曲二十日。笛、箫、筚篥、笳、桃皮筚篥一曲各二十日。小鼓一曲十日，中鸣三声十日，羽葆鼓一曲三十日。錞于一曲五日，歌、箫、笳一曲各三十日。小横吹一曲六十日。箫、笛、筚篥、桃皮筚篥一曲各三十日成。①

由此可见，这太常寺②属下的两个乐署都实施教乐的职责。太乐署所训练的雅乐应为"十二和乐"③，除此之外，所谓"大曲"、"次曲"、"小曲"同样由太乐署教习。大曲中除高丽来自东方、清乐为本土，其他多为西域进入，在太常寺属下以多部伎的形态存在，所谓九部伎以及其后十部伎的意义。换言之，这些"部伎"又可以大曲称之。鼓吹署所教亦有多种形态，其中多种乐器来自西域。这些乐曲如何为用呢？

《大唐开元礼》对宫廷中嘉礼用乐④有明确表述："奏太和之乐，鼓吹振作"；"太乐令设九部伎，位于左右延明门外，群官初唱万岁。太乐令即引九部伎声作而入，各就位，以次作如式"⑤。"太和之乐"为雅乐在场，将以"华夏正声"为特征的"十二和乐"根据不同仪式诉求选择为用；鼓吹乐这种胡汉杂陈的乐队组合以及九部伎等外来乐部主导的乐舞"以此作如式"，为唐代宫廷中固化为用的礼乐形态。这是"拿来主义"为用的模式，这多部伎可用于嘉礼仪式，却难以进入吉礼仪式，说明西域音乐虽与中原有效融合却分工有自。国家从顶层设计中将乐分为礼乐与俗乐（非仪式用乐，不拘泥于场合和形式，不固化为用）两条主导脉络为用，礼乐有核心为用（雅乐仅用于最高层级，且不能用于凶礼）和整体为用（非雅乐类型可在多层级、多类型礼乐中为用），这样类分明确的整体用乐观念，不失传统又与时俱进，这是中国传统音乐文化的特色构成，外来乐部（涵盖外来乐器、乐调乃至乐曲）多由丝路传播带以入，对中土音乐文化产生实质性影响的同时逐渐融入，可谓创造性转化与发展的意义。

---

① 《大唐六典》卷14，近卫公府藏版，昭和十年京都帝国大学文学部印，第24页。
② 太常寺是汉代以降国家掌礼的相关机构。
③ 始于南北朝，国家礼乐中的雅乐多以十二首为一套，以"和"、"安"、"平"等相称。
④ 中国礼制自周代始依照吉、嘉、军、宾、凶五类划分，每一类都有仪式，所谓礼乐，则是因应不同类型的礼制仪式与之相须为用的乐，分类可称为吉礼仪式用乐、嘉礼仪式用乐等。
⑤ 《大唐开元礼》卷97《嘉礼·皇帝元正冬至受群臣朝贺》。

"一路"交流：西方音乐教育模式渐呈主导

海上丝绸之路是怎样的情状呢？虽然海上丝绸之路经历了盛衰变化，西方音乐多有进入，但真正较大规模集中传入还是进入20世纪之后的事情。需明确，在乐谱尚未成熟之前，西方音乐自身也是要靠活态传承；当乐谱成熟，且相对精细，交流不畅也是问题，直到电力和留声机等科技进步终于导致这一切的改变，西方音乐文化通过海路终于大举进入中土。应把握进入中土的西方音乐是怎样的形态又怎样为用。

按照中土礼乐与俗乐两条主导脉络的用乐理念，这西方大规模进入的欧洲经典音乐，基本属于俗乐范畴，即在社会世俗日常生活中以娱乐欣赏审美为用的样态。但也有仪式用乐的传入，这就是传教士承载教堂用乐，如此使得西方音乐进入中土也是两分，即仪式用乐与非仪式用乐。问题在于，仪式为用的形态以实用功能的意义更多在教堂，真正进入社会主流文化的还是西方、特别是欧洲专业音乐，这些音乐形态多为学校音乐教育和社会娱乐美育以用，在这种意义上，中土以城市为中心的主流社会接受了欧洲音乐的本体以及音乐体裁、创作技法等多层面。当欧洲专业音乐进入之时，恰逢中土社会对传统文化以行"反思"，甚至出现反传统的过激行动，既有国家意义上的礼乐形态处于转型当口，宫廷雅乐消解，地方官府主持的礼制仪式及其用乐不再，转而为民间社会（涵盖城镇和乡村）所接衍。在传统国家用乐体系被打破的情状下，西方音乐迅速以城市和学校为中心，这意味着在这些区域淡化了传统的礼乐与俗乐两条主导脉络为用的方式，更多以俗乐为重，传统用乐理念在主流文化层面缺失。当我们的学校音乐教育以西方传入的键盘乐器（风琴、钢琴）主导训练，从视唱练耳等基础层面采用西方模式，在这些综合因素的作用下，一边是城市中乐从本体形态上对西方模式主动接受，一边是对传统用乐模式中特别是传统国家礼乐体系的消解。在俗乐为用的层面，学校音乐教育体系普遍推行西方模式，中国传统乐队组合也在不断尝试西方之创作技法和音乐思维的情状下为用。新中国之国家礼乐不健全，且完全采用西方乐队组合，放弃了延续三千载中国传统的雅乐组合类型以及国家礼乐的体系化为用，历史上中土既有和外来融入的乐器、乐队组合在国家层面弃若敝屣。在主流礼乐文化层面已显迷失，交流与融合定然会随波逐流。

有意思的是，作为戏曲和说唱等音声技艺形态本是由中国传统俗乐文化"裂变"以成，然而却最大程度保存了中国传统特色，诸如戏曲之生旦净末丑，曲牌体与板腔体同在（宋明之际在俗乐层面所有的专业音声形态均以曲牌体为主导，其后曲牌体和板腔体并存），这是中国的传统；由西方传入的话剧和歌剧可以争奇斗艳，但戏曲传统依旧。美术界也是如此，一方面油画进入，一方面笔墨丹青。何以中国传统乐文化之礼乐体系消解，裂变"瘦身"为用的俗乐形态多以西方为皓首？是否迷失自我即为融入世界？

反思：把握中国音乐"特色话语"创造性发展

学术研究在于知古鉴今，在对传统文化"讲清楚"的同时能够对未来发展有一定反思。当下这"一带一路"国家战略恰恰是将中国与西域和西方这两种关系都能够涵盖。历史上中国音乐文化受这两种文化的影响现实存在，我们应将中土文化在历史上与两者之间的交流与交融进行梳理，在发展过程中是否应秉持中国音乐文化传统、在把握中国话语体系的基础上前行，真是应该认真思考。

一部中国文化史，本是生活在这片土地上的多民族、多区域人群之间、与外来文化之间互动与创造性交流的历史。交流为两个以上主体间的互动，且各自文化主体特征差异性明显，在把握各自特征的前提下认知哪些为既有样态，哪些属于交流之后所产生的变异。只有将主体文化形态的特色辨清，方能在发展中不致迷失。

音乐文化涵盖艺术形态的本体和综合形态的整体。所谓本体，是构成音乐形态自身的诸种要素，即律调谱器以及在此基础上所形成的诸种音乐形态。在文明社会的早期阶段，交通与信息传播媒介不发达，相对容易形成区域特色。区域人群在亲缘、地缘、血缘关系相对稳定情状下文化渐呈固化样态或称在内核坚实的基础上发展。随着社会文明程度提高，科技手段不断进步，文化在交流发展中与时俱进，人们在音乐本体特征——律调谱器基础上创造出一系列相应的技术手段，诸如西方专业音乐创作依多声理念所有的和声、配器、对位、复调以及诸种曲式，中国音乐创作中亦依自我创作理念产生宫调、旋法、偷声、减字、借字、藏头、合尾等，可见侧重。音乐定然受语言以及区域环境之影响，在两周直至汉魏时期，中原音乐形态更多讲究对仗、工整，汉魏时期有西域音乐进入，但由于交流不广，还很难说对中国音乐传统产生整体性的实质影响。然而，当以西域乐舞为主导的多部乐进入中原，特别是进入都市进而成为国家用乐机构中的教材内容，其不同于既有的工整对仗结构、这些乐部被既被用于国家礼乐、亦俗乐为用之时，由于国家制度规定性下的使用和官属乐人承载，国家乐署对各地官属乐人"轮值轮训"、每期都是15载，其中多数回归地方执事应差，焉能对中国音乐文化不造成实质性影响？应该看到，即便西域音乐对中国传统音乐文化的两条主导脉络都造成了影响，由于礼乐核心为用的雅乐类型至少在乐队组合以及乐调等诸多层面显现坚守的意义，且传统社会中人们已然形成了这样的文化理念，总有国家意义上的专业人士不断探究与维系，因此会不断夯实。与此同时，西域音乐文化经上千年发展融入中土，渐为中国传统音乐文化整体意义上的有机构成。

在清代中叶的雍乾时期，中国传统礼乐文化体系中特别是在地方官府为用五类俱全的礼制仪式及其用乐多为民间礼俗所接衍（官属专业乐人随国家乐籍制度解体转入民间生存，由此将礼乐和俗乐两种类型的用乐带入民间发展，当下在民间的许多音声技艺形态在历史上并非属于"民间态"），或称中国传统礼乐和俗乐形态在当下依旧存在于中国广袤的乡间社会，虽然不以文化主流的方式而存在，但毕竟有其生存空间，关键是乡间社会中的民众对此有文化认同，即便在都市的边缘这一群体依旧活跃。当我们将中国历史音乐文化大传统辨清，并与当下民间礼俗中仪式和非仪式用乐的活态相接，可以把握中国传统音乐文化礼乐与俗乐两条主导脉络从形式到内容的相当部分。当下国家非物质文化遗产保护法为这些传统音乐文化活态存在助力并提供法律保障，关键在于我们如何将传统音乐文化礼乐与俗乐两条主导脉络整体为用的理念继续发扬光大，使之在主流文化层面从形式到内容上亦显中国音乐文化特色话语的前提下创造性发展。

历史上无论西域还是西方音乐文化都对中国音乐文化有着实质性影响，前者对中国音乐结构带来变化，后者从多声思维意义上影响深远，由于中国音乐文化数千年的积淀，虽然会有变化，但若全部改变也不可能。我们更愿意借鉴一些外来有益的思维理念以及相关技术手段来创造属于自己的音乐形态，我们不拒绝吸收，但也不应迷失自我。外来音乐形态融入必然给本土音乐文化带来新鲜血液，促动音乐文化发展。发展并不等于迷失自我，最为重要的是应努力辨析哪些属于中国话语、中国特色，对有生命力的东西应该从国家层面刻意保护。传统非一朝一夕所成，但丢弃却相对简单，只恐有意保护时已陷入迷失，应在国家战略实施之际"未雨绸缪"，祛除浮躁，对于既往的缺失"亡羊补牢"。只有认清自我文化特征、建立文化自信的前提下方不至于随波逐流，如此创造性吸收和转化会更有意义。历史上的人们明白这个道理，当下"一带一路"国家战略亦应在促进中国音乐文化良性发展的同时，以鲜亮、富有特色的文化名片更好地与世界交流。

创建亚洲新文明华侨华人的作用不容忽视

福建师范大学闽台区域研究中心主任　谢必震

世界上只要有人类居住，人口的移动就不会停止，海外移民是一个永恒的话题，值得研究。当下，国家提出"建设21世纪海上丝绸之路"的构想。我们知道，海上丝绸之路的构建，就亚洲而言，必将创建一个新的亚洲文明。这是一个漫长的过程，不是一朝一夕可以建成的，需要我们持之以恒地投入建设。在这亚洲新文明的创建中，华侨华人的历史地位和重要作用不容忽视，研究华侨华人在创建亚洲新文明的作用、如何发挥华侨华人的作用是一个极其重要的问题。

一、历史上华侨华人是亚洲文明的开创者、参与者

就亚洲文明发展的历史而言，华侨华人既是开创者，又是建设者。过去是这样，现在依然如此。

我们的先民很早就利用海上交通和海上资源发展经济。从中国古代的文献资料来看，汉代中国不仅开通了连系中亚、西亚的丝绸之路，同时也开辟了中国往印度的海上通道。很快在勤劳勇敢的中国人民不断实践和勇于探索之下，中国与世界各国的海上交通航线逐步形成。唐代中国以广州港为中心与东南亚诸国开展经济与贸易活动，宋元时期，福建泉州港的兴盛，渐渐取代了广州港的地位，而成为世界第一大港。尤其是意大利旅行家马可·波罗的游记，更使得中国泉州在世人的心目中是一个令人向往的圣地，许多探险家、航海家闻风出动，他们赞叹中国的富庶，而将自己的一生献给人类的航海交通事业。其中最伟大的十五世纪的航海家应该是中国的郑和。

郑和七下西洋，创造了人类航海史上的奇迹。他使得中国和世界紧紧地连系在一起。他为15世纪中国在世界的大国地位建立了丰厚的基石。继郑和之后，福州港的中琉航海交通与贸易，在中外交往的历史上显赫一时。中琉贸易的兴盛弥补了郑和轰轰烈烈壮举结束后的失落和沉寂，成为那一时期中外航海交通贸易的中心。

中世纪的风云变幻，漳州月港走私贸易的巨大旋风，一夜之间刮走了福州

港的中心地位，取而代之的是月港，因为它与马尼拉的大帆船紧紧相连，使月港从此走向了世界。

清代以降，郑成功时代的台湾海上交通与贸易，是那一时期的重头戏。台海之上，不得郑氏号令，不能行船走海。中国东南沿海的迁界与禁海，给了郑氏政权任意驰骋的机遇，在中国海上交通史上留下了浓墨重彩的一笔。

康熙统一台湾后，开四海关，海上交往盛极一时。但终因清王朝的禁令，出海之船不得超过二桅，中国的造船技术受到限制，中国航海交通的力量受到极大的削弱。当西方海盗和日本倭寇在海上游弋时，昔日航海之强国中国，只能退避三舍，拱手让出了海上大国的地位。

近代以降，华工出国历史拉开帷幕，成千上万的契约华工开始了他们苦难的历程。他们用汗水、献血和生命，构筑了那个时代中国与美洲与欧洲的海外移民史，为世界文明的建设奠定了厚实的基础。

回顾中国航海交通的历史，回顾中国的海外移民史，回顾中华文明在世界传播的历史，你就会发现所有的海外华侨华人都置身这一历史发展过程中，他们移民海外的所有活动，都是文明历史形成的组成部分，所以我们有理由说，华侨华人是亚洲文明的开创者，也是参与者。

今天，我们要建设21世纪的海上丝绸之路，要创建新的亚洲文明，我们应该从中国人伟大的航海历史中，从中国人移民海外的历史中，汲取健康的养分，探寻成功的秘笈，把握绝妙的玄机，领略历史的启迪，重振海上雄风。

二、华侨华人是创建亚洲新文明的重要依托

当前，海外华侨华人约有5000万，据厦门大学南洋研究院院长庄国土教授在《华侨华人分布状况和发展趋势》的课题研究中介绍，这一数字是迄今为止对全球华侨华人总数"最接近真实的统计"，大大低于海内外曾经的测算规模，"对准确了解和把握侨情变化发展具有重要意义"。在全球4543万华侨华人中，东南亚占比已降至73%左右，北美、欧洲、大洋洲和日本、韩国等地的华侨华人数量出现较快增长。新移民的途径主要有三类，第一类为已经超过100万人的留学人员，这些人主要集中在美国、日本等发达国家。第二类是非熟练劳动力，这些人通过各种途径取得定居身份，成为新移民。其中有少部分人选择非法途径前往海外定居，尤以福建沿海地区非法移民最为典型。第三类移民为商务移民，包括投资移民、驻外商务人员和商贸人员。20世纪90年代以后，中国逐渐成为世界制造业中心，中国加大了对发展中国家和地区的投资、工程承包的力

度，大量中国人员走出国门，海外华侨华人的数量与日俱增。以福建为例，闽籍华侨华人已超过 1500 万，分布在 170 多个国家和地区，其中东南亚国家的闽籍华侨华人占总人数的 80%。在世界华商 500 强中，闽籍侨商占 10%。据 2013 闽商百强榜、2013 福布斯华人富豪榜、2013 胡润全球富豪榜数据统计，福建在东盟国家的重点侨商有 45 家，财富总额达 1518 亿美元。主要华人企业集团有：马来西亚的嘉里集团、101 集团、云顶集团、国浩集团、杨忠礼机构，印尼的金光集团，盐仓集团、金鹰国际集团，菲律宾的鞋庄控股、陈永哉财团、环球罗宾娜、巅峰控股，新加坡的远东机构、华侨银行集团、大华银行集团等。显而易见，在创建亚洲新文明的过程中，福建这些在东南亚地区集聚的侨力资源将是重要的依托。

三、如何在亚洲新文明的创建中发挥华侨华人的积极作用

客观地说，华侨华人在中国与世界各国建立友好关系的过程中起到了举足轻重的作用。正如 2012 年习近平总书记访美时评价美国的华侨华人作用时所说的那样：华侨华人是中美友好和互利合作的亲历者，也是见证者、推动者。"中美建交 30 多年来的双边关系特别是互利共赢的经贸关系的快速发展，同广大旅美侨胞的贡献密不可分。广大旅美侨胞既为美国经济、社会和科技发展做出重要贡献，也为促进中美经济、科技、人文交流，推动中美关系发展做出宝贵贡献。"

我们都不曾忘记，在那国际环境极其恶劣的时代，海外华侨华人心系祖国，呕心沥血，殚精竭虑为中美建交，为中日恢复邦交正常化做出的巨大贡献。

在改革开放的时代，在侨资引进，在外资引进，促进中国与海外诸国的经济贸易往来的发展过程中，华侨华人的贡献也是彪炳史册的。

在传播中华文化方面，在塑造中国在海外国际形象方面，华侨华人都扮演了功不可没的重要角色。

然而，有一段时期以来，由于主观与客观的诸多原因，华侨华人的作用被忽视，还有许多地区的华侨华人工作我们并不是那么在意。更为突出的问题是近些年来，我们国家与周边国家的利益发生冲突时，中日关系因钓鱼岛争端而紧张，中越、中菲关系因南海问题而冲突，在以往的外交交涉的过程中，能够起影响作用的华侨华人的身影不见了，究其原因是多方面的。

首先是我国侨务工作的重视程度和力度的下滑。以日本冲绳地区为例，原本中日钓鱼岛争端就出现在日本冲绳地区和中国福建地区之间，加强福建与冲

绳的友好往来对中日妥善解决钓鱼岛问题应该是大有裨益的。学者们也提出诸多的建议，然而，相关职能部门置若罔闻，根本没有兴趣。上一任的冲绳知事仲井真弘多还是闽人蔡姓的后裔，这对于我们充分发挥日本冲绳地区的华侨开展工作是有百利而无一弊的事。可惜我们没有重视日本冲绳地区的华侨工作，自然在中日钓鱼岛问题上就没有更好的解决方法了。

相比之下，台湾当局在日本冲绳也有相当的华侨华人，他们在台湾当局的支持下，深入冲绳社会，开展诸多的活动，与冲绳上层社会关系密切，与冲绳民众打成一片，促进了日本冲绳与台湾地区的人文往来、贸易往来，完全取代了我们本该通过华侨华人组织在那一地区的影响力。

其次是近年来我们移居海外华侨华人的结构发生了变化。早期的华侨华人，有许多旅居海外的留学生，他们负笈求学海外，大多数人都怀着学成归来报效祖国的赤子之心，这些人名留青史，数不胜数。在老一辈的华侨华人中，饱经风霜，含辛茹苦，成功之后他们也是想到祖国的繁荣与富强，他们回国投资，造福一方。他们充当民间大使，使我们的祖国与海外诸国的关系更加密切，蒸蒸日上。

近些年来，我们看到一些移居海外的中国人，他们将大量的资产转移到海外，他们将子女送到海外，他们自己千方百计地偷渡到海外，打拼奋斗的目标仅仅是为了将自己的子女培养成人，出人头地。这样环境中成长起来的新一代华侨，这样目的移居海外的中国人，他们对祖国的认同感，他们对海外赤子的认同感究竟如何？这都使我们对此产生了深深的疑问。

再次，近些年来，关于海外华侨华人的研究也在走下坡路。许多研究华侨华人的机构名存实亡，许多原先很不错的研究机构的研究力量到了捉襟见肘的地步。这些都使得我国的侨务工作受到不小的影响。

有鉴于此，在今天创建亚洲新文明的过程中，如何发挥华侨华人的重要作用就摆在了议事日程之上。我们认为，要做到充分发挥海外华侨华人的作用，应该要做好以下各方面的工作：

（1）提高认识，强化顶层设计。

高度认识"一带一路"与亚洲新文明与华侨华人的关系，重视侨务工作。挖掘侨力资源，充分利用侨资侨智。领导层必须重视这项工作，制定规划，制定切实有效可行的政策。以侨为桥，实现跨境的经济合作，实现人文交流与合作。

（2）有效提升侨务资源，突出华侨华人作用。

不断加强与海外华侨华人社团的联系，维护海外华侨华人的利益。搭建侨商发展平台,为合理引导侨资投向,支持侨资企业的发展不遗余力。在华侨华人的素养提升方面提供最优惠的条件,譬如华侨子女归国的学习深造;强化国情、乡情、友情、亲情的联络工作等,都形成常态化的机制。尤其在各个地区,重点培养侨领人物,这也是极其重要的工作。

当然,侨务工作并非仅仅是侨务机构的单方面的工作,社会各个部门,尤其是教育机构更是重任在肩。今天坐在教室里的学生,明天也许就是新一代的华侨。因此新移民的素养,以及在漫长的亚洲文明构建中新华侨华人能起到什么样的作用,就在今天的课堂教学,人文关怀中塑造起来。强化共识,相互协作,侨务工作是社会大众共同的事务。

(3) 强化智库的支持。

必须提升华侨华人的研究,在原有的研究机构上,加大经费的投入,加大人力的投入,创设新的平台。在充分发挥海外华侨华人作用的研究方面,加强深入实际的应用型、对策型的研究,有的放矢。充分调动不同层次的研究机构,国家智库、非政府组织、社会社团等协同作战,以期凝练出一流的研究成果,为我国的侨务工作开创新局面。

两岸歌仔戏艺术合作之回顾与瞻望

中国艺术研究院戏曲研究所　谢雍君

一

本文主要通过对两岸歌仔戏合作历史的回顾，希冀对闽南歌仔戏剧团在两岸艺术合作中需要遵循的创作原则，以及对未来两岸歌仔戏的合作模式、闽南与东南亚地区（主要是新加坡）艺术交流合作的启示。

在展开论述之前，有两个概念需要界定。一是发言的题目里关键词是海峡两岸，但在具体报告里，内容不只局限于闽南和台湾地区，还会涉及东南亚，特别是新加坡的歌仔戏演剧情况。因为在促进两岸歌仔戏合作中，新加坡业余剧团曾经起到了关键性的推动作用。另一方面，两岸歌仔戏合作经验，可以运用到闽南歌仔戏与新加坡歌仔戏的交流合作中。二是在谈到大陆歌仔戏，即闽南歌仔戏时，不只是指厦门歌仔戏，也是指漳州芗剧。芗剧、歌仔戏，是同一剧种，不同的叫法。漳州芗剧与台湾歌仔戏的交流颇为频繁，但两岸歌仔戏合作的参与单位主要是厦门歌仔戏剧团，因此，厦门歌仔戏剧团与台湾歌仔戏剧团的合作经验，也会对漳州芗剧与台湾歌仔戏的合作有一定的启示意义。

二

歌仔戏是联结两岸文化血脉的代表性戏曲剧种，它的历史源流决定其在闽南戏曲史乃至中国戏曲史上具有独特的地位。歌仔戏还流播到新加坡等地，成为东南亚闽南族群认同的载体之一，是连接大陆、台湾、东南亚三地的文化桥梁，在"一带一路"的战略构想中有着其他闽南剧种不可替代的重要作用。

歌仔戏在福建诸多的戏曲剧种里具有独特的历史地位。它没有梨园戏、莆仙戏之古老悠久，只有百年的发展历史；也没有闽剧、高甲戏之流播广泛，只局限在厦门和漳州地区。在剧种发展历史和地域传播方面，与福建的其他地方剧种相比，歌仔戏的特色并不突出，但是，它是唯一形成于台湾，然后回传到闽南并在闽南扎根的地方剧种，因为这一点，它在福建乃至全国具有极其重要的历史价值和文化价值。

第一次真正意义上的两岸歌仔戏艺术合作之作，应该是2010年厦门歌仔戏剧团与台湾唐美云歌仔戏剧团合作创作《蝴蝶之恋》。以此为时间节点，在2010年之前，在两岸歌仔戏艺术合作之前，有过20多年的交流、对话的历史经验，而且，这种交流、沟通是经历从台湾歌仔戏剧团到闽南交流、演出的单向交流，到闽南歌仔戏剧团到台湾交流、演出的双向交流的变化。这种从单向到双向的转变，体现出两岸歌仔戏的交流不是一路顺畅，而是呈现出从受限制到顺畅的逐步变化的历史轨迹。

在这变化过程中，有三点需要值得特别指出：

第一，20世纪80年代末两岸隔绝的状态被打破，海峡两岸民众开始交通往来。但两岸的艺术交流尚未开始。在这个时期，新加坡民间歌仔戏剧团到台湾地区演出，在勾连和推动闽南和台湾歌仔戏艺术交流，起到了重要作用。

新加坡民间歌仔戏剧团之所以有能力创作、演出歌仔戏，又与闽南歌仔戏到东南亚演出交流密切相关。

1983年5月，漳州市芗剧团应邀赴新加坡作商业演出，这是芗剧首次到东南亚演出。这次演出开启了歌仔戏与东南亚文化交流的大门，也推动了海峡两岸歌仔戏的互动交流。

1986年，新加坡宗乡团体第一个福建戏曲组织"福建公会芗剧团"成立，聘请漳州芗剧团演员来新加坡传授歌仔戏表演艺术。4年后，即1990年，新加坡芗剧团应邀赴中国台湾参加宜兰县"台湾戏剧馆"开幕及春季艺术节演出，演出了芗剧古装剧《三家福》和时装剧《卖肉粽与卖豆浆》。这个剧团虽然是新加坡民间剧团，但它们演出的剧目，是从漳州芗剧那里学到的，所以他们到台湾演出，相当于间接担任了闽漳歌仔戏与台湾歌仔戏之间的传递者。

第二，在两岸歌仔戏艺术相互合作之前，厦门和台湾两地，曾多次举办歌仔戏学术研讨会，为两岸歌仔戏研究家们提供了探讨、交流的平台，也为两岸歌仔戏艺术的合作提供了理论的基础。

这个平台，举办的时间是没有规律的，后来固定为每两年开一次。1989年，厦门举办首届台湾艺术研讨会，针对两岸歌仔戏的历史源流、生态现状、发展前景等，做了探讨、交流。一直到1996年，研讨会没有固定，有时三年一次，有时两年一次，没有规律。但到了1997年之后，固定为每两年举办一次，而且两地轮流举办。

举办的地点，刚开始也主要是在厦门。1994年之前，研讨会的形式，还是单向的，主要是台湾歌仔戏学者来大陆开会，闽南歌仔戏学者不可以到台湾开会。但这种情形，到了1995年，也有所变化。1995年，台湾首度举办"海峡两岸歌仔戏学术研讨会"，大陆歌仔戏学者第一次赴台交流，开启了两岸歌仔戏学术双向交流的局面。

第三，1995年之前，两岸歌仔戏的研讨会和演出，是分开、孤立的，台湾歌仔戏来闽南演出，是没有组织的。1995年之后，即台湾举办歌仔戏研讨会之时，同时举办两岸歌仔戏演出，就是在这次，漳州市芗剧团首次到台湾演出。带去了传统戏《罗衫奇案》、《吕蒙正》、《包公三勘蝴蝶梦》和新编戏改编戏《五女拜寿》、《三请樊梨花》、《桃李梅》，文华奖获得者郑秀琴也赴台交流。之后，每两年的研讨会期间，都有两岸歌仔戏演出，即研讨会和演出同时举行。这样的模式，保持到现在。每次研讨会的主题是不一样的。

从以上的分析可以看出，在两岸歌仔戏艺术合作之前，相互交流、对话，也不是一蹴而就，刚开始就是双向互动，就有同台演出交流的机会，而是经历了从单向到双向、从理论到实践的变化过程，是逐步地向前推进的。在这过程中，新加坡民间剧团起到了重要的黏合和中介作用。

三

2010年，歌仔戏《蝴蝶之恋》的创作真正开启两岸歌仔戏艺术合作之旅。

在这之前，随着两岸研讨会的多次举办，研讨问题的更加深入，两岸歌仔戏交流越来越频繁，但合作的几乎没有，有的合作，属于个别演职人员的参与，参与规模也比较小。1995年，台湾学者刘南芳创作的《李娃传》，邀请了大陆的个别主创人员参与合作，漳州芗剧团陈彬担任作曲，鼓师郑松江司鼓，厦门原芗剧导演黄卿伟担任导演。也有人将这次创作演出，视作台湾、福建歌仔戏精英的首次合作。但对于厦门、漳州来说，属于个别主创人员参与，属于民间之间的合作，而不是台湾歌仔戏与闽南歌仔戏国家剧团之间的合作。

但《蝴蝶之恋》就不同了，它是厦门歌仔戏剧团与台湾剧团的合作，从闽南角度来说，是国家剧团与台湾民间剧团的合作，这个意义，与之前闽南歌仔戏导演、作曲家或者演奏人员参与台湾歌仔戏剧目演出的性质是完全不同的。所以，可以将《蝴蝶之恋》视作是两岸歌仔戏艺术合作中最具有实质性突破的一次创作。最主要的是，在这次合作里，两岸歌仔戏演员第一次同台演出同一个剧目，这也是件具有历史性突破的事件。

因为历史原因，大陆歌仔戏演员的表演方式与台湾歌仔戏演员是不同的。

大陆国家剧团的歌仔戏演员都受过良好的艺校训练，即使从老艺人那里传承的技艺，也是比较规范的，程式化的，大陆歌仔戏剧种受京剧、越剧影响很大，导演、表演甚至剧本创作，都有一定的规矩和模式。但台湾歌仔戏演员就不同了，他们主要是活跃在民间，在外台演出，演员表演、唱腔很生活化，没有一定的程式。在合作之前，大陆和台湾歌仔戏呈现出相当不同的特色，而当双方参与合作，共同创作一个剧目时，其中遇到诸多的问题，就很显然了。最主要的是，两边剧团体制的不同。大陆是国家院团，排练一出新戏，可以停下业务演出，用较长时间专心致志地磨戏，但台湾不行。他们都是私营剧团的人员，或是有一份工作，再兼职剧团的演出。没有接活就意味着没有生活来源，他们每天必须为生活奔忙。让他们专门停下演出来排演，是不可能的。为了解决这个的问题，《蝴蝶之恋》开始设有 A、B 角演员。平时训练时，由大陆 B 角演员来走台，等台湾主演有空档，就进行 A 角的舞台配合。在表演上让大陆和舞台演员按各自表演方式出发；在唱腔上，发挥各自的唱腔风格，语言上个别词句，按各自的习惯用语表达。《蝴蝶之恋》的主创人员，主要以大陆为主，所以，整体演出风格、剧作呈现出来的气质，属于大陆式。

到了今年《龙九》的合作，方式有所变化。这次创作主力以台湾著名的歌仔戏剧团明华园的创作团队为主，厦门歌仔戏剧团的演员、灯光设计、演奏人员参与创作演出。整体演出风格、剧目的气质，属于台湾式的。在这次合作演出中，厦门歌仔戏演员庄海蓉说，她为了配合台湾演员的演出风格，在唱腔方面，表演风格方面，受到台湾演员的影响，学习了他们自然表演、自然发声的方式，使自己的演出风格向台湾方面靠近，使舞台整体形象比较和谐。

不管是大陆式，还是台湾式的，有了《龙九》的合作，两岸歌仔戏艺术的合作又出现一次突破，那就是从原来的单向合作到双向合作的突破。

四

从 1995 年两岸歌仔戏艺术开始双向交流，到 2015 年的双向合作，经过 20 多年的时间沟通、对话、交流，两岸歌仔戏艺术开始迈进有意义的、实质性的合作双赢阶段，在建设"一带一路"文化合作中，发挥了歌仔戏艺术连接两岸文化、沟通两岸民心的独特作用。可以预见，有了之前合作奠定的基础，可以瞻望，未来的两岸歌仔戏艺术合作将会越来越顺利，合作模式也越来越多样。

首先，从合作模式来说，《蝴蝶之恋》、《龙九》的合作，主要是闽南国家剧团与台湾地区民间职业剧团的合作。在漳州，有不少的芗剧民间职业剧团，将来，可以进行两岸民间歌仔戏职业剧团的合作。合作中碰撞出来的火花，一定与国家剧团与民间剧团合作不同的。

第二，两岸歌仔戏艺术的合作，可以为闽南歌仔戏与东南亚歌仔戏艺术的合作提供借鉴。歌仔戏作为"家乡戏"在闽南语系区域——东南亚的流播，得到闽南族群的认同，它是连接中国与东南亚华人心灵的文化桥梁，漳州芗剧曾给新加坡歌仔戏剧团送去了火种，至今，相互间的交流没有中断，如果进行一次实质性的演出合作，不仅可以提升新加坡民间职业剧团的创作水平，而且可以活跃新加坡歌仔戏演出市场，进一步加深新加坡华人与祖国之间的情感沟通。

第三，为了实现合作共赢，优势互补，两岸歌仔戏剧团在具体的合作实践中，在吸收对方之优长补自己之不足时，要警惕自我个性、剧种特色的迷失，警惕双方歌仔戏艺术出现类同化趋势。

《蝴蝶之梦》与《龙九》的艺术风格是不同的，而且非常明显，大陆歌仔戏创作，喜欢在剧作中融入哲理性、教育性，特别是福建戏曲创作，哲理思辨，是一大特色。而台湾歌仔戏创作，主要以娱乐为主。针对闽南歌仔戏的这种特色，有台湾学者指出，大陆歌仔戏应该学习台湾歌仔戏艺术风格，不要总是高台教化。我的观点是，这位台湾学者提的意见，有它合理的地方，但不一定就得遵循。如果大陆歌仔戏完全按台湾歌仔戏学习，失去了自己的特性，那就只有一种歌仔戏了，没有闽南歌仔戏。大陆戏曲的高台教化，确实有它的不足之处，比如有时就不受观众待见，但这个缺点，正是大陆戏曲的特点之一，不仅仅是 50 年代以来是这样的，即中国戏曲的传统就是高台教化，是中国戏曲的传统。闽南歌仔戏创作可以艺术化处理高台教化的问题，但没必要放弃这个特色。可以在这个特色的基础上，进行多样化创作，甚至可以做些实验性的创作演出。

承认闽台文化多元化特点，推进闽台文化多样性发展，是当前"一带一路"合作中两岸戏曲生存和发展中需要提倡并值得遵循的一个原则。

弘扬丝路精神,深化文化交流

新疆艺术研究所 徐玉梅

公元前138年,中国汉代的张骞肩负和平友好使命出使西域,开启了中国同中亚各国友好的大门,开辟出一条纵贯东西、连接欧亚的丝绸之路。我的家乡新疆,就位于丝绸之路经济带上东西多元文化的交汇点。站在这里,回首历史,我能够感受到戈壁滩上回荡的驼铃声,看到大漠飘飞的袅袅孤烟。这一切,让我感到十分亲切。

新疆作为古代丝绸之路的重要枢纽,历经上千年生生不息。其历史文化特色为世界所惊叹,著名的东方学家、国学大师季羡林毫不掩饰对新疆历史文化的仰慕之情。他在《新疆与比较文学的研究》中写道:"在过去几千年的历史中,世界各民族共同创造了许多文化体系,依我的看法,共有四大文化体系,即:中国文化体系、印度文化体系、阿拉伯穆斯林文化体系、西方文化体系。四者又可合为两个更大的文化体系,前三者合称东方文化体系,后一者可称西方文化体系。而这些文化体系汇流的地方,世界上只有一个,这就是新疆。"经过长期的相融共生发展,形成了独特的地域文化和民族文化。境内不少少数民族都是跨界而居,双方血缘相亲,民族相连,语言相通,风俗相近,经济互补性强,传统友谊源远流长,具有开展区域间合作的独特的人文优势。千百年来,丝绸之路承载着和平合作、开放包容、互学互鉴、互利共赢精神薪火相传。

文化如水,润物无声,在建设"一带一路"的进程中,新疆文化人正以弘扬丝路精神、深化文化交流的担当,让命运共同体意识在沿线国家落地生根。

弘扬丝路精神,发挥地缘优势,促进文明互鉴。新疆地处亚欧大陆中心,边境线长、毗邻国家多,丝绸之路北、中、南三条通道贯穿全境。丝绸之路把中国和中亚、西亚、南亚、北非以及欧洲联系在了一起。从公元纪年之前,直到15世纪,在2000多年的历史长河里,它都是人类文明最重要、最繁忙的交通要道。它始终处于一个开放系统中,各民族文化艺术在这里交流、碰撞、积淀,与东西方艺术是一种双向选择、双向回授的关系,既有纵向流传,也有横向交流;贸易往来、宗教传播、民族迁徙、审美情感,等等,都左右着文化变迁和艺术的走向。在这片神奇的土地上既保存了民族传统文化的多样性,又构成了一体多元中华文化的共同特质,新疆的乐舞艺术便是在这种丰厚多元文化资源的滋养中传承发展。人类文明没有高低优劣之分，因为平等交流而变得丰富多彩。正所谓"五色交辉，相得益彰；八音合奏，终和且平"。新疆文化人始终坚持以开放包容的心态看待对方，用对话交流代替封闭隔阂，形成了不同社会制度、不同信仰、不同文化传统的国家地区和谐相处的典范。

弘扬丝路精神，发挥人文优势，夯实民意基础。"一带一路"战略构想涉及几十个国家、数十亿人口，这些国家在历史上创造出了形态不同、风格迥异的文明形态，是人类文明宝库的重要组成部分。新疆文化系统充分发掘自身文化底蕴，继承和弘扬"丝绸之路"这一具有广泛亲和力和深刻感召力的文化符号，积极发挥文化交流与合作的作用，使沿线各国都可以吸收、融汇外来文化的合理内容，促进不同文明的共同发展。现实中，我们深刻地认识到，深化文化交流与合作有助于夯实中国同沿线国家合作的民意基础。国之交在于民相亲，民相亲在于心相通。"一带一路"沿线各国历史文化宗教不同，只有通过文化交流，才能让各国人民产生共同语言、增强相互信任、加深彼此感情。近年来，新疆与沿线国家地区的文化交流形式越来越新、内容越来越多、规模越来越大、影响越来越广。民间交流频繁、合作内容丰富，在文化部的统一部署下，与不少沿线国家都互办过文化年、艺术节，连续四届举办国际舞蹈节、举办旅游推介活动等，多次举办了以"丝绸之路"为主题的文化交流项目。密切了新疆各族人民同沿线各国人民的友好感情，夯实了新疆同这些国家合作的民意基础和社会基础。

弘扬丝路精神，发挥资源优势，坚持合作共赢。国家主席习近平十分关注新疆在"一带一路"建设中所发挥的重要作用。2014年4月，他在新疆考察工作时明确提出，新疆要抓住这个历史机遇，把自身的区域性对外开放战略融入国家丝绸之路经济带建设、向西开放的总体布局中去。新疆资源富集，目前发现的矿产有139种，其中41种保有储量居全国前十位。石油、天然气、煤炭预测资源量分别占全国陆上资源量的30%、34%和40%，风能、太阳能等清洁可再生能源可利用量居全国前列，是我国重要的能源接替区。新疆是中国联通中亚、西亚以及欧洲的重要节点，具有广阔的经济增长潜力，是"丝绸之路经济带"的战略核心区；新疆地处亚欧大陆腹心，具有独特的地缘优势和区位优势，是中国扩大对外开放的西出桥头堡；新疆作为古代"丝绸之路"的交通要道，拥有不胜枚举的文化遗产。文化遗产的地域性，为"一带一路"沿线国家的平等合作提供了文化平台，展示了中华民族巨大的包容性；文化遗产的稀有性，为"一带一路"战略建设提供了独有的文化支撑，传承了中华民族优秀的传统文化；文化遗产的民族性，为"一带一路"战略建设提供了历史记忆的依托，印证了中华文明历来就是由各民族人民共同创造，巩固了中华民族共有的精神家园。申报的联合国遗产有"新疆维吾尔木卡姆"、"玛纳斯"、"新疆麦西热甫"和"蒙古族长调"，文化遗产承载着民族自豪感和自信心，在国家建设"一带一路"战略下，文化遗产保护不仅有利于解决国家的历史文化认同，还能够架构起民众心灵最深层的部分，是文化"中国梦"徐徐展开的底蕴。新疆文化遗产保护、利用与传承是实现新疆社会稳定和长治久安的重要基础，是新疆经济社会发展的独特推动力，是"一带一路"沿线国家文化遗产保护合作的枢纽。保护文化遗产能够维护世界文化多样性和创造性，是"一带一路"沿线国家打造"利益共同体"和"命运共同体"的前提。

"一带一路"文明圈是多样、共存、包容、共赢的。2500多年来，贯通亚欧大陆的丝绸之路文化是基于沙漠、绿洲、草原、游牧、高原为生活基础的特色文化，丝绸之路上的那些古老民族、文化、宗教还健在。至今，伊朗还有2万多拜火教信徒，伊朗议会里还保持着拜火教信徒的席位。丝绸之路文化崇尚自然、天人合一、热爱生活。今天，新疆阿勒泰地区的草原图瓦人和蒙古人的呼麦、突厥人的沙漠绿洲歌舞仍在争奇斗艳，竞相开放着。东来西去，东西双向开放，"一带一路"正以新疆为中心重新界定着中国与世界，我们不再是站在太平洋岸边看世界，而是以西域为出发点，站在天山或帕米尔的雪山顶上看世界，构思"一带一路"文明圈：那是一个突厥、阿拉伯、波斯、俄罗斯和汉文化并存、交流、重叠、融合的文明带。随着一带一路，特别是中巴经济走廊的开通，中国与中亚和西亚的边疆地带将成为华夏新中原、新腹地。我想，今天的中国需要通过"一带一路"文化圈的建设，形成一个与"一带一路"基础设施规划和贸易大道规划相适应的文化共同体。在这个文明圈内，最大限度地激发不同文化、不同国家、不同民族和部落的认同感、凝聚力、自尊心和创造力，整合丝绸之路文明圈内的无限资源，让"一带一路"的建设成果惠及丝绸之路文明圈的全体人民。

海纳百川，有容乃大。未来由中国这样一个以多元性、异质性、复杂性为特征的文化强国主导的"一带一路"文明圈应该是文化多元共生、包容共进的；而不是西方文明倡导的同质性和排他性的，更不是二元对立和文明冲突。让我们携起手来，弘扬丝路精神，深化文化交流，积极发挥文化的包容力和牵引力，最终实现"各美其美，美美与共"上的共生、共存，即：既保持文化差异，又能在一个文化多样性的文明圈里和谐相处。

区域性对外传播中如何做到"民心相通"
——以在滇东南亚留学生对"云南"的幻想主题分析为例

云南大学滇池学院　杨姣　澳门大学　吴玫

前　言

云南与缅甸、越南和老挝接壤,靠近印度、孟加拉国等南亚国家。边境线全长4060公里,有26个边境县市与3个邻国的6个省(邦)32个县(市、镇)接壤,其中11个县(市)与邻国城镇隔江(界)相望。全省25种少数民族中,有15种民族与境外居民同属于一个民族,跨境而居。这种区位上一衣带水的格局造就了云南与周边国家的交流源远流长。

地理优势,文化和语言优势使得自明清以后云南与东南亚及南亚国家之间的人员流动就日益频繁。新中国成立后,云南与东南亚国家间的人员交流主要体现在两个层面:一是官方层面的人员流动,二是民间层面的人员流动[①]。这一时期民间层面的人员交流主要表现为三种形式:互婚、迁居和避难[②],这种人员交流更多是以边境为基础的人员往来。改革开放以后,云南加快与邻近各国的口岸建设,目前全省有13个国家一类口岸,7个二类口岸,90个边民互市通道和103个边贸互市点。上述口岸建设加速了云南与周边国家的人员流动,经贸往来和媒体交流。同时,2013年建成使用的昆明长水国际机场,2014年底重新通车的滇越铁路,以及昆曼高速、昆缅高速和昆越高速等多条跨境高等级公路的开通,客观上拓宽了云南与周边国家人员交流的形式。

除了边境间的人员往来,改革开放后,基于商贸和文化交流需求的人员往来日益频繁和渐成规模。截止到2014年,云南共有留学生近3万人,其中有近八成留学生来自东南亚和南亚国家[③]。根据云南大学、云南农业大学、云南民族

[①] 杨姣:《1949—1990:云南对东南亚的传播交流史》,《文化与传播》2015年第3期。
[②] 《云南省志》卷53《外事志》,云南人民出版社1996年版,第200页。
[③] 《在云南留学生首超3万人东南亚南亚留学生近八成》,《人民日报》(海外版)2014年2月25日,中国教育新闻网(www.jyb.cn)。

大学三所主要的东南亚留学生目的高校 2014 年 5 月的统计数据显示,目前昆明 3000 多名来自泰国、越南、柬埔寨、老挝的留学生中,选择回国或者到北上广深等中国一线城市发展的人数与留昆就业人数比例约为 9∶1。近八成的东南亚南亚留学生选择毕业后回到所在国发展[①]。这些数据表明,了解云南风土人情和有一定中文交流能力的东南亚和南亚国家的留学生将日益成为云南,乃至中国与周边国家交流的目标人群和重要的传播载体。

虽然云南在构建区域信息交流中心上已初具规模,已经形成了"全方位,一体化"的传播格局,但是官方为主导的对外传播格局并没有实质性的改变[②]。这种传播模式是否能够起到"民心相通"的效果?云南官方在东南亚传播中试图塑造什么样的形象?而东南亚受众又是如何解读这样的本文?这是本文要深入探讨的内容。

本研究以在滇的东南亚和南亚国家的留学生为研究对象,同时引入符号聚合理论(Symbolic Convergence Theory)和幻想主题分析法(Fantasy Theme Analysis),借助两部典型的云南对外传播的视频,来引爆视频观众的符号分享,通过比较两个视频创造的幻想主题和东南亚国家留学生观影后产生的幻想主题的差距,来探究在滇的东南亚和南亚留学生是如何接收理解云南的宣传视频,以及影响他们产生相关幻想主题的因素。

一、文献综述

(一)幻想主题分析法的运用

幻想主题分析法以起源于美苏冷战研究的符号融合理论(Symbolic Convergence Theory)为基础,将抽象的主观意识符号化并转化为人们可以观察、测量、分析并施加影响的客观数据,已成熟地运用于分析传播对象的意识图景(吴玫,2014)。它试图揭示幻想主题的载体语言符号与人的行为动机之间的关系(邓志勇、王懋康,2013),也就是说,它借助于符号化的主观意识去关注人的行为变化,并试图根据"语义视野"(rhetorical vision)去预测人们的行为。

[①] 《仅一成东南亚留学生毕业后愿留昆发展》,2014 年 5 月 25 日,昆明信息港(http://daily.clzg.cn)。
[②] 吴玫、杨姣:《中国—东盟媒介交流新策略——以云南省为例》,李红、方冬莉等:《中国—东盟合作:从 2.0 走向 3.0》,广西师范大学出版社 2015 年版,第 165—182 页。

Bormann 等（2001）将已有的幻想主题的研究从"欲解决的研究问题"的角度分成六个类别：人际传播研究（Interpersonal Communication Study），小群组传播研究（Small Group Communication Study），公众传播研究（Public Communication Study），组织传播研究（Organization Communication Study），大众传播研究（Mass Communication Study）和跨文化的传播研究（Intercultural Communication Study）。

幻想主题分析法作为一种修辞学的批评方法引入中国后，研究者多结合自身的研究方向尝试将这样的研究方法运用于各类语料分析中。最常见的是以大众媒体为语言符号载体的研究，这类研究着眼于探究大众媒体对特定传播对象建构的语义视野。例如英国《金融时报》塑造的美国衰落和中国扩张的符号图景（吴玫、朱文博，2014）、飘柔洗发水电视系列广告中男女主角的语义符号研究（曾萌芽、杨洪玉，2011）、央视"关爱老人"系列公益广告中对"空巢老人"的电视符号建构（盛佳红，2014），甚至对社会亚文化群体的关注，比如网络论坛中的"同人女群体"的研究（马中红、陆国静，2012）。

除此以外，幻想主题分析方法也运用于以组织的宣传材料为语料分析对象的研究中。这类研究多着眼于探究组织意欲向外界传达的价值观。例如黄静芬（2012）通过对阿里巴巴内部刊物《阿里味儿之悟道》的幻想主题分析，认为阿里公司的价值观体系：客户第一、团队合作、拥抱变化、激情、诚信、敬业已内化成阿里成员的信念。郝捷（2015）通过对安利的内部刊物《安利新姿》进行幻想主题分析后发现，安利建构了一个"美好新生活"的语义视野。

（二）城市形象宣传片的研究及其对幻想主题分析法的运用

目前国内对城市形象宣传片的研究主要集中在两个层面：（1）城市形象宣传片制作的研究，主要包括技法的提升（周进，2015；曹静，2014；付饶，2013；雷雨晴，2013；黄安，2013；于纪胜，2012；容华朝，2009）、存在的问题（曹毅梅，2013；蔡夏梦，2010）。（2）城市形象宣传片的影响和作用（严晓璐，2015；冯菊香，2015；柳邦坤，2013；黄玉敏，2013）。

在对城市形象宣传片进行研究的时候，研究者多采纳的理论分析框架是品牌营销（张天培，2012；陈奕，2012；付敬，2014；张朝晓，2014）和符号学理论（尹迎春，2010；李元海，2012；舒心，2014）。基于符号学理论的研究者都认为，城市形象宣传片实质上是对城市资源和城市形象的符号建构的结果。

将幻想主题分析法运用于对城市形象宣传片的研究，目前国内可见的研究有傅恒倩（2013）将该方法用来分析 2011 年在美国时代广场播放的中国国家形象宣传片，以及吴玫、梁韵（2015）运用幻想主题分析法去分析广西"中国—东盟博览会"的官方宣传片。

（三）国内对东南亚留学生的研究

目前国内对东南亚留学生的研究主要集中在两个方向：

（1）以东南亚留学生作为研究对象。这类研究基本上以问卷调查为研究方法，重点关注了留学生的在中国的文化适应问题（周琬馨，2012；肖耀科，2012；唐志敏，2015），此外还有他们的跨文化身份认同和交往模式研究（杨军，2012），东南亚华裔留学生来华留学的动机研究（陈文，2013）和他们在中国的社会支持状况（周琬馨，2012）。

（2）以东南亚留学生作为研究视角。目前国内的这类研究多用调查问卷结合访谈的研究方法，以东南亚留学生作为研究视角，关注了中国的国家形象（陈文，2012），大陆电视节目在东南亚留学生中的收视效果（韩愈，2012）和云南民族文化在东南亚地区的传播效果（杨玉，2014）。

综上所述，本研究将引入以幻想主题分析法，打通现有研究中城市形象宣传片和东南亚留学生研究中的隔阂，从语义修辞的视角看区域性的对外传播中如何把握受众的价值观。

二、研究方法

（一）幻想主题分析法（FTA）

幻想主题、幻想类型和语义视野，构成了幻想主题分析的三个基础概念，同时也是幻想主题分析的三个渐进层次。它们虽有大小的区分，但并不是线性递进的关系。也就是说，幻想主题不一定先聚合成幻想类型，然后再构成语义视野。也有可能没有经过幻想类型，幻想主题就直接聚合为语义视野；还有可能是幻想主题既没有构成幻想类型也没有聚合成语义视野。以上基础概念之间的这种非线性递进关系，在一定程度上导致了幻想主题的分析过程不是一个一成不变的操作过程。

幻想主题分析法的实施步骤

按照 Bormann 的说法，幻想主题分析法并没有一个特定的分析步骤和程序。但是他在 1972 年的文章中，仍然建议了一些可能的步骤（Bormannn，1972）：

（1）收集群组成员沟通过程的相关资料，包括录影带、录音、成员的回忆或记录，或研究者自己的观察记录。

（2）分析这些资料，找出被复诵的叙事或情节。

（3）归纳重复出现的角色、情节与行动等戏剧类型。

（4）建构语义视野。

与上述的步骤建议相比，Foss（1989）提供的分析步骤更为详尽和系统：

（1）找出符号融合发生的证据，包括明显和隐藏的符号融合现象。

（2）记录重复出现的幻想主题。必须对文本逐句检查，并注意每一个可能的幻想主题。研究者可以用角色、场景和故事情节三个层面来分析。

（3）尝试建构语义视野。从重复出现的幻想主题中尝试归纳幻想类型，进而建构语义视野。

（4）界定语义视野背后的动机。

（5）评估语义视野。

从Bormann和Foss提供的步骤建议可以总结出做幻想主题分析的一些共有步骤：

（1）群组成员沟通资料的获取，依据研究对象的不同，沟通资料的形式也各异。

（2）对沟通文本做逐字逐句的检查。

（3）从角色、场景和故事情节三个层面记录重复出现的幻想主题。

（4）对幻想主题进行归类，尝试建构语义视野。

（5）探究和评估构筑语义视野的外部影响力。在以上分析步骤的基础上，林静伶和陈焕芸（1997）建议研究者依据其研究问题、文本特性、群体特性等规划幻想主题的分析步骤。应用幻想主题分析的学者都应随着上述的相关考量，做弹性调整。

在本研究中，幻想主题分析法（FTA）主要运用于三个具体的研究对象：两个云南的对外宣传视频：《七彩云南旅游天堂》和《云南的一天》，以及对东南亚留学生访谈资料的分析。

（二）研究样本的选择

1999年昆明成功申请举办世界园艺博览会后，云南多样性的旅游资源逐渐为外界所知，云南将自己定位为"中国旅游大省"的同时，也加快了发展旅游的基础设施建设。所以，对外宣传云南的旅游资源，发展云南的旅游产业成了云南对外传播的主题。本项目从中国内地最大的两个视频资源库：优酷视频和百度视频中锁定了两个典型的云南旅游宣传片，一个是《七彩云南旅游天堂》

的官方宣传片，另一个是民间制作团队完成的《云南的一天》。

1. 研究样本一：《七彩云南旅游天堂》官方宣传片

目前，云南已经将"旅游大省"的形象及定位深入人心，并树立了"七彩云南旅游天堂"的形象品牌。2010年由云南省旅游发展改革委员会牵头制作完成的《七彩云南旅游天堂》的官方宣传片正式亮相，同年推出了包括中、英、日、法、德语在内的多语言版本。另据中新网报道，2015年新年元旦期间，为更好地向世界推广中国云南的旅游资源和文化，《七彩云南旅游天堂》登陆纽约时报广场广告屏幕。

该官方宣传片的时长为22'45''，从云南复杂多样的地质地貌，多样性的气候，动植物的王国，26个民族及宗教文化和多样性的旅游选择五个方面诠释了"七彩云南"。

2. 研究样本二：宣传视频《云南的一天》

《云南的一天》获得首届"七彩云南，梦想家园"创意云南广告大赛的唯一一个全场大奖，该广告大赛由昆明国家广告产业园试点园区承办，云南省工商行政管理局、云南省旅游发展委员会、云南省广告协会共同主办。

该作品由丽江的一个名为和照工作室的民间影视制作工作室选送。该团队从2006年8月起，走遍云南129个县区拍摄，用超过6万分钟的高清影像素材剪辑成了这部5分钟的短片，被认为是"突破了传统意义上的民俗旅游的创意概念"。

该视频将云南多姿多彩的生活画卷浓缩在一天展现，以此表达"云南一天，天天精彩"的主题。

3. 对宣传视频的幻想主题分析

根据Bormann和Foss提供做幻想主题分析的步骤，本项目对上述两个云南旅游的宣传视频的分析是依照如下步骤完成的：

（1）将两个宣传视频的声画语言和解说词转换成文字稿。

（2）对文本进行逐字逐句的检查。

（3）从场景、角色和行动三个层面记录重复出现的幻想主题，即Bormann认为幻想主题分析中的最小单位。

（4）从重复出现的幻想主题中尝试归纳幻想类型，进而建构语义视野。

（三）基于符号聚合理论的焦点小组访谈（Focus Group）

焦点小组就是把一小群人组织起来讨论某个特定的话题。从20世纪50年代开始，这种方法就被广泛运用于市场营销的研究中（Cragan& Wright，1991）。

与调查问卷相比，焦点小组访谈能就某个话题或对象深入地了解被访对象态度和意见的复杂性。从这个意义上来说，符号聚合理论（SCT）和焦点小组访谈也有能够结合的可能。因为符号聚合理论是借助于幻想主题分析法来探究人们基于"符号分享"的世界观和价值观，而焦点小组访谈意欲了解的被访对象态度和意见的复杂性，也就是他们世界观和价值观的折射。

1. 焦点小组访谈问题的确定

本研究在参照前人研究，特别是梁韵（2015）对广西-东盟博览会宣传片的焦点小组访谈的问题设计的基础上，确定了本研究的访谈问题。本研究围绕"宣传视频"、"云南的旅游"、"云南（云南人）"、"昆明（昆明人）"和"中国—东盟关系"五个研究对象来设计研究问题，最终形成了17个开放式的访谈问题（访谈问卷详见附录）。

2. 焦点小组访谈对象的确定

本项目选择了云南民族大学的东南亚留学生作为访谈对象。以尽可能多地覆盖东南亚的国家为目标，经该校留学生院的汉语任课老师的推荐，我一共得到14名来自7个东南亚和南亚国家的访谈对象。但在实施访谈的过程中，两个来自老挝的女孩和一个来自斯里兰卡的男孩因为中英文沟通都无法进行，所以最后的访谈对象就剔除了这三名学生，剩余11个访谈对象。

（四）焦点小组访谈的实施

本项目组于2015年5月23日和6月3日分两次到上述11名留学生所在的授课班级进行焦点小组访谈。在访谈实施过程中，因为受到课程分班的限制，所以11名被访对象被编入3个组：第一组是编号1-5的5名泰国留学生；第二组是编号5、6、7的组员；第三组是编号9、10、11的被访对象。5月23日完成第一组的访谈，6月3日上午是第二组，下午完成第三组。

每组访谈的过程均为先给每个访谈对象发放访谈问卷，便于他们在观影过程中记录；然后请访谈小组成员观看两个云南旅游的宣传视频；观影结束后进行每组约90分钟，每人约30分钟的访谈。所有小组的观影过程及每个被访对象的访谈过程均用DV进行记录。

（五）访谈资料的幻想主题分析（FTA）

根据幻想主题分析的实施步骤，在访谈结束后，对访谈资料依据如下步骤进行了幻想主题分析：

（1）根据访谈问卷，将被访对象的DV影像记录资料转换成文字稿。

（2）按照：1）对两个视频的大致感受；2）对现实中云南和昆明的感受；3）对所在国与中国关系的认知。三个部分对访谈资料的文字稿进行分类整理。

（3）对上述的文字稿进行逐字逐句的检查，筛选出那些包含有幻想成分的典型回答。

（4）从筛选出来的回答中提炼不同的幻想主题。

（5）尝试从幻想主题中归纳出幻想类型，进而建构语义视野。

三、研究发现

本项目的研究发现共有两部分组成：第一部分是对两个具有代表性的云南旅游的宣传片进行幻想主题分析，第二部分是对东南亚和南亚留学生的焦点小组访谈资料的幻想主题分析，最后对这两部分资料提炼的幻想主题进行比较研究。

（一）对《七彩云南旅游天堂》官方宣传片的幻想主题分析

经过分析，研究者为该官方宣传片提炼出两个语义视野：一是"七彩云南"，二是"人间天堂"。

1. 语义视野：七彩云南

这一语义视野在宣传片中由两个幻想类型和四个幻想主题共同聚合而成，详见下表：

语义视野1：七彩云南						
幻想对象	幻想类型1	幻想类型2	幻想主题1	幻想主题2	幻想主题3	幻想主题4
云南的旅游资源	地质地貌复杂多样	旅游选择多样	气候多样	动植物的王国	文化多元	宗教圣地

幻想类型1：地质地貌复杂多样

	幻想对象	角色	场景	情节
幻想主题1：山的世界	云南的旅游资源：山	梅里雪山、白茫雪山、哈巴雪山、玉龙雪山、大理苍山、高黎贡山	蓝天白云、高天流云、各色雪山山峰、蓝色的平静湖面	无

续表

	幻想对象	角色	场景	情节
幻想主题2：河的故乡	云南的旅游资源：河	金沙江、珠江、怒江、澜沧江、大盈江、红河、三江并流、虎跳峡、长江第一湾	高山、蜿蜒的河流、蓝天白云、广袤的田野、平静的水面、高山杜鹃、孔雀、小熊猫、奔腾的河水	少数民族划船，一群小男孩光身子在河水里奔跑
幻想主题3：自然奇观的博物馆	云南的旅游资源：自然奇观	石林、土林、彩色沙林、老君山、白水台、腾冲火山、东川红土地、九乡溶洞、九龙瀑布	石林、瀑布、蓝天、高山、丹霞地貌	无
幻想主题4：千姿百态的高原湖泊	云南的旅游资源：高原湖泊	滇池、洱海、泸沽湖、抚仙湖、普者黑	夕阳下的金花、平静的湖面、蓝天、飞翔的海鸟	老人在湖边静坐、泛舟洱海、摩梭妇女泛舟泸沽湖、渔船泛舟夕阳中的抚仙湖、壮族女性采莲花

幻想类型2：旅游选择多样

	幻想对象	角色	场景	情节
幻想主题1：生态之旅	云南的旅游（资源）	牵马的藏族妇女、手举酥油茶的小男孩	蓝天白云、平静的湖泊、雪山流云、丹顶鹤、耕牛田野	农民耕种、年轻的藏族女孩做酥油茶
幻想主题2：民族风情之旅	云南的旅游（资源）	外国游客	赛马会、大型露天歌舞	外国游客参加泼水节、外国游客和当地少数民族歌舞、游客接受哈达

续表

	幻想对象	角色	场景	情节
幻想主题3：边地风情之旅	云南的旅游（资源）	无	湄公河、游轮、界碑、版纳、大象、吴哥、泰国	无
幻想主题4：康体之旅	云南的旅游（资源）	一群年轻女性	散满鲜花的温泉、蓝天白云下的高尔夫球场	一名年轻女性泡温泉、游客在打高尔夫、一群人在绿草地上的欢笑跳跃
幻想主题5：历史文化之旅	云南的旅游（资源）	中国游客	东巴古乐表演、怒江边马帮、剑川石宝山石窟、官渡古镇、黑井古镇、李家山青铜器、大观楼、铁索桥、元谋猿人、恐龙化石	游客走过铁索桥、游客参观博物馆
幻想主题6：随心之旅	云南的旅游（资源）	小女孩、年轻女性、情侣	海埂大坝、翠湖边、湖边的房车、蓝天白云、高山草地河流、雪地	小女孩放风筝、年轻女性晨跑、情侣骑自行车、游客在江河漂流、攀岩、溜索、骑自行车、滑雪
幻想主题7：多样的旅游交通	云南的旅游（资源）	飞机、火车、旅游大巴、航运	长水国际机场、巫家坝机场、昆明火车站、滇越铁路、城际列车、金沙江、湄公河	无
幻想主题8：多元的住宿选择	云南的旅游（资源）	中国游客、外国商务游客、背包客	度假村、星级宾馆、客栈	中外游客入住酒店

幻想主题1：气候多样

幻想主题	幻想对象	角色	场景	情节
多样性的气候	云南	老外、小女孩、花腰傣妇女、穿现代服装的女孩	雪山、森林、蓝天、湖泊、绿地、海鸥	老外弹吉他、小女孩唱歌、花腰傣采油菜花、现代服装的小女孩在蓝天下张开双臂

幻想主题2：动植物的王国

幻想主题	幻想对象	角色	场景	情节
动植物的王国	云南	丹顶鹤、滇金丝猴、大象、飞鸟、蜜蜂采蜜	阳光、树木、蓝天、白云、高山、杜鹃满山	丹顶鹤在慢步、滇金丝猴在凝望、群鸟飞起、蜜蜂采蜜

幻想主题3：文化多元

幻想主题	幻想对象	角色	情节	场景
文化多元	云南的旅游（资源）	佤族女孩、藏族女孩、摩梭女孩、苗族妇女的笑脸、街头骑车少年、唱歌的苗族女孩、正在学习的藏族孩子、眼望白塔的小普哨	佤族女孩跳甩头舞、大型街头歌舞、藏族女孩敬献哈达、摩梭女孩划船、藏族老头打高尔夫、白族对歌、白族金花撒花	跳甩头舞、葛丹松赞林寺、昆明金马碧鸡坊、泸沽湖、滇池高尔夫球场

幻想主题4：宗教圣地

幻想主题	幻想对象	角色	场景	情节
宗教圣地	云南的旅游（资源）	圆通寺、筇竹寺、葛丹松赞林寺、崇圣寺、鸡足山、巍宝山、曼飞白龙塔、卧佛寺、金殿、西山龙门、茨中天主教堂	蓝天白云、寺庙口的狮子、庙里的罗汉、寺庙群、三塔	寺庙僧侣扫地

2. 语义视野：人间天堂

在官方宣传视频中，"人间天堂"的语义视野由三个幻想类型聚合而成：（1）最大最神秘的民族风情园；（2）人间净土；（3）人间乐园。详见下表：

语义视野2：人间天堂			
幻想对象	幻想类型1	幻想类型2	幻想类型3
云南人的生活	最大最神秘的民族风情园	人间净土	人间乐园

幻想类型1：最大最神秘的民族风情乐园

幻想主题	幻想对象	角色	场景	情节
幻想主题1：彝族是创造十月太阳历的民族	云南人：彝族	彝族女性、彝族男性	太阳历广场、彝族的书籍、土掌房	刺绣、梳头、吹笛子、跳菜、打歌、祭火
幻想主题2 世代居住在苍山脚洱海滨的民族	云南人：白族	穿白族服饰的年轻金花	白族民居	一群金花唱歌、金花泡制三道茶
幻想主题3：傣族是与水相融的民族	云南人：傣族	撑纸伞的小朴哨、跳孔雀舞的傣族男性、寺庙里的小僧侣	大金塔、佛寺、吊脚楼	一群小普哨在河水中嬉戏、跳孔雀舞、赛龙舟、吃竹筒饭、骑大象

续表

幻想主题	幻想对象	角色	场景	情节
幻想主题4：纳西族是惬意生活的古老民族	云南人：纳西族	纳西族妇女、纳西族老人	玉龙雪山、东巴文书籍、小桥、流水	纳西族女性歌舞、欢笑、弹奏纳西古乐、纳西族老人晒太阳
幻想主题5：傈僳族是勇敢热情的民族	云南人：傈僳族	载歌载舞的傈僳族男女	傈僳族村寨	傈僳族大型歌舞、爬刀杆、跳火海
幻想主题6：无比奔放的佤族	云南人：佤族	载歌载舞的佤族男女	佤族村寨	大型歌舞表演、敲木鼓、跳甩发舞
幻想主题7：创造大型歌舞的景颇族	云南人：景颇族	载歌载舞的景颇族男女	景颇族村寨	大型露天歌舞表演
幻想主题8：藏族是生活在理想世界中的民族	云南人：藏族	藏族男女	蓝天、白云、雪山、草场	敬献哈达、喝酥油茶的藏族老人、跳藏族热巴舞

幻想类型2：人间净土

	幻想对象	角色	场景	情节
幻想主题1：阳光灿烂，天空纯净	云南	外国游客、小女孩、花腰傣妇女、穿现代服装的女孩	雪山、森林、蓝天、湖泊、绿地、海鸥	老外弹吉他、小女孩唱歌、花腰傣采油菜花、现代服装的小女孩在蓝天下张开双臂
幻想主题2：诗一般的地方	云南：大理	一群金花、两个渔民	晨光中的洱海	金花在唱歌、渔民泛舟洱海
幻想主题3：人间净土，女儿国	云南：丽江	两个摩梭妇女	蓝天白云、平静的湖面、湖边的村寨	摩梭妇女泛舟泸沽湖

续表

	幻想对象	角色	场景	情节
幻想主题4：田园诗意，如在画中	云南：文山	壮族妇女、渔民	蓝天白云、平静的湖面上漂浮着荷叶、湖面倒映着山	壮族妇女在荷叶丛中采莲
幻想主题5：高原水乡，惬意生活	云南：丽江	纳西族妇女	丽江四方街、丽江的雪山、小桥、流水	一群纳西族妇女跳篝火舞、三个纳西族妇女在雪山脚下跳舞、两个纳西族老人在晒太阳
幻想主题6：田园山水美景	云南：文山	游客	群山、田野、平静的湖面、金色的油菜花、转动的水车	泛舟
幻想主题7：离天很近的理想世界	云南人	藏族男女	蓝天、白云、雪山、草场	敬献哈达、喝酥油茶的藏族老人、跳藏族热巴舞
幻想主题8：田园牧歌	云南人	牵马的藏族妇女、手举酥油茶的小男孩	蓝天、白云、平静的湖泊、雪山流云、丹顶鹤、耕牛田野	农民耕种、年轻的藏族女孩做酥油茶

幻想类型3：人间乐园

	幻想对象	角色	场景	情节
幻想主题1：快乐都市	昆明（人）	外国游客、时尚白领、街头少年、女车模、外国情侣	珠宝店、近日楼、夜晚的市中心、名车店、高楼大厦、麦当劳、时装店	街头少年在玩单车、跳街舞
幻想主题2：美食天堂	昆明（人）	中国情侣、外国游客	各种全国美食和少数民族美食	家人聚会、吃火锅、过桥米线，

续表

	幻想对象	角色	场景	情节
幻想主题3：购物乐园	昆明人	年轻女孩	玉器、银饰、鲜花、呈贡鲜花基地	拎着购物袋微笑的年轻女孩
幻想主题4：当地人善良热情	云南人、昆明人	当地人、中国游客及外国游客		壮族女孩为外国游客指路、正在为客户介绍的年轻女孩、开怀大笑的苗族老人、吃 KFC 的一家

（二）对《云南的一天》创意视频的幻想主题分析

经过仔细分析，研究者认为《云南的一天》形成了一个语义视野和一个幻想类型。其中"七彩云南"的语义视野由两个幻想类型聚合而成，"人间净土世外桃源"的幻想类型由三个幻想主题聚合而成。

1. 语义视野：七彩云南

幻想类型1：自然景观的博物馆

	幻想对象	角色	场景	情节
幻想主题1：云南阳光普照	云南：气候	傣族小普哨	梅里雪山、罗平油菜地、芒市大金塔、小中甸藏族村寨、西双版纳热带植物园	朝阳照亮雪山、太阳从罗平油菜地升起、傣族小普哨在树下休息、在树林里行走
幻想主题2：湖水平静	云南		德钦属都湖	树枝植物叶子挂满晶莹的露珠、晨雾中的湖面有树林的倒影、雾气在湖面升腾

续表

	幻想对象	角色	场景	情节
幻想主题3：珍稀动物的王国	云南的旅游资源	红嘴鸥、滇金丝猴、孔雀	昆明翠湖公园、森林	一只红嘴鸥在树上张望、一群红嘴鸥飞过湖面上空、孔雀开屏、滇金丝猴在挠痒
幻想主题4：壮观的高原瀑布	云南的旅游资源	布依族女性	罗平九龙瀑布	两个布依族女性手指九龙十瀑

幻想类型2：民族风情园

	幻想对象	角色	场景	情节
幻想主题1：神奇的少数民族	云南人	女子腰鼓队、女子花腰彝舞龙队、彝族村民	香格里拉安龙堡、红河石屏、文山普者黑、楚雄咪依噜风情谷、文山西畴、楚雄双柏、东川、楚雄州	身着彝族服饰的女子腰鼓队在红土地上练习、女子舞龙队在演出、脸上画满油彩的全裸男子在跳舞
幻想主题2：欢乐的少数民族	云南人	壮族男子、傈僳族村民、佤族小伙子、藏族村民	文山广南、迪庆维西、普洱、香格里拉独克宗古城	壮族男子在跳铜鼓手巾舞、傈僳族村民正在欢跳阿尺木瓜、一个佤族小伙子在即兴打木鼓、藏民们正在跳锅庄
幻想主题3：奔放的少数民族	云南人	傣族村民、哈尼族村民	西双版纳橄榄坝、红河绿春	傣族村民在泼水狂欢、哈尼族长街宴刚刚开始

2. 幻想类型：人间净土世外桃源

	幻想对象	角色	场景	情节
幻想主题1：保持传统习俗	云南人	渔民、马帮、基诺族妇女、手工艺人、牧民	文山普者黑、怒江丙中洛、石屏异龙湖、元阳、大理洱海、西双版纳、腾冲、怒江、德宏、迪庆、丽江拉市海	普者黑渔夫开始出船、丙中洛的马帮上路、石屏异龙湖的渔民划船出海、元阳梯田人们忙着耕种、洱海开海节、百舸争渔、基诺族妇女开始织布、腾冲手工艺人正在制作传统油纸伞、腾冲民间艺人正在排练皮影戏、一对傈僳族母子正在过溜索、傣族妇女赶摆归来、依拉草原牧民赶牦牛回家、渔民正扛着鱼鹰回家
幻想主题2：喜悦收获	云南人	壮族群众、彝族年轻夫妇、摩梭家庭	文山普者黑、泸西城子村、丽江泸沽湖	壮族群众忙着收割、一对年轻夫妇正在收玉米、摩梭家庭忙着收获
幻想主题3：生活闲适	云南人旅游者	一对中国情侣、摩梭老人、摄影爱好者、一对老外情侣、一对身穿婚纱的情侣、一群佤族女孩、一对少数民族情侣	丽江、东川、腾冲和顺、会泽大海草山、丽江拉市海、沧源翁丁村、石林	丽江的柔软时光拉开序幕、东川红土地摄影爱好者正在拍照、腾冲和顺一对老外正在喝下午茶、会泽大海草山羊群在回家的路上、丽江拉市海一对情侣定了终身、沧源翁丁村佤族女孩们休息聊天、石林一对情侣在跳阿细跳月

（三）对东南亚留学生访谈资料的幻想主题分析

1. 以"云南的旅游（资源）"为幻想对象

幻想对象	幻想主题1	幻想主题2	幻想主题3	幻想主题4	幻想主题5	幻想主题6
云南的旅游（资源）	旅游的地方很多	风景很漂亮	西双版纳和泰国很像	大理和丽江是云南旅游的名片	旅游能够促进双方交流	能够发展对东盟国家的旅游

幻想主题1：旅游的地方很多

"看完这两个片子，我觉得云南旅游的地方很多。"（［泰国］甘美凤）

"一个词概括对昆明的印象是旅游点多。一个词概括对云南的印象是旅游点多。"（［泰国］甘美凤）

"我觉得这两个视频想要介绍云南的风景和少数民族，像广告片。但是我觉得第二个更好，因为对云南的介绍更具体，让我知道很多云南旅游的地方。"（［老挝］丽丽）

幻想主题2：风景很漂亮

"让我印象深刻的镜头是云南的风景，因为云南的风景比缅甸好。如果自己来拍一个这样的视频，我会想向缅甸的朋友介绍云南的风景。"（［缅甸］兴日）

"让我印象深刻的镜头是云南的风景（Environment）。"（［斯里兰卡］Kuma）

"让我印象深刻的镜头是云南的风景和自然风光。"（［老挝］丽丽）

"让我印象深刻的镜头是云南的风景和自然风光。"（［缅甸］哒哒）

"我觉得视频中描述的云南天气很好，自然风光很美，和我对云南的印象一致。"（［泰国］薇心）

幻想主题3：西双版纳和泰国很像

"让我印象最深的镜头是西双版纳和泼水节，因为建筑和泰国很像，泰国也要过泼水节"。（［泰国］薇心）

"让我印象最深的镜头是西双版纳的泼水节，因为泰国也要过泼水节。"（［泰国］王霖）

"云南的傣味和泰国的食品很像。"（［泰国］李娟）

幻想主题4：大理和丽江是云南旅游的名片

"让我印象最深的镜头是大理的古城，和白族人的生活。因为我很想去大理旅游。"（［泰国］李娟）

"让我印象最深的镜头是大理,还有大理的三塔,因为我很喜欢大理,想去大理旅游。"([泰国]甘美凤)

"如果自己来拍一个这样的视频,我会想拍云南的少数民族,还有旅游的地方,特别是大理。"([泰国]单玉婷)

"让我印象深刻的镜头是云南的大理和丽江,因为在过去两年,我和我的先生来云南旅游,大理和丽江都去过。如果自己来拍一个这样的视频,我会想向越南的朋友介绍昆明、大理和丽江。"([越南]阮恒燕)

幻想主题5:旅游能够促进双方交流

"我觉得云南大力发展旅游对泰国有影响,因为泰国人会到中国来,了解中国的生活是怎样的,可能会改变很多以前对中国的看法。"([泰国]李娟)

"我觉得云南大力发展旅游能够促进中国与泰国之间的文化交流。"([泰国]单玉婷)

"如果云南大力发展旅游,能让缅甸人更好地了解中国文化,了解中国旅游的地方很多。"([缅甸]哒哒)

幻想主题6:能够发展对东盟国家的旅游

"因为越南很多地方,比如老街省和云南相邻,所以如果云南大力发展旅游,那么想来云南旅游的越南人会很多。"([越南]阮恒燕)

"如果云南大力发展旅游,缅甸想来云南旅游的人会很多。"([缅甸]兴日)

"如果云南大力发展旅游,会对老挝有影响,因为想来云南旅游的老挝人会增多。"([老挝]丽丽)

"如果云南大力发展旅游,会对我们国家有影响,因为想来云南旅游的印度人会增加。"([印度]光祐)

2. 以"云南(云南人)"为幻想对象

幻想对象	幻想主题1	幻想主题2	幻想主题3	幻想主题4
云南(云南人)	云南是个美丽的地方	气候很好	少数民族众多	当地人生活安静

幻想主题1:云南是个美丽的地方

"我觉得泰国人看完这两部片子会对云南有美好的感受,会想来云南旅游。因为云南是一个美丽的地方"。([泰国]甘美凤)

"看完这两个视频,我觉得云南风景很漂亮,天气很好,有很多少数民族,每个民族都有不同的风俗"。([越南]阮恒燕)

"我觉得这两个视频让我对云南留下了很好的印象"（Good impression）。（［斯里兰卡］Kuma）

幻想主题2：气候很好

"我觉得我们国家的人看完这两部片子会对云南有美好的感受，会想来云南旅游。但老年人会更想来云南旅游，因为天气很好。"（［缅甸］哒哒）

"我觉得视频中描述的云南天气很好，自然风光很美，和我对云南的印象一致。"（［泰国］薇心）

"我在昆明住了两年，最喜欢昆明的天气，泰国太热了。"（［泰国］薇心）

"我在昆明住了两年，最喜欢昆明的天气，还有云南的傣味，因为和泰国的食品很像。"（［泰国］李娟）

"我在昆明住了两年，最喜欢的是昆明的天气。"（［泰国］王霖）

"我在昆明住了两年，最喜欢的是昆明的天气，没有最不喜欢的。"（［泰国］甘美凤）

"我之所以选择来昆明学习，是因为这里气候很好，学习费用比较低。"（［斯里兰卡］Kuma）

幻想主题3：少数民族众多

"看完这两个视频，我觉得云南风景很漂亮，天气很好，有很多少数民族，每个民族都有不同的风俗。"（［越南］阮恒燕）

"我觉得这两个片子都做得很好。因为民族很多。"（［缅甸］兴日）

"我觉得视频中描述的云南海拔很高，有26个少数民族。同我对云南的印象一致。"（［越南］阮恒燕）

"我印象里的昆明很美，少数民族很多，文化很多。"（［越南］阮恒燕）

"视频中有关昆明的镜头，展现了一个民族文化多，风景好的城市。"（［缅甸］兴日）

幻想主题4：当地人生活安静

"让我印象最深的镜头云南的传统艺术，比如片子里面做是纸伞，还有少数民族的歌舞，我觉得当地人生活很安静，这也让我印象很深。"（［泰国］单玉婷）

"我觉得我们国家的人看完这两部片子会对云南有美好的感受，会想来云南旅游。但是老年人更想来，因为他们喜欢安静。"（［老挝］丽丽）

3. 以"昆明（昆明人）"为幻想对象

幻想对象	幻想主题1	幻想主题2	幻想主题3
昆明（昆明人）	春城	昆明发展很快	好玩

幻想主题1：春城

"一个词概括对昆明的印象是'春城'。"（［泰国］薇心）

"一个词对昆明的印象是天气很好。"（［泰国］李娟）

"我觉得昆明天气很好，想留下来生活。"（［泰国］甘美凤）

"视频中的昆明天气很好，吃的也非常好，这个与我印象中的昆明一致，我觉得昆明是座非常好的城市。"（［泰国］单玉婷）

"视频中展现的昆明与我印象中的一致，我印象里的昆明很美，少数民族很多，文化很多。"（［越南］阮恒燕）

"一个词对昆明的印象是春城。"（［缅甸］哒哒）

幻想主题2：昆明发展很快

"让我印象深刻的镜头是云南的交通，飞机、高速铁路、城市地铁。"（［印度］光祐）

"视频中的昆明是一个发展很快的城市，交通很方便，有飞机、火车、大巴车。"（［越南］阮恒燕）

"一个词概括对昆明的印象是 Fast developing area。"（［斯里兰卡］Kuma）

"一个词概括对昆明的印象是做生意的城市。"（［老挝］丽丽）

幻想主题：好玩

"我在昆明住了快一年，最喜欢的是昆明旅游的地方多。"（［缅甸］兴日）

"一个词概括对昆明的印象是旅游的地方多。"（［泰国］王霖）

"一个词或短语来概括你在昆明的学习生活：好玩。"（［泰国］薇心）

"一个词或短语来概括你在昆明的学习生活：好玩。"（［泰国］李娟）

"一个词或短语来概括你在昆明的学习生活：好玩。"（［泰国］王霖）

"一个词或短语来概括你在昆明的学习生活：好玩。"（因为有好朋友住在一起，跟老师关系融洽）。"（［泰国］甘美凤）

4. 以"宣传视频"为幻想对象

幻想对象	幻想类型：与实际有偏差				幻想主题
	幻想主题1	幻想主题2	幻想主题3	幻想主题4	
宣传视频	风景与实际有偏差	视频中的云南与现实有差距	视频中的昆明与现实有差距	对云南特色食品的介绍太少	内容丰富

幻想主题1：宣传片中的风景与实际有偏差

"我觉得这两个片子都做得很好，因为比实际漂亮。"（[越南]阮恒燕）

"我觉得看了视频中描述的云南会想来云南旅游。但是实际上不是，旅游的地方不一样（人太多），吃的也不一样。"（[泰国]李娟）

"我觉得视频中展现的云南很漂亮，但是云南实际的风景与视频中不一样，实际风景没有那么漂亮。"（[泰国]王霖）

幻想主题2：视频中的云南与现实有差距

"我觉得视频中展现的云南很好很漂亮，但与我的印象不一致。我原本以为云南地方大，人少，天气好，但实际人很多。"（[泰国]甘美凤）

幻想主题3：视频中的昆明与现实有差距

"片子中展现的昆明和我对昆明的印象不一致。片子中的昆明是一个国际化大都市，但是除了天气好，地铁方便，其他都不是这样的，更像一个大农村。"（[泰国]薇心）

"视频中的昆明很漂亮，但是和实际不一样，有差异。"（[泰国]李娟）

"视频中的昆明天气好，风景好，城市很漂亮。但这些与自己所见的不一样，尤其是卫生间不好。"（[泰国]王霖）

"视频中的昆明很大，出名的地方很多，人也不多，但实际上昆明的人很多，所以印象不一样。"（[泰国]甘美凤）

"视频中有关昆明的镜头表现了昆明交通方便，天气很好，物价便宜，视频中昆明人很热情。但是这与我印象中的昆明不一致，因为在昆明去买东西时，昆明人对老挝人的态度不好。"（[老挝]丽丽）

"视频中的昆明交通方便，天气很好。但是这与我对昆明的印象不太一致，我印象里的昆明肉类便宜，蔬菜贵，昆明人对陌生人（外国人）问路表现出不信任，公交车司机态度不好。"（[缅甸]哒哒）

幻想主题4：对云南特色食品的介绍太少

"如果自己来拍一个这样的视频，会配上英文字幕，增加对云南特色食品的

介绍，视频时间相对要短。"（［泰国］薇心）

"如果自己来拍一个这样的视频，想向泰国人展示云南的食品，我很喜欢云南的米线。"（［泰国］甘美凤）

"如果自己来拍一个这样的视频，会想向泰国人介绍一些云南旅游的地方，和好吃的东西。"（［泰国］李娟）

"如果自己来拍一个这样的视频，会想展示云南最美最好的地方，还有最好吃的东西。"（［泰国］王霖）

"如果自己来拍一个这样的视频，我会想向老挝的朋友介绍云南的风景和吃的。"（［老挝］丽丽）

"如果自己来拍一个这样的视频，我会向缅甸的朋友介绍云南旅游的地方和吃的东西。"（［缅甸］哒哒）

幻想主题：内容丰富

"我觉得这两个视频很好，它们在宣传云南，内容很丰富，但是和老挝不一样。我觉得这两个视频想要介绍云南的风景和少数民族，像广告片。"（［老挝］丽丽）

"我觉得这两个视频很好，特别是《云南的一天》音乐很好听，心里感动，展示了云南丰富的文化生活。"（［缅甸］哒哒）

"我觉得这两个视频做得都很好。因为它们展现了云南丰富多彩的文化，是个旅游的天堂。"（［印度］光祐）

5. 幻想对象五：中国—东盟关系

幻想对象	幻想主题1	幻想主题2
中国–东盟关系	好朋友	生意伙伴

幻想主题1：好朋友

"一个词或短语来概括你们国家与中国的关系：亲密。"（［泰国］薇心）

"一个词或短语来概括你们国家与中国的关系：好朋友。"（［泰国］李娟）

"一个词或短语来概括你们国家与中国的关系：好朋友，好兄弟。"（［泰国］王霖）

"一个词或短语来概括你们国家与中国的关系：好朋友。"（［泰国］甘美凤）

"一个词或短语来概括你们国家与中国的关系：好朋友。"（［泰国］单玉婷）

"一个词或短语来概括你们国家与中国的关系：好朋友。"（［越南］阮恒

燕)

"一个词或短语来概括你们国家与中国的关系:好朋友。"([缅甸]兴日)

"一个词或短语来概括你们国家与中国的关系:Good relationship from long history。"([斯里兰卡]Kuma)

"一个词或短语来概括你们国家与中国的关系:很好。"([老挝]丽丽)

幻想主题2:生意伙伴

"一个词或短语来概括你们国家与中国的关系:很好的生意伙伴。"([缅甸]哒哒)

"一个词或短语来概括你们国家与中国的关系:中国向印度输出原材料资金和技术。"([印度]光祐)

6. 小结:在滇东南亚留学生访谈资料的幻想主题

幻想对象	幻想类型	幻想主题1	幻想主题2	幻想主题3	幻想主题4	幻想主题5	幻想主题6
云南的旅游(资源)	无	旅游的地方很多	风景很漂亮	西双版纳和泰国很像	大理和丽江是云南旅游的名片	旅游能够促进双方交流	能够发展对东盟国家的旅游
云南(云南人)	无	云南是个美丽的地方	气候很好	少数民族众多	当地人生活安静		
昆明(昆明人)	无	春城	昆明发展很快	好玩			
宣传视频	与实际有偏差	风景与实际有偏差	视频中的云南与现实有差距	视频中的昆明与现实有差距	对云南特色食品的介绍太少	内容丰富	
中国-东盟关系	无	好朋友	生意伙伴				

（四）宣传视频与留学生访谈资料幻想主题的对比分析

1. 以"云南的旅游（资源）"为幻想对象

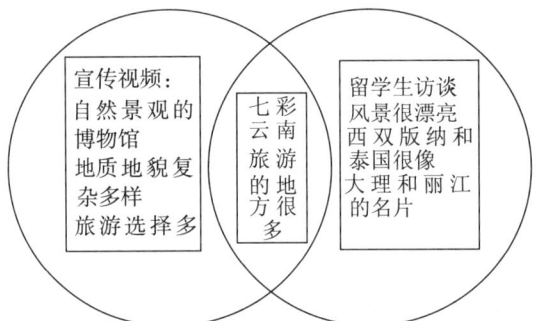

2. 以"云南（云南人）"为幻想对象

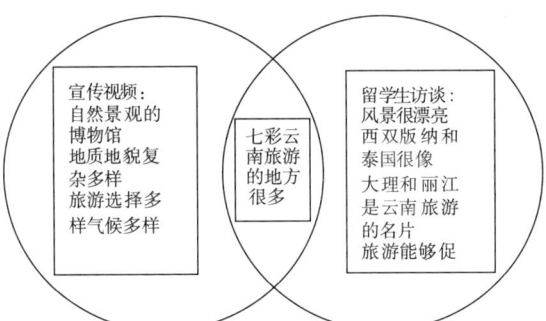

3. 以"昆明（昆明人）"为幻想对象

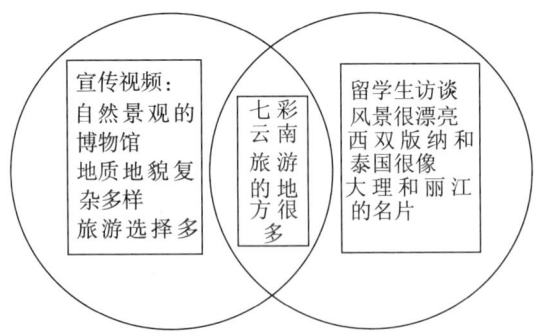

通过上述三个幻想对象的对比分析可以发现，总体上，针对每个幻想对象，宣传视频能够引爆东南亚留学生的符号共鸣是非常有限的，传播者针对云南构建的旅游图景和东南亚留学生通过观影能够形成的脑海图景，大部分时候并不

能够重合。

具体来说：

（1）以"云南的旅游（资源）"为幻想对象的情况。视频制作者立足于云南旅游的实际，从地质地貌、气候特征、特色物种、宗教文化等方面综合展现了云南丰富的旅游资源。但本质上这依然是"传播者中心"，或者是以"我想表达什么"为出发点的，因为视频中大部分的幻想主题未能引发东南亚观众的共鸣，反而是他们强调的幻想主题，比如"西双版纳和泰国很像"、"旅游能够促进双方交流"、"能够发展对东盟国家的旅游"这样一些切合观影者心理的幻想主题丝毫没在视频中得到体现。尽管这样，以"云南的旅游（资源）"为幻想对象，我们依然能够看到，传播者极力营造的"七彩云南"的语义视野确实引发了东南亚留学生的符号共鸣，虽然他们有限的中文只能表述为"旅游的地方很多"，但是这并不妨碍"七彩云南"已成功地成为云南品牌形象和对外传播符号的事实。

（2）以"云南（云南人）"为幻想对象的情况。这是宣传视频和东南亚观众的符号共鸣最多的一个幻想对象。因为"气候很好、少数民族众多"的符号共鸣得益于云南自改革开放以后持续不断的对外传播，以至于这样的符号今天几乎成为了外界认知云南的标签。

（3）以"昆明（昆明人）"为幻想对象的情况。昆明被誉为中国的"春城"，但很意外的是，宣传视频和东南亚观众的符号共鸣并不是这个早已深入人心的城市标签，宣传视频构建的语义符号"人间乐园"取代"春城"的标签，成为引发东南亚观众，特别是泰国留学生最强烈共鸣的语义符号，因为他们认为"昆明是一座很好玩的城市"。除此以外，以"昆明（昆明人）"为幻想对象，宣传视频构筑的幻想主题，比如"美食天堂"、"当地人善良热情"不仅没有引起东南亚留学生的符号分享，甚至引起了相反的传播效果，比如泰国留学生觉得宣传视频对云南及昆明的特色美食介绍太少等，关于这一点，本文的结论部分还有详细介绍，在此不做赘述。同样的，东南亚留学生对昆明的幻想主题，比如"城市发展很快"也没能在宣传视频中得到很好的体现。

综合来看，以"云南的旅游（资源）"、"云南（云南人）"和"昆明（昆明人）"为幻想对象，宣传视频的符号传达和东南亚留学生的信息接收之间确实能够有部分的重合，在上述的分析中，我们看到，这样的重合既可以来自传播方持续不断的重复传播，也可以来自受众体验和传播符号的契合。但是总体上，这样的交集非常有限，甚至有可能还会产生相反的传播效果。

三、结论与讨论

我们通常认为，与全国性的对外传播相比，区域性的对外传播具有如下三方面的优势①：

一是地理上的优势。边界地区毗邻而居，交通运输有优势，货物流通、人员往来方便快捷，各种信息汇集迅速，且可以随时验证更新。

二是有人员的优势。国界两边的人民常年生活在同一地区，交往久远且频繁，同其他地方的人相比，本区域的人民彼此双方都有更直接和深入的了解与交流，有更多交织的亲戚圈、朋友圈和生意圈。

三是文化和语言的优势。在跨国界区域，有不同的少数民族居住，在很多情况下，他们与境外的民族有相同或相近的语言、相似的文化风情和社会习俗，有着历史形成的长期的交往的文化纽带，形成一种地缘文化圈。所以，从理论上来说，这种基于地缘文化圈中的交流与沟通会更为亲近与密切。

但是本研究却认为基于地缘文化圈的优势会带来区域间跨国界人际传播的便捷，却未必能实现大众传播的无缝对接。如果传播者不能很好地洞悉信息接受者的心理，那么不仅不能做到传播，很有可能还会适得其反。

本研究以两部典型的云南旅游的对外宣传片和东南亚留学生对宣传片的解读为研究对象，借助幻想主题分析法，意欲探究宣传视频呈现了怎样的"云南"符号和东南亚留学生如何解读这样的符号。

在上文的分析中，我们分别罗列了两部云南旅游的宣传片呈现的幻想主题，以及东南亚留学生通过观看这两部宣传视频形成的幻想主题，同时确认了东南亚观众的接收和宣传视频意欲传播的意图之间确实存在明显的差距。对外传播不看对象导致传而不通，这是以往研究给出了为什么会存在上述差距的原因。本研究以东南亚留学生观看宣传视频为个案，试图从更深层次和更细致的层面去分析传播和接收之间存在差距的原因。

（一）构筑幻想主题的合法性依据存在差距

Bormann 等（1996）认为，构筑幻想主题或语义视野需要更深层次的支持性结构（a master analogue）或合法性依据，并根据其对"冷战"的语义视野分析

---

① 吴玫、杨姣：《中国区域性对外传播实践及研究的现状评析》，"全球化与区域社会发展：基于文化的视角"学术研讨会，南宁，2014年6月27—28日。

提出了三个具有普适性的合法性依据：正义性（righteous）、社会性（social）和实用性（pragmatic）。正义性强调的是做某事的正确途径；社会性强调和大多数社会成员的关系；实用性强调实用、方便和合算，或任何能够解决问题的方法。

下表显示了宣传视频构筑的幻想主题和东南亚留学生的观影后形成的幻想主题存在巨大差距的深层次原因：

合法性依据	幻想对象	语义视野	幻想类型		幻想主题	
			视频	访谈	视频	访谈
社会性	云南的旅游（资源）	七彩云南	地质地貌复杂多样自然景观的博物馆		气候多样	动植物王国、文化多元、宗教胜地
	云南（人）	无				云南是个美丽的地方、少数民族众多、当地人生活安静
	昆明（人）				春城发展很快	
实用性	云南的旅游（资源）				旅游地方很多、风景很漂亮、西双版纳和泰国很像、旅游能够促进双方交流、能够发展对东盟国家的旅游	
	云南（人）	人间天堂	民族风情园、人间净土、世外桃源			气候很好
	昆明（人）		人间乐园			好玩

上表的内容显示，无论是宣传视频还是东南亚留学生观众，都倾向于从

"社会性"和"实用性"两个方面来构筑各自的幻想主题,但是,大多数时候,宣传视频和东南亚留学生是选择不同的合法性依据来建构相同的幻想对象的。以"云南的旅游(资源)"为例,针对该幻想对象,宣传视频构建所有幻想类型和幻想主题的合法性依据是"社会性",而东南亚留学生依据的则是"实用性",这即是造成宣传视频与观众接收之间存在巨大差异的深层次原因之一。反之,以"云南(云南人)"和"昆明(昆明人)"这两个幻想对象为例,以"实用性"为依据,双方构筑的幻想主题出现了交集,而这恰恰是未来针对东南亚地区的年轻受众群可以挖掘的传播空间。

陈文(2013)对两广地区 15 所院校的抽样调查数据显示,东南亚非华裔和华裔留学生来华留学的动因都是多重的,但中国经济迅速增长所带来的个人事业的发展机会则是吸引他们的最重要因素。所以,针对东南亚的年轻受众,在传播中做利他性的价值输出才能产生预期的传播效果。

(二)宣传视频美化现实造成接受者的心理落差

舒心(2014)以成都为例,认为中国的城市形象宣传片在制作中有不真实的因素从而影响受众感知。本研究对东南亚留学生的观影访谈证实了这一点。因为,以"宣传视频"为幻想对象,东南亚留学生形成的最重要的一个幻想类型是"与现实有偏差",例如:

"我觉得看了视频中描述的云南会想来云南旅游。但是实际上不是,旅游的地方不一样(人太多),吃的也不一样。"([泰国]李娟)

"我觉得视频中展现的云南很好很漂亮,但与我的印象不一致。我原本以为云南地方大、人少、天气好,但实际人很多。"([泰国]甘美凤)

"片子中展现的昆明和我对昆明的印象不一致。片子中的昆明是一个国际化大都市,但是除了天气好、地铁方便,其他都不是这样的,更像一个大农村。"([泰国]薇心)

城市宣传片必定是以展现城市的特色和优质资源为目标,但本研究发现,如果一味美化城市而不能相对客观地直面城市发展中存在的问题,这必定会导致信息接收者的心理落差,甚至引爆相反的传播效果。

在本研究中,无论是官方还是民间的宣传视频都在极力建构的一个幻想主题是"当地人热情善良,友好好客",但正是这个幻想主题却引发了留学生的不满:

"视频中有关昆明的镜头表现了昆明交通方便、天气很好、物价便宜,视频中昆明人很热情,但是这与我印象中的昆明不一致,因为在昆明去买东西时,

昆明人对老挝人的态度不好。"（［老挝］丽丽）

"视频中的昆明交通方便，天气很好，但是这与我对昆明的印象不太一致，我印象里的昆明肉类便宜、蔬菜贵，昆明人对陌生人（外国人）问路表现出不信任，公交车司机态度不好。"（［缅甸］哒哒）

所以，在传播过程中依据传播对象的"痛点"来建构符合他们接收心理的符号图景，既展现城市美好形象的一面，又适度呈现问题，可能才是未来做区域性对外传播的趋势。

（三）东南亚留学生群体的复杂情况及其差异

信息接收者的个体差异也是造成传播差距的重要原因，特别是东南亚留学生群体之间复杂的国情差异和文化差别。

1. 对中国的总体评价及所在国与中国关系的认知

本研究中，以"中国—东盟关系"为幻想对象，东南亚留学生形成了两个幻想主题：一是"好朋友"，二是"生意伙伴"，而支持它们的合法性依据分别是"社会性"和"实用性"。除了来自印度和缅甸的留学生认为所在国与中国关系是"生意伙伴"外，其余国家的留学生都认为自己国家与中国的关系是"好朋友"。

陈文（2012）通过对两广地区 15 所院校东南亚十国的来华留学生进行调查问卷后发现，东南亚来华留学生对中国国家形象的评分高于印度，但低于美国和日本，也低于东南亚国家。总体上来自中南半岛国家的学生高于来自海岛国家学生的评分；硬实力方面，东南亚留学生对中国评价较高，且来华后高于来华前；软实力方面评分较低，且来华后低于来华前。研究者认为这与东南亚留学生来华前后了解中国的渠道、与中国人的交往程度及其所在国与中国的关系有关。

综合以上的研究结果，留学生在来华前后对中国的总体评价及其所在国与中国关系的认知是造成传播差距的一个重要原因。

2. 东南亚国家之间国情的差异

虽然早在 1961 年东南亚国家联盟（简称东盟）就已经正式宣告成立，但对于东盟成员国内的大多数普通人而言，"东盟"可能仅仅是个政治概念。东盟成员之间政治、经济和文化发展的巨大差异，可能才是个体的真实感知。比如来自老挝丽丽和来自缅甸的哒哒，提到自己的国家时会说是"小国家"，但是会说泰国是"大国"。

另一方面，云南因为自身的区位特点和自身发展的需要，必定与东南亚和南亚的多个国家之间存在亲疏远近的差别。例如，我们2012年的研究[①]发现，泰国在云南对东南亚的新闻议题设置中有显著地位。因为在中国与东南亚各民族的交往历史中，泰国对华人融入采取最为开放姿态的国家。自西人东渐，中国势力弱化以来，东南亚国家多有大规模的排华事件，但泰国鲜有这样的记录，华人社会融入当地社会的水平最高。改革开放以来，中泰两国双边往来频繁，合作的领域多样，泰国成为中国游客最喜爱的旅游地之一，也是云南人民最熟悉的东南亚国家。

所以，东南亚国家之间国情的差异也是影响在滇的东南亚留学生信息解读和符号建构的一个重要因素。

3. 留学生个体情况的差异

肖耀科（2012）、周琬馨（2012）和唐志敏（2015）分别针对广西和云南的东南亚留学生，通过问卷调查的方式研究上述留学生的文化适应问题。他们相似的研究结论指出，东南亚留学生在日常生活、人际交往和学业等方面都在一定的跨文化适应的困难。

周琬馨（2012）认为社会文化生活的参与度和跨文化适应呈正相关。东南亚留学生参与中国社会文化生活的方式主要为学习汉语、旅游、参观文化展、看影视作品和读中文报纸，学术活动和学生活动的参与度较低，所以，周琬馨（2012）认为总体上东南亚留学生参与中国社会文化生活的程度比较低，这同时导致他们对来自中国的社会支持总体评价一般。

除了个体的文化适应差异，我们的研究还发现，家族关系中华裔与非华裔的区别，也是影响在滇的东南亚留学生观影后建构幻想主题的一个潜在因素。因为总体上，华裔的东南亚留学生会对中国文化秉持相对正面积极的评价。

---

① 吴玫、杨姣：《云南与东南亚媒介交流的新策略》，李红、方冬莉：《中国东盟合作：从2.0走向3.0》，广西师范大学出版社2015年版，第8章，第165—182页。

生态文明时代的文化精神

黑龙江大学文学院院长　于文秀

近年来，人与自然的生态危机引发了思想界对现代性社会模式和生态问题的关切与思考，由此生态一词成为当今时代最为关键的词语之一，并出现了"浅生态学"（Shallow Ecology）和"深生态学"（Deep Ecology）的论争，二者就坚守人类中心主义还是反人类中心主义的争执也引发整个知识界、思想界的参与，但争论至今各执己见，莫衷一是。笔者认为，这些论争的深层问题实际上关涉的是生态文明时代的文化精神的思考。当今时代，在反思和批判生态危机时，我们要做的是不能止于对某个问题的二元对立是非此即彼的结论的探究，而是要在总体上倡扬什么样的文化精神，在笔者看来，生态时代的文化精神概括地说就是，在哲学层面上，检省极端人类中心主义、倡导有机整体观；在社会生存层面上标举后物质时代的新物质观；在价值取向上坚守现代性和后现代性相兼容；在生存境界层面上在追求诗意栖居与和谐守望。

一、倡导有机自然观

在生态时代，我们所倡导的文化精神应该首先从哲学层面上批判极端人类中心主义，倡导有机整体观，在反思生态环境危机问题上，历来存在着坚守与反对人类中心主义的理论争执，这似乎是一个绕不过去的结点性问题。浅生态学家们批评深生态学家的反人类中心主义立场和道德主体的扩大化倾向，深生态学家则指责浅生态学的功利狭隘的人类利益观不可能真正解决生态危机问题。

在评价上，深生态学的一些理论观点和主张显然是更具深度和意义的。虽然它的生物绝对平等性原则和肯定一切生物内在价值论上有待确认，但它的整体主义思想确实值得肯定的。

其实不论哪一个生态学流派似乎都不否认这一点，即不是人类中心主义，而是极端人类中心主义是导致生态危机的元凶。因为这种极端人类中心主义只有浅近的功利主义价值取向，是一种将自然看成是仅有工具作用的片面性的人类中心论。极端人类中心主义自工业社会以来一直十分强劲，甚至已内化为现代性社会发展模式的深层理念。因此在改善生态环境的当今时代，首先必须从哲学层面批判极端人类中心主义立场和价值观，倡导有机整体观。

有机整体观认为，世间万事万物是联结在一起的有机整体，它们相互联系相互依赖，整个世界是一个生命整体，认为人在自然之中，人的生存与其他物种的生存状况密切相关，其他物种的存在状况关乎人类的生存质量。因此整体的性质是首要的，部分是次要的，整体和部分之间的区别是相对的，联系才是基本的。

有机整体观体现了马克思主义哲学关于生态与自然的基本精神，在马克思主义哲学看来，人与自然的关系具有统一性和一致性，人和自然从来是一个有机整体，人是自然的一部分，自然是人的无机体，是人类存和发展的前提，"人靠自然界生活"。

二、标举后物质时代的新物质观

在检省和反思生态危机时，学者有着较为一致的看法，就是生态危机其实是现代性危机的一个集中表征，而产生现代性危机和生态危机的原因之一就是以实利主义（也称经济主义）为核心的片面意义观。因此生态时代必须批判片面实利主义人生观，在社会生存层面倡导新物质观，从而实现价值理念的转向。

实利主义将物质的繁荣和财富的聚积视为社会生活的核心和世俗社会观念的荣耀，经济的迅猛发展和物质的急剧增长成为现代文明的显著标志。

经济主义对于人的基本假设或信条就是，人是经济的动物，以此来看待人类时，无限度地改善人的物质生活条件的欲望就被看成是人的内在本质性。同时按此逻辑可以由此自然推导出人的一切行为归根结底是经济行为，个人的幸福和社会的进步与经济的增长具有内在的统一性，并坚信无限丰富的物质商品可以解决所有的人类问题。同时这种价值取向已不仅内化为社会的信念，而且也内化于个人的心灵，不仅被推崇为社会的信仰，而且成为个人的理想。在现代社会中，经济动机似乎才是决定一切的力量。因此，经济主义是现代社会的人生意义论，是具有片面性特征的人生观。

对现代社会所具有的经济主义特征，生态后现代主义者给予了深刻的批判，他们指出：经济主义或实利主义信条已经成为内化于现代文明深层的意识形态，甚至是一种"现代宗教"。"这种宗教态度和对自然的疏远增长了人们不惜一切代价地去控制自然及其资源的欲望。"[1] 经济主义顺从的是人们的贪欲，而不是

---

① ［美］大卫·雷·格里芬著，王成兵译：《后现代精神》，中央编译出版社1998年版。

与自然规律相符合的可行性。它所制导下的是生产、生活方式的不可持续性后果。

为改善人类生态环境倡导新的文化精神，一个重要的工作就是标举后物质时代的新物质观，即由注重对物质财富的无限增长转变为对生态环境、生活质量、自我实现、公民自由等的关注，尤其是生态环境和生活质量是后物质时代的新物质观的最基本的诉求，它反对资源的浪费和物质的挥霍，反对经济的无止境增长，主张更节约、更自然、更和谐、更人性化的生产生活方式，以便更符合生态文明时代的新的发展模式。当然，完善的社会福利与社会保障制度是推行后物质主义价值观的关键所在。

后物质主义时代的新物质观是 20 世纪 80 年代在西方开始流行，它之所以被逐渐接受和认同，最主要的原因是现代社会发展模式带来的生态问题。当物质商品匮乏、生存难以危机已不再是首要问题时，保护环境、拥有良好的生态才是重要任务。当前应注意处理经济发展、生活改善与保护生态的关系，以实现人与自然、人与社会的和谐和可持续发展。

三、现代性与后现代性相兼容

现代性与后现代性是两个理论范畴，并且它们之间是相互拒斥的。后现代性对现代性持有异常激烈的批判与颠覆态度。虽然它们似乎水火不容，但其实现代性与后现代性并非只有简单的对立关系，相反它们具有"家族的相似性"，后现代是现代的"亲生子"（利奥塔），有的学者和流派从后现代的立场出发在批判现代性是采取完全拒斥和否定的态度是不可取的、也是不合理的。从根本上讲，现代性与后现代性各有利弊与短长，将二者优长兼容，这应该是生态文明时代所应有的价值取向与文化精神。在这一点上，生态学的马克思主义的理论主张值得肯定并富有启示意义。

生态学马克思主义者所反对的是后现代主义，它不满于后现代主义的"超越现代的情绪"，它也反对现代化的种种负面效应，但不否定现代化本身，有着修复现代性弊端的强烈愿望，有着继续追求文化经济社会领域的现代性可能性动机。著名的生态学马克思主义者高兹认为："我们当今所经历的并不是现代性的危机，我们现代所面临的是需要对现代化的前提加以现代化。当今的危机不是理性的危机，而是合理化的（日益明显的）不合理的动机的危机，……当前的危机并不意味着现代化的进程已经走到了尽头，而是我们必须走回头路。……需要对现代性本身加以现代化，需要反身性地将现代化本身纳入其自身的行为领域,即将合理化本身加以合理化。"① 生态学马克思主义在不否认现代性这个大的前提下,它所作的是检省现代性自身出现的扭曲和变异,从而给予匡正和修复。

生态学马克思主义主张人类中心主义,反对生态中心主义,正如生态学马克思主义的重要代表佩珀所指出的那样:"生态学的马克思主义就是人类中心主义和人道主义,……它反对生物道德论和自然神秘论以及由它们所导致的任何各种可能的反人道主义体制。"② 但生态马克思主义并不完全将人与自然万物截然分割,而是强调它们之间的相互依赖,生态学马克思主义强调人类精神的重要性,但也强调"这种人类精神的满足有赖于与其他自然之物的非物质性交往。虽然不能把人与其他动物同日而语,但人也是自然存在物。"需要指出的是生态马克思主义反对人类中心主义的资本主义形式,在修复现代性的创伤和弊端等方面有积极的态度,如倡导稳态经济模式方面,积极探索减小和遏制生态危机的对策等。

马克思也指出:人与自然之间应"合理地调节他们和自然之间的物质变(交)换……在最无愧于和最适合于他们的人类本性的条件下进行这种物质变换"③。

四、和谐守望与诗意栖居

人生存于地球之上,到底应该怎样对待他所栖居的大地与自然,这是生存境界的问题,说到底,生存境界与生态有着直接的决定关系,因为"无论从微观还是宏观角度看,生态系统的美丽、完整和稳定都是判断人的行为是否正确的重要因素"。在生态文明时代,诗意栖居与和谐守望无疑是人类应有的境界与追求。

对诗意栖居与对和谐的守望一直是中外大哲共同追寻的理想。中国儒家"天人合一"、"大同社会"的理想体现了中国文化的本真追求和对和谐的向往。在马克思看来,诗意与和谐是人与自然、人与社会的崇高境界。他在《1844年经济学—哲学手稿》中就认为自然界不仅仅是自然科学的对象,而且也是"作

---

① 高兹:《经济理性批判》,伦敦,1989 年,第 1 页。参见陈学明:《评生态学的马克思主义与后现代主义的对立》,《天津社会科学》2002 年第 5 期。
② 陈学明:《评生态学的马克思主义与后现代主义的对立》,《天津社会科学》2002 年第 5 期。
③ 《资本论》第 3 卷,《马恩全集》第 25 卷,第 926—927 页。

为艺术的对象",人不能仅仅将自然界作为物质资源加以占有,还应保持一种精神上的沟通,保持一种诗意与审美关系。马克思还认为社会的真正和谐的标志就在于"人与自然界之间,人与人之间的矛盾的真正解决",共产主义无疑就是异化消除、人性复归的理想的和谐社会的最高境界,"自然主义等于人道主义等于共产主义",实质是实现了人、自然与社会的和谐。

正像国际著名的环境伦理学家霍尔姆斯·罗尔斯顿所指出的:"人类的文化有助于人类在地球上的诗意的栖居,这种文化是智人这种智慧物种的文化。存在着许多各有千秋的起居方式。诗意地栖居是精神的产物,它要体现在每一个具体的环境中,它将把人类带向希望之乡。"

人类对生态的保护不仅是人的"聪明的自利",而应是生命存在应有的超越境界,只有这样才能从根本上使人与生态达到双赢。

诗意地栖居与和谐守望不仅是改善生态环境、改善人与自然的关系,也是改变人与社会、人与人之间关系的关键所在,正如马克思和恩格斯在《德意志意识形态》中指出的那样:"人们对自然界的狭隘关系制约着他们之间的狭隘关系,而他们之间狭隘的关系又制约着他们对自然界的狭隘关系。"恩格斯还提出过两大和解,即人与自然的和解及人与自身的和解,这是人类的两大变革目标。

当代中国社会更是在社会发展战略高度上,提出了建构和谐社会和发展生态文明模式的主张,生态文明时代的文化精神所包含的四个层面的意蕴,昭示着一种新的世界观和意义观。第一,它为文明的发展提供了正确的哲学思想基础,既避免了以往机械论和二元论的偏颇,有没有像绝对生态主义那样走向反人类中心主义的迷途。第二,它所倡扬的后现代社会新的物质观,使我们在发展经济的同时,能更好地兼顾与环境保护的关系,以提高生活质量,维护生态平衡,将代价降到最低点。第三,近年来现代性与后现代性之争使我们在价值取向上异常困惑,甚至无所适从。生态文明时代的文化精神所提倡的现代性与后现代性相兼容的价值观,使我们对现代性和后现代性皆有正确而客观的认识和评价,使我们不再简单地把破坏环境与现代化运动对接和等同,从而正确运用理性和技术的力量,而不简单地拒斥和敌视。第四,对诗意的追求与对和谐的守望,它的直接意义不仅在现实层面使生态环境得到保护,而且它也是人的存在的形上境界和超越性的表征,即人不仅是生物性的存在,同时更是一种精神性的存在,标示着一种精神的向度和人的存在的独特性和创造性,正是这一点充分彰显了人的价值和意义。

闽南文化在"一带一路"中的纽带与桥梁作用

福建师范大学协和学院　袁勇麟
福建师范大学海外教育学院　涂怡弘

2015年全国两会期间，习近平总书记指出："闽南文化作为两岸文化交流的重要组成部分，大有文章可做。"[①] 这是国家领导人从国家发展战略高度出发对闽南文化寄予厚望。在21世纪经济全球化和科学技术不断创新的时代背景下，闽南文化遭遇了前所未有的机遇和挑战。弘扬优秀的闽南文化，应该用新的文化自觉和文化发展理念来展示我国的文化实力。实现闽南文化的保护和现代化发展，重点在于对传统文化从根源上进行保护、传承、创新、传播、交流和建设，强调文化资源的整合利用。同时，保护与传承闽南文化，也有利于促进"一带一路"建设。

一、本体论视角下的闽南文化特性

本体论原是一个哲学范畴，所研究的是事物存在的本质。虽然学术界尚未对本体论的定义形成统一的认识，但它已经被应用于多个学科领域。在文化保护与传承领域中，本体论指的是研究文化保护与传承的根本目的及其存在的本质。目前，许多地方政府对保护与传承传统文化的认识和方式陷入了误区，认为只有赋予传统文化新的经济价值才有利于传统文化的传播。但是，这种"文化搭台，经济唱戏"的做法，并不能真正解决文化留存问题。事实上，文化保护与传承的根本性目的是确保丰富的传统文化遗产得以代代相传、发扬光大。将文化价值转化为产业经济价值是促进传统文化传承的途径之一，而绝非唯一。

从本体论视角探寻保护和传承闽南文化的途径，了解闽南文化的特性是基础。闽南文化是从越文化和楚文化以及中原文化融合的基础上生成的。所以它具有以下特性。

---

① 习近平：《两岸文化交流大有文章可做》，2015年3月4日，新华网，http://news.xinhuanet.com/politics/2015-03/04/c_1114523227.htm。

(一) 多元杂糅性

极强的文化包容性决定了闽南文化杂糅了多种不同的文化类型特点,此在宗教文化表现得最为突出。在闽南地区,不仅崇拜玄天上帝、土地公、关帝圣君等全国性的神祇,也信奉以祭祖、普度等习俗为载体的祖先崇拜,还有以妈祖、清水祖师、保生大帝为典型的地方性信仰,形成了道家、儒家信仰与民间信仰并存的文化环境。

(二) 血缘持续性

自西晋开始,北方人民携家眷南迁,以此形成以血缘为纽带的姓氏、族群、系族关系。闽南人的先祖在开发新的生活场所时,由于缺乏外界支持而不得不依靠家族或宗族的力量与恶劣的自然环境抗争,进行生产和生活空间的开拓而得以生存,无形中增强了闽南族人间的凝聚力和族群意识。闽南文化的传承也依着"传男不传女"、"传内不传外"的系族惯例得以延续至今。如今,重视家族血脉情感,认同同宗同族的文化风气不仅存在于闽台两地闽南人的心中,旅居海外的闽南华侨也始终将闽南文化惦记在心。

(三) 传播口头性

大多数的闽南文化是无形、无像、难于保存的非物质文化遗产,主要靠人们在民间生产劳动中的口耳相传得以传播。① 这其中,闽南语成为最重要语言传播载体。然而,闽南语是"有音无字"的语言,所以众多的闽南文化主要通过讲故事、俗语、童谣、戏曲、谚语等方式沿袭下来,虽然具备口语传播形象性、生动性的特点,但终究缺少稳定性和持久性。

二、建立闽南文化生态保护网络

从本体论的视角出发探讨保护闽南文化,首先要解决的是为谁保护?闽南文化,不仅维系着厦门、泉州、漳州三个地区人民的生活和情感,也是台港澳和海外闽南华人华侨共同拥有的文化,所以保护闽南文化必须开放视野,着眼于四海内外,建立一个整体性的闽南文化生态保护网络。何谓"生态"?文化生

---

① 何小海、张静容:《闽南习俗的文化意象与主要特征》,《厦门理工学院学报》2007 年第 1 期,第 68—73 页。

态学是从生态学的视角,运用相关的理论和方法研究文化的结构、功能及其演化规律,强调的是环境变迁对文化适应性的影响。"生态"二字的内涵表明了文化是活态的,是与环境共生共存的文化形态。

(一)横向整合多元闽南文化,建立生态保护区

早在2007年,作为全国第一个文化生态保护区——闽南文化生态保护区宣告成立。对闽南文化生态保护区的认识不应局限于"实验区"的浅层格局,而应该将区域内的文化遗产及其周边环境作为一个整体,综合考虑区域特殊的历史、社会、经济、自然条件,从整体上保护特色风貌和文化遗产,从全局的角度认真研究保护区的文化特色。

1. 整体性原则

整体性原则指的是文化本身的完整性和环境保护的完整性。任何文化都不是孤立存在的,而需要与其他多种文化表现形式共生,也需要与文化所依附的环境相互依存。所以闽南文化的保护需要强调文化本身与环境联系起来保护。因此,我们必须树立整体的观念,将闽南文化的保护和营造适合闽南文化传承的环境连接起来,形成一个完整的文化生态系统。要知道,倘若以厦门地区的闽南文化消亡了,势必影响泉州地区的闽南文化传承;泉州的闽南文化消失了,漳州的闽南文化也失去了共生"伙伴"。充分发挥闽南文化的整体优势,打破厦门、漳州、泉州三个子"实验区"各自为政的碎片化传播格局,实现闽南文化资源的"整合营销"。从资源的散落—整合—共享,转化为闽南文化生态保护的启动—发展—成功,应是一条必由之路。①

2. 开放性原则

有学者认为,按照国际有关"生态保护区"的建设经验,保护区一般在具有特殊性、力所能及、便于操作的地区设立,因此闽南文化生态保护区应该限于闽南三市。②但试想,如果保护区内的文化切断了与外界的联系就会成为"一潭死水",失去了鲜活的生命。正如上文所述,闽南文化具有鲜明的血缘持续性,所以闽南文化的生态保护就不应限制于福建,而应该是一个以福建本土闽南地区为核心,以大陆其他省份和台港澳地区为两翼,以东南亚、欧美地区为辐射范围的全球性闽南文化网络,融会贯通了全球多元特色的闽南文化。充分

---

① 郑镛:《论闽南文化的特质及其生态保护》,《福建师范大学学报》(哲学社会科学版)2010年第1期,第45—50页。
② 马建华:《闽南文化生态保护的"三题论"》,《闽台文化交流》2008年第1期,第6—19页。

发挥华人华侨的力量，以高屋建瓴的战略高度传承与弘扬闽南文化。广泛而优质的文化传播，让世界看到闽南文化的魅力，必然会促进福建本土的闽南文化保护。

3. 和谐性原则

诚如上文所述，闽南文化融合了楚、越文化的共性，兼具儒家与道家的精髓。但从局部上分析，不同地区的闽南文化拥有各自丰富而独特的资源类型。如同为民俗信仰，泉州渔民多信仰妈祖，而漳州地区则更崇拜开漳圣王陈元光，台湾地区则以保生大帝信仰居多；在民间技艺方面，泉州有高甲戏、惠安石雕、德化陶瓷，漳州有提线木偶、八宝印泥、漳浦剪纸……所以对闽南文化的保护，既应该从整体上抓住共性进行保护与传承，也应该针对不同地区的文化特色，打造区域文化精品。把特色的"点"和共性的"片"整合成"网"状结构，以整体、活态的方式对文化保护区内的文化形态进行有效的保护和传承，切实维护民族文化的多样性，促进文化生态保护的和谐发展。

（二）纵向联结多方传播载体，打造动态保护流

文化生态区的建设不是一座静态的博物馆，而是一个融入当地民俗、生活之中充满活力的文化空间。早在20世纪初叶，北欧国家就开始建设"活态博物馆"，其模式是以特色文化为核心建立一个集民俗风情、文化节日、表演游戏、贸易文化、民宅建筑为一体的有机空间。① 可见，"活态"的内涵即是指将文化融入生活流中加以保护。

1. 以现代节庆为契机，复兴闽南文化

传统闽南民俗文化的保存需要依赖现代新元素的包装和带动，而节庆正是同时具备动态性和活动性的文化载体。如今，许多地区均通过举办各种各样的现代节庆，以闽南传统民俗活动、宗教祭祀等仪式文化作为主体，加入音乐舞蹈、戏剧戏曲表演、文化观光等元素，融习俗、宗教、表演与艺术为一体，形成一条活的文化生态链，增加了传统民俗的视觉效果和传播价值。依靠节庆中仪式角色的扮演强化民众对文化的感知，使参与其中的民众在潜移默化中了解文化意象，获得文化的再次认同和归属。如妈祖文化节、郑成功文化节、保生慈济文化节等，均是此类节庆的典型。

2. 以传统建筑为基地，再现闽南风俗

集合闽南风俗遗产、传统的生活方式和生活习俗，将其展示、保存在原来

---

① 马建华：《闽南文化生态保护的"三题论"》，《闽台文化交流》2008年第1期，第6—19页。

所属的闽南历史遗址、历史街区和古建筑等环境和社区中,将闽南风俗以一种"动态"的形式鲜活地展示于人们面前。大家可以参与其中,产生更加直观的感受,加深人们的印象。同时,这些保存完整、自然生态良好的街道、社区、村落和院落,则可形成经典的闽南文化旅游项目,产生较高的经济附加值。游客来到这些建筑景点,不仅可参观建筑,更多的是被该地特有的民俗文化和风情所吸引,从而形成民间民俗文化保存的良性循环体系。

3. 以新型媒体为载体,创新传播路径

文化是人所创造的,也是为了人而创造的。[①] 闽南文化保护与传承的核心就是人,只有让民众自觉地参与到文化保护的行动中,才能为闽南文化的传承提供源头活水。既然如此,让现代人真正了解闽南文化、热爱闽南文化是关键。有鉴于闽南文化的传播口语化、难于保存的特点,想要真正使闽南文化代代相传,则首先需要克服传统的口头传播方法导致变味、变形和遗失的缺陷,利用现代化电子传播媒介,将闽南文化以新型的方式传播给现代人。首先可通过网络、微博、微信等新媒体载体推送图文并茂的简介和小视频,用喜闻乐见的语言和形式让受众随时可以接触到闽南文化的精髓。其次,应致力于将闽南文化相关研究成果转化为大数据库,把图书、期刊、报纸、音视频、图片等文献整理入库,成立闽南非物质文化遗产数据库、闽南人物库、闽南文史资源库、地方戏曲库、闽南族谱库等,确保闽南文化研究资料保存完善,并通过网络平台发布获得资源共享,实现传播最大化。

三、本体论视野下正确认识闽南文化生态保护

闽南文化生态保护区的建立,其根本目的是解决闽南文化在当代的保护与传承问题。所以,从本体论视角保护与传承闽南文化应该处理好几对关系。一是保护与开发的关系。随着经济全球化、工业化和城市化的推进,要有选择地进行闽南文化的保护性开发,同时注重对开发项目的跟踪与持续性研究。二是继承与创新的关系。传统文化应与当代优秀文化融合创造出新的文化。三是政府主导与发挥民众主体作用的关系。在我国进行文化生态保护区建设的过程中,政府扮演了主要角色,但如果忽视民众参与的主体性,就无法盘活闽南文化的内在机理。所以闽南文化的传承与发展要以人为本、关注民众,才能调动民众参与的积极性。四是政府主导与发挥民间社团作用的关系。文化生态的建设同

---

① 陈东海:《闽南文化生态保护区建设的几点思考》,《闽台文化交流》2010 年第 3 期,第 55—59 页。

样需要民间社团最大限度的参与，从而建立起政府和民众的桥梁。五是城市化建设与传统文化生态保护的关系。要将传统文化生态保护的内容纳入现代城市建设的总体规划中，形成良性互动，将闽南文化的重点区域建设与城市建设、文化旅游区建设紧密结合。

随着经济的不断发展，人们的生活、生产方式不断变化，中华民族传统文化赖以生存的环境和土壤也在不断发生着变化，文化的生态环境也正经历着前所未有的冲击和考验。然而这并不意味着中华民族传统文化的保存、发展与社会的现代化进程对立。树立正确的本体论思想，充分挖掘它的文化潜力，集合社会各界的力量，在保存文化精髓的基础上不断推陈出新，经由纵向的资源整合及横向的精品开发，形成"点"、"线"、"片"、"面"、"网"层层扩张、带带丰富完整的闽南文化生态全貌，才能促使闽南文化获得不断创新与传承的动力。

四、充分发挥闽南文化在"一带一路"中的纽带与桥梁作用

"一带一路"战略构想的提出，使福建在新时期遇上了新的发展机遇，尤其是以泉州为中心的闽南地区，作为海上丝绸之路的南线起点，成为"一带一路"发展和建设的要地。而思考闽南地区在"一带一路"中的作用，可以从闽台关系、闽侨关系、闽南文化产业整合传播三个层面着眼，寻找到自身发展的定位和契机，从而以闽南地区作为桥梁，辐射至整个亚洲乃至全球范围。

（一）闽南地区作为福建与台湾关系的桥梁

闽南地区与台湾在语言、风俗、信仰方面均十分相似，例如开漳圣王陈元光，目前在台湾奉祀陈圣王的威惠庙、昭惠庙等有53座，其中以宜兰、桃园、台北数量、香火为最。在东南亚各地陈圣王庙也有二三十座之多。这种共同的信仰，是联通两地的深厚文脉。以文化、信仰为连接点，促进经济的共同发展，从而寻求一体化和互利共赢，这正是"一带一路"的基本出发和目标。以建立利益和命运共同体为切入点，从而实现福建与台湾地区的整体发展与中华民族伟大复兴交融并进。

（二）闽南地区成为中国与东盟关系的纽带

福建省海外侨胞有1512万人，归侨侨眷653万人，新侨110万人，侨乡文化底蕴深厚，是面向亚太地区的主要开放窗口之一。尤其是闽南地区，有大量华侨在菲律宾、印度尼西亚、马来西亚、新加坡等东南亚、中亚、东亚国家经

商、生活。可见闽南地区与东南亚地区渊源深厚，人文关系密切、产业互补性等优势明显。在"一带一路"的战略建设中，中国与东盟的关系无疑是关键。对于侨乡文化这棵大树，中华文化是"根"，地缘文化是"源"，充分发挥地缘文化资源，培育闽南地区的侨乡优势，可获得东南亚地区的广泛认同，在促进中国东盟关系发展中产生更加积极的作用，铺就面向东盟的海上丝绸之路，打造带动腹地发展的战略支点。

（三）闽南文化产业整合传播的辐射作用

"一带一路"的项目建设重点在于加强与沿线有关地区的合作，加大资源开发和人文交流。要让闽南文化资源更加广泛、迅速地传播至各地，首先需要做的就是为静态的文化资源注入鲜活的当代因素，使文化资源与当代人的精神生活形成一种相互接纳、相互促动的互动关系。其次，在文化资源产品化的过程中，对资源的整合是一个重要环节。具体可从以下几个方面展开：

1. 坚持请进来和走出去相结合

有计划邀请"一带一路"沿线国家官方和民间人士开展各项交流。此外，福建的戏曲、宗教、语言、风俗、饮食等方面都蕴藏着丰富的地方特色，它们广泛流行于海外华侨社会。将这些文化进行传播开发，可以获得侨乡的双向交流和共享。

2. 坚持依靠华侨民间力量和深化官方合作相结合

通过海内外共同开发，实现把地缘文化优势转化为地缘经济优势，是跨世纪培育侨乡优势的根本之策。深化与海外非政府组织、智库、社会团体和外国青年交流，增设闽侨文化中心和闽侨书屋，筹建中华文化生活馆，借助这类文化实践活动起到连接桥梁的目的。

3. 坚持国内主导和海外需求相结合，打造文化精品

地缘文化精品的开发将为侨乡和海外华人社会之间的人员往来和文化交流开创新的局面，它在繁荣侨乡和海外华人文化市场的同时，必然成为两者之间世代相传的精神纽带。（1）发挥海上丝绸之路的旅游和文化资源优势，策划闽南文化旅游项目，如南少林旅游区、惠安崇武旅游区、南安郑成功文化园、安溪茶博园等，使闽南文化成为旅游主旋律。（2）借助融合闽南风格和南洋文化的集美学村风貌建筑的保护和修建，形成新的旅游景区和文化资源，使其成为具有较高的经济、历史、艺术和科学价值的华侨文化产业资源。

闽南地区虽然从地域上看只是中国偌大国土中的一个小区域，但是在台湾同胞和海外侨胞中很大一部分祖籍都是来自于福建厦漳泉三个地区，从这点上

看，将给福建带来更多地缘优势的同时，也不断把闽南文化扩散至海外。可见，闽南文化在"侨"、"台"两方的传播是密切联系的。闽南地区与台湾地区、东南亚地区的地缘、血缘关系，在"一带一路"的发展中极大地促进了福建与台湾、香港、澳门，中国与东南亚乃至与整个亚洲的文化融合，以此为跳板，从而撬动"一带一路"沿线相关地区和国家的沟通磋商，实现中华民族文化与其他优秀文化的共同发展。

敦煌与丝绸之路文明

兰州大学历史文化学院、敦煌学研究所 郑炳林

丝绸之路是东西方文明之间碰撞、交融、接纳的通道，沿着丝绸之路产生很多大大小小的文明，丝绸之路文明是这些文明的总汇。敦煌是丝绸之路上的一颗明珠，它是丝绸之路文明最高水平的体现，敦煌的出现是丝绸之路开通的结果，而丝绸之路的发展结晶又在敦煌得到了充分的体现。因此我们谈到敦煌就涉及丝绸之路的最早开通，而证明丝绸之路的存在又离不开"敦煌"这个名字在中国历史上的最早出现的问题。研究丝绸之路的专家学者都将丝绸之路的最早开启归结为张骞，但是真正能够说明丝绸之路存在的又往往早于张骞时期。早在所谓张骞丝绸之路开启之前，中国人的地理观念中就已经知道有敦煌，只不过后来人们没有给予足够的重视而已，没有将敦煌与丝绸之路联系在一起进行学术考察。先秦人们的地理观念中已经知道敦煌和罗布泊，并将罗布泊称之为"黄河之源"。丝绸之路文明起源于丝绸之路，而丝绸之路的存在可以从以下三个方面证实，它的起源要早于张骞出使西域：

第一，为考古发现证实。首先，证实和田玉石在殷墟遗址出土，经过考古鉴定这些都是羊脂玉，出产在和田；出产于西域地区的琉璃大量使用在先秦墓葬中，特别是甘肃张家川马家塬墓葬考古发现，更证实了公元前350年外来文化的影响。其次，战国虢国墓葬出土了大量玉器，这些玉器都是出产于和田的玉石。

第二，文献记载证实中原地区与西域很早就有来往。首先是《穆天子传》的记载，穆天子西行会见西王母，西王母生活的区域根据研究，认为在河西走廊或者塔里木盆地一带，这就说明当时的中西交通是畅通的；其次就是《山海经》的记载，《山海经》记载都盐泽，以及流入罗布泊的疏勒河三条河流，表明当时中原地区对西域地区的历史地理是很清楚的。

第三，河西地区在先秦时期居住的居民是国际商业民族——昭武九姓胡人，即大月氏和乌孙人，特别是九姓胡——粟特人足迹遍布丝绸之路每个角落的商业民族，他们居住河西地区，生活在渭河流域周、秦邻近，具有通商的可能。敦煌和酒泉的大月氏于这条道路运送的商品多为丝绸，故称作"丝绸之路"。因此演变出来"海上丝绸之路"，海上丝绸之路出口的商品多为瓷器，没有出土丝

绸，所以戏称"一丝不挂"。

　　就陆上丝绸之路来说，最早贩运的并不就是丝绸，而是玉石，就是中原王朝从西域地区进口大量的玉石，这可以从殷墟墓葬以及战国虢国墓证实，其出土的玉石来自于和田，为典型的和田羊脂玉。就是说丝绸之路上最早贩运的商品不是丝绸而是玉石。白银之路，是根据丝绸之路贸易使用的货币主要是白银，因此将这条道路称之为白银之路，还可以称为丝绸之路、玉石之路、绢马之路、茶之路、陶瓷之路。如果我们根据丝绸之路的功用，还可以有很多名称。

　　丝绸之路也可以称之为艺术之路，西域地区的音乐舞蹈都是通过这条道路传入中国的，隋代的九部乐、唐代的十部乐中西凉、高昌、龟兹、疏勒、康国、安国、天竺等都来自于西域地区，也都是通过这条路线进入中原地区。佛教艺术形成自己的特色后又回传到河西、敦煌及西域地区。石窟众多，佛教艺术各有特色，著名的有麦积山、北石窟、南石窟、大像山、水帘洞、炳灵寺、天梯山、马蹄寺、金塔寺、文殊山、榆林窟、莫高窟、西千佛洞。祆教艺术通过粟特人的墓葬石刻表现出来并保留下来，沿着丝绸之路和中原商业城市分布。特别是西凉乐就是龟兹乐与传入河西的中原古乐融合之后形成的一种乐舞。所以将丝绸之路称之为艺术之路，一点也不为过，更能体现出它的特色来。敦煌是佛教最早进入的地区，敦煌汉简中就记载到了寺院，敦煌文献是关于中国佛教最为详细和真实的记载，寺院的一切表现都会重构中国寺院的面貌。敦煌文献中还保存有最早的汉文景教经典、摩尼教经典，虽然敦煌文献中没有祆教经典，但是作为官府主办祆教祭祀仪式足以看出祆教的影响力。在敦煌佛教、道教、祆教、景教、摩尼教以及儒教之间的和谐共处超过相互排斥和争斗。这种局面的基础就是敦煌多民族共聚的形成。

海丝文化概念及其生成内涵
——兼论海丝文化与闽南文化之关系

中国艺术研究院文化发展战略研究中心　郑长铃　王巨川

当前,在国家倡导发展"一带一路经济带"的契机下,国内及国外丝路沿线国家与地区积极行动起来,海上丝绸之路又一次成为世界瞩目的商贸经济与文化交流之路。从历史上看,海上丝绸之路不仅仅是中国古代时期与其他国家的经济交往活动,它同时也是中国与海上丝绸之路的沿途国家之间的一种文化交流活动,并在文化交流活动过程中形成了世界上独一无二的"海丝文化"。所谓海丝文化,即是以中国文化为母体,以地域文化为核心,面向世界的多元文化形态。它是中华民族文化大家庭中的一支重要文化力量,在古代与现代的文化交流中影响着海上丝绸之路沿途各个民族国家的文化发展。历经几千年积淀的海上丝绸之路已然不仅仅是中西贸易的历史遗产,同时,围绕海上丝绸之路所形成的"海丝文化"也是贯连着丝路沿线各国的文化象征。因而,"海丝文化"同样是人类所共有的文化遗产与文化生命。由此来看,客观审视并界定"海丝文化",便成为当前研究者尤为重要而迫切的命题。

一、海上丝绸之路由来及范围

丝绸之路作为古代横贯东西方的政治、经济、文化交流的生命大动脉,为亚欧之间的联通及其发展做出了巨大的贡献。从历史时段及地域形态来看,丝绸之路又分为陆上丝绸之路与海上丝绸之路。陆上丝绸之路与海上丝绸之路在不同的历史时段有合有聚,当唐宋时期陆上丝绸之路"道路梗绝,往来不通"[1]而逐渐衰落的时候,海上丝绸之路却日益繁荣起来。

早在12世纪初,法国汉学研究学者沙畹（Edouard Chavnnes）在《西突厥史料》中即认为"丝路有海、陆两道,北道出康居,南道为通印度诸港之海

---

[1]　陆贽:《慰问四镇北庭将吏敕书》,《全唐文》卷464。

道"。① 陆上丝绸之路是指东起中国陕西渭水流域，经河西走廊、敦煌、土库曼斯坦马里、里海，东南达姆甘、马丹、巴格达等国家而最终抵达地中海东岸安塔基亚，全程达 7000 余公里的一条陆路商道。海上丝绸之路是由陆地丝绸之路衍生而来，它是指以中国为起点的古代东方通过海运的形式，与（南亚、中亚、西亚）西方各个国家进行经济贸易所形成的交通路线。

从现有的研究来看，海上丝绸之路共有四条：一是从广州经由印度、西亚、非洲、欧洲等地往返的西洋道；二是以泉州为起点，经澎湖、琉球、菲律宾至印度支那和南海各地的南洋道；三是从明州（宁波）至日本、朝鲜的东洋道；四是登州朝日道。这条海上丝绸之路与明州并行，是中国北方与朝鲜、日本经济贸易的交通要道，但因其非政治中心及战乱频发，故此并未在海上丝绸之路中占有太多地位。因此，在学界的共识中，海上丝绸之路又有"两海四道"之说，两海即南海与东海。南海丝路有广州、泉州、宁波三道；东海丝路则是以山东登州为起点的登州朝日道。

南海丝路形成于秦汉时期，发展于三国、隋朝时期，繁盛于唐宋时期。在 2 世纪初期，罗马船只便通过印度洋驶抵南海，通过缅甸及该地区的古掸国向汉朝进献"幻人"，其"自言我海西人，海西即大秦也"，因此《后汉书》中有"掸国西南通大秦"的记载。②"至桓帝延熹九年（166），大秦王安敦遣使自日南徼外献象牙、犀角、玳瑁，始乃一通焉。"③《汉书·地理志》中较为详细完整地记载了南海、印度洋航路的贸易："自日南障塞、徐闻、合浦航行可五月，有都元国；又船行可四月，有邑卢没国；又船行可二十余日，有谌离国；步行可十余日，有夫甘都卢国；自夫甘都卢国船行可二月余，有黄支国；民俗略与珠崖相类。其州广大，户口多，多异物。自武帝以来皆献见。有译长，属黄门，与应募者俱入海，市明珠、璧琉璃、奇石异物，赍黄金杂缯而往。所至，国皆禀食为耦，蛮夷贾船，转送致之，亦利交易，剽杀人，又苦逢风波溺死，不者数年来还。大珠至围二寸以下，平帝元始，王莽辅政，欲耀威德，厚遗黄支王，令遣使献生犀牛。自黄支船行可八月，到皮宗；船行可二月，到日南、象林界云。黄支之南有已程不国，汉之译使自此还矣。"据唐代史料记载，当时往来中国的外国商船名目繁多，有称为南海舶、蕃舶、波斯舶、昆仑舶、狮子国舶、

---

① 姚楠：《海上丝绸之路与中外文化交流·序》，载陈炎《海上丝绸之路与中外文化交流》，北京大学出版社 1996 年版，第 2 页。
② 《后汉书·西南夷传》。
③ 《后汉书·西域传》"大秦"条。

婆罗门舶,等等,其长度更有"二十丈,载六七百人"①的大海舶。东海丝路起始于周武王灭纣建立周朝时期(前1046),即周武王派箕子偕养蚕、缫丝、织绸技术赴朝鲜教其民众田蚕织作,其后又传到日本,由此形成中日韩贸易与文化交流的东海丝路。唐代贾耽在《登州海行入高丽、渤海道》中详细记录了东海丝路的两条航海路线:一是由鸭绿江北航转陆路至渤海王城;二是经乌牧岛、贝江口、椒岛长口镇、麻田岛、古寺岛、得物岛、唐恩浦口至朝鲜新罗王城,而后继续向东即可到达日本。②同时,在唐朝时期,新罗统一朝鲜半岛与日本"大化革新"都使得他们与中国展开了繁密的交往活动,这些活动大多是通过东海丝路的商船往来。据日本史料记载,当时的日本不断派遣使节从海商来到中国,仅公元630—894年间,日本赴中国的遣唐使团就达到19次之多,每次达五六百人,其中除了使节之外,还有大量留学生,人数众多,规模巨大,大多分乘四艘船只往返于中日之间,进行政治、贸易、文化的交流活动。

二、"海丝文化"的生成及其意义

在人类的发展过程中,任何的物质活动与文化形态从来都是密不可分、相辅相成的,物质活动产生文化形态,而文化形态又促进物质活动。丝绸之路所产生的文化影响要远远大于经济影响,随着海上丝绸之路的形成,"海丝文化"也因各条丝路经济贸易的交往而逐渐形成。

首先,丝路沿线国家的文化输入。在海上丝绸之路的贸易活动中,西方文化输入中国有两方面的途径:一方面,伴随各种诸如明珠、翠羽、香料、象牙、犀牛角等,以及各种珍奇异物的货物输入活动中,使中国人看到了丝路沿途国家的奇彩各异的文化形态;另一方面,还有许多诸如僧侣、文人等乘坐商船与商人们结伴来到东方,他们带来了西方诸如佛教文化的新鲜血液,并把西域文化注入中华文明之中。如天竺僧佛驮跋陀罗由交趾随商船至青州、建康;罽宾僧人求那跋摩随商船至广州后往宋京祇洹寺;中天竺僧求那毗地至建康正观寺,"万里归集,南海商人咸宗事之"。再有昙善、法显等僧人都是通过海上丝绸之路来到中国,他们在学习中华文化的同时也把异域的文化传播出去,从而使原生于印度等地的佛文化在中国逐渐繁荣起来。而且,鉴于当时中国社会的繁盛,许多周边的岛国以及印度、波斯等国家重视对中国的贸易交往与文化交

---

① 元应:《一切经音义》卷一。
② 参见《求恕斋丛书》,吴承志:《唐贾耽记边州入四夷道里考实》卷二。

流，都积极发展海上交通，以便于同中国加强海上联系。正如阿拔斯王朝第二任哈里发曼苏尔废弃旧都大马士革而以巴格达为新都时所说："这个地方（指巴格达）是一个优良的营地。此外，这里有底格里斯河，可以把我们和遥远的中国联系起来。"① 与此同时，中国的许多人也往返于海丝沿路各个国家进行文化的学习。例如公元671—695年间，唐代义净就通过海路往返于中印之间，并在当时的东南亚地区政治经济中心室利佛逝学习梵文，他从印度回来后著有《南海寄归内法传》一书，其中详尽记述了印度以及东南亚地区的政治、经济、文化风貌。再如杜环的《经行记》等书都成为中国人了解、学习异域文化的重要史料书籍。

其次，中华文明的海外传播。当异域文化通过海上丝绸之路来到中国，对古老的中华文明进行补充、改造的同时，有着千年历史的中华民族文化也源源不断地通过海上丝绸之路传播到海外，伴随着中国丝绸、瓷器等商品中所附加的文化形态影响并改造着异域文化的形成与发展。如公元750年曾被大食国俘虏的杜环归国后所撰写的《经行记》中一方面记载了当时中亚、西亚的情况，同时也详细记载了有关中国的先进纺织、书法等技艺与文化传入大食国的情况。早在东吴时期，孙权就特别派遣使节康泰、朱应从海路出访扶南和南海诸国，即我国历史上著名的"南宣国化"，这也是中国首次派遣使节通过海上丝绸之路加强对外的政治、经济、文化联系。康泰、朱应出使南海诸国多年，归国后写了《吴时外国传》和《扶南异物志》等书籍，详细记述了南海各个国家的政治、经济、文化等方面的情况。这些著作虽然大部分都已散失，但还有相当部分保存于《水经注》、《太平御览》和《通典》等著作中。扶南作为当时的南海大国，其势力范围已经包括了今日的泰国、缅甸和马来半岛等地区，其位置处于东西海上交通要冲。在《梁书》中记载："吴时，遣中郎康泰、宣化从事朱应使于寻国（扶南国王范寻），国人犹裸，惟妇女著贯头。泰、应谓曰：'国中实佳，但人亵露可怪耳。'寻始令国内男子著横幅，今干缦（筒裙）也。大家乃截锦为之，贫者乃用布。"②

据汪大渊的《岛夷志略》中记载，大量中国商人从海路到中亚的安南、占城等地经商后便留居当地，成为旅居丝路沿线各个国家地区的华侨。这其中有不少人都是浸染在中华文明的传统教育中成长的，因此都有着极高的汉文化素养，他们许多人将中国的文化典籍、技术知识传授给他们留居的当地人，如通

---

① ［美］希提著，马坚译：《阿拉伯通史》上卷，商务印书馆1979年版，第401页。
② 《梁书·诸夷传》"中天竺"条。

行安南的《授时历》即是最好的证明。同时，一个又一个的华侨聚集地的形成，使中国文化在这一国家扎根播种，成为中国文化对外传播的重要基点。如《续文献通考》载爪哇"其地有杜板流寓者多广东人，漳、泉人。又东行半日至厮村，中国人客此成聚落，遂名新村，约千余人，村主广东人。藩舶至此互市，金宝充溢。又南水可行半日至淡水港，乘小艇二十余里至苏鲁马益港，旁大洲，多中国人"。《岛夷志略》中也提到华人居住的南海地区很多，如麻逸（多罗岛）、渤泥（加里曼丹）、文老古（马鲁古）、吉里地闷（帝汶岛）等地，华人与当地人相处和睦，如渤泥"其俗尤敬爱唐人，醉则扶之以归歇处"，龙牙门"男女兼中国人居之"。

再次，对海洋文化的生成与促进。海上丝绸之路的文化交流与发展，不仅补充完善了丝路沿线国家的文化内涵，同时也促进了海洋文化的形成与发展。从广义上来说，海洋文化"作为人类文化的一个重要组成和体系，就是人类认识、把握、开发、利用海洋，调整人和海洋的关系，在利用海洋的社会实践中形成的精神成果和物质成果的总和。具体表现为人类对海洋的认识、观念、思想、意识、心态以及由此而产生的生活方式包括经济结构、法规制度、衣食住行习俗和语言文学艺术等形态"①。狭义而言，海洋文化"其实也是地域文化，主要指中国东南沿海一带的别具特色的文化。同时，也包括台、港、澳地区以及海外众多华人区的文化"②。在海洋文化的生成与发展中，作为衔接内外文化的港口必然成为重要的基点，而连接海上丝绸之路起点与终点的也是作为海洋文化重要基点的港口。由于港口发展的外向性，以港口为基点的海洋文化成为一种外来文化与本土文化相互冲撞、相互激发、相互融合的产物，具有文化发展上的先导性和多元性两大特点。

综上而言，我们可以清晰地看到海丝文化的形成与发展，它是在中西商贸活动中以海洋文化为基础、以贸易文化为依托而形成的多民族、多种族共同参与的人类多元文化形态的组成部分，它具有杂糅性与多元性特征。简而言之，"海丝文化"并非是单一的民族、国家文化形态，而是一种由多个民族、多个国家的文化在交流、碰撞、吸收、融合而成的一种文化共同体。正是这样一种文化共同体形态，从而使得自我民族对其有强烈的文化认同感，同时，在海丝沿线各个国家的民众精神之中对海丝也同样有着强烈的文化认同意识。

---

① 曲金良：《海洋文化概论·绪论》，青岛海洋大学出版社1999年版，第5页。
② 李天平：《海洋文化的当代思考》，《岭峤春秋·海洋文化论集》，广东人民出版社1997年版，第39页。

三、海丝文化与闽南文化

  南海丝路因涉及地域广博、贸易量巨大和文化影响深远等因素，成为中国几千年对外交往的重要通路。而在南海丝路的三条商路（广州、泉州、宁波）中，自古就有"梯航万国"之称的泉州是西洋、南洋、东洋三路的物资交汇和集散之地，故此在海上丝绸之路中最为发达，占有重要的地位，成为吞吐港口之首。仅据南宋赵汝适《诸蕃志》一书记载，宋朝时期通过泉州与海外进行贸易关系的国家和地区总计 53 个，而到了元代汪大渊的《岛夷志略》中统计就达到了 98 个之多。这就使得泉州在元代的时候便成为东方的第一大港，它的进出口贸易额达到了世界的前列，即便是当时埃及的亚历山大港也无法与它匹敌。马可·波罗在其游记中就这样说道："印度一切船舶运载香料及其他一切贵重货物咸临此港。"还说当时外国商品集中于泉州，再由"船舶装载商品后，运到蛮子省（指原南宋统治地区）各地销售"，"刺桐（泉州）是世界上最大的港口之一，大批商人云集这里，货物堆积如山，的确难以想象"。他甚至以运到泉州的胡椒和运到亚历山大港的胡椒相比较，发现后者不过为前者的百分之一。[①] 摩洛哥旅行家伊宾·巴图达也明确指出："刺桐港为世界上各大港之一，由余观之，即谓为世界上最大之港，亦不虚也。余见港中，有大船百余，小船则不可胜数也，此乃天然之良港。"[②] 有文说："海船通他国，风顺便，食息行数百里，珍珠玳瑁、犀象齿角、丹砂水银、沉檀等香，稀奇难得之宝，其至如委。巨贾大贾，摩肩接足相刃于道。"（《多暇亭记》）形象地描绘了泉州港舶辐辏、宝货如山与"市井十洲人"、"涨海声中万国商"的繁荣景象。

  从泉州在海上丝绸之路上的历史地位来看，它一方面是中国通往海外的重要起点和吸纳海外商贸的驿站，另一方面也是调和中国文化与西方文化的场域。因此，在海上丝绸之路两千余年的发展中，以泉州为代表的闽南文化在中华文化与西方文化的交织中日益彰显出独特的人文魅力和精神风貌。从这个角度来看，海丝文化与闽南文化有着相同的文化因子与根基，在文化精神中又具有强烈的兼容性，二者之间既有叠合点又有各自独特的张力所在。

  首先是有着相同的文化基因。海丝文化的根基在中国文化的土壤之中，它是以中国文化为母体。闽南文化同样如此，从东汉时期的大规模人口迁移到西

---

① 《马可·波罗行纪》第 22 章。
② 张星烺编著，朱杰勤校订：《中西交通史料汇编》第二册，中华书局 2003 年版，第 75—76 页。

晋时期中原家族的整体迁徙，闽南文化逐渐在中原文化的浸染中孕育而生。我们可以看到，闽南人历来强调自己是中原士族的后裔，其观念中一直都恪守着"慎终追远，民德归厚"。同时，闽南的语言也历来被语言学家们称为汉语"语言的活化石"。

其次是具有强烈的兼容胸怀。海丝文化与闽南文化在传统文化的土壤孕育中，又以强烈的兼容性吸纳着异域文化的给养。在广州、泉州、宁波这三条海上丝绸之路中，泉州作为当时最大的世界性贸易港口，以世界性的胸怀迎接着所有通过海上丝绸之路来到中国的各地商贾人士，与此同时，也吸纳着包括南洋文化、东南亚文化、阿拉伯文化以及西方文化的各种品质，这种海纳百川的精神极大地促进了闽南文化与海丝文化的发展，经过漫长而复杂的过程逐渐融入到中国文化的大家庭之中，为中华文化增添了新鲜的生命活力。

再次是发展的流动性与多元性共存。海丝文化与闽南文化最大的不同之处就是前者具有强烈的流动性和丰厚的多元性特征。在海上丝绸之路的广泛交流过程中，泉州作为各种文化的汇聚地，承担着吸纳与传播的功能。比如早期的伊斯兰文化便是通过泉州为始点传入中国的，据明万历年间晋江人何乔远依据回回家言（即伊斯兰教长老或阿訇口述）所著的《闽书·方域志》中写道："自郡城南折而东，遵湖岗南行为灵山。有默德那国二人葬焉，回回之祖也……唐武德中（618—626）来朝，遂传教中国。一贤传教广州，二贤传教扬州，三贤四贤传教泉州。卒葬此山。"[①] 这种流动性与多元性是构成海丝文化的张力所在，而闽南文化则基于传统文化与地域文化的约束中具有相对稳定性。

综合而言，"海丝文化"的形成及其发展，对闽南地域的政治、经济、文化都产生了重要的影响。在当下中国政府倡导的以"一带一路"建设思想带动亚洲共同体经济文化发展契机中，对"海丝文化"内涵的意义清理与价值重估，不仅是某一地域的需要，同时也是国家经济文化发展乃至整个亚洲共同发展的需要。

---

① 何乔远：《闽书》卷7《方域志·灵山》。

第三届亚洲文化论坛论文集

分论坛外方论文

在日本正仓院仓库中新发现伊朗纹饰织锦

日本奈良文化财研究所副研究员　影山悦子

众所周知，日本法隆寺和东大寺中的珍宝体现了多种伊朗文化元素和波斯萨珊王朝艺术元素，这些文化元素早在初唐时期便传入中国，并且流行于当时的长安。最新研究发现，5世纪中期到6世纪中期的白匈奴时期，萨珊王朝的文化和艺术开始传入东方，而突厥人、丝绸之路的商人们则大量地从中亚涌入中国，成就了当时伊朗文化在长安的繁荣。[1]

20世纪70年代和80年代，根据从考古学家、历史学家和文献学家研究中发现的很多新的资料和信息，人们认为有必要重新研究一下法隆寺和东大寺中珍宝的艺术历史。该研究把伊朗影响分成三类：伊朗萨珊王朝的直接影响、白匈奴时期伊朗文化在中亚地区的繁荣、突厥移民到中国产生的影响。比如，在法隆寺发现的著名织锦上绣着一个圆形连珠纹，里面是4个骑手在射猎狮子，这样的纹饰就是中国受到萨珊王朝艺术直接影响的产物，尽管一些学者指出纹饰中的一些细节不符合萨珊王朝艺术形式。1999年以来，中国发现了几处突厥墓葬，从这些墓穴中我们了解了很多6世纪后半叶突厥部落的艺术偏向。[2] 突厥石棺的浮雕上刻着头戴王冠、身着华服的突厥骑手和带翼的马，这与法隆寺中发现的织锦纹饰非常相似。所以我们可以推测这些织锦是受到进入中国的突厥族的设计影响，而非萨珊王朝的设计影响。

在本文中，我论述的重点是正仓院仓库中发现的织锦纹饰，正仓院是东大寺的主要仓库。织锦的正面是一个连珠纹圆形，中间绣着一只鸟[3]。这种纹饰的部分片段也用作旗帜底端纹饰。连珠纹是萨珊王朝织锦的著名设计形式，随后在其他地区开始盛行，包括中国。这种对称的纹饰和高水平的绣工说明这段织锦是产于中国。

---

[1] J. Il'yasov：《"白匈奴陶俑"：丝绸之路的艺术和建筑》2001年7月，第187—200页；E. Kageyama：《从中国突厥墓葬器中发现有翼王冠和三半月型王冠：它们与白匈奴占领中亚的关系》，《亚洲内陆艺术和建筑杂志》2007年2月，第11—22页。

[2] Lerner, J. A.,：《形式的同化：居住在中国的中亚人墓葬形式和墓葬器》，《中国—柏拉图论文》2005年，第168页。

[3] 正仓院仓库宝物，10, 1997, Mainichi Shimbun, No. 161.

仔细观察连珠纹圆形中的鸟，我们可以看到在鸟的腹部有一张脸和六个圆。想要了解这一纹饰的含义，织锦片段在青海的都兰和新疆吐鲁番发现过很多[①]。两种织锦片段都是以正面的一只鸟作为代表。都兰发现的织锦片段被认为是来源于拜占庭王朝，图案显示的一只鸟，腹部有一个简化的人形。所以正仓院织锦片段上肯定也是个人形，只是由于刻画得太简单，难以辨认而已。

我们在冬宫博物馆珍藏的一只银盘上发现上面有巨鸟的纹饰，一只巨鸟抓着一个裸体女人向上飞，这应该是制作于6世纪晚期或7世纪早期的波斯萨珊王朝时期。同样的纹饰在乌兹别克斯坦南部靠近铁尔梅兹的萨尔-特帕绘画中也发现过，其时间可追溯到3至4世纪时期[②]。尽管我们不能完全破译出这种纹饰的含义，但可以确定的是这个纹饰非常重要，它在萨珊王朝文化中随处可见，在萨珊王朝银器和织锦上都有。带有这种纹饰的织锦传入中国，经过长时间的演化，逐渐变成了现在这种简化的形式。正仓院的织锦纹饰可以算是萨珊王朝艺术的直接影响。

毋庸置疑的，丝绸之路在连接东西方文化上起着重要的作用。但如果把它比作跨越中亚的桥梁则是不恰当的。因为这部分伊朗文化的影响很大，直接传入中国，但或许其中的很大一部分传入中国是因为中国包容了这些文化并且让它在中亚地区繁荣昌盛。对于七八世纪时期伊朗文化传入中国和日本，可以说中亚人民或者说丝绸之路所扮演的角色是非常重要的。

[①] J. C. Y. Watt et al.（eds.），《中国：公元200—750年，黄金时代的黎明》，纽约大都会艺术博物馆，2004年，No.246；佐川美术馆（ed），《旅顺博物馆佛教艺术杰作：中国中亚丝绸之路的珍宝》，2002年。

[②] G. Azarpay：《萨珊王朝银盘上的本生经故事》，亚洲研究所，1995［1997］年9月，第99—125页；M. Compareti：《大夏绘画中所谓的依斯干达君主的短信息"》，帕提亚，2010年12月，第95—106页。

亚洲文化合作的共赢之路

韩国韩中文化艺术 FORUM 会长　柳在沂

衷心地祝贺"第三届亚洲文化论坛"在"21世纪海上丝绸之路"的起点福建省泉州市成功举办，我认为在这里举办本次会议非常有象征意义。

1. 亚洲为文化资源的宝库

亚洲的文化资源比任何一个大陆都要丰富，相信在21世纪亚洲文化时代中，会成为最为活跃的大陆。虽然在此不能一一介绍亚洲的文化资源，但毋庸置疑，世人的目光都集中在亚洲文化。就像苏格拉底出生在雅典，成为希腊和欧洲的著名人物，最后闻名于世界一样，孔子也是出身于鲁国，成为中国和东亚之名人，现在已成为世界上著名的人物。

有位老学者说过这样一句话："东亚的汉文、儒教、佛教文明与基督教文明和伊斯兰文明，是数千年间共存并发展的，因此东亚文明就是参与到文明创造的国家及民族的共同资产。"我个人非常同意这一看法。因此，我认为基于这些丰富的文化基础，这一文化宝库充分可以吸引世人的关注并受到喜爱。

目前，灿烂的文化资源与经济相融合，形成文化产业，正在充分地发挥出其价值，而且越来越多的人已经享受着文化产业带来的幸福与快乐。今后为让亚洲文化继续发展，亚洲各国要凝聚所有的力量。

2. 重新发现亚洲文化

当今亚洲各国为保存并传承本国独特的文化，也为创造出新的文化做出很多努力。最近"一带一路"构想中提到的加强文化交流这一内容，让我们重新思考过去是否对发展文化方面付出了全力。

各国国民一方面得益于经济发展，另一方面为体验更多其他地区的文化，越来越多的人正在出国旅游。去年韩国出境旅游人数为1608万余人，访韩旅游人数也多达1420万余人次。去年出境旅游的中国人多达1亿1659万人，外国访华人数也多为2629万人。这些出国旅游的人在当地体验到独特的文化之后，会重新认识到本国文化的重要性和价值。

数千年间灿烂闪烁的亚洲文化，激发出新的活力，丰富了亚洲人的生活方式。同时也与关注亚洲文化的世人分享文化时，从中获取着更多的机遇。我们要把握好这一良机，重新评价亚洲文化的真正价值，让其价值永驻世人心中，要贡献于全世界人可以享受的人类的普遍生活。

3. 一带一路和亚洲文化的世界化

国家与民族之间的交流合作是"21世纪新丝绸之路"的核心精神，相信会给亚洲文化方面的合作注入更大的活力。我们从"一带一路"的时代背景与沿线国家之间建立的共同建设原则、发展框架思路、重点合作领域和合作机构中可以看出，都是以各国共同发展作为基础。

特别是"21世纪新丝绸之路"的友好合作精神在加深文化交流、促进学术往来、扩大人才交流与合作、加强媒体合作、增进青年与女性交流、扩充志愿者服务方面具有重要意义，相信今后亚洲各国会共同举办文化年、艺术节、电影节、绘画展等多种文化艺术活动，并且共同制作电视节目、共同申报世界文化遗产等，会在各领域深化合作。

并且通过加强旅游产业的合作，为扩大旅游产业规模，进行多种特别活动。不仅如此，还可以开发带有丝绸之路特色的国际型旅游商品。这不仅能共同促进旅游产业的发展，还能扩大并加强体育交流方面的活动，从而给重大国际体育大会注入活力。希望通过这一系列的文化艺术活动与体育大会，使亚洲文化的结晶正确刻印到全世界人的脑海之中。

4. 结尾

我期待韩中两国共同推动符合国际社会根本利益的"一带一路"构想，为在亚洲文化宝库中发掘亚洲文化的新价值，使21世纪的亚洲文化传向世界，实现世界人民的幸福生活做出贡献。"一带一路"沿线国家应正确理解对方国家的文化，并以包容的态度实现真正的友谊。我认为这就是文化交流的真正意义。

"一带一路"建设和亚洲文化对话

缅甸国立文化与艺术大学副校长　吴吞翁

亚洲是地球上最大且人口最稠密的洲，主要位于东半球和北半球。尽管亚洲仅覆盖了地球总表面积的8.7%，它却占据了地球陆地面积的30%，聚集了地球大部分人口（目前大约为60%）。

亚洲的边界是从文化层面决定的，这是因为亚洲与欧洲之间没有明显的地理划分。亚洲与欧洲共同形成一个连续的大陆，称为"欧亚大陆"。亚洲覆盖面积广，在亚洲区域中，有族群、文化、环境、经济、历史关联和政府系统。亚洲比欧洲更大，文化也更多样。亚洲的历史可被视为几个周边沿海地区的独特历史：东亚、南亚、东南亚和中东，它们由中亚大草原连接。海岸周围是世界最古老文明的发源地。

全世界有835个世界遗址，其中192个位于亚洲，由亚洲国家保存。

序列号	国家名称	编号	序列号	国家名称	编号
(a)	阿富汗	2号	(t)	蒙古	3号
(b)	亚美尼亚	3号	(u)	缅甸	1号
(c)	阿塞拜疆	2号	(v)	尼泊尔	1号
(d)	巴林	2号	(w)	巴基斯坦	6号
(e)	Bigalardach	2号	(x)	菲律宾	3号
(f)	柬埔寨	2号	(y)	卡塔尔	1号
(g)	中国	34号	(z)	韩国	11号
(h)	朝鲜	2号	(aa)	新加坡	1号
(i)	Jorgiyar	2号	(bb)	叙利亚	6号
(j)	印度	25号	(cc)	塔吉克斯坦	1号
(k)	印度尼西亚	4号	(dd)	泰国	3号
(l)	以色列	9号	(ee)	Tuyake	13号
(m)	日本	15号	(ff)	土库曼斯坦	3号
(n)	约旦	4号	(gg)	阿联酋	1号

续表

序列号	国家名称	编号	序列号	国家名称	编号
(o)	哈萨克斯坦	3号	(hh)	乌兹别克斯坦	3号
(p)	吉尔吉斯斯坦	2号	(ii)	瓦努阿图	1号
(q)	老挝	2号	(jj)	委内瑞拉	2号
(r)	黎巴嫩	5号	(kk)	越南	5号
(s)	马来西亚	2号	(ll)	也门	3号

因此，可以准确地说，文化在亚洲占据重要地位。

文化是一个特殊群体的特征和知识宝库，由诸如语言、行为、宗教、美食、社会习惯和艺术等要素来定义，此种习惯和行为会伴随他们一生。它可以分为有形文化和无形文化。人类总是不断地从一个地方迁往另一个地方，与不同的邻国做交易：交换物品、技术和思想。纵观历史，欧亚大陆的位置十分重要——它连接了许多贸易和交通要道，逐步形成我们今天所说的"丝绸之路"。

海路是该网络的一个重要部分，通过海洋连接了东方和西方。这些分布广泛的网络承载着更多功能，不仅仅是商品和贵重物品的交换，同时，人口的不断移动和混合也促进了知识、思想、文化和信仰的传播，而这种传播对欧亚人民的历史和文明具有深远的影响。

游客不仅被丝绸之路上的贸易所吸引，同时也青睐这里的知识和文化交流。这就是旅游业发展的关键。旅游业在丝绸之路沿线城市逐步发展起来，使这些城市成为文化和知识的中心枢纽。科学、艺术和文学以及工艺和技术在丝绸之路沿线的群体中得以共享和传播，同样，语言、宗教和文化也发展起来，并相互影响。因此，丝绸之路的最大价值在于文化的交流。

古代海上丝绸之路是在政治和经济的背景下发展起来的，是东西方祖先共同努力的结果。作为一个有着丰富资源和相对发达的国家，中国可以在帮助丝路沿线国家发展的各个领域中发挥自身的作用。中国在2013年提出的"一带一路"思想势必将会使丝绸之路沿线国家的文化得到更大发展。

中国提倡建立"21世纪海上丝绸之路"，帮助各国了解古代丝绸之路的独特价值和概念，在当代赋予其崭新的蕴意，从而积极发展丝绸之路沿线国家的经济合作关系，在现有合作的基础上寻求进一步合作，以实现在供应链、产业链和价值链方面的积极效果和亚洲的发展。此外，丝路的建设将提高丝路沿线人民思想文化方面的交流与合作，将带来众多的效益。

现如今，世界的经济和政治中心逐步转向亚太地区，亚太地区已经步入了一个地缘政治阶段，该阶段利益相互重叠和冲突。通过促进丝路沿线国家之间的交流，海事局将帮助建立一个代表各个国家共同关切、共同利益和共同预期的共同体，为构建和平稳定的亚太地区提供指导和支持。

亚洲基础设施投资银行（AIIB）和丝路基金是"一带一路"的两大平台，中国将提供 500 亿美元的资金。大多数国家对这一倡议表示欢迎。中国已启动 400 亿美元基金作为"一带一路"建设基金供其他建筑、投资者、贸易、金融投资和文化使用。

现在，60 个国家同意"一带一路"项目，东南亚国家联盟（Asean）和南亚区域合作联盟、上海合作组织、阿拉伯国家联盟、联合国亚洲及太平洋经济和社会委员会（UNESCAP）、海湾合作委员会、国际道路运输联盟（IRU）都支持"一带一路"项目，并宣布了谅解备忘录。

此外，海上丝绸之路将进一步联通"丝绸之路经济带"、"孟中印缅经济走廊"和"中巴经济走廊"，同时联通欧洲和亚洲。这种联通将大大促进中国和其他国家的经济发展，同时限制外来风险。海上丝绸之路将在非传统安全领域进行合作，同时维护海上安全。

中国举办了多个文化交流项目，如艺术节、文学节和电影节等。上海国际艺术节、北京联欢活动、国际节日合唱团、南宁国际民歌艺术节、国际乡村音乐节、国际舞蹈节、国际马戏节、国际杂技艺术节、亚洲艺术节、新视野艺术节、非物质文化遗产国际节等；与南亚和中亚合作在斯里兰卡、老挝、巴基斯坦和尼泊尔开设了文化中心。

在这些合作中，文化扮演着重要角色。由于文化联系是一种软实力，包括各国与各国人民之间思想、信息、艺术和文化以及其他方面的交流，以增进相互了解。亚洲各国间友谊进一步增强，并在奥林匹克运动会、世界杯、商品交易会和最高级会议中进行了合作。在举办期间完成了文化艺术的表演。此外，传统美食、民族服装和传统项目也得到了展现，促进了亚洲各国的相互理解。

一些亚洲国家有相似的美食和传统节日，如缅甸的泼水节（新年）在全世界广为人知，但在泰国、老挝和柬埔寨也举行泼水节。缅甸人说"享受美食的时候想起朋友"，意思是与朋友一起分享美好的事物。相似的文化和美食使亚洲各国间更加友好，也使他们更加相互了解。此外，亚洲著名的戏剧《罗摩衍那》表达了亚洲人民间相同的道德与人生观，世界遗产和文化艺术吸引着世界各地的游客。不仅如此，指定国、酒店、学校、宗教建筑、博物馆和住宅都装饰有艺术品，如绘画、雕塑、工艺品和音乐，这些都可以在大酒店、大厦里感受到，每个不同的地方，即使是从小小的玩具身上也能感受得到。

文化联系的目的在于培养对国家的理念和制度的认识,以为经济和政治目标提供更广泛的支持。从本质上,"文化联系反映了一个国家的灵魂"。

从亚洲文化的特性看"一带一路"合作

21世纪,国家之间通过海洋加强了在市场、技术和信息方面的交流。世界现在已进入一个重视海洋合作和发展的时代。中国提议建立"海上丝绸之路"符合经济全球化背景下的更大发展,同时也符合中国与沿线国家的共同利益。其目的在于形成政治互信、经济融合、文化包容的利益共同体。因此从多极化、经济全球化、合作和竞争并存的角度来看"一带一路"就显得至关重要。

多个区域的联通和各地区的广泛合作,21世纪"海上丝绸之路"的这一任务不可能在短期实现,相反,这一任务的实现需要中国和相关国家循序渐渐并采用务实的态度。建立海上丝绸之路将需要多种形式的合作,重点关注经济合作,并考虑所有相关方。

"一带一路"项目需要15000亿美元的建设资金,中国将投资其中的17%,沿线国家也将提供支持。

项目将基于现有的合作机制和平台,需由中国和沿线其他国家的共同推动。"21世纪海上丝绸之路"将覆盖20多个国家和地区,这些国家和地区在加强交流、增进友谊、促进发展、促进本地区及其他地区的安全和稳定方面达成了广泛的共识。因此,"21世纪海上丝绸之路"将满足多个国家的需要,将合适的政策应用至各个国家。同时,丝绸之路必须改变合作模式,并巩固新的合作模式。通过联通"中巴经济走廊"、"孟中印缅经济走廊"和"丝绸之路经济带",亚洲各国将合作建立一条开放、安全和有效的海上丝绸之路,从而推动贸易、交通、经济的发展和文化的传播。

亚洲文化的发展是紧密倚靠着各国的特点而壮大的,有些功能存在差异。但是,他们非常重视保留自己的文化。各国应努力寻求亚洲文化影响的真实证据,合作中应对其给予重视并加强文化交流,应重视繁荣与稳定和文化的可持续发展,各个国家应把重点放在这些举措上。

亚洲文化合作共赢之路径

"海上丝绸之路"符合国家经济的发展和社会福利的提高。亚洲必须重视以平等、合作、互惠、双赢、包容和和谐为特征的价值、合作和发展的新视角。"海上丝绸之路"将连接太平洋和印度洋。中国将重点关注中国—东南亚国家联盟自由贸易区，将其扩展至印度洋、波斯湾、红海和亚丁湾的沿海区域。

优化合作互通有无。除了海洋经济、海洋环境保护、防灾减灾方面的合作，还需要扩大海洋文化的合作。海洋文化是建立"21世纪海上丝绸之路"的基础，该计划同时也号召各个国家增强海洋意识、实现共同理想。亚洲各国需要充分利用海上丝绸之路的地缘政治和文化，促进海洋文化、旅游和教育的交流，使丝路成为友好交流的关键纽带。同时，亚洲国家需要进行海洋文化方面的交流与合作，如文化或艺术交流、文物交流、海洋旅游合作、教育和培训。这样，亚洲国家将能扩大海上丝绸之路的文化影响，将丝路推向新世纪并推动海洋文化多样化。

亚洲区域的友好合作，推动了该地区的和平发展。丝路项目扩展了海上丝绸之路，进而推动了各个领域的改善。

21世纪，全球化的直接或不利影响是我们共同担心的问题。高速公路的修建加深了亚洲发展中国家的担忧。我们担心全球化会侵蚀我们的文化，威胁我们的地位。因此我们一直在采取更多预防措施来保护我们的文化遗产。

在保护（有形和无形）文化遗产方面的合作，使我们更加了解文化和技术的优势。世界遗产将吸引更多旅游者，而这可以繁荣"旅游业"，带动奢侈品、工艺品（绘画、雕塑和音乐）的销售以及信息的流动。因此，如果丝路沿线各国在各个领域相互合作，寻求发展机遇，这一项目可以为他们带来益处。

总　结

今天的世界和以往的世界相比有很大的不同。各个地区有不同的自然环境和不同的文化。但是。所有人都无法孤立地存在，必须与不同的国家和文化保持和谐。这使得人们了解其他不同的文化、不同的气候、不同的环境、不同的社会道德、不同的宗教、不同的思想和东西方不同的政治等。并且人们需要接受与他人和谐共存，尊重他人，以获得更好的更安宁的生活。因此，地球村的所有居民（通过守护各自的家园和家人、国家和文化）可以促进共同体的发展。所有人将在同一片蓝天下生活。但是人与人之间又不尽相同，有些有崇高的品德和较高的道德准则。一个真正有道德的人将受到其他人的尊重。

本文旨在帮助了解亚洲"海上丝绸之路"的经济合作，可以通过国家与其社会环境的互惠关系来推动世界各种文化间的相互了解。因此，可以延伸对亚洲和其他地区合作的适当理解。

当今世界，以经济和殖民主义为根源的灾难、区域战争和世界战争不断发生。有人类自己的因素，也有自然灾害的影响。我们亲眼目睹了许多灾难事件如海啸、地震、洪水、暴雨和原子弹爆炸，过度使用农药和病毒感染也给人类带来了麻烦。我们都在试图预防这些灾害的发生。

为了免受他人的挑唆，"文化"是唯一的出路。例如，人类的贪婪、愤怒和肆意仅可通过思想来控制。"清水洗污泥"，个人的任何行为只为人类造福——正确的学习方式、正确的思考方式、正确的说话方式、正确的做事方式、真正的警觉和真正的诚实。只有这样，我们才能构建我们的文化环境和一个更加和平的世界。

今天，我的演讲就到这里。我想说"让我们通过改善我们的文化环境，共同建造一个更加和平的世界"。

丝绸之路：跨文化之融合

越南国家文化艺术研究院　越南文化、体育和旅游部　阮氏玄

丝绸之路和 21 世界海上丝绸之路

丝绸之路是连接中国、中亚、拜占庭，从东方到西方最重要的一条商路。公元前 206 年到公元 220 年中国汉朝时期，当时的朝廷为了与中亚进行政治、经济和文化交流，开通了丝绸之路，并最终连通了陆路和海上丝绸之路。几百年来，许多商队和船只穿梭于欧亚之间，他们经历了不同的政治局势、经济条件、地理环境、宗教信仰、文化特征以及人与人之间关系的发展和文化的交流与融合。因此，除了经济价值外，丝绸之路还可以看作是沿途不同国家的人们的跨文化融合的象征。

经常会有来自中国商队的丝绸、物品和文物等通过中亚的中间商运往遥远的西方——大罗马帝国。事实上，除了货物交易外，商队和中间商之间还有黄金、贵金属、玉石、象牙、珊瑚、香料、茶叶、纸、纺织品、瓷器、皮草、陶瓷、香料、肉桂树皮、青铜武器等的交易。从中国到欧亚大陆，除了商品的贸易，更重要的是人们的宗教信仰、佛教戒律、各个地方的仪式和文化活动也随着贸易活动融入到了沿途当地的生活环境中。

所以说，是东西方对贸易的需求建立了这条连接欧亚各国的丝路网，成为了联系商人、传教士、僧侣和当地人民的纽带。欧亚地区的交流也涌现了很多民间故事，有关于货物的、有关于文化的，也有关于当地人民的。这些故事涵盖了不同的宗教信仰、生活方式、不同国家不同阶级人民的文化形态，反映了沿着丝绸之路，不同国家在不同时期的社会、经济和政治关系。

丝绸之路的发展让这些古代人产生了交集，最终产生了文化、宗教、技术、艺术等的交流。丝路就像是个媒介，通过它，中西方之间传递着不同的形态、风格、时尚和音乐。中亚地区是融合多种文化和信仰的大熔炉。丝路的旅行者们被这里的知识和文化交流所吸引。沿着丝路，人们交流的同时也分享和传播各自的科学、艺术、文学以及手工艺品和技术等；同样也影响了当地人民语言、宗教和文化的发展。

丝绸之路，除了作为经济遗产，对不同国家的文化融合和人们彼此交流也有着重要作用。多元文化的互动既促进了物质交换，也是不同群体和国家之间建立关系的基础。丝路丰富的文化也让许多艺术学家、人类学和民俗学家有研究印度、伊朗、叙利亚和其他丝路国家的艺术史的绝佳机会。[1]

千百年来，丝路的精神——"和平合作、开放包容、互学互鉴、互利共赢"——薪火相传，推进了人类文明的进步，是促进沿线各国繁荣发展的重要纽带，是东西方交流合作的象征。进入21世纪，在以和平、发展、合作、共赢为主题的新时代，加强亚洲、欧洲和非洲国家之间的文化交流和彼此尊重，传承和弘扬丝路精神更显重要和珍贵。

2013年，中国国家主席习近平访问中亚和东南亚诸国，先后提出"共建丝绸之路经济带和21世纪海上丝绸之路（一带一路）"的重大倡议，得到国际社会，包括越南的高度关注。共建一带一路，习主席共谈到了五点，它们分别是政策沟通、道路联通、贸易畅通、货币流通、民心相通。

我们肯定建设"一带一路"能够促进经济繁荣，加强文化交流，不同文明交流互鉴，同时还能加强不同宗教、群体和种族群体之间的彼此尊重和对话。这有助于促进世界和平与发展，不仅仅是经济的发展，同时还有文化的发展。

2015年3月由中国国家发改委、外交部和商务部经由国务院授权联合发布《推动共建丝绸之路经济带和21世纪海上丝绸之路的愿景与行动》，文章强调了作为东盟国家的邻居，利用广西壮族自治区具有的独特优势，加速了通往东盟地区的国家走廊的开放与发展。同时它很好地利用了云南省的地理优势，开创了大湄公河次区域经济发展的新趋势。

文章还指出，中国应与东盟国家合作，在现有的双边、多边、区域和次区域合作机制的框架下，共同展开联合研究、论坛、博览会、人员培训、交流和访问等，促进大陆人民和中国周边地区和东盟国家人民的文化交流。同时，中国应与"一带一路"国家合作，稳步推进合作项目，共同确定能够符合双边或多边利益的项目，并加速项目启动。

越南和21世纪海上丝绸之路

越南是"一带一路"中不可分割的一部分，是连接福建和东南亚、北亚和欧洲的重要地方。2015年4月，越南共产党中央总书记阮富仲访华期间，与中

---

[1] http://gallery.sjsu.edu/silkroad/religion.htm，UNESCO 1997。

国国家主席习近平就"一带一路"问题进行了深入探讨。首先也是最重要的，此次会面庆祝了两个亚洲邻国建交65周年，尽管道路曲折，但两国65年来在友谊和合作之路上一路前行。两国之间的互动也雄辩地证明了，只要两国坚守承诺，必定能解决分歧，维持友好关系。两国领导人再次重申了彼此对两国关系的承诺，即"好邻居、好朋友、好同志、好伙伴"。中国明确强调"一带一路"涵盖了中国南海大部分区域，旨在促进亚洲和世界的共同繁荣和发展共赢。

21世纪的海上丝绸之路，就如同古代的贸易之路，随着更多物品的贸易和知识更频繁的交流，可以使交易双方、人民和国家之间更好地相互理解，减少紧张和冲突。越南和中国都是21世纪海上丝绸之路的受益者，这同时也反映了中国想要通过多种途径让南中国海成为一个合作和平地区的渴望。通过两国的共同努力，中越友好关系定会翻开新的篇章。中国国家主席习近平和越南共产党中央总书记阮富仲表示要共建海上丝绸之路。

越南是中国海上丝绸之路的一个重要部分——多条贸易之路都始于中国福建省，途经西南和南亚地区通往欧洲。越南海防市一个配有大型集装箱船的港口设施最早将于2017年底开放使用，运往中国内地的货物可在此装卸，无需再绕道上海或香港，大大节省了运输时间。

自从两国邦交正常化以后，本着"好邻居、好朋友、好同志和好伙伴"的精神，在"睦邻友好、全面合作、长期稳定、面向未来"的方针指导下，中越两国立志推动两党和两国向前发展。

早在阮富仲访华前，越南总理阮晋勇曾于2007年4月3日在河内市接待来访的中国交通运输部部长李盛霖，那次会面双方强调了两国曾立下的承诺"睦邻友好、全面合作、长期稳定、面向未来"。早在2004年之前，越南前总理潘文凯曾提出过"两个走廊、一个经济带"的重要计划，得到了中国政府的大力支持。2006年，中国中共中央总书记和国家主席胡锦涛访问越南，并与越南签署了该项计划。政府间的核心项目是开发一个公路和高铁系统：从南宁—谅山—海防港—广宁港；从云南—老街—河内以及东京湾沿路一带。该计划的实施进一步巩固了中越两国的传统友谊关系，也是中国和东盟合作策略的关键。随着中国积极参与到与东盟在多领域的"行动计划"，包括经济、外贸、社会—文化、技术、青少年教育等领域，中国与越南的关系也获得了全面的发展。

加强文化研究合作

随着两国机构在经济、人文和社会科学领域共同合作项目的实施，两国关系也得到了进一步加强。比如近十年来，越南国家文化艺术研究院，文化、体育和旅游部和云南省社科院签署了一系列合作项目，主要针对红河谷研究，研究对象是沿河居住民族的生态和社会文化。同时，越南国家文化艺术研究院，文化、运动和旅游部和广西少数民族文化学院，广西壮族自治区文化局，中国南方研究中心，香港科技大学共同开展了一项"针对中越边境民族和地域文化连接研究的跨国合作研究计划"。这些跨境居民们长期保持着友好的关系，他们分享了他们传统民族和文化观点。跨境研究对中越两国的"两个走廊、一个经济带"总计划的实施做出了巨大贡献。

正如上面所提到的，几十年来，越南国家文化艺术研究院与云南省社科院在多领域建立发展长期友好关系，包括学术交流、共同项目研究、联合实地考察、研究参考和图书交流。到目前为止，两个机构已在红河谷共同实施了两个大型项目。

接下来我会从学术角度和对中越两国跨境居民的理解上详细说明为何红河谷合作项目是如此的重要和及时。红河是一条国际著名河流，起源于中国云南大理的文山，途经越南北部，在太平省巴叻口入海。红河流经的地方涵盖了丰富的地域、生态系统和文化特征。研究和了解更多两河流域的文明和文化价值、生态系统、当地人民的知识，不仅仅可以帮助积累这些地方的民族文学（到现在为止我们对他们的文学了解得还很少），同时这项研究还能促进两国人民相互理解。红河是沿河居民生活和农耕的主要水源，且红河提供了肥沃的土壤，这些居民包括泰族（在中国被称为"傣族"）、哈尼族、伊斯兰民族、苗族、彝族、京族和壮族……红河同时也是沿河人们的迁徙之"路"，帮助人们迁徙到土壤更肥沃、环境更好的地方生活。因此，红河沿岸的民族有着共同的文化和农业价值观，却又说着不同的语言，有属于自己风格的文化特征、居住环境和房屋。

从红河两岸的地理区域和生态系统我们可以看到，红河是当地居民和群体的经济、文化和社会发展的强大纽带。我们以前的红河谷合作项目主要关注的是自然、文化和人类的多样性，包括丰富的自然地貌、当地知识、生态和不同的传统农业系统、原住居民对于红河和水的信仰和活动。从历史中我们可以看到，红河流向和支流的改变会造成沿河居民文化、社会和经济活动的变化。我们的合作研究是为了更多地了解红河的文化基础、价值及对人民生活和河道变化的影响。共同研究项目包括在两个国家的四处实地考察，从云南大理文山红河的上游和下游直到越南太平省的入海口。研究项目对于促进红河上下游文化理解、文化传承和生态保护有着极高的价值。

在政府层面上的大型项目，包括"两个走廊、一个经济带'及其他项目等。

云南是越南和其他东盟国家的主要项目合作地，也是红河发源地，红河承载着从云南到越南的水上贸易。历史上著名的曼耗河站是连接云南与越南老街的贸易枢纽，现在已经成为历史遗迹。我们对云南民族和红河谷三角洲的人文研究对促进当地经济和商业的发展有很大帮助。

不止是对经济领域的影响，我们的文化和人文研究也是理解红河民族、生态系统和当地知识的很好的教科书。另外，分布在云南和越南的跨境民族，比如说哈尼族、瑶族、彝族、京族、泰族……红河过去是他们迁徙的主要道路。所以对这些民族的研究也让我们了解到：每当迁徙到新的土地、面临新的当地政策时，这些民族和他们的传统文化会有哪些变化。

用两个国家的法律体制管理红河流域及其不同民族的文化和社会、两国关系和经济发展的问题上，人民和社会总是起着很重要的作用。红河研究也为越南国家文化艺术研究院与其他中国机构，如广西少数民族文化学院、广西壮族自治区文化局和香港科技大学等的合作研究打开了大门。这是对跨边境沿河居住的各族非常重要的研究，并且对东京湾经济带的发展做出了贡献。

为了加强两国今后的关系，并主动参与到"一带一路"项目中去，我所在的机构邀请中国和东盟国家的合作机构共同进行这项跨国跨边境民族研究，包括泰族、傣族、壮族、哈尼族、彝族、瑶族，等等，以及湄公河沿岸的人民。这对很多学者和研究机构来说是很好的机会，通过实地考察、组织跨国会议，以及从跨国的角度进行这一区域跨边境居民和侨居移民跨文化融合的研究。跨国主义的概念主要阐述的是加强一带一路沿线居民的无国界交流。跨国主义的本质是社会、政治和经济影响对沿途人民有哪些影响。

跨国研究能够促进人员流动，以及丝绸之路上不同地区之间的思想和商品的贸易。人们对于居民、国家主义和社群主义等的概念将会发生变化，并随着新时代的发展，这一现象也会被重新审视。跨国主义从理论上来说指的是东盟各国与其他地区的新丝路合作，也就是人与人之间的交流，并因此促进了各国和平、对话、对文化多样性的尊重，同时也是跨文化融合的典范。

求同存异

孟加拉国尼姆菲娅出版社出版人　卡伦南舒·巴鲁阿

塞缪尔·亨廷顿（Samuel Huntington）在其学术著作《文明的冲突与世界秩序的重建》中假设了冷战后的世界新秩序。冷战结束前，社会被分为各种社会意识形态，比如民主主义与社会主义之间的斗争，等等。亨廷顿的主要论点是：各国之间最主要的分歧不再是意识形态、政治或经济的差异，而是"文化"的差异。新的冲突将因文化差异而产生，各种文化本身也将更加独立。换言之，宗教信仰和国家治理等方面的文化差异的新"断层"将日趋严重。

从表面来看，亨廷顿的论点可能具有说服力，但从深层角度来看，其实他只分析了问题的表面现象。人类文明史中不仅有冲突，也包含生存与生活中各个方面的合作、理解与交流。

如果我们对这一区域，尤其是丝绸之路进行细致的研究，就能看出这条路对整合意识形态、文化理念和艺术交流起到了怎样的助推作用。

据史料记载，公元前2世纪，中国汉代外交家张骞自大夏国（费尔干纳）返程途中听说了一个名叫"天竺"（今"印度"）的国家，并讲述了他开辟的一条中亚新线路，即后来的"丝绸之路"。

"丝绸之路"成为了贸易和文化传播的成功之路，它开启了亚洲大陆各地区之间的文化互通，来自中国、印度乃至地中海的商人、朝圣者、僧侣、士兵、游牧民和居民成为了东西方交流的桥梁，同时也开放了中国、印度次大陆、波斯、欧洲、非洲之角和阿拉伯半岛之间的远距离政治经济关系。开通丝绸之路的主要目的不仅是为促进经济发展，也是为加强文化交流提供一条专门且快速的主要通道，使我们能够从中获取大量的多元文化。一千七百多年来，我们也通过丝绸之路交流了思想理念、宗教信仰和各类技术。

公元前2世纪前25年，汉朝统治下的佛教僧侣们将佛教教义带到了中国。随后，中国人也开始造访南亚次大陆，最著名的有法显、玄奘和义净。他们自公元前5世纪到7世纪来到印度和古孟加拉国。这些杰出的中国朝圣者将大量珍贵的佛教历史文学和宗教文学带回中国，为加强古代中孟两国之间的文化纽带做出了杰出贡献。在8世纪到12世纪的波罗王朝，中国僧侣和朝圣者还曾在孟加拉国的Somapura Mahavihara和Vikramshila Mahavihara等寺院学习佛学。特别是玄奘，他曾在游历次大陆期间求学于著名的那烂陀大学，并由当时的孟加拉裔校长戒贤直接监管，为期 22 个月。经过一段时间成功的特训后，玄奘带着 750 卷手稿，用 20 匹马驮回了中国。回国后，他对手稿进行了翻译，由此，中国百姓第一次了解了这种特别的佛教思想及其内涵。随着这些手稿的广泛传播，中国迎来了佛教兴盛的新时代。

10 世纪至 11 世纪，最杰出圣学者阿提沙（Atisha Dipankar Srijnan）到访西藏和中国其他地区。他向西藏人民讲授了孟加拉国、古印度与中国西藏地区、中国内地和北亚各国的宗教和文化关联。他正直的为人、渊博的学识和崇高的精神境界使他成为孟加拉国和印度最智慧的杰出人物之一。他反对当时盛行的牺牲行为和深奥难解的教义，宣扬积德行善、慈悲为怀的佛教教义，劝导人们停止迷信行为。同时，他也主张更高尚的道德生活，为人要谦卑、正直、博爱、不施暴力、友善、冥思，以修达菩提心，即慈悲成佛。在中国数以千计的僧侣，不分教派，都接受了阿提沙的教义。他传达了道德生活中应正直为人、无私奉献、坚持奉行纯粹的大乘佛教教义的思想。

近 2000 年来，自古丝绸之路开启，我们一直在通过多条陆路和水路进行文化和传统方面的合作。经过几个世纪的演变，现代孟加拉文化成为多个孟加拉社会团体组成的多元文化。19 世纪和 20 世纪早期的孟加拉文化复兴时期涌现出了一批孟加拉裔作家、圣人、科学家、研究者、思想家、作曲家、画家和电影制作人，他们对孟加拉文化发展起到了至关重要的作用。孟加拉文化具有多样性，但经过几个世纪的同化，已将伊斯兰教、印度教和天主教融为一体。这种同化现象表现在各个方面，如音乐、舞蹈、戏剧、艺术工艺、民俗传说、语言文学、哲学宗教、节日庆典，以及饮食烹饪传统。

1971 年独立战争后，我们一直在不断探索新的愿景与使命，以融合文化日趋分散化的世界格局。我们相信这种文化全球化能够为我们提供更多利于文化传承的思维模式和践行办法。尊敬的习近平主席提出的"一带一路"这一变革性倡导，不仅为连通 60 多个国家、多条经济走廊再次创造了机遇，同时也为人民沟通和文化沟通铺建了不计其数的道路。这条宽广的国际沟通隧道无疑将为我们和我们的后代提供互相沟通的渠道，并以最具活力和最多样化的方式加速我们的文化交流活动进程。这样，我们将更加了解如何与他国发展积极的伙伴关系，思考问题的角度也将更加宽阔，从而丰富自己的知识和技术，以应对世界文化多元化的趋势。

比如孟加拉和中国的文化交流始于 1979 年 11 月，为便于增加两国文化交流项目，双方已于 2014 年 5 月签订了"文化交流项目"协议（CEP），以进一步发展并加强中孟两国间的文化交流和友好关系。在最新的文化交流项目协议中，两国将于2014—2017年实施多项交流项目，涵盖众多领域，如：艺术、文化和文化遗产、青年和运动、教育、印刷和电子媒体。

我相信，中孟文化交流和合作将在中孟外交关系建立40周年之际达到一个新高度。现在正是我们审视历史关系的最佳时期，同时，"一带一路"或求同存异倡议，也是这一时期审视双方关系的最佳概念平台。我相信，在这个文化全球化的时代，深入理解和合作就是实现和平与和谐的最佳方法，而亨廷顿是无法理解的。

家庭为根,社会为本
——斯里兰卡文化发展项目

斯里兰卡内政、西北省发展和文化部辅秘　伯纳德·瓦桑塔

简　介

　　斯里兰卡内政、西北省发展和文化部下属的斯里兰卡文化事务局计划从 2016 年 1 月开始执行一个关于家庭为根、社会为本的文化可持续发展的五年国家项目——"Ape Sonduru Paula"（我们幸福美满的家庭），以解决国家现有的与家庭相关的社会文化问题。这一项目旨在提高斯里兰卡所有家庭成员的道德价值观和生活技能，培养积极的态度和增长必要的知识，同时动员和协调所有资源系统来解决家庭问题，从而开启培养优秀人才和成就幸福家庭之旅，最终创造一个包容、和平和和谐的社会。

　　世界文化与发展委员会将文化定义为"生活在一起的方式"，并认为文化是可持续发展的核心要素。世界文化报告强调了在发展中考虑文化作用的重要性。具体如下：

> 文化塑造了我们看待世界的方式。因此文化可以带来态度的改变，而态度的改变可以确保和平和可持续发展，后者是实现美满生活的唯一可能方式。①

　　斯里兰卡文化和道德价值观在逐渐弱化，这已成为事实。与此同时，忽略本土社会规范、伦理价值和文化，信仰外来文化和价值也渐成趋势。这已成为国家家庭和社会问题持续增加的主要原因。同时，这也证明了发展不仅应该包括物质层面的改善，同时应包括社会文化方面的进步。家庭作为社会的基本单元，在国家社会文化发展中扮演着重要的角色。因此，巩固家庭被作为发展本项目的手段，应对道德、伦理和精神层面给予特殊的关注。

---

①　来源：《世界文化报告——前言》，联合国教科文组织出版，巴黎，1999。

家庭的现状

毋庸置疑，斯里兰卡社会在过去几十年发生了翻天覆地的变化。与此同时，人口、社会、经济和文化的发展给家庭带来了巨大的变化。

2012年，斯里兰卡的家庭户数达到518.8万，但人口为2300万。由于人口出生率下滑和生育年龄的增加，家庭人口数从1986年的5.1个到2012年的3.9个（资料来源：人口普查统计局）。结婚年龄和生育年龄发生了改变，年轻男性和女性未婚比例大幅增加，这已成为一个重要现象。

由于许多人口、社会、文化、经济和政治因素，家庭人口数减少，家庭成员似乎也比较分散。因此，父母和孩子居住在一起的核心家庭已成为社会的典型，由三代组成的传统大家庭几乎已经消失（这在过去的50年非常常见）。由于人口老龄化、迁移、男女人口比例减少、单身者和国家社会、文化和经济的其他变化，单身家庭渐成趋势。

在斯里兰卡，年龄最大的男性被指定为户主，这是一种文化常态。与此同时，家庭以女性为户主也逐渐成为稳定的趋势。2010年，以女性为户主的家庭占23%（资料来源：人口普查统计局）。离婚是家庭单元的悲剧。很多人由于抛弃、分居或离婚等原因突然解除婚姻关系，离婚率逐渐增加，这一现象在西部省份更加常见。关系性质的改变和离婚率的增加同时导致儿童普遍在单亲家庭中长大。家庭的经济和家庭内基于性别的分工多由劳动力市场提供的机会决定。

从1978年开始，开放的经济体制为女性在劳动力市场上带来了更多的工作机会。因此，今天，越来越多的女性有了自己的工作。2012年第二季度，经济活动人口或劳动力大约为830万，其中33%为女性。（资料来源：人口普查统计局）。在过去50年，国家的熟练、半熟练的和非熟练劳动力迁移率迅速增长。20世纪80年代，迁移到中东国家的劳动力大部分为女性（母亲）。每年超过10万人移居，使他们的家庭成员存在不安全感。

斯里兰卡人口的变化导致老年人人口显著增加。2012年，老年人人口达到最高纪录。更重要的是，老年人增长率不断增加，但国家人口增长率却呈下降趋势。这一趋势与个人和家庭生活模式的主要变更相关。没有进行合法登记的男女同居也逐渐成为普遍现象，尤其是在城市地区。在21世纪初，家庭的子女人数已经下降至1—2个，这与20世纪60年代的8个多孩子相比，数量显著减少。

在过去50年，随着家庭结构和组成的变更，家庭价值观也随之发生了显著的变化。传统的家庭价值观通常指道德、宗教和辨别是非的生活之道。现在，宗教活动减少，人们更倾向于寻求更物质的生活方式。

除了消费者驱动型社会的负面影响，科技、婚前性行为和怀孕、流产、离婚、亲代抚育孩子的减少、对老年人缺乏关爱以及夫妻间婚姻关系的恶化产生的生物伦理问题也导致了现代社会传统价值观的弱化趋势。女性角色的变化也影响了男性在家庭中地位。由于越来越多的女性努力追求事业，同时兼顾孩子，许多男性开始将更多精力放在家庭中。如前所述，斯里兰卡传统家庭背景由于上述原因而被破坏。

项目目标

提高斯里兰卡所有家庭成员的道德价值观和生活技能，培养积极的态度和增长必要的知识，同时动员和协调所有资源系统来解决与家庭相关的社会文化问题，从而开启培养优秀人才和成就幸福家庭之旅，最终创造一个包容、和平、和谐的社会。

1. 项目的主要目标

通过文化遗产的保存、维护和利用，为组织国家人民的文化生活奠定基础；

帮助人民确定积极的文化特质，从而促进具有斯里兰卡特质的文化的形成；

帮助人民找到导致文化衰落的内部和外部因素，同时消灭这些因素；

向社会灌输文化是充满活力的、有挑战性的、自由的力量，文化高于爱国主义的思想；

通过认知计划，在5年内提高斯里兰卡所有家庭成员的道德价值观和生活技能，培养积极的态度和增长必要的知识；

通过动员和协调资源系统提高需要特殊照顾和保护的家人的心理、社会、文化和经济地位；

建立持续的动员体系，通过授权建立民间团体和民间组织作为当地社会体系的一部分来防止和解决家庭问题，保护每个村的个人权利；

在分区的秘书处建立331个文化发展中心，以执行服务供应计划，主要用于确保为需要特殊关爱和保护的家庭提供个案管理服务，适度执行认知计划和教育计划，管理相关服务，以监督服务的可接受度、存在的问题和取得的成功。目前斯里兰卡已经建有178个文化中心，这些中心应转化为服务交付中心；

使用文化部门和其他相关部门的员工，提高技术人员在项目运行中的专业技能，以及在未来扩展项目的能力，创建在中央、省级、地区和部门级别的技术人员网络；

通过家庭发展执行行动研究，共享国家发展的最佳实践经验。

斯里兰卡传统的家庭是充满爱、友善和和谐的家庭，本项目旨在让现在的家庭回到传统家庭状态。

2. 项目的直接目标（2016—2020 年）

每年将产生 20 万对夫妇，应提高所有结婚夫妇的认知，内容关于婚后的幸福生活，以及在出现婚姻与家庭生活问题时可获得哪些服务；

每年将诞生 35 万个婴儿，应提高所有孕妇及其丈夫的认知，内容是关于他们将有一个健康的孩子，在进行婴儿护理、应对精神和心理方面给予特殊关注（社会方面）以及在出现婴儿护理方面的问题时可获得哪些帮助；

每年将成长的 35 万个孩子，应提高幼儿园、托儿所、孩子母亲的认知，内容关于孩子的权利、儿童护理、应对精神和心理方面给予特殊关注（社会方面）以及在出现儿童护理方面的问题时可获得哪些帮助；

每年将出现的 35 万个学龄前儿童，应开始建立关于社会价值观、心理—社会技能和身体发育方面的积极态度，同时给予孩子传统的健康食物；

每年将出现 40 万个 3 岁、6 岁、9 岁和 12 岁的儿童以及经常逃学的儿童，应提高儿童和青少年的认知，内容关于精神发展、生物伦理、心理—社会技能、防止物质滥用、身体发育、儿童权利、和平和和谐，以及出现问题时可获得哪些服务。此外，还要介绍斯里兰卡传统的生活艺术－简单的生活方式；

每年大约 40 万个在高等教育机构或青年乡村俱乐部的青少年可通过文化中心参加戏剧、音乐表演，观看街头剧院电影和参与讨论。应提高中学毕业生以及青少年的认知，内容关于青少年的新兴问题、心理—社会技能和身体发育、生物伦理、人权、和平和和谐，以及出现问题时可获得哪些服务；

每年大约 24 万人通过文化中心参加乡村 Samurdhi 受益人委员会、老年委员会、女性俱乐部和其他乡村组织。应提高所有家庭成员的认知，内容关于建立以家庭为单位的亲密关系、儿童&青少年护理、健康的生活方式、本土家庭价值标准和习惯、对生活的憧憬，以及出现问题时可获得哪些服务；

为需要特殊照顾和保护的贫困艺术家庭发展生计，并提供住所；

在所有分区秘书处提供基本资源，建立 331 个文化发展中心；

通过家庭发展执行行动研究，共享国家发展的最佳实践经验。

项目需要解决的特殊问题

如上所述，由于社会经济、社会和文化演变的影响，家庭单元在过去 40 年显著减少。今天，我们已经认识到大家庭的减少，同时斯里兰卡社会体系中的核心家庭在过去几十年也在显著减少。国家经济系统不断扩张，海外不断提供新的就业机会，人民尤其是女性的教育水平也在提高，城镇化和全球化推动了国家经济的发展。但与此同时，它们也对家庭结构、男性和女性的角色、家庭的态度和价值观造成了影响。

在提出关键问题后，我们得出家庭系统演变的最终结果，即家庭单位已经破裂、国家的社会系统需要保护。

与儿童相关且会对儿童造成影响的现实问题：虐待儿童、继母、家庭破裂、儿童亲代抚育减少、缺乏对商业广告进行引导、贫困孩子、压力。

与青少年相关且会对青少年造成影响的现实问题：婚前性行为和怀孕（青少年）、流产、失业/增加收入、犯罪和攻击行为、高离婚率、吸毒、犯罪自杀、非传染性疾病、执著于不可能完成的目标。

与成年人相关且会对成年人造成影响的现实问题：内部家庭问题、离婚、自杀、非传染性疾病、夫妻间婚姻关系恶化、压力。

与老年人相关且会对老年人造成影响的现实问题：孤独、被抛弃、收入不稳定、社会不安全感。

影响家庭的常见社会问题：生理和心理疾病、人口老龄化、犯罪率增加、事故增加。

科技导致的生物伦理学问题：能否获得基本服务、能否满足基本需求、增加收入。

需要特殊照顾和保护的被排斥和被边缘化的家庭：残疾人为户主或有残疾人的家庭、单亲家庭、贫困和有需要帮助的老年人的家庭、长期 & 跨代贫困的家庭、有吸毒成员的家庭、有其他危险社会心理问题的家庭。

为了让社会回到正确的轨道上，国家迫切需要采取必要的措施防止家庭单元的减少和确保家庭美满。这些许多问题由错误的态度、意识缺乏和心理社会技能而非实体资源匮乏导致。为了尽量减少这些问题，有必要实施更广泛的认知计划，使用分区综合式和参与式方法而非特殊的认知计划提高所有家庭成员的认知。类似的，提供的服务应更系统，从而让需要特殊照顾和保护的人们和家庭得到帮助。启动关于家庭发展的"Ape Sonduru Paula"（我们幸福美满的家庭）国家计划以解决这一需要。

本项目的干预方式

本项目中使用了多种独特的方法，包括参与当地社会发展的方法，以实现这些目的和目标。这包括以下几方面：

1. 合作和协作方法

国家实现培养出色的个人、幸福的家庭和和平和谐的社会的目标不可能独自完成，所以合伙和合作显得尤为重要。这一计划旨在以协作的方式，作为利益相关者与中央政府、省级政府和地方政府、国际组织、国际非政府组织机构、民间组织和私营部门组织合作。

2. 参与式方法

参与式方法用来确保双向的沟通系统，动员目标群体执行社区动员和培育计划。项目活动包括：

整修文化中心、建立新文化中心、发展文化中心基础设施、开发文化官员和其他相关人员的人力资源、展现和保存本土知识和文化价值；

在儿童、青少年、老年以及政府官员和私营部门间开展音乐、舞蹈戏剧、短篇小说、儿童故事、歌曲创作和翻译竞赛；

保存民间艺术，包括民俗音乐、民间舞蹈和乐曲；

为学生和青少年准备民俗音乐娱乐节目；

组织年度音乐节；

执行本土糖果、特殊食品种类、饮料、食品花样和烹饪方法的认知计划；

举办针对各目标群体的会议和研讨会；

使用僧伽罗语和坦米尔语印发传单、海报和小册子；

举办区域和国家级竞赛，选择美满家庭和优秀方案运营者；

使用大众媒体（国家报纸、收音机和电视频道）；

使用视听设备（CD/DVD 纪录片 & 电视剧）；

举办国家和区域级研讨会和会议。

总 结

文化可造福一个国家的人民。文化是愿景和使命的符号表达。人民的生活方式构成了一个社会的生活方式,而社会的生活方式是人们的饮食习惯、居住场所、服饰以及所有产品和创作的标记。愿景和使命传达了人们在社会中的思维方式、人们的信念、信仰和目标,艺术基于文化,同样,表演艺术也以文化为基础。包含所有这些特征的文化在与一个国家的环境保持和谐中形成,不仅仅是社会经济环境,政治环境也对文化的形成有巨大作用。反过来,一个国家的文化也有助于改善国家的政治和社会经济环境。鉴于此,文化在一个社会中的作用尤为重要,如可以促进国家的进步、改善人民的生活条件、使人民幸福和谐等。

(资料来源:《斯里兰卡文化部项目报告》,2014年;《斯里兰卡西部省社会服务部年度报告》,2013年;斯里兰卡人口普查统计局,2011—2013年)

Proceedings of the 3rd Asian Cultural Forum

Address

The Address in the Opening Ceremony of the 3rd Asia Cultural Forum

Li Shulei
Director of Propaganda Department, Fujian Provincial CCP Committee

Hon. Mr. Ding Wei, Vice Minister of Ministry of Culture,
Mr. Wang Wenzhang, President of Chinese National Academy of Arts,
Mr. PhinijJarusombat, Chairman of Thai – Chinese Culture Culture Promotion Committee,
Mr. Moyan, experts and colleagues from academic and cultural community,
Guests, ladies and gentlemen,

Good morning!

Today, guests are gathered in Quanzhou for the 3rd Asian Cultural Forum. It is fair to say that this hall is full of talents both senior and young. Entrusted by Secretary You Quan, on behalf of CPC Fujian Provincial Committee, Fujian Provincial People's Government, I would like to express my congratulations on the convening of this forum, and my sincere greetings to leaders and guests attending this forum.

Quanzhou is the host city of this forum, so I am delighted to take this opportunity to brief you on Quanzhou. In the Song and Yuan dynasties, this city attracted businessmen from all over the world. It symbolizes the openness of Chinese culture. The openness of Quanzhou is not the one forced by exterior forces, but the one that is active, conscious, and free, which reflects the inclusiveness and progressiveness of Chinese culture. Many relics related to foreign cultures are preserved in Quanzhou, which makes us surprised and full of thoughts.

Quanzhou is the hometown of Li Zhi, a great thinker. His home is preserved in the old block. The yard, house and stone inscriptions are still kept there. Li Zhi's dynamic thinking and sharp words are attributable to Quanzhou's diverse cultures and traditions. Master Hong Yi moved to Quanzhou to spend the rest of his life. I think he loved the ancient atmosphere and virtues of this city. Master Hong Yi once copied a couplet praising Quanzhou which was originally written by Zhu Xi. The couplet goes: A land of Buddhism, Saints everywhere. This couplet inspires us to make more efforts to develop Quanzhou's culture.

Fortunately, about 6 – 7 km^2 of Quanzhou's old blocks was preserved. The streets and houses are still kept in its original layout and features. People in these blocks live a happy life by doing various businesses. These blocks are the living and dynamic embodiment of traditional Chinese urban culture. In particular, during the time of morning and evening markets, if you walk in the old streets along the river, you will feel that you have entered the history. This is the result of the concept of developing old and new blocks separately, so that the old blocks have been well protected. In Jubao Street in the south of the city, we plan to carry out protecting and renovation project. Our vision is to keep the old buildings, hutongs, and people's life in their original flavor.

We also encounter a lot of difficulties and pressure in protecting old blocks. First, we should strongly curb the impulsion of interests. We should stop developers from developing real estate projects in these old blocks. Second, we should solve the problems such as insufficient maintenance and dilapidated houses caused by unclear ownership. Third, we should find approaches to handling the newly built houses in old blocks, so as to keep the ancient characteristic to the maximum extent. These are all the questions we want to consult with experts present today.

Many old factory buildings are also preserved. They bear the memory of this city, and witness China's industrial progress in modern times. They have been transformed into bases of creative industry. With an artistic atmosphere, these plants are suitable for cultural creativity. Many young makers have been attracted there for start – up. I recommend you to visit Live Show Wonderland and Yuanhe 1916 Idea Land. These two places bring enormous vitality and energy to this ancient city. The workshops and wheat barns of the old flourmill in Yuanhe 1916 are still amazing today. The grand style can be compared with shrines in ancient Rome.

The protection of cultural heritage and cultural development give unique characteristic and charm to a city. They are the source of attractiveness and value of a city. Governments at all level in Fujian and Quanzhou, as well as our people, have been increasingly aware of cultural protection. Quanzhou's cultural protection is actually an experiment we are doing. We try to revive ancient blocks by inheriting and carrying forward traditions. We have successes and achievements, but also failures and setbacks. I hope experts present can do a case study on Quanzhou's cultural protection. Selecting a distinctive city as the object of study is meaningful and interesting.

To conclude, I wish this forum a full success.

Thank you.

The Address at the 3rd Asia Cultural Forum

Phinij Jarusombat

The Former Vice-premier of Thailand

Dear friends, ladies and gentlemen:

Good morning!

I am honored to attend "the 3rd Asia Culture Forum of the 14th Asia Arts Festival" which is held in Quanzhou of Fujian province, China, on behalf of Thailand at the invitation of the Ministry of Culture of China. And here I would express my most sincere gratitude to the Chinese organizers!

The purport of this cultural forum is to build a high – level platform for the cultural exchanges between the Asian countries, by taking the opportunity of making joint efforts to build the Silk Road Economic Belt and the 21st – Century Maritime Silk Road, to promote understanding, mutual trust and friendship. Located in the Indochina Peninsula of Southeast Asia, Thailand is only more than 200 kilometers away from the land of China as the crow flies and also one of the countries along the Maritime Silk Road. Since Han Dynasty, our country has started to frequently interact with China, and the Chinese porcelain, silk and handicrafts as well as the traditional festivals and customs have exerted important influence on enriching and promoting Thai culture. At present, Thai – Sino relation is going through an all – round and deepening development and Thailand ought to actively participate in the construction of "the Belt and Road" and make a due contribution for the promotion of the peaceful development and cultural exchanges between China and Thailand and among other Asian countries.

I have served as the vice – premier of Thai government for 2 terms and as the minister for 7 terms and was in charge of economic work. Any farsighted statesman full of wisdom knows that it is the starting point and principle in the foreign relations to safeguard the national interests. However, one country cannot find the foundation for international cooperation or achieve real development to benefit its people until it integrates its national benefits into the international community. The initiative of "the Belt and Road" proposed by His Excellency the Chinese President Xi Jinping on behalf of the Chinese Government complies with the trend of peace, development, cooperation and win – win situation in our era, so it has received wide attention and support from all the countries along the line.

"The Belt and Road" cross over vast land and date back to one thousand years ago. It has been a road for trade and business since ancient times and also served as a journey of culture. Economy is closely related to culture. The economic development cannot be sustained unless it is linked with culture. I have been engaged in politics and trade & business in the past and attached less emphasis on culture. My understanding of and focus on culture began after I was appointed as the President of Thai – Sino Culture and Economy Association and President of Thai – Chinese Cultural & Friendship Council. After I held and participated in a series of Thai – Sino cultural exchanges jointly with the Ministry of Culture of China, China International Cultural Association, Chinese Embassy in Thailand and Bangkok Chinese Cultural Center, I really feel that the soft power of culture has exerted unique important function in promoting the relations between the two countries and deepening the friendship between two peoples. It is not overstated that the essence of the exchange between two countries lies in the exchange of culture and communication of the soul even if they talk about politics and do trading and business. Today, we representatives from Asian countries attending the Asia Cultural Forum are to discuss and exchange ideas on how to give play to the function of culture when we build "the Belt and Road". The cultural exchanges among Asian countries should also board on the fast train of "the Belt and Road" as taking the high speed train of China to seek new opportunities and paths for accelerated development of Asian cultural and tourist industries.

Here, I want to propose some advice for the Thai – Sino cultural exchanges:

1. Accelerate the establishment of cultural centers in China and Thailand. Thailand will set up Thai Cultural Center in Beijing as soon as possible. The Chinese Cultural Centers built in Asian countries need to expand their functions by expanding the audience and coverage through such means as the new media.

2. Establish the mechanism for sharing the historical archives, information and materials among the Asian countries. China has many orderly inherited historic relics and archives over her long history though she went through the chaos caused by war. Thailand and some neighboring countries have been affiliating with China frequently all the time in history and they learnt from each other and became integrated in fields like nationalities, religion, culture and customs, and their friendship can date back to the ancient times, but they lack in materials for study. If the Chinese side can offer help, it will further narrow the gap among

the peoples of China and the countries along the route of "the Belt and Road", especially the neighboring countries, promote the cultural identification and tamp the social and historical foundation of the interests community of "the Belt and Road".

3. The Asia Cultural Forum works well. We can list some projects for discussion separately under the big frame of the forum to help the experts and scholars of various countries study and solve the practical problems existed in some exchanges in a more pertinent and concrete manner.

4. Under the support from the government, we should further exert the function of non – governmental cultural organizations and social forces and hold more bilateral and multilateral cultural exchange activities. The brand projects of great influence such as "Happy Spring Festival" held in Thailand and "Sino – Thai Kin" advocated by Princess Chulabhorn Walailakand held by the two governments should be operated as ever before. On November 16 of this year, the friendly motorcade of Thai – Sino tourist culture with the slogan of "New Journey on the New Silk Road" will depart from Xinjiang and end in Bangkok of Thailand after travelling for 7, 500 kilometers, which will offer a new channel for publicizing the Chinese and Thai tourism and culture. In next year, Thailand and China will co – produce an entertaining TV show with the theme of giant pandas and participated by Thai and Chinese TV stars, in which the panda Lin Bin which was born in Chiengmai will also show up. This is a TV show made for people in both countries especially the young population, and it has received support from the Vice – premier, the Thai National Tourism Bureau and 3 TV stations in Thailand. Whether the motorcade or the panda and stars TV show, they are both the innovation of the traditional cultural cooperation. We hope they could be the model projects among the cultural cooperation between Thailand and China, even in "the Belt and Road" project, to start a new journey for cultural exchange.

Dear representatives participating in the Forum and friends, the construction of "the Belt and Road" in the new era has already gone under way and it is a common mission for the big family of Asian countries. The cultural exchanges can go ahead when we need to plan and prepare some projects in the cooperation of economy and technology. Let's cooperate hand by hand to expect a more brilliant and beautiful future in the development of Asian culture.

Thank you all!

Proceedings of the 3rd Asian Cultural Forum

Key-note Speech

My View on Asian Cultural Exchange

Mo Yan
Honorary Chairman of Art Creation Academy of Chinese National Academy of Arts

I In all cooperation dialogues among Asian countries or among countries of the world, political dialogues are to handle relations of countries and economic trade is to reap profits for own, while cultural exchange is to enrich the life of people of each country and even all mankind.

There are no simple political dialogues and political games which are for economic benefits. All economic trade includes cultural exchange at the same time. As silk is not only a kind of textile that can make clothes, and ceramics are not only vessels that can hold articles, all economic trades bear the cultural exchange. Many commodities themselves are carriers of culture, and boutique of art. Therefore, the Silk Road is a road of culture fundamentally, whose economic benefit is temporary, while culture significance is far - reaching.

II Traditional culture is our precious and inexhaustible treasure. The cultural exchange shall be based on their own tradition. We should show the people of other countries with our most brilliant and classic traditional culture.

III Cultural exchange is a process of mutual attraction and mutual leaning. Cultures of countries in Asia have long been well blended and inseparable.

IV The radical purpose of cultural exchange is innovation of culture. It is inheriting their countries' own valuable tradition, learning the excellent culture of other countries and creating new culture forms that can reflect the reality in today's world and meet people's spiritual needs, to make people's emotions richer and people's lives better.

Outline of Speech on Japanese Tea Culture

Genshitsu Sen

15th-generation Grand Master (Iemoto) of Urasenke, Japan

As written in Shennong's Classic of Materia Medica, "Shennong tasted a hundred herbs, met with 72 poisonous substances in a day, and detoxified them with tea." This was the first step human beings tried with tea. In around 780 A. D., Lu Yu of the Tang Dynasty, in his The Classic of Tea, provided a complete introduction to the history, origin, current situation and technologies of tea production, as well as the feats of selecting water and drinking tea. It was in this period that the custom of drinking tea spread from China to Japan. About 400 years later, in the Kamakura period, the tea – drinking culture was truly passed on around Japan.

Matcha reached its peak in the Tang and Song dynasties. In the Song Dynasty in particular, China had cultivated a complete ceremony of matcha and diancha in temples. Since the Ming Dynasty, it came into vogue to brew leaf tea in little teapots in China. To date, tea – tasting modes have been developed to cover six types of tea, which are green tea, yellow tea, white tea, oolong tea, black tea and dark green tea. The ancient methods of matcha and diancha gradually got lost.

In the end of the ninth century (the mid of the Heian period in Japan), matcha was brought to Japan by Japanese diplomats to China. Diancha was thus accepted and admired by Japanese people. In 1191, Japanese monk Yosai took tea seeds back to Japan from China, ushering in large – scale cultivation of tea in Japan. In 1259, the late period of the Song Dynasty, monk Nampo Shomyo from Japan went on a pilgrimage for Buddhist scriptures to Jingshan Temple in east China's Zhejiang. He witnessed the complete ceremony of tea banquet in the temple, and for the first time introduced the Chinese tea ceremony back to Japan. He was the earliest spreader of Chinese tea ceremony in Japan. Encyclopedic of Tea Utensils kept a record of this event, "as for the origin of tea ceremony, Nampo Shomyo returned to the country from the Song Dynasty, and brought with him tea table and tea ware to Sofuku – ji Temple."

Later, during the General Ashikaga Yoshimitsu period, there was a record of "Uji Six

Gardens", suggesting that tea cultivation began to take shape around Uji. During the Muromachi age, Chinese-style life and culture developed fast in Japan. Murata Shuko, Takeno Jōō and Rikyū appeared to push Japanese tea-drinking culture into the tea-soup culture, popularly known as "bowl-shaped compressed mass of tea leaves". This laid a solid foundation for today's Japanese tea ceremony. People of later generations summarized the tea ceremony ideas of Rikyū into harmony, respect, pureness and tranquility. And they summed up the following seven experiences in the practice of launching tea ceremonies.

Diancha should have good taste. Charcoal is added to burn water. Flowers must be the same as blooming in the wilderness. Tea must be served warm in winter and cool in summer. Keep time. Take precautions beforehand. Show solicitude for fellow diners.

In the meantime, the craftsmanship of making matcha got matured in the later Edo period. It started in mid April each year. Farmers shaded tea plants with rice straws, reeds or cold-resistance fabrics for about 30 to 40 days, till tea leaves were picked in mid May. This helped to increase the contents of chlorophyll and amino acids in tea, and reduce astringent taste. Matcha was picked for the first time in May, and by hand in traditional tea gardens. Having been plucked, tea leaves were steamed to stop fermentation, and then rapidly air-dried for dehydration and processed into rough Tencha. Tencha was refined when stored for a period in refrigerated compartment. In the end, it was ground into powder products with a stone mill.

The tea ceremony was improved as ever after Rikyu, and spread by his descendants and disciples. The complete tea ceremony is known as the tea culture, finished in about four hours. It includes many steps, such as adding charcoal, serving Kaiseki meals, intermission, offering thick tea, adding charcoal again, and enjoying thin tea. It is an integrated art of living comprising chinaware, calligraphy, architecture, flower arrangement, smelling fragrance and diet. By means of studying tea and drinking tea, we may have a glimpse of many sides of Japanese traditional culture.

Tea ceremony is not a philosophical concept, nor an aesthetic theory. We may extend the practice of tea ceremony to our daily life, to open our sense organ, experience natural beauty, and hold in awe the greatness of life. The art of tea stems from showing consideration for the greatness of life. We will learn in the practice of tea ceremony that we should apply ourselves to one thing, and in the meanwhile do not think or do other things. We may find out in a cup of tea a corner to soothe the soul. Thank you again for spending time together with tea.

Keynote Speech at the 3rd Asia Cultural Forum

Bundit Limschoon

Secretary General of the Asia Cooperation Dialogue

His Excellency Ding Wei, Vice Minister of Culture of China,

His Excellency Wang Wenzhang, Former Vice Minister of Culture of China, and President of the Chinese National Academy of Arts,

Distinguished Delegates,

Ladies and Gentle men:

On behalf of 33 Member States of the Asia Cooperation Dialogue or the ACD, it is indeed my honor and privilege to deliver a statement on the role of the New Silk Road as an alternative forum for Cultural Globalization.

Excellency,

Since the beginning of human civilization, culture has never been static. With the interactions between human beings as agents of culture, culture is constantly changing. Human societies across the globe have established closer contacts over many centuries, but recently the paces have dramatically increased.

Currently, with the advent of communication and information technology, globalization contributes to the exchange of cultural values throughout the world. With the development of modern means of transport and economic relations, and the formation of transnational corporations and the global market, globalization of culture accelerates the integration of nations in the world system. Yet, the speed of change under the flow of globalization has been so rapid and intense that it causes concern for cultures to become vulnerable to homogeneity.

The phenomena of Macdonisation, CocaCola – nisation, or Modernisation, created potential impacts to the loss of cultural identity and cultural diversity; and it was the 'weaker' cultures of the developing nations which have been most threatened. Depredations of globalization, causing cultural vulnerability is hazard to every cultural identity but the developing world is particularly at risk. Consequently, people in our region become much more concerned about the preservation of uniqueness and identity of their own cultures.

Nevertheless, the fear that globalization advances homogenization should not preclude cultures from social interactions because the beauty of cultural exchange can create tremendous synergy and foster maximum constructive engagement. Instead, strategic plan should be implemented to enhance mutual understanding, strengthen cross – cultural communication and collaboration among nations.

For this reason, there have been many endeavors to find alternatives to balance local cultures from the fall under the mainstream culture or westernisation.

As a consequence, the New Silk Road initiative, revived by H. E. Xi Jinping, President of the People's Republic of China, is befitting of alternative to globalization. The significance of the New Silk Road is absolutely not limited to only trade and economic cooperation because the cultural dimension in the Silk Road will also play a very important role to increase a regional harmonisation.

The implementation of the New Silk Road in the cultural perspective would help create constructive engagement where minor cultures could express their identities, interact equally and eventually survive the influence of dominant culture.

Take the ancient Silk Road as an example. Retrospectively 5000 years ago, Silk Road was not a simply trade route but also a mean to connect communities surrounding it. Businesses occurred between strangers as well as the infusion of foreign and local cultures along the Silk Routes. This connectivity was the spirit of peace and harmonious development of which some consequences are still persisting in the modern days.

This Silk Road or Silk Route, reflects the web of a unique link that not only became a source of prosperity and trade relations, but had also promote the exchange of knowledge and inventions as well as wisdom and culture, including art and music among different communities. For me, the Silk Road was more than an international trade, it portrayed the interactions of human civilizations, which created the uniqueness of Asia or the so – called Asianess.

Land routes along the Silk Road, unlike the maritime, compelled caravans to interact with other communities and different cultures on the way to their final destinations. As a result of trade – driven interactions, even the smallest villages in the desert were exposed not only to the products of advanced civilizations, but also to the exchange of ideas, knowledge, experience and beliefs.

Accordingly, Silk Road was not merely a trade route but a road with plenty of economic and cultural activities in between. Silk Road commerce brought otherwise hostile communities into interactions based on a peaceful manner; the peaceful connectivity.

Thus the historical Silk Road offers a template for modern international commerce "a modern metaphor for sharing and learning across cultures, art forms and disciplines."

Now, in these present days, to bring the regional cooperation to the ultimate benefits, the Silk Route would need a platform to support greater cultural interactions among Asian communities.

With the purpose of promoting prosperity and understanding among human civilisations, my Organization, the Asia Cooperation Dialogue or the ACD, is a perfect platform with the geological proximity advantage for regional cultural communication. The regional cooperation of the ACD is an essential mechanism to accelerate not only economic but also social progress. Along with cultural interaction based on spirit and culture of the Silk Road, we could create a cultural bridge that connects people with different religious beliefs and backgrounds. With deeply connected ties between Member States, collaborations and talks become easier, less offense and less conflict. ACD's role in cultural cooperation will be vital to help accelerate the collective approach in gathering and garnering support to empower the Asian Culture.

In this regards, Members of ACD have set up a cultural cooperation to enhance cultural ties Asia – wide. A mechanism to review the in – depth discussion on the wide variety of cultural issues is the establishment of an ACD Cultural Coordination Centre. The proposal was initiated by the Islamic Republic of Iran, who also proposes to host the 4th ACD Ministerial Meeting on Cultural Cooperation in Tehran in 2016. The gathering of Ministers of Culture next year will ensure materialising and implementation of cultural initiatives and projects and ultimately establish coordination and coherence in cultural policy – making among Asian Countries.

The close cooperation and constructive engagement will lead Asia to sustainable economic prosperity and to counter the hegemonic globalisation. In this connection, I would like to refer to Speech by H. E. Xi Jinping, President of the People's Republic of China, at UNESCO Headquarters, which mentioned that

History proves that only by interacting with and learning from others can a civilization enjoy full vitality. If all civilizations are inclusive, the so-called clash of civilizations' can be avoided and harmony among civilizations will become a reality.

Excellency,

I would like to end my statement by signifying that Asia is the cradle of ancient civilisation. From Middle East to Far East, regions' prosperity has been gracefully cultivated because of the well – preserved local fine – cultural identities. The uniqueness of Asia is our diversities. Countries, big or small, developed or underdeveloped, are respectful of local distinctiveness and any attempts to guard and maintain national's prides have not held back Asia from its peaceful coexistence.

While Asia is blessed with the beauty of interactions despite diversity, I believe that if we advocate more shared comprehension and tolerance among distinctive civilizations and urge for communication and mutual understanding as well as the synergy among various cultures, Asia, through the Belt and Road and the ACD forum, will be an essential tool to build a harmonious world with heterogeneous cultures on the basis of mutual respect and equitable communication.

Harmony with Diversity: Great Wisdom of Chinese Culture

Liu Mengxi

Director of Chinese Culture Research Institute and Lifetime Research Fellow of Chinese National Academy of Arts

Chinese culture intends not to intensify interpersonal relations, and not to believe that matters in the world are incompatible. "Harmony with Diversity" is the general principle with which Chinese people look at the world, and also a great wisdom that Chinese culture contributes to the human being. The key of Harmony first lies in recognizing diversity. If everything is uniform, there is no harmony. The implication is that matters are different but they can exist in a community.

However, what I want to know is the difference between people. Is the difference between northerners and southerners, between Chinese and foreigners so much? In scientific principle, I think such difference is the second, while their sameness is the first. The Book of Changes, a very old Chinese philosophy classic says, "In the universe, all roads go to the same destination, and all thoughts go to the same conclusion." Its meaning is that methods and paths may be different, but people will finally go to the same place.

Cheng Hao and Cheng Yi, two philosophers in Chinese Song dynasty believed, whether people pursue the sameness or the difference is a question to seek public or private interests. They said, "Being public results in the sameness, while being private results in difference." (Collected Works of Two Chengs, p1256). They also commented, the sameness is the heart of heaven, namely, the decree of the God. In another section, they pointed out, "The philosophy of sages is to seek sameness of the majority but maintain difference of the minority. If a person can't seek sameness of the majority, he acts against truth and law; if a person can't maintain difference of the minority, he goes with the stream blindly." (id. P. 1264) In other words, Two Chengs believe, if a person doesn't admit difference in people and matters, he must lack of knowledge and be telling nonsense. By contrast, if a person denies "sameness of majority", he acts against the universal law, and is behaving absurdly. As far as fallaciousness is concerned, Two Chengs believe he who can't seek sameness of the majority is more wrong.

Qian Zhongshu, a great modern Chinese scholar, wrote a book in his early years, Notes on Literature and Art. In 1948, when the book was published, he wrote in the preface:

East sea or west sea, mentality is the same;

South school or north school, truth never parts.

In the eyes of Qian Zhongshu, cultures in the east and west are different, but psychological response and orientation of people, no matter where they live, are the same.

Mencius says, "Mouths have the same love for taste; ears have the same desire for sound; eyes have the same wish for beauty." From here, Mencius retorts, "Are human hearts so special that they share nothing?" In other words, is it true that people's mentalities don't have the sameness? Mencius concludes, "People have the same mental processes, and this is the universal truth and natural law" (Party One of Gaocius) . He believes that people have similar senses and consciences. The Chinese saying supports the same truth that all people have the same heart, all hearts agree with the same reason. The original emotions and expectations of human beings should have been like this. However, interweaving of intentions and behaviors leads to all kinds of conflicts. Sages and gurus teach us we should look through confusion of interwoven conflicts in human life and see that people have the same expectations and sameness lies behind differences.

From 1999 to 2000, I did research at Harvard University. I had conversations with many professors there, one of whom was professor Schwartzin Fairbank Center of Harvard University. He was a French Jew, and knew seven or eight languages. At early years, he studied Japan, and later China. Mr. Lin Yusheng told me, when you saw Schwartz, you would know how great western scholars looked like. One of his major academic concepts is "cross – cultural communication", which advocates that different people, different cultures and different ethnic groups can communicate. In our conversation, he raised a theory that the impact of language on thinking was not as so great as people had imagined. I had never heard of such a statement before. Language is a tool for thinking. Without language, can people think? Nevertheless, we all know that babies who can't speak can draw pictures, and drawing picture is a kind of thinking. In order to advocate cross – culture communication, Schwartz tried to create a new theoretical structure. His theory intended to prove that language barrier is not insurmountable for human communication. At that time, I said I could give him an example to prove that two persons who couldn't communicate with language could fall in love with each other. Of course, language barrier may lead to some problems in their romantic experience. Anyway, two lovers without language barrier will have problems too. Therefore, the major cause is not necessarily language.

Different cultures can communicate and may not be so seriously antagonistic. This is a traditional idea of Chinese culture. Zhang Zai, a very great scholar and philosopher in Song Dynasty had written four famous sentences, "Set heart for heaven and earth, settle life for the populace, inherit great knowledge of past sages, and create peace for thousands of generations." The four sentences are very great. Let's imagine, "set heart for heaven and earth, settle life for the populace", what an immense heart one should have! We know that in Chinese culture there is a human – oriented tradition, and concerning interests of populace is what each scholar and each official should do. For this reason, in the past a county magistrate is called a "parent official". As a parent of the populace, he surely should take care of people's interests. "Settle life for the populace" advocated by Zhang Zai comes from Mencius thoughts. Mencius preaches "Right Life", advocating that people should get a right birth, live a right life, and reach a right death. People should not make abnormal life. This is the point to "settle life for the populace". The final goal is to "create peace for thousands of generations". These are the four famous sentences from Zhang Zai, also titled "Four Teaching Sentences of Hengqu".

However, Zhang Zai has another set of four sentences, which I call "Four Philosophical Teaching Sentences":

Every image has an opposite; the opposite must move differently; different movement results in conflicts, but conflicts will be harmonized at last.

The four sentences state a philosophy and a universe outlook, which covers all phenomena of the whole universe. In this world, there are numerous individual living entities, which can be named "images", including animals and plants. Each "image" is an individual entity, and the world gets colorful. Every image has two parts, suggesting that images are different. For instance, beautiful women have different characteristics. Therefore, ancient people say "beautiful girls have different figures and different faces." Westerners have similar sayings that there are not such two living creatures that are completely the same.

"The opposite must move differently" suggests that various "images" are not still but move. Different images move in different directions, and sometimes they are poles apart. So conflicts occur. Zhang Zai used "hostile" in Chinese to describe conflict in the sentence. The ancient Chinese character "hostile" consists two parts, each of which is a bird in meaning separated by "word" in the middle. The bird in this "hostile" is a bird with a very short tail. The original meaning of the character "hostile" here represents two birds are fiercely discussing, debating or quarreling. Human beings have languages, and birds also have their speeches. The "hostile" is also used for "revision". We all have revised some articles or books, which is a very difficult task. However, we often say there is not a book without mistakes. In the ancient time, revision was a big business. You take a copy, and I take a copy. We read slowly and carefully. We have to discuss debate or quarrel about problems. However, the two short – tailed birds discussing, debating or quarreling will not swallow the other. They have to reach an agreement or a compromise. They seek sameness and maintain difference, which is "settle by harmonization".

Our world has difference, but difference does not necessarily lead to conflicts, and conflicts don't necessarily lead to life – and – death battles. They can surely be settled by harmonization. If we look at the world with this principle, will we avoid many unnecessary troubles? Of course, this can't be done by one party. It needs mutual efforts from two or more parties. Therefore, communication and discussion of multiple parties is very important. "Opposite movement leads to conflicts" is a process for communication, conversation, consultation, discussion and revision.

However, dialogues need wisdom, and dialogists should be tolerant. Confucius says, "Do not unto others as you would not have them do unto you", which reflects the tolerance of Chinese culture. Both "Harmony with diversity" and "Do not unto others as you would not have them do unto you" are words Confucius said when he lived about 500 B. C. It was a hub period of the world culture and history. I think we have every reason to take the two sentences of Confucius as a big wisdom for human survival.

The 20th century can be regarded as a combat century as two world wars occurred in it. Now, the 21st century has turned over 15 years. Will human beings be gulped by similar disasters in this new century? Can human beings change the world better by using their reason and wisdom? Both "Harmony with diversity" and "Do not unto others as you would not have them do unto you" request us to correctly look at the living conditions in the world, and to correctly look at human beings. They have in essence given solutions to crises. I think the world can be more beautiful, more harmony. There should be no fear, and we solve all conflicts with friendly dialogues.

Here, I'd like to mention the two keywords again: Harmony and diversity. Harmony is a situation that all people are happy to expect and accept. Diversity is the prerequisite for harmony. We should admit diversity, tolerate diversity and appreciate diversity so that we can reach harmony. If everything is the same, and all people with the same clothes, same gestures, same thoughts, same speeches, the world will make us breathless. Mencius says, "Fulfillment is beauty, and fulfillment with brilliance is greatness." Just imagine, are things that can be fulfilled completely the same? Combination of different things can be called fulfillment. Combinations that agree with aesthetic rules can create beauty. Therefore, "Harmony with diversity" is the original form of the world, and also the source for creation. It is the starting point of beauty, and also the starting point for fulfillment and brilliance.

We should not forget there is another sentence, "Do not unto others as you would not have them do unto you", which is a rational and most natural method to solve human conflicts.

To Attend the 3rd Asia Cultural Forum on "the Belt and Road"

Samraing Kamsam

Secretary of State, Ministry of Culture and
Fine Arts, Kingdom of Cambodia

Excellency, Ladies, Gentlemen,
And Dear Friends:

It's a great honor and privilege for me to be here, on behalf of the Ministry of Culture and Fine Arts, Kingdom of Cambodia, to attend the 3rd Asia Cultural Forum, a high-level platform for Cultural Exchange and communication among Asian Countries, providing more channels and opportunities for Asian experts, scholars and art organizations to increase their mutual understanding, trust, communication and cooperation in Quanzhou, Fujian Province, People's Republic of China.

First and foremost, I would like to take this special opportunity to express my deep appreciation and gratefulness to the People's Republic of China, especially to the Ministry of Culture of China for organizing the 3rd Asia Cultural Forum on the theme "the Belt and Road" in this auspicious occasion. Our gratitude goes also to the Organizing Committee for its warm welcome and hospitality.

As one of the attending countries, Cambodia firmly supports Chinese Government who has recently put forth the Silk Road Economic Belt and the 21st Century Maritime Silk Road Initiatives also known as "the Belt and Road", to urge relevant countries to build the community of common interests for mutual benefits and win-win outcomes. And at the same time, these initiatives build the community of common destiny for cohesive progress and prosperity.

Cambodia fully agrees with the concept that a future-oriented approach "the Belt and Road" will strengthen our connectivity, promotes peace, cooperation and mutual benefits which are the spirit of the century and also the sole intention of the people of the world.

Hopefully, Cambodian Delegation is strongly convinced that our cultural dialogue on:

— The Role of Asian Culture in Asian Cooperation,

— The Interpretation of "the Belt and Road" cooperation from the Cultural perspective of Asia, and

— The Roads to partnerships and win – win outcomes in Asia, would be successfully materialized.

Excellency, Ladies, Gentlemen, and

Dear Friends,

Taking this auspicious opportunity, would you please allow me to share with you, in this crucial Forum about the Current Cultural Cooperation in preserving, protecting of Cultural Heritage in Cambodia:

Within the framework of cooperation and preservation of Cultural Heritage, as one of the world abundant country of Tangible and Intangible Cultural Heritages, Cambodia has been making so many efforts in generating the National Cultural Policy, the Strategic Objectives and Action Plans to preserve, restore and revitalize our Cultural Heritages such as Cambodian cultural, historic cities, ancient temples, religious monuments and cultural expression and diversity.

Indeed, the effective preservation and restoration of ancient historical sites and the protection of Intangible Cultural Heritage have also been accomplished through people 's educational programs as well as the inspiration of the people's participation and the establishment of the regulations and legal frameworks.

Towards this end, strengthening cultural Cooperation among Asian friendly countries has been made very closely and cordially.

At last but not least, on behalf of Cambodia's Delegation, I would like to call upon the 3rd Asia Cultural Forum to firmly carry out the fruitful outcomes of the 3rd Asia Forum with following recommendations:

1. To firmly maintain our commitments towards strengthening our Cultural Cooperation for mutual understanding, common benefits, trust, communication, stability, peace and prosperity of Asia and the World as a whole.

2. To work together for the protection of our Cultural Heritages against illicit, trafficking and negative impact of Globalized Culture.

3. To support the outcomes of the 3rd Asia Cultural Forum in order to build our community of common interests for mutual benefits and win – win outcomes.

4. To deeply enhance our community of common destiny for Peace, Cohesive Progress and sustainable development.

In conclusion, once again, on behalf of Cambodia's Ministry of Culture and Fine Arts, I wish to extend my deep thanks, profound gratitude and good wishes to all of you, Excellency, Ladies and Gentlemen: Be Happy, Healthy and Lucky!

Thank You Very Much for your kind attention!

Three Characteristics and Three Responsibilities

Yu Qiuyu
Famous Cultural Scholar

In the various cultures of the world, the Asian culture shows three common characteristics and hence generates three common responsibilities.

First, Asian culture has a long history. Asia keeps three of the world recognized four ancient civilizations of mankind. They were the Mesopotamia civilization, Chinese civilization and Indian civilization. Besides, Asia also had the Hebrew civilization, Persia civilization, Arab civilization, and Mongolia civilization, which left significant impacts on the world. Their rising to the power, decline and struggles provided numerous positive and negative historical experiences that should be told systematically to the world today.

Second, Asian culture is extremely diversified. Since its ecological environment is much more complex that Europe and America, Asian culture has the richest, most peculiar and self – sufficient cultural patterns. Therefore, Asian culture is most qualified to prove that cultural diversity is not the source of conflicts. All the major vicious conflicts in history which might appear in the banner of "civilization", all sprang from the opposite of civilization. In consequence, when I attended a seminar discussing the Human Development Report of the UN in 2004, I, along with some other scholars, disapproved the "Clash of Civilization" theory of Huntington, and concluded my report with a phrase from Archbishop Desmond Tutu that we should "delight in our differences".

Third, Asian culture calls for further elaboration. Compared with the European and American cultures, the Asian culture, long and diversified, is largely short of modern global recognition. It is often hunted for novelty, misread, and demonized. Therefore, it is a weighty responsibility for us to explore the precious contents of Asian culture, and make it overflow with the shared values of mankind. In this process, trans – boundary circulation of Asian culture will be the best solution. The ancient Silk Road has set a good example for us in this aspect and we have reason to unfold a grander modern form.

The Role of Culture in Asian Countries and "the Belt and Road" Co-operation

Md. Altaf Hossain

Director General Department of Archaeology

Ministry of Cultural Affairs, Bangladesh

Introduction

More than two millennia ago the diligent and courageous people of Eurasia explored and opened up several routes of trade and cultural exchanges that linked the major civilizations of Asia, Europe and Africa, collectively called the Silk Road by later generations. For thousands of years, the Silk Road Spirit- "peace and cooperation, openness and inclusiveness, mutual learning and mutual benefit" -has been passed from generation to generation, promoted the progress of human civilization, and contributed greatly to the prosperity and development of the countries along the Silk Road. In the 21st century, a new era marked by the theme of peace, development, co-operation and mutual benefit, it is more important for us to carry on the Silk Road Spirit in face of the weak recovery of the global economy, culture and complex international and regional situations.

Culture is the instrument which takes people closer to different countries and it is the things which do not have any territory like border, religion and society.

Before going to interpretation of the Belt and Road co-operation from the cultural perspective of Asia we have an idea of the silk road, silk road economic belt and the 21st century maritime silk road. We also have to understand closely related networks i. e. The China – Pakistan Economic corridor (CPEC) and the Bangladesh – China – India – Myanmar (BCIM) economic corridor officially classified as "Closely related to the Belt and Road initiative".

Silk Road

Silk Road, also known as SILK ROUTE, ancient trade route that, linking China with the West, carried goods and ideas between the two great civilizations of Rome and China, Silk came westward while wools, gold and silver went east. China also received Nestorian Christianity and Buddhism (from India) via the road.

Originating at Sian, the 4, 000 mi (6400 km) road, actually a caravan tract, followed the Great Wall of China to the north – west, by passed the Takla Makan Desert, climbed the Pamirs (mountains), crossed Afghanistan and went on to the Levant; from there the merchandise was shipped across the Mediterranean Sea. Few persons travelled the entire route and goods were handled in a staggered progression by middlemen.

With the gradual loss of Roman territory in Asian and the rise of Arabian power in the Levant, the Silk Road became increasingly unsafe and untraveled. In the 13th and 14th centuries the route was revived under the Mongols and at that time Marco Polo used the road to travel to Cathay (China).

The road now partially exists in the form of a paved highway connecting Pakistan and Sinkiang Uighur China. The old road has inspired a U Nations plan for a trans – Asian highway.

The Belt and Road

The Silk Road Economic Belt was unveiled by Xi Jinping at Nazarfayev University on September 7, 2013 as part of his state visit to Kazakhstan. The new Maritime Silk Road was announced before the Indonesian Parliament Of Xi Jinping state visit to Indonesia.

These two concepts envision the creation of a highly integrated, co – operative and mutually beneficial set of Maritime and land – based economic corridors thinking European and Asian markets as well as cultural co – operation. "Vision and Actions on Jointly Building Silk road Economic Belt and 21st Century Maritime Silk Road" states that : –

The Belt and Road run through the continents of Asia, Europe, and Africa, connecting the vibrant East Asia economic circle at one end and developed European economic circle at the other, and encompassing countries with huge potential for economic development. The Silk Road Economic Belt focuses on bringing together China, Central Asia, Russia and Europe (the Baltic); linking China with the Persian Gulf and the Mediterranean Sea through Central Asia and West Asia; and connecting China with Southeast Asia, South Asia and the Indian Ocean. The 21st – Century Maritime Silk Road is designed to go from China's coast to Europe through the South China Sea and the Indian Ocean in one route, and from China's coast through the South China Sea to the South Pacific in the other.

The belt and Road initiative consists of several economic and some non – economic elements where culture is an important part. Perhaps the most frequently mentioned economic element is a Chinese commitment to invest heavily in a wide variety of infrastructure project in order to strengthen the economic capacity and "connectivity" among the nations with in the Belt and road area and with china's western regions. Xi Jinping stated that China must make common efforts with relevant countries to accelerate the pace of infrastructure and connectivity construction and built well the silk road economic Belt and the 21st Century Maritime Silk Road. After making connectivity of these countries, culture of the country automatically spread with in these area.

The initiative to jointly build the Belt and Road, embracing the trend towards a multipolar world, economic globalization, cultural diversity and greater IT application, is designed to uphold the global free trade regime and the open world economy and culture in the spirit of open regional cooperation. It is aimed at promoting orderly and free flow of economic factors, highly efficient allocation of resources and deep integration of markets; encouraging the countries along the Belt and Road to achieve economic, culture policy coordination and carry out broader and more in – depth regional co – operation of higher standards; and jointly creating an open, inclusive and balanced regional economic, cultural co – operation architecture that benefits all...

The Belt and Road Initiative aims to promote the connectivity of Asian, European and African continents and their adjacent seas, establish and strengthen partnerships among the countries along the Belt and Road, set up all – dimensional, multi – tiered and composite connectivity networks, and realize diversified, independent, balanced and sustainable development in these countries. The connectivity projects of the Initiative will help align and coordinate the development strategies of the countries along the Belt and Road, tap market potential in this region, promote investment and consumption, create demands and job opportunities, enhance people – to people and cultural exchanges, and mutual learning among the peoples of the relevant countries, and enable them to understand, trust and respect each other and live in harmony, peace and prosperity.

Great practical significance for further developing China's relations with Central Asian nations and for deepening regional cooperation. By strengthening policy communication, road connectivity, trade links, currency circulation, and connections among their peoples, the countries involved can tighten their economic links, deepen co – operation among them, and expand the space for development. The Silk Road, the world's longest economic and trade corridor with the greatest development potential, would be revived, with countries along the road poised to gain new momentum for economic development as well as cultural co – operation and new opportunities for sharing the fruits of co – operation.

Principles

The Belt and Road Initiative is in line with the purposes and principles of the UN Charter. It upholds the Five Principles of Peaceful Coexistence: mutual respect for each other's sovereignty and territorial integrity, mutual non – aggression, mutual non – interference in each other's internal affairs, equality and mutual benefit, and peaceful coexistence.

The Initiative is open for co – operation. It covers, but is not limited to, the area of the ancient Silk Road. It is open to all countries, and international and regional organizations for engagement, so that the results of the concerted efforts will benefit wider areas.

The Initiative is harmonious and inclusive. It advocates tolerance among civilizations, respects the paths and modes of development chosen by different countries, and supports dialogues among different civilizations on the principles of seeking common ground while shelving differences and drawing on each other's strengths, so that all countries can coexist in peace for common prosperity.

The Initiative follows market operation. It will abide by market rules and international norms, give play to the decisive role of the market in resource allocation and the primary role of enterprises, and let the governments perform their due functions.

The Initiative seeks mutual benefit. It accommodates the interests and concerns of all parties involved, and seeks a conjunction of interests and the "biggest common denominator" for co – operation so as to give full play to the wisdom and creativity, strengths and potentials of all parties.

Framework

The Belt and Road Initiative is a way for win-win co-operation that promotes common development and prosperity and a road towards peace and friendship by enhancing mutual understanding and trust, and strengthening all-round exchanges. It promotes practical co-operation in all fields, and works to build a community of shared interests, destiny and responsibility featuring mutual political trust, economic integration and cultural inclusiveness.

The Belt and Road run through the continents of Asia, Europe and Africa, connecting the vibrant East Asia economic circle at one end and developed European economic circle at the other, and encompassing countries with huge potential for economic development. The Silk Road Economic Belt focuses on bringing together China, Central Asia, Russia and Europe (the Baltic); linking China with the Persian Gulf and the Mediterranean Sea through Central Asia and West Asia; and connecting China with Southeast Asia, South Asia and the Indian Ocean.

History of Cultural Exchanges between Bangladesh & China

New opportunities for China – Bangladesh cooperation

Chinese President Xi Jinping meets with Bangladeshi Prime Minister Sheikh Hasina in New York, the united states, Sept. 26 – 10 – 2015 and the two leaders agreed to strengthen bilateral co – operation in various areas.

Calling Bangladesh "a good neighbor, good friend and good partner," Xi said Beijing regards Bangladesh as an important co-operation partner in the South Asia-Indian Ocean region and stands ready to maintain high-level exchanges with Dhaka and expand bilateral co-operation in such key areas as trade, production capacity, energy development and infrastructure construction.

He urged the two countries to make a success of the activities marking the 40th anniversary of bilateral ties, boost up co-operation in education and radio and TV services and between universities, and facilitate personnel exchanges.

The two countries should also maintain communication and coordination on major international and regional issues, Xi said, adding that China will provide assistance within its capacity for Bangladesh to cope with climate change.

Noting that the Chinese people are endeavoring to realize the Chinese Dream of national rejuvenation and have launched the Silk Road Economic Belt and 21st-Century Maritime Silk Road Initiative, Xi said China hopes to share the development opportunities with its neighbors and friends, including Bangladesh.

He added that the two sides have agreed to encourages Chinese companies to invest in Bangladesh and is willing to provide financial support for major co-operation projects the two sides have agreed to.

Also, China values the constructive role that Bangladesh plays in promoting the construction of an economic corridor connecting Bangladesh, China, India and Myanmar, and will work closely with all other sides to achieve results as soon as possible, added the Chinese president.

Prime Minister Sheikh Hasina, for her part, said Bangladesh and China have built a close partnership since the establishment of diplomatic relations 40 years ago and Dhaka is grateful to China for its long-time assistance for Bangladesh's social and economic development. Bangladesh is willing to strengthen co-operation with China in such areas as trade, finance, infrastructure construction and culture, and will actively participate in co-operation programs under the framework of the Bangladesh-China-India-Myanmar corridor.

Since the establishment of diplomatic relations in 1975, China and Bangladesh have been good neighbors, friends and partners based on equality, mutual respect and mutual trust. In 2010, the leaders from the two countries announced that they committed to establishing a "Closer Comprehensive Partnership of Cooperation". In 2013, the bilateral relationship has maintained a good momentum of development:

Furthermore, the Initiative of Bangladesh-China-India-Myanmar Economic Corridor has made substantial progress.

Six friendship bridges in Bangladesh have been built, and the Seventh is under way. Many other mega infrastructure projects are under construction with Chinese fund and technical support.

Since Bangladesh locates geographically close to China, has cheaper labour force, friendly investment environment and beautiful landscape like Cox' bazaar, it deserves to have more privilege to make good use of "Chinese opportunities". With completion of the BCIM Economic Corridor, Bangladesh will take an even more favourable posture.

The four countries agreed that the priorities of BCIM Economic Corridor should focus on, among other things, the following areas: regional connectivity, including transportation, telecommunication, and power & energy, trade and investment, sustainable development and people-to-people exchange. Therefore, China and Bangladesh should intensify interaction and co-operation with each other in the following aspects:

Promoting regional connectivity. Ancient Silk Road had connected us in history. Bangladesh should work together to restore the road link in the region and explore railway, waterway and airline connectivity as well. Recently, Bangladesh Government has decided to fast-track 6 projects, including the Padma bridge, a deep-sea port and the metro rail. This clearly showed determination to improve communications and Bangladesh, which is sandwiched by South Asia, Southeast Asia and East Asia, has the potential to become the regional transportation hub.

Widening people-to-people exchange. As traditionally friendly neighbors, China and Bangladesh should pursue transportation connectivity as well as understanding and friendship between the two peoples.

Improving cross-border transportation infrastructure, widely known as connectivity, is a major agenda of Bangladesh for economic benefit. There was a proposal on Bangladesh-China road connectivity through Myanmar. How do you assess its progress made so far? During Bangladesh Prime Minister visit to China in 2010, China and Bangladesh agreed to continue to discuss the possibility of building road and rail links between the two countries. Since then, the two sides have kept close co-operation in this regard. In May, 2013, China and India jointly raised the proposal of establishing the Bangladesh-China-India-Myanmar Economic Corridor which is based on better connectivity and ultimately boost trade, economic and cultural exchanges within the BCIM region. The road connectivity between China and Bangladesh would be one of the priority projects under the framework of BCIM-EC. And the Chinese side is willing to work with Bangladesh side to put it into fast-track implementation.

Cultural Charms of the Belt and Road

The Belt and Road Initiatives were put forward by Chinese President Xi Jinping during his overseas visits in 2013, which includes the Silk Road Economic Belt and the 21st Century Maritime Silk Road.

The initiative has been seen as Beijing's plan to revive the ancient "Silk Road", which linked Europe to China as a major trade route more than a thousand years ago, boosting the economies and cultural interactions of all the peoples along the way.

The Belt and Road possesses rich Chinese cultural connotations and activates the essence of harmonious Chinese culture in the new historical circumstance. The bright future of the Belt and Road initiative is closely related to its historical origin and cultural charm.

Firstly, the Belt and Road pursues peace. Peace is the common aspiration of all peoples across the world. The Silk Road Economic Belt and 21st Century Maritime Silk Road involve more than 50 countries, 4.4 billion people and 21 trillion yuan in aggregated regional economic largesse. They are mostly developing countries of different histories, conditions and levels of development. Their infrastructures are poor and communication between these countries is not so smooth. But they have strong late-mover advantages and big promotion space.

For these countries, the biggest appeal is to win development opportunities in a peaceful international environment. The Belt and Road Initiative is conducive to enhancing international relations and to maintain geopolitical stability. Undoubtedly it provides favorable conditions for these countries to enjoy economic prosperity and their peoples to lead happy lives.

Secondly, the Belt and Road means cooperation. No country can develop without cooperation. Of all the countries involved in the Belt and Road, some have excess capital, others excess resources. Some have sufficient labor, others huge market potential. In short, they have complementary advantages and it is urgent for them to build a diverse platform for cooperation.

In recent years some countries have strengthened co-operation through the Shanghai Co-operation Organization (SCO), China-ASEAN (10 + 1) and BRICS platforms. These bilateral, regional and multilateral co-operation mechanisms between China and the Belt and Road countries have been continuously improved. China took the lead in boosting infrastructure construction by establishing the Asia Infrastructure Investment Bank and Silk Road Fund which provide genuine help for developing countries involved in this initiative. Meanwhile, the buildup of other financial platforms such as the BRICS

New Development Bank and SCO Development Bank have been steadily pushed forward and guarantee implementation of the Belt and Road initiative.

Thirdly, the Belt and Road initiative advocates win-win cooperation. Win-win cooperation has become a trend in global development. The Belt and Road not only links up the East Asia economic region with its strong development momentum, but also connects it to the developed Europe-North America economic powerhouse.

The Belt and Road advocates communication of policy, connection of facilities, smooth trade, accommodation of funds, the common aspiration of people and adheres to principles of joint discussion, construction and sharing. The Belt and Road initiative is open and inclusive. Along with the gradual implementation of the initiative, the Belt and Road will open channels along the New Silk Road and promote common development of regional economic entities. It will facilitate the building of a new maritime order. The Belt and Road will exert influence on the global geopolitical structure and the establishment of a new future world order based on win-win cooperation.

In Chinese civilization's several millennia of history, there has been long-term peace and prosperity. The Chinese people have a deep grasp of peace and win-win cooperation. Through the guidance of these concepts full of historical wisdom and traditional Chinese culture, the Belt and Road will certainly inject powerful positive energy into world peace, stability, development and prosperity.

Measures to Promote Cultural Diversity and Protect Cultural Heritage in Asia

Asia has a rich diverse and ancient ensemble of tangible and intangible cultural heritage sites. Notably south Asia, particularly Bangladesh, Bhutan, India, Nepal and Srilanka, have 35 UNESCO Cultural Heritage sites. 15 of them are Buddhist heritage sites that includes birth place of Lord Buddha at Lumbini in Nepal.

The Indian sub-continent (including Bangladesh and Pakistan) along with Srilanka, Myanmar and Other adjacent countries has a unique ancient cultural heritage which dates back from 5000 years. Among all the heritage sites of this area, Hinduism plays a vital role. There are so many ancient temples and monuments of Gupta, Sen, Pal and other dynasties. Besides, during the Muslim Empire, particularly in Moghul period, there are hundreds of wonderful monuments, forts and buildings which represent the Islamic culture in this region. A huge number of mosques with an excellent architectural design and concept reveals the wonderful culture and creative sense of those periods.

The Role of Culture in the Asian Countries

We should hold culture years, arts festivals, film festivals, TV weeks and book fairs in each other's countries; cooperate on the production and translation of fine films, radio and TV programs; and jointly apply for and protect World Cultural Heritage sites. We should also increase personnel exchange and co-operation between countries along the Belt and Road.

We should enhance co-operation in and expand the scale of tourism; hold tourism promotion weeks and publicity months in each other's countries; jointly create competitive international tourist routes and products with Silk Road features; and make it more convenient to apply for tourist visa in countries along the Belt and Road. We should push forward co-operation on the 21st-Century Maritime Silk Road cruise tourism program.

Promote Cultural Diversity and Protect Cultural Heritage in Bangladesh

Dept. of Archaeology, under the Ministry of Cultural Affairs deals with the tangible heritage sites in Bangladesh through "Antiquities act in 1968". (Amendment in 1976).

At present, there are 451 protected heritage sites and monuments in Bangladesh. Some of the most important sites are

- PaharpurMahavihara, Noagaon.
- Mahasthangarhfortified City, Bogra
- ShaitGumbad Mosque& Its adjacent mosque, Bagerhat.
- Kantajiu Temple, Dinajpur.
- Lalbagh fort, Dhaka.
- Panama City, Sonargaon
- ChotoSona Mosque, ChapaiNawabganj.
- Megaliths, Sylhet.

· Armenian Church, Dhaka.

· JagaddalaMahavihara

· LalmaiMainamati, Comilla.

Dhaka was declared as Islamic Cultural Capital (Asia Region) in 2012 by ISESCO. As a member country of ISESCO, Bangladesh is working to protect and preserve the ancient and historical mosque and monuments.

Recently 2015 Ministry of Civil Aviation and Tourism, Bangladesh in co-operation with United Nations World Tourism Organizations (UNTWO) arranged3 day International Conference on 'Developing Sustainable and Inclusive Buddhist Heritages and Pilgrim Circuit in South Asia's Buddhist Heartland'. This will promote the cross border Buddhist circuit as pilgrim tourism, peace and harmony among the people in this region. Besides, it will help people bringing the sense and urge to protect the Buddhists heritage sites.

Bangladesh Tourism Board with the help of Bangladesh Parjatan Corporation and Department of Archaeology is promoting nature and culture-based tourism providing supports to private sectors and international tourist's organizations.

Awareness programs are being taken for the local people residing at the heritage sites.

A project entitled South Asia Tourism Infrastructure Development Project has been launched in 2010 under south Asia Economic Co-operations (SAEC) framework. Through this project Department of Archaeology conserving four important heritage sites and their infrastructures to promote and facilitate culture-based tourism.

Concluding Remarks

The Belt and Road Initiative is a systematic project, which should be jointly built through consultation to meet the interests of all, and efforts should be made to integrate the development strategies of the countries along the Belt and Road. Symbolizing communication and co-operation between the East and the West, the Silk Road Spirit is a historic and cultural heritage shared by all countries around the world.

To take the principle of "joint discussion, joint building and joint sharing" to promote "the Belt and Road" construction, should not only actively promote the regional economic exchange and cooperation, but also appreciate the cultural heritage and humanistic spirit. Further deepen the friendly, non-governmental and practical co-operation between countries along the Silk Road. Countries along the Silk Road economic belt and Maritime Silk Road can promote the ideas of communication, integration, dialogue and win-win for flourishing and peaceful Eurasian regions by cross-border and cross-civilization activities.

"The Belt and Road" construction should break the traditional regional economic mode, and rebuilt a new and efficient one. Guided by concepts and principles recognized by different countries, need to promote a higher level co-operation of the broadened contents, including industrial transformation, further trading, deep investment and cooperation. Also need to deepen co-operation in the fields of humanity, education, culture, science and technology, ecology, environment, etc. to achieve normalization of policy communication and liberation of trade and investment.

In an age that features in the ever deeper integration of knowledge and economy, higher education has become a key force to promote social and economic development. To promote a better communication of education among countries along the roads, especially the exchange of higher education, is of great significance for the construction of "the Belt and Road". The countries along the road should further encourage all forms of the personnel exchange among higher educational sectors and, by the way of educational resources sharing in more frequencies and of higher level, scientific and technical co-operation and personnel exchanges, provide more experts and intellectuals for the construction of "the Belt and Road".

Strengthen Transcultural Studies and Enhance the Reciprocity Understanding among Asian Civilizations

Wang Mingming

Beijing University

Since the proposal of the strategic vision of the "Silk Road Economic Belt" and "21st-Century Maritime Silk Road", building a community of shared interests, destiny and responsibility that cross region, ethnic and nation has become a call with characteristics of the times.

The form of a community of shared interests, destiny and responsibility that cross region, ethnic and nation depends on the political mutual trust and economic integration. However, it is never easy to realize political mutual trust and economic integration without culture inclusiveness. Therefore, it is highly necessary and urgent to open up the situation of confidence, inclusiveness and prosperity of culture (as the famous Mr. Fei Xiaotong said, "achieving one's own goal yields gratification, lending a hand to consummate others' goal doubles satisfaction, goals of self and others can be unified, thus the world can be harmonized") and promote the mutual respect between different civilizations, different cultures and different religions.

Confidence, inclusiveness and prosperity of culture not only require the further attention of nation and the society, but also the intensive study and extensive elaboration by humane social science circle.

The mutual understanding of cross culture appeared early. There were rich cases on it in ancient knowledge and religious domains. However, the transcultural studies based on the cultural anthropology and the method of culture study were formed in Europe in 1990. It aims to seek reciprocal knowledge and mutual understanding in space between cultures (said by Alain Le Pichon) . For me, "reciprocal knowledge and mutual understanding" make up certain reciprocal understanding, i. e. , understanding formed or partially formed in the mutual cognition between cultures which is conducive to the involved parties' self-identification and mutual identification.

During its spread in the past two decades, transcultural studies have gradually evolved into a comprehensive knowledge of humanistic and social science (for example, University of Heidelberg Germany has established a research degree for transcultural study). There were scholars participating in the activities held by European Transcultural Research Institute.

However, as a comprehensive academic branch, transcultural study is in the ascendant in domestic.

Look ahead of the future of academic development, we have faith to believe that the cooperation and communication between Asian countries shouldn't only depend on the Self-cognition, we need to enhance the transnational cultural exchange to achieve the confidence, inclusiveness and prosperity of culture.

Speech

K. P. Bernard Vasantha Silva

Additional Secretary of Ministry of Internal Affairs,
Wayamba Development and Cultural Affairs, Sri Lanka

Let me extend my thanks, first to the Government of Peoples Republic of China, Ministry of Culture of China, Fujian province and also Chinese National Academy of Art for inviting us for this important forum. The relation between China and my country, Sri Lanka traces back as far as Centuries. It gives me great pleasure to say that relation was sincere and cordial always as it is at present. Whenever Sri Lanka was facing hardships China was supporting Sri Lanka without any hesitation.

I am happy to say that in addition to China there are many friendly Countries especially India together with Sri Lanka here to participate in this forum.

I am here to represent the Ministry of Cultural affairs of Sri Lanka. As we know culture is a tool that builds powerful relationships. Ministry of Cultural affairs in Sri Lanka has signed a number of memorandums of understanding (Mou) with foreign Countries to have cultural relationships.

Though we all who are meeting here are from different Lands, speaking different languages and having different faiths and religions, but we all have come from one or two or many cultural origins. We can't forget Indo valley civilization and we can't forget Mohendejaro Harappa civilization and also Howangho civilization.

Ministry of cultural affairs of Sri Lanka has singed 58 Memorandums of understanding (mou) up to now with the foreign countries to have cultural relationships. In keeping with the said memorandum of understanding arrangements are made for Sri Lankan cultural troupes to attend ceremonies of those particular Countries and the cultural troupes of those Countries for Sri Lanka ceremonies is a matter of happiness that this cultural exchange has paved the way for strength and cordiality among those countries.

At the same time I would like to say that there are more programs that can be implemented on those memorandums of understanding (mou). Here may I mention some of them.

1. Exchanging of Cultural Knowledge.
2. Exchanging of Folk Arts.
3. Creating programs aiming at Cultural promotion.
4. Sharing the knowledge of languages.
5. Organizing various International conferences for cultural Development.
6. Organize visits for foreign experts in the field of Culture.
7. Hold Culture exhibition on foreign soils.
8. Organizing international Cultural pageants.
9. Officers and delegates participate in the foreign training courses and workshop.
10. Widening the knowledge and understanding of each other through the exchange of children and youth.
11. Having opportunities for the academics of the friendly countries to study the valuable historical document lying in the archives of the member countries.
12. Enhancing tourism to acquire cultural and religious knowledge of the member countries.

As I mentioned above those memorandum of understanding have been signed not only with the Asian countries such as India, Pakistan, Maldives Islands but with the countries which are out of the Asian region.

On the consent of government of Sri Lanka is willing to sign mous with other countries that we have no such relationship at present and widen the existing cultural relationships with the countries we have already singed mou.

Further I like to mention about a special project implemented in the year 2014 under the cultural relationship extension endeavour. A museum Gallery was designed in memory of the Chinese navigator Admiral Zheng He who landed in Sri Lanka in the 15th century and it has been located in the Galle Museum in my country. Many Chinese tourists visited Sri Lanka in 2014 and this year to visit the above Admiral Zheng He gallery at Galle Museum. The gallery has been displayed that Zheng He and his counterparts landed from their huge vessel and also display the social and cultural situation of Sri Lanka in the Southern province in Galle.

Funds for that was processed by the Sri Lanka government and the statue of the Navigator Admiral Zheng He was given by the Chinese government The minister of National Heritage of Sri Lanka and the Governor of Southern province in Sri Lanka and also higher officials of the Government of peoples Republic of China participated in that opening ceremony. The Chinese tourist in Sri Lanka may have an enthusiastic experience by visiting that Zheng He gallery in the Galle museum.

Further I would like to express anther project implemented by the Ministry of Cultural affairs in Sri Lanka in 2012 in Andre Pradesh in India. That project is the famous Sri Lankan statue of the Lord Buddha's replica been established in Cultural theme park in Andre Pradesh.

We are engaged in several projects and programs with Nepal and Thailand under the our bilateral and cultural relationships

A special project has been planned to enhance the performance of Sri Lanka cultural centers. It will be implemented from the year 2016. We are looking forward to build up a better society by bringing back the traits that the Sri Lanka culture had inherited.

I believe that the other countries, participating in this forum have similar endeavors. Further I express that the friendly Countries could implement similar programs like the above for the Cultural ties among the Asian countries.

The role of "Culture" can play in a country for its betterment is monumental, the forums like this is very vital to share the experience of that nature and, let me express my gratitude to the people's Republic of china, Fujian province, Chinese National Academy of Arts and the organizers'and finally all participant for giving me this opportunity.

Thanking you all.

Protection of Intangible Cultural Heritage and Construction of "the Belt and Road"

Tian Qing
Research Fellow of Chinese National Academy of Arts

"The Belt and Road" refers to "Silk Road Economic Belt" and "21 – Century Maritime Silk Road". "The Belt and Road" is an innovative concept on cooperation and development proposed by Chinese government. It aims to borrow the history symbol of the ancient "silk road", hold high the banner of peaceful development and actively develop partnership relations with countries along the route, so as to build a community of shared interests, destiny and responsibility that features mutual political trust, economic integration and cultural inclusiveness.

Relevant countries along the "the Belt and Road" boast a long historic culture, and abundant intangible culture heritages. It is a special significance to protect these intangible culture heritages well. They are the common treasure of human, the important sign of national spirit and culture, and the DNA of a country and a nation's culture life which contains the ethical thinking mode, imagination and culture consciousness. They not only show the rich creativity of people all over the world, but also reflect the diversity of world culture. During the progress of globalization and modernization, the world's cultural ecology is going through tremendous changes. Especially in most developing countries along the "The Belt and Road", their intangible culture heritages which imply the national spirit have been influenced by the fierce shock of western powerful culture, facing the risk of extinction. Therefore, it is extremely important and pressing to propose and well protect the national intangible cultural heritages of "the Belt and Road".

Though China started late in protecting the intangible culture heritages, but China has made big progress. Chinese government and society have accumulated many ways of protecting the intangible culture heritages, which are the "Chinese experience". It is important to share the experience with countries along "The Belt and Road", to let the century-old great creation of human ancestors along the "silk road" and "maritime silk road" which have passed today be revalued and re-appreciated and to continue inheriting and carrying forward the unique national culture in the tide of "modernization".

The Role of the Culture in Building Economic Belt for the Marine Silk Road in the 21st Century and the Dialogue of Civilizations

Ramadan AlSharrah

Professor of Management and Economic Sciences Secretary General of the Union of Investment Companies Kuwait

The paper deals with the following topics:
- New Silk Road and the reasons for calling it with this name.
- Economic and political importance of the project.
- The feasibility of the project on the economic level: Global-Local.
- SWOT Analysts for the project.

The road extends for about 11 thousand kilometers (8,000 miles) starting from Shanghai in China and ending in the German capital Berlin, but there has been an update on the project suggesting expanding the road until the Iberian Peninsula in Spain.

The Chinese President, "Xi Jinping" has announced the idea of reviving this road in early 2013, followed by announcing the launch of the World Bank for Infrastructure Asian (AIIB) in 2014 initiative with the participation of about 58 countries, including 12 member state of the North Atlantic Treaty Organization (NATO), to provide the initial funding for the project amounted to an initial contribution of Chinese – US $ 47 billion.

The origin of naming the Silk Road goes back to the woven silk in China, which has been able to develop its industry in terms of weaving, embroidery types of high – end technical duties in about the third millennium BC, which made it a commodity needed in the rest of the world and the highest prices.

The project includes about 65 countries and the importance of its main objectives lies in promoting political relations, infrastructure, increasing the flow of goods, the matter that leads to increase income and to encourage interaction between the peoples. Also, the project is important for land transport, as well as the importance to sea transport, and the importance of the project in terms of air transport.

The project economically feasible on a global level as well as at the level of the State of Kuwait.

Following the course of events on the economic level in the State of Kuwait, we can find a link between the project of the Silk Road city and the city of silk in Kuwait. In our perception, we have a strategic vision for the state extends to 2035, which passes through a five – year implementation plans carries mega – projects, including the Silk City group. The place of this strategic project of the city of silk has been chosen carefully, as it connects both of Mubarak and the new airport, which would make it crossing for a number of countries in the Gulf region, Iran, and Central Asian countries point. This will be enough for finding a city that helps neighborhoods of historic Silk Road, which restores Kuwait's role as a center of global financial and commercial and will make it a crossroads linking East and West.

The project "Silk City" is not just an investment project. This vital and strategic project is accompanied by the establishment of a number of projects on all levels including trade, tourism, investment projects and business development. It has already been designed as a free zone, which will provide through better facilities to companies and regional businesses to open centers have its location in Kuwait, which is located in the business hub of the Arabian Gulf and Central Asia.

The philosophy and the vision of the project "Silk City" and its future prospects came to mimic the philosophy of linking investment and culture, this is evidence that there is a contact point between the past, present and future in the "Silk City" project, which will restore the spirit of the Silk Road in the communication and dissemination of culture.

Break through Isolated Culture, Build Cultural Community

Yin Hong
Professor and Deputy Director of School of Journalism and Communication of Tsinghua University

The initiative of "the Belt and Road" is to develop economic partnerships with relevant countries, build interest community, fate community and duty community that are politically trustful, economically integrated and culturally compatible by following the tradition of Silk Road, upholding a banner of peace and development. In this plan, culture plays an important role in exchanging emotions, facilitating mutual trust, and promoting public connection so that the road will be smooth and the belt will be harmonious.

I. Current Situation: We should respect cultural difference and break through cultural islands. The strategy of "the Belt and Road" involves dozens of Asian, European and African countries, especially countries of East Asia, Middle Asia, West Asia, North Asia and South Asia. They are of a vast region, but have met communication obstacles and cultural islands because of six reasons.

The six reasons are: 1. Difference of economic levels; 2. Difference of social systems; 3. Difference of religious beliefs; 4. Difference of geographic relationships; 5. Difference of languages; 6. Difference of ethnics and traditions.

On one hand, there are cultural islands in Asian countries that are isolated in different levels; on the other hand, due to its overall cultural superiority in development, European culture is exerting more and more impact on Asian countries. Therefore, in Asian countries, there have appeared various cultural groups, including local and foreign cultures.

II. Strategy: Develop commerce with culture by utilizing resources of large markets.

"The Belt and Road" is firstly a trade road. The ancient Silk Road is a trade and commerce road, along which science and technology were spread together with cargoes and products. Because of their practicality, necessity and lack of ideology, physical goods were easily communicated. Therefore, culture should be spread with commercial means.

1. Stress should be place on building of commodities with culture. For instance, in the ancient times, Chinese porcelain wares and tea products were not only substantial cargoes, but also items involving aesthetics, calligraphy, lifestyle, philosophy and concepts.

2. Cultural elements should be infused through fashion, tourism, leisure, design, trade of industrial and handicraft articles so that mutual communication and understanding can be facilitated.

3. Priority should be given to creative design, instruction, training and brand building, and Chinese traditional culture and modern lifestyle should be reasonably combined to manifest nationality with modern senses.

III. Development: Cultural exchange develops into cultural transaction, and cultural products develop into cultural industry.

1. Cultivate market demand through cultural exchanges, and maximize cultural communication through cultural transactions;

2. Cooperate in products first, and then form joint ventures and multi – national enterprises;

3. Explore and share cultural resources, and build regional cultural community;

4. Establish complete cultural chains with commodity culture, cultural products, minority culture and public culture.

Proceedings of the 3rd Asian Cultural Forum

Speeches of the Sub-forums from China

Role of Overseas Chinese in People's Communication of "the Belt and Road"

Chen Yiping
Professor and Peputy Director of School of International Relations/
Overseas Chinese Institute of Jinan University

In September and October 2013, when visiting Kazakhstan and Indonesia, Chinese President Xi Jinping proposed the initiative to jointly develop the "Silk Road Economic Belt" and the "21st century Maritime Silk Road", which is usually simplified as "the Belt and Road". The Belt and Road initiative proposed by the Chinese government intends to develop a "Destiny Community" through policy exchange, facility connection, trade smoothness, fund integration and people communication. The key to develop Destiny Community is people's communication, the basis of which is cultural communication, mutual understanding and respect. The ancient Silk Road is both a commercial road and cultural communication road. The common historical memory, cultural heritage and win – win trade cooperation of relevant countries are the basis of the Belt and Road development. How to promote cultural communication and cooperation, and how to facilitate people's communication are important projects for decision – makers and scholars. This article will explore cultural communication ways, mechanisms and platforms through roles of overseas Chinese in Chinese cultural communication and national image creation.

Roles of Overseas Chinese in People's Communication of the Belt and Road

At present, there are over 60 million overseas Chinese across 198 countries and regions, among which 40 million are in the Belt and Road regions. They have lived locally for generations, and have developed impressive economic power, extensive human relation, and cultural advantage to connect China and foreign countries so that they can play special and important roles in people's communication of the Belt and Road.

(Ⅰ) Communication of Chinese Culture

As the bridge and linkage between China and residence countries, overseas Chinese have been actively communicating traditional Chinese culture, creating and maintaining positive international image of China by establishing various social organizations, founding Chinese schools and media, creating Chinese literary works, and promoting Chinese educational activities. At the same time, overseas Chinese also develop Chinese culture by absorbing local cultural elements so that unique overseas Chinese literature and art atmospheres are formed and popularly accepted by local people.

Overseas Chinese inherit and develop Chinese culture in three major levels. The first comes superficial utensil culture such as tea sets, lanterns and couplets. Second, behavioral and custom culture such as Spring Festival, Lantern Festival, Qingming Festival, Duanwu Festival, and Mid – Autumn Festival, and Chinese marriage ceremony. Third, traditional Chinese cultural and value concepts embodied on overseas Chinese. [1]

(Ⅱ) Introduction of China's Actual Conditions and Way of Development

After 30 years of reform and opening, China's economy has been developing rapidly with an amazing average annual GDP growth rate of 9%. The key of China's rapid economic development lies in Chinese economic system and the way of development. The Chinese government has conducted various programs and has made some achievements in introducing Chinese national conditions and developing way. However, the huge potential of overseas Chinese and returned overseas Chinese or their relatives in this aspect hasn't been appropriately stressed. In fact, "overseas Chinese media, Chinese societies, cultural centers and Chinese activists have been introducing Chinese actual conditions and development patterns at different levels and in different ways. In recent years, overseas Chinese media have universally increase reports on Chinese news with increasingly enlarged volumes and intensities to present Chinese political conditions, economic develop-

---

[1] *Harmony and Win – Win: Overseas Chinese and China's Soft Power*, edited by Chen Yiping, Jinan University Press, September, 2012, p. 192.

ment, cultural prosperity and social stability[①]."

The overseas questionnaire survey directed by the author has also confirmed this. In Malaysia[②], in order to investigate roles of Chinese Malaysians in introducing China, we designed two sets of questionnaire for overseas Chinese and other nationals (mainly Malays). "Have your friends, neighbors or colleagues ever inquired the following matters about China from you?" "Have you ever inquired the following matters about China from your Chinese friends, neighbors or colleagues?" The survey indicates that Chinese Malaysians play an important role in introducing Chinese culture or art, economic development or situation and communicating Chinese values. It should be noted, possibly due to sensitivity, Malaysian Chinese are not very passionate in introducing Chinese political conditions and development. (See Table 1.1)

Table 1.1 Roles of Chinese Malaysians in Introducing China

	Have your friends, neighbors or colleagues ever inquired the following matters about China?	Have you ever inquired the following matters about China from your Chinese friends, neighbors or colleagues?
Chinese culture or art	72.8%	82.7%
Chinese economic development and situation	46.6%	62.5%
Chinese political development and situation	38.4%	42.8%
Chinese values (e.g., emphasis on education and family, filial respect to parents)	76.8%	73.5%

[①] *Harmony and Win – Win: Overseas Chinese and China's Soft Power*, edited by Chen Yiping, Jinan University Press, September, 2012, p. 7.
[②] In 2011, the research group led by the author gave out questionnaires when we were having academic exchange, and we also asked Malaysian professors to help distribute questionnaires. In total, we received 429 valid questionnaires, among which 242 and 187 copies were from overseas Chinese and Malaysian interviewees.

(III) Public Diplomacy of Overseas Chinese, Understanding, Support and Explanation of Chinese Diplomatic Policies

Public diplomacy has long been stressed by the Chinese government, and by now it is an important part of Chinese overall diplomacy. On July 17, 2009, on the 11th diplomatic envoy meeting, Hu Jintao clearly requested, "China should enhance public diplomacy and cultural diplomacy, and execute various foreign cultural communications to effectively promulgate excellent Chinese culture. [1]" The report of the 18th National Congress of the Communist Party of China clearly requests, "We will actively promote public and cultural diplomacy, and safeguard our overseas legal rights. We will friendly communicate with political parties and organizations of different countries, and enhance foreign communications of NPC, CPPCC, local and civil groups to lay social solid foundations for international relation development."[2]

The history and practice of Chinese development have manifested that overseas Chinese is an important and indispensable bridge or linkage for diplomatic communication between China and the world. They are also important pioneers, carriers and maintainers for Chinese overseas interests. Overseas Chinese made significant contributions to the new China in opening diplomatic situations and solving diplomatic deadlocks. For instance, Chen Xiangmei contributed much to the development of Sino – US relationship. In the past decades, she has frequently traveled between the two countries and has done a lot of work to promote Sino – US friendship. Zeng Yongsen, a Chinese Malaysian whose ancestral home is Beiliu, Guangxi, made an "ice – breaking journey" to promote Sino – Malaysian relationship. He made invaluable contributions to the diplomatic relation establishment, and was recognized "Kissinger of Malaysia".

---

[1] Hu Jintao and other central leaders attended the 11th diplomatic envoy meeting, Xinhuanet, July 20, 2009, http://news.xinhuanet.com/politics/2009 – 07/20/content_ 11740850_ 1. htm.

[2] The 18th Congress Report (full text), Nov. 19, 2012, http://www.xj.xinhuanet.com/2012 – 11/19/c_ 113722546. htm

Path and Mechanism for Overseas Chinese Participating in People's Communication of the Belt and Road

(Ⅰ) Channels and Paths that Overseas Chinese Communicate Chinese Traditional Culture

1. Channels of Behavior and Concept Culture of Overseas Chinese

Channels of behavior and concept culture for overseas Chinese, including those such as overseas Chinese festivals and customs, business concepts, management patterns, help to demonstrate special charm of Chinese traditional culture in local and international communities. As the saying goes "Wherever there is sea water and sun shine, there are Chinese", overseas Chinese spread all over the world, who are messengers of Chinese culture. China towns, Chinese restaurants, traditional Chinese medicine clinics, Chinese language schools and Chinese Kungfu clubs all over the world have become important venues and paths to demonstrate Chinese culture, and Spring Festival, Mid – Autumn Festival, Chinese marriage and other customs enable westerners "Zero – Distance Contact" of Chinese culture.

2. Channels of "Three Treasures" of Chinese Society

Chinese organizations, Chinese media and Chinese schools are called "Three Treasures" of Chinese society, which are significant platforms to communicate Chinese culture.

In Spring Festival, overseas Chinese will organize dragon or lion dancing, Spring – Festival parade, float performance, gourmet festival and celebrating parties. In the Spring Festival of 2010, the temple fair organized by the Greater Washington native association in Washington D. C. attracted many people, when various Chinese gourmet foods was supplied and national dances were performed. Songs, short plays, operas, martial arts and folk music were played and drove the celebration to a climax.

Activities organized by overseas Chinese are not limited to China towns. In the past, spring festival celebrations by overseas Chinese were unconscious and self – entertaining activities for missing homeland, educating children. Therefore, the activities are restricted to overseas Chinese communities. With the improvement of their impact in residence countries, to demonstrate Chinese long history and unique culture, various celebrations extended beyond their residence quarters and went to landmark venues.

Overseas Chinese media have been undertaking promotion of Chinese culture as their important missions, and become substantial channels for communicating Chinese culture. With the rise of China and the promotion of its international status, overseas Chinese media have also entered into a new epoch. Zhao Yang, the former vice director of The Overseas Chinese Affair Office of the State Council said on the closing ceremony of the Fourth World Chinese Media Forum in 2007, "Overseas Chinese media are in their flourishing period, and overseas Chinese media have a very bright future." "Overseas Chinese media is an important force to communicate Chinese culture, and is a cultural messenger to expand the exchanges between China and the world." [1]For instance, the 678 reports on Chinese Mainland of the Southern Chinese Daily includes 185 reports on politics, 196 of economy, 226 on society and 71 on culture. [2]

Overseas Chinese schools play a major role for overseas Chinese societies. Since 1980s, due to the increase of Chinese impact, stress of Chinese government on Chinese language education and needs of overseas Chinese of Chinese education, Chinese language education has entered a flourishing development period. Overseas Chinese education has cultivated Chinese talents for their residence countries, supplied important platforms and means for maintaining and enhancing national recognition and cultural identification of Chinese communities. It has also supplied significant channels for inheriting and promoting Chinese culture. The research group led by the author have visited many Chinese schools in US, Canada, France, Myanmar, Philippines, Malaysia and Indonesia, and have personally experience their efforts and outstanding effects in inheriting and promoting Chinese culture. For instance, the Wenqiao Trilingual School of Bali, Indonesia organizes spring festival parties every year. Under instructions of teachers, little English and Chinese anchorpersons well cooperated for students from kindergartens to middle schools to participate and perform, including dance, singing, handwriting, poetry recitation and music instrument performance. Parents also actively participated, and attract a lot of local audience.

---

[1] *Promising Overseas Chinese Media are in Their Flourishing Period*, Zhao Yang, www.chinaqw.com, Sep. 4, 2007.
[2] *Study on China National Image Reports by Overseas Chinese Media-A Case Study with the Mainland Section of Southern Chinese Daily*, Yan Huan, Wang Linlin, Press Circles, vol. 15, 2012.

3. Channels of Overseas Chinese Businessmen and Chinese Elite

Overseas Chinese businessmen are also significant messengers for Chinese culture. In this article, overseas Chinese businessmen refer to overseas Chinese organizations on the world economic stage. The total asset of global overseas Chinese businessmen is several trillion US dollars. They have become an important economic force in the globalization period, they are an important bridge and a driving force for economic cooperation between China and the world, and also a driver to manifest and communicate Chinese culture. Unique business concepts and management culture of overseas Chinese businessmen originate from Chinese traditional culture. Chinese enterprises stress values of "faith", "human – orientation", "harmony brings wealth", "diligence and saving", and "keeping expenditure within income", which are "undoubtedly helpful to family harmony, enhancement of enterprise engagement, social stability and development". "Overseas Chinese enterprises have established extensive relations through blood ties, family relations, and geographic relations, which have contributed much to the growth and development of overseas Chinese enterprises", and modern commercial networks are gradually founded in this way. [1]Many overseas Chinese businessmen are eminent on the international stage, being not only key objects of our national overseas Chinese work, but also objects closely pursued by governments of many countries.

Many overseas Chinese elites communicate Chinese special thoughts, philosophical concepts, moral standards, literary and art values through their academic works, activities and articles on media, and actively discuss and promote the role of Chinese culture in driving human civilization. For instance, Du Weiming, a representative of modern new Confucian school, has long been engaged in Confucian research and promotion, interpretation of Chinese culture, reflection on modern spirit, advocacy of civilization dialogues. Therefore, he was highly recognized in the world. In Feb. 2013, on the fifth global forum of UN Civilization League, Du Weiming became the only keynote speaker, demonstrating "value of cross – culture dialogues to our era". The high recognition he received reflected the increase of speech right and impact of overseas Chinese scholars in the international community.

---

[1] *Overseas Chinese Businessmen in China-Advantages in ASEAN FTA Development*, Chen Weiping (Chairman of Anda Holdings International Limited), July 26, 2004. http://www.chinaqw.com/node2/node116/node119/node162/node2222/node2542/node2545/userobject6ai184523.html

(II) Communication Channels and Paths of Chinese Road and Foreign Policies

Communication channels of Chinese culture are also communication channels for Chinese road and foreign policies.

First, overseas Chinese introduce Chinese situations, development patterns, foreign policies and overseas Chinese policies through their personal channels, overseas Chinese media, overseas Chinese education, works and speeches of overseas Chinese elites. Chinese national cohesion is the biggest soft power of China, and the culture of 5000 years offers them strong identification sense, and they are very proud of the development of their homeland. Since the establishment of P. R. China, especially in the 30 years after reformation and opening, overseas Chinese have played very important roles in promoting foreign exchanges, and assisting our diplomatic work. They introduce and explain China to the world through their personal channels, overseas Chinese media, overseas Chinese education, works and speeches. Therefore, they become "civil ambassadors" to enhance communication and understanding, and to facilitate friendship and cooperation.

Second, overseas Chinese organizations, especially world organization networks and association activities such as the regularly held World Chinese entrepreneurs Convention, which have tightened relations between overseas Chinese and their homeland, and facilitated exchanges and cooperation between their residence country and China.

In recent years, many overseas Chinese organizations are being globalized, and a number of world Chinese organizations and networks have been formed. These world Chinese organizations are not only platforms for trade cooperation and cultural communication of overseas Chinese, but also important channels for them to understand and cooperate with China. World Chinese Entrepreneurs Convention (WCEC) founded in 1990s is such an organization, the first convention was held in Singapore in August 1991. After over 20 years of development, WCEC has been held in Singapore, Hong Kong, Bangkok, Vancouver, Melbourne, Kuala Lumpur, Seoul, and Kobe. Its scale and impact increases steadily. In September 2013, the 12th WCEC was held in Chengdu, with 3000 representatives form 104 countries attended the convention. WCEC has become "the bridge and linkage for overseas Chinese around the world to promote economic and trade cooperation, which has effectively facilitated local economy and development of countries and regions where they live."[1] The convention has tightened relations between overseas Chinese and their homeland as well as understanding of China.

Elements Influencing Overseas Chinese to Participate in the Belt and Road Development

Overseas Chinese possess very important roles in cultural exchanges of the Belt and Road, and building of our national image. However, there are some difficulties and challenges for them to play these roles.

1. International relations directly impact survival and development of overseas Chinese. Whether the relation between their residence country and China is friendly, frustrated or worsened, their survival and development will be influenced.

2. Policies to Chinese of overseas Chinese residence country. For instance, policies to Chinese of Southeast Asian countries, European countries and US impact their survival environment. Even Southeast Asian countries have different policies to overseas Chinese, and their political statuses are different.

3. Due to historical reasons, overseas Chinese have different viewpoints on many issues among themselves. Cross – strait relations influence the relation between overseas Chinese from Taiwan and Chinese Mainland. Different Chinese organizations may be separated, and old and young generations may have different opinions on Chinese culture.

4. Identification difference between overseas Chinese and Chinese with foreign citizenship. The Chinese government has repetitively stressed overseas Chinese, whether they are of Chinese or foreign citizenships, are all our service objects but with distinct difference in policy definitions. As Chinese citizens, overseas Chinese are obliged to protect our national interests, and should contribute to the development and friendly cooperation between their residence countries and China. However, overseas Chinese with foreign citizenships will be naturally loyal to their citizenship countries. How to balance, maintain, develop relations with overseas Chinese with foreign citizenships are closely related to scientific and sustainable development of our national work for overseas Chinese affairs.

---

[1] The World Chinese Entrepreneurs Convention, Xinhuanet, Jun. 25, 2003.

Policy Advice

1. Cooperation and Win – Win Thoughts: Principle of People's Communication

Realistic power outlook emphasizes competitiveness and exclusiveness, and pursues relative benefit. Even the soft power theory in Europe and US intends to hold a competitive point of view towards the development and application of Chinese soft power [1], but "most people hold a zero – sum opinion, looking at the development of China's soft power with negative rather than positive attitude."[2] "Our focus should be placed on reminding western country governments of appropriate responding to China's soft power as well as any relevant problems."[3]

The performance and influence of overseas Chinese in their residence countries is an important link of the appeal and influence of their homeland country, and one foundation to facilitate cultural identification. However, to play roles of overseas Chinese, win – win thoughts are necessary. In the past, we excessively stressed the contributions of overseas Chinese to our economic and technological development. However, with the development of China, some western countries and populists always look at China with tinted spectacles, exaggerating Chinese threat, and overseas Chinese are sometimes are slandered as the Fifth Column members or "Yellow Spies". [4]In order to refute such slanders and eliminate governmental and civil doubts of their residence countries, we should emphasize the win – win[5] nature of overseas Chinese resources-they contribute to

---

[1] Overseas Chinese and China's Soft Power: Roles, Mechanism and Policy Ideas, Chen Yiping and Fan Rusong, Institute of Overseas Chinese History Research, 2nd issue, 2010.
[2] The Rise of China's Soft Power and Its Implications for the United States, Joseph Nye and Wang Jisi, *World Economics and Politics*, 6th issue, 2009.
[3] Comparison of Chinese and US Soft Powers and Implications for China, Fang Changping, *World Economics and Politics*, 7th issue, 2007.
[4] Overseas Chinese and China's Soft Power: Roles, Mechanism and Policy Ideas, Chen Yiping and Fan Rusong, Institute of Overseas Chinese History Research, 2nd issue, 2010.
[5] Overseas Chinese Resources under Soft Power Perspective, Gao Weinong, Xuelin Bookstore, Kuala Lumpur, Preface, July, 2010.

multiple parties, including other overseas Chinese, their residence countries and China[①]. At the same time, we should pay attention to difference of expression and communication on soft power inside China and around the world.

In fact, the Chinese government has always stressed the "three – beneficial" principle – beneficial to long – term survival and development of overseas Chinese and local social, economic and cultural development, beneficial to the friendly and cooperative relation between the residence country and China, and beneficial to China's modernization development and country unification.

2. Cultural Identification: Basis for People's Communication

Cultural identification is a kind of identity recognition that recognizes the cultural identity and produces deep psychological deposition in mind. By using the same cultural symbols, obeying the same cultural concepts, upholding the same thinking and behavioral standards, people develop affinity and sense of belonging.

During long – term of life in residence countries, overseas Chinese have developed their unique culture, which is different from the original Chinese culture. However, they are of the same origin, and have close relations. The excellent Chinese culture is the spiritual pillar to support permanent development of Chinese people, and is an important linkage to contact overseas Chinese. Overseas Chinese are important carriers and transmitters of Chinese culture, and positive force to promote international friendship and communicate Chinese culture. Therefore, they play an important role in increasing the influence of Chinese culture in the world.

Of course, we should know that most overseas Chinese have become citizens of the residence countries. Therefore, in politics they should be loyal to the residence countries. In practice of overseas Chinese affairs, we should respect their political identification and loyalty to their residence countries, and guide them to promote local economic development and enhance their social statuses, and thoroughly integrate into the local society. Under these conditions, overseas Chinese can contribute more to the improvement

---

① The first UN High – Level Dialogue on International Migration and Development held in 2006 stated clearly, the goal that "different countries cooperate to ensure win – win of migrants, their homeland and accepting country" has been recognized by more and more countries at political levels. See General Assembly of United Nations, Globalization and interdependence: international migration and development, A/60/871, 18 May 2006, http://www.un.org/esa/population/migration/hld/Text/Report% 20of% 20the% 20SG (June%2006) _ English. pdf, p. 5

of relations between their residence countries and China.

3. Public Diplomacy: Acting Point for People's Communication

To facilitate popular connection, overseas Chinese should first play their bridging function. Marrha Finnemore and other constructivist scholars pointed out: International organizations and non - country behavior entities transmit and expand international regulations, and persuade countries to assess functionality of national interest goals[1]. In interactions, people have constructed common concepts, conceptual shaping and change foreign policies of country behaving entities. Therefore, interpersonal positive interactions can set up communication bridges for two countries. [2]

Overseas Chinese public diplomacy is an important part of Chinese special public diplomacy, which serves the overall national diplomacy, and is a distinct sign for increasingly expanded resources of the national entity. Overseas Chinese public diplomacy stresses public diplomacy with overseas Chinese affair as work channels, and its goal is to reflect the true image of China and Chinese government. It should also eliminate confusions, mistakes and objectively express our opinions. We believe, under the current complex international conditions, it is a new task to promote friendly exchange and cooperation, eliminate diplomatic deadlocks, truly introduce China and build positive images of China through overseas Chinese public diplomacy. Relevant departments involved in overseas Chinese affairs should take it an important task.

4. Building National Images: Key for People's Communication

National image building is the core part of national soft power construction. Building positive national images is an important national policy of China. Building new images of a large country needs efforts of all parties of the society. As a cultural voice to reflect Chinese requirements and promote Chinese culture, overseas Chinese media used to focus on alleviating homesick emotions of the Chinese people in early years. By now, it has become an important force in promoting participation in political election, and has much more influence on local social life and local politics. Under complex international politics and globalization conditions, it strives to reconstruct the sensitive and complex ethnic re-

---

[1] National Interests in International Community, Marrha Finnemore, Zhejiang people's publishing house, Hangzhou, pp. 6 – 7, 2001.
[2] Juyan Zhang, Exploring Rhetorie of Public Diplomacy in the Mixed – motive Situation: Using the Case of President Obama's nuclear – free world's Speech in Prague, *Place Branding and Public Diplomacy*, 2010, (6): 294.

lations between the Chinese and local people. To some degrees, it has maintained Chinese national images, and promoted political relations between China and overseas Chinese residence countries.

Two Paths of Chinese Culture Influencing the World: the Important Civil Culture

Chen Zhiping
Institute of Chinese Classics of Xiamen University

In recent years, with the deepening of China's reform and opening and rise of international status, when people are searching the impact of Chinese culture on the world civilization, many have sighed the weakness of Chinese culture in the world layout in modern history. Study of collisions and exchanges of Chinese culture and the world civilization of Ming and Qing dynasties until the Republic of China, and historical process and experience from the said collisions and exchanges, will sure be helpful for us to comprehensively understand the contribution of Chinese culture to the progress of the world civilization, and understand the mutual impact and historical statuses between Chinese culture and the world culture since Ming and Qing dynasties.

By now, the study of Chinese culture in the world has been habitually limited to the communication of the upper culture of Chinese classic culture – Confucianism – in the world civilization, and has neglected the role of Chinese civil culture, especially that of Southeastern coastal regions of China. Therefore, this is quite unreasonable. In fact, since Ming and Qing dynasties, external communication of civil culture from southeastern coast Chinese region has been the major force in the entire communication of Chinese culture with the world.

In the middle and late periods of Ming Dynasty, Chinese merchants actively responded to the collision and integration between the east and the west, and emigration of Chinese people became a constant phenomenon. As these emigrants had family or hometown relations, they must maintain ancestral lifestyles in their new settlements in foreign countries. Therefore, family settlement, townsman inhabitation, heritage of civil and religious culture, maintenance of customs and languages, education and entertainment have been passed generation after generation in oral and behavioral manners, and have been survived.

Since Ming and Qing dynasties, the popular lifestyles and cultural communication spread in civil groups have become special Chinese cultural signs in foreign countries. Therefore, when we review the Confucian classic – centered ideological communication to Western countries since the end of Ming dynasty, we should never neglect the role and value of civil cultural communication in mid and late periods of Ming dynasty, namely, impact of lifestyles of the populace on western civilization.

See "the Belt and Road" from the Perspective of Culture

Fang Changping

Professor and Deputy Director of the College of International Studies, Renmin University of China

Fields of economy & trade and safety are mainly focused in the study of "the Belt and Road", while academic circle and press circle seldom study it from perspective of culture. The author plans to study the construction of "the Belt and Road" from perspective of culture. There are three views on this issue from China's diplomatic tradition: first, public products shall be provided during the construction of "the Belt and Road" and in Chinese diplomacy. The public products are not only material things, but also include things of culture type like concept and system. That is to say, we should spread our culture and value to the outside world in forms of public products. Second, relative to the above viewpoints, the nature and vitality of culture shall be its diversity. Integration cannot be applied in culture; cultural diversity shall be more stressed under integration of economy. Therefore, during construction of "the Belt and Road", we shall avoid talking about cultural integration. Especially in China, cultural transmission shall be shunned. Unlike the above two viewpoints, the author holds that cross-cultural communication and people-to-people exchange are indeed important in the construction of "the Belt and Road", which can link the peoples' hearts. The final result is not assimilating other culture by culture of one country and one nationality, but forming something with common value during the equal exchange of culture, like peace, opening up, equality, inclusiveness, corporation, win-win, etc, which are proposed by us, but they surpass the state and nationality, and they reflect the common value of human kind. Seen from cultural exchange mode, cultural exchange shall not be impacted by the mode of "developing culture industry on the economic basis" in domestic China, but shall have its own internal law and autonomy. It shall not overstress the utilitarian of cultural exchange in promoting the development of the economy.

Integration Development of Asian Culture Seen from the Formation of Dunhuang Culture

Gao Dexiang
Professor of Dunhuang Culture Society

Dunhuang culture, so broad and profound, has a very long history. Such kind of multicultural product has developed into its unique charm of culture form after experiencing over 2000 years.

Dunhuang, located in the westernmost place of Gansu province, China, is the throat on the ancient Silk Road and the only way for the ancient East-West exchanges. Here is the intersection of four great cultural systems in the world (China, India, Greece, and Islamic), and here realizes the complete exchange and integration of various cultures. Therefore, profound Dunhuang culture is created eventually.

Represented by Dunhuang Mogao Grottoes, the grotto art displays a variety of culture forms in the ancient Silk Road. At the beginning of 20th century, the Library Cave of Dunhuang Mogao Grottoes was found, and about over 70, 000 pieces of precious historical relics was unearthed, which shocked the world. Besides the Buddhist classics, the literature also includes the books on Manichaeism, Nestorianism, Daoism, and Confucianism. In addition, the books on astronomy, calendar, military, geography, folk custom, surname, account book, directory, correspondence, letter, poetry, lyrics, dialect, travel note, and miscellaneous writings are also contained in it. Accordingly, a new subject-Dunhuang Studies is created due to the discovery of library cave.

The formation of Dunhuang culture is the aggregation of multinational and multiregional spread and combination on the Silk Road. If the ancient Silk Road is not opened, if the combination development of East-West multicultural product is not existed, it is impossible to produce such world-famous Dunhuang culture. This shows that the development, innovation and prosperity of culture must go the way of exchange combination. Today, the proposal of "the Belt and Road" again provides an unprecedented opportunity for the development and prosperity of economic culture. In this era, Asia will spur with long accumulation and also have certain regional advantages. The economic development and cultural prosperity need to strengthen the cooperation, enhance the exchange, and learn from each other for common development. Meanwhile, Asia is a residence of many nationalities, and the cultures vary from each other, with rich contents and various forms, such characteristics and advantages of Asian culture can also be a good base for Asian cultural exchange; through extensive exchanges, it is bound to produce a profound influence on the promotion of Asian economic development, cultural prosperity, social progress, and the development of human history.

Historical Background for the Formation of Dunhuang Culture

The formation of Dunhuang culture has gone through a long process and has had a very complicated historical background, mainly including three reasons from the current situation: smoothness of the Silk Road, introduction of Buddhism, and mixture of multinational culture.

1. The Unimpeded Silk Road

According to the history, China has had so close contacts with many countries in Central Asia, South Asia, West Asia and Europe by road traffic since long time ago. In 138 BC, under the order from Emperor Wu of Han dynasty, Zhang Qian and over 100 persons led by him went to the Western Regions for the first time, and returned to Chang'an in 126 BC, lasting 13 years. In 119 BC, he and over 300 persons led by him were ordered to the Western Regions again, to further understand the economic and cultural development condition throughout the West, which provided Western Han dynasty the important basis for the opening of the Silk Road; therefore, Western Han dynasty set up the Dunhuang County in 111 BC, as well as Yangguan and Yumen Pass, specialized in the management of East-West passers-by. Because of its special location, Dunhuang at that time was the only way for the communications between Central Plains and Western Regions; with the commercial circulation, various cultures were also under the broad communications. The music-accompanied dance in the ancient Western Regions was developed very well, and around the Northern and Southern dynasties period (third century AD), the influential Kangguo music, Anguo music, India music, Qiuci music, Gaochang music, Shule music, and Xiliang music were introduced into the Central Plains from the West, which had a great impact in Sui and Tang dynasties, the flourished "Ten musicians" in Tang dynasty was formed based on the absorption and mixture of exotic music and dance. "Huxuan dance", "Huteng dance", and lute, upright Konghou, tartar pipe, five-string pipa, shie drum, and waist drum were also introduced from the West. Hu dance, Hu music, Hu clothes, and Hu meals became a fashion of the royal court. At that time, the culture of West Regions had the great influence on the traditional culture of Central Plains.

The cultures no matter from Central Plains or Western Regions would be introduced in Dunhuang at first. In addition to a large number of Chinese documents, the documents in Dunhuang also include quite a number of Sanskrit, Sogdian, Turkic, Khotan, Uighur, Syriac, Xixia, Mongolian, and ancient Tibetan scripts. These precious historical documents fully proved the real condition of cultural exchange in Dunhuang.

2. Introduction of Buddhism

It can be said that Dunhuang art is the product of Buddhism, and the Dunhuang Grottoes art will never be generated without the introduction of Buddhism, so Buddhism plays a decisive role in the generation of Dunhuang art.

Buddhism was generated in India at about five or six century BC, and then introduced into China in about the initial stage of Eastern Han dynasty. Dunhuang was one of regions receiving the earliest Buddhism spread. With the development over times, Buddhism produced increasingly great effect in Central Plains, and the believers became more and more. Under such situation, the building of Buddhist grottoes had sprung up since Northern and Southern dynasties. As the throat of the Silk Road, Dunhuang has become the distributing center of economic culture. With the quick spread and development of Buddhism here, the grotto building and Buddha creating had naturally become a spiritual pursuit, and accordingly, the world-famous Mogao Grottoes, Western Thousand-Buddha Caves, and Yulin Grottoes were created successively in Dunhuang. Since the creation in 366 AD, Mogao Grottoes had experienced more than 10 dynasties, including Northern Wei, Western Wei, Northern Zhou, Sui, Tang, Five dynasties, Song, Western Xia, Yuan, and Qing, going through over 1000 years. In 492 grottoes currently existed, over 45,000 square meters of ancient mural and over 2000 painted sculptures are preserved, which is the greatest Buddhist art treasure from the existing scale in the world. In 1988, Mogao Grottoes was included in the World Cultural Heritage List by UNESCO. In June, 2014, the Silk Road was also included in the World Cultural Heritage List by UNESCO, while the Xuanquan Post and Yumen pass in Dunhuang, two sites of Han dynasty, was included in the important cultural sites of the Silk Road.

Now, Yulin Grottoes has 42 caves while Western Thousand-Buddha Caves exists 16. A lot of murals and painted sculptures are also preserved in these two caves, whose contents and forms are basically the same as those in Mogao Grottoes, belonging to the same type of construction style.

Besides the Buddhist themes, the contents of Dunhuang mural also reflect many real-life scenarios, such as harvesting, plough, travelling, hunting, weddings, funerals, acrobatics, martial art, song and dance performances, and even the teeth brushing, tonsuring, baby carriage and such nuances of life are vividly depicted in the mural.

We can see clearly from the Dunhuang mural that the drawing lines in the early mural are rough and uninhibited with simple composition; no matter heavenly musicians, flying musicians or character images, dressing and clothing all reflect the Western style (see Figure 1). However, the painting style in Sui and Tang dynasties changes completely, the things of Western style fades gradually while the traditional painting style of Central Plains is quite obvious with smooth lines, delicate composition, and lifelike character image, which not only pursues the similarity in form, but also the similarity in spirit (see Figure 2). This is the fundamental change occurring over hundreds of years since the Buddhism is introduced into Central Plains, which fully displays the diversity and inclusivity of Dunhuang culture.

It is worth thinking that, the original purpose to build the Buddha grottoes is just a kind of spiritual ballast for believers, their spending of great time and property is not to pursue the art creation, but to obtain the afterlife. In fact, these grottoes seems to leave away from the original purpose of initial builders, no longer the single Buddhist shrine, but becomes the worthy art treasure grotto, and such ending cannot be imaged by any builder at that time. The ancient Buddhist grottoes become the precious art treasure today, and its art value is far beyond the meaning of Buddhism. This is really a dramatic change! Since ancient times, so many people have dreamed to create the art, but eventually disappeared with nothing; however, many things not for art creation initially become the unique art creation in the world after thousands of years. There are many such examples in history, such as Mogao Grottoes of Dunhuang, Terra-Cotta Warriors in Xi'an, Badaling Great Wall, and Forbidden City in Beijing, which are not built for art, but finally become the important world cultural heritage with the development of history. Such examples show clearly that the formation of any culture is not determined by the subjective will of people, but needs long-term exchanges, integration, and accumulation.

3. Multinational living condition is the basis of the generation of Dunhuang culture

We can say that the cultural history is the human history, and the cultural history of a place is also the nationality development history of such place. Dunhuang has always been a place living with many nationalities, so the integration of multinational cultures is an important factor for the formation of Dunhuang culture.

As early as the Neolithic age, Sanmiao nationality had always lived here. In Qin and Han dynasties, Dunhuang was the nomadic place for Yuezhi and Wusun people. Yuezhi was a branch of the Qiang people, and Wusun was the shifted sound of "Rong in Chinese. Until the first year of Emperor Wen of Han dynasty (179 BC), the Northern Xiongnu became powerful and expanded to the South gradually, and Yuezhi and Wusun people moved to the westward successively. Vast land of Dunhuang and Hexi Corridor was occupied by Huns.

Zhang Qian was ordered to the Western Regions twice and provided Han dynasty with certain knowledge, so the Emperor Wu selected only 20-year Huo Qubing to lead the army against Huns in the spring of the second Yuanshou year (121 AD). Huns were defeated. Dunhuang and Hexi area were included in the territory of Han dynasty. Moreover, a large number of people immigrated to Dunhuang, reclaiming the land and developing the agriculture, which changed Dunhuang into a place consisting of mostly Han nationality mixed with minorities from the original minority nomadic place. This was a significant historical change occurred to Dunhuang culture.

After the Han dynasty, the nationalities in the North area lived together, and various cultures were blended here, so at that time, a unique music and dance Xiliang Music was formed here, which not only had great influence in the North, but also was popular for a long time in the royal count of Sui and Tang dynasties, attracting high attention and love from the emperors. As for the formation of Xiliang Music, it is recorded in Book of Sui, Music Records: "Xiliang (music) arose from the end of Fu family. Lu Guang and Juqu Mengxun occupied Liangzhou district, and changed Qiuci music into it, called Qin-Han dancers". Also, it is recorded in Old book of Tang, Music Records: "(Xiliang Music) is the music to mix the music in Qiang and Hu nationalities into former music of Liang people spread to China." From the documents, the popular Xiliang Music was actually an integration of Qiuci Music in the Western Regions, national music in northern area and the traditional music in Central Plains, which was just a multicultural product. Dunhuang was the place to generate and spread Xiliang Music, which was far-reaching and widely loved by people; it was even painted in Buddhist murals, and so far, the good performance scene of Xiliang Music could be seen in the mural at the north wall of No. 220 Mogao Grottoes (early Tang dynasty) (see Figure 3).

In 755 AD, Dunhuang was occupied by Tibetan. Though most local residents were from Han nationality over 70 years of Tibetan rule, their forcible implementation made Tibetan culture become the mainstream of local culture. During such time, not just a large number of Tibetan was appeared in the translation of Buddhist scriptures, but great changes had taken place in people's basic necessities of life, and even the long-lasting Xiliang Music was replaced by Tibetan music and dance. The travelling picture painted in the south wall of No. 156 Mogao Grottoes reflected the grand scene that Zhang Yichao, the Military Governor of Hexi, defeated Tibetan and reoccupied the Hexi region. Dunhuang and Hexi district again belonged to the dynasty in Central Plains, and people sang and danced to celebrate it. However, over 70-year reign of Tibetan penetrated the Tibetan culture into the traditional local culture, which was difficult to be changed, so the dance performed in the grand team was also the Tibetan kind (see Figure 4). It is clear that the alternation of nationality will impact greatly on the culture.

In 1036 AD, Dangxiang nationality in the north area became powerful quickly. Dunhuang was occupied by the Western Xia dynasty for more than 190 years. The Western Xia dynasty created the Xixia characters and tried their best to create a new cultural pattern, so as to consolidate its sphere of influence for a long time and completely change people's traditional cultural values. Therefore, the contents and forms shown in Dunhuang murals at that time were clearly different from the previous generation, which were with distinctive characteristics of the Western Xia culture (see Figure 5).

In the 13th century, another northern nationality rose. In 1227, Dunhuang was under the jurisdiction of Mongol-Yuan Empire, so the culture of northern nomadic nationalities was again combined into Dunhuang culture. Then, Ming dynasty was established in 1368 AD. For various reasons, Ming dynasty built the great wall in Jiayuguan for defense, relinquished the jurisdiction to Dunhuang, and all original residents in Dunhuang had to move eastward. Therefore, Dunhuang culture was temporarily interrupted with the migration of population during this period.

Dunhuang was recovered again by Qing dynasty. At the fourth year of Emperor Yongzheng in Qing dynasty, the people from 56 counties of Gansu province moved to

Dunhuang, making Dunhuang become a place living with multiple nationalities. Once again, various cultures exchange and combine here, and another type of culture types was formed.

We can see from its over 2000-year development process that the formation of Dunhuang culture has gone through a very complex and long historical process, which is also the main reason for the formation of diverse cultures in Dunhuang. To summarize the historical reasons for the formation of Dunhuang culture will help us further understanding of Asian culture integration development.

Potential of Asian Culture Integration Development

Among several continents in the world, Asia is with the largest population, longest history of traditional culture, most complicated nationality composition, and great multicultural patterns. Buddhist culture, Taoism, Confucianism culture, and Islamic culture form the basic forms of Asian cultures. The traditional folk cultures from different races and different areas greatly enrich the spiritual and cultural life of the nationalities. In today highly developed information era, the proposal of "the Belt and Road" again links the people in Asia closely, and the era of multicultural exchange is imperative and unstoppable; the exchange and combination of Asian cultures will not only greatly enrich the culture connotation of Asia, but will also have important influence on the development of human civilization.

1. Population advantage is the basis for the development of Asian culture

Two-thirds of the world's population lives in Asia, the country with largest population in the world is also in Asia, and there are many nationalities, beliefs, social systems, and various culture patterns. Asian countries are closely linked, friendly and connected for centuries; only through the mutual exchanges, mutual reference, and mutual reliance can promote the economic development and social progress. The influence of culture spread often depends on the quantity of the audiences, so the population resource is the greatest advantage for the exchange and development of Asian culture. Culture is a product created by human spirit, different human populations will create different cultural patterns, and culture is also the bridge and link for the human thought communications; therefore, much wider cultural exchange is required for Asia, and "the Belt and Road" needs to be built to improve the development of Asian culture to a new height.

2. Long history is the advantage for the integration development of Asian culture

Asia is one of the earliest birthplaces of human civilization; its various culture patterns, rich content, long history, and thousands of years of civilization history create many enduring culture essences. Chinese culture, ancient India culture, and Islamic culture create their own systems, spread widely and far-reaching, which have a significant impact on the human development and make great contributions to promoting the progress of human history. From a historical perspective, Asian countries have begun a wide range of exchanges as early as the opening of the Silk Road, East to West, constant and continuous, and multiple cultures have been mutually integrated and penetrated here. The formation of Dunhuang culture can prove it fully.

Culture reflects people spirit. In different nationalities and different times, people will have different culture concepts, which will be changed with the development of times. The unchangeable culture pattern is not existed in the world in fact. The cultural tradition in Asia is with long history, but during its development, mutual exchange, mutual reference, and integration development are existed all the time actually, that is, not only keeping their own culture tradition, but also injecting with new culture connotation, which is the important reason to keep the Asian culture ever-lasting and flourishing.

3. Imperative for integration development of Asian culture

History is developing, human is progressing, culture is innovating, and this is the history inevitability of human development. The vitality of culture lies in the innovation, or it cannot be inherited. Asian culture is with a long historical tradition, which has laid a good foundation for the innovation and development of Asian culture under new historical conditions. With the joint efforts of Asian countries, "the Belt and Road" is implemented well to strengthen the contact and cooperation. In this way, Asian culture will certainly create new brilliance again, and a kind of rich and diverse Asian culture will be displayed in front of the world.

Cultural Dialogue: Management of Cultural Difference

Guo Huimin

Professor and Deputy Dean of University of International Relations

In the first thirty years after reform and opening up, China embraced a new round of international economic globalization led by new computer network technology. There is no gainsaying that China is the beneficiary of it. However, China has been making more and more contributions to world economy. In 2014, China's economy contributions to the world's and Asian economic growth were 30% and 50% respectively. China is becoming an important force of maintaining world peaceful, safe and steady development.

In 2014, China became a net capital exporter for the first time. From product output to capital export, the era of "China capital" is coming. China's oversea investment and merger have showed the new features of this round due to the fact that China's economic development is highly reliant on energy and resource and world economic crises bring opportunities, and our overseas interests are also booming. With the implementation of the national initiative "the Belt and Road" and the formal establishment of Asian Infrastructure Investment Bank, China's enterprises is expected to go out on a large scale; meanwhile, China will be more closely integrated with the world.

The main risks facing the future China's enterprises when going out: geopolitical economic risk, rules risk of the commercial game and cultural difference & conflicts risk. The world is filled with uncertainty due to sharp changes, and it is common to see the anxiety, alienation, rupture, gap and conflicts caused by cultural difference. It is no strange for the existence of difference due to the diversified culture. We should vigorously advocate dialogism and solve conflicts and rubs through conversational mechanism to manage cultural difference and reduce the conflict risk. We should promote the dialogue and collaboration between people, communities and states, in a bid to realize maximum consensus cohesion and build mutual trust, which are conducive to the establishment of the sound and win-win international ecology. Here, in the logical frame "risk-dialogue-trust", the focus is mutual trust.

Trust is rooted in dialogue. The core proposition of dialogism includes: first, dialogue is the purpose "dialogue is the final purpose. Single voice can't conclude or solve anything. Two voices are the minimum requirement"; second, the essence of human thought is dialogue. To have the idea become the real concept, it is a must to have themselves be placed in active interaction with others; third, dialogue does not seek the permanent structure and the same thought, instead, it is the interweave of different voices and debates, and the "polyphony" formed by different comments and thoughts; fourth, the premise of the dialogue is difference. The dialogists are independent without mix or assimilation. No one is the absolute owner of truth, or the monopolist of words. Fifth, the direction of the dialogue is that people wish one can listen to their voice and understand them. It makes dialogue an open and unaccomplished dynamic process which is not necessary to have the final conclusion. The "unaccomplishment" of dialogue carries profound philosophy and historical significance, which requires people to select, create and transcend in a constant manner.

The greatest enlightenment dialogism rendered us is that in this era, when facing cultural difference, we should abandon traditional binary opposition thought , i. e. not conquer unitary with another, or overlook nihility, finality and even other disastrous consequence caused by opposition and split, but seek growth in wide gap, promote mutual understanding (understanding is not equals to acceptance) in flexible, balanced, long-lasting, multivariant and multifaceted dialogue, promote reciprocity and value consultation, express and realize multivariant and own interests, so as to create a diverse and well-ordered world.

New Relations between "the Belt and Road" and Asian Cultural Spatial Order

Hu Huilin
Professor of National Cultural Environment and Policy Research Center, Shanghai Jiaotong University

Spatial Relationship and Cultural Traits of "the Belt and Road"

"The Belt and Road" construct the spatial relationship and cultural traits of ancient Asia with the world: mainland civilization merges with maritime civilization, openness and inclusiveness, mutual learning among civilizations and unity in diversity.

The silk road-the way of conversational mode of culture in ancient Asia: the silk road is formed between the economic and trade contact and cultural exchange between China, continent of Europe and Arabic world. Yet, it belongs to Asia.

Silk-the unique language and expression of Chinese civilization: the spiritual relation and culture order between human and nature, between human and society.

Silk-the achievement of civilization China contributes to Asia and the achievement of civilization Asia contributes to the world;

Silk-the common language and aesthetic carrier of dialogue between human civilization and Asian civilization;

The silk road-it is the road of communication and intercourse between Asian civilization and world civilization, linkage and integration, mutual appreciation and mutual reference, achievement sharing and common development constitute the intrinsic nature of it.

Spatial Composition and Culture Order of Asia

As the composition of system of civilization: Confucian civilization and Islamic civilization make up the basic spiritual space order of Asian culture.

As the composition of civilization form: Chinese civilization, Indian civilization and Arabic civilization made up the basic source forming Asian culture.

As the composition of civilization subject: the multinational fusion and cultural diversity made up the basic history of Asian cultural diversity.

New Relationship between "the Belt and Road" and Evolution of Asian Culture Order

"The Belt and Road" proposes new proposition for the development of Asian culture, brings new opportunity for Asian culture exchange and innovate the new form of Asian culture dialogue.

The old form and contemporary value of "the Belt and Road";

The old form and contemporary conversion of "the Belt and Road";

The modern form and communication revolution of "the Belt and Road";

New relationship between "the Belt and Road" and promotion of modern evolvement of Asian cultural relation & reconstruction of Asian culture.

Research of the Silk Road and North-west Ethnic Art History

Li Qing
Professor of Xi'an Academy of Fine Arts

For the past century, with the deepening of investigation and research of the northwestern silk road by Chinese and overseas scholars and explorers, an array of works on the nationality, history, archaeology, art and culture of the silk road were published, which laid a foundation of the research on the ethnic art history of north-west silk road. Seen from the perspective of history and reality, this research is undoubtedly an academic project which worth exploration and which is to be solved urgently in contemporary Chinese art history. The art of each ethnic of the East and the West forms a unheard-of new pattern of exchange and bumping, which plays an immeasurable role in the development of the art of the East and the West. The diversified cultural traits which hidden in the national art sites of north-west silk road and the open and perky spiritual nature are the precious heritage of both China and human arts. The research of this topic also shows the self cognition and self-confidence of contemporary Chinese culture, which is of far-reaching significance for the development of "the Belt and Road."

I. The concept of the silk road/ II. Brief introduction of academic history/ III. The significance of research/ IV. Main relics/ V. Research methods/ VI. Nationality and religion/ VII. Research difficulties.

Rebuild the Relation between Art and Life
——Re-recognize the Future Value of Oriental Art Culture
Li Xinfeng
Secretary of Graduate School CCP Committee of
Chinese National Academy of Arts

Asian culture and oriental culture have their distinct characteristics, which are conspicuous when they are compared with western culture, especially western modern culture. Let's take art as an example. As far as I am concerned, "Art Culture" outlook that stresses internal relations between art and nature and human life is the essential artistic concept with distinct oriental cultural characteristics. It forms sharp contrast with the "self-discipline" art concept prevailing in western world in modern times.

The oriental art culture stresses cultivating culture with art, approaching culture with art, understanding culture with art, carrying culture with art and seeking culture with art. Professor Lou Yulie of Peking University says, "culture dominates art", and "improve culture with art". We can see, art and culture can't be separated, namely, art should not separate from natural and social laws. In other words, culture is embodied by art, art is brightened by culture. Therefore, art and culture should be combined and integrated. We can also say that art is culture. This art culture outlook has been fully represented in Daoist and Confucian art concepts. Daoism stresses natural culture, and Confucianism stresses social culture. In Buddhism and Chinese localized Buddhism (Zen Buddhism), in Japanese traditional art concepts, this outlook is clearly represented. This outlook is rooted in the natural and indivisible relations between art and nature and human life, which conforms to art creating practices, and is helpful to art creating activities. This art concept has formed powerful oriental art traditions such as life transformed art, art functionality, art transformed life and aesthetics transformed life. In addition to creations of professional poets, this concept also produced a lot of other art forms, including calligraphy culture, tea culture, and flower culture. This theory has very clear rationality and superiority.

However, when modern society comes and western wind flows to the east, Asian countries strived to introduce western modern art ideas and methods into their cultural systems. At the same time, these Asian countries began to review or re-evaluate or re-build their cultural traditions. Many oriental traditional ideas and concepts were challenged and criticized or abandoned. The most important was the "self-discipline" art outlook that was represented by Kant, that subjectively divided art with the truth, the good and the beautiful values, and that clearly disconnected the internal relations between art and nature and human life. Therefore, the oriental art outlook was denied. Under this general background, the oriental traditional art culture was in fact treated as a negative heritage, and hence was criticized, denied, rejected and abandoned.

Nowadays, the Western "self-discipline" art outlook that subjectively disconnects relations between art and nature and human life is being reviewed and re-assessed in the world (including Europe and America). Its subjectivity, artificiality, fabrication, arbitration, and ignorance of internal and real relations between art and nature and human life have been gradually seen by people, and its alienation of art creation has also clearly been disclosed. By contrast, the oriental traditional art culture will be recognized and evaluated for its revelation of real relations between art and nature and human life, and it will play an important role in the restructuring of human art outlook in the future.

Significance of Integrating Mother Tongue Culture of Yunnan Cross-border Ethnic Groups in "the Belt and Road" Initiative

Li Ying
Professor of Yunnan Minzu University

Abstract: Yunnan, a key province in the southern Silk Road, has 16 ethnic groups living across borders. The mother tongue culture, a direct and important expression of ideology, has important role and significance in the country's strategic Belt and Road Initiative. First, it extends the mother tongue cultural development, elevates the mother tongue cultural status, and promotes harmonious development and social stability in border areas. Second, it strengthens the sense of identity and history of cross-border ethnic groups, demonstrates the great home-bound power of the mother tongue culture, and serves as a spiritual foundation for national identity and economic development in border areas. Third, it contributes for achieving positive interactions of cross-border ethnic group mother tongue culture and diplomacy in Yunnan, and deepen China's friendly ties with countries in South Asia and Southeast Asia.

Key words: Yunnan cross-border ethnic groups, mother tongue culture, Belt and Road Initiative

Yunnan province, facing towards Southeast Asia, South Asia and West Asia, and shouldering the Pacific Ocean and Indian Ocean, has been a land corridor connecting China and countries of South and Southeast Asia since ancient times. With over 20 outbound roads, Yunnan is an important province in the Silk Road in South China. It has important significance and role in the national strategy of the Belt and Road Initiative.

Yunnan is known for the long history, profound culture, pluralistic religious culture, and distinctive ethical characteristics. In China's 56 ethnic groups, 25 have lived in Yunnan for generations. Yunnan is home to 15 ethnic groups living exclusively in the region, as well as 8 ethnic groups with small population. And 16 ethnic groups live cross borders. Yunnan borders on Myanmar, Laos and Vietnam, and is geographically joined with Thailand, Bengal, Cambodia and India. It is a province with the largest number of cross-border ethnic groups[①]. The 16 cross-border ethnic groups (Dai nationality, Jingpo nationality, Miao nationality, Lahu nationality, Wa nationality, Zhuang nationality, Lisu nationality, Hani nationality, Yi nationality, Dulong nationality, Buyi nationality, Yao nationality, De'ang nationality, Achang nationality, Nu nationality, and Bulang nationality) live on the borders with a total length of 4,060 kilometers, which are separated into 1,997km with Myanmar, 710km with Laos, and 1,353km with Vietnam. They "share the same mountains, rivers, common ancestry and cultural roots." For instance, the Dai-Tai nationality comprises the Dai ethnic group in China, Tai in Thailand, Shan in Myanmar, and Lao in Laos, who live in the valleys of Lancang River and Mekong River. The cross-border distribution of numerous ethnic groups has a significant impact on the construction and development of the border areas of Yunnan. It is precisely in this sense that we may see the important link between national development and ethnic minority works.

Cross-border ethnic groups is a special phenomenon relating to the ethnic minority issue. Though they live in different countries with various national institutions, ideologies and living environments, the cross-border ethnic groups keep great influence among themselves, interconnected rather than separated in language, culture, religion, folk customs, economy, ties of blood and geographical relationship. The cross-border ethnic groups in Yunnan, the gateway of southwest China, play an irreplaceable role in the Belt and Road Initiative, including building the economic corridor, improving technical application, tourism development and ecological protection, protecting tangible and intangible cultural heritages, inheriting and promoting ethnic traditional culture, and safeguarding national unity and world peace. The native language culture, in particular, plays a greater role in exchange, communication and influence, as it is the most direct and important manifestation of ideology. It is bound to be melted into the Belt and Road Initiative and play a positive role.

1. Mother tongue communication strengthens emotional bond and good-neighborliness. It is a good measure to extend and elevate the cultural status of mother tongue, promote harmonious development and social stability in border areas.

Though they are unbalanced in development domestic and abroad, the cross-border

---

[①] Geographically, cross-border ethnic groups refer to all the ethnic groups that live across borders whose political boundaries do not match ethnic distributions.

ethnic groups have abundant native language cultures in Yunnan. The Zhuang ethnic group has the Zhuang language instituted under the help of the Chinese government and ratified for promotion. The Zhuang nationality in Vietnam also has a language of its own, created under the assistance of the government spelling with the latin alphabets. In China, the Miao ethnic group is mainly distributed in Guizhou, Hunan, Yunnan, Sichuan and Guangxi, while that overseas are found mainly in Vietnam, Laos, Thailand, Myanmar, the United States, France, Canada, Australia, Germany and Argentina. The Miao ethnic group keeps dialects and sub-dialects. Miao people in China speak several dialects and sub-dialects, while those overseas apply only the dialect popular in Sichuan, Guizhou and Yunnan, and the sub-dialect adopted in Sichuan, Guizhou and Yunnan. Miao ethnic people home and abroad adopt a number of written language forms, which comprise the Miao language of western Hunan, Miao language of eastern Guizhou, Miao language of Sichuan, Guizhou and Yunnan, old Miao language of northeast Yunnan and new Miao language of northeast Yunnan in China, and Vietnam Miao language, Laos Miao language, and Yang Songlu Miao language in overseas areas. Most of the Yao ethnic group people in China and abroad use the Yao language. They have the tradition of applying square scripts of Yao, in imitation of the Chinese characters. They have also created latin letter-based spellings, accepted home and abroad. People of the Yi nationality mainly spread in Yunnan, Sichuan, Guizhou and Guangxi in China, and in Vietnam and Laos in overseas areas. All these Yi people share a common Yi language which is further separated into six major dialects of great differences. The Yi ethnic group keeps an old Yi writing system, which is seldom learned and used now. The provinces of Sichuan, Yunnan and Guizhou have standardized the old Yi writing system in areas under their jurisdiction, and promoted the application. The Hani ethnic group is distributed in Honghe, Simao and Xishuangbanna of Yunnan in China, and in Vietnam, Laos, Myanmar and Thailand in overseas areas. The Hani language consists of the three major dialects of Haya, Bika and Haobai. The Chinese government has helped the Hani people to create the Hani writing system. Overseas, some Hani groups have their writing system, while others do not. The Dai people are mainly found in Dehong, Xishuangbanna and Simao of Yunnan in China, while overseas they are classified as the Shan in Myanmar, Tai in Thailand, Tai in Laos and Leren in Thailand. The Dai people use the Dai language which is divided into Daina and Daile dialects. In China, Dai people apply the Daina writing system in Dehong, Daile writing system in Xishuangbanna, Daibeng writing system and Jinping Dai writing system. The Shan people in Myanmar use the Daibeng writing system, and the Tai people in Vietnam adopt the Jinping Dai writing system, as well as the recently created latin-based Dai writing system. The Jingpo nationality are found in Dehong of Yunnan in China, and in the Kachin and Shan of Myanmar. The Jingpo people use the Jingpo language and Zaiwa language, with respective writing systems. The Jingpo language was created in Myanmar in the late 19th century. It was reformed in China in 1957. People in Myanmar continue to adopt the original form of the language. The Zaiwa language was established in China in 1956, which is promoted and applied in China alone. The Lisu nationality is distributed in Nujiang, Lijiang and Diqing of Yunnan in China, and in Myanmar and Thailand overseas. The Lisu language comprises Nujiang and Luquan dialects. In China, the Lisu people use the old Lisu and new Lisu writing systems, while those overseas adopt only the old Lisu writing system. The Lahu ethnic group is based in Simao and Lincang of Yunnan in China, and in Myanmar, Thailand, Laos and Vietnam overseas. The Lahu language comprises the Lahuna and Lahuxi dialects. Lahu people kept a writing system previously, which was reformed and further promoted in the country in 1956. The writing system remained untouched overseas. The Wa ethnic group is mainly distributed in Lincang and Simao of Yunnan in China, and in Myanmar, Thailand and Laos overseas. The Wa people use the Wa language. In the old days, British missionaries created a Wa language for the Wa people, known as the "Sarah language". In 1956, China created another set of Wa language. Christians home and abroad remain using the "Sarah language". The De'ang nationality is based in Dehong of Yunnan in China, and in Myanmar overseas. De'ang people speak the De'ang language, without a writing system in China, and using the Myanmar and Shan writing systems overseas. The Dulong nationality lives in Gongshan county, Nujiang of Yunnan in China, and in the downstream area of Dulong River of Kachin in Myanmar overseas. Dulong people use the Dulong language. In the past, missionaries created a latin-based spelling system for Dulong people in Myanmar, known as Riwang language, which is still applied by Dulong people in Myanmar. Because of the phonetic difference, China designed a spelling program for the Dulong language for trial implementation in 1983.

All these languages mentioned above are still actively used by people of the cross-border ethnic groups. They are important, effective and realistic modes to keep in touch with each other. When they visit relatives and friends, go to market, participate in folk-custom festivals and singing contests, they would use their mother tongues for small talks and stories. Over time, they have been interrelated in emotions, connected in economy and inter-penetrated in culture. An important idea of the strategic Belt and Road Initiative is for China and neighboring countries to make construction and development together. The mother tongue culture of cross-border ethnic groups of Yunnan has laid a solid foundation of language and culture for all-round communication.

2. Mother tongue literature strengthens cross-border ethnic group's sense of identity and history, demonstrates great home-bound power of mother tongue culture, and serves as spiritual foundation of national identity and economic development in border areas

The mother tongue literature of Yunnan cross-border ethnic groups is a major carrier and important content of the mother tongue culture. It is revealed in three layers, which are oral literature, ancient documents and mother tongue creations of writers. The oral literature, including myth, epic, legend, story, poem, ballad and proverb, is widely spread home and abroad. Some folk culture varieties have declined and got lost in China, whereas well preserved in neighboring countries. In reverse, some are well inherited in China, but lost in neighboring countries. Besides, plenty of ancient works with written records are historical expressions of the mother tongue culture, such as the palm leaf manuscripts of Dai nationality and ancient books in Yi language. They amount to tens of thousands of volumes, which could be said as museums of ancient works of ethnic groups. The long narrative poem Ashima of Yi nationality has been listed into the first batch of national intangible cultural heritage directory. Whether they are oral literature or ancient works, the mother tongue narrative tradition are "of the same origin and school" for cross-border communication. They not only facilitate frequent cultural contacts of ethnic cultures home and abroad in the Belt and Road construction, but also stimulate economic ties of cross-border ethnic groups. They build a sound cultural environment for all ethnic groups in China and neighboring countries to work together for common development. They are an important content of constructing Yunnan into a center spreading its influence to Southeast Asia and South Asia.

Compared with the oral literature and ancient works, mother tongue creations of cross-border ethnic group writers of Yunnan started in the early days of the founding of the People's Republic of China in 1949. It has developed fast in the past two decades. In the 25 ethnic groups living for generations in Yunnan, 22 have their own languages, and 14 have their own writing systems. They have laid a solid foundation for diversified development of ethnic minority mother tongue literature in Yunnan. The mother tongue creations of cross-border ethnic group writers include the Jingpo nationality, Dai nationality and Lisu nationality of Dehong prefecture; Dai nationality of Xishuangbanna prefecture; Lisu nationality of Nujiang prefecture; Hani nationality and Miao nationality of Honghe prefecture; and Miao nationality of Wenshan prefecture. The mother tongue literary works feature unique aesthetic styles and artistic characteristics. They are of special role and significance to facilitate cultural harmony and national identity in the multi-ethnic regions of southwest China borders. The mother tongue works of cross-border ethnic group writers have manifested the specific humanistic spirits of border areas. They help to elevate the status of mother tongue culture, deepen and develop friendly ties of China with people of South Asia and Southeast Asia, contribute to the implementation of the strategic Belt and Road Initiative. In particular, as the geopolitical layout has changed in Southeast Asia and South Asia, cross-border ethnic group writers of Yunnan, with their respective mother tongue creations, leave great impacts on ethnic groups of neighboring countries. They are spiritual weapons for national identity and reunification. The mother tongue works of great many writers, like a bridge of cultural exchange of cross-border ethnic groups in border areas, shoulder the important mission of harmonious cultural construction in border areas. They are of far-reaching significance. The original mother tongue works of writers of cross-border ethnic groups in Yunnan are quite influential among local people. They are also of magical power to touch same ethnic groups overseas. Miao ethnic group poet Zhang Yuanqi recited his Miao language poem Our Name is Miao Nationality in the Spring Festival Gala in Wenshan People's Radio in 1987. The following is the literal translation:

Why we speak our own language/Why we wear our own clothes/It's not for anything else/But because we have a name - Miao nationality/Why should we learn our own characters/Why should we never forget our own history/It's not for anything else/But because we have a name - Miao Nationality/Why should we pass on our own culture/Why should we keep our own customs/It's not for anything else/But because we have a name - Miao Nationality/We have our own bloodline/We have our own flesh and blood/We have our own thoughts/We have our own missions/We are a race in the world/We have an equally long history/We are industrious/We are brave/We have the right to life/We have our idea on development/We live in this world/Our footprints spread from the east to the west/We are not afraid of anyone/We will not be slaves/We do not bully the weak/We love peace/Along with other ethnic groups/We create a harmonious, beautiful world/Wherever we go, we are Miao nationality/No matter how long it has passed, we remain Miao nationality/We will never forget our own name --/Miao Nationality! Miao Nationality! Miao Nationality!!!"①

The poem was applauded by the broad masses of Miao people. It was later composed into a song by Miao composer Tao Yonghua from Wenshan, popular in Miao ethnic communities in Vietnam, Laos, Thailand, the United States and France. It leaves a positive impact on promoting friendly communication between Miao people of Wenshan and their overseas counterparts, as it evokes strong national identity of Miao people scattering in various parts of the world for centuries.

3. Southeast Asia and South Asia have played a significant role in China's foreign policy. Yunnan, located in southwest border areas, enjoys unique regional competiveness. To date, China highlights interconnection with neighboring countries, and strengthens economic cooperation and cultural exchanges with countries along the ancient Silk Road. Yunnan cross-border ethnic groups share the same origins with many ethnic groups of neighboring countries. Hence, in virtue of the natural bond of cross-border ethnic group mother tongue literature between Yunnan and Southeast Asia and South Asia, the province may fully display the soft power of the cross-border ethnic group mother tongue culture, enhance mutual trust, facilitate cooperation, deepen friendship, and create a sound social and international environment for the Belt and Road Initiative. Therefore, the protection and development of the mother tongue literature in the national level, and all-round demonstration of the real condition of multi-layer co-existence of cross-border ethnic group mother tongue life tally with the cultural conception and spiritual appeal of the contemporary Belt and Road strategic development.

In 1956, Premier Zhou Enlai approved the establishment of the Unity newspaper in Dehong Dai and Jingpo autonomous prefecture in Yunnan. The newspaper was circulated in the five ethnic languages of Dai, Jingpo, Lisu, Han and the later added Zaiwa of Jingpo, showing the foresight and sagacity of the great statesman. In addition to publishing works of writers for the development of mother tongue culture of cross-border ethnic groups of Yunnan, the media, like a propeller with its carrier and communication func-

---

① Yang Guilin, Remarks on Contemporary Literature of Miao Ethnic Group in Southern Yunnan – Review of Contemporary Literary Creation of Miao Ethnic Group in Wenshan, Yunnan, Collected Papers of Miao Ethnic Academic Seminar in West China, edited by Wenshan Zhuang and Miao Autonomous Prefecture Miao Science Development Society, published by Yunnan Nationality Press, 2011 edition

tions, has spread to neighboring Southeast Asian countries. In 1982, the Literary Federation of Dehong prefecture founded literary periodical Yong Han in Dai language, literary periodical Wen Bang in Jingpo language, and periodical W—Ny in Lisu language (suspended publication later). The Literary Federation of Xishuangbanna founded the literary periodical Banna in Jingpo language. These periodicals have published literary works of ethnic minority writers over a long time. They are favored by Chinese readers as well as overseas readers. In addition to released in China, and circulated widely among Jingpo people of Dehong, the Jingpo language literary periodical Wenbang has been officially issued in Kachin, Myanmar, leaving great impacts on overseas Jingpo people. Yunnan provincial radio and television station set up special channels for ethnic minority language programs. So far, the radio programs have covered the Jingpo, Dai (including Dehong and Xishuangbannan dialects), Lisu and Lahu ethnic groups. Many prefectures have also set up ethnic minority language radio stations, such as radio programs in Miao, Zhuang and Yao languages by Wenshan People's Radio Station, covering Tuyen Quang province, and parts of Kien Giang and Lao Cai provinces of Vietnam, with over one million audiences. Minnesota State University professor Yang Dao, an American of Miao nationality, heard of a Miao language song of Wenshan radio station in Kunming city in 1987. He said with emotion, "There are seven to eight radio stations in Miao language in the world. Wenshan station is the best. I hope Wenshan station Miao language programs could spread welcome news of friendship to worldwide audiences. " Hou Zongkua, kmuoy Miao village head in Phichit province, Thailand, known as Dramana in Thailand, started to listen to Miao language programs of Wenshan radio station in the early 1980s. On March 13, 1991, when Wenshan was not yet opened to the outside world, Hou, with nice wishes of 200 Miao households in his village, paid a special trip to Wenshan radio station, via Kunming, to call on Miao language program staff. " [1]In 1997, Dehong prefecture founded the "Dehong Ethnic Minority Language and Culture TV Translation and Production Center", an exclusive service for TV programs of Dai, Jingpo and Zaiwa languages. The best known services include the "Dai famous opera appreciation " program. The center is designed to serve about 1.5 million audiences with ethnic

---

[1] Publicity Management Department of Yunnan Radio and Television Bureau, "Asphalt Felt Spirit" Burst Into National Blossoms – Outstanding Deeds of National Language Channel of Wenshan People's Radio Station, September 20, 2010

minority programs. They are accessible for people in neighboring Baoshan prefecture and Myanmar border areas. Following the social, economic and cultural progress, county-level radio and TV administrations have edged into the rank along with provincial and prefectural organs to tap the mother tongue radio program production. In September 2012, Pingbian county people's radio station officially broadcast Miao language programs.

Without doubt, there are problems in developing cross-border ethnic minority mother tongue culture. They include the application of writing systems home and abroad. Data from Yunnan provincial language authority shows that in the 16 cross-border ethnic groups in Yunnan, 12 (Dai, Jingpo, Yi, Hani, Zhuang, Miao, Yao, Tibet, Lisu, Lahu, Wa and Dulong) have corresponding writing systems in overseas areas. The overseas writing systems are growingly demonstrating their impacts. For instance, many people home and abroad remain using the old Lisu writing system created by foreign missionaries. But since the 1950s, China pushed forward a new set of Lisu writing system to replace the old one. Now, the two systems are applied simultaneously, to trigger some conflicts. In another case, some people want to use the overseas writing systems in China to influence the domestic ethnic minority languages with newspaper, radio and VCD materials. Surveys show that in Dehong prefecture alone, hundreds of varieties of newspapers and books are imported applying overseas Dai, Jingpo, Zaiwa and Lisu writing systems. There are dozens of radio stations providing ethnic minority language programs, including the Tibetan language, Dai language, Jingpo language, Zaiwa language, Lisu language, Miao language, and Yao language. And over 200 varieties of VCD products, totaling 400,000 pieces, are found everywhere in border areas of ethnic minorities. Many ethnic minority people in China often read newspapers and journals of overseas writing systems, listen to overseas ethnic minority radio programs, watch overseas VCD discs, much affected by them as a result. The cross-border ethnic minority mother tongue culture has been listed by some ill intentioned people overseas in human rights platforms to affect stability in border areas.

Consciousness, and the guidance and influence of cultural exchanges home and abroad, in the first place, depend on our efforts in the languages. Following the implementation and construction of the strategic Belt and Road Initiative, our efforts to advocate and promote mechanisms for exchanges and dialogues of cross-border ethnic group mother tongue languages in Yunnan, domestic and foreign, and for the protection, continuation and development of the mother tongue cultures will make for enhancing national cohesion, realizing positive interactions of Yunnan cross-border ethnic mother tongue culture and diplomacy, and deepen friendly ties with South Asia and Southeast Asia countries, with far-reaching significance.

Research on Folk Literature and Ethnic Relations along "the Belt and Road"

Lin Jifu

Professor of Minzu University of China

By borrowing the historical symbol of the ancient "Silk road", "the Belt and Road" aims to build the community of interests and destiny of cultural inclusiveness. When construct "the Belt and Road", the concept of "culture construction first" has become the consensus of statesman and scholars. In the cultural construction of "the Belt and Road", the folk literature has played an important role in the nationality development and national contact as the most active wide-spread traditional culture in life with longest history and profound influence.

The folk literature along "the Belt and Road" is the life culture crossing nation and region. They exist in folk's life with diversified way, and have special power traversing different ethnics and regions. Different ethnics tell the same story, which is spreading in different ethnics. It implies that the folk literature contains the circulation and culture borrowing of different ethnic emotions under the shared value and morality of ethnics, thus highlighting that the folk literature boast functions like culture exchange and ethnic communication hidden behind the multi-ethnic culture elements.

The folk literature along "the Belt and Road" contains rich contents of ethnic communication relations. In history, different ethnics have selection and tendency when narrating the folk literature. In terms of real life, as the ethnic communication relation, the particularity of the folk literature along "the Belt and Road" is constantly deduced. We should tap in the psychological convergence feature of the folk literature, discuses the significance and mental structure of the folk literature, and trace the same popular sentiments and the common structure relation of multi-ethnic folk literature along "the Belt and Road".

The folk literature is related and inherited orally. This kind of literature is the record of life and the representation of the emotion. Therefore, the folk literature along "the Belt and Road" has become the memory of multi-ethnic life relation and culture relation, lubricating the communication relationship between different ethics.

Maritime Silk Road, Maritime Silk Culture and Southern

Liu Denghan

Research Fellow of Fujian Academy of Social Sciences

The East and the West have different marine conceptions and marine value orientations. China is not only an inland country, but also enjoys long coastline and offshore islands, especially the territories in the east and south. Thus, rich marine culture resources are available. However, China never avails of ocean as the means to expand her territory and plunder her wealth, which is quite different from the western countries. Previously, China aimed to increase her political influence, good-neighborliness and reciprocal relations (in terms of the tributary trades, China gave more gifts to other countries) through the oceangoing foreign trades. Such marine conception and marine value orientation could create Maritime Silk Road as a way of trading, cooperation, friendship and peace.

Here, the marine spirit in the southern Fujian culture and their historical traditions of going to the southeast countries are crucial to the extension and development of Marine Silk Road. As neighboring sea, the people in southern Fujian previously went to sea for business and survival. So, you could always find the footprint of people in southern Fujian for that purposes in the countries along the Marine Silk Road. The people in southern Fujian value feelings and have strong patriotism. Due to the tradition of believing in God and worship ceremony since the ancient times, the people in southern Fujian always set up temples to worship their ancestors when taking root in the countries along Marine Silk Road. Also, such tradition was mutually blended with local cultures and a new type of culture evolved. As one of the important cultural rendering in the Chinese culture for inheriting the marine silk culture, the southern Fujian culture is the indispensible element. Thus, when studying the marine silk culture, we should pay attention to the extension and development of southern Fujian culture abroad.

Win-win Paths of Sino-Korean Film Cooperation

Liu Fan

Associate Research Fellow of the Cultural Development Strategy Research Center of Chinese National Academy of Arts

Ways of the film cooperation between China and Korea are diversified and involve the upper and lower streams of the industrial chain. At present, major cooperation ways are: 1. Investment of cinemas, for instance, cinemas invested by CGV under Korean CJ Group; 2. Importation of films from the other country. For instance, Korean commercial films such as *Assassination* and *Battle of Myeongryang* have been introduced into China, and Chinese films such as *Red Cliff* and *Finding Mr. Right* are exported to Korea; 3. Cooperation in shooting films where art and market are fully cooperated, such as *A Wedding Invitation*, and *Mr. Go*; 4. Talent exchange between the two countries. China used the Korean production team in *Assembly*, and Korean directors Jae-young Kwak in *My Girlfriend is Sick* and Kang Je-gyu in *The Broken Sky*. Exchanges of actors are more frequent. Korean actor Kwone Sang Woo acts in *Chinese Zodiac*, Jang Dong Gun acts in *Dangerous Liaisons* and *The Promise*, and So Ji Sub acts in *Sophie's Revenge*. Many Chinese actors or actresses have acted in Korean films, include Li Xinjie and Ren Dahua in *The Thieves*, Zhang Ziyi in *The Warrior*, and Shu Qi in *My Wife Is a Gangster* 3; 5. Reference and cooperation in story. Korean director Ui-seok Jo produced *Cold Eyes* on basis of Hong Kong film *Eye in the Sky*; *Return to 20 Years Old* is the sister film of *Miss Granny*, and *Chronicle of a Blood Merchant*, the work by Yu Hua, was adapted into a Korean film; 6. Equity cooperation. At the end of 2014, Huace Media acquired 15% equity of Korean Next Enter tainment World company, and became its second largest shareholder; 7. Special cooperation. Korean companies train Chinese actors or actresses with Korean styles. For instance, Wu Yifan and Lu Han cultivated by Korean institutes have become popular young actors in China.

In the above cooperation ways, the jointed produced films by Chinese and Korean teams should be firstly studied, as this cooperation type can directly promote cultural exchanges and populace communication.

Unity of Heaven and Man in Square Inch World
——Artistic Features and Cultural Functions of Chinese Seal-cutting Art

Luo Pengpeng

Research Fellow and Director of China Seal Cutting Academy under Chinese National Academy of Arts

Chinese seal-cutting art is a traditional art of Chinese characteristics that takes stones as the carriers, and Chinese characters as the images, developed from the ancient Chinese seal engraving feats. In ancient days, seals were tokens to exercise and authorize state organ powers and testify personal identity. They were mainly produced by craftsmen under metal casting and engraving methods. The art has a history of more than 3,000 years.

This is not unique, but has its counterparts. In the long history of human civilization development, utensils similar to Chinese seals appeared in other ancient civilization countries, with similar functions. But it is only in China that the art of seal cutting has developed as an independent art over the past 3,000 years. As a result, China seal-cutting art takes a key position and plays an important role in the cultural development and progress of human civilization with its characteristic cultural functions.

Chinese seal-cutting art boasts the beauty of miracle, beauty of abstraction and beauty of nature. It integrates the way of cutting, calligraphy and art of composition in the techniques. It combines the beauty of materials, buttons and stamps. It maintains unparalleled good standing. It keeps inherent practicability and artistry. It possess unique aesthetic functions to "reveal the universe in a square inch world". And it holds the cultural attribute and natural quality of "unity of Heaven and Man". Chinese seal-cutting art has been an important channel for Chinese people to cultivate their moral character, expound their ideas in writing, and improve personal quality since the ancient time. It is an effective mode to enhance human communication, and cultural and artistic exchanges.

Heritage Preservation Studies on the Cultural Route —Marine Silk Road: Fujian Historical Sites

Luo Wenwei

Associate Professor of School of General Education, Huaqiao University

Thanks to the great initiative of "the Belt and Road", Fujian will become the core area of the 21st Century Maritime Silk Road. This should be a once-in-a-life-time opportunity for the protection of Marine Silk Road legacies in Fujian. "the Belt and Road" highly coincides with "Cultural Routes" in terms of connotation, concept, features and development tendency. As a brand new concept of remains, the cultural routes should be the new philosophy for the protection of "Maritime Silk Road: Fujian Historical Sites".

Firstly, the concept of new normal thinking should be available. The "New Normal" refers to nine-city alliance that applies for world cultural heritage for historical sites along the Maritime Silk Road. Also, the "New Normal" could include other important port cities which produce the decisive influence to "Maritime Silk Road". Secondly, the concept of "Overall Protection" should be advocated. The heritage protection campaign should protect not only the single cultural relic, but also the whole town, village, block and even linear landscape with unique culture. The regional or even international collaborative innovation mechanism should be established to create a new and complete nationwide network for protection of cultural heritage from Marine Silk Road. Thirdly, the "Protection First and Rational Exploitation" should be followed. In terms of the connotation and features of cultural route, we should follow the principle of "Protection First and Rational Exploitation" and "Co-existence of Social-cultural Benefits and Economic Benefits, so as to soundly carry out such basic work as the museum construction, scenic spot interpretation system, marine Silk road tourism planning & development, laws and regulations formulation, heritage application documents preparation, protection policy issuing and project demonstration. Fourthly, the public participation should be encouraged. The popular propaganda of heritage resources should be launched to arouse the public participation awareness, so as to form the peripheral " Protective Belt" and enjoy popular support. Particularly, the youth should be educated in such fields as heritage, ocean, Maritime Silk Road and history of overseas Chinese. Fifthly, the symbiotic idea should be available: I. the multiplex symbiosis of religion and culture; II. the symbiosis of urban modernization and historical & cultural heritage; III. the symbiosis of culture survival, natural environment and intangible cultural heritage

Revive Traditional Oriental Colors

Niu Kecheng

Director and Research Fellow of the Fine Arts Researth
Institute of Chinese National Academy of Arts

    The cognition and expression of oriental colors are long-standing and well-established. There are a large number of color terms recording ancient oriental's identification and feeling about color in the tales of legendia and epic poems of Asian countries. The application of colors in painted pottery, dyeing and weaving, apparel and accessories and painting in histories of Asian countries shows the richness and exquisiteness of oriental's color sense. However, in modern times, the western color names and color matching ways were introduced into Asia along with the import of European synthetic dyestuff, thus weaken the oriental colors sense which had lasted since ancient times. On the other hand, oriental colors knowledge system had been covered gradually by western color science which was brought by "the East Meeting the West". In 1920s-1930s, the concept and system of books on color science authored by Lv Cheng, Shi Yan, Li Weici, Liu Yixiang and Yu Jifan were basically from western color science. The introduction of western color science to Japan, Korea, India and other Asian countries was similar to the introduction to China; some were even earlier. Color Science (1928, published by Commercial Press) written by Chen Zhifo is the paraphrase of western color science with Japan as the intermediary. Since then, western color science has become the color science we learnt and applied. From cognition to expression, we have been relying on the terms, concepts and knowledge frame, while oriental traditional color sense, color concept and color matching experience have been gradually ignored and neglected. In 1992, National Museum of Modern and Contemporary Art, Korea published Korean Traditional Standard Color Name and Color Sample; many traditional color names in it are hard to be understood by modern people. In China, color names like Xiang (light yellow), Jiang (deep red), Cheng (red) and Zi (black) as well as the subtle color sense have been gradually faded. This phenomenon implies that in the progress of modernization, serious fraction has been incurred in layer of concepts and cognition with tradition, just like the utensils, which causes the uncertainty of traditional subject consciousness on oriental colors.

The color cognition in oriental style is concluding the complex colors of everything in nature into several primary colors related with the basic materials. These primary colors form various colors. It emphasizes the propor color the object itself, and pays attention to the base color quality of color itself and the structure relations like comparison and antithesis of different colors. This is quite different from the western color science system with light color principle as the starting point which was formed through analysis of spectral color by Newton in the mid-17th century, and it came down to the difference of the thinking modes of the east and the west. Western color science is a scientific and analytical system, which is supported by western scientific thought, namely, the conception of nature and methodology with analysis of formal logic system and system experiment as the main and the formal logic axiom system established through experimental study, quantitative analysis, reasoning and proof. By contrast, in oriental colors tradition, the quintessence of thought of overall harmonious organicism and comprehensive, vague, instinct and comprehending thinking characters are reflected.

However, we have been admiring and adoring western. As an Asian, we know little about Asia. We had been focusing on what happened to the color science in western research circle, while caring less on the color research progress in our surrounding countries. We would compare our color resources and condition with those of western, but seldom make horizontal comparison with those of our surrounding countries'. Thus, the incoordinate contrast between a single color system of Asian countries and the whole western color science is formed.

Therefore, to revive traditional oriental colors, we should first be proud of Asia, and should learn to appreciate our surrounding countries for their color history experience and their color research condition. On this basis, we shall strengthen the academic exchange among scholars in Asian countries, and thus facilitate the overall depth of oriental colors research by publishing papers through the association journals and the anthologies, translating color works and introducing color science research results and borrowing the concepts and methods. We shall find out the commonality of each other in terms of color conception and expression by comparing the color traditions between Asian countries, and thus realize the reconfirmation of oriental subjects on color cognition and expression system. Currently, Asia has a relatively large-scale "Asia Color Forum", but the subject terms of each term is limited to the application and market of color in Asia. Parallel with the application research, construction work of the basic concepts, category, and system of oriental colors tradition is more urgent for the color application of oriental shall be supported by oriental culture.

Reviving traditional oriental colors is not just the carding of academy of the color history resources of Asian countries, or the value revaluation of oriental colors tradition, in fact, it is more related with an important issue of contemporary culture: in the progress of modernity, how should we excavate the oriental wisdom with a long history to contribute it to the contemporary culture of Asia and even the whole world in the new century?

French Concept and Operation Practice of "Silk Road"
——Take "Ninth Biennale de la Danse de Lyon" as a Case
Ou Jianping
Director and Research Fellow of the Dance Research
Institute of Chinese National Academy of Arts

French Major Contributions to World Culture and Art

In the history of world culture and art, the French have made significant contributions. According to the four volumes of French Cultural History, "the most important event in the history of the French' culture in 5th- 10th centuries is to create the French, which is the oldest language in Romance languages". In terms of the history of world literature art, the 18th and 19th centuries are called "the centuries of the French". In the history of the world dance, so far there have been no major changes to the academic ballet stylized language since it was named in French in 1700. In world literature trends, the Romantic Movement originated in the 19th century in France. The "art for art" theory and practice with an emphasis on the ontological aesthetics are also from France of the same period. Since the romantic ballet "Fairy" made its debut at the Paris Opera in 1832, pirouette technology still is the "legal technology" of the traditional women's ballet so far.

For more than 200 years, many famous French writers and artists stand out, such as writers Balzac, Stendhal, Hugo, George · Sang, Merimee, Flaubert, Dumas, Dumas Fils, Baudelaire, Daudet, Zola, Romain · Rolland, Gautier, painters Delacroix, Monet, Manet, Degas, Renoir and Cezanne, sculptor Rodin, musician Berlioz, Gounod, Debussy and Adam, dramatists Voltaire and Moliere, dancers Norvell, Westley and his son, Taglioni, Petipa etc. They can be described as illuminating as heavenly stars and numerous!

Even in the 20th century, French writers and artists are also still star-studded. In 1901, French Laign Sully Prudhomme won Nobel Prize for Literature for the first time. In

1985, Frenchman Claude Simon again won the prize. In the history of more than 80 years, a total of 12 French won this award, called the world's first, more than double those of other European cultural powers including England, German, Italy, Spain, Russia, etc. In the history of the world dance in the 20th century, the French are also famous, such as choreographer Roland Petit who is known for uniqueness and rehearsed a total of five classic works for Chinese ballet like "Carmen", "Youth and Death", "The Girl From Arles", "Pink Floyd Ballet" and "Bat"; dance thinker Maurice Bejart who had come to China to perform ballet epic "The Dance of Life", with amazing stage tension; performer Yvette · Xiaoweilei with superb artistry from Paris Opera and Sylvie Guillem known as "the First Leg in the World", etc. The strong potential of French art and culture is evident, which is precisely the root cause that the French cultural soft power continues to rise.

In addition, in the international academic community, the number of sinologists among French people and French cultural circle is said to equal the sum of those around the world. In terms of translation and study into the "Book of Changes", there is the French edition that is first printed in 1889 and translated by sinologist Charles de Harlez among two of the earliest Spanish translation. In 1998, the French President Chirac put forward a detail question at the opening ceremony of the ancient Chinese bronzes in France, and even the archaeological experts of our delegation could not answer it; the Chinese and foreign media have reported. In 2006, during my fourth study to France, when looking for information on the Pompidou Cultural Center Library, I met a French young scholar named Allen who took the initiative to say hello to me. It turned out that he had been an undergraduate in the Department of Archaeology, Peking University and watched my lectures on dance in CCTV for several times. Later, he returned to the University of Paris, studying as a graduate student of Chinese cultural relic archaeology. These seemingly accidental but inevitable cases not only illustrate the French people's high interest in the study of Chinese culture but also prove that this nation's own aesthetic taste is extraordinary.

Looking Back at "Biennale de la Danse de Lyon" Over the Past 30 Years

"Biennale de la Danse de Lyon" was founded in 1984 by Mr. Guy Darmey, director of the dance palace in Lyon. From the very beginning, it has gotten generous help of the government at all levels from the city of Lyon, Rhone-Alpes, and the French Central Culture and Communication Ministry. Until 2014, it has been successfully held 16 sessions. Dance teams participating in the performance, international coverage, the specific content of the dance festival, number of various performances, audiences, and its tremendous impact both at home and abroad are constantly expanding.

From the second session, the Biennale de la Danse embarked on a series of development path, namely that each has a different theme. In 2000, 2002 and 2006, I was respectively invited by French Ambassador to China, Cultural Counselor and the dance festival to visit here for three times. In addition to watching performances and making comments, I interviewed President Darmey and carefully studied the concept of the dance festival, mode of operation and promotion methods. The specific circumstances are summarized as follows:

The first Biennale de la Danse was held in 1984, without a theme, with only 14 dance teams, 66 times of performance and 39, 800 audiences.

The second was in 1986 and started to make the Lyon citizens familiar with the world dance as the goal, setting such a theme: "German expressionist dance and its impact", which whereby traces the Enlightenment-style influence of the German dance on French modern dance; with 18 dance teams and 42, 350 audiences; in addition to performances, around this theme, it also organized many activities including exhibition and film broadcast.

The third was in 1988, with the theme of "400 years of French dance", which recalls the entire history of the French dance from ballet to modern and contemporary dance, with 20 dance teams. It began to hold open-air performances and dance around urban areas in Lyon, therefore making the number of audiences increase to 54, 737.

The fourth was in 1990, with the theme of "American Story", aimed at tracing back a major impact of the United States' modern dance on the French contemporary dance. It invited all the world-renowned American dance teams, with the number up to 23. A number of directors were found. The number of audiences soared to 72, 974.

The fifth was in 1992, with the theme of "Spanish Passion", which let Lyon citizens enjoy the country's passionate dance traditions and colorful contemporary development; 27 dance teams participated and the number of audiences continued to grow to 89, 000; at the same time, according to the Spanish customs, the fair with folk dance as the theme was held in Lyon city center, which attracted 150,000 Lyon citizens.

The sixth was in 1994, with the theme of "Mama Africa". 20 dance teams were from Africa and American New York's Harlem, with the number of audiences up to 75,500; the big parade "colorful Festival" at African rhythm attracted 120,000 enthusiastic Lyon citizens.

The seventh was in 1996, with the theme of "The Brazilian Colors". 31 Brazil dance teams participated in the performances. 500 dancers, singers, musicians, stunning modern creators and popular music tradition defenders all gathered in Lyon, attracting as many as 82,559 audiences. The first of its kind "Le Défilé" mobilized thousands of professional and amateur dancers who performed various Brazilian dances in six months, attracting as many as 200,000 audiences.

The eighth was in 1998, with the theme of "Mediterranean hot air". 35 dance teams were from 12 Mediterranean countries, performing a large number of dance styles. The number of audiences increased again, reaching 85,000.

The ninth was in 2000, with the theme of "Silk Road". Along the ancient Silk Road route, 31 deputations and two solo performers were selected from China's Beijing, Shanghai, Guangzhou, Hong Kong, Taipei and other Asian countries including South Korea, Japan, Thailand, India, Mongolia, Syria, Iraq, Algeria in Africa, European Uzbekistan, Croatia, the Netherlands and France and so on.

The tenth was in 2002, with the theme of "Latin Land". 600 directors, dancers, singers and musicians of 36 dance teams were selected from 11 countries including Argentina, Bolivia, Brazil, Chile, Colombia, Costa Rica, Cuba, Mexico and host France, with a total of 37 performances and 93,000 audiences.

The eleventh was in 2004, with the theme of "Europa". After years of negotiation, the European countries failed to reach a consensus on the establishment of the European Union. This dance festival invited dance teams of 21 European countries to dance in Lyon. 10 performances were premiered in the world, including the performances by the popular British contemporary dance choreographer Wayne McGregor and the Netherlands' artist Jan Fabre, aimed to perform the great power and charm of the European countries' collaboration in the form of dance.

The twelfth was in 2006. The theme ended the geographical division series, and turned their attention to the urban population accounting for 50% of all mankind, thus being named as "Urban Dance", aimed to show urban people's significant contributions to the progress of human civilization through the experimental and exploratory performances of 29 urban dance teams of four continents.

The thirteenth was in 2008. The theme turned to fully provide a stage for the contemporary dance, and began the new series of the "dance focus". It launched a total of 16 new works. Choreographers included German Susanne · Linke, French Montalvo · Aierweie, Angelin Preljocaj, American Caroline · Carlson, Chinaese Wenhui and so on.

The fourteenth, fifteenth and sixteenth were respectively in 2010, 2012, 2014. The themes continued to be "dance focus," but the emphasis was respectively placed on the support of the new generation director, promotion of amateur dancers, and dances neglected by Portugal and previous biennales.

To sum up, there are 5 items of successful experience in Biennale de la Danse de Lyon over the past 30 years:

First, it is held once every two years, in order to have sufficient time to do the preparatory work for the next, including doing research work earnestly, personally going to theme countries and regions to select dance teams and programs, signing feasible performances, even agreeing work contract;

Second, each year it selects a country, region or Europe, the city as a theme, in order to vividly disseminate the colorful globalization to the Lyon citizens and deepen people's awareness for the establishment of the European Union and the development of urban cultural;

Third, with Lyon Dance Palace as a base, establish a permanent organization of Biennale de la Danse, to ensure that each detail of the contract is implemented before and after the opening of the dance festival;

Fourth, around the theme, hold the activities including the universal performances, exhibitions, movie player, free open-air performances, open classes, dance, Le Défilé for young people on the weekend afternoon to ensure that the dance festival becomes the Lyon citizens - the taxpayers' holiday;

Fifth, increase publicity and coverage work of media at home and abroad, making Biennale de la Danse de Lyon become an international activity of global significance, which not only greatly strengthens Lyon and France's international influence, but also effectively promotes the mutual understanding among peoples. As I said when giving an interview to "New York News" in New York in 1988: "If people understand each other, there will be no war."

"Ninth Biennale de la Danse de Lyon" with "Silk Road" as the Theme

"Silk Road" is the trade route across the Eurasian continent. From Zhang Qian's travel to western countries, it starts from Chang'an, the capital of Western Han Dynasty, via the Hexi Corridor, continues westbound through two routes, and finally enters Europe and Africa, which greatlypromotes economic and cultural friendly exchanges between China and the countries of Asia, Europe and Africa. At the time silk exports are the most representative. In 1877, the German geographer Ferdinand von Richthofen put forward it in the book China for the first time. It was subsequently endorsed by Chinese and foreign historians and is still used by people of all countries, with far-reaching influence.

As the first stop of Chinese Silk into France, Lyon has a sizable Silk Museum. Coincidentally, "Biennale de la Danse de Lyon" rented its space as the headquarters during the opening each time. Therefore, the dance festival with "Silk Road " as the theme in 2000 can be described as well-prepared and very successful; Chairman Mr. Guy Darmey said in an enthusiastic and poetic way in the program booklet " opening speech: "East, West Asia, Europe, 2000 Biennale de la Danse de Lyon will take us on Silk Road. For 2000 years, this narrow Silk Road' leads mankind from the depths of Samarkand to the gates of Venice, and from both sides of Rhone across Lyon to both sides of Aegean Sea. When different world just begins to learn from each other, "Silk Road", through the silk and gold trade and the exchange of ideas, ties a variety of skills and culture together. 'Biennale de la Danse de Lyon' invites you to depart from Xian in China to go westward all the way, crossing Central Asia, West Asia, until silk factory in Lyon and Port of Alexandria, Egypt. 800 Asian dancers, musicians and singers' performances will include drummers' prolonged rumbling, lovely Chinese classical dance, Japanese Kabuki's perfection, Thai shadow play's fun, and Indian Kathak classical dance's barefoot tapping sound. These artists will share their creative passion with artists in the French Rhone - Alpine area. I invite you to come to meet them and share their own culture and religion, art and talent. "Silk Road" will open the doors of knowledge for everyone. Let's work together to bring the knowledge to our home…

On the Ninth Biennale de la Danse de Lyon, 31 deputations and two solo performers along the ancient Silk Road routes were selected from China's Beijing, Shanghai, Guangzhou, Hong Kong, Taipei, other Asian countries' South Korea, Japan, Thailand, India, Mongolia, Syria, Iraq, Algeria in Africa, European Uzbekistan, Croatia, the Netherlands and France and so on; as many as 10 teams are from all over China. The only two solo performers are also from Hong Kong, China (Mui Cheuk-yin, Daniel Yeung, both choreographing their own modern dance) - Chinese people and Chinese culture are in the limelight on the international dance festival.

It has the historical reason -it is well known, "Silk Road" originally began in Xi'an of China, namely Chang'an. Therefore, the Netherlands' international folk dance is called "Golden Xi'an". 16 dance programs include six Chinese-style programs: the first is "Tai Chi". Captions to the media read: "Xi'an is China's ancient imperial city and also the starting point of the Silk Road. As many as 6000 Terra-Cotta Warriors are unearthed from the tomb of Qin Shi Huang. Their imperturbable expression and the unity of body and mind may be represented by Tai Chi, a kind of art with the most Chinese cultural characteristics." The second program is "stilts", captioned as: "stilts are major folk activities in Shaanxi Province and Xi'an during the Spring Festival every year, including a clown- 'old woman' that can add humor to the whole show, "Lion Dance" with virile style and dragon dance praying for good weather." The third program is "Fan Dance", captioned as: "as fan is made of silk, fan dance can best embody the silk culture and the charm"; the fourth program is "long silk dance". The organizers believe, "This dance not only carries forward silk culture and charm but also fully displays the spirit of classicism in the Chinese opera and dance." The fifth program is "Tibetan Dance", which mainly shows the passionate nation character of Tibetan compatriots living in the land south "Silk Road" and the "Roof of the World" through two representative dances such as "Zhuoxie" (round dance) and "Duixie" (tap); The program list noted, this is written and directed by a Chinese dancer Liu Youlan. The sixth program is Kashgar's sanam, which is specifically noted to be directed by China's Xinjiang Uygur dancer Pasha Umer in 1999. It vividly reproduced Uighur ethnic nature of singing and dancing. Xinjiang was the only way which must be passed on "Silk Road". Dance festival organizing committee's interpretation of the relationship between keywords like "Silk" and "Silk Road" and a variety of dance can be described as fresh and concise. It not only can help French audiences to better appreciate this show, but also allows performers and commentators to draw inspiration. Subsequently, this show also along the

Silk Road performed the traditional music and dance across the Eurasian nations of Asian ethnic groups including Mongolia, India, Tajikistan, Uzbekistan, Pakistan, Afghanistan as well as the Caspian Sea and the Caucasus Avar, Armenia, Russia. The audiences seem to depart from the ancient capital Xi'an of China to Europe in just 135 minutes. They not only re-take this ancient "Silk Road" but also witness the costumes and customs along the way, so that they could not help but appreciate the world cultural diversity and the long history of human civilization.

With the sense of history, the program list also provides a "map of Asia" drawn by Antwerp, Belgium in 1570. 16 programs of the whole dance party were marked one by one in accordance with the track of "Silk Road", which let the audience see the respect for history.

In the Biennale de la Danse with "Silk Road" as the theme, the opening performances are composed of "long silk dance" and "Terracotta soul" by Beijing Dance Academy, solo dances by Li Hongjun of Guangdong Modern Dance Company and Hong Kong dancer Mui Cheuk-yin as well as Japanese drum dance team and South Korea's song and dance troupe. Then the Chinese party includes Dance fashion show "Golden Dance Silver" of Shanghai Song and Dance Ensemble and "Chinese folk dance show" of Shanghai Normal University student troupe. Three of them showcase the profound Chinese traditional dance culture and all make the French audience dazzling, relaxed and happy. They all went to the background, asking for dancers' signature.

There are both historical and realistic reasons for Chinese dance's uniqueness in this session. China Taiwan, Hong Kong, Guangzhou and Beijing's modern dances spread good news rapidly in recent years.

On the whole dance festival, Mr. Lin Huaimin and his "Cloud Gate Dance Theatre" are dominant. As the flagship troupe of Asian modern dance, "Cloud Gate" was the only qualified to launch the "Song of Vagrant" (video) and "Moon Water". The intrinsic tension of overcoming hardness with softness and floating clouds and flowing water produced by "Tai Chi guide" matches with the visual effects of simplicity, dignity and unity of heaven and man make the audiences amazing.

Taiwan's three outstanding groups also performed: "Sumptuous Feasting Song", created by Chen Meie for "Han and Tang Yuefu", is considered by the French media as "indoor dance of the most oriental humanistic spirit and Western modern concept"; "Flora Worship" performed by Lin Lizhen for Legend Lin Dance Theatre is one of the few commissioned works funded by Biennale de la Danse de Lyon, with simple and bright colors and very peculiar Chinese ritual beauty; the inspiring epic "Sound of the Ocean" by U Theatre can be described to make the strong sound of nature.

Hong Kong's program is also colorful- first, modern dance epic "Nine Songs" by the City Contemporary Dance Company is marvelous. Choreographer Li Haining takes Chinese-American composer Tan Dun's distant and grieved music as an opportunity to release a long depressed feeling and perform a life drama of parting forever, allowing Westerners to experience the Chinese culture and aesthetics' deep background and inner tension different from the West's; as the second generation representative of Hong Kong modern dance, since her "return" Mui Cheuk-yin has been popular on the big stage all over the world with her own identity as well as the contemporary representative of Chinese traditional culture; This time, she participated in the opening ceremony of the entire Biennale de la Danse; Daniel Yeung, graduate of Chinese University of Hong Kong, student of evening classes of the City Contemporary Dance Company and show director, is now the representative of the third generation of Hong Kong modern dance and has been active on the international stage; his multimedia new works "human nature paradise" skillfully blend his carefully recorded video with his flexible body and mind, which meets the psychological needs of self-appreciation and also indulges in singing the infinite wisdom of the human body.

Mainland show is always magnificent - established in 1992 during "reform and opening up", Guangdong Modern Dance Company becomes China's first professional modern dance company. Under great help of a large number of experts and scholars at home and abroad, especially founder Yang Meiqi and artistic director Willy Tsao, a large number of superb modern dance elite emerged. Among them, Qiao Yang, Qin Liming, Xing Liang, Sang Jijia, Li Hongjun successively won four gold medals for China in Paris international modern dance competition and created "Chinese modern dance miracle" that made the French people puzzled. Therefore, Li Hongjun was also invited to perform his solo "I Want to Fly" at the opening ceremony that won a gold medal in Paris, which received high praise from French audience and media;

Since it was taken over by Zhang Changcheng and Willy Tsao in 1999, Beijing Modern Dance Company frequently appeared on the international dance scene and has achieved a lot to shape the ancient capital Beijing's modern new image. Their party includes Willy Tsao's "Bird Song", "Two Worlds" by Gaoyanjinzi and Teng Aimin,

"Mumbling" by Teng Aimin, "Call of the Wild" by Li Hanzhong and Ma Bo, which let Westerners appreciate the enormous potential of the Chinese modern dance.

In other Asian countries, the Dance Festival also invited dance companies and orchestras of Japan, South Korea, India, Thailand, Mongolia, and Uzbekistan, including four of Japan: the first is "Intangible Cultural Heritage" project- Kabuki originating in the 7th century as well as three modern dance companies: Shonen-Shojo Boys & Girls by Kim Itoh and The Glorious Future, Kyoto Scene by Monochrome Circus; but the most impressive performance was Absolute Zero by Japanese modern dance master SaburoTeshigawara. As director, actor, musical co-director, set designer, costume designer and lighting designer, SaburoTeshigawara firmly grasped the audience's attention one night only through freely limbs, proper comparison, a little video projection and a girl's occasional appearance, without feeling tired.

South Korea's performances include Chang Mu Dance Company's performance by senior dancer Jin Meizi and Hong Shangyu's modern dance performances.

India has three performances by two classical dances of New Delhi Borneo and Madras Odissi as well as modern dance group led by Narendra Sharma, student of New Delhi modern dance master Udey Shankar.

Thailand selected the traditional narrative ballet, and the theme is the Indian poem "Ramayana."

Mongolian side invited Kilina Cremona who once danced in Lyon in the 1980s, later served as director of Split Croatian National Theatre Ballet Group and now is director of Ulan Bator to create the dance party paying respects to Lyon silk manufacturer Jacques · Brochier.

Uzbek has dance concert "Voice of Uzbekistan" performed by folk band from Samarkand.

Iraq invited the famous Baghdad Maqam Ensemble, and the name is "desert caravan on the Silk Road."

Host France has four modern dance performances, with themes in different ways, which were directly or indirectly related to the "Silk Road". This perspective can provide a reference for us:

The first is the contemporary ballet "Les Larmes de Marco Polo", which is created by the famous French contemporary dance choreographer Jean-Claude Gallotta for his National Dance Center in Grenoble. I read it twice in a row, and at the invitation of Liu

Lihua, cultural counselor of the French embassy in China, interviewed choreographer Gallotta, screenwriter Claude - Henry · Bouffard, composer Xu Shuya in France, Chinese flute player Zhang Weiliang, cellist Vincent · Deburena, Marco Polo actor Ludwig · Galván. I persuaded the French embassy in the form of a written argument, so that this very avant-garde contemporary dance was performed in Beijing and Shanghai of China in the fall of 2001.

This ballet was inspired by the world-famous "Marco Polo Travels" - in 1254, Marco Polo was born in Venice, Italy, and came to the East in 1271. He won Kublai Khan's trust, so he was an official for 17 years in China and travelled through China; in 1292, he left China, after three years of travel fatigue, and finally returned to Venice, but he was taken prisoner in jail in war with Genoa. Misfortune may be an actual blessing. He had a chance to settle down, recalled and dictated his own rare experience in the East, especially in China, which was recorded into a book. In 1299, he was released to return home, but this travel was translated into many languages and widely circulated in various countries, resulting in a significant impact on the opening of the new route and Silk Road. The significance of Gallotta's ballet is that facing the fact that the same theme of opera, ballet, movies and television came into being, he easily went out of the errors of telling the "story", and boldly focused on the rough clues according to the plot development.

The second French work was the contemporary dance drama "Bombyx Mori" created by Lyon local contemporary dance choreographer Miss Delphine Gaud for her dance team. As France's earliest capital of silk production, the subject of this ballet was from a real but extraordinary story happening in early 20th century in Lyon: a group of female workers of a silk factory were obsessed by silk and even cocoons, so they began to produce a fetish type of sexual addiction. Then they ventured to steal silk, and eventually were put in jail or sent to a madhouse... for convenience for dancing, choreographer personified the transparent white silk to the fifth character. Four women crawled on the ground like cocoon sometimes and became the legendary figures sometimes. This story has been widely circulated in the Lyon people. Therefore, the audience's applause and even cheers prove that they did not have any obstacles in the understanding, so they were able to concentrate to watch the choreography and dancing. On the action, Miss Gaud's approach apparently broke the narrative habits of classical ballet, mainly conveying the protagonist's mental state, Therefore, it was close to Gallotta's Les Larmes de Marco Polo in style. This work is also the dance festival's agreed production to reflect support for local dance development.

The third French group was also from Christiane Blaise in Grenoble. The style is contemporary. The works was called Alerte La Soie! Different with the previous two works, this works doesn't tell stories, but talking philosophy - we must beware of the soft and beautiful things such as silk. For example, "the mother of modern dance" Isadora · Duncan died of that long and flowing scarf! All these concepts transform into a feeling through sharp contrast of the actions in efforts, time and space.

The fourth performance was "Dance of man and God" that French Besancon and Saint-Priest's RAP integrated Western hip-hop dance and Indian Kathak classical dance, reflecting the "Silk Road" spirit of a combination of Chinese and Western elements and ancient and modern blend.

During the dance festival, it also held a variety of activities, including 11 performances held by the Netherlands international folk dance groups and Shanghai Normal University's students for the social people from all walks of life and students, photographic exhibition, exhibition of cultural relics, silk opera costumes exhibition of the countries along "Silk Road", "Tai Chi guide" open class of Cloud Gate Dance Theatre, film screenings, square dances of port of Alexandria, Egypt and Venice, Europe's largest Le Défilé participated by 4, 500 masses of various immigrant communities in the region of Lyon.

"Ninth Biennale de la Danse de Lyon" has a total number of 79, 060 spectators. Excluding free audience and participants of exhibition, "Tai Chi guide" open class and other demonstration lectures, the number of audiences who buy tickets are as many as 71, 531, 11% more than those of the last. 7, 529 audiences got free tickets. The theater attendance average was 90 percent, which includes adult packages and teenager packages of four performances and three performances; in addition, Le Défilé spectators are up to 200, 000. French national TV III live had attracted an additional 150, 000 audiences, with a total of 350, 000 spectators. Meanwhile, the Dance Festival also invited 249 overseas correspondents. Foreign reporters including me were up to 96. 19 TV channels at home and abroad reported at different depths.

When the Chinese government proposed the grand strategic vision of building "One Belt and One Road", and gradual implemented it, I would like to share French "Silk Road" concept and operation practices that I experienced in person as well as the beautiful pictures with you . . .

Thank you for listening and watching!

Reference:

1. [French] M Soto, J. -P Boudes, A Guerreau-Jalabert, Yang Jian, Fu Shaomei, Qian Linsen translating, French Cultural History [M] Shanghai: . East China Normal University Press, 2006.

2. [Canada] J. -B Nadeau, J Barlow, He Kaisong, Hu Jilan translation Sixty Million French People Cannot Be Wrong [M] Beijing: Oriental Press, 2005.

3. [USA] W Sorrell and Ou Jianping translation. Cultural History of Western Dance [M] Beijing: China Renmin University Press, 1996.

4. Ou Jianping, History of World Art · Dance volume [M] Beijing: Oriental Press, 2003.

5. Ou Jianping "Les Larmes de Marco Polo": a deep sense of poetic dance [N] People's Daily (overseas edition), September 18, 2001, 7th edition.

6. Ou Jianping, Les Larmes de Marco Polo and Poetry of Dance Language [J] Today Art, November 2001: pp. 22-23.

7. Ou Jianping. Open to the world -Biennale de la Danse de Lyon Commentary 1 [N] . Dance information, 15 January, 2003 (Fourth edition).

8. Ou Jianping. Introducing the Silk Road to France-Biennale de la Danse de Lyon Commentary 2 [N] . Dance information, February 1, 2003 (Fourth edition).

9. Ou Jianping, Latin American Dancing Popular in Lyon-Biennale de la Danse de Lyon Commentary 3 [N] . Dance information, February 15, 2003 (Fourth edition).

10. Ou Jianping, Latin American Dance Popular in Lyon-Tenth Biennale de la Danse de Lyon Commentary [J] Sino-Foreign cultural exchanges, February 2003: pp. 54-55.

11. Ou Jianping, spectacular Latin American Dance [J] Dance, March 2003: pp. 23-24.

12. Ou Jianping. Latin American at Pinnacle of Modern Dance-Biennale de la Danse de Lyon Commentary 4 [N] . Dance information, March 1, 2003 (Fourth edition).

13. Ou Jianping. Concept pure dance & projection-Biennale de la Danse de Lyon Commentary 5 [N] . Dance information, March 15, 2003 (Fourth edition).

14. Ou Jianping. Performance Art & Environment choreography -Biennale de la Danse de Lyon Commentary Six [N]. Dance information, April 15, 2003 (Fourth edition).

15. Ou Jianping, zebra dance company and others in Biennale-Biennale de la Danse de Lyon Commentary 7 [N]. Dance information, June 15, 2003 (Fourth edition) .

History and Prospect of Drama Exchange in "the Belt and Road" Frame

Song Baozhen
Director and Research Fellow of the Drama Research
Institute of Chinese National Academy of Arts

The "New Silk Road Economic Belt" and "21st-Century Maritime Silk Road" were put forward by the Chinese President Xi Jinping in September and October 2013 respectively.

As the frame of modern idea and cross-cultural development, "the Belt and Road" aims to promote the political consultation, economic prosperity and cultural tolerance between China and surrounding countries and to achieve the dialogue, exchange and cooperation between different civilizations from Asia, Europe and Africa on the basis of community of interests, as well as to realize the peaceful development of China and the joint negotiation, sharing and co-building of interests of surrounding countries.

The economic development and cultural prosperity are very important to guarantee the peaceful rise of China. The economic takeoff conceived in the "the Belt and Road" can't realize without the cross-cultural communication, cooperation, reciprocity and integration. In such background, it is the realistic proposition worthy to be considered that how the Chinese drama grasps the opportunities and deals with challenges for development and progress. This article will comb the relationships between Chinese drama and foreign culture in over hundred years of historical development of Chinese drama, in order to learn from the history and face up to the future.

Encounter and Exchange between Chinese and Foreign Dramas

China is a drama giant. After over eight-hundred years of development, the traditional Chinese opera art has been developed into over 300 types of drama and distributed throughout China. However, in early 20th century, a modern stage artistic form originating from the west - spoken drama was appeared.

The artistic form of Chinese spoken drama is different from traditional drama, which presents the story mainly by dialogues, physical movements and stage set to create the stage illusion of reality, instead of song and dance.

Without the fusion of Chinese and western cultures, there would be no Chinese spoken drama.

As a modern form of art, spoken drama is also a carrier of cultural creativity and exchange. In the frame of "the Belt and Road", it shall play its role in enhancing friendship, expanding understanding, developing cooperation and seeking consensus among nationalities

The performance of western drama in China can date back to the end of 16th century based on existing records. According to the Annuals of Macao St. Paul's College, the teachers and students in the college once performed western drama on the steps of St. Paul's Cathedral (the Ruins of Saint Paul's Cathedral today) on January 16, 1596:

"On the Assumption Day, a tragedy was performed in public. The protagonists were acted by the first-grade teachers and other roles were acted by students. The drama is about how the belief defeats Japanese's persecution. The performance was on the steps of our college, which attracted the entire citizens to watch. The street in front of the St. Paul Temple was packed by the crowd… The performance was very wonderful and not inferior to the level of any university. Because the main story was performed in Latin, the Chinese dialogues were made especially for audience who didn't understand Latin… It was accompanied with music and accompany at the same time, which made all people very satisfied." (Quoted from Study of Macao St. Paul's College, written by Li Xiangyu, Macao Daily, July 2001, page 1.)

It is mentioned in the article that it is about the "belief defeats Japanese's persecution", so we can deduce that this drama might not be a simple religious drama, but a story reflecting the Macao people's fighting against Japanese, which might be one of the reasons why it attracted wide attention of the citizens. It is also recorded that there were "Chinese dialogues" in the performance, which indicated that the teachers and students in the St. Paul's College were already good in Chinese, or Chinese people might participated in the production and performance activities of the drama.

In the Annuals of Macao St. Paul's College, the content and process of a comedy performance were recorded in detail. The performance of students of St. Paul's College even began to cross the wall of the college and enter the life of citizens in Macao society. The record mentioned the social effect of the performance: "Originally, this comedy was performed to welcome the arrival of Chinese bishops, as always in previous years. But this year it seemed to entertain the citizens in the city, who were depressed for the loss caused by the Dutch. The Dutch plundered three cargo ships recently…" (Quoted from Study of Macao St. Paul's College, written by Li Xiangyu, Macao Daily, July 2001, page 90.)

For the two performances mentioned above, the drama audience included the Macao citizens, which indicated the nature of "public performance". So far, it is the earliest performance of spoken drama in China recorded.

After the Opium War, China was compelled to open the border and the eastern and western cultures began to be blended. At the end of 19th century, the Qing Government began to send people to the west for travelling. The first man travelled far to Europe was Bin Chun, who was known as "the first oriental to the east".

Bin Chun was one of the first Chinese sent by Qing Government to "Taixi" (Europe) for travelling. He was a bannerman, who was not intelligent since childhood and was "more pedantic" when grew up. However, he was also a "freak", a traveler liked travelling. He said: "I have travelled most place of the country and I'm proud of my rich experiences." At that time, it was regarded as a dangerous journey to travel overseas. However, the 63-year-old Bin Chun "was willing to travel there". Someone worried about him, but he wrote "the God wants to test the courage of scholar, but I just regard the vast sea as a little pit" and travelled overseas resolutely. After returning home, he wrote the Chengcha Notes, recording the new things observed by his curious perspective.

Bin Chun reported the performance scene of western drama to the Chinese for the first time. In the theater, he saw nobilities and socialites coming slowly wearing gorgeous, bold and back-long robes and precious jewelry and he was felt more novel for the scene on the stage and praised: "There are 50 to 60 female performers on the stage, half of which are very beautiful and all of which are half-naked when dancing. There are mountain, water, fall, sunshine, moonlight and figure of Buddha or dozens of goddesses falling from the sky suddenly with dazzling auspicious light, which are fantastic and marvelous. (Zhong Shuhe: Openings, page 69, 1985 edition, Zhonghua Book Company) Obviously, he was fascinated by the marvelous and mysterious western drama.

In the initial contact with foreign dramas, what Chinese most interested was always not the drama itself, but the most sensitive parts caused by cultural differences, which can be easily found in the books written by some earliest Chinese diplomatists, such as the Western Magazine (Li Shuchang), Diary of Visiting Britain, France and Russia (Zeng Jiyi), Recording of Traveling (Wang Tao), Sketches on Visiting France with Others (Zhang Deyi), etc.

They were most interested in the architecture of foreign theaters, for example, the Paris Opera House was "like the imperial palace for short stays, "the scale is grander than imperial palace", etc. ; and the differences between Chinese and foreign performers, for example, "the British performers are artists, who are not humble as Chinese actors and actress, so the owner of theater can contact with government officials". They even felt "it is really inconceivable that performance is studied by idlers in China but mainly by schoolchildren in western countries, and the people there all appreciate that without any objection". Contacting with the drama itself, people felt surprised most by the real and marvelous stage set of western drama: "diversified and realistic sets", "the audience is immersive in the scene, which is very amazing". But the initial summary of spoken drama is: "dialogues without songs" and "without songs and sets". The western style of drama entered in the east and the foreign form of art was gradually accepted by the Chinese.

Growth and Birth of Modern Drama with Modernity and Nationality

The Chinese drama experienced a "western trend" in the contemporary history during the May Fourth Period.

The Chinese theater struggled against imperialism and feudalism and absorbed nutrition from foreign cultures to explore the development direction of national drama. When people exploring the new development direction of drama, Ibsen and his drama not only came into the view of Chinese, but also became the ideological banner and example of art at that time.

In the 1920s, not only Hu Shi persisted in "Ibsenism", some youths aspiring to create modern Chinese drama, including Hong Shen, Tian Han, etc. also regarded "being a Chinese Ibsen" as their ideal of life. Meanwhile, the western modernism, including symbolism, expressionism, aestheticism, futurism and various schools of drama spread into China, opening the view of modern life for Chinese dramatists. However, Chinese people couldn't understand and even were unintelligible to the performances directly translated from western dramas, which compelled the Chinese drama to explore the drama road of nationality.

In the middle 1920s, the "national drama movement" once appeared in the Chinese theater. The "national drama movement" actually was that some overseas returnees wanted to seek for the development road of national modern drama for feeling the decline of Chinese crude stage play and set off a discussion of drama thought. In 1926, Yu Shangyuan, Hsu Chih-mo and some others initiated to found the Morning Paper – Drama and established a grand plan including plans to establish drama school, theater, etc., but many plans fell through. Only the Drama was realized with the support of Hsu Chih-mo and about over 20 articles about drama were published in total, written by Hsu Chih-mo, Yu Shangyuan, Wen Yiduo, Zhao Taimou, Zhang Jiazhu, Xiong Foxi, Deng Yizhe, Liang Shiqiu, etc. Their own artistic ideas and theoretical perspectives were not the same, but obviously they had a common goal of creating Chinese own drama style.

Based on the comparison between Chinese and western dramas, Yu Shangyuan, Zhao Taimou and others thought that Chinese traditional drama's "focus-on-meaning" was different from western drama's "focus-on-reality", therefore, Chinese should absorb the advantages of Chinese and western dramas to create a "national drama". However, for what is "national drama" and how to create "national drama", they were still in the stage of exploration in theory.

The breakthrough achievement in drama practice was made after the 1930s.

Going through the ideological emancipation and cultural integration during the May Fourth Period and on the basis of wide absorption of western drama's essence, Chinese spoken drama became mature based on local drama. The drama results represented by Cao Yu's excellent Thunderstorm, Sunrise, Champaign, Pekingese, Home, etc. appeared. These dramas are with modern consciousness and reflect the national spirit and Chinese style by employing native subjects. They also are regarded as the classic works of Chinese drama for their profound meaning, consummate skills, successful images and perfect structures.

Sino-Russian Drama Exchange and Establishment of Chinese Performing System

After the establishment of the People's Republic of China, the whole Chinese theater has begun to learn the Stanislavsky performing system (Stanislavsky system for short) since 1953.

First, theatrical workers were recommended to learn Stagecraft, An Actor Prepares and other Stanislavsky's works in art management way. Second, the Soviet experts (普·乌·列斯里鲍·格·库里涅夫 and 格·尼·古里也夫) were invited to give lessons in China. Third, the training class and refresher class were held in The Central Academy of Drama and Shanghai Theatre Academy during 1953 to 1957.

The promotion of Stanislavsky system plays a positive role in improving Chinese stagecraft level.

In 1957, the spoken drama Teahouse was created by Lao She, and then performed in the Beijing People's Art Theatre, becoming a milestone and masterpiece in drama creation of new China. The thirty-thousand-word drama describes the story of three "dynasties" (generations) within 50 years, depicting 70 characters vividly. It created an epic picture with highly artistic condensation, strong national features, large history contents and strong flavor of life. The Chief Director Jiao Juyin explored the road of performance-nationalization. He had deep understanding and mastery of Stanislavsky system, but he was more interested in applying the essence of Chinese operas to spoken drama and discovering the moment for its fusion with Stanislavsky system to open up the way for the combination of Chinese opera and western drama. He agreed the "inner experience" and "vividly reproducing life", but he pursued more the stage of dramatic poem, highly artistic reality and highly artistic condensation.

In 1958, a creation upsurge of historical drama appeared marked by Tian Han's Guan Hanqing, characterized by many old-generation dramatists participating in the creation, such as Guo Moruo's Cai Wenji and Wu Zetian, Cao Yu's Gall and Sword, Ding Xilin's Meng Lijun, Liu Chuan's Tragedy of Dou E, Lao She's Righteous and Harmonious Fists, Tian Han's Princess Wencheng, Zhu Zuyi's Naval Battle in 1894, etc. Some of these historical dramas are quite wonderful and were highly praised by audience after the performance, among which the Guan Hanqing could be called the masterpiece of

Tian Han. He composed a paean of Guan Hanqing by the language, tone and conception of poetry, showing his remarkable brilliance as a dramatist and passionate and romantic poet. The strongly lyric coloring of Guan Hanqing and its romantic charm and rhythm of Yuan opera present strong poetic romance and tragic significance.

In 1959, Guo Moruo created a 4-act historical drama Cai Wenji for Beijing People's Art Theatre, presenting the image of an ancient talented lady over 2,000 years ago on the Chinese modern drama stage. Directed by Jiao Juyin and acted by Zhu Lin, the drama caused a sensation after the performance and is still the repertoire of Beijing People's Art Theatre now.

Drama Development after the Reform and Opening-up

After the reform and opening-up, various philosophic concepts, artistic ideological trends and genres of modern western countries were introduced into our country. Modernism's concepts regarding the exploration of human beings, the human heart and the ulterior soul hidden deeply inside the human beings, Expressionism and Symbolism techniques, the artistic characteristics of Stream of Consciousness and Absurdist, and Brecht's idea of Verfremdungseffekt, Epic Theatre, Theatre of Cruelty and Poor Theatre and the like all have brought a new feeling and inspiration to the people engaged in the drama. These modern ideas are incorporated into the modern drama stagecraft, and are gradually nationalized by continuously being absorbed and transformed, and are also accepted by the Chinese people little by little.

In order to broaden the view of the drama and demonstrate the outstanding dramatic achievements of our human beings, the Chinese theatrical circles have conducted a wide range of artistic cooperation with the dramatists from other countries and regions by virtue of their broad and open cultural mind and unique aesthetic insight.

Since the beginning of the new era, Beijing People's Art Theatre has provided a huge number of foreign dramas with good quality script and high artistic level, such as Justifying Public Opinion (Romania), The Visit (Switzerland), Butcher (Austria), Death of a Salesman (U.S.A), A Woman's Life (Japan), The Gin Game (U.S.A), Amadeus (UK), Schwejk In Word War II (Germany), Major Barbara (UK), Mutiny (U.S.A), Seagull (Russia), Hamlet (UK), Don't Touch (France), It's A Long Way Home (UK), Desire Under The Elms (U.S.A), etc.

For a long time, Beijing People's Art Theatre has invited many foreign drama experts to the theater to conduct artistic cooperation and exchanges, and has formed multiple drama achievements: in 1981, British famous theatre director Toby Robertson directed Shakespeare's famous play Invitation to a Funeral for Beijing People's Art Theatre. In 1983, American famous dramatist Arthur Miller directed his own famous play Death of a Salesman for Beijing People's Art Theatre. In 1988, Charlton Heston, Academy Awards winner and president of American Film Institute, directed Mutiny for Beijing People's Art Theatre. In 1991, Director Oleg Efremov from Moscow Art Theater directed Seagull for Beijing People's Art Theatre. In 2013, Director Petrov from Moscow Art Theatre directed the Italian writer Luigi Pirandello's famous play Sei personaggi in cerca d'autore together with Young Director Wang Peng from Beijing People's Art Theatre.

From September to November of 1980, Beijing People's Art Theatre was invited to give a visit performance of Teahouse in Germany, France and Switzerland with a total period of 50 days, visiting 15 cities and giving 25 performances. Wherever we arrived, there would be strong repercussions among the foreign audiences, and they were all impressed by the superb performances of Chinese actors, cheering that Teahouse is a miracle of oriental stage.

In 1983, we were invited to perform Teahouse in Tokyo, Osaka, Kyoto, Hiroshima of Japan.

In 1986, we performed Teahouse in Hong Kong, Singapore and Canada.

In 2006, the rearranged Teahouse was performed in John F. Kennedy Arts Center and went on tour in other cities of the U.S.A.

Since its establishment in 1995, Shanghai Dramatic Arts Center has been focusing on expanding cultural exchanges with other countries in the world, learning outstanding drama creation experiences from them. During the past decade, the Center has been staged more than 100 ancient, current and modern works successively, and has carried out all kinds of cooperation and visit performances with the artists from the United Kingdom, the United States, France, Australia, Russia, Japan, Singapore, South Korea, Ireland, Egypt, Germany and other countries as well as Hong Kong and Taiwan of China, gaining high praises from the cultural circles at home and abroad, and arousing a strong reaction in the audiences in different countries and regions.

National Theatre Company of China (NTCC) is the national performance arts group of People's Republic of China. It was founded based on the former China Youth Art Theater and Central Experimental Theatre on December 25, 2001.

NTCC is incorporated with a number of the best drama stage artistic talents and television artistic talents. It is a production base that inherits traditions, hard work, and is full of exploration with the pursuit of high-level drama performance arts, creating drama masterpieces.

NTCC treats the creation and performance of high-quality, high-grade elite dramatic arts at home and abroad as its mission, while continuing to pursue classical and experimental theater stage, and always reflects the advanced cultural achievements of the world and the nation.

In 2002, it created and performed the five dramas: The Crucible (USA), The Dawns Here Are Quiet (Soviet Union), Return of the Native woman (Switzerland), Head without Tail and "Call Me Brother, I'll Tear Drops Like Raining", organized some repertoires to perform in Shanghai, Hong Kong, Macao, Japan and other regions, and also participated in the stage performance of international art festivals and exchange activities of foreign and domestic dramas.

From 2004 onwards, NTCC established the biennial International Theatre Season together with China Arts and Entertainment Group and other units. The first two International Theater Season has focused on the stage performance of domestic and overseas dramas in honor of Chekhov, Ibsen, Shakespeare, Colorful Asia, Colorful Europa and international performance season, promoting the exchange of domestic and foreign theater circles, and facilitating the development of Chinese drama career.

In recent years, the new features of the exchange of domestic and overseas dramas are as follows:

1. Changing from performing overseas dramas to inviting foreign directors, until introducing the western famous dramas with market prospect and social influence.

2. Drama Performance Season, Masterpiece Performance and Internal Theatre Festival that aim to co-perform the domestic and foreign dramas obviously increase and first class foreign dramatists and their teams frequently come to perform in China.

3. Chinese modern dramas begin to spread abroad and participate in the festivals like Chekhov Theatre Festival, Avignon Theater Festival, China, Japan and South Korea Drama Festival and Edinburgh Festival, etc.

From November 1, 2014 to December 25, the 6th Olympic Drama was held in Beijing. The theme of this Olympic Drama is dream with the slogan of Chinese dream &

World stage, which brings together 46 works created by thousands of dramatists from 22 countries, and gives hundreds of performances in 17 theaters of Beijing.

Olympic Drama is the visual feast of stage artistic charm. President of Olympic Drama and Greece director Teer Zuo Boras that directs Prometheus Bound makes Prometheus' tragic stand out by prostrate body of the chorus actor within the stone circle, and realizes the docking and interaction between the ancient and the modern times by the chanting of the director at the edge of the stage and the explosions from the outside.

With the increasing of exchanges between the domestic dramas and foreign dramas, the development of Chinese native dramas will be ever-increasingly popular.

According to the statistics by Beijing Trade Association for Performances, there are various business performances totaling 24, 595 in Beijing in 2014, and drama performances totaling 4519 with an increase of 5% over last year; children's drama performances totals 3134, and other types of performances and small theater performances totals 3200. Among them, drama, children's drama, comic dialogues, acrobatic performances and other language performances account for 67.8% of total screenings. By audience demographics, drama audiences reach to 1, 471, 000; children's drama audiences reach to 1, 015, 000, and other types of performances and small theater performance audiences reach to 1, 061, 000.

Outlook on the drama exchange under the Framework of the Belt and Road:

1. The strategic conception of the Belt and Road is the powerful measure aiming to facilitating the rising of Chinese economy and the prospering of national cultures; the modern drama will exert important role as the carrier of cultural exchange.

2. Good drama has no national boundaries; in today's integration of world's economy, the exchange of domestic dramas and foreign dramas will be normalized, ordering and continuous.

3. Chinese modern dramas are basically "imported goods" and its artistic form and developing gait has the affinity and convergence with the arts of other nations.

4. Under the circumstances of mutual respect, mutual benefit and win-win strategy, cross-cultural drama exchanges will be broadened with its forms increasing and effects better.

French Absurdist Dramatist Eugene Lonesco once said, "Drama is the essence of human needs". We hereby wish the human drama and the civilization development of the world will become better and better.

Take an Example of Translation in *A Dream of Red Mansion* to View the Interaction between Scholars in China and Japan

Sun Yuming
Director of the Dream of Red Mansion Research
Institute of Chinese National Academy of Arts

By now, Japan has appeared four translation versions of 120-chapter A Dream of Red Mansions. Versions by Matsueda Shigeo andIto Sohei were published before the Normalization of Sino-Japanese relation, so they were not influenced by the academia of Mainland of China. After the normalization, especially at the beginning of 1980s, after Matsueda Shigeo andIto Sohei visited A Dream of Red Mansions Research Institute of Chinese National Academy of Arts, Ito Sohei revised his first translation version, and his notes were much influenced by us. Lizuka Akira's full translation version and Inami Ryoichi's full translation version published last year are clearly influenced by us. Taking Futile Frowning in the Fifth Chapter as an example, we can see clear influence. The first and second revision noted by A Dream of Red Mansions Research Institute of Chinese National Academy of Arts assigned the song Futile Frowning to Baoyu and Daiyu, which is obviously against the fact. In the third revision, we accepted opinions of some scholars and assigned it to Daiyu and Baochai. Inami Ryoichi has clearly adopted notes in the first two revisions. If he revises his translation, we don't know if he adopts our changes in the third version.

Cultural Genes and Dialogues in Chinese Traditional Operas

Wang Kui
Director of Chinese Opera Research Institute of Chinese National Academy of Arts

Cultural dialogues need some preconditions: the cultures are self-confident and self-sufficient, tolerant and compatible, creative and developing. In the development of "the Belt and Road" initiative, it is necessary to expose a national culture outlook that is confident, tolerant and open, which are important cultural tradition and historical experience China has achieved. Mulian Saving His Mother originates from the reincarnation belief of Indian Buddhism, and is represented in Chinese Buddhist ceremonies and folk operas. It suggests that Chinese culture is tolerant to accept cultural genes from foreign countries, and is creative to develop richer art forms.

In the Buddhist flower ceremony of Hakkas in Guangdong, the most touching is the unfolding of Mulian saving his mother. Along the Silk Road that goes from west to the east of China, the story introduces the Buddhist Karma into traditional ethical systems of China. It exhibits the ultimate truth that cause and effect never fail, and is combined with Buddhist worshiping merits and civil saving ethnics. In addition, it integrates Chinese traditional family ethnics and human concern. With travelling of Chinese people along the Maritime Silk Road, the story of Mulian Saving His Mother was spread to overseas Chinese communities of Southeast Asia. At the same time, operas combined the story with Chinese traditional ritual music systems, and became an important play on Chinese opera stages. With rich national creation, geographic creation and ethnic creation, various performance forms with different styles have been developed.

The evolution of the story has connected various regions with different cultures and traditions, and has created rich and diversified cultural forms, which effectively reveals oriental wisdom. In the cultural space of "the Belt and Road", the cooperation and win-win mechanism of Asian cultures will be clearly displayed through the cultural exchange history reflected in this story.

Impact of Silk Road Art Exchanges on Development of Ancient Chinese Music Dance
—Case Study of Court Music Dance
Wang Ningning
Research Fellow of Dance Institute of Chinese National Academy of Arts

In 138 B. C. , Zhang Qian went on a diplomatic mission to the Western Regions under the order of Emperor Wu of the Western Han Dynasty. The action, with an original intention of resisting Xiongnu, an ancient nationality in China, and strengthening national defense and diplomatic ties, opened up the ancient Silk Road towards the Western Regions. It hence connected China to the rest of the world, where civilizations of the east and west collided. Following the opening of the Silk Road, China and the states of the Western Regions made exchanges in economic and trade, political and cultural sectors. They also communicated constantly in the art of music and dance.

During the Han Dynasty (206 B. C. – 220A. D.) , Khotan Music was introduced from the Western Regions, while acrobatic "Illusion Man" (similar to today's magic) was brought from East Rome and India. The Emperor and nobilities in the capital city were fond of the "Hu music", "Hu dance" and "Hu clothing" of the Western Regions.

As it came to the Period of Wei, Jin, and Southern and Northern Dynasties (220 – 581), the exchanges remained as ever along the Silk Road, despite the national secession, separation and turmoil. This period witnessed most impressive exchanges among ethnic groups, and cultural diversity in ancient China. The music-based dances introduced from the Western Regions in this period included the Qiuci Music, Xiliang Music, Tianzhu Music, Gaochang Music, Kangguo Music and Shule Music.

The Sui and Tang period (581 – 907) marked the most prosperous and powerful times in ancient China. The unified empire kept more frequent contacts with the Western Regions. As recorded in the preface to the Illustrated Book of Western Regions, by Pei Ju of the Sui Dynasty, the Silk Road went straight to Persia, India and Rome. Chang'an, the capital city, was not only the political, economic and cultural center of China, but also a world famous center for cultural exchanges between the east and west. As shown in history books, over 50 countries, including 25 states from the Western Regions, maintained ties with the Tang regime. Diplomats from various ethnic groups and foreign countries gathered in Chang'an, marking unprecedented prosperity in exchanges of Chinese and western cultures and cultural diversity. In the era of Sui and Tang, featuring national unity, social stability, liberal politics, and developed economy and culture, the music-based dances previously introduced from Western Regions states, and various ethnic groups were well sorted out and preserved in the new historical environment.

The court banquet music of Sui and Tang absorbed many foreign music-based dances, including Xiliang Music, Tianzhu Music, Anguo Music, Qiuci Music, Shule Music, Gaochang Music, and Kangguo Music. It integrated music dances of various countries and ethnic groups into large-scale banquet music of grand scenes and diversified styles, in an open, tolerant attitude, "embracing all with wide heart". Thanks to the long-term exchanges of Chinese and western music dances, people of this period changed quietly their notion of dances. They started to pay close attention to the body movements and expression of artistic styles. The court music dance institutions were separated to focus specifically on singing and dancing. Dance began to break through the traditional pattern of "skillful in dancing with long sleeves", and expressed the art in richer space. The opening of the Silk Road towards the Western Regions, exchanges of Chinese and western culture and art, and collision of diversified cultures facilitated ancient Chinese music dance to develop in depth and breadth. Meanwhile, it also promoted development of the art in Asian countries in terms of university and complementarity.

QianZhongshu Interprets "The Health Status of the Elderly is Unstable, like Spring Chill and Autumn Heat"

Wang Ren'en

Professor of School of Literature of Jimei University

"The health status of the elderly is unstable, like spring chill and autumn heat" came out of Zijuan in A Dream in Red Mansions. The Dictionary of A Dream in Red Mansions quoted materials of Brocade in Sleeves for annotation, believing Zijuan said it in reference of Grandmother Jia, a metaphor that the health of the elderly is like spring chill and autumn heat that could not last long. It is roughly correct to explain it in such a way, though not having attained to perfection, or pointed out the earliest source. Mr. Qian Zhongshu, in his Notes on Literature and Art, quoted from many sources, including letters, traditional Chinese operas, novels, proverbs, poems and essays, to unveil the origin, circulation, and quotation of "The health status of the elderly is unstable, like spring chill and autumn heat". It traced to the source to provide precious material for annotation and research of A Dream in Red Mansions. Qian made clear to the later generations a valuable advanced research technique.

Point of Cultural Convergence for Marine Silk Road and Land Silk Road in Yuan Dynasty
——Take the Example of Eastward Flowing of Hellenism to Quanzhou

Wu Youxiong

Professor of Quanzhou Normal University

In Yuan dynasty, Quanzhou of Fujian was the famous trading port in the East and the center of Jiangzhe and Huaihu Trading Zone in China. Also, it was the provincial capital of Jiangzhe Province and Fujian Province. At that time, the middle and lower reaches of Yangtze River was both the rear base and imported products sales area for the traded goods from Quanzhou Port. Also, with the economic and cultural exchange between the world and China, Quanzhou became the region where various religions were and introduced and propagated. Now Quanzhou is provided with many Gandhara-styled sculpted stone in Yuan dynasty, which respectively belongs to Buddhism, Hinduism, Islam, Christian and Catholicism. Also, such Gandhara-styled sculpted stone was introduced by land and ocean. In Yuan dynasty, there were a lot of religions in Quanzhou. Prevail of Gandhara -styled sculpted stone should be contributed to Quanzhou which was the largest harbor in the East and the center of Jiangzhe and Huaihu Trading Zone at that time.

In this paper, the Buddhist sculptures from Yuan dynasty left in Quanzhou are adopted to verify the eastward flowing of Hellenism to Quanzhou through Maritime Silk Road by means of Gandhara-styled art. Meanwhile, the legacies of Christian tombstones in the Syriac language show that the Hellenism was introduced to Quanzhou by Christians through land Silk Road. So, we conclude that Quanzhou of Fujian in Yuan dynasty was the point of cultural convergence for Marine Silk Road and Land Silk Road. Here, the religious remains from Yuan dynasty were used to verify the introduction of culture and art of Greece to Quanzhou of Fujian through the Marine Silk Road and Land Silk Road.

Exchange and Integration of Chinese and Foreign Music: Reflection on History and Development of "the Belt and Road"

Xiang Yang
Provisional Director and Research Fellow of the Music Research Institute of Chinese National Academy of Arts

China is initiating the "the Belt and Road" national development strategy. It can be predicted that the economy of the countries and regions along this belt and road will get substantial growth, and a win-win situation can be expected. At the same time, economic exchanges will drive cultural communication, which involves many aspects, including music. In Chinese history, the most important exchange of music and culture occurs in the West Regions and Europe. Since Han and Tang dynasties, music from the West Regions exerted much influence on Chinese music when many music works came to China and were integrated into local ritual and civil music. The influence from the Maritime Silk Road on Chinese music happened in Ming and Qing dynasties, and reached the apex in the 20th century. China experienced a process from passive to active acceptance of western music, which involved a number of complex elements. At the national level, China began to actively accept western music in the 20th century, the Chinese traditional music formed in the past thousands of years has gradually changed from its ontology-centered nature (tune and instrument).

We should clarify what the original Chinese music traditions are, or when we want to enhance historical research of Chinese traditional music, we should grasp its original characteristics, and clearly state its profound cultural connotation. Under these conditions, we can study the historical and substantial impact of western regions and European music on Chinese traditional music. In the implementation of the "the Belt and Road" national development strategy, after tradition is clearly defined from the top, we should make sure what specific measures should be taken in future cultural exchanges. Therefore, we can have clear objectives.

It should be noted, during Han and Tang dynasties, although music works of the

Western Regions introduced through the Silk Road could be used in rites, they couldn't enter the core part of ritual ceremonies, which suggests that the Western Region music and the local music had effectively integrated but had different functions. When China gradually released restriction of music on national rites, ritual and civil music was not strictly classified, and civil music was stressed. In other words, when ritual and civil music application was not subjectively classified, although people might feel the clear difference between the western and Chinese music, they would not plainly refuse western music from entering solemn occasions as when China first communicated with the Western Regions. We may say that the distinguishing concept has vanished. Therefore, little barrier may be met during music exchange and integration, which should be reflected by us. When self is missed, what value exchange and integration will bring about?

The Role of Overseas Chinese is Crucial to the Creation of New Asian civilization

Xie Bizhen
Professor and Director of the Research Center of
Fujian-Taiwan Area, Fujian Normal University

The migration of population will never cease if the people live in the world. So, it is an eternal topic on overseas immigrants. At present, China proposes the construction of the 21st Century Maritime Silk Road. As we all know, the construction of Maritime Silk Road will create the new Asian civilization. This should be a long process and cannot be done in one day, so we should insist on it. During the construction of new Asian civilization, the historical status and role of overseas Chinese are crucial. Therefore, it is very important to study the role of overseas Chinese in the construction of new Asian civilization.

In history, the overseas Chinese are the pioneers and the participants of Asian civilization. At this moment, the overseas Chinese are also the important support for the creation of Asian civilization. Here, we should bring the role of the overseas Chinese into full play from several aspects as below: firstly, we should highly recognize the relationship among "the Belt and Road", new Asian civilization and the overseas Chinese, and value the overseas Chinese affairs. Secondly, we should continuously enhance the relations with the societies of overseas Chinese to safeguard their interests. Thirdly, based on the existing research institutes, we should further make research on overseas Chinese affairs, i. e. both funds and labors are increased to set up a new platform.

Review and Expectation of Cross-strait Cooperation in Hokkien Opera

Xie Yongjun
Research Fellow of the Chinese Opera Research Institute of Chinese National Academy of Arts

Hokkien Opera is a representative opera to connect cross-strait cultural veins, and its historical evolution has determined its special role in Minnan operas and Chinese operas. In addition, it plays an irreplaceable role in "the Belt and Road" initiative. The exchange of Hokkien Opera on both sides of Taiwan Strait began at the end of 1980s. Since then, a number of Hokkien Opera symposiums were held in Xiamen and Taiwan, and a solid theoretical foundation was laid down for cooperation. In 2010, Xiamen Hokkien Opera Troupe and Taiwan Tangmeiyun Opera Troupe cooperated to create Butterfly Love. This cooperation was termed an "Ice-Breaking Journey", and was a pioneering exploration for cross-strait opera cooperation. This year, the play Longjiu jointly created by Taiwan Ming Hua Yuan Opera Troupe and Xiamen Hokkien Opera Troupe has driven the cross-strait cooperate forward with a large stride. Recognition of cultural diversity in Taiwan and Fujian, and promotion of cross-strait cultural diversity, is a principle that should be advocated and followed for survival and development of operas on both sides of the strait under the general background of "the Belt and Road" initiative. For win-win cooperation and advantage complementation, troupes on both sides of the strait should absorb advantages of the other to complement its weak points. However, necessary caution should be given to avoid missing of individuality and characteristics of their own troupes, and to prevent assimilation of performing art on both strait sides. Only in this way can national emotions, relations and peaceful development be effectively facilitated.

Building of "the Belt and Road" and Xinjiang Music and Dance Art

Xu Yumei

Director and Research Fellow of the Research
Department of Xinjiang Art Research Institute

As the important hub of the ancient Silk Road, Xinjiang has been growing all along with wonderful people. Its historical culture features are exclaimed by the world. China's famous orientalist and great masters undisguisedly expressed his love for historic culture of Xinjiang. He wrote in his Research of Xinjiang and Comparative Literature "during the past several thousand years, each ethnic of the world has created many culture systems. For me, they can be concluded into four systems, namely, Chinese cultural system, Indian culture system, the Arab and Muslim culture system and western culture system. The four can be integrated into two greater culture systems, with the former three integrated into oriental culture system and the last western culture system. There is a place in the world where converges these culture systems, that is Xinjiang." Xinjiang will play an irreplaceable role in the initiative of "the Belt and Road" proposed by President Xi.

There were 3 Silk Roads in Xinjiang. The Silk Road connects China, Central Asia, west Asia, South Asia, North Africa and Europe. From B. C. to 15th century, it is the most important and the busiest vital transportation line of human civilization in 2000 years. It has been open all along, cultures and arts of each ethnic exchange, collide and deposit here. It interacts with arts in the East and the West. The trade contacts, religion transmission, ethnic migration, aesthetic emotion and other factors are influencing the culture change and the direction of arts. In this magic land, diverse traditional national culture is preserved, the common traits of Chinese culture with integrated diversity is formed. The music and dance art of Xinjiang is inherited and developed under the nourishment of these profound and diverse culture resources.

How to Achieve "People-to-people Bonds" by External Communication in the Region?

Yang Jiao/Wu Mei

Lecturer of the Communication Department of Dianchi College of Yunnan University/ Associate Professor and Vice-dean of Department of Communication of the University of Macau

Yunnan borders on Myanmar, Vietnam, and Laos, close to India, Bangladesh and other South Asia countries. Its advantages of geography, culture and language allows it to have more communication with other Southeast Asia and South Asia countries on personnel, material, technology and information between Ming and Qing dynasties. Now an image of regional communication center has begun to take shape in Yunnan, which has constitute a "all-directions and integrative" external communication pattern, but the pattern led the authority hasn't change substantially.

So this paper will try to find out if the pattern above be effective on "People-to-People Bonds", what kind of image has been shaped by official media in Yunnan to Southeast Asia, and how the Southeast Asia audiences interpret such symbols?

More specifically, this paper studied two typical promotional videos about tourism in Yunnan and interpretations of Southeast Asian students in Yunnan by virtue of Fantasy Theme Analysis (FTA), in order to explore what 'Yunnan' is in promotional videos and how the Southeast Asian students decode the symbols about Yunnan in these videos.

Finally, the result shows that the commercial made by Yunnan Tourism was trying to create a semantic vision of "heaven on earth" which is consisted of four fantasy types - colorful Yunnan, historical inheritance, ethnic harmony, and culture diversity. But there is an obvious gap between information received by audiences and intention expressed by the promotional videos, which due to three main reasons: 1) Similar fantasy themes base on different master analogues. 2) The promotional videos beautify excessively the people's life in Yunnan, which creates a strong psychological gap of Southeast Asian students in Yunnan. 3) The complexities of Southeast Asian students, as well as individual differences.

Cultural Spirit in an Era of Ecological Civilization

Yu Wenxiu
Professor and Director of the College of Literature of Heilongjiang University

The eco-crisis between man and nature has led to ideological circle's concerns and thoughts on modern social patterns and ecological issues in recent years, which made ecology one of the most crucial words in today's world. The entire intellectual and ideological circle have also been involved in the dispute over anthropocentrism and anti-anthropocentrism as a result of dispute over 'shallow ecology' and 'deep ecology', which remains unresolved today. In my opinion, the underlying issues of those disputes lie in thinking on the cultural spirit in a time of ecological civilization. In this day and age, we should focus on the cultural spirit to advocate as a whole instead of end up with discussion on simple binary opposite conclusions to certain issues when reviewing and criticizing the ecological crisis. I believe the cultural spirit in a time of ecological civilization can be summarized as reflecting on extreme anthropocentrism and advocating organic view of holism from philosophical perspective, advocating new view of matter in the era of post-materialism from the perspective of social existence, persisting in the integration of modernity and post-modernity in terms of value orientation, and pursuing poetic dwelling and harmony from the perspective of existence status.

Advocacy of Organic View of Nature

In a time of ecological civilization, the cultural spirit we advocate shall firstly animadvert on extreme anthropocentrism and encourage organic view of holism. As for reflection on the problem of eco-environment crisis, there has always been this theoretical dispute over anthropocentrism and anti-anthropocentrism, which seems like an inevitable issue at a certain point. Shallow ecologists blame deep ecologists on their stance of anti-anthropocentrism and the tendency of expansion of moral subjects, while deep ecologists criticize that shallow ecologists' utilitarian and short-sighted view of mankind's interests will never truly solve the problem of eco-crisis.

From the perspective of evaluation, some of deep ecology's theoretical views and propositions are obviously more profound and meaningful. Although its theories on the principle of the equality of all creatures and intrinsic worth of all creatures are subject to confirmation, its holism thought is truly remarkable.

As a matter of fact, no genre of ecology denies that it's extreme anthropocentrism that caused eco-crisis rather than anthropocentrism. This kind of extreme anthropocentrism, which has simple-minded utilitarian value orientation, is a one-sided anthropocentrism only treats the nature as a tool. Extreme anthropocentrism has maintained a strong momentum since the establishment of industrial society, and even become a deep-seated idea for development mode of modern society. Therefore in this era of eco-environmental improvement, the stance and values of extreme anthropocentrism must be animadverted from philosophical perspective, and organic view of holism must be advocated in the first place.

The organic view of holism believes all kind of things in the world, which are interconnected and interdependent, constitute an organic whole. The entire world is a whole of life, the existence of man is closely related to existence status of other species in the nature, and the existence status of other species can affect the quality of mankind's existence. Hence the nature of whole is primary, and the nature of parts is secondary. Differences between whole and parts are relative, while their connections are fundamental.

The organic view of holism reflects Marxist philosophy's fundamental spirit on ecology and nature. From Marxist philosophy's angle, man and nature has a unified and consistent relationship, man and nature have always been an organic whole. Man is a part of the nature, while the nature is the inorganic matter of man as well as the premise for the existence and development of man. In a word, 'man lives on nature'.

Advocacy of New View of Matter in the Era of Post-materialism

When reflecting and rethinking on eco-crisis, scholars have reached a consensus that the eco-crisis is indeed a main superficial characteristic of modernity crisis, and the one-sided materialism (also known as economism) oriented view is one the causes of modernity crisis and eco-crisis. Therefore, one-sided materialism philosophy must be criticized in a time of ecological civilization, and new view of matter must be advocated from the perspective of social existence to realize shift in values.

Materialism treats material prosperity and accumulation of wealth as the essence of social activities as well as an honor in the eyes of conventional society, and the rapid economic development and the dramatic growth of materials have become a remarkable sign of modern civilization.

Economism's fundamental hypothesis or belief is that man is economic animal. From this perspective, the desire to consistently improve the material living conditions of mankind is deemed as the inherent nature of human beings. By this logic, it can be naturally concluded that all human behaviors are economic actions after all, and there is an inherent unity in the happiness of individuals, social progress and economic growth. It believes infinite material goods can solve all problems of human beings, and this kind of value orientation has penetrated into the belief of the society and the mind of individuals, which made it both a belief of the society and the cause of individuals. In modern society, economic motivation looks like the force decides everything. Therefore, as the theory of meaning of life in modern society, economism is the most distinctive one-sided view of life.

Ecological postmodernists have given in-depth critique of the economism characteristics of modern society, and pointed out that: the creeds of economism or materialism have become an underlying ideology of modern civilization, and even a 'modern religion'. 'This religious attitude and alienation from the nature have increased people's desire to control the nature and its resources at all costs.' [1]Economism serves the greed of human beings instead of chances for compliance with laws of nature. It'll lead to unsustainable consequences in terms of production and lifestyle.

To improve mankind's ecological environment and advocate new cultural spirit, one of the most important works is to advocate new view of matter in the era of post-materialism, in other words, shift from focus on infinite growth of material wealth to attention to eco-environment, quality of life, self-actualization, civil liberty and etc. Eco-environment and quality of life are particularly the most basic demands of new view of matter in the era of post-materialism, which is against waste of resources, waste of materials and

---

[1] D. R. Griffin, *Spirituality and Society: Postmodern Visions* translated by Wang Chengbing, Central Compilation & Translation Press, 1998.

infinite economic growth, and promote more economical, natural, harmonious and humanistic production and life style to better suit new development mode in a time of ecological civilization. Sound social welfare and security system is surely the key to facilitate the values of post-materialism.

New view of matter in the era of post-materialism has become popular in western countries since 1980s, and the ecological issues arising from development mode of modern society are the main reasons for it to be gradually accepted and recognized. Environmental protection and the maintenance of excellent ecology will be an important task once shortage in material goods and problem to survive are no longer primary concerns. At the moment, attention shall be paid the relations between economic development, life improvement and ecological protection to realize the harmonious and sustainable between man, nature and society.

Integration of Modernity and Post-modernity

Modernity and post-modernity belong to two theoretical categories which are repulsive to each other. Post-modernity holds a strong critical and denial attitude towards modernity. Although they look like incompatible as fire and water, actually they are more than simply opposite to each other, they have 'similarity of a family', and post-modernity is the 'son' of modernity (Lyotard). Therefore, it's not wise and rational for some scholars and genres to hold completely repulsive and denial attitude towards modernity from the stance of post-modernity. Fundamentally, modernity and post-modernity have their own strengths and weaknesses, and integration of their strengths shall be made the value orientation and cultural spirit in a time of ecological civilization. To this end, theoretical claims of ecological Marxism are positive and quite inspiring.

Ecological Marxism is against postmodernism, and it's unhappy with postmodernism's 'idea of going beyond modernity'. It's also against different negative impacts of modernization without denying modernization itself, and it's highly motivated to fix the drawbacks of modernity and pursue the possibilities of modernity in the field of culture, economy and society. The well-known ecological Marxist Gorz believes that 'what we are experiencing today is not a crisis of modernity, we are facing the need to modernize the precondition of modernization. Today's crisis is not a crisis of rationality, it's a crisis of rationalized (increasingly obvious) irrational motive... Today's crisis doesn't mean modernization drive has come to an end, it means we have to go back... We have to modernize modernity itself, and reflexively include modernization itself into its own area of actions, i. e. rationalize the rationalization itself.' [1]What ecological Marxism does is to reflect on distortion and variation of modernity itself, and thus correct and fix it on the premises of not denying modernity.

Ecological Marxism advocates anthropocentrism and opposes ecocentrism, as Pepper, an important representative of ecological Marxism indicated, 'ecological Marxism is anthropocentrism and humanism... It is against the theory of ethics of creatures and natural mysticism as well as different anti-humanism mechanisms may derived from them.' [2] However, ecological Marxism does not completely separate man from all living things in the nature, instead it emphasizes their interdependence. Ecological Marxism attaches importance to the importance of human spirit, but it also emphasizes 'the satisfaction of such human spirit relies on other non-material contacts with other things in the nature. Although other animals are incomparable with human beings, but man is also a natural existence.' It needs to be pointed out that ecological Marxism opposes the capitalism form of anthropocentrism, and holds positive attitude towards fixation of traumas and drawbacks of modernity, such as advocacy of steady state economy as well as active exploration on countermeasures to minimize and curb eco-crisis.

Marx also indicated that man and nature should 'reasonably adjust the exchange of matter between man and nature... and conduct such exchange of matter under conditions live up to and best suit their human natures'. (Capital, Vol. 3, Collected Works of Karl Marx and Friedrich Engels, Vol. 25, pp. 926 - 927)

Pursuit of Harmony and Poetic Dwelling

As for people live on earth, the way for them to treat the earth they live on and the nature is an issue of existence status. After all, existence status and ecology have direct decisive relations, because 'from both micro-perspective and macro-perspective, the

---

[1] Gorz, Critique of Economic Reason, London, 1989, pp. 1. Chen Xueming, Remarks on Opposition between Ecological Marxism and Postmodernism, Tianjin Social Sciences, 2002, Vol. 5.

[2] Chen Xueming, Remarks on Opposition between Ecological Marxism and Postmodernism, Tianjin Social Sciences, 2002, Vol. 5.

beauty, integrity and stability of ecosystem are important factors to judge the correctness of human behaviors.' In a time of ecological civilization, poetic dwelling and harmony undoubtedly should be the status and pursuits that mankind should have.

The pursuit of poetic dwelling and harmony has been the cause of great philosophers at home and abroad. China's Confucianism's pursuit of 'unification between human beings and nature' and 'society of great harmony' has reflected Chinese culture's pursuit of truth and longing for harmony. In Marx's opinion, poetic dwelling and harmony is a high status between man, nature and society.

In his work of Economic and Philosophic Manuscripts of 1884, he said that nature is both an object of natural science and 'an object of art'. Man shall not only take nature as material resources, but also maintain a spiritual communication as well as a poetic and aesthetic relationship with nature. Marx also believes the genuine harmony in society lies in 'the genuine resolution of conflicts between man and nature and between man and man.' Communism is undoubtedly the highest status of an ideal and harmonious society characterized by elimination of alienation and restoration of humanity. The theory of 'communism, as fully developed naturalism, equals humanism' has actually realized the harmony between man, nature and society.

As the internationally renowned environmental ethicist Holmes Rolston said, 'human culture can facilitate mankind's poetic dwelling on the earth, this culture is the culture of the intelligent species of homo sapiens. There are many ways of living with their own advantages. As a spiritual product, poetic dwelling shall be reflected in each specific environment, and it will bring mankind to the land of hope.'

Mankind's protection of ecology shall be a proper higher status for life existence rather than just a 'smart selfishness' of man, only by doing so a win-win situation can be achieved fundamentally between man and ecology.

Poetic dwelling and pursuit of harmony are not only the key to improve eco-environment and the relations between man and nature, but also the key to change the relations between man and society and between man and man. Just as Marx and Engels pointed out in The German Ideology, 'the shallow relationship between man and nature restrains their shallow relations, while their shallow relations also restrain the shallow relationship between man and nature.' Engels also mentioned two great reconciliations of the reconciliation of mankind with nature and with itself, which are two major objectives of mankind's changes.

Contemporary Chinese society has proposed to build a harmonious society and develop the mode of ecological civilization as a social development strategy. The connotations of cultural spirit in a time of ecological civilization in four aspects have shown a new view of world and meaning. Firstly, it has provided the right philosophic foundation for the development of civilization, which avoided the biases of mechanism and dualism, and never went on the wrong path of anti-anthropocentrism like absolute ecologism. Secondly, the new view of matter in postmodern society it advocates allows us to do a better job in environmental protection during economic development to improve quality of life, maintain ecological equilibrium, and minimize the cost. Thirdly, the dispute over modernity and post-modernity has made us quite confused and even lost in value orientation. The values of integration of modernity and post-modernity that cultural spirit in a time of ecological civilization advocates allow us to have objective understanding and evaluation of both modernity and post-modernity. It made us no longer simply associate environmental destruction with modernization drive, and allowed us to properly take advantage of rationality and technologies instead of simple repulsion and hostility. Fourthly, as a pursuit of poetic dwelling and harmony, it allows eco-environment to be protected in reality, and it also reflects the metaphysical status and transcendence of man's existence. In other words, man is both a biological existence and a spiritual existence. It indicates the spiritual dimension as well as the uniqueness and creativity of man's existence, which fully reflect man's value and meaning.

Southern Fujian Culture Functions as the Bond and Bridge in "the Belt and Road"

Yuan Yonglin / Tu Yihong
Professor and Director of Concord College/ Professor of Overseas Education College, Fujian Normal University

Since the ancient times, Southern Fujian has been closely associated with Southeast Asia, particularly Indonesia, Malaysia, the Philippines, Thailand and Singapore, so that strong human network is available as the bond and bridge for "the Belt and Road", especially "the 21st Century Maritime Silk Road".

For the initiative of "the Belt and Road", the relationship between ASEAN and China is crucial. Also, Southern Fujian culture is rooted in the Chinese culture and sourced from geo-culture, so we should fully unearth geo-culture resources and bring the communication advantage of Southern Fujian culture into full play. When being widely accepted in the Southeast Asia regions, more positive influence could be produced to promote the relationship between ASEAN and China. Here, the Maritime Silk Road could be extended to the Southeast Asia regions and become the strategy support for economic growth. In particular, when questions "the Belt and Road" are raised, we should further give the reins to the soft power of cultures and create the benefit community and development community with the countries along the "the Belt and Road", to realize peace, cooperation, harmony and win-win solutions. From this point, we are well enlightened by the transmission and fusion of Southern Fujian culture with that in Southeast Asia.

When giving the government's leading role into full play, we should also sufficiently arouse the enthusiasm of common people, so that exchanges could be made at both governmental and non-government levels. We should stand fast to "inviting in and going out policies", rely on the overseas Chinese and deepen governmental cooperation. Through the joint efforts at home and abroad, the advantages of geo-cultures could be transferred into those of geo-economics. Along with the development of "the Belt and Road", the cultural fusion between Southeast Asia and Fujian, or even China could be substantially boosted. Therefore, we should seize this opportunity to friendly communicate with the countries along "the Belt and Road" and realize the jointly development of the Chinese culture and other excellent cultures.

Dunhuang and Silk Road Civilization

Zheng Binlin

Director of School of History and Culture, Lanzhou University

The Silk Road was a channel for the collision, integration and acceptance of eastern and western civilizations. There emerged many civilizations, large or small, along the Silk Road. The Silk Road civilization was an aggregation of these civilizations. Dunhuang, a bright pearl in the Silk Road, embodied the highest level of civilization of the Silk Road. Dunhuang developed into a key town exactly because of the opening of the Silk Road. The development achievements of the Silk Road were fully reflected in Dunhuang. As a result, when we speak of Dunhuang, we must relate to the opening of the Silk Road. Proving the existence of the Silk Road could not do without catching the earliest appearance of the name of Dunhuang in Chinese history. Experts and scholars of Dunhuang attributed the opening of the Silk Road to Zhang Qian. But materials indicating the existence of the Silk Road were usually earlier than the days of Zhang Qian. Long before the story that Zhang Qian opened up the Silk Road, Chinese people had known Dunhuang as a geographical concept. People of later days did not pay enough attention to it, or connect Dunhuang with the Silk Road in academic research. In the pre-Qin period, people were aware of Dunhuang and Lop Nor as geographical concepts. They called Lop Nor as the source of the Yellow River. The Silk Road civilization derived from the Silk Road. The existence of the Silk Road may be testified in three aspects. Its origin was earlier than Zhang Qian sent on a diplomatic mission to the Western Regions. First, archaeological discovery proved that Hotan jades were unearthed in the Yin Dynasty ruins. The jade articles were identified through archaeology as mutton-fat jade, produced in Hotan. Colored glaze produced in the Western Regions appeared in large quantity in the tombs of the pre-Qin period. In particular, archaeological discovery of the Majiayuan Tomb in Zhangjiachuan, Gansu, proved the influence of foreign culture in 350 B. C. Besides, many jade articles were unearthed in the Guo State tombs of the Warring States Period, which were jades produced in Hotan. Second, historical documents showed that the Central Plain area had connections with the Western Regions long ago. It was recorded in the Biography of Emperor Mu. Emperor Mu went west to see Queen Mother of the West. The region Queen Mother of the West lived, as research showed, was believed to be along the Hexi Corridor or Tarim Basin. It explained the traffic between China and the west was unimpeded. It was also recorded in the Classic of Mountains and Seas, which noted Du Yanze and Shule River that flew into Lop Nor. It showed that people of the Central Plain areas were quite familiar with the history and geography of the Western Regions. Third, the residents of the Hexi area in the pre-Qin period were international business people, known as the Northern barbarian tribes in ancient China. They were also remembered as Darouzhi, Wusun and Sute people, among others, leaving footprints in every corner of the Silk Road. They lived in the Hexi Corridor area, near the states Zhou and Qin in the Wei River basin, with capability for trading. Those in Dunhuang and Jiuquan were known as the Darouzhi people. Since the commodities delivered in the road were largely silk, it was referred to as the Silk Road. There hence evolved the maritime Silk Road, which mainly exported porcelains, without any silk. It thus won a trick word as a road without a rag. As for the land-based Silk Road, the commodities transported in the earliest days were jade rather than silk. They were imported by royal courts of the Central Plain areas from the Western Regions. It was testified in the tombs of the Yin Dynasty ruins and State Guo tombs of the Warring States period. The jade articles unearthed in the tombs came from Hotan, typical mutton-fat jade over there. It explained that the goods trafficked earliest in the Silk Road were not silk, but jade. It was also known as the Road of Silver, because the currency applied in Silk Road trade was mainly silver. It might also be referred to as the Road of Silk, Road of Jade, Road of Silk and Horse, Road of Tea and Road of Ceramics. We may give it many names, considering the functions of the Silk Road. The Silk Road may also be termed as the Road of Art. Music and dance of the Western Regions were introduced to Chinese inland via this road. The nine-part music of the Sui Dynasty and the ten-part music of the Tang Dynasty that stemmed from western regions of Xiliang, Gaochang, Qiuci, Shule, Kangguo, Anguo and Tianzhu entered the Central Plain areas through the route, mingling and converted into Chinese. The Buddhist art, establishing its own features, was passed back to Hexi, Dunhuang and Western Regions. The regions had multiple grottoes, with Buddhist art showing distinctive features. The most famous sites included Maiji Mountain, North Grottoes, South Grottoes, Daxiang Mountain, Water Curtain Cave, Bingling Temple, Tianti Mountain, Mati Temple, Jinta Temple, Wenshu Mountain, Yulin Grottoes, Mogao Grottoes and Western Thousand Buddha Caves. The Zoroastrianism art was revealed and reserved through stone inscriptions of the tombs of the Sute people. They were distributed along the Silk Road and business cities in the Central Plain areas. In particular, the Xiliang music was a dance music created by integrating the Qiuci music and Central Plains music introduced to the Hexi areas. As a result, it was no exaggeration to call the Silk Road as the Road of Art. It could even better display its characteristics. Dunhuang was an area to greet Buddhism earliest. The bamboo slips of the Han Dynasty found in Dunhuang kept a record of Buddhist temples. Dunhuang documents furnished the most detailed and genuine records of Chinese Buddhism. All performances of the temples would reconstruct the looks of Chinese Buddhist temples. Among the Dunhuang documents were the earliest sutras of Nestorianism and Manichaeism in Chinese language. Though no Zoroastrianism sutras appeared in the Dunhuang documents, the sacrificial ceremonies sponsored by feudal officials for Zoroastrianism were enough to show the influence of the religion. In Dunhuang, Buddhism, Taoism, Zoroastrianism, Nestorianism, Manichaeism and Confucianism maintained harmonious coexistence than mutual repulsion and fight. This situation was attributed to the formation of the multi-ethnic co-existence in Dunhuang.

Concept of Maritime Silk Road Culture and the Connotation

—as Well as the Relation between Maritime Silk Road Culture and Minnan Culture

Zheng Changling / Wang Juchuan

Deputy Director and Research Fellow/ Associate Research Fellow of
The Cultural Development Strategy Research Center of
Chinese National Academy of Arts

Nowadays, Chinese government initiates to develop "The Belt and Road" economic belt, which is actively responded by countries and regions along the Silk Road. Thus, the maritime Silk Road has become the world-famous road for trade economy and culture exchange once again. From history, the maritime Silk Road is not only a route for trade economy between ancient China and other countries, but also a road for cultural exchange between China and countries along the road. And the unique maritime Silk Road culture is thus formed. The so-called maritime Silk Road culture is a kind of global multi-culture with Chinese culture as the basis, and the regional culture as the core. It is an important cultural power in Chinese culture. After several thousand years' accumulation, the maritime silk road is not only the historical heritage of the trade between the East and the West, but the maritime silk road culture formed through centering on maritime silk road has become the cultural symbol linking each country along the silk road. Therefore, the maritime Silk Road culture is also the common cultural heritage and culture life of human. Thereby, objectively review and define the maritime Silk Road culture have become the important and impending proposition to be studied by researchers.

Proceedings of the 3rd Asian Cultural Forum

Speeches of the Sub-forums from Foreign Countries

Newly Identified Iranian Motif of Brocade in Shosoin Storehouse in Japan

Etsuko Kageyama

Associate Fellow, National Research Institute
for Culture Properties, Nara, Japan

It is well known that the treasures of Horyu-ji Temple and Todai-jiTemplein Japan represent various elements of Iranian culture and art of the Sasanian Persia which were brought to China and populated in Changan in the early Tang period. Recent studies has demonstrated that the Sasanian culture and art was introducedinto the East during the Hephthalite period from the middle of the fifth century to the middle of the sixth century, and that the Sogdians, Silk Road merchants, which immigrated in great number from Central Asia into China contributed the flourishing of the Iranian culture in Changan[①].

It is the time to reconsider the art historical study onHoryu-ji and Todai-ji treasures in the 1970s and 1980s using the new materials and information acquired by archaeological, historical and philological studies. Such examination enables classification of the Iranian influence into the following three sub-groups: direct influence from the Sasanian Iran, influence of Iranian culture flourished in Central Asia during the Hephthalite period, influence of the Sogdian immigrants in China. For example, the famous brocade of Horyu-ji with a design of four riders shooting lions circled in a pearl roundel is usually considered to be produced in China under the direct influence of the Sasanian art, although a few scholars pointed out somedetails which were different from those of the Sasanian art. Since 1999 several tombs of the Sogdian immigrants have been discovered in China, and they have given us a lot of information about the art favored in the Sogdian

---

[①] J. Il'yasov, "The Hephthalite Terracotta", *Silk Road Art and Archaeology* 7, 2001, pp. 187-200; E-. Kageyama, "The winged crown and the triple-crescent crown in the Sogdian funerary monuments from China: their relation to the Hephthalite occupation of Central Asia", *Journal of Inner Asian Art and Archaeology* 2, 2007, pp. 11-22.

colonies in the second half of the sixth century①. A crowns, clothes of a Sogdian rider and winged horses represented on the reliefs of the Sogdian stone sarcophagi are much similar to those found on the brocade of Horyu-ji Temple. Therefore it is supposed thatthe brocade was produced after designs known among the Sogdian immigrants in China rather than after Sasanian designs.

In this paper I would like to focus on a motif of brocade stored in Shosoin, the main storehouse of Todai-ji Temple. The design of the brocade is a front view of a bird circled in a pearl roundel②. Some fragments with the motif were used for the end of banners. The pearl roundel is the famous design of Sasanian brocade and it became popularin other regions including China. Symmetrical pattern and high level of weaving techniqueof this brocade indicate that it was produced in China.

Observing carefully the bird represented in the pearl roundel, we can see something like a face and six roundels on its belly. To understand this image, brocade fragments from Dulan in Qingjhai and from Turfan in Xinjiang are of great use③. Both fragments represent a design of a frontal view of a bird. The fragment from Dulan attributed to the Byzantine Empire shows a simplified depiction of a figure on the belly of the bird. The unclear image of Shosoin fragment must be a depiction of a personal figure which is too simplified to be understood.

The motif of a giant bird flying up with a naked woman in its clawsis found on a silver plate stored in the Hermitage Museum, which is supposed to be made in the Sasanian Persia in the late sixth or early seventh century④. The same motif is found in the painting from Zar-tepa near Termez in southern Uzbekistan, dated to the third or fourth century. While the meaningof this motif is not fullyidentified, it is clear that this motif was so important and popular in the Sasanian Persia that it was used as a design of the Sasanian silver vessels and brocades. The brocades with this motif were brought to China

---

① Lerner, J. A. 2005, *Aspects of Assimilation: The funerary practices and furnishings of Central Asians in China*, Sino-Platonic Papers 168.
② *Treasury of Shosoin Storehouse*, 10, 1997, Mainichi Shimbun, no. 161.
③ J. C. Y. Watt et al. (eds.), *China: Dawn of a golden age, 200-750 AD*, Metropolitan Museum of Art, New York, 2004, no. 246; Sagawa Museum (ed), *Buddhist art masterpieces of Lushun Museum: treasures of the Silk Road in Chinese Central Asia*, 2002.
④ G. Azarpay, "A Jataka tale on a Sasanian silver plate", *Bulletin of the Asia Institute* 9, 1995 [1997], pp. 99-125; M. Compareti, "A short note on a so-called IskandarDhu'l-Qarnayn in a Bactrian painting", *Parthica*12, 2010, pp. 95-106.

and the imitations were produced there for a certain period which were enough long to cause the simplification of the figure. This brocade of Shosoin can be classified into the sub-group representing a direct influence from the Sasanian art.

It goes without saying that the Silk Road played an important role to connect the East and the West. But if we compare it with a long bridge over the Central Asia, it is not correct. Certainly a part of Iranian influence was so important that it was directly transmitted to China, but probably most parts of it transmitted to China only because they were accepted and flourished in Central Asia. For the transmission of the Iranian culture to China and Japan in the seventh and eighth centuries, the role of the peoples in Central Asia or Silk Road regions cannot be overemphasized.

The Win-win Solution for Asian Cultural Cooperation

Ryoo Jae Ky

Chairman of Korea-China Culture & Art Forum, ROK

I'd sincerely congratulate the success of the 3rd Asia Cultural Forum held in Quanzhou of Fujian Province, where is the starting point of the 21st-Century Maritime Silk Road. I think the venue for this forum is of great symbolic significance.

1. Asia is the treasury of cultural resources

Asia boasts much more cultural resources than any other continents in the world, so I am convinced that Asia will be the most vibrant continent in the times of the 21st century Asian culture. Although Asian cultural resources can't be introduced at large, Asian culture catches the eye of all walks of life. Just like Socrates, who was born in Athens and renowned in Greece and Europe and has been well-known around the whole world eventually, Confucius was also born in the Kingdom of Lu, renowned in China and East Asia and has become the notable in the world nowadays.

An elder scholar once said that "Han culture in East Asia, Confucianism and Buddhism coexist with Christian religion and Islamic civilization in the past several thousands of years, so the East Asian civilization is the joint assets of the nations that take a share in the creation of civilization". I very much agree with this idea, so I think that this cultural treasury can fully catch the eye of the people and be appreciated based on these prolific cultures.

At present, gorgeous cultural resources are blending with the economy as a kind of cultural industry, which is bringing full play of its value. In the meantime, more and more people are indulged in the wellbeing from the cultural industry. In a bid to keep developing Asian culture, the countries in Asia shall gather all the powers together.

2. The Asian culture shall be rediscovered

Great endeavors have been exerted by the countries in Asia, for the purpose of conserving and inheriting the unique cultures respectively and creating new cultures. As mentioned in the conception of the Belt and Road, to strengthen cultural exchanges makes us ponder whether we've spared no efforts in the cultural development.

On the one hand, the people can benefit from economic development; on the other hand, more and more people are traveling abroad to experience various cultures in other places. The outbound Korean tourists reached 16.08 million last year, while the tourists to Korea amounted to over 14.2 million person-time. Moreover, the outbound Chinese tourists amounted to 116.59 million last year, while the foreign tourists to China reached 26.29 million. These outbound tourists will rethink the significance and value of their own culture with the experience of unique local cultures.

In the past several thousands of years, gorgeous Asian culture is reviving and enriching the Asian's lifestyle, while more opportunities are created during the culture sharing with the people who pay attention to Asian culture. We should seize this good opportunity and reevaluate the real value of Asian culture, laying emphasis of its value in the mind of common people and contributing to the life of the masses around the world.

3. The Belt and Road and the globalization of Asian culture

Exchanges and cooperation among the countries are the core essence of the 21st Century New Silk Road, so I am convinced that more vitality will be brought to the development of Asian culture. It can be seen that the context of the Belt and Road, the principle of joint construction with the surrounding countries, the thinking of development framework as well as the key cooperative fields and organizations are based on the co-development.

Particularly, the essence of the friendly cooperation of the 21st Century New Silk Road is of far reaching significance for more cultural exchanges, more academic contact, more talent exchanges and cooperation, more media cooperation, more contacts with women and more volunteer services. I have the faith that the countries in Asia will jointly organize a variety of art activities, for example, the year of cultural exchange, the art festival, the film festival and the paint exhibition. What's more, cooperation in multiple fields will be made, for example, the joint production of television programs and the application of the world cultural heritage.

With more cooperation in the tourism industry, a variety of special activities will be launched to scale up the tourism industry. Furthermore, the international tourism commodities with the characteristics of the Silk Road can be developed, which will not only promote the development of tourism industry, but also strengthen the exchanges on sports and revitalize the major international sports activities. I hope that such cultural, art and sports activities will have the essence of Asian culture properly engraved in the mind of the people around the world.

4. Conclusion

I expect that Korea and China will jointly promote the conception of "theBelt and Road" in the fundamental interests of the international community and make contributions to the discovery of new values in Asian cultural treasury, the communication of Asian culture in the 21st century and the wellbeing of people around the world. In addition, the countries along the Belt and Road should correctly understand other cultures and make real friends in an inclusive manner. That is the true meaning of cultural exchange in my mind.

The Building of "the Belt and Road" and Cultural Dialogues in Asia

U Tun Ohn

Pro-rector (Admin) of National University of
Arts and Culture, Yangon, Myanmar

Introduction

1. Asia is the Earth's largest and most populous continent, located primarily in the Eastern and Northern hemispheres. Though it covers only 8.7% of the Earth's total surface area, it comprises 30% of Earth's land area, and has historically been home to the bulk of the planet's human population (currently roughly 60%).

2. The boundaries of Asia are culturally determined, as there is no clear geographical separation between it and Europe, which together form one continuous landmass called Eurasia. Asia varies greatly across and within its regions with regard to ethnic groups, culture, environments, economics, historical ties and government systems. Asia is more largerand more culturally diverse than Europe. The history of Asia can be seen as the distinct histories of several peripheral coastal regions: East Asia, South Asia, Southeast Asia and the Middle East, linked by the interior mass of the Central Asian steppes. The coastal periphery was home to some of the world's earliest known civilization.

3. 835 World Heritage sites have in the world and 192 sites have been established in Asia and there are preserved by Asia Nations:

4. Thus it can say exactly that Culture hold important part in Asia.

5. Culture is the characteristic and knowledge of a particular group of people, defined by everything from language, custom, behavior and religion, cruising, social habits and arts. That behaves and acts from their cradle to death. It can define as Tangible Culture and Intangible Culture. Human beings have always moved from place to place and traded with their neighbors, exchanging goods, skills and ideas. Throughout history,

Eurasia was crisis - crossed with communication routes and paths of trade, which gradually linked up to form what are known today as the Silk Roads;

6. Maritime routes were an important part of this network, linking East and West by sea. These vast networks carried more than just merchandise and precious commodities however: the constant movement and mixing of populations also brought about the transmission of knowledge, ideas, cultures and beliefs, which had a profound impact on the history and civilizations of Eurasian peoples.

7. Travelers along the Silk Roads were attracted not only by trade but also by the intellectual for cultural exchange. It is the main key and brings to tourism business. That was taking place in cities along the Silk Roads, many of which developed into hubs of culture and learning. Science, art and literature, as well as crafts and technologies thus shared and disseminated into societies along the length of these routes, and in this way, languages, religious and cultures developed and influenced each other. Therefore the greatest value of the Silk Road was the exchange of culture. The ancient Maritime Silk Road was developed under political and economic backgrounds and was the result of cooperative efforts from ancestors of both East and West. If rich resources and developed nation, China would establish and more improve in every sectors the countries situated along the Silks Road. China forecasted and made proposal in 2013 that it would be more improved in culture alone the road.

8. China's proposal to build 21st century Maritime Silk Road to get at the unique value and concepts of the ancient road, enriching it with new meaning for the present era and actively developing economic partnerships with countries situated along the route. It seeks to further integrate current cooperation in order to achieve positive effects and develop the Asia in Supply Chain, Industry Chain and Value Chain. Moreover, People situated along the route will improve in cultural exchange, ideas and cooperation. It purposed leading the good results.

9. Nowadays as the world's economic and political center shifts towards the Asia Pacific, the region has stepped into a stage of geopolitics characterized by interesting, overlapping and conflicting interests. By facilitating communication between countries along the road, the Maritime will help build a community that represents the common concerns, interests and expectations of all countries. The community is expected to guide and support a peaceful and stable Asia Pacific landscape.

10. The Asia Infrastructure Investment Bank (AIIB) and the fund of Silk Road are

the two platform of B&R and China will provide $ 50 Billion. Most countries welcomed this proposal. China has launched a $ 40 Billion for B&R fund and others Building, Investors, Trade, financial investment and culture.

11. Now, 60 countries consented upon the project of B&R and Asean and South Asian Association for Regional Cooperation, Shanghai Cooperation Organization, League of Arab States, United Nations Economic and Social Commission for Asia and the Pacific, U. N Economic and Social Commission for Asia and the Pacific (UNESCAP), Gulf Cooperation Council, International Road Transport Union (IRU) were supported and declared the MOU on the project of B&R.

12. Moreover, the Maritime Silk Road will further bring together the "Silk Road Economic Belt", the "Bangladesh - China - India - Myanmar Economic Corridor" and the "China - Pakistan Economic Corridor" that together connect Europe and Asia. Such connection will greatly enhance China and other countries' to develop economically while limiting external risks. The Maritime Silk Road will also cooperate in non-traditional security areas while maintaining Maritime security.

13. China celebrated the culture exchange programmes, such as Arts festivals, literary Festival and movie festivals. Shanghai International Arts Festival, Meet in Beijing Arts Festival, International Chorus Festival, Nanning International Folk Song Arts Festival, International Country Music Festival, International Dance Festival, International Circus Festival, International Acrobatic Arts Festival, Asia Arts Festival, New Vision Arts Festival, International Festival of the Intangible Cultural Heritage are celebrated in China. Cooperating with South Asia and Central Asia opened the culture centers at Sriyalinka, Loas, Parkstan and Nipal.

14. In these cooperation, culture plays an important role. Because cultural relations is a type of soft power that includes the "exchange of ideas, information, art and other aspects of culture among nations and their people in order to foster mutual understanding. Friendship ties more relationship among Asian Countries and lead to cooperation in Olympic Games, World Cups, Trade Fairs and Summit. During celebrating times it performed with cultural arts. Moreover, treads with their traditional foods and showed their national dress and also played with traditional games. There lead to more understanding among Asia Nations.

15. Some Asia Nations have similar food and traditional festival, example: Myanmar's Water Festival (New Year Festival) is widely known in the World it also

held in Thailand, Loas and Cambodia. Myanmar says the "Remember friends while eating good foods" means to share the good things to friends. Similar Culture and food should become more friendly and understanding among the Asian Nations. Moreover, Famous Ramayana Drama in Asia expresses the similaring ethics and philosophy among Asia People. World heritage Sites and Cultural Arts will attract the Tourist. Moreover, the Landmarks of the designated countries, Hotels, Schools, Religious buildings, Museums and Home are decorated with artistic works such as painting, sculpture, art works and also Music. It can feel in grand hotels big buildings, such as Telephone and every place even the toy can feel.

16. The purpose of cultural relations is to develop an understanding of the nation's ideals and institutions in an effort to build broad support for economic and political goals. In essence "cultural relations reveal the soul of a nation".

The Interpretation of "the Belt and Road" Cooperation from the Cultural Perspective of Asia

17. In the 21st Century, countries have become more inter-connected by the ocean in conducting market, technological and information exchanges. The world now is an era that values maritime cooperation and development. China's proposal to build a Maritime Silk Road conforms to larger developments in economic globalization and taps into common interests that China shares with countries along the route. The goal is to forge a community of interest with political mutual trust, integrated economies, inclusive culture and inter - connectivity. It is thus great important to view it from the perspective of multipolarization, economic globalization and the co-existence and balancing of cooperation and competition.

18. Connecting multiple regions and uniting wide areas of cooperation, the tasks put forth in the 21st Century Maritime Silk Road will not be achieved in the immediate future instead, these task call for China and relevant countries to work in a step-by-step and practical manner. Building the Maritime Silk Road will require diverse forms of cooperation. With a focus on economic cooperation, the Road will give consideration to all parties involved.

19. China aims to invest 17% needed the nations along situated the Road and will provide US 1500 Billion in the project of B&R.

20. It will be based on the existing cooperation mechanisms and platforms and be promoted by China and other countries along the route. The 21st Century Maritime Silk Road will cover more than 20 countries and regions that share a broad consensus on enhancing exchange, friendship, promoting development, safety and stability within the region and beyond. Therefore, the 21st Century Maritime Silk Road will accommodate various countries' demands and apply suitable policies to each country. Meanwhile the Road must change and consolidate new patterns of cooperation. By virtue of connecting the "China-Pakistan Economic Corridor", the "Bangladesh - China - India - Myanmar Economic Corridor" and the "Silk Road Economic Belt", Asian cooperation will build an open, safe and effective Maritime Road that can facilitate trade, transportation, economic development and the dissemination of culture.

21. Asia Culture developed and Strong according their designated nations culture and some functions have differences. However, there is one solemn that is to preserve their own culture. There should attempt to express real evidence the impact of Asia culture constellation. It should be valued on cooperation to strengthen it. It prefers prosperity and stability come together and draw attention for the sustainability of the cultural development. These initiatives to be undertaken will be the milestone for each nation.

The Road to Cultural Partnerships and Win-win Outcomes in Asia

22. The Maritime Silk Road is in line with the development of national economies and the improvement of welfare. Asia must follow the new perspective on value, cooperation and development featuring equality, cooperation, mutual benefits, win / win results, inclusiveness and harmony. The Road will connect the Pacific and Indian Oceans. China will focus on upgrading the China-ASEAN Free Trade Area and extending it to the coastal regions of the Indian Ocean, the Persian Gulf, the Red Sea and the Gulf of Aden.

23. By prioritizing cooperation in inter-connectivity, the maritime economy, maritime environmental protection and disaster protection and mitigation, it will call for expanding cooperation in marine culture. Marine culture is the foundation of building a 21st Century Maritime Silk Road. The plan will also call on countries to increase marine awareness and achieve common aspirations. Asian needs to make full use of the geopoli-

tics and culture of Marine Silk Road to promote exchanges in marine culture, tourism and education to make the Road a key link for friendly exchanges. At the same time, Asian needs to carry out exchanges and cooperation in marine culture, in areas such as culture or art exchanges, archaeological exchanges, marine tourism cooperation, education and training. In such a way, Asian will be able to expand the cultural influence of the Maritime Silk Road, push the Road into the new century and promote general marine cultural diversity.

24. Cooperation Asian regions make more friendly and lead to promote peace in this areas. The Silk Road project extended the maritime Silk Road, then drive to improve every sectors.

25. As the 21st century sets in our common fear of direct or side effect of globalization through IT super high-way is deepened among developing Asian countries. We are worried that globalization would erode our culture and undermine our identity. So we have been taking more preventive measures to protect our cultural heritage.

26. Cooperation in preserving of cultural heritage (Tangible and Intangible) more understands the advantage of culture and skills. World heritage sites would bring in many tourists which could flourish "Tourism Business". That attaches to work luxury things for people, artistic works, (Painting, Sculpture, Music) and information's. Thus, this strong project can provide to improve the nations situated along the Silk Road. So, should cooperate by Asia Nations for new opportunity in every sector.

Conclusion

27. The world today is very different from the world in the past. Each region, having different natural environment, many have different cultures. However, all people who live in the world today cannot exist in isolation to keep in harmony among different nations and the cultures. This enable people to understand other different cultures, different climates, different environments, different social ethics, different religions, different thoughts, and East or West's different political isms etc., in the world today and should accept their co-existence, then respect them for better way of life and peaceful better existence. Therefore, all villagers in the global village (by taking care of one's house and family, one's country and culture) will be able to promote the community in which they live. All human beings are sheltered by the same sky and they all live in the world. But

all man are not the same. Some have great virtues and high moral principles. A truly virtuous person is greatly respected each others.

28. This paper is aimed to contribute through the proper understanding of the Maritime Silk Road Economic Cooperation in Asia, it can be gained of the true concept in reciprocal relations between the countries and their social environment and promote the mutual understanding among the various cultures of the world. Consequently, it could be expected to extend the proper understanding of the cooperation in Asia and outside region.

29. In this world there are disasters, regional wars and world wars based on economy and colonialism. Because of human being's instigation and also because of natural disasters, we have seen many distasteful scenes like Tsunami, earthquake, flood, storms and explosion of atomic bombs. Using insecticide extremely and virus infections are also giving trouble to mankind. We all are trying to protect and prevent these disasters urgently.

30. To protect from men's instigated things, "Culture" is the only way. For example, men's greediness, anger and naughtiness can only be controlled by the mind. "Mud which is formed of water can only be cleaned by clean water". Practice individually for the wellbeing of mankind- the right way of knowing definitely, the right way of thinking, the right way of saying, the right way of doing, the right way of mindfulness and the right way of integrity. By this way, we can build our cultural environment and a more peaceful world.

31. So, to conclude my presentation I would like to say, "Let us build a more peaceful world by improving our cultural environment".

The Silk Road: Multicultural Integration

Nguyen Thi Hien

Associate Professor, Vice Director of Vietnam National Institute of Culture and Arts Studies Ministry of Culture, Sports and Tourism, Vietnam

1. The Silk Road and the 21st Century Maritime Silk Road

The Silk Road has been the greatest East to West trade route between China and Central Asia and Byzantium. It was established during 206 BC to AD 220 in Han Dynasty of China for the political, economic and cultural contact with Central Asia. The Silk Road eventually formed the network of both land and sea routes. Many caravans and ships went through Eurasia over the centuries and they adapted to different political situation, economic conditions, geographic environments, religious beliefs, cultural traits as well as development of people-to people relationships and cultural exchanges and integrations. Thus, besides the economic values, the Silk Road could be seen as the symbol of the multicultural integration of the peoples along the route.

From time to time, there had been the exchanges of silk, goods and cultural objects among the Chinese caravans and middlemen in Central Asia to the far West, Roman Empire. In fact, besides the trades of goods, the caravans and middlemen exchanged gold, precious metals and stones, ivory, coral, spices, tea, paper, textiles, and chinaware, furs, ceramics, incense, cinnamon bark and bronze weapons. On the top of the exchanges of merchandises, the different religious beliefs and Buddhist precepts, local rituals and cultural practices had integrated into the living environment of the area on its ways from China to Eurasia.

Thus, the demands of merchandise exchanges between East and West had constructed the network of Silk Road, linking Eurasian countries that connected traders, missionaries, monks, and local people. The exchanges across the Eurasia had emerged the various folk narratives in association to the goods, cultures and people. The stories included various religious beliefs, live styles and cultural patterns of various classes of people in many countries, reflecting the social, economic and political relationships between countries at different times along with the Silk Road.

The development of the network of the Silk Road enabled people in the past to interact with each other that resulted in the exchanges of culture, religion, technology, arts and so on. The Silk Road was the medium of which, forms, styles, fashion and music been transported between the East and West. The Central Asia was the melting pot of different cultures and beliefs. Travelers along the Silk Roads were attracted by the intellectual and cultural exchange. Science, arts and literature, as well as crafts and technologies were thus shared and disseminated in the communities along the routes, and in this way, languages, religions and cultures developed and influenced the local people along the route.

In addition to the economic legacy of the Silk Road, it also played its role in connecting cultures and peoples in contact with each other, and integrating in each other. Multicultural interaction was the tool for material exchange as well as the rapprochement among communities and peoples. The rich culture along the Silk Road has enabled researchers of arts, anthropology and folklore to study the art history of India, Iran, Syria and other countries along the route. (See http: //gallery. sjsu. edu/silkroad/religion. htm, UNESCO 1997)

Therefore, for thousands of years, the Silk Road Spirit – "peace and cooperation, openness and inclusiveness, mutual learning and mutual benefit" – has been passed from generation to generation. The Road promoted the cultural dialogue and in the sake of prosperity, dialogue and development among peoples throughout the continents. In the 21st century, a new era marked by the theme of peace, development, cooperation and mutual benefit, it is all the more important for us to carry on the Silk Road Spirit in the cultural dialogue and respect among the Asian, Eurasian, African countries.

When Chinese President Xi Jinping visited Central Asia and Southeast Asia in 2013, he raised the initiative of jointly building the Silk Road Economic Belt and the 21st Century Maritime Silk Road (the Belt and Road), which have attracted close attention from all over the world, including Viet Nam. There are five points that have been pointed by the President, namely policy communication, road connectivity, trade facilitation, monetary circulation and people-to-people exchanges.

We acknowledge that building the Belt and Road can help promote the economic prosperity, strengthen exchange, mutual learning as well as enhance the respect and dialogue between different regions, communities, and ethnic groups. This promotes world peace and development not only through the economy, but also the culture.

In Vision and Actions on Jointly Building Silk Road Economic Belt and 21st-Century Maritime Silk Road, issued by the National Development and Reform Commission, Ministry of Foreign Affairs, and Ministry of Commerce of the People's Republic of China, with State Council authorization, March 2015, it states that the neighbor of ASEAN countries takes the unique advantage of Guangxi Zhuang Autonomous Region, speed up the opening-up and development of an international corridor opening to the ASEAN region. Also, it makes good use of the geographic advantage of Yunnan Province, and develops a new trend of economic cooperation in the Greater Mekong Sub-region.

China shall be in collaboration with ASEAN Countries that together carry out joint research, forums and fairs, personnel training, exchanges and visits under the framework of existing bilateral, multilateral, regional and sub-regional cooperation mechanisms in terms of culture and promote cultural rapprochement among the peoples in mainland and cross borders of China and ASEAN Countries. This document also emphasizes that China shall work with countries along the Belt and Road to steadily advance collaborative projects, jointly identify programs that accommodate bilateral and multilateral interests, and accelerate the launching of programs.

2. Viet Nam with the 21st Century Maritime Silk Road

Viet Nam is an integrated part in the Belt and Road, in the network from Fujian to Southeast Asia, Northern Asia and Europe. It is one of the topics that the Party General Secretary Nguyen Phu Trong of the Communist Party of Viet Nam and Chinese State President Xi Jinping discussed during his visit to China in April, 2015. Firstly and most obviously, it comes as the two Asian neighbors celebrate the 65th anniversary of their diplomatic relationship, which has generally been moving ahead on the track of friendship and cooperation despite various twists and turns. Their interaction has eloquently proved that as long as they adhere to the consequences of their actions in mind, they can resolve their differences and remain good neighbors. The two leaders reaffirmed the commitment to a relationship that is defined as "good neighbors, good friends, good comrades and good partners." China has made it clear that "the Belt and Road" covers large areas in the South China Sea with its aims at promoting common prosperity and win-win development in Asia and beyond.

The 21st Century Maritime Silk Road, just like with similar trade routes in the past, it will also reduce the tensions and conflicts as more frequent exchanges of goods and ideas will lead to better mutual understanding among trading partners, peoples and countries. Viet Nam shares the opportunities of the Maritime Silk Road in the 21st century with China, as also reflects China's aspiration to use a variety of ways to make the South China Sea an area of cooperation and peace. With efforts from both sides, new chapters will be added to the China-Vietnam friendship. Chinese President Xi Jinping and Vietnamese Communist Party General Secretary Nguyen Phu Trong have agreed to work together on the Maritime Silk Road trade initiative. (See Pang Xinglei, 2015, and Scott Kennedy, David A. Parker, 2015)

Viet Nam is a key part of Chinese plans for the Maritime Silk Road - a series of trade routes that would originate from China's Fujian Province, passing through Southeast and South Asia toward Europe. A port facility accommodating large containerships could open as early as the end of 2017 in the northern Vietnamese city of Haiphong. Cargo bound for inland areas in China could be unloaded there instead of Shanghai or Hong Kong, greatly speeding up its journey.

Since the normalization of ties, Vietnam and China have set a vision to push ties between the two Parties and countries forward in the spirit of "good neighbors, good friends, good comrades and good partnerships", and under the motto "friendly neighbors, comprehensive cooperation, long-term stability and future vision".

Long before Nguyen Phu Trong's visit Prime Minister Nguyen Tan Dung in the reception of the visiting Chinese Communications Minister Li Shenglin in April 3, 2007 in Hanoi emphasized the commitments made by the two countries' leaders under the motto "Friendly neighborhood, comprehensive cooperation, long-standing stability, and look toward the future". Before that time, in 2004, the former Prime Minister Phan Van Khai proposed the most important project "Two corridors, one economic belt", and was supported by the Chinese government. Then in 2006, when Chinese Party General Secretary and President Hu Jintao paid a visit to Vietnam, this project was signed by the two countries. The core of the intergovernmental project was to develop a road and express railway system: Nanning-Lang Son_ Hai Phong-Quang Ninh; Yunnan-Lao Cai-Hanoi and the belt road in the Gulf of Tonkin. The implementation of this project would help cement the Vietnam-China traditional friendship. It is also a key point of the important strategies in the collaboration between China and ASEAN. The relationship between the two countries becomes more fulfilled when China encourages "Action Plans" in the relation with ASEAN in many fields such as economics, foreign trade, social-culture, technology, youth education. (See Deng Yushan, 2015)

3. Strengthening the Cultural Research Collaboration

The relationship between the two countries especially has strengthened by the joint projects that have been carried out by institutions from both countries not only in economics, but also in humanities and social sciences. For instance, for about a decade, Viet Nam National Institute of Culture and Arts Studies (VICAS), Ministry of Culture, Sports and Tourism signed a number of joint projects with Yunnan Academy of Social Sciences (YASS) on Red River Research on ecological, social cultures of ethnic groups who live along the rivers. Also, Viet Nam National Institute of Culture and Arts Studies, Ministry of Culture, Sports & Tourism and Guangxi Academy of Ethnic Minority Culture, Cultural Bureau of the Guangxi Zhuang Nationality Autonomous Region and South China Research Center, the Hong Kong University of Science and Technology have jointly carried the project entitled "Transnational Collaborative Research Plan for the Study of Cross-border Ethnic Groups and Regional Cultural Connections on the Sino-Vietnamese Border". These cross border communities have maintained and developed their friendship and share their ethnic and cultural traditional values. The cross-border research is a great contribution to the overall joint project between China and Vietnam "Two corridors, one economic belt".

As aforementioned, Vietnam National Institute of Culture and Arts Studies has developed a long term relationship with the Yunnan Academy of Social Sciences (YASS) for decades with various activities including scholars exchange, joint projects, joint fieldtrips, research reference and book exchange. So far the two institutions have developed two big joint projects on the Red River.

I will elaborate why and how the joint Red River research is crucial and timely in academics and in the understanding of the people who live cross borders in China and Vietnam. Red River is identified as an international river that comes from Weishan, Da Li, Yunnan, China, goes through the northern part of Vietnamto the sea at Ba Lat mouth, Thai Binh province. Red River runs through various geographical areas, ecological systems and cultural features. To study and get to know more about the civilization and cultural values, ecological systems, local knowledge of peoples who live along the reaches of the two Rivers are not only to accumulate the ethnographic literature about these peoples and regions that are actually still a few, but our research result is also to contribute to the mutual understanding among peoples. The Red River is the main source in terms of water and fertile soil for peoples to cultivate and to live, including the Chinese, the Tai, the Hani, the Islamic, the Meo, the Yi, the Jing, the Zhuang... The river also serves as a "road" for the peoples to immigrate to their new land for better cultivating land and suitable environment. Thus, the ethnic groups live along the Red River share common cultural, agricultural values, but also distinguish by their languages, own cultural features, living environment, and living houses.

Along the Red River through geographical area and ecological systems, the river has strong connections with the economic, cultural, social developments of the peoples and local communities. Our past collaborative project on the Red River research focuses on native, cultural and human diversity, including rich native landscapes, local knowledge, ecological and different traditional agriculture system, folk beliefs and practices related to the river and water. Through history, the change of river in its flows and currents probably causes the change of cultural, social and economic practices of the communities who live along the river. Our joint project is to understand more about the river's cultural foundation, its values and effects on the life of people and current change. The joint research includes four fieldtrips in the both countries, in upper and lower reaches of Red River in Weishan, Da Li in Yunnan and down to its mouth in Thai Binh province in Vietnam. Our joint research is seen high valuable to promote the cultural understandings about the reaches of Red River, cultural heritage and ecological system protection.

The upper scale project at the governmental level including but not limited to the project "two corridors, one economic belt" in which Yunnan is the most important location for this project to cooperate with Vietnam and the other ASEAN countries. Yunnan is known as the source of the Red River and the trading waterway from Yunnan to Vietnam is on the river. In history, the famous river station of Manhao became a historical place where the commercial goods from Yunnan were shipped to Lao Cai, Vietnam and vice-versa. Our humanities research of the ethnic groups in Yunnan and in the Red River delta would contribute to the agenda of economists with their better ideas how to promote the local economy and commerce.

Not only the influence in terms of economic sector, our cultural and human research also serves a tool for understanding the ethnic peoples who share the same river, ecological systems, and local knowledge. Furthermore, the same ethnic people live cross border in both Yunnan and in Vietnam such as the Hani, the Yao, the Yi, the Jing, the Tai... The Red River used to serve as a road for their immigration. Thus, research of these peoples along the river helps to see the changes of the peoples as well as their traditional cultures when they immigrated to the new land with the new local policies.

Together with the legal frameworks of the two countries to manage the river basins as well as the culture and societies of the ethnic groups, the human and social always play their important role in the economic collaboration as the relation between the two countries. The Red River research has opened up the other collaborative research between VICAS and the other Institutions in China, Guangxi Academy of Ethnic Minority Culture, Cultural Bureau of the Guangxi Zhuang Nationality Autonomous Region, and Hong Kong University of Science and Technology. This is very important research of the Jing who live along the cross border coastal area and it will contribute to the economic belt of the Gulf of Tonkin.

To strengthen the relationship of the two countries in the coming years and to participate actively in the Belt and Road, my institute invites its institution partners from China and ASEAN countries to work together on the transnational research on the cross border ethnic groups such as the Tai, Dai, Zhuang, Hani, Yi, Yao, so on as well as the peoples along the Mekong River. It will be a great opportunity for scholars and research institutions to work together by doing field work, organizing international conferences, and joint publication on the multicultural integration of the peoples who live in the interregions, cross border areas, and diasporic immigrants from the transnational perspectives. The concept of transnationalism concentrates on the enhancement of the interconnectivity between people along the One Road and One Belt routes without the boundaries between countries. The nature of transnationalism has social, political and economic impacts that influence on the peoples along the routes.

The transnational research will facilitate the flow of people, ideas and goods between regions along the Silk Road. Concepts like citizenship, nationalism and communitarianism of the peoples are being changed and reexamined with this phenomenon of the modern age. Transnationalism can be used as theoretical analysis that refers to the new Silk Road co-operation between ASEAN countries and other regions, the exchanges between peoples, and thus promote peace, dialogue and respect for cultural diversity and as well as demonstrate multicultural integration.

Unity in Diversity

Karunangshu Barua

Publisher of Nymphea Press, Bangladesh

In his seminal work The Clash of Civilizations and the Remaking of World Order, Samuel Huntington hypothesized a new post-Cold War world order. Prior to the end of the Cold War, societies were divided by ideological differences, such as the struggle between democracy and communism. Huntington's main thesis argues, "The most important distinctions among peoples are no longer ideological, political, or economic. They are 'cultural.' New patterns of conflict will occur along the boundaries of different cultures and patterns of cohesion will be found within the cultural boundaries. In other words, the new 'fault line' between cultures are going to be deep-seated differences in areas such as religious beliefs and how people are governed.

On the face of it, Huntington might seem to be convincing, but looking it from a deeper perspective, it will appear he is focusing only on the surface of the issue. The human civilization is not only about conflicts, it is also about cooperation, understanding, and exchange in different areas of life and living.

If we turn our focus to this part of the globe particularly the Silk Road, we will see how this road has played the role of a catalyst in integration of ideology, cultural ethos and artistic interchange.

Records describe that Chang Ch'ien, a Chinese diplomat of the Han dynasty, on his return from Ta-hsia (Ferghana), in the 2nd century BC, heard of a country named Tien-chu (India) narrated his travels of a new route towards Central Asia which later known as the "Silk Road".

"Silk Road" emerged as a successful network of trade and cultural transmission routes that initiated cultural interaction through regions of the Asian continent connecting the West and East by merchants, pilgrims, monks, soldiers, nomads, and urban dwellers from China and India to the Mediterranean Sea. This opened up a long-distance political and economic relations between the civilizations of China, the Indian subcontinent, Persia, Europe, the Horn of Africa, and Arabia. Though the "route" was fabricated mainly for economic advancement, but this was also a major, distinct freeway for cultural exchange that had endowed us with enormous cultural diversification. Depending on the rapports through the silk road, we also traded syncretic philosophies, religions, and various technologies for more than 1700 years.

Under the patronage of Han dynasty, Buddhist monks transported Buddhism teachings to China in the first quarter of the 2nd century BC. With the passage of time, several travelers from China visited this South-Asian sub-continent. Most notably, FaHien, Hieun Tsang, and I Tsing travelled India and ancient Bengal from fifth to seventh century. These eminent Chinese pilgrims took back wealth of historical and religious literature pertaining to Buddhism to China and remarkably contributed to the forging of cultural ties between China and Bangladesh in ancient times. During the Pala dynasty in Eighth and Twelfth centuries, Chinese monks and pilgrims also studied at the Buddhist institutions like Somapura Mahavihara and Vikramshila Mahavihara in Bangladesh. I may specially mention here, Hieun Tsang, during his travels in the sub-continent, studied at the famous Nalanda University under direct supervision of the then Bengali principle, Silabhadra for 22 months. After a successful period of specialism, Hieun Tsang returned to China with more than 750 manuscripts carried on 20 horses. After returning to China, he translated the manuscripts and for the first time, the unique sayings and messages of Buddha were introduced to the mass people of China. With the successful circulation of these manuscripts, a new era of religious upsurge took place in China.

At the end of the second quarter of 11th century, Atisha Dipankar Srijnan, the most outstanding saint-scholar of 10th-11th century, visited Tibet and China. He provided the religious and cultural link of Bangladesh and ancient India with Tibet, China and northern Asian countries. He is among the brightest luminaries of Bengal and India by virtue of his character, scholarship, erudition and spiritual eminence. He fought against prevailing practices of sacrifices, esoteric manuals and preached Buddha's doctrine of good ethical lives, morality and compassion to liberate the masses from superstitious practices. He advocated higher moral life, humility and purity of existence, universal love, non-violence, amity and need for meditation to achieve Bodhicitta, the common name for enlightenment and compassion. In China, thousands of monks, irrespective of sects accepted the teachings of Atisha. He brought the message of moral purity and selfless sacrifice for others, of the virtuous life and to the adherence to pure Mahayana teachings.

For almost 2000 years now, we have been in cooperation on culture and heritage through several roads and waterways, the practice that was initiated by this ancient Silk Road. In modern times, the culture of Bangladesh has evolved over the centuries and encompasses the cultural diversity of several social groups of Bangladesh. The Bengal Renaissance of the 19th and early 20th centuries noted Bengali writers, saints, scientists, researchers, thinkers, music composers, painters, and film-makers have played a significant role in the development of Bengali culture. The culture of Bangladesh is composite and over the centuries has assimilated influences of Islam, Hinduism, Buddhism, and Christianity. It is manifested in various forms, including music, dance, and drama; art and craft; folklore and folktale; languages and literature; philosophy and religion; festivals and celebrations; as well as in a distinct cuisine and culinary tradition.

After the War of Independence in 1971, we have been continuously reaching out, with newer vision and mission, to meet the potential dispersive cultures the world had been offering. We believe this cultural globalization can enrich our mode of thinking and methods of implementation for cultural succession. With the revolutionary "the Belt & Road Initiative", (YíDàiyílù) Honorable President Xi Jinping has not only recreated opportunities to reach multiple economic corridors encompassing more than 60 countries but also opened myriad ways of connecting people and cultures across the route. This vast channel of international communication will definitely let us and our future generations to reach out for each other and accelerate our cultural exchange activities in dynamic and most diverse way possible. This way, we will learn more to develop positive relationships with others, understand a broader range of perspectives, and develop the knowledge and skills needed for participation in our multicultural world.

For this instance, I may add here, Bangladesh and China have signed "Cultural Exchange Program" (CEP) back in May 2014 to pave opportunity for exchanging more cultural programs in order to further develop and strengthen cultural exchanges and friendly relations existing between Bangladesh and China, which was primarily initiated back in November 1979. Under the latest Cultural Exchange Program agreement, the two countries will undergo several executive programs for the years 2014-2017 that will cover many areas such as arts, culture and cultural heritage, youth and sports, education, and print and electronic media.

On the 40th anniversary of the establishment of diplomatic relations between China and Bangladesh, I believe, this cultural communication and cooperation will attain a new height. It's the high time for us to review historical cooperation and in such time the "One Belt, One Road" or in other words Unity in Diversity initiative is the perfect conceptual platform to do so. I believe in this age of cultural globalization, better understanding and cooperation is the answer for peace and harmony that Huntington failed to understand.

Family Based Socio-cultural Development Project in Sri Lanka (Role of the Culture with Sri Lankan Experience)

Bernad Vasantha

Additional Secretary of Ministry of Internal Affairs,
Wayamba Development and Cultural Affairs, Sri Lanka

Introduction

The Department of Cultural Affairs in Sri Lanka coming under the Ministry of Internal Affairs, Wayaba Development and Cultural Affairs has planned to implement a 5 year national project on family based socio-cultural enhancement for sustainable development namely "Ape Sonduru Paula" (Our happy and perfect family) from January 2016 to address the present socio-cultural issues relating to the family in the country. This project aims at improving moral values positive attitudes, life skills and necessary knowledge of all family members of Sri Lanka and also mobilizing and coordinating resource systems to address the family issues, so as to start a journey towards shaping up an excellent person and happy family, finally to have an inclusive, peaceful and pleasant society.

The world commission on culture and development define culture as "ways of living together" and argued that this made culture a core element of sustainable development. World cultural report stresses the importance of considering culture in development as follows.

"Culture shapes the way we see the world. It therefore has the capacity to bring about the change of attitudes needed to ensure peace and sustainable development which, we know, form the only possible way forward for life on planet Earth:.

Source: Preface, World Culture Report, UNESCO Publishing, Paris, 1999

It is a fact that there is gradual decadence of culture and moral values in Sri Lanka. As well there is an increasing trend of neglecting indigenous social norms, ethical values and culture to the embrace of foreign culture and values. This has been a major cause to increase family and social issues in the country. As well this proves that development must include not only material progress but socio-cultural dimension as well. Family as the basic unit of the society plays a major role of socio-cultural development of the country. Therefore, strengthening the family is used as a means of development in this project giving special attention to moral, ethical and spiritual dimension.

The Existing Situation Concerning the Family

Sri Lankan society has undoubtedly changed significantly over the last few decades. Meanwhile demographic, social, economic and cultural evolutions have brought about considerable changes with reference to the family unit.

By the year 2012 number of households in Sri Lanka stood at 5.188 million while it's household population was at 20.3 million. As an inevitable outcome of declining fertility rates and increasing age at first birth, family size has been reduced from 5.1 in 1986 to 3.9 in 2012. (Source: Department of Census and Statistics) Here it is considered household size as family size. Age at marriage and age at first birth has changed and a substantial increase of the proportions never married among both male and female at young age is a significant phenomenon.

Due to many demographic, social, cultural, economic and political reasons, the number of the family members has been reduced and members of the family seem to be scattered and dispersed. Consequently the nuclear family with its parents and children became the model of society and the traditional extended family usually constituting three generations has almost disappeared. This could be seen significantly during last 5 decades. As a result of population ageing, migration, decrease in sex ratio, unmarried persons and other social and cultural, economic changes occurring in the country, an emerging trend of single person household can be seen.

In Sri Lanka, the oldest male is designated as the head of household as a cultural norm and in the meantime female headed households have become a steadily growing phenomenon. By the year 2010 female headed households was 23%. (Source: Department of census and statistics) Marriage dissolution is a tragedy concerning to the family unit. A considerable proportion of marriages are disrupted suddenly for reasons such as desertions, separations or divorce. The incidence of divorce is increasing and this phenomenon is more prevalent among women in the western province. Changing nature of the relationship coupled with the increase in divorce has also led to a situation where children have one parent in common. The economics of the family and the sexual division of the labour within the family are very much determined by opportunities in the labour market.

The open economic system has facilitated more job opportunities since 1978 for women in the labour market. Therefore today more women are employed than ever before. Economically active population or labour force was about 8.3 million in the second quarter of 2012, of which 33 percent were females. (Source: Department of census and statistics) The migration of skilled, semiskilled and unskilled labour from the country has rapidly increased in the last 5 decades. Women (mothers) migration to Middle East countries predominate among labour migration from 1980s. In every year over 100,000 persons migrate allowing their family members under insecurity.

The changing demographic scenario in Sri Lanka has led to a significant increase in the proportion of older persons. The highest proportion of older persons is reported in 2012. More significant is the progressive upward trend in the growth rate of older person and declining trend in national growth rate. This trend has interacted with major changes in patterns of individual and family life. Cohabiting couples without legal marriage are an emerging phenomenon especially in urban areas. According to the general observation number of children of a family has fallen to 1-2 in 2000s which is considerably lower than the figure of 8 or above children in 1960s.

In the last 5 decades family values have undoubtedly changed significantly alongside the change of family structure and composition. Traditional family values often refer to morality, religions and a way of life that recognizes right from wrong. Today adoption of religious practices has declined and people are much more inclined to follow a more materialistic lifestyle.

Apart from the negative influence of consumer-driven society, bioethical issues arising from science and technology, premarital sex and pregnancy, abortion, divorce, decline in the parental care of the children, lack of love & care for elders and erosion of marital bond between husband and wife also have contributed for the declining trend of traditional values in the modern society. Changing role of the women is affecting the role of the male in the family. As increasing number of women strive to pursue a career as well as look after children, many men are converting to a more domestic role in the home. As its mention before Sri Lankan traditional family back ground has been damaged due to the above recent.

Goal of the Project

Improving the moral values, positive attitudes, life skills and necessary knowledge of all family members of Sri Lanka and also mobilizing and coordinating resource systems to address the present socio-cultural issues relating to the family so as to start a journey towards shaping up an excellent person and happy family, finally to have an inclusive, peaceful and pleasant society.

Main Objectives of the Project

1. To pave the way to organize the cultural life of the people of the country through preservation, maintenance and utilization of cultural heritages.

2. To motivate the people to identify positive cultural characteristics and thereby to promote a culture with distinct Sri Lankan identity.

3. To help the people in identifying themselves the external and Internal factors causing cultural downfall and in exterminating these factors.

4. To pave the way to inculcate in the society the fact that culture is an energetic, challenging and a free force preceded by patriotism.

5. Improving the positive attitudes, life skills and necessary knowledge of all family members of Sri Lanka within 5years through awareness programmes.

6. Enhancing psycho, social, cultural and economic status of families which need special care and protection through mobilizing and coordinating resource systems.

7. Establishing a continuous mobilization system to prevent and solve family issues and protect persons' rights in every village by empowering civil society and civil society organizations as a part of the local social system.

8. Establishing 331 cultural development centers in the of Divisional Secretariat division to implement the service provision programme mainly to ensure case management service for families which need special care and protection, awareness and education progrmme in the proper use and the management of the services and to monitor the acceptance, problems and successes of the delivering services. Already 178 cultural centers has been established in Sri Lanka those centers should be converted to the services delivery center.

9. Improving the professional capacity of technical personnel in project operation and to have the ability to extend the project by themselves in the future and create a network of technical personal at central, provincial, district and divisional levels using staff from cultural sector and relevant other sectors.

10. Conducting action researches and sharing experience on best practices of country development through family development.

11. Traditional Sri Lankan family is living with love, kindness and harmony and this project urge to recent family convert to like the traditional Sri Lankan family.

Immediate Objectives of the Project

1) To increase awareness of all couples entering matrimony about happy & success married life and making available information about services available to get help in the issues of marriage & family life, during the period 2016 - 2020about 200, 000 couples annually.

2) To increase awareness of all pregnant mothers and their husbands on having a healthy child, infant care, giving special attention to spiritual and psycho - social aspect and information about services available to get help in the issues of infants care, during 2016 - 2020about350, 000 annually.

3) To increase awareness of all preschool and day care children's mothers on child rights and improving child care in the family giving special attention to spiritual and psycho - social aspect and information about services available to get help in the issues of child care, during 2016 - 2020about 350, 000 annually.

4) To initiate establishment of positive attitudes on social values, psycho - social skills and posturing resiliency in all preschool children, during 2016 – 2020 about 350, 000 annually. Also give traditional healthy foods to children.

5) To increase awareness of children and teenagers on spiritual development, bio-ethics, psycho-social skills, Substance abuse prevention, posturing resiliency, child rights, peace and reconciliation and information about services available to get help in the issues of them during 2016 – 2020 about 400, 000 annually for children in year 3, 6, 9, 12, and children with irregular school attendance.

6) To increase awareness of children and teenagers on positive attitudes, bioethics, psycho - social skills, Substance abuse prevention, posturing resiliency and information about services available to get help in the issues of them during 2016 – 2020 about 400, 000 annually for children in year 3, 6, 9, 12, and children with irregular school attendance and also introduce simple life style specialty traditional Sri Lankan life art.

7) To increase awareness of school leavers and youngsters on emerging issues in youngsters, psycho - social skills and posturing resiliency, bioethics, human rights, peace and reconciliation and information about services available to get help in the issues in the young, during 2016 – 2020 about 400, 000 annually at tertiary and high education institutes and village youth clubs the youth can be engage in drama arts, music, street theatre films and discussion in the cultural centers.

8) To increase awareness of all family members on developing family as a unit with intimate bonds, child & youngsters care, healthy life style, indigenous family values norms and customs, vision of the life and information about services available to get help in the issues, during 2016 – 2020 about 240 000 annually at the village base, getting participation of village Samurdhi beneficiary committees, elders committees, women's clubs and other village societies through the cultural centers.

9) To develop livelihoods of poor artistic families which need special care and protection, during 2016 – 2020.

10) To provide shelter for poor artistic families which need special care and protection during 2016 – 2020.

11) To provide basic resources and establish 331 cultural development centers in all divisional secretariats.

12) To conducting action research, sharing experience on best practices of country development through family development, during 2016 – 2020.

Specific Problem to be Addressed by Project

As explained above the family unit has declined significantly over the last 4 decades as the effects of economic, social and cultural evolution in the society. Today decline of the extended family is well recognized as well as the nuclear family is also declining significantly over the few decades in Sri Lankan social system. The expansion of the country's economic system, the opening up of new employment opportunities in overseas, increasing education level of the people especially in women, urbanization and globalization have brought about greater improvement physically in the country. As well they have affected the family structure, role of the women and men, attitudes and values of the family.

As the final outcome of the evolution of family system, following critical issues have raised and the family unit has broken down and the social system of the country needs to be protected.

Existing issues relating to and affecting children
- Child abuse
- Child mothers
- Broken family
- Decline in the parental care of the children
- Miss guidance by commercial advertisement
- Child poverty
- Stress

Existing issues relating to and affecting Teen and Youth
- Premarital sex and pregnancy (among teen & youth)
- Abortion
- Unemployment / income generation
- Crime and aggressive behavior
- High rate of divorce
- Drug abuse
- Delinquency
- Suicide
- Non communicable disease

- Stay attached with non-achievable expectation
- Stress

Existing issues relating and affecting adult
- Internal family problems
- Divorce
- Suicide
- Non communicable disease
- Erosion of marital bond between husband and wife
- Stress

Existing issues relating and affecting to Senior citizens
- Loneliness
- Abandon
- Income insecurity
- Social insecurity
- Stress

Common social issues affecting to families
- Physical and mental illnesses
- Ageing population
- Increasing in crimes
- Increasing in accident
- Bioethical issues arising from science and technology
- Accessibility to basic services
- Accessibility to basic needs
- Income generation

Excluded and marginalized families which need special care and protection
- Families headed by persons with disabilities and families with persons with disabilities
- Single parents' families
- Families with needy and affected elderly persons
- Families with chronic & generational poverty
- Families with persons of substance abuse
- Families with other critical psycho social problems

In order to bring the society to correct path it is an urgent need to take necessary steps at national level to prevent the decline of the family unit and have the perfect family. Many of these issues arise as a result of wrong attitudes, lack of awareness and psycho social skills rather than lack of physical resources. To minimize such issues it is necessary to embark on an extensive awareness program to make aware of all family members, with an incorporating sectorial integrated and participatory approach instead of ad-hoc awareness programs. Similarly the services provision is also to be made more systematic so as to empower person and families who need special care and protection. "Ape Sonduru Paula" National Project on Family Development was started to address this need.

Mode of Intervention in Terms of this Project

A combination of distinctive approaches including participatory local social development approach is used in the project in order to achieve these goals and objectives. This includes followings;

Partnership and Collaborative Approach

The goal of shaping up an excellent person, a happy perfect family and a peaceful, pleasant society in the country can't be achieved working alone, so partnership and collaborative is more important. This program is planned to work with the partnership of central government, provincial governments and local governments, international organizations, international non-government organizations, civil society organizations and private sector organizations as stakeholders in collaborative manner.

Participatory Approach

Participatory approach is used to ensure a two way communication system and mobilize the target groups for tasks in community mobilization and empowerment programmes.

Project Activities

1. Renovation of Cultural Centers.
2. Build the new cultural centers.
3. Infrastructure development of cultural centers.
4. Human resource development of cultural officers and other relevant officers.
5. Revealing and preserving of indigenous knowledge and culture values.
6. The competition of music, dancing theatre, short stories, children's stories, song writing, translation among the children, youth and elders as well as both officers of government and private sector.
7. Conservation of Folk arts including Folk music and Folk dancing as well as music melodies.
8. Folk music entertainment programme for the students and youth.
9. Organize annual music festival.
10. Awareness programme of the indigenous sweet, special food items, and beverages, food pattern, cooking methods.
11. Meeting and workshops for each target groups.
12. Publish Leaflets, Posters and Booklets in Sinhala and Tamil Languages.
13. Competition to select perfect family and excellent project operator at divisional district and national level.
14. Use of Mass Media (National Newspapers, radio and T. V. Channels.)
15. Audio visual instruments (CD/DVD documentary & Tele drama)
16. National and regional Seminars and Conference.

Conclusion

The culture has a role to play for the people of a country. Culture denotes the vision and mission, based on the pattern of living style of the people that constructs a society the pattern of living is a sign of people's foods habits, houses clothes, wearing's ornaments, all their productions and creations. Vision and mission denotes their way of thinking, the creeds, belief and objectives existing in a Society Contribute for their vision and mission. Not only that the fine arts and performing arts also based on their culture. The culture including all these features is formed in keeping with the environment of a country not only the nature given environment by the socioeconomic and political factors are also contributing largely for the formation of culture. At the same time the culture of a country is instrumental largely to brighten the political and socio-economic spheres of a country. In view of this, the function of "Culture" is vital and ample in a society, i. e. Contribution towards the forward March of a country, Having impression for the betterment of the living condition of people, Keeping up the people is happiness and in harmony.

Abstracts and Sources:

1. Project reports of Department of Culture in Sri Lanka, 2014.

2. Annual report of Departments of Social Services in Western Province in Sri Lanka, 2013.

3. Department of Census and Statistics in Sri Lanka. 2011, 2012, 2013.